LISA SUZANNE

VEGAS ACES
THE COMPLETE SERIES
© Lisa Suzanne 2022

Published in the United States of America by Books by LS, LLC.

ISBN: 9798839349902

Cover Designed by Najla Qamber Designs

CONTENTS

BONUS MATERIAL

Home
GAME

LISA SUZANNE

DEDICATION

To the three who make my *Home Game* the most fun.

CHAPTER 1

"Come on, Todd," I murmur. "It's fine. Nobody will ever know."

"Not at work," he mutters. He shuffles some papers on his desk just after his eyes flick to my chest. He wants this too, clearly, and his words of protest are more along the obligatory line than the sincere one.

I'm not usually the girl who comes onto her colleague at work, but we've been dating for the last few months, and last night he railed me good and hard, so this girl is back for her seconds.

I walk around his desk, and he looks up at me. I look down at him. That moment of *yeah this is happening* passes between us, and I take that as my signal.

I hike up my skirt and climb onto his lap.

His hands settle onto my ass, and he shifts me around a little, letting me know he's into it too. Gone are the weak protests of a moment ago, instead replaced by the tiny kisses he's trailing up my neck.

I lean back to give him more space to work with, and I shiver a little at how good it feels. He shifts his hips up toward me, and I buck mine down, and that's the good ol' signal that we're about to bang.

"I don't have a condom," he whispers. His eyes dart toward the door.

"I do," I say, but it's in my purse tucked into my desk drawer in my office. I nip a kiss on his lips. "Be right back."

I climb off him and scurry to my office, grab the condom out of my purse, and rush back.

Belinda, our boss, is standing in the doorway when I return. Her eyes fall to me, and I tighten my fist around the condom in my palm. I wish I wasn't wearing a dress with no pockets today. Why do I even own a dress without pockets? How terribly inconvenient.

"How's the Montgomery account coming?" she asks, raising a brow at me.

"Excellent," I lie. Truth be told, I've barely even glanced at the Montgomery account. She just slid it into my inbox this morning. I had some other things I was wrapping up and then I wanted to wrap up Todd and *then* I was going to dig into it.

She purses her lips like she doesn't believe me, and I smile. She doesn't like me. The feeling is mutual.

"What are you doing in Todd's office?" she prods.

"I just wanted to run a few things by him regarding the construction company you gave us," I say. It's not a total lie. That's what brought me here in the first place, but sex—or at least the promise of it—is what kept me here a little longer.

"Fine. Then back to your office, and I want a summary of your plans for Montgomery before you leave today."

I smile sweetly even though I'm now seething on the inside. Before I leave today? That'll make for a long night, but most nights at this job are long. At least I like what I do...even if I don't like my boss. "Of course."

She stomps off, and I look at Todd and make a face. I kick the door shut behind me and stalk toward the guy who's about to make my eyes roll to the back of my head.

"Now where were we?" I ask, settling back onto his lap and linking my arms around his neck.

He chuckles. "I was just getting back to work. I've got deadlines and as much fun as this sounds, I don't think we should do it at work. Let's save it for later when we can take our time."

I thrust my hips down on him again. "You sure about that?"

He groans, and then he mutters, "Nope. Not even a little." And then he gives me what I want. I produce the condom from my palm and shift back. He glances at the door, and then he sighs, unzips his pants, pulls himself out, and rolls on the condom.

I feel giddy as he reaches toward me and hooks his finger around my panties to shove them aside before he thrusts up into me.

I moan—loudly—and he presses his mouth to mine in some misguided attempt to quiet me, and then he really starts moving.

It's hot and illicit doing this here in his office. It's bright outside so no one can see in, especially not up here on the fifth floor, but I can see out there, and I see cars moving and people walking while I'm up here getting screwed in a desk chair.

I throw my head back and close my eyes, giving into the heat and passion that burns between us.

"Oh God," I moan. "Oh yes, yes, yes!" He clamps a hand over my mouth, but it's too late. I'm yelling because holy hell he's good at the sex stuff, and he keeps hammering into me because neither of us are done yet, except I'm just about done because he feels so damn good. I start yelling as everything goes black and pleasure is just about to sweep over me. "I'm so close, so close!"

And then he gasps and everything stops as I'm about to fly into my orgasm. I'm dying for just a teeny-tiny little more friction to really send this bliss to that sheer level of perfection, and he's thick inside me but completely still.

I open my eyes to see just why the hell he thought it was a good idea to stop moving as my body is literally tipping over the edge of ecstasy, and I see his wide eyes pinned toward the door.

My heart stops for a beat as my brain catches up, and then my head slowly turns to see what caused him to stop.

He shifts as I turn, and it's just enough of a shift to tip me into the throes of my climax as my eyes meet Belinda's across the room.

I cry out as I fly headfirst into my orgasm. I close my eyes tight and come and come as I grip onto Todd, and then it all stops, and I'm pretty sure Belinda saw the entire thing.

And now what?

Do I just, you know, climb off him? Because then that big, hard thing will just be hanging out for Belinda to see.

"I'll give you a minute," she says, and then the door slams shut.

"Do, uh..." I pause. "Do you want to finish?"

"Um, no." He gently pushes me off, but I was really just thinking of him. You know, blue balls and all that. "Dammit, Ellie. I told you we shouldn't do it at work."

"Oh, so now this is *my* fault?" I fire back as I smooth my dress back into place and attempt to balance myself as my knees still shake from that orgasm.

He pulls off the condom and tucks himself back into his pants. He grabs a tissue to get rid of it. "I didn't say that, exactly, but yes. It's absolutely your fault. You didn't even bother to lock the door?"

I lift a shoulder. "Guess not. But you could've put up a fight if you really didn't want to do it."

"Are you serious right now? If I did put up a fight, you would've badgered me until you got your way anyway. I love this job, and you didn't lock the door, and now we'll probably both be fired for having sex in the workplace during working hours, and man you didn't just fuck me, but you somehow managed to fuck me over, too." He heaves out a breath when he finishes his speech.

I stare at him with wide eyes, not really sure what to say to that. "Really, Todd?" My comeback is weak, but the truth of the matter remains: Todd is no Prince Charming, and it looks like our relationship was no fairy tale.

There's a knock on the door.

"Come in," Todd yells.

Belinda shakes her head in disgust when she opens the door.

I've been working here for three years, starting as an intern fresh out of college and working my way up to account manager. Belinda was brought over from a competing company a few months ago and we sort of got off on the wrong foot.

"Well, he's right," she says, not hiding the fact that she heard our entire conversation through the door. "You're both fired."

I guess it looks like Belinda and I will be *ending* things on the wrong foot, too.

CHAPTER 2

"And that's the story of how I lost my boyfriend and my job in the same day," I finish.

My brother laughs. "Only you, Ellie, I swear."

I hold the phone between my ear and my shoulder as I grab my suitcase down from my closet shelf.

"Are you still coming Thursday?" he asks.

"Yep," I say. "I need a weekend away now more than ever, to be honest. I'm not really all that sad about Todd. He was hot, and I had hope for us at the start, but it turns out he was just a crush. It's not like I saw myself marrying him or anything. And the job...well, I've never been fired before, so that kind of stings. But I'll find something."

"Move to Vegas," he says softly.

My older brother and I are close—or, we were before he was traded and moved from Chicago, where we've both lived our entire lives, to Las Vegas to play for the Vegas Aces last year. His fiancée, Nicki, is one of my best friends, and they're getting married this weekend. I'm the maid of honor, and they're flying me out Thursday for the bachelorette party before all the wedding festivities begin.

Work obligations have kept me from visiting very often since they moved there. In fact, I've only been out once, and it was just for a quick weekend. We hit a nightclub on the Strip and drank too much, but mostly we hung out at their house since they'd just moved in and I offered to help with the unpacking.

I never really considered actually moving to Vegas, but the idea of starting fresh has a nice ring to it.

"I don't have a job there," I say.

"Well, not to be the dick reminding you of this, but you don't have a job in Chicago, either," he counters.

"Ouch. Okay, fine, but I don't know anybody there." I already know this is a losing argument. If Todd was right about me badgering people about things until I get my way, well, it's because I learned it from Josh.

"You know Nicki. You have me. And you know that if we're both in the same city, Mom and Jimbo will eventually come too."

I roll my eyes. He always calls our dad, whose name is Jim, *Jimbo*. "Ah, the ulterior motive unmasked. You want Mom and Dad close by so when you and Nicki start shitting out babies, you have sitters nearby."

"Well, let's start with A, that's a disgusting way of putting it. B, we have no child plans on the current radar. I just miss having you all within a few miles, that's all."

I blow out a breath. He's being vulnerable, and it's starting to soften me. "I don't have anywhere to live." He starts to say something, but I interrupt. "And before you get any crazy ideas, I'm not living with you and Nicki. Living with newlyweds sounds frickin' awful, and I also don't want to stay alone in your huge-ass mansion while the two of you are off on your honeymoon. I'm almost positive it's haunted."

He laughs. "We're having some renovations done while we're out of town so you wouldn't want to stay here anyway. I have a good buddy who you can stay with until you find somewhere permanent. He's on the team, and he's a real stand-up kind of guy. He's got this huge house so you wouldn't really even have to see him, and it isn't haunted. The best part is that he lives across the street from me, so you won't actually be in the newlywed's house, but you'll be close. No flirting, though. He's recently single and not looking."

"Ha," I say without actually laughing the word. "Same here. No worries, I'm not in the market right now either. Unless he wants a fling. And he's hot. Then maybe. Is he hot?"

14

"Gross, Elle. God, you've always been so damn boy crazy. No hooking up with my friends."

This time I do laugh. "Okay, okay."

"You'll do it?" he asks.

"Do I really have a choice? Live in a mansion with your hot friend in a tropical paradise with mountains, palm trees, slot machines, and new opportunities...or stay here in Chicago where we haven't seen the sun in the last twenty-one days and I just got dumped and lost my job in the same damn day?"

"He's not *hot*," Josh argues, but he's missing the point.

I laugh. "What the hell. It's worth a shot, and if it doesn't work out, I can just come back home."

I can hear his smile in his voice. "Yes! We'll have so much fun. I'll introduce you to all the guys on the team, and you and Nicki can hang by our pool all day. She's missed you so much. And we'll find you a job in public relations out here. I've got tons of connections and you know I'll do anything to help."

"I know you will. I love you, big bro."

"Love you, too, little sis."

We hang up, and I get moving. I've got some packing to do, and it's not all going to fit in the one little suitcase I just pulled down from my closet shelf.

I call my mom next. My mom and I are close, but she tends to err on the side of critical, and while most often I just brush it off as something my mom does, sometimes it digs in a little deeper. "Josh just talked me into moving to Vegas," I blurt when she answers.

"What?" she gasps, and I laugh.

"Well, it's kind of a long story," and one you don't tell your mom, "but today I was fired and Todd and I broke up."

I pause just long enough to hear her mutter something about how she's going to have to wait even longer for grandchildren now, and I rush ahead with my speech.

"Josh told me to come live there while I get back on my feet, and I don't really see a reason not to." Except all the ones I named when Josh first brought it up, but admitting all that wouldn't exactly sell this idea to my mother.

"So you're just...leaving?" she asks, and I can tell she's totally flabbergasted but it's my life and I'm at the point where I need to stop living it as a way to please my parents.

"Yep. Oh, and can I leave my furniture in your basement for a while until I decide if I'm staying there or coming back?" I ask.

Okay, I don't *ask*. I plead.

"Of course you can, Ellie, but are you sure about all this?" Her tone is doubtful. "Aren't you sort of making a snap decision here?"

"Absolutely," I admit. "But what's the worst thing that could happen?"

What's the worst indeed.

By the time I'm boarding the plane to Vegas two days later, my brother has arranged for movers to pick up my essentials and move the rest of my furniture to my parents' place. Thank goodness for that fat pro-football paycheck and a generous big brother, am I right?

I said my goodbyes to my parents, which weren't really goodbyes as much as they were *see you tomorrow* since they're heading to Vegas for Josh's wedding too.

I said my goodbyes to my friends, but let's be honest. Everyone I was *really* close to either scattered after college or was left behind when I was fired from my job. Even Brittany, the girl who I would consider my best friend at the office, pretty much abandoned me over the last few days, citing an overwhelming amount of work since two people on the team were fired in the same day.

Okay, so maybe it's a little my fault she's overworked right now...but I could still use a friend.

The only close friend I have left is Nicki, who is engaged to my brother. I'll finally have the sister I always wanted, and I found her in someone who has been like a sister to me since we were in high school.

I'm ready for this move. It feels right even though it's a little scary. At least I'll have my brother, which means I'll also have all the Vegas Aces football players he's close to. They're a tight-knit bunch, a real family according to Josh, and he assured me over and over that I'll be included in that equation, too.

And I'm not just ready for the move. I'm also ready to meet the hot stud of my dreams...but just for a little fun. I did just get dumped by Todd, and I don't know how permanent this move is going to be.

When the wheels touch down and I look out the window to see the famed skyline of Las Vegas Boulevard, something pulls in my stomach as dreams and magic collide with that feeling of *home* for the first time in my life. I love this city. I've loved it every time I've visited, and it's not just the bright, flashing lights or the neon signs or the excitement of the Strip. It's not just the beautiful weather or the gorgeous scenery. It's a feeling, some inexplicable thing inside me that I want to keep experiencing over and over again.

My head keeps telling me this isn't a permanent move, but I think my heart just might have other plans.

CHAPTER 3

"Ahh, you're getting married in two days!" I yell when I see my brother. He grabs me up in a big hug, and we both laugh.

"Is that Josh Nolan?" someone nearby says as they pass us.

My brother lets me go and smiles at the passerby. "It is," he says. "Pleasure to meet you." He sticks out his hand and the guy shakes it vigorously.

"We're huge Aces fans," he says. "That pass you caught in the third quarter in that last game was inhuman."

Josh laughs, and I just stand by as I smile awkwardly. It *was* a great catch, but they ended up losing the game, so the Aces technically finished in third last season. They didn't make it to the Super Bowl, but they have high hopes that they will this year.

And I need to be honest for a second.

I literally know next to *nothing* about football.

I'm just repeating shit my dad said.

The quarterback passes the ball and they run into the end zone. Someone kicks a ball and they can score points that way too. They wear lots of padding because it's a violent game and they wear tight pants that look better on some players than others.

That's about the extent of my knowledge.

I watch all Josh's games, of course. I'm a supportive sister. But I'm not really paying attention to the *game*. I'm watching the fans in the stands go crazy for their team. I enjoy the fanfare even if I don't really understand it. My dad has tried to explain it to me hundreds of times, but usually I tune out.

I'm still a huge Aces fan, though. In fact, I'm wearing my favorite women's Nolan 18 jersey, in part because it's my own last name and in part because it's my brother's jersey and in part because I'm here in Vegas and it's fun when people start chatting me up about how great the team did last season.

I think I've heard *worst to almost first* at least a dozen times since I got to the airport this morning in my jersey. It was the Aces' tagline last season after a dismal performance the season before. They brought in a ton of fresh blood and a whole new coaching staff, and suddenly they're a top contender to head to the big game next year.

The fan chats him up a while longer, we grab my suitcases, and he leads me out to his boat of a car, a Nissan Armada—something he claims he needs because of his height and bulkiness.

"So what's the plan?" I ask once I'm buckled in.

"Nicki's getting ready now so she can just go to the hotel with you." He maneuvers out of the parking deck and toward the exit. "You can borrow one of my cars, and you'll go check in, party it up, watch my girl so she doesn't get too wasted, and then tomorrow we'll have breakfast with Mom and Dad, the men will go golfing, and then we'll have the rehearsal dinner."

"Are you ready for all this?" I ask.

One side of his mouth lifts as he glances over at me. "I've been ready to marry that girl since the day I told her I had feelings for her. Maybe even before that."

"When does football start back up?" I ask after he's paid for his short term in the parking deck.

"I have to report back for training camp at the end of July," he says. He signals a lane change and then we're off toward his mansion. "So we've got the wedding, then a few days later we leave for three weeks in Fiji, and then a little over a month to enjoy married life."

"You liking it out here?" I'm partly asking as a way to check up on my brother, but I'm partly asking because I genuinely want to know if he likes it. If he's happy. If *I* will like it.

"I fucking love it, Ellie," he says, and then he begins this impassioned speech like I've never heard out of him. "The weather, the palm trees, the blackjack tables, the food, the entertainment. It's all incredible. Unbeatable. But most of all, I love the Aces. I loved playing for the Bears, too. They're our hometown team. But this new coaching staff at the Aces is incredible. They've managed to bring us together in a way where every single guy on the team is a brother to me. In fact, I don't know if I told you this, but one of the guys who has been on the team longer than me is my best man."

I raise a brow. As maid of honor, that'll be the guy escorting me. "So I'll be walking down the aisle with a football friend?"

He nods. "Not just a friend. My best friend. And, incidentally, the guy you'll be living with since you refuse to live with me. So be nice to him."

I laugh. "I'm always nice. Maybe you should tell him that, too."

"Oh, don't worry. He's been fully warned about you."

I narrow my eyes at my brother in a *what the hell is that supposed to mean* kind of way, but he just laughs.

He pulls into his four-car garage that's actually a six-car garage with the lifts he has in there. He's a car guy. I am not. "Which one do you want to borrow?"

I glance over at the collection. I'll be driving one of these cars down Las Vegas Boulevard, and that's more than a little daunting. "Which one's the least expensive in case I wreck it?"

He laughs. "Don't wreck it. The Mercedes is probably the closest to your style."

"Do you mean because of my little Camry?"

He lifts a shoulder. "I just mean a sedan. It's yours while you're here. Except seriously, Elle." He shortens my name by a syllable. "Don't wreck it."

We're both laughing as we walk into the house, through an expansive laundry room, and into the even more expansive kitchen that's something right out of an architectural magazine. Or a kitchen magazine. Some magazine. "This place is ridiculous," I mutter.

"You're here!" Nicki yells as she walks into the room. She looks like she just stepped off the pages of some other kind of magazine with her long, blonde hair cascading in perfect waves down her shoulders and a cute white romper that would look totally ridiculous on me.

"Oh my God, it's the bride!" I gush, and she giggles as she beelines for me and grabs me into a hug. "Happy wedding weekend."

She squeezes me tight. "Thank you. I'm so happy you're here. Now let's get to the hotel and get the party started."

I laugh, but we don't waste time. She already has her little overnight bag packed with make-up and hair supplies, the dress she's planning to wear is in a wardrobe bag, and she has another bag filled with liquor. "Ready?"

Josh puts everything in the Mercedes, including my suitcases, and then we're off for the Cosmopolitan. It's only a twenty-minute drive, but it's filled with excited chatter not just for the night ahead but the entire weekend.

I'm at the check-in desk and Nicki is at the clerk beside me checking in when my clerk says, "Okay, Miss Nolan, we have you in one of our wraparound terrace suites for three nights. Is that correct?"

"Well, yeah, the three nights thing is correct," I say, a little confused. "I'm checking out Sunday. But did you say a suite?"

"Yes, ma'am," the clerk replies. "The reservation here requests a suite."

Nicki elbows me. "Just take it. It's the least we could do for our maid of honor."

I narrow my eyes at her, and I'm about to put up a complaint when I stop. If they want to treat me to a suite, who am I to take that away from them? I nod. "Thank you," I murmur, and she smiles.

"We got the penthouse, so don't thank me until you make the comparisons."

I laugh, and then we're on our way to wait for our luggage and get ready for our night out. The penthouse is where she'll get ready for her wedding on Saturday, and it's also where she'll be spending the night for the next few nights—tonight after the bachelorette party, tomorrow after the rehearsal dinner, and Saturday after the wedding.

She comes with me to my room first, and after my suitcase arrives, I grab the dress I'm wearing tonight and we head up to her room, where we'll get ready for our night out.

And then the fun begins.

CHAPTER 4

I haven't had a strawberry daquiri since I was in high school, and I think I'm getting brain freeze.

It's preventing me from actually getting drunk, if I'm being totally honest. The frozen concoction is slowing the intake, but Nicki treated us all to those dumb yard drinks that are a pain in the ass to carry around. She's all classed up with a tiara that has penises hanging off it, and it's our job to do what she says tonight. She and I lead the pack as we walk through a mall to get to the restaurant she chose for dinner, and her six other bridesmaids trail along behind us.

Nicki worked in finance when she lived in Chicago, but when they made the move to Vegas, she started doing charity work with the wives of some of Josh's teammates. The bridal party is a mix of friends from Illinois and the friends she's made out here, and so far, everyone seems to be getting along well.

Thankfully the restaurant doesn't allow the yard drinks, so we all ditch them in a garbage can out front before we head in to eat. Since I started with rum in my daquiri, I order a mojito.

It goes down fast.

I order another.

Now I'm starting to feel it, that tipsy feeling where everything is funny and I don't feel sick just yet. I luxuriate there a while as we wait for our dinners, listening to the conversations around me. Some of the ladies are talking about what it's like being a football wife, giving Nicki advice about how to maintain her own identity and still support her husband. A woman named Leah says, "Yep, you need to lift your husband up or else you'll end up single and some woman half his age will swoop in on him."

"Oh my God, that reminds me! Ellie, tell the story of how you just ended up single," Nicki demands out of the blue.

My eyes edge over to her. "Uh...what?" I was actually sort of content just listening in on the other stories.

"Tell them what happened," she urges me, and I sigh.

"I lost my job and my boyfriend," I mutter. And then I look up at all the women whose eyes are fixed on me. I let out a laugh. "On the same day."

Once I laugh, it seems like that's the go-ahead for everyone else at the table, too, so I continue.

"It was just this past Tuesday!" I say, and okay maybe I'm a little more than *tipsy* because I start laughing so hard at that I have to actually wipe tears from my eyes.

At least they're tears of laughter. I haven't shed any *real* tears over Todd...though I do miss the sex. And my job.

"What happened?" Krista, one of the football wives, asks.

"Well, we were, you know, *getting busy* in his office and our boss walked in." I air quote *getting busy* and my face would probably be burning with embarrassment if I wasn't a few mojitos deep and this wasn't a bachelorette party where these sorts of stories are pretty run of the mill. I mean, for God's sake, Nicki's wearing a dick-shaped necklace that matches her tiara.

"She fired us both, and he blamed me and dumped me on the spot."

"Oh, Ellie, that's awful," Jen, a girl Nicki and I went to college with, says.

I lift a shoulder. "Eh, Todd was good in bed but I never really saw him as part of my forever story. For a while I thought maybe he was my Prince Charming, but he turned out to be just another frog."

"We need to get this girl laid tonight!" Nadine, another football wife, says.

I giggle and hold up a hand. "It's fine. I'm fine. Everything's fine."

Everyone at the table laughs, and then Nicki says, "Bridal mission one. Get the maid of honor laid. Hey, maybe we'll find someone for you at the Man Mansion we're heading to next."

"Yeah, hook me up with a male stripper," I say, my voice dripping with sarcasm. "Because what happens in Vegas stays in Vegas."

"Except STDs," Jen sings, and everyone laughs. Then she asks, "While we're on the topic, who here has had a one-night stand?"

"Oh wait!" Nicki says. "Before you answer, let's make it a game!" She glances around the table. "Okay, everyone has a drink. Let's play *I Never*. I will start, and if you've done it, you have to take a drink. We'll go around the table until our food gets here."

I haven't played a drinking game since...okay, since last weekend when Todd and I watched a movie and drank every time the main character said *fuck*, but still.

Nicki looks giddy, and it's such a stupid, immature game, but we're here for the bride. "I never had sex outdoors." She takes a sip of her drink, and I shoot her a look that says *gross* since I'm sure she's talking about her sex life with my brother.

I take a sip. I've had my fair share of outdoor sex. Everyone else at the table drinks, too.

"I'll go next," Jen says. "I never had sex in water."

Everyone drinks, and Nicki looks at Nadine next.

"I never had sex with a pro football player."

Nadine, Krista, Leah, and Nicki all drink, and the rest of us all look at them with a touch of jealousy. Maybe now that I'm here in Vegas, Josh can introduce me to some of his hot football friends and next time I play *I Never*, I can drink to that question.

"Ellie, you go," Nicki says.

"Okay, I never had a one-night stand," I admit, and I don't touch my glass.

Every other woman at the table takes a drink.

Including Nicki, who has been with my brother for the last seven years and who has been my best friend since high school...but I already knew about her one night. She was seventeen and a virgin, and it was the summer before we left for college. She wanted to get it over with, and she never talked to the guy again. She also has zero regrets about that.

"Seriously?" I yell. "I'm the *only* one who hasn't?"

The women all laugh, but it's Delia, one of Nicki's old work friends, who speaks up first. "Mine was on my twenty-first birthday and I just wanted to have some fun."

"Mine was after a work happy hour and it was really awkward when we ran into each other the next day at the office," Brianna, another former work friend of Nicki's, says.

Each woman tells her story. It was in a corner of a nightclub. It was a Tinder date. It was on a vacation. Some are happier with the outcome than the others.

"And after tonight, you'll be able to tell your story about your one night with a male stripper," Nicki says.

"Oh please," I mutter. "Like I'm going to bang a stripper. Maybe a hot guy at the club afterward, though..."

Our dinners arrive, and we barely even got the game off the ground.

But now that this one-night stand idea is in my head, I can't pretend like it doesn't sound like one hell of a good time.

After dinner, we head to the strip club, where we stick dollar bills in thongs, yell and scream uncontrollably, and drink some more.

I most definitely don't hook up with a stripper, though I can't deny some of them are *hot*. But the oil...there's a lot of oil. Like *a lot*. I think I'd just slide right off some of them.

Laughter is rampant as the eight of us pile into a car to head back to the hotel, where we'll go to the nightclub and dance before we officially call it a night. Nadine and Leah bow out as soon as we get back to the hotel, and Krista heads out with them since they're her ride.

But Jen, Delia, and Brianna are all here in town visiting from Chicago, and they're all staying at this hotel. They're here for a good time just like I am, and we're here to shower our bride to be with attention, drinks, and dancing.

We head into Marquee Nightclub, where the music pounds and drinks are quite a bit more expensive than the restaurant—but, according to Nicki who is now slurring, "It's all good because Josh is footing the bill."

And speaking of my brother, we've only been dancing for what seems like five minutes when he saunters up behind Nicki and laces his arms around her waist. He says something in her ear, and she giggles, and I look away because this might be my best friend, but it's also my *brother*. He must've ended his bachelor party at the same club as us, and clearly those two drunken lovebirds will shortly be heading up to the penthouse to use that suite to their advantage.

A second later, they're making out, and I just keep dancing with Jen, Delia, and Brianna, and then it's time to break the seal, so to speak.

Jen comes with me to the bathroom because of that unspoken rule that girls don't use the restroom alone, and as we're walking down the hallway back toward the dance floor, she asks, "Find anyone for that one-night stand yet?"

I hear some guy say, "I volunteer!"

I shoot Jen a look and the two of us laugh as we practically run back to our friends. When we get back, though, two of those friends are gone. Josh and Nicki must've headed up to their room, and Delia and Brianna seem to have found some boys to talk to.

I look at Jen. "Another drink? Or head up to bed?"

"Another drink," she says, and we head to the bar. We order and wait.

"Let's not forget the bride's orders that I'm the sole woman left with the mission to find you a guy to sleep with," she says. She's kind of drunk, and even with the loud music, she's still loud. I was pretty drunk at the strip club, but all the dancing has driven me back from drunk to tipsy.

"I'm gonna need another drink for that," I say.

"Did she really just say she wants to find you a guy to sleep with?" someone to my left asks.

I shiver. The voice is deep and husky and too close to my ear, tickling me and somehow turning me on at the same time. I should turn and slap the guy, but I don't.

Because I'm just tipsy enough that sleeping with a guy just to earn my one-night stand banner still sounds like fun.

And when my eyes meet his...

Holy. Shit.

This is most definitely my candidate.

CHAPTER 5

A ripple of desire travels all the way down my spine and back up again.

His eyes are a dark blue and hold an air of mystery. I don't know if I've ever found bone structure sexy before, but man, this guy's is one hundred percent perfect. He looks like he might be fake, maybe a sculpture or a painting—you can't be that hot and be *real*—but the little bit of scruff on his jaw makes him human again. He's got these lips that I want to drown in and this magnificent, short hair I want to run my fingers through and the actual physical attraction I have the moment I see him is a crazy tangible thing.

He wears a white t-shirt and jeans, and it's so simple yet so ridiculously hot. The shirt stretches across a broad chest with muscled biceps peeking out the sleeves.

I want those arms wrapped around my body. I want those lips on mine. I want to see the goods hidden beneath the shirt and jeans.

I can't help it when I sigh with lust and an ache pulses between my legs.

If ever there was a candidate for a one-night stand based solely on looks alone, I'd tag this guy in a heartbeat.

"Why?" I ask, somehow keeping my cool despite the fact that I'm talking to hands down the hottest guy I've ever seen in my life. And then I say something stupid. "You volunteering?"

My eyes widen after the words slip out. He laughs, and it's this musical sound that I want to hear again and again. I want to record it and make it my ringtone. Is that weird?

"No," he says, and I'm filled with disappointment.

Wait a second.

I'm filled with disappointment?

I don't even know this guy, and I'm disappointed that he's not volunteering to sleep with me tonight?

"Well, not yet, anyway," he clarifies. "I like to at least get to know a girl's name before I sleep with her. And maybe hit her with a bad pick-up line."

I laugh as the disappointment dissipates. And then I basically let him know I'm game for sex by telling him my name since that's one of his two prerequisites for sleeping with a stranger. "Ellie," I say.

"Nice to meet you, Ellie. I'm Luke."

"Go ahead and hit me with the bad line." I can't help the twinkle in my eye as I wait for it.

He grins. "Hey good lookin'. You come here often?"

I giggle. "That's pretty bad."

Hot Luke waves to the bartender when he sets the drinks in front of us to indicate that he'll treat.

"You don't have to do that," I say. I'm about to tell him my brother is rich and he's paying for my drinks, but I stop myself.

"I want to," he says.

"Why?" I ask.

He shrugs. "I don't know. I'm not usually the guy who buys random women drinks at nightclubs. I'm not even the guy who *goes* to nightclubs."

"And yet you're here," I point out. "And, for the record, I'm not the girl who accepts drinks from strangers. I'm not even from Vegas."

He laughs. "So what are you doing here?"

"You know, my entire life has turned upside down in the last few days, and I guess I'm turning over a new leaf."

Hot Luke lifts his glass to mine. "I'm working on some new leaves, too. Let's get drunk and see where the night takes us."

I clink my glass against his, and I spot a hint of sexy danger in his eyes. "Getting drunk with you probably isn't my smartest move."

I turn and look at Jen, who shrugs. "He's hot, Ellie. Go for it."

I laugh. "You're a big help."

She holds up both hands. "Hey, my mission is complete. Now it's up to you."

"What was her mission?" Hot Luke asks.

"I'll tell you, but only after we dance and drink and then find a quiet place to talk that isn't a hotel room so you can prove you're not a bad guy."

"Whoa," he says. "That's a lot of pressure. But I think I'm up to the task."

I laugh. "We'll see, Hot Luke."

"Hot Luke?" he asks.

I smile a little sheepishly. "Sorry. That's what I heard in my head when you said your name, and clearly that's how I will reference you when I talk about this night from now until the end of time."

He laughs, and his genuine smile makes him even hotter. "Okay, then, Sexy Ellie. Let's dance."

I glance at Jen, who gives me the *go on, shoo* signal, and I head with Hot Luke to the dance floor.

We start out a little awkwardly, but it only takes about the length of one song before we get comfortable with one another.

He moves in a little closer.

I fling an arm around his neck.

His fingers dig into my hip.

I grind on his leg.

We dance, and we talk, and we laugh, and we dance some more. We throw inhibitions out the window thanks to our drinks.

He's got moves.

"I read once that the way a person dances is the way they bone," he says after we get drink refills and we're heading back to dance some more.

"Bone?" I tease.

He laughs. "Yeah. What do you call it?"

"Bang."

"Okay, so the way a person dances is the way they *bang*. I'll forever use that word now instead of *bone*."

I giggle at the lasting impact I'll clearly have on Hot Luke. "Deal. And where are you going with this fun fact?"

"I took dance lessons."

I laugh. "Did you take sex lessons, too?"

He shakes his head and shoots me maybe the slyest smile anyone has ever shot anybody before. "Don't need lessons for that when you start out at expert level."

I'm getting closer and closer to the point where I'm ready to find out if that's true.

I'm hot, and I'm thirsty, and, above all else, I'm freaking *horny* for this guy. I know I met him literally a half hour ago, but let's call a spade a spade. I want a one-night stand, and it's not like those are all about finding some deep connection with another person.

It's about attraction, lust, and animal instincts, and all three are on-fucking-point for me at the moment.

We dance a few more songs when he nods toward the door. "Let's get out of here and find somewhere to get to know each other," he suggests, and I nod even though I don't know if he means get to know each other or *get to know each other*. Like, literally? Or, you know, in the carnal sense?

I follow him out of the club and through the hotel, and we end up near one of the hotel's three pools. One of the other pools here turns into a nightclub on the weekends, and that's the one Josh and Nicki reserved to hold their wedding the night after tomorrow.

He settles onto a lounge chair, stretching his long legs out in front of him, and I take a beat to really look at him. He's glowing blue from the pool lights, but he's still definitely the hottest guy I've ever seen in my life.

Why is he talking to *me*? He could have any girl in that place.

34

And then a dart of reality hits me. Right. My friend screamed about how she wanted to find a guy I could have sex with, and Hot Luke was the one who overheard. He thinks I'm a sure bet, and even though I'm still pretty tipsy, that thought leaves me a little hollow.

I haven't had a one-night stand before because sex means something important to me.

But just for tonight...maybe I need to let that go.

When else am I ever going to have the chance to sleep with someone who looks like Hot Luke?

The answer is *never.*

I force myself to get out of my own head and enjoy this time. I slide onto the chair next to Luke's and lean back.

Jeez, this chair is comfortable. It's padded and sturdy and I could freaking sleep out here.

It's quiet down here near the main pool, but Vegas is never *really* quiet. The bass from some speakers not too far away pounds, and I feel the beat in my chest. There aren't any people here, though, where the club was pulsing with the constant hum of bodies. Out here, it's just the two of us, and between the shadows moving with the water and the relative quiet, the setting provides an almost romantic tranquility.

"God, I hate nightclubs," he mutters as he rubs his temples, and I laugh.

"Why were you at one, then?"

He flashes me a grin, and butterflies start battering around in my stomach. "Because of fate." When I roll my eyes with a laugh, he admits, "I went for a buddy."

"I don't like them, either," I say, thanking God for the tipsiness that allows me to talk to someone who has a smile like that. "I'm more of a *grab a few drinks at a bar with friends* kind of girl. I guess I liked them more when I was younger."

"So why were you there?"

"I went for my best friend." I leave it at that instead of getting into the whole bachelorette party thing, which will get into the reason why I'm here, which will lead to the wedding and the fact that my brother plays professionally and it's all just details I don't want to share.

I want this stranger all to myself.

"Ah, something in common," he says, nodding sagely. "That's surely the way to prove I'm not a bad guy."

I laugh. "We're getting there. Are you single?" I ask it because I feel like you should know these details about your one-night conquest.

He spits out the fewest possible details. "I broke up with a long-term girlfriend a few months ago."

"Why?" I ask.

He sighs. "We were together a little over a year when she moved in. And then I realized there was no future for us."

My brows dip down. "Why?"

"She would put sugar in her coffee, stir the coffee, and then leave the used, wet spoon in the jar of sugar."

I laugh. "That's an interesting reason to dump somebody."

"There were little clumps of cold coffee sugar all the time. I even made a jar of sugar that was just for her. But that was sort of the tipping point where I started to notice everything else that made us completely incompatible, you know?"

I nod. "What else?"

He shrugs. "She didn't brush her teeth until bedtime some days. She was a mess in the bathroom, make-up and hair shit everywhere. Oh, plus she was manipulative as fuck."

"She sounds awful."

He chuckles. "Yeah, she pretty much was."

I glance over at him. "Are you over her?"

"Yeah. It had been over a long time. You know?" He shrugs. "My buddies tonight told me I need to get laid. I just guess I'm not ready to jump back into something after the mess my last relationship turned out to be." He's quiet for a beat, and then he says, "Your turn for the hot seat. Why are your friends trying to get you laid?"

"Apparently I'm the only one of them who hasn't had a one-night stand," I admit.

"I could definitely help you out there now that I know your name."

I giggle. "Oh, and I should probably also tell you, this past Tuesday, I was dumped and lost my job on the same day."

He sits up and swings his legs so he's facing me. He leans forward with his elbows on his knees and clasps his hands in front of him. "Now this is a story I want to hear." His eyes twinkle. They *glow* at me, actually, and I get a little lost in them for a beat.

I know this is only meant to last one night, but for just a second, I think there could be more with someone like him. I realize I'm not ready for all that after starting fresh in a new city, but my chest aches for a second as, the connection we seem to share plows into me.

I twist my lips and debate how honest to be, and then I go for it. Hell, everyone else knows the story by now. I may as well be honest with a stranger. "I seduced the guy I was seeing while we were in his office and our boss caught us."

"Oh God, that had to be awkward."

"It gets worse. I was just about to, you know..." I trail off, and he looks confused, so I spell it out even though my cheeks are burning with embarrassment. "Orgasm. I was about to orgasm when she walked in. And then he shifted when he heard the door, and it shot me over, and then I had an orgasm while my boss watched. And then she fired us both."

"At least tell me you had your clothes back on when she fired you." His voice holds just a hint of teasing, and I can't help my laugh.

"Yeah, I did. I was wearing a dress so I hadn't taken anything off. She gave us a minute to compose ourselves."

"Did he finish?" he asks, genuinely curious and invested in my story at this point.

I throw up both hands. "No! He didn't even want to!"

"That guy is fucking insane. He was banging a girl as hot as you in his office and he didn't even finish?"

I shrug nonchalantly but it doesn't escape my attention that he just called me *hot*.

Me.

Hot.

He thinks I'm hot.

That's right.

And he used my word.

"Good use of *bang*. And right?" I ask, somehow maintaining my cool as I let the word slide by. "So the boss comes back in, fires us both, leaves, and then he tells me something about how this isn't working for him."

"Ouch."

"It's fine," I say with the flip of a hand. "We'd only been casually dating a couple months. It's not like I was in love with him or anything."

"So you're over him, and I'm over my ex, and we're just two single people sitting by the pool and dancing around the fact that we want each other just for tonight while I try to prove to you that I'm not a bad guy."

I smirk. "I think you've proved it. You didn't even try to kiss me in the club, not even when I was practically humping your leg." Yeah, alcohol tends to make my filter disappear. I'd *never* say that to someone if I was totally sober. Particularly not to someone as gorgeous as this guy. I wouldn't have given him all those details about Todd if I was sober, either.

I mean, *probably* not, anyway. My brain to mouth filter has been known to malfunction upon (frequent) occasion.

We're quiet for a beat, and then he says in a voice so husky it's dripping with sex, "Oh, Sexy Ellie. I wanted to. I was just trying to prove I'm a good guy."

My chest swells and the ache between my thighs pulses.

"I wanted you to." My voice is low and it's a clear invitation.

He unclasps his hands and stands, and then he moves with caution toward my chair. I look up at him, and maybe he should look dangerous out here since he's a total stranger, but he doesn't. There's something intrinsic between the two of us that makes me trust him. I feel it deep in my bones. He's *not* a bad guy, and I want this. He wants this. We're two consenting adults.

I'm still stretched out on my chair, and he reaches down with both hands. I set my hands in his, and he pulls me up to standing.

Then he sits, and he pulls me back down so I'm straddling his lap. All memories of straddling Todd in a desk chair are easily replaced with this, the new memory I'll have of the hottest moment I ever straddled someone. He looks up at me, and I look down at him, and it isn't just the Vegas heat that's passing between us.

The sexual tension drips thickly all around us, too thick to cut with a knife. It's this palpable thing I can feel, and then he reaches a hand under my hair as he cups my neck with his big palm.

His eyes are still hot on mine, and I read all the lust that surely he must see reflected back at him. And then he pulls my neck down until our lips touch.

I move both hands to his jaw, at once out of passion and to hold his face and feel the roughness and remind myself that this moment is really happening.

His lips are firm and tender at the same time, and when he opens his mouth and his tongue brushes against mine, I lose all sense. From out of nowhere comes this sudden feeling like I need this kiss in order to breathe, like if it stops so will my oxygen.

His hand remains on my neck, big and warm, and his other holds me at my waist. His fingers dig into me there, like he wants to feel my skin but my dress is in the way—like he's trying to rein in the passion but he just can't.

His body is warm and hard beneath mine, and all this kiss is serving to do is make me want this one night with him more than anything in the world.

I shift my hips down, and he shifts his toward me, too.

He wants this. He wants *me*.

The brush of his tongue turns into something hotter and more intense, and even though it's just a kiss on a patio by a pool, it feels like so damn much more. It's melting me into a puddle of lust for this man, and the way he's kissing me back tells me he feels it, too.

I finally pull apart from his mouth. Our eyes meet, and his are hooded with lust.

God do I want him.

"Come up to my room with me," I murmur, mostly because it would be indecent to do the things with him that I want to do right here on this pool lounge chair even though it's deserted out here.

His lips are swollen as he nips another kiss to my mouth, and then he pulls back with a lazy smile. "Let's go."

CHAPTER 6

As soon as the elevator doors seal us into privacy, he backs me up into the wall with his hips. He pins me there and kisses me like he's starved, like he can't wait until we get to my room. He drives his hips toward me, and I can't wait, either.

Lust presses thrills all the way through me, starting at the tips of my toes and exploding, fuzzing my brain and muddying my senses. I hold onto his arms not because I'm caught in the moment of lust but because I *need* to. I need him to hold me up and balance me, because just his kiss is enough to bring me to my knees.

If he bangs anything like he kisses, well, I'm in for a real treat.

His fingers start trailing up my torso. They stop short of my breast, and my nipple tightens with need.

We practically jog down the hall once the elevator doors open, and of course since it's a wraparound terrace suite, it's at the far end of the hallway.

"Nice place," he says once I let us into my room, and then he kicks the door shut behind him.

A brief beat of awkwardness falls between us.

We're here in my room now, and it's time for the sex, and...shit. I don't have any condoms.

"Uh," I start. "I just realized that I don't have any condoms."

He chuckles, and then he reaches into his pocket and produces a handful.

My eyes widen, and I press my lips together and tilt my head as I try to think through the best response to the fact that the stranger I just invited to my hotel room to sleep with has a pocketful of condoms.

"I don't typically carry this many around," he protests before I even get a chance to say anything. "My buddies wanted me to get laid tonight and they kept throwing them at me during dinner. Jokes on them, though, since I actually need one."

I raise a brow and lift a shoulder. "Maybe two."

He grins, and it's that smile that absolutely kills me.

"So how does this work?" I ask stupidly. I want him to kiss me again, but I don't know him well enough to read his signals.

His brows dip down. He shoves the condoms back in his pocket, and then he makes a circle with a finger and a thumb on one hand and pokes a finger from his other hand through it. "Insert tab A into slot B."

I laugh and rest my hands on my hips.

"Do you really not know how it works?" he asks, his brows drawn together in confusion. "Weren't you fired *while* you were having sex?"

"I know how *sex* works," I say with a touch of exasperation. "I just don't know how one-night stands work."

"Pretty much the same as regular sex, I think."

"Have you had one before?" I ask.

He lifts a shoulder and has the grace to look a little sheepish. "Yeah."

"All right, then. Get over here and pop my one-night stand cherry."

He doesn't waste any time before he pounces. He practically rips my dress over my head and sends it flying in one direction, and I kick off my heels then reach for the bottom of his shirt.

I'm a little slower. A little more nuanced.

And it's like unwrapping the sexiest present I've ever received.

As I pull his shirt up, I reveal muscle after muscle after muscle and then a solid, expansive chest. I toss his shirt on the ground and stare at his physique. It's muscled. It's ridged. It's hard. It's glorious.

I may drool a little.

My eyes flick up to his, and he's watching me carefully. "I, uh, work out a lot."

I laugh. "It would appear so." I run a hand up and down my torso sort of like I'm one of those models on *The Price is Right* and I'm showing off the merchandise. "I do not."

His eyes flick to my chest, over my stomach, and to my panties. "You're gorgeous," he murmurs, and then he takes a step toward me, and another, and then he reaches for me and pulls me against him. His skin is smooth and warm as he crushes my body to his, and then his mouth crashes back down to mine. He flicks the snap on my bra and it falls open in the back. He runs his fingertips up my spine until they tangle up into my hair, and my chest lights with anticipation.

He moves back and I shimmy out of my bra, and then he slides my panties down my legs. He moves slowly, and he runs his tongue along the inside of my thigh as he does it.

I shiver.

He pushes me back until my knees hit the bed, and I sit. He kneels between my legs and looks up at me for a beat, like he's checking whether it's okay to do as he pleases with me, and I offer a small smile through the lust. Looking down into his eyes when he's like this—his body lean and powerful, his eyes heavy—causes need to pulse through me. The ache between my legs grows nearly unbearable.

And then he dives in face-first. I grip the comforter with both hands as he licks his way through me, dipping his tongue inside before flattening it over my clit, and holy shit it feels so damn good. Pleasure courses through me as one carnal thought that I need this man inside me plagues my mind.

I mutter incoherent words of encouragement as my moans of pleasure fill the silence in the room. He adds a finger to what he's doing, and I grip onto his hair, that thick, luscious hair that I've wanted to touch since I first saw him. It's like his tongue was made to pleasure my body. The coil springs loose and I see a million fireworks and stars as I squeeze my eyes shut and my body flies into an intense, mind-blowing climax.

When it starts to slow and I realize I'm pulling on his hair, I let go. "Sorry," I murmur as I collapse back, my eyes closed as I try to recover from the high.

He laughs as I pant. I open one eye and see him still kneeling between my legs. He wipes his mouth with the back of his hand, and why the hell is that so damn sexy? Maybe because the back of his hand will smell like me now, like in some way I've marked my sex territory.

But he's not my territory—at least not beyond tonight. And that thought is somehow very freeing after everything that happened this week.

I want Hot Luke to slam into me from behind while I claw at the window. I want to do whatever he wants me to do so I can please him the way he just pleased me.

He's already made me come once, and he's still wearing his jeans.

That's just not okay.

So I sit up and tug his arms with the signal that he should stand. I'm eye-level with his stomach, and I lean forward and kiss that gorgeously ridged abdomen of his. Then I trail kisses down toward his jeans. I unbuckle his belt and pop the button. Before I reach in and see the goods, I rub my hand along the outside of his pants.

My heart races when I feel the thick steel hidden in there.

He doesn't make a sound, but when I glance up at him, his neck is corded and his head is tipped back as he relishes the feel of a woman touching him.

I lower his zipper and then I reach in. He groans as I pull him out, and then just like he dove face first into pleasuring me, I lick my way down his long shaft before I take him all the way to the back of my throat.

I pull back and then suck him back in, and his fingers tangle in my hair. When I repeat the motion again, this time he holds my head in place for a beat. A guttural growl rises out of his chest, and then he lets my head go.

Holy shit.

That was hot.

I lick up and down his shaft, and then he reaches under my arms and pulls me to standing.

We're eye to eye when he says, "If you keep doing that, I'm gonna lose it. If I lose it now, I won't get to fuck you."

His eyes are heated, and he leans forward to kiss me before he lets me go. He kicks off his shoes and pulls his jeans and boxers off, and I take in his fully naked body for a beat.

It's perfect.

Gorgeous.

Stunning.

Something from a dream.

And it's the first time I feel like it's too damn bad this is just one night. But that's all it is. Sex with a stranger. My one-night stand with the hottest guy I've ever seen in my life.

The girls will be so proud of me tomorrow when I get the chance to brag about my conquest.

We're definitely on the same page because after he rolls on one of the thirty condoms he pulled out of his pocket, he walks me over to the window. "Bend forward and use the glass to brace yourself," he says, his voice husky.

I do what he says, and I feel him close behind me. He swipes his dick through my slit before he shoves himself inside me. My body expands and adjusts to his size, and I don't know if I've ever felt so full...or so horny.

I claw at the glass as he starts moving. My hotel room is on a pretty high floor, but I see traffic as it's jammed on a Thursday night down on the Strip. People move about their night like everything's normal while I'm getting fucked from behind in a hotel room by a stranger.

I groan when he hits a particularly hot rhythm with me. When I glance up, I see his eyes hot on mine in the reflection of the glass.

The very best part of doing it like this is seeing his face as he does what he's doing to me from behind.

He holds my gaze, grunts and groans filling the room as I listen to the sounds of sex and his body slapping against mine.

Between the sounds and his eyes and the heat between us as he pleasures me in a way no man has ever managed to before, I feel the start of another orgasm edging its way toward me. I squeeze my eyes shut.

"Open your eyes," he demands, and I do.

He leans forward, his eyes on mine the whole time, and he reaches around to brush my clit with his fingertips.

And that's when I lose it completely.

I thrash around as I come, my body squeezing him inside as it contracts and pulses all around him, but I keep my eyes on him the whole time. His hot face screws up as he watches me, and then he picks up the pace, shoving hard into me with little growls that tell me he's right there with me.

He mutters a curse as he comes, and when his body starts to relax, he pulls out of me. My body immediately misses his, and even though he's already satisfied the ache twice, I feel it pulsing again. I want him again. I want *more*.

He helps me straighten to a stand, and we both pant for a beat before he sweeps me literally off my feet and into his arms. He kisses me as he carries me over to the bed, and it would potentially be the most romantic moment of my life if this was more than just a one-night thing.

He gets rid of the condom then collapses beside me as we attempt to recover from what was definitely the hottest few moments of my life.

I catch my breath and take a beat to breathe him in. I memorize the scent—it's fresh and clean and manly all at once, and I want to breathe it in forever.

I break the silence once I catch my breath. "Well that was..." I trail off as I try to find the right word. I fail.

"Hot," he finishes.

"Yeah. Hot."

He laughs, and he leans over and kisses the top of my head, and I giggle, and it feels like so much more of a *boyfriend* move than what this is.

I want to do it again, but the alcohol and the physical activity from tonight catch up with me. I'm about to drift into sleep when he mutters, "Shit. I have to go."

My eyes pop open, and a dart of sadness pulses through me. I push it away. "So soon?" I was hoping for another round or two before morning. I try not to think that it's *me* that's the reason why he's darting out so quickly.

He presses his lips together and nods as he clicks off his phone. I hadn't even realized he was looking at it since my eyes were closed. "I'm sorry. I have some stuff I need to take care of and an early morning."

He's clearly giving an excuse to get the hell out after we banged, and that's fine. We were both aware of the stakes going into it even though a huge part of me is disappointed and really, really wishes we could exchange numbers or at least Instagram handles, but that's not what this is supposed to be about.

We were destined to meet for one hot night, and now we've had it.

And that's that on that.

He gathers his clothes and I find a t-shirt and shorts to toss on while he dresses. And then with a heavy heart that makes me realize I'm just not cut out for these one-night deals, I walk him to the door, grabbing my phone on the way by. He kisses me once more at the door, and I swear my toes curl and my heart melts.

I snap a quick selfie of us before he can protest because obviously I need proof for the ladies that I spent the night with the hottest guy I've ever seen in my life—not at all because I want it for spank bank material.

Okay, maybe a little because I want it for spank bank material.

God, I could stare into those eyes for-damn-ever.

He presses his lips together in a sad smile. "Bye, Sexy Ellie. Thanks for the best one-night stand ever."

I brave a smile back. "Bye Hot Luke. Thanks for breaking my one-night stand cherry with the hottest sex of my life."

His sad smile widens to a grin, and then he opens the door and walks out of my life.

CHAPTER 7

"Why the hell would they do breakfast so damn early the morning after the bachelorette party?" I grumble to myself as I try to scrub away the gross feeling that seems to coat me from head to toe.

It's a little after eight, and Hot Luke left my room last night a little after two. My parents got into town on an early flight and headed right to Josh's place to make us all brunch, which is a lovely idea even though the timing sucks.

But we had to do it early-ish because Josh has a tee time with my dad and some of his groomsmen at eleven.

I slept like shit last night.

I don't think the gross feeling comes from my night with Luke, though maybe it should. I feel gross from the strip club, like maybe some oil dripped on me and I can't quite scrub it away. Or maybe it *is* Luke I feel gross over.

I don't really know how I'm supposed to feel the morning after a single night with a guy that was only about sex. But now I have the badge of honor, and I'll wear it proudly as I show off the selfie I've already stared at a billion times.

God, we're cute together.

My heart ripples every time I open my photos and see his gorgeous smile.

My chest tightens as I touch his face on the screen and recall the feel of the stubble lining his jaw as it scratched along my leg.

I had sex with that guy.

And I won't get to have it again.

That's the cost of the one-night thing, and I realize this morning that I'm not really cut out for that lifestyle. I want more. I want to see him again. I want to kiss him some more. I want to have sex with him again.

But I can't because all I really know about him is that his name is Hot Luke and he bangs like a sexpert.

And he busted out of there so fast after we banged that clearly he wasn't interested in anything else. To be fair, those were the parameters set forth when we met...but it still feels a little icky. He seemed like a good guy, but then he just ran out, and I don't really know how to feel about that other than a little sad.

I do my best to brush those feelings away. It was what it was, and it's over now.

After I try to scrub away all the feelings and fail, I get out of the shower. I have a missed text from Nicki.

Nicki: *I'm heading home with Josh this morning. Your parents are already there cooking. Meet us there when you get up. Thanks for the best night last night! Oh and bring me something if you stop at the Bux.*

I laugh. She knows I'll stop at Starbucks on my way—especially after a night like last night. I need the caffeine that fuels me in a way regular, homemade coffee just doesn't.

I search the area for a Starbucks on my app and find one close to my brother's house, and then I gather my wet hair in a ponytail, toss on a baseball cap since Nicki has hired in a team to get us ready for the rehearsal tonight, and head for valet to pick up my brother's car.

The Starbucks is only about fifteen minutes from the hotel, and Friday morning traffic in Vegas is relatively light. I'm battling a slight hangover and my body is still a little warm from what Luke did to it.

I sit in my car in the parking lot and place a mobile order on my app. I don't get my favorite nonfat white chocolate mocha with extra whip. I opt instead for one of the most caffeinated beverages on the menu—a nitro cold brew, which, according to my favorite barista back home, isn't the top most caffeinated drink on the menu, but the caffeine hits you quicker because of a little bit of carbonation. I punch in Nicki's favorite drink, a skinny latte, and I order a little something for Josh and my parents, too.

I stare at the picture of Hot Luke one more time for good measure, set it as my wallpaper because I'm totally going to play a joke on Nicki and tell her the guy is my new boyfriend, and then I get out of my car and head inside to pick up my drinks.

They aren't ready yet.

I stand by the counter to wait, and I slip my phone out of my pocket. I'm scrolling Instagram mindlessly, wondering if I should put up the picture of me with Hot Luke when I know I won't, when I hear a voice behind me.

A bragging voice.

At least it's low, but not low enough that I don't hear every word of his conversation. I'm the only one in hearing distance, and I probably look occupied as I scroll my phone.

"Oh, yeah, I banged her real good."

My brows dip down. What kind of asshole brags at the Starbucks mobile pickup area about the girl he had sex with last night?

"I spent all night screwing her brains out up against the window, and then I bolted."

His voice is still low, but I still hear it.

Up against the window?

My brains were screwed out up against a window last night.

And that voice...

It's low, but it's still deep and husky.

It's familiar.

But it can't be.

The heat of an arm brushes mine as someone beside me grabs a drink from the mobile pick-up area. I finally glance up from my phone.

The drink is labeled simply *Luke*.

Not *Hot Luke*, but when I look over and my eyes meet his, it's definitely Hot Luke.

He glances over at me like I'm in his way—or maybe it's to apologize for getting in *my* way—as he turns to leave, and when his eyes lock with mine, even beneath my baseball cap, I spot immediate recognition in his eyes.

And some regret...probably for the words he just said.

"I'll call you back." He hangs up his phone and slides it into his pocket, his wide, very confused eyes never leaving mine.

"Were you just *bragging* about last night?" I accuse at the same time he says, "What are you doing here?"

I don't have the energy to even answer him, so I set my hands on my hips and wait for his defense.

"I know that's how it sounded, but I swear to God, I'm not an asshole. He's just been badgering me to get laid, and I *know* I told you that last night, and he asked me if I hooked up, and I may have exaggerated a little for his benefit. Give me your number. I'll make it up to you, I promise."

He's rambling, and it would be cute if I didn't feel so...grossed out by his conversation.

I feel like I was a conquest that he could use to brag to his friends.

Granted, that's exactly what it was for me, too, so maybe I don't have a reason to be angry—especially since I was about to run to Nicki and tell her all about my night with a stranger...but somehow this taints what happened between us. I wasn't about to brag every detail about my hands clawing the glass while he gave me the hottest orgasm of my life, but clearly he didn't leave the room with those same secrets.

"Order up for Ellie," the barista says, and she pushes a tray with four drinks plus another drink on the side across the counter.

I hold up a hand to Luke. "I'm good. Last night was..." I trail off.

"Hot?" he asks a little hopefully, repeating the same word he used just after we had sex.

I shake my head. "It was one night, and that's all." I pick up my five coffees. "One perfect night that I refuse to let you taint this morning. We weren't supposed to run into each other again, so I'm just going to pretend we didn't."

With those as my parting words, I spin on my heel and practically run out the door.

And just as I move in front of it to try to open it with one finger since my hands are full, someone on the other side pushes it open and right into me.

All five coffees tumble down to the ground.

I draw in a deep breath as I ward off the tears.

So *that* is how today's gonna go. Got it.

Hot Luke rushes over in some attempt to help me, but it's futile. The girl behind the counter yells, "Remake mobile order for Ellie!"

One of the workers rushes over with a mop and some paper towels from the back, and Luke picks up the five cups, and I stand there apologizing over and over and over as I blot at my shirt that will definitely smell like coffee for the rest of time.

Luke's eyes meet mine once the mess is cleaned. I press my lips together.

"You sure we can't at least exchange numbers?" he asks...*pleads*.

I shake my head. "Bye, Luke," I say, and then I turn toward the pick-up counter to wait for my remake.

Maybe he stares after me, or maybe not. I don't turn around to check as I sigh again. I can't deny that I felt a lot of things when I saw him. I can't help but wonder why he was at the same Starbucks as me at the same time. Serendipity, maybe? Fate? Or just a coincidence?

Whatever the case, he's gone when I finally do turn around. As I exit the store and carefully slide the drinks onto my passenger seat, I can't help but wonder what fate has in store and whether we'll run into each other again.

CHAPTER 8

I force myself to forget about Hot Luke and our Starbucks encounter as I pull into the driveway, and then I text Nicki to let her know I'm here since I won't have a free hand to ring the bell. I grab the five drinks and walk them up to the massive, imposing front door.

Nicki throws it open, and I go into immediate *Woo Girl* mode even though my heart most definitely isn't in it today. "Ahh! You're getting married tomorrow!"

You'd never guess she was drunk as hell last night based on her screaming reply: "Woo!"

I giggle, and she helps me with the drinks before I drop them *again*—probably since she knows that's totally my style.

"And how did your night end up?" she asks as she leads me into the house.

I giggle, and then I whisper (because my parents are two rooms away), "I did it."

Her head whips in my direction, and her eyes are wide. "You did what?"

"*It*," I whisper yell. "You know. A one-night stand."

"Oh my God!" she practically screams, and my parents are *definitely* going to want to know what that's all about. I motion with my hand that she really needs to take it down a notch, and she starts whisper yelling too. "With who? Holy shit, I'm so proud of you! What happened? How did you meet him? Did you exchange numbers?"

"I'll give you every detail later," I say as we walk through the house. I lower my voice to a whisper. "He was some random guy

I met at the club. He was tall and had all these muscles and, ugh, he was just the hottest guy I think I've ever seen in my life. It was hot. No numbers, just one night." And then we're nearing the kitchen and I give her a look that clearly means we'll talk about it later because there's my dad, and hell if I'm going to brag about my one-night stand in front of my *dad.*

"There she is!" he says, and he steps over to wrap me in a hug while Nicki sets down the drinks. My mom is right behind him.

"Oh, honey, your eyes are all puffy," she says, and I roll those eyes for her benefit. "Did you drink a lot last night?"

No, mom, I got my brains screwed out up against a window and I was up kinda late after flying in yesterday and attending a bachelorette party. "Yeah," I say instead, which really isn't a lie.

She tuts disapprovingly. "Brunch is almost ready," she says, and she heads back to the stove to stir some scrambled eggs.

Can we really call it *brunch* when it's not even nine o'clock yet? Isn't that still in the breakfast zone? I guess it's almost eleven Chicago time, so I let it slide without saying anything—something I tend to do a lot around my mother.

We sit down to bacon, sausage, pancakes, and my mom's famous scrambled eggs, chatting about the wedding and today's activities. Josh and my dad leave for the golf course, and a short while later, the rest of the bridesmaids start to show up as well as Nicki's mom. Then a team of nail techs rings the bell and gets to work on us.

We're pampered with manicures and pedicures, with stylists who do our hair and make-up, and with racks of dresses to choose from.

By the time the boys get back from golf and take their showers, it's just about time to head back to the Cosmopolitan for the rehearsal.

I drive my brother's car back, valet it, and stop at my room to drop off my purse. I take a beat to look out the windows at the view. I spot a handprint on the window.

My handprint.

The terrace wraparound suite is just how it sounds. It's a corner room, and windows literally wrap around the entire suite, giving me a beautiful view of the Strip. I remember looking down over that view last night when Hot Luke was pounding into me, and a well of regret rises over me.

We could've exchanged numbers. Last names. Career details.

Okay, maybe not career details since at the moment I don't actually have one, but anything that would help identify the other.

I wish I could really pretend I never overheard his conversation at Starbucks this morning like I told him I would...but I can't. It replays in my mind, an endless loop where I wish I could see him again followed by rising anger that he spoke about me the way he did.

That he wrote me off so easily.

But I know he's been to that Starbucks at least once, so maybe when this weekend is all over, I'll go hang out there for a bit on the off chance I might run into him again. I sigh, and then I brush it off. I have to, because it's time to head toward the pool for the rehearsal.

A different pool than the one I sat near last night when Luke first kissed me, thank God.

I step on the elevator car, the same one I was in last night when I made out with Luke—back when there was the promise of sex in the air but we hadn't done anything more than some intense kissing.

I'm not alone, so I stare up at the digital numbers as they change with each passing floor as one does in crowded elevators.

I get off on the fourteenth floor and head toward the Chelsea Pool. I spot our small group standing near the entrance, and some of the groomsmen have joined us. I check them out from a distance as I approach. Tall, lean men with tight butts in suits. Mostly football players. Scratch that...mostly *hot* football players.

I wipe the corner of my mouth in case a little drool escaped as my eyes zero in on one with a particularly cute butt.

I don't know any of Josh's groomsmen. They're all his teammates on the Aces and I didn't meet any of them the one weekend I visited Nicki and Josh, but as he's told me over and over, they're like brothers to him after only a year of playing here. He's talking to the small group of them, and after my one-night stand last night, I'm feeling a little overdose of confidence. It's not that I think I'm going to hook up with any of my brother's friends—not that I'm not opposed to the idea—but I have a little swagger to my walk just in knowing that someone as hot as Hot Luke wanted to spend some time in my bed.

Obviously that was purely about physical attraction.

Clearly he's an asshole who touts his conquests in public.

I shake it off and my confidence takes a little tumble as I trip when my heel stubs the sidewalk all at the same time. I don't fall, thankfully, but I do realize how much I have to let last night and subsequently also this morning go. I need to focus because when I don't, well, I trip and I drop coffees and it's usually a disaster.

"There she is," Josh says, looking over the shoulder of the super cute butt guy he's talking to. "My sister, the maid of honor," he announces, and he takes a step toward me to introduce me to the groomsmen.

The guy with the super cute butt turns around as Josh passes by on his way toward me.

My eyes flick from my brother to the guy in the suit.

No.

My eyes widen.

My heart stops.

It can't be.

My stomach twists.

It's just not possible.

My knees nearly give out on me.

"Ellie, this is my best man, Luke Dalton," Josh says.

Oh shit.

"Oh, and, by the way, he's the one who lives across the street from Nicki and me. He can't wait to have my little sister as his houseguest."

58

I swear to God, I'm the physical embodiment of the facepalm emoji.

You have got to be freaking kidding me.

CHAPTER 9

"Honey, you look pale. Do you feel all right?" my mom asks, walking over and pinching my cheeks to give me some color like she's done ever since I was a little girl.

Uh, no Mother, I actually *don't* feel all right. The guy who screwed my brains out against a window last night and was supposed to disappear without a trace is apparently not just my brother's best friend, but also in some crazy twist of fate...he's my new roommate.

I draw in a deep breath as I try to reconcile this new information. "I'm fine," I murmur, and Luke is definitely smirking and I want to slap that smirk right off his damn sexy face.

"Nice to meet you," I say to Luke, and I stick out my hand to shake his. His eyes find mine as he takes my hand. His grip is warm and firm. Just like other parts of him.

Of course Hot Luke is my brother's best man. Of-freaking-course he is. This is my life, so it just couldn't have happened any other way.

"You too," Luke says, playing the part just like I am. "Like your brother said, I'm happy to have you stay with me. Any little sister of Josh's is a little sister of mine." His words are thick.

He bangs my brother on the back, and some lightbulb clicks on in my brain. That's why he was at that club last night. My brother was there, too. I bet all the groomsmen were, but I didn't know any of them. I watch the games, but who the hell knows who's who under those helmets and when half of them are wearing those black stripes under their eyes?

Okay, fine.

I have the games *on*.

I don't really *watch* them.

I cheer when everybody else does. I boo when I hear others booing. But mostly I get work done on my phone while I pretend like I'm paying attention.

That's why I had no idea who Luke Dalton was when I bumped into him at the bar.

If I thought he was hot in jeans and a white t-shirt last night, well, he looks ridiculously re-fuckable in the suit today. And tomorrow in a tux? Forget about it.

Game over.

I don't know how the hell I'm going to survive this wedding weekend without giving in again.

And why shouldn't I give in again?

It was supposed to just be one night, but what if we were destined for more than that?

Oh God.

A horrible thought plagues me, and all the color drains from my face again.

When he was bragging on the phone...was he talking to *my brother*?

I feel like I might be sick.

"Now that everyone's here, allow me to introduce myself," some lady in a pantsuit says. "I'm Stella Porter." She pauses for dramatic effect like everyone should recognize the name. "I'm Nicole and Joshua's event coordinator, and tonight we're going to run through tomorrow's festivities."

Is *event coordinator* a fancy phrase for *wedding planner*?

I almost ask that question out loud, but I manage to stop myself.

"I need the bride and groom," she demands, and Nicki and Josh move to her side. "Nicole, you and your father will walk down the aisle. You can stand over there until we're ready for you. The bridal party?" she asks, and then she arranges us in order.

Jen is in front of me with another of Josh's football friends, and the rest of the bridal party is lined up in front of them.

Josh walks first up toward the place where an altar will be set up tomorrow.

The wedding isn't set up yet since hotel guests will be using the pool most of the day tomorrow, but I can imagine how gorgeous the whole effect will be with the shimmering water bouncing shadows off the buildings surrounding us.

Like something out of a bridal magazine, a platform will jut out over the pool, and that's where the bride, groom, and officiant will stand. The rest of us will stand on stairs, each one of us one level down from each other. After the ceremony, the platform will be transformed into the head table, which means the entire bridal party will sit over the water looking out over the tables filled with guests.

It's beautiful, but something tells me water and bridal gowns don't really mix. Or bridesmaids' gowns.

Stella cues the next couple when it's time to walk, and I feel like I have some things to say to Luke, but Jen is right in front of me and the last thing I want to do is fuel gossip at my brother's wedding.

So instead, I focus on the scenery. It's technically considered a rooftop wedding since it's on the top of the building where it's located, but it's the fourteenth level of the hotel, so towers stand tall all around us.

It's a perfect Vegas evening as the palm trees around the pool area sway with a gentle breeze. The heat of the day is setting with the sun, and the wedding will take place around this same time tomorrow night. It'll be perfect.

Each of the couples makes their way slowly down the aisle, and soon Jen and her escort head off.

That leaves Luke and me semi-alone.

"Your brother can't know," he murmurs to me as Jen and her guy slow their pace at Stella's command.

"Nobody can," I whisper-yell.

"Elbow out, Best Man, and Maid of Honor, arm through his. GO!" Stella yells even though she's not that far away from us. I wonder how much Josh and Nicki are paying this broad. Clearly they went for the cheaper package since she didn't even bother to learn our names.

Luke juts his elbow out, brushing my rib cage in the process. A dart of need pulses through me.

I shoot him a glare, and he holds in a laugh as I slide my arm through his.

I both love and hate being this close to him again.

I want him.

God, do I want him.

"No, I mean he *really* can't find out. He warned us all off when he invited you to move out here, and he specifically said he trusts me to take care of you the same way he would." He's whisper-yelling, too.

I glance over at him, and his eyes are focused forward. "You're supposed to be like an older brother to me?"

He glances at me, too, and there's a certain heat that passes between us. He's about to respond when Stella screeches at us. "Eyes forward!"

I turn toward the altar to appease her. This must be the longest damn aisle in the history of aisles.

He exhales. "Ellie, last night was..." he trails off, and I wish he wasn't whispering so I could hear his tone. "Hot," he finishes. "But it can't go beyond last night. You're my best friend's little sister, so that makes you off-limits."

Off-limits?

He just made it even hotter. Now it's forbidden. Now I definitely want it again.

I sigh. "I suppose it was him you were bragging to this morning?"

"Who else would it have been?" he asks wearily. "And I wasn't bragging."

"Like hell you weren't!" I exclaim the best I can in a whisper.

"Less talking!" Stella yells at us, and then we're nearing the altar and we're forced to let go of each other to move our separate ways.

But that conversation sure doesn't feel like it's over.

"What's going on with you two?" Jen whispers to me once I take my place next to her.

"With who?" I whisper back, playing dumb.

She rolls her eyes. "Isn't that the guy from the club you were dancing with?"

Oh shit.

In my little plan to keep this a secret, I totally forgot that Jen was there, too, and that she may have been lucid enough to remember the hot guy we met by the bar.

I blow out a breath. "I don't want anything to distract from Nicki's weekend," I say.

Her eyes get super round and her jaw falls open. "So something *did* happen."

"Ladies, quiet!" Stella yells at us, and Nicki shoots me a look like *come on, dude, just help me get through this.*

"We'll talk later," I say, hoping it's enough to brush her grilling off forever but knowing it definitely isn't.

When we're done with the actual rehearsal for tomorrow, we're ushered toward a restaurant where a whole section is dedicated to our little party.

And, of course, just like tomorrow night, Nicki and Josh sit in the middle of the table, and the rest of the bridal party sits in order on either side of them. That means the bride and groom separate Luke and me when I feel like I have a lot more to say to him, and Jen is on my right currently waiting for me to tell her what happened last night.

"You can't tell anyone," I say softly once I see Nicki and Josh talking to Stella. Jen's eyes go round again.

"Okay, but before you say anything at all, isn't this so exciting and totally cliché? The maid of honor and the best man are, like, *supposed* to hook up, aren't they? Isn't it some unwritten rule?"

I stare at her like she's stupid. "No! What if the maid of honor is married?"

"Then she'd be the *matron* of honor, and no such rule exists to my knowledge."

I roll my eyes. "Okay, fine. What if the best man is married?" She thinks for a minute. "Affair." She cracks up like it's the funniest joke ever, but cheating isn't really all that funny to me.

"We did the one-night thing. I had no idea he was Josh's best man. And neither of us wants anyone to know, so keep your trap shut."

She looks offended as her hand flies to her chest. "I won't tell anybody!"

"Tell anybody what?" Nicki asks, looking at the two of us.

I'm positive I look guilty, and Jen has never been much of a liar.

"About your present!" Jen says almost gleefully, and thank the Lord, Nicki buys it.

"Oooh, what is it? Tell me, tell me, tell me!" Nicki says, her eyes lighting up.

Jen shakes her head then mock zips her lips and pretends to throw away the key, and man I wish I could find that key and hide it so she can't unzip.

Nicki's attention is called away again, and I glare at Jen. "Keep them zipped."

She holds up two fingers as if to say *Scout's Honor*, and then dinner is served and we focus on that.

My dad gives a surprisingly emotional speech about Josh and how he always imagined what kind of girl he'd marry, and then Nicki's dad gives a similar speech for his daughter.

And then it's Luke's turn.

"I'm Luke, the best man and also the better receiver," he begins, drawing a big laugh from the small crowd. "I couldn't be happier for my best friend and the woman who will become his wife tomorrow. Josh and I have only been playing together a year, but he's like a much younger brother to me."

Another laugh.

Great, this guy's not just ridiculously hot and fantastic in bed. He's also charming and hilarious.

"As someone who once sat in the same seat where Josh is sitting now, I have a word of advice."

Wait a minute.

He sat in Josh's chair?

Like, literally?

Or is he saying he's been in the chair as the groom at a rehearsal dinner?

Has Luke been *married* before?

Man, when I go in on a one-night stand, I really go all in. I know literally nothing about this guy.

I didn't even know he played football professionally, though I could see why he'd leave out that particular detail to someone who didn't immediately recognize him. Maybe that's one of the things he liked about me.

"I saved the good stuff for tomorrow's speech, but I'll end tonight with this: Never go to bed angry. Stay up and fight," he says, drawing roaring applause from the room.

The maid of honor is not expected to give a speech, for which I'm grateful since I don't really want to follow funny Hot Luke with something lame of my own.

Josh talks next, and he thanks everyone for coming and gets emotional as he looks at Nicki and talks about the life they're going to share.

And that's it. The night's still young, but the rehearsal is about over.

People mingle and drink, and Nicki is briefing the bridesmaids on the plan for tomorrow while I try to keep my eyes on her rather than edging over toward Luke. Nicki is called away by Stella, and I let my eyes feast for a beat.

He looks over at me, and our eyes lock for a second when I look away.

I blow out a breath, and then I head back to my seat to grab my phone where I left it on the table when I overhear Luke say to Josh, "Will Pepper be a problem for your sister?"

I glance up as I see Josh shaking his head. "She won't care."

I won't care about someone named Pepper?

Who the hell is Pepper? Isn't that a nickname for Penelope?

Is Luke seeing somebody? Does he *live* with somebody? Is that the ex-wife? The current wife? The ex-girlfriend? A kid? Did he sleep with me when he's involved with someone else? I'm so confused.

These are the questions that roll through my mind in a split second, and I have no idea when I'll get the answers.

Not tonight, apparently, because Nicki's ready to finish her briefing, and by the time we're done chatting, all the men have cleared out except for Josh, who's waiting to bid his fiancée goodnight.

But Hot Luke is gone, and the next time I'll see him is tomorrow when he's wearing a tux and I'm torn halfway between lust and animosity.

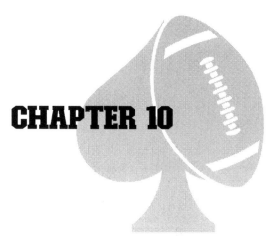

CHAPTER 10

As I go to bed alone, I can't stop thinking about Luke. If I close my eyes and concentrate, I can still smell him in this room. I can still feel his tongue on my body.

I blow out a breath and force my eyes open. That's not helping.

I do an Instagram search for him and come up blank after sorting through fifty or so accounts with the same name. There are a few photos tagged with a hashtag and his name, but there's no user by the name of Luke Dalton that matches Hot Luke. Though there is one who appears to be obsessed with fish and another who looks like he's about ten years old.

He's not on Twitter, either, or Facebook.

I stop my search there.

So he's not a social media guy. Not everybody is, though I'd think if he wanted the status as a fan favorite, he'd need to let people into his life a little more.

Maybe he doesn't want that status, but based on his looks alone, he probably *is* a favorite of the ladies.

And I had sex with him.

I glance over at the windows.

Right there up against those windows.

I let out a soft sigh as it all comes back to me. It was just last night, but somehow it feels like ages ago.

I'm nervous for tomorrow. I don't like keeping secrets from my brother or from Nicki, but neither Luke nor I want them to find out, especially not this weekend when they deserve the focus.

And so I'll pretend.

I'll pretend like I didn't have sex with Hot Luke.

I'll pretend like I don't want to do it again.

I'll put on a little act.

It shouldn't be that hard. Right?

It's another fitful night's sleep. I can't stop thinking about Luke, or the fact that I'm supposed to *move in with him* for a while until I can find a job and a place to live. My brother would surely help me out financially on those fronts, but he's a little busy, you know, *getting married*, and then he'll be on his honeymoon. His top priority at the moment certainly isn't helping his little sister find living arrangements.

I can't even stay at Josh and Nicki's because of their renovations, but even if they weren't having work done, it would be weird at this point to back out of this arrangement to live with Luke. My brother would want a reason why I suddenly had a change of heart, and I'd have to admit why I did, and then I'd be doing the one thing Luke requested in keeping what happened between the two of us.

So I'm stuck.

All the girls are meeting up in Nicki's room for breakfast followed by a day of getting ready, so after my shower, I head in that direction. Nadine throws open the door. "Happy Nicki's wedding day," she says with a smile.

I laugh. "Same to you." I beeline for the bride, who's holding a mimosa and standing by the window while she talks on the phone.

I lace my arms around her from behind and give her a hug.

"No, I said *gardenias*. That doesn't sound anything like *stargazers*! They smell awful!" She's yelling at the poor florist. "Just fix it!" She ends the call and tosses her phone onto a nearby table before taking a long sip of her mimosa.

"Happy wedding day!" I squeal, and she takes a deep breath.

"Thanks," she murmurs.

"I'm here to handle those calls from here on out, my friend. You just focus on marrying my brother."

Her eyes dart to me, and she looks a little...guilty?

"What's wrong?" I ask.

"I'm just so nervous." Her voice is a whisper.

Okay, well, I'm probably not the best candidate to listen to her say all the reasons why she's nervous to marry *my brother*, but I'm also her best friend, so I tough it out. "About what?"

"He's, like, the last guy I'll ever have sex with," she says, and she's starting to wail a little. "And what if I hate being a football wife? It's always going to be about him and his career, not about me and mine."

I feel awkward for a beat as I really have no idea what to say. I don't know what being a *football wife* entails, and I've honestly never really thought about it apart from what the ladies at the bachelorette party mentioned. I know what it's like being a *football sister*, and most of the time it's not a big deal. Nolan is a common enough last name that people don't stop me and ask about my brother.

But she's my girl, and I try to come up with some words of support.

Someone else beats me to the punch, though. It feels weird not being the one who is there for her in this moment after I've been there for her every step of the way since we were sophomores in high school and became fast friends at volleyball camp.

"Honey, it's true," Nadine says, sidling up next to her and wrapping an arm around her shoulder. "But football careers are short. Retirement is long. It may be about him and his career for the next few years, but then you have the rest of forever together to do whatever you want."

"Is that what you're banking on?" Nicki asks, and Nadine nods.

"You've known him since before his football career took off, right?" Nadine asks.

"Yeah," Nicki says.

"So you know the real *him*. The guy inside. He'll be that guy regardless of what he's doing for a career. Besides, having doubts on your wedding day is natural. It's like a rite of passage."

Nicki nods and sniffles. "You're right." She draws in a deep breath. "Okay, thanks. I'm good now."

"Every bride deserves at least one meltdown on her wedding day." Nadine winks. We're in the middle of getting ready when my phone buzzes with a new text. We've had finger sandwiches and laughed a lot as the mini-meltdown has been put to rest. My make-up is perfection, my hair is getting the royal treatment from someone named Daisy, and showtime begins in under ninety minutes with pictures in less than an hour.

I pick up my phone to check it in case it's something wedding-related. I don't recognize the number.

Unknown: *I need to talk to you.*

Me: *Who is this?*

Unknown: *The best man. It's about the wedding. Best man and maid of honor shit.*

Me: *How did you get my number?*

Luke: *Your brother gave it to me.*

Okay, well that makes sense and I don't even know why it matters.

Me: *I'm in the middle of getting my hair done but I can meet you in twenty minutes or so when I go to my room to change into my dress.*

Luke: *Same room as the other night?*

I blush. Hard.

Me: *Same room.*

Luke: *See you then.*

Daisy finishes curling my hair, and then she does some wavy thing to it and pins only part of it back so my dark blonde locks flow freely down my back.

"I'm going to go put my dress on," I say to Nicki, and she grunts some response as her make-up artist works on her eyes.

I rush down to my room, slip into the pale pink dress that makes my skin look a golden tan, and check myself in the mirror. The warm tones they used make my blue eyes pop, and I might just have to order the colors and brands they used because *damn* I look good.

A knock at my door pulls me away from the mirror, and my heart beats double time.

He's here.

When I open the door, my knees nearly buckle beneath me.

Luke stands there in a tuxedo. My eyes travel from his feet in his dress shoes, up his powerful legs to the hips that were slamming against my backside, to his abdomen that has those fine cuts of muscle, to his broad chest and shoulders made stronger from his athletic background, to his handsome face with eyes that heat as they meet mine.

"Holy fuck, Ellie. You're...that dress..." His eyes dip to my cleavage and back to my face. "And your hair..."

My lips tip up in a smile. He's flustered, and the fact that I'm the one who's making him that way makes me feel the same way. "Right back at you, Hot Luke."

He grins, and my knees actually do buckle a little.

An ache throbs between my legs.

The bed is *right there*. And the windows...we could just do it against the windows and then he won't mess up my hair.

I lean on the doorframe for support. "We, uh, have like five minutes if you want to..."

He chuckles, and then he sighs as he averts his gaze from mine. "As much as I'd love to, I already told you, I can't take advantage of my best friend's little sister."

"It's not *taking advantage* when I'm the one offering," I say, a little exasperated as the sting of rejection bites at me. "Besides, my brother is marrying *my* best friend. Why does he care if one of his friends hooks up with his sister?"

Luke laughs. "Trust me, Sexy Ellie, I want to. But this is bro code. I work with your brother, and I'm not the right guy for you anyway. Besides, I thought you were still mad at me for bragging about our night."

I sigh and cross my arms over my chest. I know it's both making me look angry and pushing my breasts together, which is exactly what I want. "That's right. I *am* mad."

I earn the intended effect as his eyes flick down to my chest again. He laughs. "I'm not convinced. You just tried to seduce me."

"Whatever. So why are you here, then? What did you need to talk about?"

"Uh," he says a little dumbly, and I try not to laugh. "Oh, right. Your brother is having this whole thing. He isn't sure he wants to get married."

"What?" I screech. I just sat through calming the bride down as Nadine convinced her she does want this. Now the groom, too? Maybe they *shouldn't* get married if they're both having doubts.

"Something about how he'll only get to bang her for the rest of his life. And I think it might sort of be my fault," he admits.

I open my door wider and motion for him to follow me. I stop near the foot of the bed, and he stops a few paces away. Good Lord this man is a real treat to look at, and he smells divine, too. Some sort of cologne he definitely wasn't wearing when we hooked up.

Did he wear it for me?

I somehow doubt it, but a little part of me hopes he did.

"So why is this your fault, and why are you telling me?" I ask.

"Those are two complicated questions, so I'll start with the easier one. You're her best friend and his sister. You know both of them probably better than anyone. Do you think they should get married?"

I nod. "They belong together. Nicki just went through a whole thing this morning, too. I think it's natural to have doubts." I repeat what Nadine said.

"It is," he says. He clears his throat. "I, uh, did when I got married. But the difference is that I should have listened to mine."

God, I'd love to dig more into that...

But the wedding is in an hour. We need to get my brother's head on straight and get them down the aisle.

And if Luke is about to become my roommate, I'll have time to learn more about him.

Even though now I'm dying to know if the ex he just broke up with is this wife he's talking about.

"He keeps harping on the fact that I had a one-night stand and he won't get to have those anymore. Do you know how fucking hard it is to hear him talk about *my* one-night stand knowing it was with his *sister?*"

"Uh...sorry?" I say, not exactly sure what he wants me to say to that.

"It's not your fault," he mutters. "Sorry. It's been a long day already. Can you help me? Tell me what to say to him to convince him he wants this, because I'm not entirely convinced people *should* get married."

"You don't want to get married again?" I ask, surprised.

"Focus, Ellie," he says with a touch of frustration, and somehow he's even sexier when he's just a little frustrated. It might even be sort of fun to poke at him. "That's not the issue at hand."

He's right.

"Okay. Take me to my brother and we'll get this straightened out."

He nods once, and I put on my shoes and grab my clutch. I slip my phone, room key, and lipstick in, and then we head toward the groom's suite so I can do some damage control.

CHAPTER 11

"She's waiting to walk down that aisle toward the man she loves more than anything in the world. Are you going to be there?" I ask my brother.

He looks up at me, and I can see the uncertainty in his eyes.

"You can't do this to her," I whisper. "She loves you, you big idiot. I know it's scary, but everyone is scared on their wedding day."

"Yeah, I know. Ask Luke," he says, and I narrow my eyes at Luke for a beat because what the hell did he say that might've put these doubts in my brother's head, and for the love of God, why would Josh choose him as his best man?

"Luke and I talked. We both know how right you two are for each other. Luke and his ex just...weren't. They didn't have that same spark you and Nicki do." I'm talking out of my ass, but it seems to be working. "She's your soul mate, Josh. You know that. She's had a crush on you since we were in high school, and she's been there for you since the two of you first got together. You know she loves you for who you are, not because you play football or because you have money in the bank."

He nods. "Yeah." He scrubs a hand along his jaw as he thinks it through. "I love her. So much that it scares me sometimes."

"I know," I say, and I squeeze his hand. I glance up at Luke, and our eyes catch. My chest aches. I want what Nicki and Josh have—maybe minus the wedding day jitter doubts. Part of me thought I could've had it with Todd, but that didn't pan out. "And that's why I know you're both ready for this."

He nods. "Thanks, Ellie Belly."

LISA SUZANNE

My cheeks burn at his term of endearment as I pray Luke somehow missed it and won't call me that forever now.

Josh blows out a breath. "Okay." He squeezes my forearm. "Let's do this thing."

"You better get moving, Osh Kosh ba-Josh," I say, glancing at the clock. "You're not even wearing shoes, and you've got pictures by the pool before the ladies get out there. You know you're not allowed to see Nicki until she walks down the aisle."

"I've got it from here," Luke says.

"See you out there," I say to my brother, and Luke walks me to the door.

"Thanks for your help," he says, and the sweet feeling of victory—of overcoming a little obstacle with him that pulled us a little closer together—rushes through my chest.

"No problem," I say softly. And then I punch him in the arm. He grabs the spot and makes a face like it really hurt even though I know it didn't. "But next time, let me know it's a freaking emergency before I blow you off for a half hour while I get my hair done."

He laughs. "Next time? You really think this might happen again?"

I giggle, too, and then I shrug. "Maybe not *this exact situation*, but you know what I mean."

His eyes twinkle, and then he opens the door. "See you out there, Ellie Belly," he says. I shoot him a glare, but it fades as his eyes linger on me for a beat. My stomach flips, and then I seem to snap out of it as I realize I need to get moving. But, *damn*, do I want his eyes to linger like that again.

Like they did Thursday night.

I don't have time to dwell on it, though.

I run back to the bridal suite.

"Where the hell have you been?" Nicki demands when I walk in.

"I went to talk to Josh after I got dressed," I admit, without actually admitting the reason why. I take a beat to study my best friend. She's the perfect portrait of a glowing, beautiful bride. "You look gorgeous."

She ignores my compliment as her eyes widen. "Why'd you go talk to him? Is everything okay?"

I nod and smile. "Everything's fine. Just wanted to see my big brother," I lie. Neither of them ever has to know the other freaked out. It's part of the maid of honor and best man's duties to ensure a smooth day, and making sure the groom is waiting there at the end of the aisle when the bride walks down it seems to fall under that umbrella.

Pictures are taken and smiles abound, and before I know it, the bridesmaids are lining up to make our way down the aisle. When Luke steps into place beside me, that cologne pulls at my senses and nerves flitter through my chest.

"You still look beautiful," he murmurs, and my cheeks redden at his words as my chest tightens.

It isn't fair.

I don't want him to tell me things like that when he's vowed not to act on this steamy attraction between us. And he's right. I'm still mad at him for bragging about us. *To my brother.*

I slide my arm through his elbow. We probably have some time before I *really* need to do that, but I like being close to him, and he smells good, and he isn't exactly pushing me away. "You still look like Hot Luke," I whisper back, and he keeps his eyes forward but his lips tip up with a smile.

Stella directs Nadine and her husband, Richard, to make their way down the aisle. She signals the next bridesmaid and groomsman, and soon enough, it's our turn.

I feel like there's so much I want to say to Luke, but I don't dare say a word as all eyes assembled in the crowd seem to turn toward the two of us.

Do we look good walking down the aisle together?

Well, duh. It's *Luke.* He'd look good escorting a clown down the aisle.

LISA SUZANNE

Could this be us someday, with him already waiting at the end of the aisle like Josh is as I wait to walk down with my dad? Doubtful, but damn, a girl can dream.

Our eyes meet more than once as we each watch our best friends marry, and I wish I could decode what he's thinking. I still know next to nothing about him...except now I know that he was married before.

Hot Luke is kind of a mystery, and that sort of makes him...dare I say...even hotter?

Once the ceremony is over, the bridal party meets in a conference room for a quick celebration and toast to the newly married couple while the guests are ushered to another area outside for a cocktail hour. I help Nicki in the bathroom, by far the worst part of my duties as MOH and a feat that's sort of comparable to peeling an onion to get the juice in the middle without messing up any of the layers. I lose track of Luke until we head back outside, where the aisle, altar, and guest chairs have been transformed into a banquet area.

A long table for the wedding party sits on the platform over the pool, lights twinkling in the near twilight as the sun begins to set behind the tall buildings circling us. It's romantic and gorgeous, somehow merging a *spare no expense* feel with a casual, intimate vibe. The whole thing just perfectly sets the scene for the reception of these two lovebirds.

We line up and the deejay who's serving as emcee calls Nadine and Richard first to make their way toward their seats. They walk up, and he twirls her, and it's all very cute. I watch as the other couples go, all doing equally cute things even though some of them only met last night, and my heart picks up speed as nerves set in.

I'm about to be introduced, and I have to walk out on Luke's arm, and we don't have anything cute planned like everyone else had.

"What should we do?" I whisper-yell.

Luke glances over at me with his brows dipped. "What do you mean?"

80

"The maid of honor, Ellie Nolan, with the best man, Luke Dalton!"

"Spin me," I whisper yell as we walk to the center of the reception area. He doesn't quite get my meaning, and he spins us both, and I grab onto his hand and twist myself around.

And, because this is *my* life, my heel gets caught in a crack along the cement walkway. The heel doesn't break completely, but it's not quite glued to my shoe the same way it was before.

Great.

Just what I need.

A broken shoe at the start of the reception as I trip in front of the hottest guy I've ever seen in my life and, of course, the entire group gathered to celebrate my brother's wedding.

Luke catches me at the last second, and it *almost* looks like I didn't totally take a spill as I wind up tight in his arms. I cling to his shoulders, and our eyes meet—his worried as I nearly topple to the ground, and mine probably rabid like a damn wild animal as I look upon the object of my lust who just saved me from a really embarrassing fall.

Now I'm in his arms and I want to kiss him but every-freaking-body in the room is watching us.

I'm shaky, somewhat from the almost-fall but more from being so close to Luke. He straightens me. "You okay?" he murmurs as I suck in a deep breath, still clinging to him and really just getting a mouthful of his cologne.

It sounds grosser than it is. It's fucking magic.

I want to lick his neck.

"Fine," I gasp, and then we're supposed to part so we can each walk up the stairs toward our seats on the platform over the pool.

Thankfully there's a railing behind our chairs, because I sure as hell would fall right into the water with the way my knees are trembling.

I glance over and find Luke smiling at me as we each take our place, and *God* that smile just gets me every time. I can't tell if he's smiling at me or laughing at me. I tell myself it's a reassuring, friendly smile. If I tell myself he's laughing at me, well, I'm not sure my fragile ego could actually take that.

My knees bang together as I think of his smile. I grip the back of the chair in front of me as I stand, and then the bride and groom are announced so eyes aren't on the two of us anymore. Thank God.

I exhale a long breath and try to regain my composure, but literally falling into Luke's arms sure threw me off balance. I keep my eyes on Nicki and Josh even though I want to look over. I feel like he's looking at me. The side of my face burns with his gaze, but when I glance over, he's looking at the happy couple dancing their way across the floor just as he should be.

He said I'm off-limits to him...but he's not off-limits to me.

He's about to become my new roommate. I'm going to have to just get past the bragging thing, though it still sort of makes him out to be an asshole. But he's not. He seems like a good guy, barring that one indiscretion of bragging about a one-night stand in the middle of a Starbucks.

Which was even dumber on his part considering he's a professional football player and anyone could've overheard. He's lucky it was just me.

We already know we're fire beneath the sheets...though I still want to know why he jetted out afterward.

And maybe, just maybe, I'll have a drink or two tonight and get up the nerve to actually ask him.

CHAPTER 12

He holds me as we sway to the romantic song, and I'm about a millisecond from resting my head on his shoulder, but I force myself not to.

Dancing with him just feels so...right.

Except when my heel keeps catching on the dance floor. It still hasn't broken off completely, but it's not doing well. I'm doing my best to ignore it.

I'm clouded by the wine I've had, which is just about the perfect place to be, and I *want* him again. So badly I can taste it. Or him.

Our bodies move in tandem, sort of like they did when he had me shoved up against a window (except not naked and not from behind), and the whole setting is a backdrop for the start of something really romantic.

I draw in a deep breath, and then I move back and look him in the eye. His are heated, but maybe that's just how they always look and I'm imagining things. Or it's possible the wine is clouding my judgment. "Can I ask you something?" I say softly.

One of his brows dips and it's freaking adorable. "Sure." His tone is hesitant.

"Why'd you run out on me after we had such a nice time?"

"On Thursday?" he asks.

I nod.

"I needed to get home to take care of some things."

Well that's sure as hell a non-answer if I've ever heard one.

"How long ago did you and your ex end things?" I ask next.

He said a couple months, and even though he said he's over her, he might just need more time. And if he needs time, it's probably out of the question to even entertain the idea of being with him...not that he's given me any indication at all that he's on board with that idea.

He looks down at me, his face blank. "You're full of questions."

"I guess I just...I don't know." I blink, and then I confess, "I'd like to get to know the guy I'm about to be living with."

"Your brother kind of made it sound like we'd each stick to our own sides of my house." His eyes are on mine, and maybe I don't know him at all, but I can still see a little twinkle there. He's teasing me even though his words indicate otherwise. He seems like he's hard to read, but I think I'm starting to figure him out.

"Is that what you want?" I ask, my voice low as I'm not really sure how he'll answer.

He hitches up a shoulder, and maybe I'm not figuring him out at all. Then he sighs. "My divorce was official a little over four years ago. My most recent ex and I ended things a few months ago."

Aha! So an ex-wife *and* an ex-girlfriend. That answers that question. "Well, you already know about my most recent ex."

He chuckles. "Yeah, you mentioned him."

"I was twenty-one when your divorce was official. Possibly twenty."

He chuckles. "You're young. You never mentioned your age before."

"How old are you?"

"Thirty-one. Fucking ancient for a football player."

I raise a brow, and then there goes my filter because why the hell would I want to point these things out to him when I'm trying to convince him we belong together? That's right. Because of wine. "You're six years older than me. That means when you started high school, I was around eight. When you started college, I was probably twelve."

"And when I was drafted into the league, you were learning how to drive a car," he finishes.

84

"It's not *that* big a difference. Not now, anyway. I feel like once you start your career and become an adult, ages don't really matter."

"That's when life experience starts to matter instead. I've been in the league nine years. I've been married and divorced. I've had multiple relationships that have shown me what I want out of life. What do *you* want out of life?"

Would it be inappropriate to say *you* here? Probably so. I'm showing my age and my sheltered life. I barely know this guy and the hopeless romantic in me is already head over heels. I need to put a pin in that. I open my mouth to answer when the song changes and the bridal party dance is over. Josh slings an arm around Luke's neck, forcing me out of his arms.

I don't know if I'll get the chance to be back in them.

"The groomsmen are heading outside," Josh says, and I roll my eyes. It's his secret code for letting Luke know it's time to go to the other side of the pool area to smoke cigars, which is about the grossest thing in the world.

I wrinkle my nose in disgust, and to my surprise, Luke does, too.

"We already *are* outside, dude," he says.

Josh laughs. "I knew you'd say that, but come anyway. You don't have to smoke."

He heaves out a breath. "Fine. But when I'm coughing at workouts Monday morning, I'm telling coach it's your fault."

"Coach isn't expecting us on Monday," Josh says.

"I'll still be there."

"Of course you will," my brother mutters, and it's another tiny insight into Luke's personality.

He's the kind of guy who will show up no matter what. He cares about his body—both what he puts into it and taking care of it. That's probably why it's utter perfection.

He heads off with my brother, and I take it as my cue to head back to my chair to sit for a few minutes. As I walk up the steps toward my seat, though, I forget about my semi-broken heel.

I stumble on a step and completely lose my balance. Instead of falling backward into the railing, though, I fall forward.

And falling forward off the steps means I don't just trip and fall onto the stairs. No, of course not. That would be too easy. That would be too *dry*.

Instead, I fall right into the damn swimming pool.

I hear the gasps from dry land only when my submerged head finds the surface.

I wipe the water out of my eyes, smearing my make-up beyond recognition. One of the fake lashes I was wearing is on my fingertips when I pull my hand away. I feel the other one sticking right to my cheek, and I peel it off.

Someone else yells, and a few people start laughing, and then a crowd gathers to watch the clumsy, very wet maid of honor as she frantically and futilely tries to make her way toward the stairs to get out of the pool.

It's not like it's deep. I'm only in three or four feet of water, and I can stand.

But what I didn't think I even needed to account for was how freaking heavy the layers of tulle and silk would become when submerged in water.

I'm still wearing my heels, and one is definitely broken now, as I try to walk across the pool, but it's like I'm stuck in quicksand. People are watching, but no one seems to know what the hell to do to help the idiot in the water without getting wet themselves.

And then I'm engulfed by a wave as someone else splashes into the water.

When I wipe the water and the surprise away from my eyes, I spot who it is.

And when he comes up out of the water—still in his tux, though he removed the jacket to jump into the pool to save me— our eyes meet. Mine must surely be racoon eyes with makeup bleeding in every direction, but he looks worried. Well, and he also looks like a goddamn fairy tale merman as he emerges from the water, the water glistening on his glowing skin like droplets that want to cling on for dear life because once they drop off, they don't get to be close to him anymore.

I know the feeling.

He reaches for me and hooks an arm around my waist, and then he helps me walk over to the steps. He gathers the weighty part of the dress in his arms, and then he squeezes it to get some of the moisture out with each step I take up and out of the water.

I feel this weird mix of completely awful that I ruined my brother's reception and totally elated that Hot Luke was the one who jumped in to save me.

I'm leaning more toward elated, though.

Because the moment I met Hot Luke, I'm pretty sure my fairy tale began.

I can't wait to see where it leads next.

CHAPTER 13

The guests all clap when we're both out of the pool, and some attendants who work for the hotel bring us towels to dry off.

"Are you okay?" Nicki asks as I wrap a towel around my wet hair and use another one to rub away some of the bleeding makeup under my eyes. I look at the towel where I did my work. It's black. I must look like a freaking disaster right now.

"Yeah, I'm okay," I mutter. "I'm so sorry."

I glance over at Luke. He does *not* look like a freaking disaster. In fact, he looks somehow even more gorgeous. Water drips from his dark hair, which is semi-slicked back but too short to hold the slick so it just sticks up in perfect disarray, and his white shirt clings to his stomach, showcasing his washboard abs for everyone lucky enough to catch a glimpse.

My one-night stand.

My brother's best friend.

My hero.

My new roommate.

I sigh softly.

"What the hell happened?" Nicki asks. "Did someone push you?"

"No, no, nothing like that," I say. "I tripped. My heel was a little wobbly and I fell while I was walking up the stairs."

"Only you, Ellie, I swear," Josh says as he laughs, and it's total déjà vu as I'm transported to the last time he said those exact same words to me less than a week ago when Todd dumped me and I was fired in the same day. To be fair, it's a phrase he uses quite a bit around me.

"The bride and groom will now be cutting the cake," the deejay announces, and thankfully that takes the eyes off Luke and me.

I don't want to miss them cutting the cake or any of the other traditions at a wedding, but I'm soaked and this dress isn't getting any lighter and I'm fucking mortified. "I'm going to go dry off and change," I tell Nicki, and I start heading in toward the hotel.

"Wait up," Luke says from right behind me. "I'll go, too." He grabs his shoes, which he took off to dive in to save me, and we walk together toward the building.

"You okay?" he asks softly.

"Yes, I'm fine," I say. "Just embarrassed. Thanks for helping me."

He laughs. "Someone had to. You were flailing around in there, spinning in circles like you didn't know which way was out."

"Yeah, well, could've been anyone, and it had to be you," I mutter. The automatic doors open and we step through and head toward the elevator.

"What's that supposed to mean?" He presses the button for the elevator.

I blink, and I debate how much to say, and then I realize...screw it. I'm starting over in a new city. I have no job, no place of my own, no friends out here. I have nothing to lose by being perfectly honest except for some awkwardness with my new roommate, but you know what? Awkwardness never killed anybody. Did it?

I shake my head. He glances down at me with furrowed brows, and hell if it isn't the cutest thing I've ever seen. "I like you, Luke. And you keep doing things and saying things to make me like you more. But you already told me I'm forbidden fruit, and I'm trying so damn hard to act like you're not the Prince Charming of the ultimate fairy tale, but you just keep proving that you are."

I'm babbling, and I realize that.

He pulls me into his arms. "It's okay," he soothes, rubbing circles on my back.

My face is pressed to his chest. His hard, firm chest. "See?" I say, my face smashed against his wet shirt, muffling my voice. "Even this is Prince Charming material."

"Oh, sweet, Sexy Ellie," he says softly. He presses a soft kiss to the top of my head. "I promise you, I'm no prince."

The elevator doors open, breaking up our intimate moment, and we pull apart to step on. It's a fairly full car, and we draw curious glances from the others as two wet people dressed up in their finest hop on board.

"Can you believe *I* fell in the pool and *she* jumped in to save me?" he says to the quiet car full of strangers, and awkward laughter erupts.

I smack him in the shoulder, laughing at him. The doors open and he gets off on the forty-third floor. "I'll come get you when I'm done," he says before the doors close, and I ride up to floor forty-seven as I wonder how long I'll be waiting for him—or if he'll move quickly and be waiting on me.

When I get to the mirror, I find that the damage is even worse than I imagined.

I scrub my face clean. I can start over on my make-up once I get this damn heavy dress off.

I take a quick body shower to get the chlorine off, not daring to mess with the rat nest that's my hair. I'll need a little time to get the pins out of the wet mess.

I'm just toweling dry when there's a knock at the door. I think we can all guess who it is.

Of course I'm in my towel and not dressed yet when he shows up. Why would it be any other way?

But you know what? I want him, and I want him to want me back.

And seeing a girl that he had sex with clad only in a teeny-tiny hotel towel has to be at least a *little* tempting, right?

I see the fluffy hotel robe on my way by the closet to answer the door, and I take all of a millisecond to ignore that it's even there. A flimsy towel that barely covers the goodie bits versus a huge fluffy robe? If I'm going for temptation, the flimsy towel wins.

I throw open the door, and it's not Luke at all.

Guess those little peephole thingies come in handy.

It's.

My.

Dad.

"Oh, gosh, Ellie!" He shields his eyes. "I'm sorry!"

"No, Dad, don't be," I mutter. "I'm the one who's sorry." My face burns as I realize I nearly flashed my own father all the goods, and *that* is when Hot Luke decides to show up at my door.

Dry as a bone.

Hair restyled perfectly.

Wearing a suit that's not a tux but that still makes him look hella delish.

And once again, catching me in a completely and totally embarrassing situation.

"Were you expecting someone else?" my dad asks, completely oblivious to the fact that Luke is standing directly behind him.

"No!" I exclaim, trying to think fast. "I, uh, figured it was Nicki or one of the other bridesmaids checking up on me."

"Well it's me checking up on you," he says.

"I came to check on you, too," Luke says smoothly, finally alerting my dad to the fact that he's standing there.

"I'm fine. But please, everyone, come on in." I open the door, and both my dad and Luke walk in. My cheeks burn as Luke's eyes move straight to the window where he had me bent over as he banged into me from behind.

He glances at me and raises a brow, and I want to just curl into a ball and die right about now.

I rummage through my suitcase and I find dry underwear. I turn to the closet for the black dress I packed as a just in case, and then I lock myself in the bathroom.

So much for seducing Luke.

I put on a light smattering of make-up, unpin my hair as quickly as I can, spray about a gallon of detangler on it, and try to comb it out. Ultimately I twist it into a bun and call it good. The pictures have already been taken, so it's not like I'll be ruining those with this fresh new look straight from the depths of hell.

I pair my dress with black flats because hell if I'm getting back into heels, and then I turn to my dad and Luke, who seem to be shooting the shit, and I say, "Ready?"

This is not exactly how I planned for the last ten minutes to go, but it is what it is.

The elevator ride down to the reception is not quite as exciting as the ride up, and when we emerge back into the pool area, everyone has basically forgotten the poor girl who fell into the pool and the hot football megastar who saved her.

But I didn't forget.

He may have told me he's no prince, but I beg to differ. Or, at the very least, I want to find out for myself.

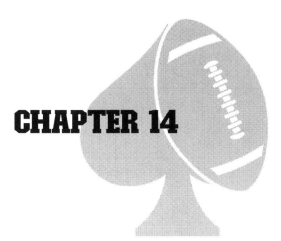

CHAPTER 14

Luke runs off to be with the guys, and there aren't any more organized dances where I get the shot to be close to him, so instead I hang with Jen. She's also here without a date, so we're just two single bridesmaids chatting about when in the hell it'll be our turn to wear the white dress.

We eat cake and we drink wine and we fight over the bouquet when Nicki tosses it. I'm not the one who catches it, for the record. Delia is.

So at least one fairy tale cliché skips past me.

By the time I slide into my bed (all alone, as planned from the start even though I had hope things would turn out differently), I'm freaking exhausted.

I wonder where Luke is. I wonder if he's still awake.

I wonder if he's thinking about me the way I'm thinking about him.

I force the thought away. But he did save me today, and it felt like more than friendship.

I shoot off a text since I have his number now.

Me: *Thanks for saving me today.*

His reply comes a few minutes later.

Luke: *Happy to help.*

I try to decode some hidden meaning in those three words, but I'm pretty sure there isn't any. He's just a nice guy who was helping out the clumsy girl who fell in the water.

I'm not sure why that makes me a little sad.

In the morning, my first thought when I wake is of Luke. I think I even dreamed of him.

I wake up with a new tenacity. He told me no—multiple times—and maybe it's time I actually listen. I do, after all, still have to live with him, and it would probably be in my best interest to respect his wishes even though I'm still sure we belong together.

I can't be the only one who feels it.

That one night we shared was more than a spark. It was a freaking volcano.

What I'm feeling now is the aftershocks, I think. Sparks here and there from the fiery lava that isn't even starting to cool.

I don't imagine I'll see him this morning since immediate family is supposed to gather for brunch. It's being held in a special suite where the staff brought all the presents last night so we can watch the happy couple open their gifts. I'll also be responsible for recording who got them what so they can churn out their thank you cards after the honeymoon.

When I get to the suite and knock on the door, want to venture a guess as to who opens it?

Not someone in my immediate family, that's for sure.

Thank God I opted for a shower this morning, though if I'd have known Hot Luke was going to be here, I might've put forth a little more effort.

"What are you doing here?" I ask.

"I'm supposed to help with the gifts," he says.

"I'm the sister." The words tumble out of my mouth, and it's about the dumbest thing I can think of to say, but it's also the *only* thing I can think of to say.

"Yeah, I sort of got that. And the bride's best friend. So you're basically doubly responsible for being here."

I laugh. "I don't know why I said that. I just...wasn't expecting to see you this morning, I guess."

He shoots me a tight, fake smile. "Well surprise!" He holds his hands out and waves them around before he opens the door wider to let me in, and I practically run past him. In one corner there's a table overflowing with gifts. This is going to take all damn day.

Nicki and Josh are giggling with their heads bent close together near the buffet table, and my mom and dad are talking to Nicki's parents. Nicki's little brother has his face in his phone on the couch, and the only other people here are Luke and me.

So even if I *wanted* to talk to someone aside from Luke Dalton, it looks like my only options are interrupting the newlyweds, walking into a conversation between parents, or sitting next to the seventeen-year-old kid who came along as a *surprise* eight years after Nicki was born.

I heave out a breath and opt for the simplest answer: the buffet table.

"Good morning," I say brightly, interrupting newlywed giggles which are probably sexual in nature given Nicki's rosy cheeks, but I don't ask, and I don't want to know.

"Hey," Josh says, his eyes never leaving his wife.

His *wife*. God, it's weird that Josh is freaking *married* now. He's a *husband*.

That's going to take some getting used to.

"Okay, I'll just sneak past you and grab some food," I say wholly to myself since they're still wrapped up in their own little world.

I fill my plate with eggs and fruit, and then I sit by myself at one of the little tables.

I glance up and see Luke approaching.

I can't seem to escape this guy. I'm also not sure I want to, but he's made it pretty clear he's not interested beyond the one night we shared.

"Looks like we're each other's best option for brunch entertainment," he says softly as he pulls out a chair beside me and slides into it.

I give him a wry smile. "Thanks for checking everyone else off the list first."

"To be fair, you definitely did the same thing but also eliminated me from your list when you came over here to sit by yourself with your lonely plate of food."

I narrow my eyes to a glare and stick a giant piece of watermelon in my mouth. I'm sure I look very attractive as I attempt to chomp it down to a normal sized piece of food.

His brows dip down. "Why the change of heart?"

I raise a brow. "You liked it better when I kept tripping over myself to get to you?"

He glances down at the table. "I wouldn't say that, exactly, but yesterday you were at least friendly toward me."

"I'm still friendly. I just realized that you don't like me the way I like you, so I need to put a pin in it." I help myself to another huge piece of watermelon.

"Yeah, I do like you the same way, Ellie," he says, and there's something really illicit about the way he says the words in a quiet, husky voice that's just for me. He glances around, and everyone else is still occupied in their own conversations. Over here, we just look like we're two people having a chat.

But it feels like a lot more as my heart races at his words.

My eyes meet his, and his burn at me with the same fire they did on our single night together.

"I'd go back on my word to your brother if I thought I was right for you," he says softly. "I think most of what he said was in jest, anyway. But that's the thing. I'm *not* right for you. You're young, and you want the fairy tale happy ending with your Prince Charming. I'm a divorced, slightly older and definitely more cynical guy who thinks those make-believe stories are for children."

My chest feels hollow at his words. "Oh." The single word is all that comes out of my mouth, though my mind races.

"It'll be easier to live together if we're just friends," he says.

I nod. "Yeah. I know. Friends. And we still think this living together thing is a good idea?"

"I thought it was a terrible idea from the start, but I agreed anyway since it was for your brother," he says, gently pushing my shoulder the way an old pal would. "And I think if we back out now, they'll know something's up. So we're kind of stuck, don't you think?" He pauses as he lets me mull that over, and then he says, "I'm going to go grab some food."

I press my lips together and stare down at my plate while he gets up. I brush away that deflated feeling that pings through my chest.

He's cynical and he thinks fairy tales are make-believe stories for children?

Enter Ellie.

We may not end up together, but that doesn't mean I can't help him lighten up a tad in the meantime. He said it'll be easier to live together if we're friends, and I intend to become his actual friend...not just his best friend's little sister.

He returns with his plate of food that's mounded with more calories than I eat in a day and sits. "So, *friend*, which football team do you scream for on Sundays?"

I raise a brow. "The Aces?"

He chuckles and shovels in some eggs. "Right answer, but I doubt the sincerity when it sounds like a question."

"I'm not actually a football fan," I admit.

He looks at me in horror, like he didn't know such a creature actually existed.

What can I say? I'm a freaking unicorn.

I glance around to make sure everyone else is out of hearing distance. "Probably also the reason why I didn't know who you were the night we met."

"Ah, yes, it all makes sense now. Everyone knows Luke motherfuckin' Dalton."

I laugh. "What position do you play?"

"Wide receiver."

"So the same as Josh?" I ask.

He nods and raises a brow. "Impressive that you know that. Do you even watch the games?"

"I do," I say. "But, like, I have them *on*. I wouldn't say I *pay attention* to them. I guess I've just been around it my whole life. Josh has played since peewee league and my parents dragged me along to every game. I think I rebelled a little and decided from a young age that I just didn't care. Then he had to go pro and put my knowledge of the game to embarrassing shame."

"I'll teach you," he says.

"I don't want to learn," I fire back.

He laughs. "You're so...feisty. It's charming, hilarious, and hot all at the same time."

"Getting a little close to the line there, *friend*," I warn.

"Touché. My apologies. But I *will* impart some knowledge on you whether you like it or not."

"Fine," I challenge. "Then I'll teach you not to be such a cynical non-believer of fairy tales."

"So what do you do while the game's on, then?" he asks.

I laugh. "Usually I work. Now that I don't have a job, I'll probably read."

"Let me guess...something where they all live happily ever after?"

"Naturally," I say lightly. He's teasing me, but I refuse to be embarrassed for liking what I like.

My dad clinks a glass with a spoon to get everyone's attention. "Thank you all for being here this morning," he begins. "Josh and Nicole are ready to open their gifts. If you could all take your places, we can get started."

I glance at my plate. I've barely eaten anything, favoring instead the conversation with the hot guy sitting next to me. But maid of honor duties call.

Luke's shoveling in the sausage left on his plate, so I shovel in some eggs before I head over to Nicki. She hands me a pad of paper and a few pens. "Write what the gift is on the back of the card. The paper's for notes if you need to make any or if we can't find a card. And thank you."

"Of course. Happy to help." I repeat the words Luke texted to me last night after I thanked him for saving me in the pool. I sit back in the chair by my food, lonely now beside Luke's half-empty plate. He's talking to my mom in a corner of the room.

He comes back and sits to eat some more.

"What's your job here?" I ask.

"Help move the heavy stuff."

We watch as the happy couple tears the paper off wineglasses and kitchen utensils and picture frames. It's all the standard, cliché stuff they registered for even though they already have everything they could ever need due to my brother's healthy paychecks. But, according to Nicki's mom, everyone likes to bring a present to a wedding, so they still registered.

Once it's all over and my hand is stiff from writing every gift on the back of every card, it's time to check out of this hotel and the room where I was banged up against a window by Hot Luke.

And that means it's time to move in with my new roommate.

CHAPTER 15

The presents are split between five different cars, and we're all heading back toward Josh and Nicki's house to help unload before I move into Luke's place.

I still can't believe I'm doing this.

My heart thumps harder and faster with each present we unload. I'm getting nervous about actually moving in with him. Before, it was just this abstract idea set sometime in the future.

It's real now. And it's happening.

It's a temporary solution, but it's not like I'll move out in a few days. I don't even have a job yet. I haven't even *looked* for a job yet.

And it's not just all that making me nervous.

I recall him saying something about someone named *Pepper*. I'm still wondering who the hell that might be and whether the hell I'll get to meet her today.

Once everything is unloaded and we're standing in the driveway after saying goodbye to all the parents, who headed back to the hotel for a day of relaxing by the pool, Josh grins at me. "You ready to see your new place?"

I raise a brow, and Luke walks *literally* across the street and holds his arms out wide in a driveway that leads up to another stately mansion.

First things first. What the hell does a single guy need a house like *that* for? It's as big as my brother's.

And second, well, when Josh first told me his friend lived across the street from him, I sort of assumed he meant across a major cross street...not literally ten steps away. Not where he could look out his window and have a peek into Luke's place if the blinds are open.

"Wow, you weren't kidding about *across the street*," I say.

"Close enough to hear the construction on our renovations that'll surely start at the crack of dawn, but far enough that you won't be able to hear Nicki and me banging it out before we head to Fiji." Josh shoots me a smirk.

"Gross, Josh," I say, wrinkling my nose.

He grins and holds up his hands innocently. "Let's get you moved in."

It doesn't take much—just rolling my two suitcases across the street, really, which I could do by myself, but Josh and Luke each take one.

Luke opens the heavy wooden front door, and I hesitate on the front porch.

"You need anything else?" Josh asks beside me. Clearly he's anxious to get back to his new wife, who's probably already naked on their kitchen counter or something even more disgusting I don't want to think about.

I shake my head.

"All right, then. You two have fun, and if you need anything, I'll be busy across the street so find someone else to bother." He laughs and Luke flips him the bird just before he turns to walk away. He flips it back. "I love both of you," he says as he runs back across the street to his house.

"Come on in and I'll show you around," Luke says, but before he opens the door, we both hear a voice.

"Luke?"

It sounds like an elderly woman, and Luke faces the door and closes his eyes for a beat. He draws in a deep breath with his nose and exhales out his mouth before he turns around.

"Hey, Mrs. Adams," he says.

"Oh, Luke, you know I want you to call me Dorothy," a petite older woman with short white curls on her head and glasses perched on her nose says. She walks with a cane and moves just short of the bottom step of Luke's porch.

"Dorothy," he corrects himself. "How are you today?"

"Just stopping by to see who this pretty lady is and why she's walking into your house with suitcases."

I giggle. This woman is nosy, and she ain't shy about it. "I'm Ellie," I say.

Her eyes dart to me and seem to narrow a bit, like she's checking me out and judging whether I'm good enough to be in Luke's presence.

"She's Josh Nolan's sister and she's going to be staying with me a while," Luke says. "She's new to town and you better be nice to her."

"I'm nice to everybody!" she protests, and Luke laughs. "Why aren't you staying with Josh if he's your brother?"

I laugh. "They're doing some renovations." It's the simplest answer for a nosy neighbor, and it'll give her something new to spy on.

"What are your intentions with my Lukey?" she asks me.

I'd love to bang him into oblivion.

I don't say those words. Obviously.

"He's been generous enough to offer me a place to stay for a while. That's all," I say.

Dorothy raises a brow. "That better be all," she says, pointing her cane at me. "Because I'm the only lady allowed to sit on that lap."

My eyes widen and Luke coughs uncomfortably. "Okay, Mrs. Adams, we need to get inside. But we'll see you soon."

"Yes, dear. My granddaughter will be in town in a couple weeks and she'd love to see you again."

Luke shoots her a smile and nods, and then he rushes to unlock the door and open it.

"Nice meeting you," I say to Dorothy, and I wiggle my fingers.

"I'm not sure about that," she mutters, and Luke ushers me in and closes the door before she gets a chance to say more.

I step into a round grand entry, and this house is just as ridiculous as my brother's. A staircase with fancy iron railings sprawls in front of me, circling up to the second floor. When I look straight up, though, there's a circular skylight letting the sunshine into the entry, giving the effect of daylight inside. It's bright and white and not at all what I was expecting.

"So that's my neighbor, Dorothy Adams," he says.

"Yeah, I gathered that. She gets to sit on your lap?"

I swear his cheeks turn a little pink, and he shrugs. "She's always been a little, uh...openly flirtatious with me. She's always asking me to fix shit at her house or open a jar of pickles. Then she either moans or makes comments the entire time I'm working."

"Doesn't that make you uncomfortable?" I ask.

"Incredibly. But she's a little old lady with no family around, so I do what I can to help."

Aha! Another insight into Luke Dalton.

He's not a douchebag. He helps old women even though they're inappropriate with him.

Instead of harping on that point, I glance around at the entryway. "Why do you need such a ridiculously enormous house?"

He laughs. "I don't. Brutal honesty, my ex-wife picked it out. She was always much more into showing her status than I was, only a small part of why we're no longer together."

"And she didn't get to keep it?"

He raises his brows and shoots me a sly smile. "I'm here, aren't I?"

"Why haven't you moved?" I ask.

He hitches up a shoulder. "Mostly for convenience, to be honest. But also for the backyard." He points awkwardly. "So this is the staircase, and that's upstairs."

I giggle. It's about as stupid a statement as when I said *I'm the sister* earlier. "I figured. How many bedrooms are up there?"

He squints as he looks up. "Technically there's six, but I've converted a few of them. Follow me." We walk through the massive entry to a hallway that leads into the kitchen.

This isn't just a kitchen, though.

If I was a chef, this kitchen would be a freaking dream. Hell, it *is* a dream, and while I'm not a chef, I sort of know my way around the kitchen.

"Wow," I breathe as I look at the endless black quartz countertops with little sparkles in them and the white cabinets and the gray walls with a white subway tile backsplash. It's just so...massive. Imposing. Beautiful.

He points toward the room connected to the kitchen. "That's family room number one."

"Number one?" I ask, and he nods.

"I have two. Plus a massage room, a fitness room, a home theater, a study, two offices, a yard overlooking the mountains with a pool, a pool house that doubles as a weight and workout room, and some sports courts."

I stare at him with my jaw hanging open. I'm sure I look like an idiot, but this is where I'm *living*? No wonder why Josh said I wouldn't even have to see Luke. I probably *won't* with all this space.

"Sports courts?" I echo...never mind the freaking *massage room*. Does that come staffed? I'm not opposed to Luke just rubbing some oil on me.

He nods. "A full basketball court, a tennis court, and I had a customized field put in with turf so I could run drills in the off-season. The patio has some workout equipment, too. You're welcome to use anything. I have a small house staff. Sheila comes in Monday and Thursday to clean. Debbie comes by a few times a week to cook. Handyman Cam swings by once a week for pool maintenance and whatever else I need him for. So if you see these people around, they're all supposed to be here."

I follow him through the house as I try to gain my bearings. This is like a freaking orientation.

We stop in front of a closed door. "Ready for this?" he asks, and I shake my head as my eyes widen. I don't know exactly what I'm supposed to be preparing for.

He opens the door, and a wild beast lunges at him. Okay, maybe not a wild beast, but an adorably cute puppy who's very excited to see her owner.

Luke just laughs as the dog licks his arms, and then he says, "Pepper, sit."

Pepper.

Oh my God. Pepper wasn't some side chick at all! She's his freaking *dog*!

I feel a little better. I survey the room. It's the other family room, and it has a few couches and a television. Dog beds and toys are scattered around the room with a crate in the corner, dog bowls, and a doggie door that looks like it leads to a fenced side yard with grass. It's a dog's paradise, honestly.

"Ellie, I'd like to introduce you to Pepper, the current love of my life." He scratches her under her chin, and the dog sits patiently and wags her tail. "Do you like dogs?" he asks me.

I nod and kneel down. "How old is she?" She lunges for me, but Luke holds her back.

"Calm, Pepper," he says to the dog, and then he turns to me. "She's four months."

"And what kind is she?" I try to guess, but I'm at a loss. She's some kind of mix with multi-colored black, tan, and white fur, and she has blue eyes. She's possibly the cutest little thing I've ever seen...but she's actually not so little.

"A Goberian," he says, like I'm supposed to know what the hell that is.

"A Go-what now?"

"Golden Retriever mixed with a Siberian Husky. She could get up to ninety pounds, but she's supposed to have all the best traits from both breeds."

"How long have you had her?"

"Just picked her up a few weeks ago. Josh talked me into getting her." He laughs and shakes his head, like he's blaming my brother but actually isn't so mad about it. "And, incidentally, she's the reason I needed to jet out so quickly after our night together.

My dog monitor app showed me she got out of her cage and this room was a damn disaster."

I blush as he brings up that night, and I wonder if I'll always feel a little embarrassed about it. It was a night that should've only left one impression, but neither of us had any idea that we'd meet again. Or that we'd end up as roommates less than seventy-two short hours after we met.

God, what a whirlwind three days it has been.

He shows me the sports courts and the outdoor living space and he takes me through the rest of the house. He leads me up the stairs, past some closed doors, and to the last room on the left. "This will be your room," he says.

He opens the door to a pristine and lavish guest room that overlooks the pool and the mountains. It has a huge bed with white sheets, a walk-in closet, and its own bathroom.

"Will this work?" he asks, and he almost seems a little...shy. Maybe even nervous. Like I'm judging his house.

"Will it work?" I repeat. I skip around the giant room and use one of the poles holding up the canopy over the bed to spin around—which probably makes me look like I'm a stripper rather than the whimsical look I'm going for. "Uh, hell yeah it'll work. How long did you say I could stay?"

He laughs, but before he can answer that, I chime back in.

"I'm kidding. I'm planning to start looking for a job tomorrow, and as soon as I get that squared away, then I'm hoping to find a place and get out of your hair ASAP."

"That's not necessary," he says softly, and his eyes burn from across the room by the door where he stands. "Take your time. It's a big house and most days it feels pretty empty."

Hence the reason for a dog, I'm guessing. Josh is definitely the meddling type who would make sure his friend didn't feel all alone in the gargantuan mansion across the street.

"You want something to eat?" he asks.

I nod, and then I follow him through the long hallway, down the marble and iron staircase, across the foyer, and finally to the kitchen. I note that he only showed me *my* bedroom. He didn't show me his or any of the others that had closed doors.

"Hey Pepper girl," he says to the dog, who's lying in the sun by the huge breakfast nook that's more like a dining room. "Let's see what Debbie left for us."

"Why'd you name her Pepper?" I ask.

"It's the leading lady in my favorite movie," he says.

My brows dip down. I can't think of any movies with Peppers in them.

"*Iron Man*," he clarifies. He rummages through the fridge and I pull out a stool on the other side of the counter from him and plop down. "We have bacon turkey ranch wraps or chicken salad sandwiches."

"Either. Can I help?"

He shakes his head and pulls out a container with the wraps in it. He grabs some plates and puts one in front of me and one in front of the spot next to me. "Drink?"

"Water is fine."

He grabs water, too, and then he sits next to me.

"So, Ellie, what kind of job are you looking for?" he asks.

"Public relations. Or, that was my field, anyway."

"What's the end-goal there?" He sips some water, and my eyes move to his lips as his tongue darts out to catch a drop.

An ache presses between my thighs.

I blow out a breath. "I mean, ultimately I would have loved to work my way up to higher profile celebrity clients."

"Well your roommate is a pro football player," he casually points out.

I roll my eyes. I suppose he wants free PR in exchange for offering me a room? I guess it's something I could offer, but certainly the team has a PR staff...right? "I mean *real* celebrities."

"Ouch," he says, patting his chest over his heart.

"You know what I mean," I say.

"Not really," he teases with an easy laugh. "Athletes aren't celebrities?"

My brother is an athlete. Is he a celebrity? I've never considered him one, but I guess the truth is that he *is* one. "I just mean like actors, musicians, that sort of thing. I don't know enough about sports to represent an athlete, though if the price was right, I'd learn."

"So money is what it'll take for you to learn football?" He raises a brow as he takes a bite of his wrap.

I lift a shoulder. "We all have our motivations, right?" Though when it comes to Luke Dalton, money is hardly the motivator. A quick flash of a smile would be enough for me to do just about anything.

And the more I think about it, the more interested I'm becoming in seeing him run around the field in those tight pants on Sunday afternoons.

Maybe I *am* suddenly interested in football.

"Speaking of which, I looked you up on social media and couldn't find you. Don't you have a PR manager or publicist?" I ask. I realize I just gave myself away, and that's my filter malfunctioning again, but I've embarrassed myself around this guy so much already that I feel like I can't really be any more mortified than I already have been.

He glances over at me with arched brows. "You looked me up?"

"Well, yeah. I had to know what I was getting into when I found out you were going to be my roommate." It's a lie. I totally looked him up because I couldn't stop thinking about him and I wanted to see his face again in a picture other than the one I memorized of us from the night of our hookup. "So why couldn't I find you?"

He lifts a shoulder. "I'm private."

"You can still be private and have social media."

He takes another bite of his wrap and lifts a shoulder. "I don't need it. I've gotten by fine for this long without it."

"So you're private, but you're willing to have a one-night stand with a random chick from a nightclub *and* you're willing to let your best friend's little sister live with you without ever having met her?"

He chuckles. "Those events are unrelated."

"Except they're the same person."

"Well, yeah, but..." he trails off. "I didn't know who you were that night, just like you didn't know who I was. It wasn't supposed to go past that one night, and I could tell you had no idea who I was, so that's why you ended up being the perfect candidate. Plus that sweet ass of yours."

I roll my eyes, but on the inside, butterflies batter around as my thighs clench together.

"And I trust Josh implicitly," he says. "I don't need to have met you to know you're trustworthy to stay here for a bit if you're cut from the same cloth as him."

I twist my lips, conceding. "Okay. But I'll get you to change your mind on social media."

"Then I'll get you to change your mind on football."

"Guess we've both got work to do," I say, and I take a bite of my wrap.

But the truth is...I don't mind one little bit being the *work* he has to *do*.

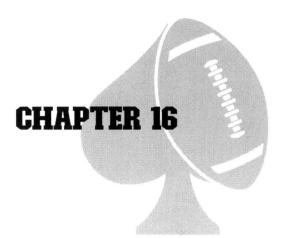

CHAPTER 16

Luke brought my suitcases up to the room that's mine and told me to make myself at home, and so I do.

I unpack, setting some clothes in the dresser and hanging others in the closet. I even unpack my toiletries, making the bathroom mine because it sure as hell beats living out of bags.

I toss the empty suitcases in the closet and move toward the window.

I sigh as I look out over the view of the mountains. I glance down at the yard. The sun shines down on the pool surrounded by palm trees, and this Chicago native *always* viewed palm trees as vacation.

But this is home now. For now, anyway.

Some movement near the patio catches my eye, and when I glance in that direction, my heart races and my brain basically malfunctions.

Luke.

No shirt.

Abs.

Sweat.

Muscles.

Running on a treadmill.

Focus and discipline and heat.

Drool. (That's me, not him.)

I blow out a breath.

So he's not a prince? Okay, maybe I can bend my fairy tale a little.

So he's already written me off? Okay, but if he can run on a treadmill right under my window without a shirt on, then...What? I can walk in front of the window without a shirt on? Maybe.

Or I can come up with other ways to tempt him. I did, after all, already share a bed with him once, and we both admitted how hot it was. I'm not saying it has to be forever, but he was into me enough to give me one night.

But it was just one night. He didn't want more than that, and I still don't know why.

I get it—he's a private guy. But we're living together now, and I'm going to get to the bottom of this.

I force myself away from the window. I can't sit here and watch him all day or I'll go crazy.

I reorganize my makeup in the bathroom and then I head down to the family room. I toss my phone on the counter and head to the fridge for some more water. And then I look at the television. I see some remotes on an end table, and I pick one up.

I stare at it. I can't figure out which button is the power button, and I don't even know if the thing I'm holding in my hand is the right remote to turn on the television.

"Television on," I say, hoping that by some miracle that in the fanciness that is this house, technology will be on my side.

Nothing happens, but Pepper looks at me like I'm insane, her head tilted to the side and her ears perked up.

"Don't tell your daddy I just did that," I whisper to Pepper, and she just lets out a little whimper before resting her head on her paws.

I plop on the couch, and Pepper jumps up next to me. She settles onto the cushion beside me, turning in three circles before lying down with a heavy sigh, and I laugh at her even as I realize I have no idea if she's supposed to be up on the furniture. She looks so cozy, though, that I don't have the heart to make her get down. She settles her head on my thigh, and I stroke her soft fur.

Luke walks into the room through a door from outside that I honestly thought was just a big window. He's a little sweaty and he still isn't wearing a shirt. He chuckles when he sees me with his dog.

"You know," he says casually, "you're only the second woman who has met Pepper since I brought her home, but she did *not* like the first."

"Who was the first?" I ask.

"My ex-wife."

I giggle. "Sounds like you don't much like her, either."

He grabs a sports drink from the fridge and chugs a little of it down. "I don't," he says, and before I can dig a little deeper there, he offers a little more information. "We just don't share the same values."

"What does she value?"

"Money," he says, his answer firm and immediate. She seems like she scarred him a little.

"And you?" I ask.

"People. Hard work. Dedication. We were opposites in that way. She didn't care about the hard work it took to earn money, she just wanted to show off mine." He clears his throat, chugs some more of his drink, then lowers his voice a little. "What about you, Ellie? What do you value?"

"Well, I'd say work, but I don't have a job. But I did love what I used to do. I love when someone hands me a project and I get to take my creativity to solve a problem, so I guess I value creativity. I value my family, of course, and love."

"Fairy tales," he murmurs, and I chuckle. His phone rings, and he pulls it out of the band still attached to his arm. "Fuck," he mutters. "Speak of the devil."

He answers the call and heads out of the room, and he returns a few minutes later while I'm still petting (and conversing with) Pepper (who really hasn't given me any insights into her hot dad). He's freshly showered and sadly wearing a shirt.

He slides into a recliner across the room, and Pepper jumps down, leaps across the room, and jumps onto his lap.

"Traitor," I mutter.

Luke chuckles as he pets the dog. "I can't help that I'm her favorite human."

"We'll see about that. Just wait until she's fully grown and still leaping on you like that."

An easy silence passes between us, and then I ask, "So which remote actually turns the TV on? You didn't train me on those during orientation."

He laughs, and then he picks up Pepper and sets her on the floor. He stands, grabs all the remotes sitting there, and tells me what each one does—something I will never, ever remember, which I admit.

My phone starts to ring on the kitchen counter, and as I move to stand, he says, "I'll grab it for you."

"Thanks," I say as I juggle the remotes and set them down on the couch beside me.

He returns a few seconds later, and when he hands me my phone which he most certainly just saw, the image of the two of us that I snapped the night he left my hotel room shines brightly at me and he has a look on his face that clearly says he thinks I'm absolutely a crazy, insane stalker.

"Oh my God," I mutter in total mortification. Yep, that's right. I just told myself that I couldn't get embarrassed in front of this guy again because I'd already reached my limit, yet here we are again. "I swear to God, I put that picture on there as a joke before I even knew who you were. I was going to show it to Nicki and brag about my one-night stand and then I found out you were the best man and I just haven't changed it back yet."

I'm babbling and my phone is actually still ringing—it's a Chicago number I don't know but it has the same first three digits as my old office, so it's probably HR or something calling to tell me I won't get my last paycheck just to put the cherry on top of this shit sundae, and he's totally uncomfortable as he continues to look at me like I'm possibly dangerous.

I send the call to voicemail because I can't just answer a call when I need to fix this. I change the photo on my phone to the same picture I had on there before, which was just a pretty purple design, and then I flash my phone at him. "Better?"

"You're a little terrifying," he finally croaks.

"Yeah, I know."

He laughs, and then he sits back in the same chair which I will call *his chair.* Pepper jumps back on his lap. "So let's see...you stalked me on social media, you changed your phone wallpaper to a picture of us, and now you're living with me."

"Yep, that about sums it up." I twist my lips. "Okay, subject change. How's football going?"

"Well, we're in the offseason, so right now it's pretty stagnant. But the upcoming year is a contract year."

"What does that mean?" I ask stupidly.

"It means I have to play my ass off so my contract is renewed." He scratches Pepper behind the ears.

"How long do you want to keep playing?" I set my phone down next to me.

He lifts a shoulder as he keeps his eyes on the dog. "Forever? Football's just...everything to me. It's been a constant in my life since I was a little kid. I'm from a football family. My dad was a college coach and it was just sort of expected of me. It's all I ever wanted to do." His voice holds vulnerability that he hasn't shown me before. Apparently football is the thing that makes him emotive. I lean a bit in his direction as he opens up. "The Aces just drafted this kid right out of college, and that tells me they're looking at the future of the team. He's young and fast and he's going to slide right into my slot."

"You don't know that," I say, but maybe he does.

"I'm the oldest receiver on the team. The average age for receivers in the league is twenty-six. I'm thirty-one. The average career is two years. I've been playing for nine. It's only a matter of time." He doesn't seem at all like he's okay with that. In fact, that vulnerability has taken a turn to something else. A little bit of sadness mixed with some despondency.

"So what's your plan?" I ask, my public relations background forcing its way out. I'm not one to sit around and complain. I'm more likely to find the solution.

"To keep playing until I can't," he says.

"And then what?"

He twists his lips. "Nothing definitive."

"Broadcasting?" I ask.

He shrugs.

"Coaching?"

"Maybe."

"Okay, you need a plan, dude. You need something to look forward to. Isn't there something you've always wanted to do?" I ask.

"Yeah. Play football. I don't want to talk about what happens when I can't anymore."

Okay, so this guy is stubborn. I tap my chin and change the subject, but I don't forget about it. I just push it to the back of my mind for now. "Would you consider playing somewhere else?"

He shakes his head. "I've played for the Aces my entire career. I'd love to finish my career here, too."

"What if you were traded?" I ask.

He looks at me in horror. "We don't speak the 'T' word in this house," he says, and I think he's joking but I'm not totally sure.

"Then you make yourself essential," I say, as if the answer was obvious all along.

His brows push together. "How do I do that?"

"Simple," I say, suddenly feeling very comfortable in my own shoes. "We put together a PR strategy. And I know just the girl to do it."

CHAPTER 17

He rubs the back of his neck and tilts his head. "What sort of strategy?"

I shrug. "You already know I know nothing about football, but I know a little something about proving your worth. Off the top of my head, and I'm just thinking out loud here, but community outreach is a good first step. Charity work. Meeting fans, shaking hands, holding babies, that sort of thing. Becoming the fan favorite that brings money to the team will keep you around. Obviously you'll need to let people in via social media to do any of that."

He shakes his head and holds up his hands. "Nope. I'm out."

"Why?" I demand.

"Being a *fan favorite* won't secure my spot," he says.

"You don't know that."

"Uh, yeah, I do," he says. "I've been in this business a long time, and that's the thing, Ellie. It's a *business.* I'm just a pawn in the league's game, and there are thousands of men waiting to snatch my position away from me."

"But it couldn't hurt to step up your presence, could it?" I press, wondering why he's so against this. "Wouldn't that only help?"

"My *social media* presence? That's a hard no."

"Why are you so against social media?" I pry.

He glances away and doesn't answer.

"Look, you can still maintain your privacy. I'm just saying, post a picture of you and Josh from this weekend to show how your relationship translates off the field. It's not like you need to post my phone's wallpaper as you brag about your one-night stand conquest." My cheeks redden even as the words tumble out of my mouth.

Why, exactly, am I reminding him of this?

I press on. "A picture of your pool with your hand holding your Gatorade. No face."

"Then I look like I'm endorsing Gatorade," he says.

"Do you have a contract with Powerade?" I ask.

He shakes his head.

"Some other sports drink?"

He continues shaking his head.

"Then who cares? You like Gatorade, and you drink it after a workout. Cover the label if that makes you feel better. Post a picture of you working out on that treadmill on your patio. Post a picture of yourself playing basketball on your backyard court. You at practice. Your uniform. Hell, even a shot of your shoes for next season. It doesn't matter what it is. People want to feel like they have an inside pass to your life, and *that* is how you become a fan favorite. You want to be that guy that will cause a fan revolt if the 'T' word is even mentioned in this city."

He narrows his eyes at me. "Okay, well, for one thing, no, but for another thing, how would I even get any of those pictures to post?"

I give him a look like he's stupid.

I may be dumb when it comes to football, but clearly Luke is dumb when it comes to public relations.

"Uh, you have a roommate who's basically volunteering to help you, Luke. Social media is a key part of PR, and if you want me to be your expert, it'll be my job to curate your content, post it, and stimulate engagement." I pull my phone out and open Instagram. I search one of the clients I worked with back in Chicago and toss him my phone. "This is one of my former clients, and this is their Instagram feed. You can see the types of things I posted on their behalf."

"This looks great," he says as he scrolls through the photos and stops to glance at some of the captions. "But it's a restaurant. I'm an athlete."

I nod. "Yeah, those are two different things for sure, but the principles are the same. My job with the restaurant was to make it irresistible. I had to post pictures that made the food leap off the page. I had to show people having a great time. I had to make sure anyone scrolling would stop and feel the vibe I wanted them to feel. And those are the exact same things I'd do with you, but I'd use the word *indispensable* instead of *irresistible*."

I refrain from mentioning that he already *is* irresistible.

"I'd make people want to stop scrolling to get to know a piece of you that you've worked so damn hard to keep hidden. I'll make them feel the vibe that the Aces are nothing without Luke Dalton, and they won't continue to be a fan of the team if you're not on it. Their loyalties move with you, not with the team. Sort of like all these new Tampa Bay fans now that *you know who* moved," I say, speaking about one of the most famous quarterbacks in the league. I'm no expert but even I heard about that.

"By posting pictures of me on a treadmill?" He seems doubtful.

I smile. "Seems like you're starting to get it."

He's quiet as he mulls over my idea, and eventually he heaves out a long breath. "What if I agree to it?"

"Seriously?" I ask, my eyes wide in total shock at his complete one-eighty.

"Okay, forget it." He shakes his head and moves to stand.

"Wait!" I say, a little desperation there in my voice as I realize I need this job just as much as he needs me to do it. "If you agree to it, then I draft out a real plan, you approve it, and we get moving."

"What do you charge?" he asks.

For Luke Dalton? Nothing. The chance to get this insider view of his life? Priceless. "How about room and board?"

He chuckles. "Don't be ridiculous. You need a job, and you just pitched yourself to me. I wasn't looking to hire, yet you've somehow convinced me that I need you to keep my job. So I'll ask you again, and I mean apart from room and board since you'll have those here as long as you need them. What do you charge?" I'm just supposed to come up with a number? I had a salary at my last job. I guess I could charge him a portion of what I took home every two weeks, but I had more than one client.

I also had a team of others behind me, including my ex. I won't have that here.

"Okay, how about this," he says to my silence as I weigh what the hell I should say. "I throw out a number, and you agree or disagree. Sound fair?"

"I need to draft your strategy first so you can determine what you think I'm worth," I point out.

"I think I know your worth," he murmurs, and I can't tell if he's flirting with me again or if he's accidentally dropping his thoughts aloud—sort of the same way I do sometimes. "But fine. Strategize and let's talk when you have it. How long do you need? A week or two?"

"I literally have nothing else going on. I can probably have it to you by morning."

He laughs. "Okay, roomie. Take the night off and work on it tomorrow. If you want, we could order something for dinner and just hang here with Pepper and maybe a movie. Sound okay? Good times with someone who's becoming a good friend."

My heart balloons during the part where he basically asks me on a date, but he manages to pop it just as quickly there at the end with his final word: *friend*.

That's all we are, and that's all he'll allow me to be.

For now.

I nod. "Sounds great. I've never seen the movie with Pepper's namesake, so maybe *Iron Man*."

He shoots me a look like I'm crazy. "You've never seen *Iron Man*?"

I shake my head.

"Then that's definitely what we're watching."

A few hours later, we're sprawled on the couch with Chinese food. Pepper lies on the floor by our feet with a chew toy, and the movie plays while we eat.

It feels like a date night in with my boyfriend.

But, I remind myself, that's not at all what it is.

In fact, depending what he thinks about the strategy I'm thinking about when I should be concentrating on the movie, it's sort of like a night in with my potential new boss.

CHAPTER 18

I stare down at the blank sheet of paper.

I swear, last night when we were watching that movie, I had about a million and one ideas for what to do, and now that I'm ready to draft the plan, I'm drawing a total blank.

It's not because Luke's out on the treadmill in his short runner's shorts and no shirt again. That's not what's distracting me except it totally is and my eyes keep moving toward the window because good God I could sit here and watch this show all damn day.

I make a list of food I want to keep around the house. Luke told me last night to add whatever I want to the general list and Debbie will pick it up. It's a great distraction when I'm supposed to be working.

It's quite the system here at Casa de Luke, and while I actually enjoy cooking, I'm certainly not the pro Debbie is. I basically add popcorn, extra bananas, and Smirnoff Seltzers (since Luke apparently only keeps beer and hard liquor around this place) to the list and call it a day.

"Focus, Ellie. Focus," I say aloud, and Pepper tilts her head at me in the same way she did yesterday, like she's trying to understand what I'm saying.

I draw in a breath, and then I pull up the worksheet I used to use at my old company whenever I'd draft a strategy. I immediately recall the acronym I always used when strategizing: SLUTS, or Situation assessment, Landscape trends, Usable data to help develop a plan, Timeline for the client, and, last, Setting goals.

He needs a lot of help. I'm going to start with social media, but he'll need a spokesperson who can handle interview, sponsorship, and collaboration requests, a publicist who can identify ways to get him out into the community, and a media relations specialist who can get the media to the same events he's at to ensure coverage. I'll need access to his agent and anyone else representing him. My specialty was always social media, but I have experience in the other areas, too.

When I think about assessing Luke's current situation and what he can do to change or improve...well, we're starting at zero. Literally. He doesn't even have an Instagram account, so anything we do will be an improvement.

I look at the landscape next. I search the top wide receivers, including my own brother, and study what types of things they post. I research other popular players and what makes them popular. I'll need more information there, and I write out all the questions I have for Luke as well as other areas to research so I can gather the most relevant usable data once I get the green light on this project.

I create a content calendar of what Luke will be posting for the next few weeks, but a lot depends on his schedule. I jot down some more questions for him. He admitted that football is his life, and when I look at what similar athletes are posting, I see a lot of collaborations and brand representing, lots of pictures of kids and families, pictures from professional events, and plenty of game day or practice action photos. I jot down a ton of notes, and I see what he means about taking a photo with a product because then he looks like he's repping that product. I'm sure once his page is verified as real, the offers will start pouring in.

And, finally, I set some goals. I note the average number of followers the most popular receivers have, which lands right around a million. And, most notably, our goal here is to make the fans fall even more in love with him by getting to know him so the entire organization will think twice about forcing him into an early retirement, though from what I've learned, his performance this season is the one thing that'll really prove he deserves to stick around. As much as I know he's attached to the Aces because it's the only place he has played, it's still a business, and if he doesn't perform to the level they need, well, they'll let him go.

All this from a few hours of research.

I glance over my plan, and I'm pretty proud of myself. I've never represented an athlete before, but if he agrees, this is going to look freaking amazing on my resume.

I bring my notes and questions to the kitchen, where I find Luke—or, rather, Luke's backside—rummaging through the fridge.

"I'm ready," I say.

He glances at the clock, surprise in his eyes when they return to me. "I figured you'd need all day."

I shrug. "I'm a fast worker, but also, I definitely have about ten thousand questions to ask you before I can finalize the strategy, so this is mostly preliminary and what I discovered through some quick research and data gathering."

"Okay," he says, pulling out a bag of baby carrots and popping one in his mouth. He crunches down on it. "Hit me with the plan."

I run through a quick presentation, sharing each part of my SLUTS acronym with him without actually calling it *SLUTS*, going over a few ways he can give back to the local community and build a brand for himself, and by the time I'm done, his brows are raised and he looks fairly impressed.

He nods. "Okay, I can get on board with building a brand. I like your community outreach ideas. And I can even approve photos of myself, or what I'm eating, or practice. Things like that. But my personal life is off-limits and my privacy remains intact no matter what."

"Of course. It's your social media even though I'm running it. I'll control it as much or as little as you're comfortable with," I say. "But can I ask why you're so worried about privacy?"

He stares at me for a beat as if he's weighing what to say, and then he doesn't really say anything at all. "It's just important to me.

At the start, I'll need to approve everything, including captions and those stupid little number sign things."

"Hashtags?" I ask, and he nods. "Okay, micromanager."

He chuckles. "If you don't mind me asking, what were you making at your last position?"

"What is all this worth to you?" I ask rather than answering. "I'll tell you, but I'm just curious."

"Having you post for me a few times a week?"

"Daily," I say. "Not just to your Instagram profile page, but also to your stories. It's best to choose one platform to focus on, but I'll also get your Facebook and Twitter up and running. If you want Snapchat or Tik Tok, we can talk about that, too. I'll curate everything, maximize each post for your audience, and slowly build your engagement and your followers. But bear in mind that this isn't just me posting on your social media. I will sort of be your personal assistant when it comes to building your brand. I'll handle scheduling interviews, working on collaborations, and finding opportunities for you. So I'm not just your PR expert and your assistant since I'll need to basically run your calendar, but I'm also your spokesperson, social media manager, and publicist all for the price of one hot girl."

He laughs. "Definitely hot," he murmurs. "I've never had a personal assistant. I've never needed one."

"Do you think you need one now?" I ask. "Because you better believe it'll be my job to be up in your business all day every day."

He wrinkles his nose.

"I'll be in your face with a camera, and I'll expect you to be completely open and honest with me," I say. I lay it all on the line because what's the worst that can happen? He'll say no? Okay, then I'm right back to where I am now, and I'd rather be honest about what he can expect from me than surprise him later.

"I'm liking this idea less and less," he mutters. "But I want to stay with the Aces. I know I need to prove myself this season, as you mentioned, but none of this other stuff can hurt me. I have no idea what that's worth. Four hundred bucks a day, presuming you'll be working basically twenty-four-seven?"

My eyes widen at his number. That's, like, over a hundred grand a year. I try to mentally calculate it. Almost a hundred fifty.

Well over double what I was making before, but I wasn't *living* with my clients before, either. I didn't have any clients that were single entities that I had to brand.

Still…that's a lot of money, so I give him my honest answer. "That's more than double what I was making in Chicago."

He lifts a shoulder. "From your presentation here, I think you'll be well worth it. Let's try it for a week or two and see how we mesh, but I think we'll make a great team."

"Team Dalton," I say, and he laughs and holds up his knuckles.

I bump his knuckles with mine, and he agrees. "Team Dalton. Let's do this. Set me up on Instagram."

CHAPTER 19

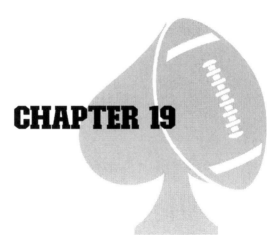

A knock at the door pulls Luke's attention from my explanation of stories on Instagram, which, let's be honest, he was half-listening to anyway. It would be better if *he* took on the stories since I probably can't literally be with him every second of every day (even if I wish I could be), but it is what it is. Even better, I'd love to see him going live there or tossing up some video footage from practice or from charity events or whatever, but he has to actually listen to my training in order for any of that to happen.

"Excuse me," he says, and he heads toward the door. A few beats later, he yells, "Ellie! Your stuff's here!"

I jump down from the stool and head toward the door. A moving truck sits out front, and the excitement that my clothes and bullet journal supplies and blankets and shoes are all here rams into me. I came here with a couple of suitcases, but this...this is what makes a *home*.

"Where do you want this?" one of the men standing on the porch asks.

"Clothes and shoes in the bedroom, and anything else can go into one of my offices," Luke says. "We can move the rest from there."

"Are you sure?" I ask. "They can just put everything in my room."

He shakes his head. "It's fine. You don't want your room overflowing with boxes, do you?"

I shrug. I sort of figured that's how I'd live until I find a place of my own, but this works, too. I'll still have boxes overflowing *somewhere*—they'll just be out of sight.

"Thank you," I murmur, and the movers set to unloading boxes from the truck.

I left my furniture in my parents' basement just in case I decide to return to Chicago. I can find a furnished place out here, and once I decide whether I'm staying here permanently, we can figure out how to get my furniture here. Everything else I own is on the truck sitting at the curb.

"Bullet journal box one?" he reads off the side of one of the boxes stacked on the mover's hand truck. "How many bullet journal boxes are there, exactly?"

"Three," I admit with just a touch of embarrassment.

His brows dip. "Three?"

"Being creatively organized is *not* a crime," I say, and he just laughs.

My bullet journal boxes are stacked in his spare office, and my clothes and blankets and shoes are up in my room. I feel more at home with this stuff here even though I had the essentials with me. It only takes the movers about an hour to unload everything, and we head back to the counter to finish our Instagram training. I've only gotten about a minute into my explanation when the doorbell rings again.

Luke sighs and gets up to answer it. A few beats later, I hear him say, "What are you doing here?"

His voice sounds...tired. Weary. Annoyed.

I glance toward the direction of their voices, and if I lean back just a little, I can see his back from where I sit perched on a stool at the kitchen counter without making it totally obvious that I'm trying to spy.

It's just a totally different Luke than I've heard before.

"I just want to talk," the voice says, and it's a woman. "Can I come in?"

"No," he says. "If you want to talk, you can call or text me."

I lean back a little more in my stool to try to get a glimpse of the woman who's annoying Luke, but I lean a little *too* far back.

The stool topples backward with me still on it. I try to grab onto the counter to save myself, but I go right down with it. The fall toward the ground feels like it happens in slow motion, and it ends with a loud crash as my ass hits the floor at the same time as the stool.

"Oh, shit, Ellie!" Luke says from the front hall. He rushes back toward me to help me up, and my cheeks are absolutely *burning* with embarrassment as I stand. "Are you okay?" he asks. He picks up the stool and pushes it in at the counter.

"I'm fine," I mutter. Holy. Shit. I cannot believe I just did that. My ass took the brunt of it. I rub at it, and that's when he chuckles just a little.

Is he laughing? At me?

The woman he was talking to through the doorway rushes in behind him. She looks like she stepped off the pages of *Vogue* with her long, dark hair falling in a stick-straight curtain and dark eyes that are full of lust for Luke...and then there's me, the dork who just fell off a stool like some idiot.

Clearly Luke doesn't like her, made obvious by the way he told her she couldn't come in on top of the way he's looking at her like she should get the hell out of his house lest she stain something while she's inside it.

I'm glad he's never looked at me with that sort of wrath, but remind me to stay on his good side.

Is this the ex-wife? The ex-girlfriend? The ex-*something*?

"Who is this?" she demands, plopping her purse down on the counter.

"I'm Ellie," I say stupidly. I think of all the ways I can identify myself. His best friend's sister? His roommate? His one-night stand? His...

"My fiancée," Luke supplies.

Wait.

What?

That definitely wasn't one of the words I just thought of.

My eyes meet his. The way they silently beg tells me that I need to agree to this.

I need to fake this with him in this moment, and he can explain later.

And so I do what I've wanted to do every second I've spent with him.

No...not that. There's a woman watching us with her mouth hanging open just a tad in complete and utter disbelief, so I can't do *that*.

I lace my arm around his waist and press a kiss to his cheek. The stubble there is rough under my lips, transporting me back to a hotel room on the Strip, and I'm so close that I feel his heat against me. He smells familiar with that fresh, manly scent that I memorized in those few beats where we collapsed on the bed together and I breathed him in.

Our night flashes back to me. It's almost painful how much detail flashes back.

Being so close to him...it's just the slightest hint that makes me crave so much more. An aching pulse throbs between my legs, and I am royally screwed.

I want my brother's best friend who just told some woman we're engaged even though he vowed that I'm off-limits to him.

And I want him *bad*.

He tosses his arm around my shoulders, and I flex my fingers where they're wrapped around his torso. Good God, I feel a little dizzy this close to him. Focus, Ellie. Focus.

"Your fiancée?" the woman repeats. Her disbelieving voice matches the expression on her face.

"Yeah," Luke says. He pulls me in closer.

"Weren't you not even dating someone like five minutes ago?" she asks snidely.

"It's actually none of your business. So what did you want to talk about?"

His fingers dig into my shoulder, and clearly this woman makes him tense. I'm sure I could find ways to relax him...

"She isn't wearing a ring," she accuses, her eyes flashing to my left hand.

"She doesn't need one to proclaim her status to the world like some people I know," he retorts.

Yes! Go Luke.

"Well whatever," she says, clearly trying to pretend like this doesn't throw her for a total loop.

"Why are you here?" Luke asks.

"Aren't you going to introduce us?" she asks slyly, ignoring his question and acting like she already has a game plan for overcoming the wrench in her plan that is me.

I stay as quiet as I can while Luke handles this situation however he wants to. I'm just along for the ride at this point.

"Ellie, it's my sincerest regret to have to introduce you to my ex-girlfriend, Michelle."

"Oh, I'm more than his ex-*girlfriend*," she says snidely, like she hates the very word. "We were lovers. We were connected in every way two humans can be connected."

Luke rolls his eyes. "And yet we're not anymore."

"I've heard so much about you," I lie smoothly, giving her my fakest, most sugary smile as I stick out my hand to shake hers.

She doesn't return the handshake, so I'm just standing there with my hand out like an idiot.

So, rather than feel like an idiot, I turn to Luke and ask, "Is she the coffee spoon in the sugar bowl girl?"

He barks out a laugh, and my chest is positively *glowing* from making him laugh like that.

She narrows her eyes at me. "I've heard nothing about you. She's not your usual type, Luke." With those words, she spins on her heel and heads toward the door, both of us following her. "Looks like I've got a big story for Savannah, so you should let me know when you can fit me into your very busy schedule." She presses her lips together in a fake, tight smile.

"Oh, fuck you, Michelle. Expect a call from my lawyer."

"I'll be looking forward to it." She winks at me, unruffled by this entire exchange—or at least pretending like she is. "His lawyer is a hottie, am I right?" She wiggles her fingers and says, "Ta-ta for now." She sashays out the front door like she still lives here.

Luke slams it closed behind her, and he sighs deeply as he stands there facing it. When he turns back toward me, I'm wide-eyed and silent as I look at the weary expression on his handsome face. I may not know him all that well, but clearly this woman does things to him that both age and exhaust him. I'm inclined to give him a hug, but we definitely aren't at that stage of our friendship yet.

Even though I'm apparently engaged to him.

"I'm sorry," he mutters.

"For what?"

He glances over at me. "For using you in my lie." He balls his fists. "For telling her you're my fiancée. I shouldn't have put you in that spot. She just makes me so goddamn angry that it just slipped out."

I clear my throat. I have a lot of questions, but there's one that's sort of pounding in my chest with every beat of my heart. "Who's Savannah?"

He draws in a long breath, and his eyes meet mine for a beat before he answers. "My ex-wife. Michelle's apparent new best friend...and a journalist."

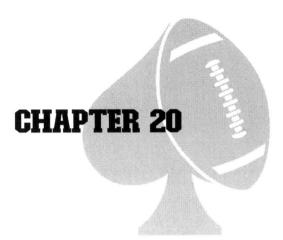

CHAPTER 20

"Well, I think I get why you're so private now."

He chuckles mirthlessly, and then he walks through the house and collapses on the couch like the entire encounter with Michelle took more out of him than his morning runs on the treadmill. He draws in a heavy breath. "Savannah is technically a sports reporter, but she found fame reporting on the personal lives of athletes. I was not exempt from that during our marriage, and that's a big reason why we're no longer married. Well, that and she's an insufferable nightmare."

I laugh as I sit a cushion and a half away from him. "Tell me how you really feel. What did she publish that got your panties all twisted up?"

He glances at me for a beat before he leans back and stares up at the ceiling in contemplation, like he isn't sure how much to tell me. And then, maybe because he trusts me, maybe because he's paying me for publicity, or maybe because I've made a fool of myself hundreds of times in the short period of time we've known each other, he spills some tea.

"She asked me if she could write what she called a tell-all series of articles based on my brother and me."

"You have a brother?" I ask.

He nods. "Jack Dalton. Current starting quarterback for the Broncos, but he's also played in Dallas and San Diego, back when the team actually *was* in San Diego. On his way to the Hall of Fame. God, you really don't watch football."

I laugh and hold up a hand. "Sorry. So what did these articles say?"

"I didn't love the idea, but I wanted her to find success in her career. And she did. Those articles *made* her career. The first few were great, but then she started to paint this rivalry between us. And there *was* always a rivalry there, but she made it worse. It became less of a sports report and more of a tabloid exposé."

"That's awful," I murmur, even though I'm insanely curious to find those articles. "So why is Michelle running to her?"

He rolls his eyes. "Attention. Plus I'm sure Savannah will pay her for the gossip, and tomorrow our engagement will be everywhere."

"Is that why you threatened her with your lawyer?" I ask.

He nods, and then he shrugs. "It's useless, though. That type of journalism isn't illegal, even though it should be. Unethical, yes, but not illegal."

"Well that sucks. So why'd you tell her we're engaged if you knew she'd run to Savannah?"

"I don't know," he mutters. "It just slipped out before I even gave it a second thought. I wanted to hit her with something I knew would hurt her because she hurt me, too." He glances over at me and shoots me a wry smile. "See? I told you. I'm no prince."

I let that last comment slip past. "So am I supposed to pretend we're engaged?"

He rubs the back of his neck. "Maybe?" He tilts his head as he thinks it over, and he shakes his head resolutely. "No. Your brother would *kill* me."

"Why not? Would it help get her off your back?"

"I can't ask you to do that," he says. "I shouldn't have said what I said. I put you in an awkward position, and I'm sorry."

"Why can't you ask me to do that?" I ask, genuinely curious.

His brows dip down. "You're young and single and gorgeous. You could have any guy who's looking for a relationship, and I can't be the guy who holds you back from finding that. Not when it's not what I want."

I roll my eyes, but it doesn't escape me that he just called me *gorgeous*.

"What?" he asks.

"Dude, I'm not looking." I laugh. "Let me spell it out for you. I just got out of a thing, I'm brand new to Vegas, I'm trying to figure out my job situation with my roommate boss. I'm handling enough shit right now, so trust me when I say that hunting for a boyfriend isn't a priority for me at the moment."

"But what about your brother? And how long will you fake this with me?" he asks. "Eventually you'll want to move on."

And by that point, I'll have Luke so in love with me that it'll all just magically fall into place for us.

Right?

Yeah, I doubt it, too.

"We can cross that bridge when we get to it," I say instead. "And we'll explain everything to Josh. If he knows it's fake, he won't get mad. Right? Besides, he married my best friend. Why can't I marry his?"

He sighs. "I don't know, Ellie..."

I reach over and give his forearm a gentle squeeze, ignoring the way just touching his skin with mine lights a fire in my belly. "I saw how awful she was," I say. "You're giving me a place to stay and you're giving me a job. I want to help you, too."

He presses his lips together as he thinks about it, and then he nods.

"Okay," he says. "Let's fake it." He twists his lips, crinkles his nose, and shrugs, and it's about the cutest thing I've ever seen. I laugh, and we're both quiet for a beat.

And then I ask softly, "What did she do to hurt you?"

"Aside from the coffee spoon in the sugar bowl?" he quips, and I smirk.

"Yes, aside from that."

"She's just...not a nice person. She said things that dug deep when we broke up."

"Okay, so then we're definitely engaged." My brows draw down. "Were you ever engaged to her?"

He shakes his head. "She begged me for a ring. *Begged.* I can't even admit some of the things she tried to get me to commit. But I held strong."

"Because you knew she wasn't right for you?"

He sits up and shakes his head. "No. Because I don't plan to ever get married again."

I feel like I'm getting whiplash here. "But you said we're engaged...and being engaged usually leads to a wedding..." I'm trailing off my sentences as I try to put the pieces together.

"Right. It's fake, Ellie. Remember?"

I nod even though I feel a little deflated.

Wait.

I feel...*deflated?*

Because he just reminded me that he told his ex a lie about being engaged to me?

In what world should that *deflate* me?

"So what's the next step, then? A fake wedding?"

His brows dip down a beat, and I wish I knew him well enough to read those facial expressions, but I don't. Not yet, anyway.

"Your brother would kill me on that one, so no. If we get married, it has to be real."

My eyes widen. "What?"

He laughs. "I'm kidding. I already told you, I'm not getting married again."

Right. And I'm the one who wants the happily ever after with my Prince Charming. More reasons he isn't right for me...and yet every little piece of him I'm getting to know makes me want to learn more.

This is starting to go deeper than a simple attraction or the lust of wanting him on top of me naked again.

I'm starting to genuinely like this guy, and that's a real problem considering he's not interested. Even though he did just tell his ex-girlfriend that I'm his fiancée.

"So...I'm confused. Do you really want to play that we're engaged or what?"

He shrugs. "Well, yeah. In front of her, at least."

"So what happens when she blabs to Savannah?"

"That's an extra bonus since that's another woman who's always trying to squeeze more money out of me." He sighs. "I guess we're doing this."

He really hasn't had a lot of luck finding a nice lady.

Enter Ellie.

CHAPTER 21

When I wake up the next morning, I check my email just like I always do.

And my mouth drops the fuck open. All the way to the floor.

I was expecting the story to hit...but I was *not* expecting *this*.

I rush down to the kitchen. It's empty.

I dart around the first family room, where I find Pepper on the couch, who just looks at me like I'm an idiot (like she always does), and then I look out the window.

Sure enough, there's Luke running on the treadmill on the patio.

No shirt.

I realize I haven't even looked in a mirror yet after rolling out of bed and I prefer to look my best particularly when I'm about to see the object of my crush...but the news on my phone is more pressing than how I look right now.

It's more pressing than what he's doing.

I run outside and wave my phone at him. He's concentrating and focused as he runs, and it takes him a beat to even notice I'm standing there. Once he does, he slows to a jog and slips out his earbuds as his brows dip down.

I wish I could just take a minute to stare at the perfection that is the man on the treadmill.

Okay, I do it even though I have something important to say. I stare shamelessly, my eyes flicking to his abs and to his legs and back to his handsome face. He's sweaty and I don't even care because he's freaking gorgeous. I lament the fact that I'm the one who has to break this news to him since he has no clue as he runs without a care in the world on his treadmill.

"Ellie, what's wrong?" he asks. His eyes are wide. Clearly I've frightened the man with my freshly just rolled out of bed look.

"She ran to the media," I say, more out of breath from running through the house looking for him for the last sixty seconds than he is from running on a treadmill for probably the last hour.

His eyes flick to my chest covered by the flimsy white material of the tank top I slept in. I'm not wearing a bra. It's bright out here. I'm dying of embarrassment as I realize he can probably see my nipples. Why didn't I think to at least change my shirt? Maybe run a brush through my hair?

Oh, right.

Because of the headlines that cluttered my inbox this morning.

He narrows his eyes at me, but he slows his jog to a walk, and eventually he shuts the thing off and steps down. He grabs a towel and wipes the sweat from his face then slings it around his neck.

"You have to see the headlines." I hesitate for a second since I don't want to be the one breaking this news to him, and then I hand him my phone.

He glances at the headline.

Aces Receiver Luke Dalton Set to Wed Amidst Baby Scandal

And the byline? Savannah Buck.

He looks back up at me, but his expression is unreadable. He has to feel *some* way about that headline. "How did you find this?"

"I set up an alert so any time an article is published about you, it goes to my email. And before you get any crazy ideas that I'm some kind of stalker, it's a standard part of being a public relations manager."

He heaves out a breath, and I wish he was more forthcoming with what he's thinking. He's schooled himself to hide his emotions, and he does a good job of it. I just haven't figured out *why* he does it. But I will.

"Well, alright then," he says. "Looks like the news is out. We're engaged."

"And the rest of the headline?" I prod.

"Shit like this gets printed all the time." He shrugs like he's blowing it off.

"Luke, there's only *one person* in the entire world who thinks we're engaged." I'm trying to impress upon him that this is more serious than he realizes. My gut tells me this isn't some joke. This is his ex. She was here yesterday saying she needed to talk to him, and he blew her off, and she ran to the press with her news since he didn't take the time to listen. "Just read the article."

He scans it. Michelle didn't just run to Savannah to let her know Luke is engaged. Michelle also ran to Savannah to let her know that she's pregnant.

With Luke's baby.

To be continued in Book 2, **LONG GAME**.

Long
GAME
LISA SUZANNE

DEDICATION

To the 3Ms who are part of my Long Game.

CHAPTER 1

"Fuck." He sighs, and *dammit* I wish I could read him better. Is he muttering curses because of the article? Because he believes it? Because of how it's going to affect his image?

And then it's like something flips. He blinks as he stares off into space for a second. "Oh, shit."

"What?"

He grabs the towel from around his neck and hangs it over the side of the treadmill. "We had a bonus night." He avoids eye contact as he stares down at his towel as realization seems to crash into him. "Fuck."

"A bonus night?" I ask, my brows furrowing.

He nods and rubs the back of his neck. "Yeah. Two months ago maybe? It was after we broke up." He tries to think back as he turns and stares out into his yard. "I was out with a group of buddies, and we drank way too much, and she showed up at my place. I was drunk and we...well, you know."

"Banged?" I fill in the blank, and he's the one looking all awkward now.

He clears his throat. "Yeah."

I wave my phone around. "You think what's in the article is true?"

He nods as he grips his hair with both hands, the first real emotion he's shown during this conversation apart from some cursing. "She's manipulative, but she wouldn't lie about something like this to the media." His hair is sticking up as he punches one fist into the palm of his other hand. "Dammit. I should've known she was going to find some way to trap me. And to run to Savannah..." He shakes his head. "That's just bullshit."

"This doesn't mean you're trapped, Luke. Plenty of parents raise kids just fine without being married."

"Yeah, but you don't know Michelle. She's the kind of person who would get pregnant on purpose to find a way to keep me in her life." He grips the railing of the treadmill, and then he sits on the belt. He hangs his head as anger melts into wistfulness. "Jesus. I'm going to be a father. This is not at all how I expected today to go."

I kneel on the ground across from him so we're eye level. "She can manipulate all she wants, Luke, but you don't have to be with her even if you're having a baby with her. You can be *there* for her. You can *support* her. But you don't have to be her boyfriend or her husband."

He glances up at me, and he has this torn look in his eyes. He wants to do what's right, but he also wants to live his own life. He wants to be happy. He doesn't want to be trapped by someone he doesn't see in his life forever...even if she *will* be in his life in some capacity if she really is carrying his baby.

And I don't believe for a second that it's really his. He can believe her all he wants, but I don't have to.

"All right, publicist," he says. He glances up at me, and when our eyes connect, even amid this scandal that I'm going to have to sort for him, I feel the heat between the two of us. "Prove your worth."

My eyes widen, and I nod. "I've got this."

"I'll get you a ring today," he says. "A bigger one than the one she wanted."

I laugh at the sheer pettiness in his tone, but I'm not sure I quite get what's happening. "So just like that...we're engaged?"

He presses his lips together. "Looks like it."

"But it's fake," I clarify.

He stares at me a long beat as if he's contemplating his next move, and then he shrugs before he speaks the words that knock my knees out from under me. "It doesn't have to be...not if we actually get married."

My jaw drops and my eyes widen as I stare at him in stunned silence. When I finally manage to form words, I stammer. "Uh...what?"

He chuckles.

"Are you suggesting we really get *married*?" I ask.

"With that reaction, I'll slowly back away and say *no*, that wasn't what I was suggesting. It was just a thought." He lifts a shoulder.

My brows dip as I think about it. "I thought you didn't want to get married ever again."

"I don't. But our engagement's public now. It's in black and white," he says nodding to the headline on my phone. "Michelle plays games. I've never played back, but you know what? I thought a lot about what you said yesterday, and I think you're right."

"What *I* said?" I ask. My cheeks are all hot just from having this conversation. I'm pretty sure I'm sweating, and I'm still in that damn flimsy tank top and shorts. "What did I say?"

"That what she does isn't fair." He pauses, and then he shakes his head. "You're right. It isn't. If I want things to change with Michelle, then I have to make them change. I need her to see I'm committed to somebody else, that this trick she's trying to pull won't work. If she's carrying my kid, I'll be the best dad I can be. But I can't be *with* her. This engagement plan is crazy enough to work...if you're still on board with it."

"I'm still on board with the *engagement*," I say.

I may need a minute on the *actual marriage* topic of conversation. I'm pretty sure he was just kidding, anyway. Wasn't he?

My eyes fall to his abs.

Is it really such a crazy idea?

That's clearly the lust talking, but still...

The thought of his hips slamming against my backside as I clawed at the floor-to-ceiling windows in a hotel room on the Las Vegas Strip flashes through my mind.

Did it just get a little hotter out here?

I blow out a breath.

I don't know about the marriage thing, but as far as a fake engagement is concerned, I have nothing to lose here. I'll help him however I can.

Not because he's hot (though he is), and not because I have a huge crush on him (though I do), but because he's letting me stay here and he's giving me a job and he's my brother's best friend. It's really not a big deal to pretend to be engaged to the hottest guy I've ever laid eyes on.

"Get back on that treadmill," I say. I need to change the subject. "We're about to set some thirst traps on your Instagram."

"Thirst traps?" he asks as he gets back on the treadmill as requested.

"Oh, my sweet husband to be, you have so much to learn. Start running."

"Right now? Don't we need to deal with this pregnancy thing first? Shouldn't I call Michelle or something?" he asks.

"That's exactly what she wants, isn't it? I'll handle the media angle, but we need a second to think it through. Let's take a deep breath and draft a plan before you run to the phone. And in the meantime, I'll take some photos so we can get your Insta-campaign moving."

His brows furrow and God he's adorable, but then he does what I ask. I relish my job as his amateur photographer, snapping different angles of him as he runs on the treadmill. I blush even harder as I think how I'm building quite the spank bank.

And that's when I remember I literally rolled out of bed to come down here. My hair is a mess, I have morning breath, I'm not wearing any make-up, and I'm donning that awful tank top with a pair of short, barely-there shorts.

As he looks over in my direction, though, and his eyes flick down the length of my body...it doesn't appear that he cares that I just rolled out of bed.

In fact, he almost seems to like it.

The heat in his eyes makes me feel that way, anyway.

I chalk that look in his eyes up to him sweating on his treadmill. I take a few more photos, let him know I'm heading inside, and I go up to my bedroom to shower.

After I scroll through all the images I just took, of course.

Once I'm dressed and my teeth are brushed, I find Luke in the kitchen pouring Lucky Charms cereal into a bowl. "Want some?" he asks.

I shake my head and move toward to the massive refrigerator to check out Debbie's breakfast options.

"There's a fresh pot of coffee," he says.

"Do you have any flavored coffee cream?" I ask from the depths of the fridge.

He nods. "Top shelf on the left."

Once I have my coffee, I carefully slide onto the stool and pull up the photos I took of Luke on my phone. I pick out one of my favorites, do a little light editing, and whip up a caption that mentions how he loves his job and works hard to keep his body field ready even in the offseason.

"Ready for your first post to Instagram?" I ask him.

He glances over at me, and I snap a picture of him pouring milk into his cereal bowl. It's such a normal, everyday thing for a guy to be doing in his kitchen, but it shows him in an element very few people have ever seen him in. He looks warily at me for a beat then grabs a spoon and steps toward me. "Show me what you've got."

I slide my phone over to him, and he looks at the picture and then up at me.

I grin. "That, my friend, is what we in the business call a *thirst trap*."

"Yeah, you said that before and I still don't know what it means."

"It's when you post a hot pic with the intention of getting attention," I explain. "The more likes and comments you get on a photo, the more Instagram will see that you're a worthwhile user, and the more they'll show your account to other people."

"And that picture of me, a sweaty mess from running all morning...that's a thirst trap?" He looks at me with disbelief, and I giggle.

"You have no idea how hot you are, do you?" I ask.

He raises his brows. "I worked up a pretty good sweat, so yeah, I have some concept of how hot I was."

I roll my eyes. "You know what I meant."

He laughs. "That doesn't make it any less weird that you're telling me how hot I am like it's no big deal before I've even had my cereal. It's a big deal, Ellie."

"Why?" I challenge. "You already told me I'm off-limits. I work for you now, and my goal is to show the world how hot you are, how kind you are, and, above all, how essential you are to the Aces. It all starts with thirst trap number one. So do I have your approval?"

"God, you really like making me step out of my comfort zone." He sighs heavily, and then he shrugs. "Go ahead. Do what I'm paying you to do, and if I live to regret it, well, then that's on me."

"You won't live to regret it. Just trust me." I click the post button and cross my fingers that I'm doing all the right things to help him and that neither of us will live to regret my words.

CHAPTER 2

Prove your worth.

Despite all the other words he said to me—like the fact that he's going to get me a (huge-ass) ring so we can really be pretend-engaged and maybe really get married even though I still think he was just kidding about that—those three are the ones that keep playing on repeat.

I need to figure out how to spin this news.

It's now my job to make him look like the good guy for being engaged to one woman when he knocked someone else up.

I sigh as I stare at the blinking cursor on a very blank screen.

I've got my work cut out for me.

No matter what way I spin this, he comes out looking like a horny douchebag.

Unless it isn't really his baby.

I need to find out how far along she is. I need some sort of concrete evidence that it might be his. "Luke?" I yell across the house.

"Yeah?" he yells back. I think he's in his office, and he walks into the kitchen a few seconds later. "What's going on?"

"When was your bonus night?"

His brows push together, and then he squints like he's trying to think back and I see the moment it clicks almost like a lightbulb going off above his head. He pulls his phone out of his pocket, opens an app, and counts. "Seven weeks ago this past Saturday. We went out for Bryant's birthday."

"Who's Bryant?"

He gives me a you-can't-be-serious kind of look, but he answers anyway. "Jaxon Bryant? Star running back of the Aces?" He says them like questions, and I just shrug because I still don't know who he is.

He shakes his head and laughs. "I've never met anyone who didn't know a thing about the game, let alone a blood relative of a player."

I hold up both hands. "Sorry! Josh has only been playing here a year. Ask me about a player on the Bears and maybe I'd know." That's a lie. I wouldn't know.

"Was that your only question?" he asks. "I'm going through some paperwork from my agent."

"When did you break up?" I ask.

"I don't know. A few months ago?"

"Not good enough. I'm trying to figure out your spin here, and you're not giving me much to work with. So unless you want to come off looking like a d-bag who can't keep it in his pants, I need a date."

He stares at me for a beat in a bit of shock, and then he raises a brow and shoots me a sly smile. "I like when you get all authoritative over me even if what you just said was really kind of mean."

I know I'm blushing, but I force myself not to react to his words. Instead, I raise my brows in a silent way of asking what his answer is.

He blows out a breath, and then he looks at his phone again. I peek over and see him scrolling through his calendar, and I bet if I asked Michelle when they broke up, she'd have a date and time down to the minute.

"It was January, right after we lost the playoffs. She thought she was being cute when she called me a loser, and that was it. I was done."

"What a bitch," I say. "And you still gave her a bonus night?"

"I was so fucked up I don't even remember it," he says. He slides his phone back into his pocket. "She was there when I woke up in the morning. We were both naked. I put two and two together."

"You were wasted, banged a woman you can't stand, don't remember it, and she shows up claiming she's carrying your baby a convenient seven weeks later?" I ask. It's not adding up, and I don't trust Michelle. But I have to find a way to make Luke look like a good guy without tearing down a pregnant Michelle to the press. Public sympathy will be on the pregnant lady's side regardless of how I spin it.

"Yeah, that about sums it up," he says. "What are you suggesting?"

"Maybe a paternity test? I don't know how these things work, but I can research it for you."

He clears his throat. "I might have some experience there."

I raise a brow, and he sighs.

"Total transparency, after my divorce, I made some really dumb decisions."

I have some questions about all that, but I log them and push them to the back of my brain because I have a problem to solve here.

"Okay, before I send out your statement, you need to talk to her," I say. "Call her right now. Demand proof that she's pregnant and that it's really yours."

He stares at me for a beat, and then he slides onto the stool next to me. "I'll demand evidence she's really knocked up, but I can't just call her and demand a paternity test."

"Why not?"

"It's complicated." He doesn't wait for me to reply to that. Instead, he dials her number and puts her on speaker so I can listen in.

"Luke, my darling," she answers. "I've been waiting for your call."

He rolls his eyes, and I stifle a giggle. "I need proof you're really pregnant."

"I had my first doctor's appointment two days ago," she says. "I'm seven weeks along. They put my date of conception on April fifth, and that's the night we slept together. I came by to tell you about the baby but you didn't seem interested in conversation."

"So you ran to Savannah?" he sneers.

"I had to do something to get your attention, my dear."

I want to reach into the phone and rip her head off.

"I want proof you're really pregnant," Luke says again.

"I'll screenshot the paperwork from my doctor over when we hang up. Maybe me smiling with my little stick of pee. Will that be good enough for you?"

"It'll do for now, but I want proof from your doctor."

"Yes, sir. God, I miss when you used to get all dominating on me." Her voice comes out in a moan, and I guess this is her way of coming onto him.

I raise a brow at him. Dominating? Interesting.

My thighs clench at the thought of him demanding things from me while we're both naked. Thoughts of sex up against a window in a hotel room crash into me.

Again.

I blow out a breath. That night really turned all this into a complicated mess. If I was just living with my brother's best friend and I had a crush on him, that would be one thing.

But I can remember his body against mine. I remember him sliding in and out of me. I remember kissing him.

Butterflies batter around in my stomach.

This isn't good.

"Well I'm marrying another woman, so you'll just have to go on missing it." He ends the call, and I raise my hand up for a high five.

He twists his lips as he slaps my hand with his, like he doesn't really want to celebrate the call.

"Good work, my darling Luke," I say.

He narrows his eyes at me. "You better watch it. I haven't forgotten that your brother calls you Ellie Belly."

My cheeks burn and I change the subject. "What's our story?"

He looks confused, so I clarify.

"What will we tell people when they ask how we met?"

"We met through Josh," he says as he starts sorting our pretend meet cute. "Maybe you were out here for a weekend when he first moved here and we met and kept in touch. You decided to move here more recently because I proposed."

I shake my head. "My ex, Todd, the one who I got fired for banging in the office..." I trail off when he winces.

Why did he wince?

Is it because he feels some sympathy over me getting fired?

Or is it because he doesn't want to think of me having sex with somebody else?

Add the wince to the list of things I'll overanalyze tonight when I'm trying to fall asleep.

"Yeah?" he says with a tone that urges me to continue.

"I feel like he's pretty pissed at me over what happened and I wouldn't put it past him to blow that story up," I say, trying to think through all the angles. "We need something more airtight."

"Okay, then we met through Josh about a year ago. Does that part work?" he asks. I nod, and he continues. "We kept in touch. We got to know each other over the distance. We both had feelings but the timing never worked out so we were just good friends. And then you came out here for the wedding, we were both finally single at the same time, and within days, we knew it was right and we got engaged."

I lift a shoulder. "It could work. Some people won't believe in the insta-love, though."

"Insta-love?" His brows crunch together.

"Like we instantly fell in love."

"We didn't," he says, shaking his head. "We'll say we met a year ago. We kept in touch. We both fell in love over the course of time, and when we finally had the chance to be together, we grabbed it. That's not instant love."

"Insta-love," I correct, and he laughs and holds up both hands. "Okay, okay. Whatever. Does that story work for you?"

I nod slowly, my lips pressed together. "I think it could work."

"Good." He glances at the clock. "I need another hour in my office, but want to do dinner after?"

"Sure. And if you're looking at endorsement stuff from your agent, be sure to run it by your publicist first." I smirk at him, and he chuckles before he leaves the room.

LISA SUZANNE

Before I even get the chance to let that blinking cursor intimidate me some more, someone starts banging on the front door, clearly forgoing the doorbell.

Luke exhales heavily, turns around from the hallway he started down, and moves toward the door instead. He peeks out, and then he opens it.

"You're engaged to my sister?" It's Josh, and he's pissed.

I chuckle from my spot in the kitchen even as I start to realize how big this story is. I've worked with the press before. I know how fast news spreads...I've just never been the subject of that news before.

He comes storming into the kitchen.

"Hey Josh," I say with a wide smile.

He glares at me. "Don't you hey Josh me," he says, pointing a finger in my direction.

Luke rolls his eyes. "Will you please tell your brother that it's all fake?"

My brows dip down. "What's all fake?"

"Our engagement," he says, air quoting the words.

I stand and fold my arms across my chest. "What?" I say sharply. "This is all just fake to you?"

His jaw falls open as he sputters with something to say, and Josh is almost gloating for a beat.

I can't watch Luke sputter any longer. I start laughing. "Yeah, I'm just kidding. It's fake." I slide back into my chair.

Josh sighs. "Why are you doing this?"

I'm not sure if he's asking me or Luke, but Luke fields that one. "It just slipped out when Michelle stopped by. I said we were engaged to get a rise out of her, and your sister very kindly played along. And by the by, Ellie is also handling my PR."

"Nicki mentioned she saw your thirst trap on Instagram," Josh mutters.

"Am I the only one who didn't know what a thirst trap is?" Luke asks.

"Yes," Josh and I say adamantly at the same time.

Luke huffs, and I giggle.

"Who does your social media?" Luke asks my brother.

160

"Uh, me," Josh says, inflecting his tone at the end to make it sound like he's asking a question. "I may not be the sharpest tool in the shed, but I'm not a complete idiot."

"Apparently I am," Luke says. "Got any more thirsty traps to post?"

"Thirst," I correct.

Josh laughs. "We leave for the airport in a couple hours, but I couldn't leave for three weeks in Fiji without straightening this out first."

"Have a good honeymoon." My eyes return back to my screen.

"Don't forget to pack that really tight and small Speedo you modeled for me," Luke says. "Show off the goods, man."

"Already in the bag," Josh jokes. Then he turns serious for a second. "Before I head out, though, I just want to be clear about one thing." I stop looking at my screen and turn back to my brother. "From where I stand, neither of you is ready to get into a relationship. I know you're faking it or whatever, but just be careful, all right? I don't want to see whatever this is go up in flames because you wanted to help," he says, pointing at me, "and because you took advantage of that." He points at Luke.

"He's not taking advantage," I say. "I volunteered."

"Well that was stupid," Josh says.

"Uh, thanks for your unsolicited opinion." I flash him a sarcastic smile, and he smirks back at me.

"I just care about you both. Have you thought about what happens when Michelle finds out the truth? Won't that give her even more ammo against you, especially if she's really carrying your kid?" he asks Luke.

"For the record, she did send me evidence that she really is knocked up." He holds up a picture of her smiling as she holds a positive pregnancy test toward the camera. "And I haven't thought about her finding out the truth. I guess we'll cross that bridge when we get there."

"You realize you will get there eventually, right?" Josh asks. "At some point, you'll each meet someone and then this arrangement won't work anymore. Or someone will find out the truth. This just isn't a great idea."

We both nod. God, if Josh only knew that Luke and I had sex the night of his bachelor party. I think he'd kill both of us...not that it's really any of his business. I know he's just looking out for the two of us for different reasons, and I know he's coming from a place of love.

But one thing Josh hasn't considered—one thing I've ruminated on pretty much continuously for days—is whether the person I'm supposed to end up with...is Luke.

CHAPTER 3

When I walk into the kitchen the next morning, there's a woman at the stove stirring something in a pot and the kitchen smells like a damn bacon dream.

"You must be Debbie," I say, and the woman turns around with a smile.

"And you must be Ellie," she says. She wipes her hands on her apron and moves around the counter. "Luke told me all about you." She leans forward and gives me a little hug.

"He did?" I ask. What the hell did he say about me?

She smiles. "Congratulations on your engagement. It seems so fast, but Luke's the kind of boy who knows what he wants. I just think it's so sweet that he fell for his best friend's little sister. Isn't that just the thing romance novels are made of?"

So we're faking it even for the house staff. Noted.

"I'm a lucky girl," I say, still wondering exactly what Luke told her about me.

Maybe I need to move bedrooms. Won't it be weird if they're here and see that we're not sleeping together? Is that even something they'd notice, or am I just really searching for ways to sleep with Hot Luke?

And I literally mean *sleep*. Just share a bed.

For now, anyway.

I can't help but wonder what insider info she has on the enigma that is my husband-to-be. How long has she cooked for him? How well does she know him?

"He's outside on the treadmill," she says. "Breakfast should be ready in about ten minutes if you want to let him know."

I nod. "I will. Thanks, Debbie. It's a pleasure to meet you."

"You too," she says, and she gives me a little wink.

I head out to Luke, snap a few more thirst traps that are making me thirsty as all fuck, and chat away while I work. "Debbie congratulated me," I say.

His lips press together.

I lower my voice. "Are we, um, faking for everyone?"

"I don't know, Ellie." He seems a little frustrated. "I hate lying to people." He slows his running and then stops. He gets off the treadmill and starts stretching. "Maybe we just, I don't know...have a very public break-up or something."

"Yeah," I say softly. "Maybe." I hope not, especially not after I put out a press release this morning where Luke takes full responsibility for the baby and also full responsibility for his own happiness.

I head back inside because Luke is crabby. Maybe he just needs some of Debbie's home cooking to cheer him up.

"Is Luke taking you to the ball tomorrow night?" Debbie asks.

Ball?

What ball?

I don't say that. In fact, I don't know *what* to say. I'm about to stammer out some non-response when he walks in.

"Debbie was just asking me about tomorrow night's ball," I say to him, my eyes wide as if to ask him *what ball is this and why didn't you mention it and are we going* all in one look.

Clearly we're not at the place where he can read my nonverbal communication.

"I was planning on skipping it," he says.

"Why?" Debbie asks. "Aren't they expecting you?"

He nods. "Yeah, but I don't have a..." he trails off as his eyes widen, and I'm pretty sure he was about to end that sentence with *date*.

He's really *not* a good liar.

"Tux," he finishes. "My, uh, tux isn't clean."

"Oh, Luke, I can take care of that for you," Debbie says.

Luke blows out a breath. "You're not letting me get out of this one, are you?"

She shoots him a smirk. "Nope."

I stand and look back and forth between the two of them, a little unsure as to whether I should admit I have no idea what ball they're talking about. And then Luke fills in the blanks for me.

"Would you be my date for the seventh annual Beating Hunger in Vegas Charity Ball?" he asks.

"I'd love to," I say. "And, for the record, this is one of those amazing opportunities to post on your social media."

And then I do a mini-freak out on the inside.

Hot Luke just asked me out on a date.

Okay, okay...so he was kind of forced into it, and we're putting on an act...but still.

We're going to a charity ball together.

Tomorrow night.

Oh shit. I need to find a dress and shoes and figure out what the hell to do with my hair.

"Social media?" Debbie asks. "Like Facebook?"

I nod. "I got him all set up."

"She's doing some public relations stuff for me."

Debbie beams as she looks between the two of us. "Oh my goodness, Luke. I already *love* her for you."

He laughs as my insides warm. "Ellie, I know it's short notice for the ball, and I'm sorry about that. But don't worry. We'll get it all sorted."

We better. That's all I have to say about that.

Debbie leaves not too long after that, and my questions start immediately over a pancake and bacon plus Lucky Charms breakfast at the kitchen table instead of the counter, where we usually eat our meals.

That's right. I have a *routine* with Hot Luke.

"Okay, first things first," I say. "Lucky Charms *again*?"

He shrugs. "Get used to it. It's my personal obsession."

"Noted. Second, Debbie thinks we're engaged. Does the rest of your house staff know? And is it weird that we sleep in separate bedrooms?"

He glances up at me. "Yeah, I've been thinking about that, too." He looks down at his plate. "We should probably just move you into my room for now unless that's too weird for you."

"It's fine," I say maybe just a tad too quickly. "Next, what the hell am I supposed to wear to the ball tomorrow night? The bridesmaid's dress I ruined when I fell in the pool?"

He laughs. "You can borrow my card and take it shopping. Get whatever you want. Dress, shoes, jewelry. I don't care."

Okay...well that sounds like fun.

After we clean up the breakfast dishes, Luke says, "Should we move your stuff into my room?"

I shrug even though my heart is beating in triple time at the thought of actually sleeping beside this man. I didn't even get to do that the night we had sex since he bolted so fast. At least now I know the reason for the bolting was Pepper, not me.

We each grab a load of clothes from my room and walk down the hallway toward the double doors of the master bedroom, and my heart races as I realize this is the very first time I'm seeing his bedroom even though I've lived here for the last four days.

He opens the doors.

His bedroom is masculine. The bed linens are a charcoal gray, the furniture is dark wood, and one entire wall is made up of a puzzle of reclaimed wood. It's the perfect backdrop for more thirst traps. And while I liked the view from my bedroom, the windows in here are much larger and offer a gorgeous view of the mountains and the Las Vegas Strip off in the distance beyond my brother's house.

It's incredible.

It's sexy.

It's luxurious.

And, for now, even if it's pretend...it's mine.

He takes me through an expansive bathroom and into his closet, which is neat as a pin and larger than the bedroom in the apartment I lived in back in Chicago. His clothes are mostly black, white, and gray, with the odd splash of red here and there to represent the Aces team colors, black and red. A huge, framed Aces jersey rests on one wall with DALTON and the number eighty-four on it. His clothes only take up one side of the closet. The other side is completely empty, almost like he was waiting for someone...waiting for me.

He nods to some drawers built into the wall. "You can put your stuff in those drawers. They're all empty."

I want to ask why they're empty, but I have a feeling I know the answer. When Savannah moved out and then Michelle, he just never refilled them. He probably never needed to. His side of the closet is fairly sparsely used, so there was no need to change up his system of organization.

Sort of like the bathroom, which I find also has empty drawers just waiting for my stuff.

After I fill the drawers, I glance at the bed as I think about what *could* happen in there versus what likely *will* happen.

Being around him is almost too much for me as it is. And now he's going to be sleeping mere inches away from me in the same bed every single night.

This is going to be the most beautifully difficult situation I've ever found myself in.

"Fuck," he mutters, clicking something on his phone.

"What?"

He collapses on the bed and heaves out a sigh, and then he holds his phone up for me to take. I read the headline on his screen.

Is Dalton Lying? His New Fiancée's Ex Spills the Tea.

It's from some celebrity gossip vlog, and I click to watch the video. "Billy Peters here with your latest *Celebrity Snaps!*"

I raise a brow over the phone as I look at Luke. "Looks like someone thinks athletes are celebrities."

He chuckles even though this isn't funny.

"Breaking news, gossip mongers," the flamboyant host declares on the screen. "Sin City is heating up and not just from the sunshine. The Luke Dalton scandal is full of all the tea, and I'm here to spill it today."

He snaps his fingers and the screen flips to a photo of Luke in his football uniform. And *fuck* does he look delicious.

"Hottie football star Dalton knocked up his ex and then got engaged to another woman. His press release from this morning makes it sound like he'll be there for the ex while he's planning his wedding to the woman he loves—side note, his *teammate's sister*—but...are you ready for this tea?" He pauses, and the picture flips to an image of a fish. "Something's fishy!"

It flips back to the host. "Luke's new fiancée split from her ex *less than a week ago*. He's claiming there's no way she could be engaged already." He makes a huge round O shape with his mouth. "Somebody's lying! Stay tuned for all the latest on this juicy tale."

The video cuts there, and I blink at the screen.

Fucking Todd.

I heave out a breath. "I'm sorry," I mutter.

"For what?" he asks.

"For dating that douche-bucket in the first place."

Luke laughs.

"How can you laugh at a time like this?"

He sits up and lifts a shoulder. "Douche-bucket." He chuckles again. "What else can we do? We can laugh or we can commiserate. I choose laughter. And then we take action, right?"

I nod, and then an idea forms.

Take action.

I draw in a deep breath as a lightbulb seems to click on over my head. When he first mentioned it, my initial reaction was hell to the no. But now...

I lift a shoulder. "Maybe we should just get married. That would shut up Todd *and* Michelle."

He freezes. Then, as if moving in slow motion, he looks up at me. "What?"

"Let's just get married. We're in *Vegas*. It's like the land of quickie weddings, isn't it?"

He narrows his eyes. "You didn't seem too into the idea when I first mentioned it."

"I wasn't," I admit. I'd always planned to get married only once in my life. In fact, as someone who fully believes in fairy tales, I admit that marriage is both serious and sacred to me, yet something about doing this with Luke seems right.

I want to help him even though I've only known him for a few days. I have these urges to protect him and I don't even know why. My body knows his body, and that's a language the two of us were fluent in that one night. My heart has been introduced to his heart.

I fully expect this *marriage* sham will only last a few months, maybe a year. But I'm at a point in my life where it's one adventure after another, and what bigger adventure could I embark upon right now other than dedicating my entire life to becoming a football wife? I'm already devoting a huge chunk of my time to this man as his public relations manager. Why not just take it another step (okay, a few thousand steps) further?

At the worst, it's maybe a year out of my life. Even if Luke and I end up hating one another, if we agree to just one year, he has a big enough house that we could basically avoid each other. I could go live in the damn pool house if I need to. And there's a lot of potential in that it might open doors for my career. It might give me a whole new network of people—*celebrities*, which, I'll admit now, even includes athletes—to meet and potentially work with.

"I've got nothing else going on," I say instead of any of that, and I realize it makes me sound both desperate and incredibly sad.

He presses his lips together. "I had a hard enough time coming to terms with you agreeing to be my fake fiancée. But my fake wife?" He shakes his head and glances away from me. "When I said it at first, it just sort of slipped out. But I just...I don't see myself getting married again. Not after Savannah destroyed me the way she did."

I nod even though I feel a little defeated. He's the one who brought it up first. "Okay. It was a stupid idea. Forget it."

He drums his fingers on the table beside him where he stands, and then he heaves out a huge breath. "What if it's not a stupid idea? Am I stupid for actually considering it?"

My brows shoot up. "You're considering it?"

"Josh will kill us both."

"This isn't about my brother," I say. "I don't really care what his opinion is. If I'm in and you're in, isn't that all that matters?"

He nods. "I don't know if I'm in."

"Okay, so we're trial running me as your PR manager for the next week or two, right? What if we trial run me as your fiancée, too?"

He nods and steeples his fingers in front of his mouth. "Okay, I like where your head's at, but what do *you* get out of it?"

"I get to be married to a hot ass football star."

He laughs and shakes his head modestly and with a touch of embarrassment. "I'm insane for even considering this," he breathes, and he pauses. "You'd need to get something out of it. I could double what I offered to pay you for my PR. And, no offense, we'd need an airtight prenup. I don't know you well enough to fork over half of everything I own when we know there's an end date on it."

I pretend his words don't kill a little piece of me. I fully know what I'm getting myself into here. I'm under no illusion that he'll magically fall in love with me and we'll navigate our very own fairy tale as we find our way to our happily ever after.

Even though a girl can still hope and dream.

CHAPTER 4

Luke's watching ESPN to catch today's sports highlights while I flip through the selection of dresses on the mobile sites of some local stores, and then he clicks for the recorded shows on his DVR and starts a football game.

It's the Aces against the Bears. I glance over at him with pursed lips, and he laughs at my expression.

"Listen, babe. If you're engaged to me, you better understand the basics of what I do." He clicks a button on the remote.

I huff out an annoyed breath and give him a look with raised brows. I hold out my hand toward the television as if to say, *all right, let's get on with it.*

"Lesson one," he begins. "This is just a quick overview of the game."

He starts telling me about quarters and downs and yardage and blitzes, and the way he's so passionate as he talks is both endearing and incredibly sexy. He clearly *loves* the game. He loves what he does, and as he shows me examples of each part of the game he explains, I actually start to get it.

All the times Josh and my dad have tried to explain this damn game to me were absolute failures. But after one session with Luke, I finally understand what a first down is.

I even know the little thing the fans do with their arms to indicate a first down.

I see him in his uniform. I watch for number eighty-four. I see him catch the ball. I see him *run.*

It's really freaking hot.

He's fast and agile, and watching him play the sport that's everything to him sort of peels back another layer of who he is. I can see it in the way his eyes study the screen before they light with passion when he glances at me to explain what something means. I can hear it in the inflection of his voice, both excited to talk about the game and patient as he explains what must be the most rudimentary aspects of it.

He *loves* this game. It's the most important thing in his life. I get why he's scared going into the last year of his contract. He doesn't know what comes next because he's never really had to think about it. He's been too busy living his dream to worry about the next stage even though it looms closer and closer every season.

It's not just that, though. He's not just looming closer to the end of his career...but he's doing it *alone*. When he got married, surely he didn't expect to get divorced. Nobody goes into marriage with that mindset—unless you're doing it as a sham, I guess. He must've seen her in his future so that when his career was over, he'd have someone there beside him as he entered into whatever phase of life came after the game.

And maybe that's why I fell into his life. Maybe part of my job here isn't just to help him continue playing for the team he loves so damn much. Maybe it's also helping him discover what the next phase of his life is going to be once it's time to transition...because that time *will* come whether he's ready for it or not. He can't play football *forever*.

I can't help my yawn as the clock strikes eleven.

"Sorry," Luke says, his eyes still animated as he watches the game. "I'm boring you now."

I laugh. "Actually, not at all. I could listen to you talk about football forever." I realize how much I mean those words when they tumble out of my mouth. Watching how excited he gets about a catch is something lovely to behold. "It's just getting late."

He glances at the clock. "Yeah. Sorry, I get caught up when I'm talking about the game. You ready to go to bed?"

I nod. It's our first night sharing a bed, and that thought is a little daunting. "I think I'll head up."

"You go ahead," he says. "I'm just going to watch a little more film."

"Film?" I ask.

He chuckles. "It's just what we call it. An older word leftover from another time. I'm going to watch a little more of this game and study it. Look at what I did, what I could have done differently, what those around me and on the other side of the ball did, that sort of thing."

"Okay," I say, and I have this strange and totally natural urge to lean over to kiss him goodnight. But I don't. I somehow stop myself. "Have fun watching your film."

His laughter follows me out of the room, and I'm kind of glad that I'm heading to bed first tonight. That way I can pretend to be asleep when he comes in because I sure as hell know I'll be too nervous to actually fall asleep as I'm just lying there waiting for him.

I get ready for bed, and then I stand in front of the mattress as I realize we didn't pick *sides* when we talked about this arrangement. I assume he'll want the side the clock is on, so I go to the other side. I don't use a bedside clock since I sleep with my phone next to me. Maybe he's old school with this whole clock thing he's got going on. I snap the light off and slide down into the bed.

It's fucking luxurious. The sheets must be a billion-thread count, and the mattress is firm and cool.

His sheets smell like him, and suddenly I'm incredibly horny lying in the bed of the man I'm crushing *hard* on.

Okay, maybe not *suddenly*, but smelling him as the cool sheets lie over my body is making the ache between my thighs rage for him.

I'm just about to dip my fingers into my panties to find some tiny measure of relief when his bedroom door opens.

He's quiet as he closes it behind him, shutting himself into the dark room. He uses the flashlight on his phone to move around the room, and I lie as still as I can, my hand resting just under the elastic band of my panties.

He disappears into the bathroom, and I ease my fingers out before I get caught.

That was close.

I probably shouldn't even consider fingering myself in someone else's bed.

But he just...does that to me. He makes me want to make bad decisions.

He's only in the bathroom a few minutes before he emerges and slides quietly into the bed beside me. I force my breathing to stay even because I don't know what the hell to say to him. We're sharing a bed. It's all for pretend. My massive crush on him seems to be getting exponentially larger by the millisecond, but it doesn't matter because he's already written me off.

I'm sure he thinks I'm fast asleep.

And then he whispers into the darkness. "Sweet dreams, Sexy Ellie."

Oh, that's just great.

One more thing for my overactive brain to overanalyze.

I must fall asleep at some point because when I open my eyes to the bright morning, Luke isn't in bed. He's an early bird, obviously, and he's already catching the worm.

Except when I glance at my phone, I see that I've slept in...and I have a missed call and voicemail from my mother.

It's already nine—later than usual for me, but I was up pretty late trying to figure out why he'd call me Sexy Ellie when he's made it so clear that he doesn't want to be with me. What a confusing guy.

I blow out a breath as I click through to my mother's voicemail. I'm not looking forward to this already.

"Ellie Marie Nolan, how in the world could you get *engaged* and not even tell your mother? What is going on with you? How well do you even know this guy? You've only been there a few days! Are you crazy? Are you pregnant? Is it Todd's? Am I going to be a grandmother? Call me!"

She's a handful.

And I'm neither caffeinated nor drunk enough to answer any of her questions. Not any of the fifteen thousand of them.

Instead, I take a shower and head down for breakfast. I slept too late to catch the morning show better known as Hot Luke's Workout, but he's just coming in from the patio, a towel around his neck and his skin glistening with sweat. His hair is wet and his face is flushed and his abs are practically calling my name but I'm apparently not allowed to answer that call.

"My, uh, mom called," I say, trying my damnedest not to be distracted by those abs. I'm trying not to even think about them, but it's impossible. The more I try not to, the more the only thing I can think of is them. My eyes flick down of their own accord, and when they wander back up to meet Luke's, his are a little heated...and not from the workout. At least I don't think that's what it's from. I've been wrong about these things before, though. "It seems she saw our news. Are we keeping the lie up to our families—apart from Josh since he already knows—or do they get the truth?"

Luke sighs and glances away from me before he answers. "I'm not telling my family but I'm not going to tell you what to do with yours."

I nod. "Okay. Can I ask why?"

"My brother will go straight to the press and blow our whole cover." He glances away from me like he's hiding his true emotions about all that.

We may not have known each other long yet, but I *will* find a way to get him to open up. He doesn't need to screen his emotions around me.

"Do you have any other siblings?" I ask.

Pepper walks over to Luke with a ball in her mouth and drops it at his feet. He tosses it into the family room, and she runs to get it. "Yeah, a sister, Kaylee. She's still in college. She was a surprise ten years after I came along."

"Are you close with your siblings?"

He lifts a shoulder. "Not really. I really only see them on our annual family trip."

"How come?" I ask.

"We don't see each other on the traditional holidays because my brother and I can't make it. I talk to my parents maybe once every three or four months. Jack and I occasionally shoot off a football-related text to each other. Kaylee texts me a few times a week." He shrugs with nonchalance, like it's not a big deal he isn't close with his family when to me that's a totally foreign concept.

"Is that hard?" I ask, and I move toward the fridge.

"It's actually easier that way." He leaves it at that, and I don't press despite the strong desire to.

I look in the refrigerator and find some little egg muffins Debbie left. I take two and put them on a plate. "The annual family trip sounds fun."

"It's fine." He nods at my egg muffins. "Can you make me two of those?" Pepper returns and he tosses the ball again while I arrange more on the plate, and then he walks over to the pantry and grabs the box of Lucky Charms. "It's always nice to escape the Vegas heat in the middle of summer."

I'm about to ask a follow up on the weather when I realize that's exactly how Luke manages to keep himself private and why I've been living with him for a week now and I still don't know much about him. He brings up topics that we can explore in our conversation that have nothing to do with him. I can look up the weather later.

What I can't look up is Luke Dalton.

Although the thirst traps have been working. His Instagram account is building quickly, and I can tell his fans want more.

Even though a tiny part of me wants to keep him all to myself. That's not what he's paying me to do, though.

"Where do you take your family trips?" I ask after I stick the plate in the microwave.

"Always somewhere different, and we rotate who picks the location. Last year my brother chose New Zealand."

"Oh wow. How was it?" I grab another plate and some forks.

"It should have been amazing, but Michelle was there." He pours himself a bowl of cereal and holds it up in my direction as if to ask if I'd like some. I shake my head, and then he mutters, "She managed to find ways to make it miserable."

"What about this year?" I ask.

"Kaylee has chosen Hawaii."

"Mm," I murmur. "That sounds nice. Where was your pick?"

"Two years ago we did an Alaskan cruise." He grabs some juice from the fridge and holds it up in my direction. "Want some?"

I nod. "How was that?"

"Same answer as New Zealand." He fills two cups as he talks. "My family didn't care for her, so it ended up not being a very family-oriented trip, which is sort of the whole point."

The microwave beeps, and I take out the muffins. I arrange two on a plate for myself and meet Luke on the other side of the counter. "I bet this year you're looking forward to Hawaii without Michelle and just your family," I muse.

His answer shocks me.

Shock isn't a strong enough word.

I'm fucking obliterated.

"Just my family and my fiancée."

My jaw falls open dumbly, and I can't seem to form words.

"Yeah." He nods and gives a little laugh as he elbows my arm. "That's you."

"You want *me* to come to *Hawaii* with you on your *family* trip at the end of this month?" This is his *family* trip. The one he takes annually. The only chance he gets to see his family each year.

And he wants me to come? Why? To keep up the ruse?

His brows raise and he presses his lips together and nods. "That about sums up our conversation. It's on me if you want to go. We'd probably have nice backdrops for your hungry traps."

"Thirst traps," I murmur, but is he for real offering me a free trip to Hawaii where I'll spend days upon days with *his entire family*? I'm floored. And I'm nervous. I know literally nothing about his family other than the fact that he and his brother have some intense sibling rivalry.

"Is that a yes?" he asks.

"Oh my God, Luke!" I toss my arms around his neck and press a kiss to his mouth without even thinking twice about it. He's hot and sweaty but I could not care less. I'm crushed against Luke Dalton and it's exactly where I want to be. He presses his fingers to my hips for just a beat like he's about to give into this pull between the two of us...but then he backs away. He chuckles, and my cheeks burn. "Yes it's a yes!"

They're the only words I can think to say after I just totally embarrassed myself by kissing him, but I try to play it like it was a thank you kiss.

Though that does beg the question of what I'll be willing to do as a thank you when he actually takes me on the trip. There's not much that wouldn't be on that list, if you catch my drift.

"Do you have any champagne?" I ask after we sit and start eating.

"To celebrate your upcoming trip to Hawaii?"

I shake my head. "Mimosas are one of the few acceptable breakfast drinks, and I'm gonna need a little something before I call my mom back."

He laughs. "Is she really that bad?" He stands and walks over to one of the lower cabinets near the refrigerator. He opens the cabinet door to reveal a wine cooler. He grabs a bottle, pops the cork, and hands it over.

"Thanks," I say. "Impressive little wine refrigerator."

He laughs. "It's a wine *cooler* and a complete beverage center, actually."

"You drink a lot of wine?"

He shakes his head. "Next to never. Beer or whiskey for me. But I keep a stock of it for entertaining. Now tell me about your mom."

I let that *entertaining* comment slide even though I want to know if it's because he has big parties or if it's because he's entertaining different *women*. I hope it's not a wide variety of women...but I also remember my brother was working hard to get him laid the night of the bachelor party, so maybe not any recent conquests. At least I hope not.

I brush those thoughts away and heave in a breath as I think about my mom. She's equal parts critical and loving mixed with a little old-fashioned.

"She's a handful. She usually means well enough, but let's just say Josh is her favorite and I'm the disappointment."

"I doubt that," he says softly, and then he dumps some champagne into his orange juice, too.

"He gets a pass on everything. When Todd dumped me, her first words were literally about how she's going to have to wait even longer for grandchildren when her son was getting married a few days later. Can't he produce grandchildren?" I say it lightly because it's just the way she is. I'm not damaged or scarred from it, and if anything, it's a big joke between my brother and me—something that, over the years, has drawn us closer if nothing else than for the laughs.

"If it makes you feel any better, my brother is my dad's favorite and my sister is my mom's favorite. I'm just on a lonely island," he says. He flashes me a smirk, and we don't dig further into it even though I want to know why he hid behind the smirk.

After breakfast, I finally make the call to my mom—even though the champagne wasn't nearly strong enough.

And I lie through my teeth—the same damn lie we'll be telling everyone.

She buys it.

This might be easier than we think.

CHAPTER 5

I stare at myself in the mirror.

I found the perfect dress exactly three minutes after I walked into the first store, and they had shoes and jewelry that work as the perfect accessories. The dress fits like it was made for me. His tux is black so I had a pretty wide palette of colors to choose from. I settled on a gorgeous purple that makes my skin glow. I took an hour to curl my hair into loose waves that cascade around my shoulders, and I spent extra time perfecting my make-up. I feel like a different person.

I feel like the future wife of a football player.

I glance at the clock and see that I'm officially out of time. Luke wanted to leave no later than six forty-five, and that gives me two minutes to get downstairs where he's already waiting for me.

I move toward the top of the stairs and start my descent made a little slower in these tall heels. I'll get used to them—I hope. I think back to what happened at the wedding.

God, please don't let me fall into any pools tonight.

When I walk into the kitchen, Luke looks up, and our eyes meet.

My heart races.

His dark eyes sweep along my entire form, and I grip onto the counter because I feel like my knees might buckle at the sight of Hot Luke in his hot tux.

He looks much the same as he did at my brother's wedding in a different tux less than a full week ago, yet at the same time...he looks totally different to me.

He looks like a man I could potentially fall for. A man I *am* falling for. Every second we spend together, another little piece of me belongs to him.

And I'm afraid the more time I spend with him, the more I'm going to keep falling. Then what? What happens once I'm done falling and I'm already there...but he isn't?

I force the thought away.

I have to. I can't go into a night like tonight and play the part with those thoughts plaguing me. But it's still a very real and very scary concern.

"Wow," he says softly, and he takes a step toward me. He reaches around my waist and pulls me into him. I grip onto his bicep. It's hard and freaking huge and I need to keep holding on or I might fall over. "You look beautiful."

My heart hammers and my stomach flips being so close to him. I breathe in the same cologne he wore at the wedding—something he doesn't wear every day, just for special occasions. It's a little peek into who he is, and it makes me want more. It makes me *crave* more. I want to know *everything* about this man. What he likes, what he dislikes, what makes him tick, what makes him smile.

What makes him moan.

And maybe I'll get that chance.

It certainly feels like I could when I'm this close to him.

I close my eyes and breathe him in.

He presses a soft kiss to my cheek, the dark scruff on his jaw scratching my face and forcing memories of our single night together back to the surface of my mind. I want him to kiss me. I want his mouth on mine. I want all of him wanting all of me again.

"Our ride is waiting out front," Luke says, breaking up the intimate trance we find ourselves in.

I follow him to the front door, and he asks, "Is purple your favorite color?"

"Yeah," I murmur.

"It looks nice on you," he says softly, and then he locks the front door before he helps me into the backseat then gets in on the other side. His eyes meet mine once he shuts the door, and a little heat passes between us before he looks away first.

He's not in the right place to get into a relationship, and especially not with someone who wants the fairy tale ending. I have to keep reminding myself of that...but when he looks at me the way he just did, I have to wonder *why*.

We're quiet in the car on the way to the event—or rather *he* is quiet and I'm wrestling with what to say the whole way. I finally break the silence with a question. "Will any of your teammates be there?"

He shrugs. "Yeah, there will probably be at least a few guys there. Any big ticket event like this one always has local celebrities. I wasn't planning on going so I didn't ask around."

"We should have snapped a few pics by your pool before we left," I muse. More thirst traps with this guy in a tux. "Well, if you're ready to unveil me as your fiancée."

"I think we're past the point of whether I'm ready," he says dryly.

Twenty minutes later, we pull up to the venue and the driver lets us out. Other couples dressed like we are emerge from similar chauffeured cars and walk through the doors presumably for the same event we're attending.

I feel out of place as soon as we walk into the room after we check in and receive our dinner table number. My arm is firmly planted through his, and that seems to be about the only thing keeping me steady at the moment.

I recognize faces I've seen before just about everywhere I look. An actor here. A television host there. A famous singer here. A model there. Some seem to know Luke, friendly greetings and head nods going back and forth, and I feel even further out of my element.

I grip onto Luke's arm a little more tightly, and I almost feel like he's holding a little more tightly onto me, too. It must be my imagination.

I'm just a normal girl, a public relations manager from Chicago, and suddenly I'm on the arm of a very handsome man as his fiancée at a fancy soiree where the dinner plates cost upward of a few hundred dollars. Maybe even a thousand. I haven't gotten up the nerve to ask, and I won't.

But this whole event is to raise money, so I'm sure it didn't come cheap.

"So you paid for two dinners and you just...weren't going to show up?" I ask under my breath as I look around the classy room and the elegant people moving about it.

He lifts a shoulder. "I wrote it off as a donation."

I glance over at him, and he looks stiff. Uncomfortable. Out of his element, too.

"Are you okay?" I ask.

He tugs at his collar and clears his throat. "These events aren't my thing. Savannah forced me to go to the first one with her because she liked rubbing elbows with the rich and famous."

"Have you come every year?"

He nods as we stop in a short line near a bar. "This was the first I was planning to miss, actually." He glances down at me, and I try to figure out what's in his gaze. I don't know him well enough yet to interpret it.

"I'm glad we came," I say softly.

One side of his mouth tips into a smile, and then it's our turn to order. He opts for beer, and I order some wine. We keep it simple, and I start to feel an idea forming as I watch him tug at his collar again.

I need Luke to do more for the community, but I want him in a setting where he feels comfortable. The idea hasn't quite formed yet. It's just the start of the snowfall, but I feel like it might be starting to roll into something that resembles a snowman.

"Dalton!" a deep voice behind us says.

We both turn around, and I see someone who looks familiar. I think he might've been one of the groomsmen at my brother's wedding, but let's face it, I sort of had tunnel vision for Luke so I can't really be positive on that one.

"Fletcher!" Luke says in the same tone of voice. "I didn't know you'd be here."

"And yet here I am." He flashes Luke a smile and then his eyes edge over to me.

"This is Ellie," Luke says. "Ellie, this is Brandon Fletcher."

"Nice to meet you," I say, sticking out my hand, and he gives me a look like we've met before.

"You're Nolan's sister," he says, and I nod.

"And my future wife," Luke adds.

Brandon's brows both shoot up. "Your *future wife?*" He doesn't hide his shock for my benefit. "I didn't even know you were dating anybody since that train wreck with Michelle."

Luke shrugs. "We've known each other a while and the timing was just never right." He glances at me, and hot damn he's a good actor because hell if I don't see all the adoration in his eyes that I'd expect him to have when he's looking at his fiancée. "And then it was, and now here we are."

"Well congrats, man," Brandon says, slapping him on the back.

Luke presses his lips together in one of those *thanks* sort of smiles.

"When's the wedding?"

Luke and I exchange a glance, and I field this one. "We just got engaged, so we haven't had time to plan anything yet."

"Before camp, though, right? I'd love to get fucked up on your dime." Brandon booms out a laugh, and I gather that he plays for the Aces, too.

Luke offers a casual shrug. "We haven't made any decisions yet." It's both the closest to the truth and the easiest way to get out of committing to anything.

A beautiful woman with really huge boobs saunters up beside Brandon. She practically hangs herself on him, clearly proving that she's here with him and he's going home with her.

Okay, honey, we get it. He's your guy.

"This is Lauren," he says, nodding to the woman without really looking at her or acknowledging her. "My date," he adds, and the way he says it tells me that she's way more invested in whatever is going on between the two of them than he is.

We wait for them to order their drinks, and as they order, Luke quietly informs me that Brandon is the quarterback for the Aces.

I should probably have known that considering my brother plays for the team and my future husband does, too, and I've even watched *film* with Luke...but I didn't.

185

Once they get their drinks, we mingle around the room with them. We run into one of the defensive coaches and some other people he knows, and Luke introduces me to everyone as his *future wife*.

I guess that makes it pretty official.

And then we run into an older man who looks like he bleeds money.

"Mr. Dalton," he says. He side-eyes me, and Luke seems suddenly nervous—quite a different look than I'm used to on the guy with all the confidence I've started getting to know.

"Mr. Bennett," he says, and he turns to me. "This is Ellie Nolan. Ellie, meet Mr. Calvin Bennett, the owner of the Vegas Aces."

Okay, now I get it. He's nervous because he's worried about his future with the Aces. He's scared that the younger players are going to replace him, and the owner is the one who gets the final say in all that. That's basically the highest boss at his company...if you don't count the fans.

"Mr. Bennet, lovely to meet you," I say, reaching out a hand to shake his.

He nods once. "You're Josh Nolan's sister and Luke's fiancée," he says. Yeah, I'm aware of that, thanks. I'm not sure where he's going with that until he delivers his next sentence. "You're connected to more than one of my men."

I give him my warmest smile, and Luke blanches. I reach over and squeeze Luke's hand in solidarity. "I am. And I love them both so much." I give him a giggle. "In very different ways, obviously."

I glance over at Luke, who looks like he wants to be anywhere but here, and then Calvin's smiling eyes turn a little serious as they edge to my future husband. "Luke, we need to talk. I'll expect you in my office Monday morning, and I'll expect the press taken care of by then. Remember where your priorities are."

Luke nods. "Yes, sir. You know where my top priority is."

Calvin gives him a long stare, and I almost think for a second that he's about to say something more. Maybe something about how families should be his top priority...that football is important, obviously, but that as long as his head's on straight where the game is concerned, maybe other things—particularly in the offseason—can also be priorities in his life.

They're not, for the record, and I can't help but think that maybe that's another part of the reason he's had two failed relationships in the last few years. You know, in addition to the fact that the women he chose were nightmares.

But he doesn't say any of that. Instead, he simply nods and moves along to a different conversation, and Luke lets out a breath with a muttered curse as he guides me to our table.

"What does he need to talk to you about?" I ask. "The baby headline?" I can't imagine why he'd really care about that. I'm sure football players have done far worse than impregnating one woman when they're about to marry another, but I guess I can kind of see how Luke's behavior might reflect poorly on the organization as a whole.

Luke clears his throat, and he looks a little pale as he glances over at me.

"Hey, are you okay?" I ask, reaching over to squeeze his hand.

He shrugs. "I could fucking kill Michelle and Savannah for that goddamn article, but yeah, I'm okay."

"Your boss seems..."

"Nice?" he deadpans, and I chuckle.

"He seems like he really cares about you guys."

He raises a brow at me as he pulls out my chair. "You got that from what he said to me?"

I take my seat, and Brandon immediately pulls his attention so I don't get to answer, and then the first of our seven courses is served.

We listen to the keynote speaker during our dessert, and then we're told that the dance floor is open.

Lauren drags Brandon out there, who looks helplessly at Luke and flags his hands in the *come here* signal.

Luke laughs. "Care to dance?" he asks me.

"I'd love to," I say, and the truth is there's no way in hell I'm missing my chance to get closer to Luke Dalton.

The first song is a faster dance song, and Luke seems uncomfortable. It transitions into a slower song, and he looks awkwardly at me. I lift a shoulder and smile as an invitation to let him know it's okay to dance, and he smiles back before he takes me in his arms.

My body is crushed to his. My heart races, and my legs turn to jelly as I breathe him in.

There's nothing I want more than for all of this to be real.

"The only reason he's even dancing with her is because he knows it's his ticket to getting laid," he says softly to me.

I giggle. "Is that why you're dancing with me?" I ask.

His eyes flash with some hot combination of danger and slyness. "That night was certainly something."

I want him to say more. It was *certainly something*? Does this guy, like, *rehearse* lines that he can throw at me that'll cause me to overanalyze and overthink them later?

"Yeah," I murmur. "Something..." I trail off, leaving the door open for him.

"You know how I felt about it," he says softly.

Do I, though?

Not really.

I lean back and look in his eyes to say just that, but more heat passes between us and my train of thought goes off the rails. I think he's about to lean in to kiss me, but then he doesn't.

He heaves out a sigh. "God, I hate tuxes." He yanks at the neck of his shirt again.

I clear my throat. "So if you could hold a charity event, it wouldn't be black tie with a seven course meal and after dinner dancing?"

He shakes his head. "Fuck no. It would be casual. People would be encouraged to show up in running shorts and t-shirts. There would be a buffet table with appetizers and another with desserts and you could dance if you want but it would be because you're drunk."

And that's when the snowflake from earlier forms right into that snowman in my mind. "Oh my God," I murmur. "That's it!"

"What's it?" His brows dip down and he looks epically confused.

"A charity event. Hosted by you. Casual, fun, beer, running shorts. It can be whatever you want it to be, and it's the perfect start to get you moving in the community like we talked about."

He tilts his head a little as he thinks over the idea. "But I don't have time to plan an event."

My face is the picture of sarcasm for a second, but I force my wrinkled brow and twisted mouth straight again. "Okay, well it seems like you have a bunch of free time right now in the offseason to plan something, but whatever. I can do it, or we can hire somebody."

He chuckles. "Okay, so then what would I even do? What charity would it be for?"

"What's important to you?" I ask.

His shrugs as he thinks, and then he says, "I'd want to help either dogs or kids."

"There are tons of things you can do for kids. You can create your own charity for whatever's important to you. Or you can give back to someone else. There are charities for kids who are sick, for foster kids, for dropout prevention, for spending time with kids, for granting wishes, for sex trafficking, for drug abuse, for helping those in poor communities, for building playgrounds..."

I trail off as that last one seems to spark an idea in his eyes.

"Building playgrounds?"

I nod. "I worked with a charity in Chicago where they refurbished and modernized old playgrounds to make them usable for kids again. Is that something important to you?"

The song changes and it's another slow one, so we keep moving together as we have what feels like an important conversation.

"Something close to that," he says. "I was always outside when I was a kid. I've thought about doing something to help build athletic fields in the community. As part of that, though, I also want to create a scholarship fund for young kids whose parents can't afford to put them in sports." His eyes start to light with the fire of passion as he talks.

"I love that idea," I say, and my arms tighten a little around his neck. It's an involuntary move, almost like I'm hugging him while we're dancing, and his fingertips press into my back, sending flutters right through my stomach. "I think it totally fits who you are while it also gives you the chance to do something positive here in the community. And not just for the media attention you'll get, but because it's something you're passionate about."

He looks thoughtful for a beat. "Let's look into it. So I have the idea for what I'd want to do to help the community, but what kind of event would we do?" He glances around and lowers his voice. "It can't be like this. It's not me."

I laugh. "So you've indicated. I don't know, what would be a fun event? You could do a celebrity softball tournament, or one of those football games where you just mess around for fun—what's that called?"

His brows dip down. "Scrimmage?"

"Yeah, that."

He laughs. "But I thought you said athletes weren't celebrities."

I lift a shoulder. "I stand by that."

He laughs again.

"I'm kidding. I didn't mean for it to sound how it sounded when I said that. You just...I don't know. You make me nervous," I admit.

"I make you nervous?" he asks, a sly little smile playing at his lips. My eyes flick there for a beat and between his lips and how fantastic he smells, my knees nearly give out on me.

I nod. "Incredibly."

"Huh," he says in wonder, and my eyes move back to his. "That's interesting because the feeling's sort of mutual."

My tummy somersaults as he holds my gaze for a beat longer than we should as *friends*.

But we're not friends...not really. I'm working for him. I'm his fake fiancée. I'm his roommate. I'm his best friend's little sister. At this point, we hardly know each other, but I'm getting to know him. And every new piece of Hot Luke that I discover presses my feelings for him just a little deeper.

He clears his throat. "Cornhole."

His single word breaks the daze I started falling into.

"Um...excuse me?"

"Cornhole," he repeats, like I just didn't hear him the first time. No, I definitely heard him, but what the fuck is cornhole?

Is he...

No. I shake off the thought.

Wait a minute.

Is he offering me butt play?

"Right. Okay." I nod like I get it.

"You have no idea what cornhole is, do you?" he says, and it sounds less like a question and more like a statement.

"No," I lie, because I'm pretty sure a cornhole is a butthole. "Not a clue."

He laughs. "It's a game where you have two wooden platforms placed a certain distance apart and they have holes in the top of them. Then you throw beanbags and try to get them into the hole. That could be my charity event. Celebrity cornhole."

"Oh!" I say, a little flustered that I thought he was talking about something completely different. "Yes! Bags. That's what I call it. But yes, I love that idea!"

And I take that as my green light. He's got a charity, he's got an event, and he's got the passion.

As soon as this ball is over, I've got work to do.

I'll just push my feelings for him aside. That shouldn't be too hard...right?

CHAPTER 6

We grab one more drink before last call, and we dance a little more, and with every step we take on the dance floor, my heart beats a little more strongly for him.

The way his eyes light up when he's passionate about something is beyond endearing. It's pushing my feelings for him into another place that's both dangerous and scary for me considering how adamant he's been that he isn't right for me.

I want him to kiss me.

I want to share a bed with him but for it to be real.

It's too soon, yet I want our engagement to mean something for *us*, not just for the media.

Brandon leaves with his date still plastered to the side of his body, and Luke asks if I'm ready to go not too long after that. He bids his farewells to the people that he knows, and before we slide into the town car waiting for us out in front, I tell him I need to use the restroom. He does, too, and tells me we'll meet in the lobby when we're each done.

I'm riding the high of the night with Luke combined with my ridiculously good idea for a charity event when I'm blindsided in the ladies' room.

I'm washing my hands when the woman at the sink beside me says, "No ring on that third finger."

Is she talking to me?

She's right. I don't have a ring on my finger...even though I'm *engaged*.

"Pardon me?" I say politely. I glance up at the mirror to get a look at her, and she's absolutely gorgeous. Stunning blue eyes and wavy dark hair that cascades down to the middle of her back. Her skin glows and her dress looks like it was made to fit her petite frame. I'm immediately intimidated by her just from the way she's narrowing her eyes at me. She has that resting bitch face thing going on even though she's smiling at me. Is that smiling bitch face?

I grab a paper towel to dry my hands, and she does the same. "I said you're not wearing a ring. Aren't you engaged to Luke Dalton?"

I'm confused. Who is this woman and how does she know who I am? "Yes, we're engaged," I say.

"So why aren't you wearing a ring?" she presses.

"We haven't had time to pick one out." The lie rolls smoothly out of my mouth and I just want to get out of this bathroom and get back to Luke, who's waiting for me in the hallway. I toss my paper towel in the trash, and this woman is right behind me every step of the way, her paper towel going in right on top of mine.

I don't like fielding questions alone. When we're together, at least we can make sure we're telling the same stories.

"When did you get engaged?" she asks, and I'm still walking toward the door to exit this damn bathroom and it must be the biggest bathroom in the history of bathrooms because it feels like this is taking forever.

"A few days ago." I'm about to rush out of there, but then I realize that makes me look like I have something to hide.

"How long have you been together?"

You have a lot of questions for someone who hasn't introduced herself.

I wish I had the guts to say something like that...but I don't. I'm intimidated by this woman, and Luke didn't train me on how to handle rabid fans or whoever this is. I'm a big girl, though. I can handle this.

"We've known each other a while but the timing was never right." I lift a shoulder. "And then it was, and we grabbed our chance."

"Luke said he would never get married again. How did you manage to tie him down?"

My brows dip, and I finally open the door. "I'm sorry, but who are you?"

Luke is standing just down the hallway, and his eyes move toward the two of us.

When he spots the woman beside me, his eyes widen and then he looks just plain angry.

I look over at the woman again, and she flashes me a smirk as we reach Luke.

"Savannah," he says, and the word comes out with venom.

My heart races as I finally realize who she is.

The ex-wife.

After all the research I did, you'd think I would've come across her picture *somewhere* to recognize her, but Luke did a good job keeping his past hidden. I've been so busy learning about wide receivers that I haven't had time to really get into Luke's personal history.

But this is the reporter.

She was digging at me for a story back there in the bathroom.

What a bitch.

"Luke," she says back, entirely too sweetly.

"It's my extreme displeasure to introduce you to my ex-wife, Savannah Buck," he says to me.

"Maybe in a few months when this is all over, we can start an ex-wives club," she says, circling her finger between Luke and me.

"Get the fuck outta here," Luke mutters, and it's clear they did not part amicably. "Why'd you print that lie the other day?"

She raises a perfectly manicured brow. "The *lie*? Excuse me, Mr. Dalton, but I only tell the truth."

He laughs, a hearty and fake laugh filled with malice that I've never heard from him before. "You print whatever's convenient for you that also manages to fuck with my reputation."

Savannah's hand flies to her chest in an act like she's deeply offended. She makes a noise of disbelief, but I don't buy her act for a second. Neither does Luke.

"So if you only print the truth, where's your proof that Michelle is really carrying my child?"

"Big difference in what you're asking there, Captain." Her eyes twinkle like she's enjoying this banter, but Luke looks like he's about to pop a blood vessel in his forehead.

"What, you mean a story versus a story with evidence?" he shoots back, and it's clear he's flustered by this entire conversation while she maintains her cool, and I fucking hate her in that moment. I hate what she's doing to Luke. I hate that she's getting under his skin. I hate that she can stand there and do that to him with such calm confidence.

"You didn't ask for evidence. You asked why I printed a lie, and I didn't. A woman came to me with her claims, and nowhere in the article does it say that there's evidence she's carrying your child. That's why we use words like *alleged*. I know it's hard for your overly concussed brain to grasp, so I'll break it down for you. Lady said she's knocked up with your kid and you're marrying some side chick you've known four seconds."

"Oh fuck you, Savannah," he spits, rolling his eyes. "Come on, Ellie. Let's go home."

She holds up her hands innocently. "Bye bye," she says, and then she winks at Luke as she starts to walk away. "Looking forward to your check, my sweet benefactor." She tosses that final line over her shoulder.

Luke exhales heavily as we head toward the exit. "So that's another reason I didn't want to come tonight, you know, just in case you were wondering."

"Why did she call you her benefactor?" It's a stupid question but apparently the only thing I can think of to say.

"Alimony, although not as much as she'd like and certainly not as much as I'd have to pay if we'd have gotten married now versus seven years ago."

"How long were you married?"

"About a year. I was young and stupid and thought she was hot. Hot does not equal marriage material."

Sage advice indeed. It would probably do me well to remember that.

"Why didn't you contact her boss and demand a retraction?" I ask.

"It's sensationalism. It's unethical, but it's not illegal. She prints her little stories at the expense of accuracy, and unless there's libel or slander involved, it's not illegal."

"Isn't it libel if that baby Michelle is carrying isn't yours?"

He lifts a shoulder and twists his lips a little wistfully. "There's more to it than that. They're both backing me into a corner, and I don't have a choice but to sit back and take it."

The car is waiting for us when we get out front, and it feels very much like the end of that conversation as we slide into the back of the car...but I want to know *why* he doesn't feel like he has a choice.

We're well on our way back to Luke's place, silence blanketing us as he seems like he's deep in thought while I'm not sure what my role is. Should I try to distract him? Let him think it out? Talk? I go with lighthearted small talk. "Did you have fun?"

He shrugs and glances over at me. "As much fun as I always do at these things. Capping the night with my ex-wife wasn't the ideal way to end it."

"Then let's pretend that didn't happen. We can find our own way to cap the night." I wink at him. "At least you had a hot date." Okay, maybe I'm a *tad* tipsy after all the wine.

He chuckles and moves his gaze to the window. "That I did," he says, and it's under his breath so I almost miss it.

But I don't, and I think back to when he called me *Sexy Ellie* when he thought I was asleep.

"So tomorrow I'll look into what it takes to start a charity and how to make it happen," I say, mostly to change the subject and a little because I don't think he realizes I heard what he just said. But honestly...I don't even have a clue as to where to start my research. I don't even know what I don't know.

"I can put you in touch with the charitable contributions department at the Aces to see if they have any guidance," he says almost as if he's reading my mind.

"That would be amazing," I gush.

"Erin's great," he says. "She helped Brandon get his charity off the ground."

"What's his charity?" I ask.

"Fostering Fletch. He raises money that goes to help foster kids," he says. "He can be kind of a douchebag when it comes to women, but deep down he's a pretty good guy."

We pull into Luke's neighborhood.

"How did my brother end up across the street from you?" I ask.

He chuckles. "I had the receivers over one night for beer and poker, and he saw the sign in the yard across the street. We got to talking, laughed about how fun it would be, and he made a lowball offer the next day. They accepted, and the rest is history."

"Do you like Vegas?" I ask.

He nods. "I've been here nearly a decade now. It's home."

"Where'd you grow up?" I ask as we pull into the driveway.

"Michigan. I was recruited by Wisconsin and drafted right out of college by the Aces."

"Lucky Luke," I say.

"My grandfather used to call me that." He chuckles. "Hence the Lucky Charms. But honestly it was luck combined with a little hard work." He opens the door and runs around the car to my side to help me out. He bids goodnight to the driver, and then we walk together up to the front door.

We stand there on the porch for a beat. He watches the driver as he backs out of the driveway, and he hasn't moved to open the door yet.

The light breeze in the night air makes me shiver.

My eyes meet his, and he takes a step toward me. He's close enough for me to feel his heat.

"This is the part of the night where I'd usually kiss my date goodnight," he says softly.

I look up at him as nerves rattle around in my chest.

We've kissed before.

I mean, we've had *sex*, so of course we've kissed too.

I think back to that first kiss in the lounge chair by the pool at the Cosmopolitan, and another shiver runs through me. This one isn't from the chill in the evening air, though.

He reaches beneath my hair to cup my neck, his fingers curling around me as the heat in his eyes turns to an inferno.

He moves a centimeter closer, and my heart races as my knees start to shake.

I want this.

God, do I want him to kiss me.

He moves in even a little closer, his big hand warm on my skin. That fresh scent of his plows into me.

Kiss me, kiss me, kiss me, I chant in my own head.

And just when I close my eyes to wait for his lips to meet mine, he sighs and pulls away.

He unlocks the front door, and I follow him into the kitchen. He loosens the knot in his tie and unbuttons the first button of his collar, revealing a delicious peek of skin.

I want to lick it. I want to lick *him.* Everywhere.

I want that kiss we missed out on...but I'm afraid the spell has been broken. Whatever drove him to nearly kiss me appears to have evaporated, and I can't recreate the quiet peace that nearly brought us there.

"I'm uh..." he begins. "I'm sorry. I realize I'm sending confusing signals, and I think it's because, well, I'm confused. I like you, Ellie. A lot." He clears his throat as he looks away, and I wish I could get inside his mind and figure out what he's thinking.

"I like you, too." My brows dip down.

He blows out a breath. "This is all just so complicated."

"What is?" I ask.

"I feel like I keep doing all the wrong things. What happens when this is all over?"

"My brother is your best friend. If we fake this engagement for another day or another year, it doesn't matter. He'll still be in your life, which means maybe it's okay for me to be, too."

He nods. "What if I push you away and you hate me?"

"Come on, Luke," I say a little more loudly than may be completely necessary. "You're grasping at straws here. You're finding ways to sabotage our arrangement before it even gets off the ground."

"That's not what I'm doing," he counters. "I'm just being realistic. I'm analyzing. I'm looking at it from all the different angles and perspectives." Just like he does when he studies film.

Looks like I'm not the only one who overanalyzes things.

"What are you so scared of?" I ask.

He doesn't answer, but I think I already know. He hasn't healed from his past relationships. His ex-wife and his ex-girlfriend were manipulative. They scarred him, and now he's scared to get into something with another manipulator, so he's written off relationships.

He wants to focus on his career, and that's an awfully big hurdle for someone like me to overcome...especially when he's so damn stubborn.

"Look, I won't lead you on," he says. He presses his palms to the counter, his elbows straight as he hangs his head down a bit, his eyes focused between his hands. "I like you, and you like me, but I can't give you the kind of future you want."

"You don't know that," I say softly...hopefully. And for the tiniest flicker of a second, I think about a friends with benefits sort of situation. Whatever he decides next, we're faking this thing together for at least the short term. I could get *some* pleasure out of it. But a friends with benefits thing won't work. I'm already falling for him, so adding sex to the mix (again) will only push me there faster.

"Yeah, I do." He presses his lips together a little sadly as he looks up at me. "I'm going to go take a shower. Goodnight."

He turns and heads out of the room at that, shattering that tiny ray of hope he gave me when he almost kissed me.

CHAPTER 7

On Monday morning, Luke gives me specific instructions for how to find Erin at the staff offices located inside the practice facility.

"Why are the offices at your practice facility and not at the stadium?" I ask.

"The team doesn't own the stadium," he says.

This is one of those times I don't even know what I don't know. Same with his directions. It's the kind of thing you can't find on your phone's GPS as he explains how to navigate the hallways of the building, and I stare at him like he has two heads.

He glances at his watch. "You want to just go together?"

I nod. His meeting with Calvin starts an hour after my meeting with Erin. "Pretty please?"

He chuckles. "Of course. Let's take two cars, though, because I have a workout planned with Tristan and I don't want you to have to wait around for us to finish."

"Who's Tristan?" I ask.

"The new guy," he says, giving me that look like I know nothing about football again. "Tristan Higgins."

I shrug. "Maybe I could stop by your workout to snap a few pictures for Instagram. Imagine how good it'll make you look. You're extending goodwill toward the new guy, you're confident about your place on the team, you're introducing him to what you do. Plus it would give your fans an insider look of where you work out with the team. They'd love it."

"I'm not doing it to look good. I'm an actual decent guy," he says.

"Yeah," I say softly, thinking of my history of men who really weren't such good guys versus this man who gave the girl he doesn't even know a place to live and a job. "You do seem like you're one of the good ones."

He joins me for my meeting, and there are multiple reasons why it's actually a good thing to have him with me. For one, I *never* would have found Erin's office without him. And for another, I end up looking to him to answer a lot of the questions Erin has. I don't want this to be *my* event. I want it to be his. I want it to be something he can carry with him beyond our time together, however long that might last.

And then I glance over and see how excited he is about this whole charity idea. He can't wait to start raising money to ensure every kid has a fair shot to play sports, that they won't get left behind just because they can't afford the team uniform...that they have a sufficient place to practice and play.

My heart pitter patters.

My stomach flips.

Oh shit.

I knew it was happening.

I could feel it coming, and there was little I could do to stop it.

It's as we sit in this meeting with Erin, excitement lighting his face and passion burning in his eyes that I realize something. That feeling in the pit of my stomach is the low burn of fire as my body tried to warn me. *Stop! Alert! Stop!*

But it's too late. I went and fell for him, and now I'm pretending to be engaged to him while privately he keeps pushing me away.

I've gotten myself into quite the jam.

He transitions into a bundle of nerves as the clock ticks closer and closer to nine-thirty, and then he excuses himself to meet with Calvin while Erin and I work out some more details on our own.

I'm dying to ask him about the meeting once he returns a half hour later, but I don't get the chance, and this isn't the place for him to talk about it, anyway.

Instead, we head to the gym. That fire in my stomach only burns hotter as I take pictures of him working out with the Aces' newest team member.

And it's not until a few hours later as he signals his way onto the highway that I finally ask the question that has been burning in my mind since ten this morning. "How was your meeting with Calvin?"

He clears his throat. "Not great."

"What did he say?"

"He ripped me a new one for knocking up Michelle, and then I had to explain how I'm not the right man for her but I'll be there for her and the baby every step of the way." He's quiet and flat as he speaks, and I can tell the conversation did a number on him even though the workout must've helped him categorize his feelings. "He also reminded me more than once that I'm not the only wide receiver in the league."

"That's awful," I say, reaching over to squeeze his hand.

But I don't get it. Why does Calvin care what Luke does on his own time?

He presses his lips together and keeps his eyes focused forward on the road. "He's right, though. I'm not. I'm easily replaceable, and that's why I need you." He pauses, and my heart races. He *needs* me. Except then he adds, "It's why I need your help with both my image and my brand to make me someone who isn't so easily replaced." His words are a reminder that this is nothing more than a business deal to him...even though it's more than that to me. "He asked me how I'm going to make things right with Michelle. I told him I'm engaged to somebody else now. I hope you're still okay with pretending with me for a while."

I'm still okay with it even if I don't really get why Calvin is so invested.

I just find myself wishing more and more that it wasn't pretend.

CHAPTER 8

After my shower the next morning, I head down to the kitchen with my laptop and grab some coffee before I get to work. I slide onto one of the stools at the counter and I'm munching on a banana when Luke walks in.

"I have something for you," he says.

I glance away from my screen and over at him, my brows dipped down. "What is it?"

"Come with me."

I abandon my laptop and toss the banana peel in the trash. We walk through the house, and he stops at a closed door. It's the office where my boxes have been stacked since the movers dropped them off.

Maybe this is his way of telling me to move my boxes or unpack my shit or just get the hell out because it isn't working for him.

"Open the door," he says softly.

My heart pounds as I do it, and I gasp as I look around.

Gone is the dark wood, replaced with a fresh and completely opposite look. A huge, white desk sits in the middle of the room with a very comfortable looking white chair. Two white chairs sit opposite the desk. Empty white bookshelves line one wall, and floor to ceiling windows give me a gorgeous view into his backyard.

In the center of the room is a fluffy purple rug.

The desk is filled with office accessories.

They're all glittery purple.

A large purple couch sits on the wall across the room from the desk, a place where I can relax and create.

Hanging on the walls I see all sorts of artwork with phrases like *hustle* and *lady boss* and *grind* in glitter. Another one says *work work work*, and another says *I'm not bossy* with its twin photo hanging next to it that reads *I'm the boss.*

It's all purple and white with silver sparkles, and the boxes that were stacked along the wall are gone.

"This is for *me?*" I ask.

Tears fill my eyes as I look at Luke, who looks proud of himself. He nods with that lady killer grin of his.

I move toward the fluffy purple rug and spin in a circle. The fabric is soft on my feet. "When did you do all this?"

"I've been at it a while. Everything was delivered while we were at the ball and I've worked on it the last couple days with Debbie's help."

"But you asked me my favorite color the other day..." I trail off.

He chuckles. "Like I didn't already know. Ellie, your phone is purple. So is your suitcase and most of your clothes."

"And all the glitter?"

"I don't think you've gone a single day without wearing something that sparkles, whether it's your watch band or your shirt or your bright smile."

I melt into a pile of lust for him as my knees feel a little weak. "You noticed all that?"

One side of his mouth lifts. "Of course I did," he says softly.

I can't help when I automatically move toward him and toss my arms around his neck. I want to kiss him. Every urge inside me is telling me to kiss him.

And I do...but I go for his cheek, and then I untangle myself from him. I walk over to the desk and open one of the drawers. A bunch of my bullet journal stuff is in there, all organized neatly. "Thank you. This is incredible."

"I figured if you're going to be here working for me, you deserve to have your own space. Even if it's just temporary. I'm sure you love the kitchen counter, but that ergonomic chair will be a little easier on your back than the barstool."

"This is the nicest thing anyone has ever done for me," I say softly.

We stare at each other as heat passes between us.

He's agile and athletic, his black shirt clinging to his broad chest and his charcoal shorts making his legs look lean and muscled. His eyes are on me, and he almost looks a little nervous.

"Can we, uh, talk a second?" he asks, and a dart of anxiety rushes through my chest as I wonder whether the gift of this office is about to be tainted by this conversation.

"Of course," I say, and neither of us moves from where we stand.

"I know we haven't exactly figured out the logistics of our fake engagement, but between running into Savannah at the ball and my conversation with Calvin...I feel like we need to push forward with this idea if you're still okay with it."

"Push forward with what?" I ask. I'm confused as to what he's getting at. We've already agreed to faking this, so it's like he's a step behind me and he can't quite catch up.

"I don't even know how to ask this, or what the hell I'm doing, and your brother is going to fucking murder me...but I mean an actual fake marriage." He shakes his head and looks out the window. "I can't believe I'm even suggesting it."

My brows dip. "I thought you were against the idea. What changed your mind?"

He sighs. "Getting reamed by my boss got me thinking, and I'm not sure I see any other solution. And, obviously, I'd make sure you walk away with a healthy payday."

"Why does your boss care so much about your private life?"

He looks at me in confusion for a beat like it's a silly question, but then a light seems to dawn in his eyes. "Oh, you don't know." He clears his throat. "Michelle's last name is Bennett. She's Calvin's daughter."

My eyes widen. "She's his *daughter?*"

Well, I guess that explains Calvin's investment in this whole thing. Suddenly everything falls into place.

Now I understand why he feels backed into a corner...and why he isn't demanding a paternity test just yet. He can't make a big public stink about this or he risks pissing off the team owner in a contract year. It makes much more sense for him to just lie low and let the media frenzy blow over.

Man, he really is stuck between a rock and a hard place.

"I think an actual marriage might be the only way to shut Savannah up and keep Michelle from trying to squeeze the life out of me while also getting Calvin to understand that even though I'll be there for both her and the baby, marriage isn't in the cards for Michelle and me."

"But what if it doesn't?" I ask, and I'm not sure why, exactly, my dumb ass is trying to talk him *out* of this idea where I get to marry a hot football player who happens to be my brother's best friend and also the guy who I have a raging, massive crush on.

He blinks in surprise. "What if it doesn't...what?"

I lean my ass on the edge of my brand-new desk. "What if it doesn't shut Savannah up? What if it doesn't keep Michelle off your back? What if it doesn't prove anything to Calvin? We haven't given it much of an effort, but it doesn't seem like being *engaged* has worked. Why do you think marriage will? Maybe I need to get knocked up, too." I say that last part as a joke, but Luke pauses and raises his brows like he's considering the idea. My heart falls into my stomach. "Oh Jesus. I'm kidding, Luke."

He laughs. "Gotcha."

"Dude." I walk across the few steps between us and smack his shoulder. "Not cool." I take a second to look out the window and regroup. I can't stare at Luke's hot face and make a rational decision.

I haven't thought this through.

It's stupid. Everyone would tell me that.

And yet...it feels somehow like the right thing to do. He offered me a place to stay before he knew a damn thing about me, and so I'm offering him this as a way to help him out of his own mess. Plus, you know, that whole *healthy payday* thing. It would give me the chance to find my own place and maybe even start my own PR firm.

I like him a little more every second I spend with him. It's not like this is *all* bad.

And that's why I'm leaning toward a yes here. It's my job to clean up his image. To make him indispensable to the Aces. To prove to the world that he's as amazing as I think he is. And if I need to be his wife to do that...then it's sort of part of my job description, isn't it? And as his wife, I don't think it's necessarily outside my wifely duties to demand a paternity test from his pregnant ex since he doesn't feel like he can.

God, I'm riding a fine line here. I really need to be more careful about what I wish for.

I'm going with my heart, clearly not my brain, as I speak my next words. "I don't know. It isn't the *worst* idea in the world, is it? If you really think a fake marriage is going to help you, I'm still in."

"Maybe we should leave it up to fate," he muses.

I raise a brow. "Fate?"

He shrugs. "Let's hit the casino tonight."

"That's not fate," I point out. "That's a gamble. I prefer to be in charge of my own life decisions."

He laughs. "We're in Vegas, baby. Let's gamble."

I don't like the idea of this, but I'm starting to find that when Luke asks, I agree. And so, after dinner, we head to the Strip.

He navigates to the valet parking of Caesar's Palace, and he grabs my hand. A tingle buzzes around my chest and my stomach does a little flip. I don't know if he does it because we're in public or if he does it because he wants to hold my hand. I hope it's the latter, but I have a sinking feeling he's just trying to show off our relationship should he be recognized by anyone.

We head inside and walk through the expansive casino toward a bar. He glances at me. "Want anything?"

I'm not sure if this is a *get wasted* kind of visit to the bar or more of a *have one and we'll head home* kind of visit, but I order a glass of white wine and he opts for a whiskey sour.

He pays, and we take our drinks toward a room marked *High Limit.* I may be new to Vegas, but I'm pretty sure they're not talking about alcohol.

The room is empty except for one older couple playing a slot machine in the corner. He pulls out his wallet, grabs a hundred dollar bill, and sits at a poker machine. I sit in the open chair next to him.

"You go first," he says. "If we double our money or more, we get married."

I stare at him for a beat.

He's serious.

And I'm not going to be the one to back down.

I push the button to deal the cards, my heart thumping so loudly in my chest that I'm afraid he'll hear it. It's five card draw, so I get five cards, I can discard as many as I want, and I'm dealt enough to make it five again. If I get a pair or higher, I win...or, at least I don't lose.

I get a two, a four, a six, an eight, and nine. All shit cards. I press the button to get all new cards, and I get about the same shit I had on the first hand.

He tries next, and it's the same shit, different hand. My heart is still thumping, but the initial nerves over this whole idea are starting to dissipate as I realize there's no way in hell we're going to win.

He nods for me to go, and I lose. Zero cards go together to attempt to make any sort of hand.

He goes again, and he loses.

We go back and forth, and when we get down to our last ten dollars, he says, "Let's push the button together."

I nod, lean in so close I can smell him, and set my finger on the button. He places his on top of mine and pushes down.

The cards seem to flip in slow motion.

King of hearts.

Ten of hearts.

Queen of hearts.

Ace of hearts.

And a fucking four of spades.

He looks at me with wide eyes, and I'm sure my gaze back mirrors his.

If we snag a jack of hearts, that's a royal flush, and that's the top jackpot payout on this machine—twenty-five thousand dollars.

That's more than *doubling* our money.

He saves the ten, queen, king, and ace, and then I set my finger on the button.

He presses my finger.

I squeeze my eyes shut because I can't look. I'm too damn nervous.

"Holy fuck," he murmurs close to my ear, and that's when I know.

My eyes pop open. "Oh my God!" I squeal when I spot the jack of hearts in the place where that four was sitting before. The machine starts going crazy, and the jackpot song plays as a big, blue stripe across the center of the screen screams, "JACKPOT! Hand pay required."

We're both in shock. We stare at the screen, and then we look at each other, and then we look back at the screen, and holy shit we let fate decide and fate is absolutely pushing us together—for this fake marriage, at least. He leans in and presses a soft kiss to my lips, and I want to hold on for more. I want to straddle his lap and hump him right here as we celebrate our big win, but it's a quick celebratory kiss because we just won twenty-five thousand dollars in a public place.

"I guess we've got our wedding budget," he says, and I burst into giggles.

CHAPTER 9

We're both a little drunk by the time the Uber drops us back in Luke's driveway, and when we get into the kitchen, I drop my purse on the counter and kick off my shoes.

So we're really doing this.

I have hundreds of questions, but I have no idea where to even start and all the celebratory wine I had mixed with coming down off the thrill of winning is making me sleepy. We can deal with the questions in the morning.

To my surprise, though, Luke steps closer to me and grabs my hand. He links his fingers through mine. "Thanks for a fun night, Ellie. You're making me see that not all women are evil."

I laugh, but he doesn't.

"I'm serious." He pulls our joined hands up and presses a feather light kiss to my knuckles.

My knees go weak.

"I'm not like them," I whisper. "I won't manipulate you. I won't hurt you. I'll just be here for you. However you need me to be."

He leans a little closer. "You're definitely going to hurt me." His warm whiskey breath mixes with his Luke scent so close to me, and it overwhelms my senses.

"Why do you think that?" I ask, genuinely curious as I wonder whether whiskey is some sort of truth serum or if it's just a horndog pill and he's coming onto me.

"You already have." He leans even closer, and his nose brushes mine. I think he's going to kiss me, but I'm not sure.

My chest buzzes with excitement, and my legs nearly give out as my hands start to tremble. My body responds even though my brain is trying to do the right thing. I don't even know what the right thing is at this point. We just let a fucking poker machine decide we're getting married.

And I want him.

God, do I want him.

My mind races back to our night together. Snippets here and there—his hand on my ass as he pounded into me from behind. A stolen kiss on a lounge chair by the pool.

"How?" I ask, my breath a whisper just inches from his mouth.

"By being you. By being everything I want but nothing I can have." His lips brush mine, and everything inside me lights with fire as rockets explode in my chest.

"But you *can* have me, Luke," I argue softly against his lips.

He shakes his head as if my words sober him for a beat. "No," he says. "I can't. I'll only hurt you in the end. It's what I do. My past relationships that ended...there were two people involved, and I'm not innocent. You're too good for that." He brushes his lips across mine again. "You're too goddamn good for me." He kisses me just for a second where it's more than a brush of lip on lip, it's a tender press of his mouth to mine, but then he pulls back from me. He backs up a step.

"Goodnight," he says softly, and then he strides out of the room.

I'm not sure where he goes, but I give him some time in case he went upstairs to the bedroom we're sharing.

When I finally go up to bed, though, he's not in there. My heart drops with disappointment.

He must be sleeping in one of the guest rooms, which is probably a good thing considering the amount of alcohol we both had tonight.

Drunk or not, I want another night with him.

I want all the nights, but I'd settle for one.

* * *

I'm in *my office* working on some community outreach for Luke when he knocks on the doorframe.

"You can just walk in," I say a little more testily than I intend to. "It is your house, you know."

"I know," he says. "I just wanted to say I'm sorry about last night."

"Which part?" I ask a little flippantly, my eyes returning to my laptop screen. Does he mean the part where he let a slot machine decide our fate, the part where he kissed me and then bolted, or the part where he said he's no good for me? It appears he has much to apologize for.

"All of it, but mostly for kissing you."

"I'm not." My eyes flick to his. "Anything else?"

He sighs. "Do you still want to do this thing with me?"

"First, don't call it a *thing*, and second, I have no idea why, but sure, why not."

His brows both rise in surprise, like he was sure I was going to back out. "I still don't understand why, either, but if you really are on board, then I'm not going to question it."

I glance up at him, and he seems conflicted where he stands as his gaze falls to the window. "Did you want to win on that machine?" I ask.

His eyes slide over to mine. "I've never lost on it," he says softly.

I'm glad I'm sitting, because my knees would freaking give out if I wasn't.

"So I guess we should make it official." He draws in a shaky breath, and then he shifts as he moves to get down on one knee. He grabs something from his pocket, a little box, and he flips open the lid.

I gasp.

I'm still sitting at my damn desk.

"Ellie Nolan, will you be my wife?" he says.

Of all the scenarios I imagined upon receiving a ring for the first time from the man of my dreams, faking it was never part of the story. Sitting behind a desk while he asked was also not part of the story.

Yet here we are.

I stand up, my demeanor softening, and I walk around the desk to where he kneels.

I smile down at him. "I'd love to," I say, and I'm a little scared at how very much I mean those words.

It's only going to mean bad news for me when it's all over.

He slides the rock onto my hand, and I can't help when I bring it up a little closer to inspect it. It's gorgeous and the diamond is almost heavy it's so big. Way too big.

But beautiful.

And mine.

It's square with smaller diamonds surrounding it set in a platinum band. It must've cost a fortune, and it sparkles in the bright white office where we stand. I already know I'll always look at the spot where Luke kneels and think of this moment.

I just have no idea how I'll *feel* when I look at this spot.

In all those scenarios I imagined for my engagement moment, I also never really thought the guy who just proposed to me would seal the deal with a quick hug and a whispered *thanks*, but that's exactly what happens.

"When are we doing this?" I ask, in part because I'm afraid I'll change my mind if I have too much time to think about it and partly because I'm worried *he* will change his mind. I back up and lean against my desk since my knees are still a little shaky.

He stands as he draws in a breath, and then he collapses on my couch. *My* couch. The one he got for me and put in *my* office. I'm still a little awestruck over that. "Probably before your brother gets back from his honeymoon."

I nod. That only gives us about two and a half weeks. Holy cheese and crackers. "Definitely. And are we having a wedding or is this a City Hall affair?"

"Well..." he says, and then he trails off like he just had an idea. "What?"

"We're supposed to go to Hawaii in a couple weeks. What if we surprise my family with a wedding while we're there?"

"You'd be okay getting married as a lie in front of your family?" I ask.

"It's not a lie that we're getting married," he points out. "We *are* actually getting married. It's just the whole, you know, barely knowing each other thing that we can leave out of the conversation."

I press my lips together. If he's okay with it, I guess I'm okay with it, too.

"And what'll we tell people is our reason for the rush?" I ask, trying to cover all the angles as I glance down at my ring again.

I can't help it.

"Love." He says the word so simply that I almost believe him.

My eyes flick over to his. "How long will we stay married?"

He lifts a shoulder, and I can't help but think he looks a little sad sitting there on the couch. I have this strange urge again to hug him, and even though I'm going to be his wife, I'm still not sure we're there. "A year? I don't want to tie you up any longer than that but it should give me enough time to deal with all this." He waves a hand through the air.

To deal with all this. That's why we're doing this.

I'm still not exactly sure why I agreed. I have literally nothing else going on when it comes to career, abode, or my love life. Whatever the case, I'm going to be someone's wife in three weeks.

Or less.

Suck on that, Todd.

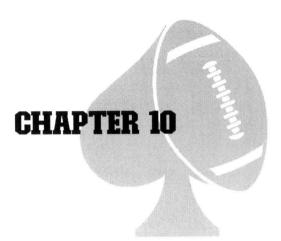

CHAPTER 10

The feelings I've now identified that I'm having for him are exacerbated further when I show him the selection of tuxedoes he can pick from for our surprise wedding in Hawaii. And it's physically painful as I scroll through wedding dresses as I try to find a good destination option that'll travel well and still be perfect for our day.

I push those feelings down, down, down. Ignoring that I'm falling for him is my only option.

He sets up the cornhole boards in his backyard and challenges me to a tournament, and, never one to back down from a challenge, I agree.

That was my first mistake.

As I may have mentioned, I'm not the most coordinated person on the planet.

He explains the rules to me, positions me next to the board he will toss his beanbags to, and tells me to toss my bag onto the board he will be standing by. He tells me the goal is to try to get my beanbag right into the hole, and I nod him off since I've played this game before and just didn't know it was called *Cornhole.*

And my first toss of my beanbag toward Luke's board hits him right in...well, his beanbag.

He doubles over and grabs his crotch in pain, and I rush the thirty-or-so feet across the yard to check to be sure he's okay. "Oh my God, Luke! I'm so sorry!" I put my arm around his shoulders awkwardly as he moans and falls to the ground, still grasping himself.

"Are you okay?" I yell, and I don't know why I'm yelling except maybe I'm panicking a little that I actually hurt him.

He chuckles and sits up, his hands not moving from covering his crotch, and dammit I can't pretend like I don't wish those were my hands there. "I'm being a *little* dramatic, but damn, girl, you've got quite an arm on you."

I smack him in the arm, and he moves one hand to rub that spot. "You had me really worried about you!"

"Sorry. But seriously, where the hell did you learn to throw like that?"

I lift a shoulder then sit on the grass beside him. "The force or the aim?"

He laughs. "I'm talking about the force since the aim could use a little work."

I shrug. "From Josh? I mean clearly I have no idea of my own strength since I really thought that would sail right into the hole."

"Maybe we need a little more practice before the event," he says.

"Speaking of which, when do you want to actually hold the event?"

He glances over at me. "Before the season starts if we can. If not, we'll need to wait until it's over."

"Preliminary research tells me we can have the event without the proper paperwork on hand so long as we disclose our tax status to donors ahead of time." I cross my legs crisscross-applesauce and pick at a blade of grass.

He finally lets go of his crotch, and he stretches his legs out in front of him. "So we could have it next week if we wanted."

"Theoretically, yes. But bear in mind the woman planning it is also planning a wedding and managing your public relations and doesn't think she could handle the stress of executing a charity event in a week."

He laughs. "What the fuck am I paying you for?"

It's a clear joke, and I giggle. "When do you report back for training camp?"

"End of July," he says.

"And what's that like? Could we hold it then?"

He gives me a look like I'm insane. "Uh, no."

"Why not?"

"It's grueling. Harder than the actual season. It's where we show what we're made of. We arrive at six in the morning and don't get home until ten or eleven most nights. I get three, maybe four days off for the entire month of August. There just wouldn't be time."

"Then we do it before training camp," I say. "Year one can be a trial run with just the people in your circle, and next year we can plan for a huge blowout."

He catches his bottom lip between his teeth, and God I wish I could catch that lip between *my* teeth, and then he nods. "Okay. Let's do it."

I grab the calendar, we pick a date that falls the weekend before training camp begins...and then I get to work.

* * *

"A little closer," I say, and his body is nearly pressed against mine.

Oh yeah, baby. Right there.

I try not to sigh as I click the remote in my hand to snap a photo of the two of us. My phone is on a tripod a few feet away from us. The palm trees surrounding his pool are behind us, with the mountains as a backdrop beyond those, and the sun at the perfect angle as it starts to set. We're smiling in the background of this photo as I hold my ring up to the camera after a fresh manicure this morning.

"Now one of us kissing," I say, and I turn toward him.

Any excuse to get those lips back on mine.

This is for my job, though. I need to stir up a little publicity, to show that he's in love with me, to make him look like he's heading toward his happily ever after and that he really is engaged to silence people like Savannah. Posting a ring pic seems like a good start.

He brushes his lips with mine, and I get so lost in the feel of his mouth on mine again that I nearly forget to click the remote.

He stops it first, and I turn away and walk toward my phone to check our work. I pretend like I'm unaffected by his kiss...but I'm not.

I'm *totally* affected by it.

I wish he felt the same. I wish I could understand why he was so adamant this can't work between us because the more time I spend with him, the more convinced I become that it *would* work.

I clicked the button three times in the short window I had, and I love all three options. There's no way to choose the best one. Studying those three pictures later as I try to decide which one to post will definitely not be the worst part of my day.

Except maybe it will. I'm only hurting myself here. I have the option of walking away, but when I think about that, my stomach seems to turn over with knots. Maybe that's an option because that's *always* an option, but it's not one I'm willing to take. Now that I've met Luke Dalton, I want to be a part of his life.

Even if I have to get hurt in the process. Just being a player in this game will have to be enough for me. Well, that mixed with the hope that someday he'll feel the same way I do.

Time seems to pass in the blink of an eye between working on getting a charity off the ground, planning a wedding, and managing a celebrity's public relations—a celebrity who, by the way, is in the spotlight because of this baby news, and suddenly it's the night before we leave for Hawaii.

I've been shopping for days, and I've managed to get all the outfits I need for a wedding plus fun in the sun...and even a *just-in-case* negligee should the opportunity present itself on our wedding night. Or any other night of our trip.

We met with the lawyer and the paperwork has been signed. We even got our marriage license, so we'll be legal once the ceremony is performed. It all came together incredibly quickly, and now it's time to pack.

The wedding gown is in a garment bag along with a few other dresses I decided to bring along, and it's hanging unzipped on my side of the closet when Luke walks in.

I jump up from where I'm kneeling on the floor as I survey my clothes, and I zip the bag shut.

He laughs. "I don't think the whole thing about it being bad luck to see the dress before the wedding applies when it's fake."

I purse my lips. "While that may be true, I don't want to tempt fate."

"Suit yourself," he says. He grabs a suitcase down from the top shelf and starts tossing clothes into it. While I have an outfit for each day laid out on the closet floor beside my suitcase, he's literally just tossing in a handful of shirts, a couple pairs of shorts, some swim trunks, and jeans.

"Don't forget your wedding tux," I remind him, and he nods toward a garment bag similar to mine hanging on his side of the closet. I slide back down to my knees in front of my clothes. I stack three outfits I'm definitely taking with and set them gently into my suitcase.

"Got it." He's quiet a beat while he organizes the clothes he tossed into his luggage, and then he asks, "Are you ready for all this?"

I turn around and find that he's sitting on the floor, watching me as I sort my clothes. He's leaning against the shelving unit on his side.

I sit back and lean on my own shelves directly across from him. We're maybe eight feet apart, and it feels too far. "Ready for what? Being Luke Dalton's wife?" I tease with a smile.

He lifts a shoulder and doesn't crack a smile like I expect him to. "Meeting my family. Getting married. The media frenzy that'll surely follow."

My smile fades. "What's your family like?" I've gotten snippets here and there, but I don't really know Luke all that well...and yet I've agreed to marry him. "I'm at a slight disadvantage here considering you know my family pretty well."

He shoots me a sad smile that's a little hollow, a rare glimpse into what he's thinking. "Sometimes I wish I was born into a family more like yours."

My brows dip. "You do?"

"Yeah." His tone is a little wistful. "We're not close. I wish I had the kind of dynamic you and Josh share."

"Didn't you say Kaylee texts you a few times a week?" I ask, recalling one of the few times he's talked about his family.

"Yeah, but she's a decade younger than me. She's in college and I've been in my career for almost ten years. She wasn't even old enough to go to a bar and have a drink with me until a couple months ago, and I've been married and divorced and now I'm getting married again." He blows out a breath and shakes his head. "We're just at very different stages of life."

"That doesn't mean you can't be close," I point out.

"I know," he concedes softly. He picks at the plush carpet, and it strikes me that it's kind of odd to be having such a deep conversation with him in his closet. "I just don't put in the effort. It's easier to keep myself closed off."

"Even from them?" I ask immediately even as I realize that while it's in his nature to keep himself closed off, he's actually opening up to me right now. The thought sends a buzz through my chest.

"Especially from them. Kaylee and my mom are close. Jack and my dad are close. Kaylee would run to my mom with any tidbit about me, my mom would tell my dad, and it would get back to Jack. It's stupid family politics bullshit. I can't be myself around them. I have to put on an act."

"That's awful. I'm so sorry," I say, and I mean it. I can't imagine having a relationship like that with Josh. He's my best friend, and he married my best friend, and I love them both so much. I'm so grateful I have them in my life.

But every family is different, and sometimes I wonder what my relationship with Josh would be like if there was another sibling in the picture. Would all three of us be close? Or would one of us always feel left out? Luke seems to feel left out of his own family even though he hasn't actually admitted that.

"Why don't you want things getting back to Jack?" I ask.

"Jack is..." he trails off as he searches for the right words. "He's complicated. He's the kind of guy who always gets his way, and I've been burned more than once because of that."

I'm curious to know more about that, but I don't want to interrupt when he's in the middle of letting me in. I haven't even met Jack yet and I already don't like him just based on the few things Luke has said. I just hope I can keep my feelings to myself when we do meet in a few days.

"So what's a typical Dalton family vacation like? What can I expect?"

He shrugs. "We usually meet for dinner the first night, and then it sort of depends. Since this was Kaylee's choice, she gets to pick a few family outings and the rest is usually free time. Based on how well I know my sister, I'd guess we'll be doing things like sunset dinner cruises and whatever typical tourist traps we can find."

I'm starting to get a little nervous about meeting his family...and what this trip has in store for us.

CHAPTER 11

The car pulls up in front of our hotel, and I can see straight through the open lobby and out to the beach. The white marble floors paired with massive arches, gorgeous greenery, and a ginormous fountain right in the middle of the lobby tell me this hotel is a paradise oasis...and it's mine to enjoy for the next ten days. You know, with the guy I have a huge crush on that I'm actually going to marry while I'm here—the guy who doesn't return my feelings even though we shared that one spectacularly hot night.

I sigh as that old cliché of a warning haunts my thoughts. *Be careful what you wish for.* I wished for a one-night stand. Sure, that's what I got...but somehow I also got a roommate, a boss, and a fiancé. Funny how that worked out.

And in a couple days, I'll be meeting my future in-laws. I'll have to put on an act like the two of us are so in love when this is nothing more than a publicity stunt. My chest aches at the thought.

We're promptly lei-ed with fresh orchids when we get out of the car, and we check in and head to our room— a corner wraparound suite, incidentally, but this one has a separate bedroom unlike the one in Vegas. I take a quick glance out the windows at our view of the beach as I fight off the memories of my hands pressed up against the glass while he took me from behind.

The view is different, but the urges are the same. I wanted him in that hotel room in Vegas when he was nothing more than a stranger, and I want him even more now that I've had a few weeks to get to know him.

I'm falling for him.

Actually, that's not true. It's even worse. I've *fallen* for him.

I turn from the windows and bump right into Luke.

"Oof," I mutter, and he grabs onto my biceps to steady me. "Sorry. I didn't know you were right behind me."

I glance up at him, and our eyes lock. His twinkle down at me as he lets off a soft chuckle. "Nice view," he says, his eyes still on me.

A beat of heated silence passes between us, and is it thick with sexual tension or is that totally just my imagination?

He finally flicks his eyes to the window, and I step out of his grasp because I have to. I was seconds from reaching my hand around his neck and pulling him to me. Seconds from stripping naked and pressing my hands on the glass and sticking my ass out so he could take me again.

Okay, so it's getting warm in here. I step toward the air conditioner and set it cooler, and then I slip my lei over my head and set it on the desk. I check my phone, and then I glance back at Luke, who's staring out over the water deep in thought.

"What's on your mind?" I ask softly.

My voice seems to startle him from his thoughts. He turns from the window back toward me. He exhales, and he offers a small smile. "Nothing. What time's our meeting with the wedding coordinator?"

I glance at the clock. "We've got an hour."

"Are you hungry?" he asks.

I lift a shoulder. "Not really." I do have a wedding dress to fit into in just a couple days, after all.

"Me neither," he mutters. "Want to explore the hotel?"

I nod, and we set off on a walk of the grounds. This particular resort was voted the best luxury accommodations in Maui, and it offers six restaurants, four bars, and three pools. It sits directly on Polo Beach, and we walk around the gorgeous, plush hotel before we slip off our shoes to walk on the sand. People sunbathe all around us as it's a little before three in the afternoon, and soon they'll head inside to shower and get ready for a romantic night out.

I want to reach for his hand because there's something about a beach that's *always* romantic to me...but this is just pretend. I can grab his hand in a few days when it's for the benefit of his family watching us. While there's always the chance there may be paparazzi around somewhere, right now we're just two people walking side-by-side down the beach.

We walk toward the ocean and dip our feet in. The water is warmer than I was expecting, but I've learned lately that my expectations rarely meet reality.

We rinse our feet and head back inside to the lobby, where Alana, our wedding planner, told us to meet her.

"Luke and Ellie?" a woman with long dark hair wearing a flower-patterned dress asks. "I'm Alana," she says when we both glance up at her, and I can't help but languish in the sound of our two names side by side.

Ellie Dalton.

If I had a notebook and a hot pink gel pen and I was ten years younger, I'd be doodling my new name and hearts all over the page.

"How'd you know it was us?" Luke asks.

"You have that soon-to-be-wed glow," she says warmly, and while her sentiment is meant to be sweet, it just makes me feel sad.

Luke laughs, and I offer a smile.

"Let's start with where your ceremony will take place," she says, and we make small talk with her as we follow her out to the beach we just walked in from. She shows us the general area and explains how it'll be set up and how we'll have privacy for our ceremony.

"The bride will stand here," she says, and she stands in place and motions for me to come over because I'm the *bride*.

It's all more than a little surreal. I was dating someone else what feels like five minutes ago and suddenly I'm marrying this guy I've known four minutes. What the hell am I doing?

"The groom will go here," Alana says, and Luke moves into place beside me.

"Take her hands in yours, Luke," she instructs, and he does.

"Manny will be presiding over your vows, and he'll stand here where I am," she says. "Your only job will be to hold one another's hands and look into each other's eyes as you listen to his words, repeat after him for your vows, and then you'll be husband and wife."

Luke's eyes are on mine as she speaks, and my heart pitter-patters. He's only doing it because she's telling us to, but a girl can still wish there was more to it, right?

Alana shows us the restaurant where we'll have our rehearsal dinner and another restaurant where we'll have our reception with Luke's family there to celebrate our new titles as husband and wife. She takes us back to her office, where we review all the details, and then we're done, and while I should be elated that this is going down in just a couple days, instead I feel...hollow.

My family isn't here to celebrate.

I don't even have any friends here. The only people who will witness our vows are people he doesn't really even want at his wedding.

"Are you hungry now?" Luke asks as we stand in the hallway and I debate whether I should tell him my thoughts. "The place where our reception is going to be looked pretty good."

"That's fine," I say, and we head in that direction.

The hostess seats us in a quiet corner booth, and once we've both had a chance to look over the menu and placed our drink orders, he glances across the table at me. "You've been quiet since Alana told us where to stand for our wedding. Are you okay?"

I lift a shoulder and glance away, and then I pick up my wineglass to have something to do with my mouth rather than answering.

"If you're having second thoughts, it's okay to back out," he says quietly. "I know we signed the paperwork, but we don't *have* to do this."

I raise a brow. "Are *you* having second thoughts?" I ask.

"Second...third...fourth." His voice is low as he speaks candidly. "I haven't thought this was a great idea from the start, but I don't know how else to get Michelle and Savannah to back

down and also appease Calvin to show him and the world I'm not some horny playboy who fucked around on his little girl."

I chuckle at his assessment but it's not really all that funny. "It just feels weird that no one's here from my family," I admit. "Won't that look kind of strange?"

He shakes his head. "We take this family trip every year and we're doing it as a surprise. Can't we just spin it that we wanted to keep it secret so it was private for the two of us?"

"We can spin it however we want. I guess that's the direction I was planning to go anyway," I say, but his words are just another reminder that this is all for show.

A beat of quiet passes between us as he takes a sip of his beer, and then he says, "Thank you for all you're doing for me. I just want you to know that you always have an out."

"I know I do," I say softly, and I think back to the contract the lawyer drew up. It protects his assets, obviously, but it also protects me. Luke specifically wanted it that way, and it was just one more thing about him that dropped him decidedly into the *prince* category.

The waiter comes by with some bread, and I keep my hands busy by tearing a piece into shreds. "Have you been to Hawaii before?" I ask, changing the subject.

He nods. "Savannah and I came here on our honeymoon. But not Maui. We went to Oahu."

"What was that like?"

"Beautiful beaches, but a totally different pace than here. Maui seems more...I don't know. Relaxing. We stayed in Honolulu and it just has more of a bustling city vibe even right there on the beach. The shopping, the hustle and bustle...that's Savannah's style."

"What's your vacation style?" I ask.

"I like a mix of adventure and relaxation."

"What sort of adventure?"

He shrugs. "ATVs, snorkeling, scuba diving, ziplines, horseback riding. Any kind of tour where I can learn about the place I'm visiting. What's your vacation style?"

"More the relaxing on the beach side, but I'm always up for an adventure. Not, like, adrenaline junkie stuff like ATVs and ziplines, and certainly not horseback riding, but tours or dinner cruises. I read about a submarine outing here in Maui and there's this black beach I'd love to go check out," I say.

"Why not horseback riding?" he asks.

I narrow my eyes and hold up my hands. "You've already started converting me into a football fan, but I have to put my foot down at horseback riding. I *hate* horses."

He laughs. "Why?"

My cheeks heat. "I fell off one when I was younger. I guess I never got over the fear that he was going to trample me."

His brows dip, and it's a rare serious moment from the usually lighthearted girl I am. He reaches across the table and squeezes my hand. "We don't have to go horseback riding. There are plenty of other excursions we can plan before my family gets here."

My heart twists as he inches his hand away from mine, but I pretend like I don't feel it. "I'm sure excursions will provide some amazing backdrops for thirst traps, too," I say, trying to err on the side of professional since if I don't, I might just reveal how I'm starting to feel about this guy.

He chuckles. "We're on vacation, babe. Let's just have some fun." He sips his beer, and I chug my wine, and goodness gracious I'm in a heap of trouble.

CHAPTER 12

His side of the bed is empty when I wake, and the bedroom of our suite is still dark thanks to the heavy curtains blocking out the sunlight. I brush my teeth and use the restroom and then I head off to find my fiancé.

The main living area of our suite is swathed in sunlight, and I spot Luke out on the balcony sitting in a chair with a cup of coffee as he stares out over the ocean. I snap a picture from inside. It might not be a thirst trap, but it's an awfully gorgeous view as far as I'm concerned.

I grab my own cup of coffee from the little pot he made and join him out on the balcony. "Good morning," I say as I push the slider door closed. I sit in the open chair beside him.

"Morning," he says. His eyes are shaded by sunglasses.

"Sleep good?" I ask.

He shrugs. "Sure. You?"

"Yep." I take a sip of coffee and wonder why things feel a little awkward between us this morning, but then I remember that we hardly know each other and maybe this is just him on vacation in the morning. "You ready for your family to get here?"

He chuckles. "No. Not at all. I'm grateful for the next two days we have of actual vacation before the family political matches begin."

I'm quiet in response to that.

"It'll be nice to see Kaylee," he concedes. "A week is just a long time."

"At least you have me," I say with a big, cheesy grin, and he laughs.

"You're right there. You've sort of slipped right into the slot of my best friend over the last few weeks."

"Same goes for you, Hot Luke." My eyes widen as I call him the nickname I usually reserve for my inner thoughts.

He glances at me but doesn't say anything before returning his gaze to the water. I wish I knew what he was thinking, but I *never* know what he's thinking.

I clear my throat awkwardly. His quiet demeanor and pensiveness are throwing me off this morning. "You wanna grab breakfast or something?" I finally ask.

Rather than answer my question, he poses one of his own. "Why are you marrying me?"

I turn to look at him, but he keeps his gaze focused out on the water.

I'm quiet a beat before I answer. "You're giving me a place to live. You're my boss. You're a good guy, Luke, even though you pretend like you're not. You're my brother's best friend. You're becoming *my* best friend. My job is to help turn your image around, and I'm nothing if not dedicated to my work."

And I'm falling in love with you and I think you're falling for me, too, but you're too scared to admit it so you're pushing me away, but maybe over the next year I can make you see how right we are for each other.

I leave that last part out, obviously.

He presses his lips together and nods. "Thanks."

I'm not sure exactly what he's thanking me for—whether it's my explanation or the fact that I'm going to go through with this marriage—but I say, "You're welcome."

"Do you want to just eat up here?" he asks. "Can't beat the views."

I don't even need to glance out over the water where he's looking. I keep my gaze trained on him instead. "You're certainly right about that," I murmur.

"Pick out what you want from the room service menu and I'll call in an order."

A half hour later, our omelets and bacon are delivered.

"No Lucky Charms?" I ask.

234

"Not even on the menu." He shakes his head and rolls his eyes. "What kind of second-rate place is this?"

I laugh as we keep our eyes on the water and make small talk. Hot coffee sits in a carafe on the tray, and I tip the bottle of vodka I found in our room over my orange juice.

He holds up his glass, too. "Hook me up, future wife," he says lightly, and I giggle as I pour.

"What do you want to do today?" I ask.

"I was just about to ask you the same," he says. "You first."

"I'd lie on the beach and float in the ocean, or we could go to that black beach we talked about. What about you?" I sip my vodka. That's right. My orange juice is gone, so now it's just straight vodka. I'm on vacation.

"What if we do what you want today and what I want tomorrow?" he asks. He tips some vodka into his empty orange juice glass, too.

"And then we meet your family the next day?" I ask.

"Yeah," he murmurs. "Guess we better do what you want both days."

I laugh. "I'm all for equal opportunity. What's on the agenda for tomorrow?"

"Guess you'll find out tomorrow." He raises a brow in my direction, and I purse my lips. Then I shrug, take another sip of vodka, and head in to take a quick shower while Luke gets our tour booked.

When I emerge, Luke is waiting with a backpack. "Our tour is booked, and it's a full day thing, so we need to get our asses downstairs because our tour guide is already waiting for us."

"That was quick."

He smiles. "They were able to slip us in at the last minute, so we got lucky."

I can't help but wonder if we got lucky or if we got Luke-y...as in money talks, and Luke knew how much I wanted to see the black sand.

Our tour guide, Marcus, clearly loves everything about Hawaii. He's enthusiastic while he tells us all about the Road to Hana in our private Jeep tour as he takes the twists and turns toward the historic town of Hana. It's about five hours one-way, and we stop at different beaches along the way...including the Wai'anapanapa black sand beach.

It's not soft, fine sand like we're traditionally used to when we think of beaches, but these are small black pebbles and rocks formed from the volcanoes. Marcus treats us to the history of the area, we snap about a million pictures of each other, and then we head back toward the hotel—another five hours in the Jeep, so by the time we get back, it's a little after nine at night.

We're both exhausted from fresh air and sitting in the car all day, but as Luke showers before I fall asleep, I study the pictures I took of him. I mark a few as favorites and potential thirst traps on Instagram, but really what I'm doing is looking at his smile.

In the first few from this morning, it starts out small.

By the time we got to the black sand, it was wider.

And by the time we hit our last stop as the sun started to set, it was a genuine, happy smile.

He's loosening up as we find a rhythm with each other. We spent the entire day together enjoying the scenery, laughing at the crazy things that came out of Marcus's mouth, and bonding. I'm not quite sure yet if we were bonding as friends or as a couple, but it certainly felt like the latter.

There were times today I thought he was going to kiss me, and then he backed away. There were times I had an urge to grab his hand, but I didn't. We keep getting so close to this imaginary line, and then we both seem to back away. I'm not sure why *he* backs away, but I know why I do.

I'm afraid he'll only reject me like he's already done before. A girl can only try so many times before she gets the hint and stops, and I'm almost to that point.

I may be falling for him, but he keeps sending signals that I'm the only one. And so, before I fall down a path from which I'll never be able to get up, before I get in too deep with him emotionally...I need to stop. I need to back slowly away or I'm going to get burned. In fact, the heat is already starting to smolder. It won't be long before that heat turns into a flame that has the power to scorch me.

* * *

Two days in the sun have wiped the two of us out. We're both exhausted at the dinner table as we dine at the same restaurant where our rehearsal dinner will be held in a couple nights. The days may have been exhausting, but they were also fun. Thrilling. Adventurous. Filled with things of beauty—and I'm not just talking about the landscape, though that certainly gave my eyes many treats. We shared little moments that only served to bond the two of us. We built memories, things we can take with us even when this is all over. And that thought has me feeling a little melancholy tonight.

I put on the mask, though. I keep up the ruse like this is a good idea. But the more time I spend with Luke, the more I can see *this* as our future. I see Jeep tours and ATVs in Maui, or mountain climbing or skiing or relaxing in whatever other locations we visit.

I see hot days and sweaty nights, adventurous excursions followed by fists clenching sheets and fingerprints on windows.

"So ATV or zipline?" he asks, interrupting my internal musings. "Which did you like better?"

"I'm never going ziplining again," I mutter. "I still can't believe you talked me into doing it." He was very convincing. The fact that he took off his shirt might have had a little something to do with it, too. Hell, I might even do something crazier like bungee jumping from a bridge or skydiving out of a plane when he isn't wearing a shirt. My brain short-circuits and I can't make rational decisions when my eyes fall onto those abs.

He laughs. "And I even took pictures for evidence." He pulls out his phone. "Look at your face in this one. Priceless."

I look at myself and the sheer look of horror in my eyes and my mouth in a wide *O* shape as I started my ride across the beautiful plantation. Honestly it was prettier from the platform. I couldn't see it while I rode the line because my eyes were squeezed shut for the entire duration of the terrifying ride immediately after he took this picture.

"I'm posting the one of you throwing the devil horns with your fingers while your tongue is hanging out," I say. His abs are on-freaking-point in that one. Talk about a damn thirst trap.

He laughs. "Do what you need to."

I raise a brow. "Hawaii seems to be loosening you up. A few weeks ago, you never would've let me post that one."

"It's the rum," he says, nodding to the drink special of the night, a traditional Hawaiian mai tai.

I giggle. "I better post it before you change your mind," I say, taking out my phone. He stops me with a hand covering mine, and I can't help but feel the same pull of electricity I always feel when his hand is on mine.

"Before you post, just remember that as soon as you do, the seven hundred thousand people who've already found my account will all know we're in Hawaii," he says.

Damn. Being the publicist...that's definitely something I should've thought of. "I will also blame the mai tais on that one."

He laughs. "Let's take whatever pictures we want and save the posting for when we're back home."

I narrow my eyes at him. "Good call. Especially since your whole family will be here. Between you and your quarterback brother, there'd be a flood of sold-out flights heading toward Maui."

"Don't forget my dad. He coached college for years."

"Where'd he coach?" I ask. I take another sip of my drink. This is my second, and I'm already feeling the buzzing effects.

"Michigan. And Jack played for USC."

"So Wisconsin, Michigan, and USC? I don't know anything about college football but it sounds like big school rivalries."

He lifts a shoulder. "None are each other's biggest rival, but I played Jack when I was in college. I played my dad, too."

"Was that weird?"

He stares at his drink before he glances up to meet my eyes. "Not weird, exactly. But both Jack and I know a lot about my dad's coaching style, just like he knows a lot about our playing styles, so in some ways there were advantages and in other ways there were disadvantages. You always study your opponent, though, no matter who it is."

Our dinners are served, and a little food helps the buzzing in my head start to dissipate.

"What time do they get in tomorrow?" I ask.

"They're all getting in at different times. Kaylee made reservations tomorrow night so we'll just meet for dinner once everyone's here," he says. "I don't want to tell them about the wedding until the night before. That way no one has time to fuck it up."

I'm from the kind of family where I'd be waiting in the lobby with hugs for everyone's arrival. Clearly Luke is not from the same type of family, and not for the first time I can't help but wonder what, exactly, I'm marrying into.

Does it matter when it's all for show? I guess time will tell.

CHAPTER 13

I check myself in the mirror one last time. My skin glows from a few days in the sun, and the yellow dress I chose for tonight just enhances that glow. I draw in a deep breath. I'm nervous. I want them to like me even though it doesn't matter. I'm a people pleaser by nature, though, the kind of person who wants *everybody* to like her. And from the few snippets I've gotten about Luke's family, I'm not feeling too confident that they'll even care about me. Except maybe Kaylee.

I emerge from the bathroom and find Luke sitting on the chair in the corner, eyes trained on ESPN as usual. He wears jeans and a button-down shirt and even though he's totally casual, he looks dressy and delicious. My mouth waters as I drink him in before his eyes flick to me. And when they do...well, it seems like ESPN just doesn't matter anymore.

Something about the way he looks at me causes my knees to knock together. The heat in his gaze makes my stomach twist with even more nerves. It makes me wish this was all real...that he was feeling the same things I am.

He clicks off the television and stands. "Wow, Ellie," he says, his eyes sweeping down my form.

"Is that a good *wow*?" I ask, clearly fishing for a compliment.

"It's an incredible wow." He takes another step toward me, and then it's like he realizes what he's doing and stops short. He blows out a breath and finally glances away from me and toward the clock. "Should we head down?"

I nod as I try to push away the disappointment. "You ready for all this?" I ask.

He chuckles. "Nope. Not even a little."

"At least I won't be alone, then."

His mouth lifts in a small smile. "You're not alone."

I twist my lips and bite the inside of my cheek to keep the tears that seem to spring to my eyes at bay. That's the problem, isn't it? I'm very much alone in all this, and the thought is rather devastating.

We head toward the elevator, take it down to the lobby, and just before the doors open, he grabs my hand in his. My heart immediately lifts until my brain catches up. It's for show. This is what we'll do now. We'll play the parts. We'll put on the act. Meanwhile, my heart will take its beating and hopefully I'll be able to recover it by the time this whole thing is over.

Why am I doing this to myself?

I didn't allow that question to form in my mind until today. This moment. Right now.

Why am I putting myself through all this?

What am I getting out of it?

At first, it sounded fun. Marry the hot football guy, my older brother's best friend. That was back when this was all some big crush. But that big crush has become actual feelings, and he's been pretty clear that even though there's definitely something there between us, he's not going to act on it. This is nothing more than a business arrangement to him. To me, though, it's more than that.

I clutch his hand in mine as we walk toward the restaurant, and he mutters something under his breath as we get closer.

"What?" I ask.

"Jack's not here yet," he says through gritted teeth, and when I glance up at him, a smile is plastered across his lips. I may not know him *that* well, but I can tell the difference between real and fake. This one's fake. I force one of my own as we approach a party of three.

"Lu-Lu!" a gorgeous girl says. Long, dark hair cascades in pretty waves down to the middle of her back, and her blue eyes glow as they edge quickly to me. I see an immediate family resemblance between her and Luke.

His hand doesn't leave mine as his fake smile turns a bit more genuine. "Hey, Kay-Kay," he says, wrapping an arm around her shoulders as she tosses her arms around his neck. When he pulls back from their hug, he nods toward me. "I want to introduce you to someone," he says to his sister. "This is my fiancée, Ellie." He turns to me. "Ellie, Kaylee."

"So nice to meet you," I say, letting go of Luke's hand as I reach over for a hug.

"You too," she says. "I can't wait to get to know my future sister-in-law."

"This is the fiancée?" another female voice asks, and as I pull out of my hug with Kaylee, I'm faced with an older version of Kaylee except with a short, bob haircut and a few lines around her eyes. I smile as my eyes flick to the man who is obviously his dad. The resemblance is strong.

"Mom, Dad, this is Ellie," Luke says. He doesn't greet either of them with a hug, which surprises me.

"Carol Dalton," the older version of Kaylee greets me with her hand extended out to shake. I take hers in mine, and hers is cold.

"Nice to meet you," I say.

"Tim," his dad says, and we shake hands, too, which is followed by an awkward beat.

"So this is the girl you're marrying even though you got another girl pregnant?" Carol asks, her eyes appraising me shrewdly.

I choke on something at her question, and I glance over at my fiancé, who looks livid. "Mother," he says sharply, his voice a clear warning.

She raises a brow and purses her lips, but she doesn't say anything.

She doesn't apologize, but her son does. "I'm sorry, Ellie. That was out of line."

I shake my head, and I'm about to say it's fine when Tim pipes up. "Jack's on his way down now. We can go ahead and get our table."

Kaylee greets the hostess and we all follow along to a table in a private room, which is nice since I'm breaking bread with three celebrities, a younger sister, and my future mother-in-law. Luke clutches my hand as we walk, and when I glance over at him, his eyes are turned down to the ground. I can't tell if he's clutching my hand for show or if it has something to do with the fact that he just needs someone right now. And I'm someone. Enter Ellie or whatever.

I squeeze his hand, and he glances over at me. I see the gloom there in his eyes, one of the first times I can really read him well, and my heart aches for him. Seeing family should bring joy...not whatever this is. I give him a smile, and I squeeze his hand again just to let him know I'm right here for whatever he needs. We'll get through this together.

As far as first impressions go, Kaylee seems sweet, I haven't made up my mind on the dad, and the mom is basically terrible. I can't wait to find out where Jack falls in line with the rest of them.

Carol sits first. It's a rectangular table, and she chooses the chair at the head of the table. Tim settles at the other head of the table. Is that the tail?

Luke and I are facing the door, and he keeps glancing toward it as we all wait for his brother. I'm glancing through the menu when I hear a sharp intake of breath beside me as Luke seems to stiffen.

I look up at the doorway, and I draw in my own sharp intake of breath.

Sure enough, another member of this incredibly attractive family stands in the doorway. Intense navy eyes seem to hold a thunderstorm of emotions behind them, dark hair styled precisely, a strong jaw that's currently clenched with just enough groomed scruff to give him a bit of a mysterious edge, the same full lips his brother has.

Jack Dalton holds an air about him that commands attention, and he certainly has mine...as well as everyone else's at the table. He surveys his family, his eyes just sweeping past me like I'm of no importance to him, and he strides with self-assurance into the room. "Hello, Daltons," he says, his voice similar to Luke's deep and rich tone.

Tim stands to shake his son's hand, and my eyes fall to their connection. His hands are big like Luke's, and his fingers are long.

I wonder how many footballs he's thrown in his life. I wonder how many women he's pleased with those hands. I shake that thought away as Tim claps Jack on the back. Carol stands, too, and she gives Jack a hug. Kaylee and Luke don't get up and it's just such a weird dynamic to me. Jack takes his seat.

"This is Ellie," Luke says. "My fiancée."

"I saw the headlines," Jack says shortly rather than something like *nice to meet you* or *welcome to the family*.

He doesn't introduce himself. Instead, he moves toward his seat like I'm just supposed to know who the hell he is. Well, newsflash asshole, I wouldn't have known a couple weeks ago.

"So, Luke, how'd you two meet?" Kaylee asks, clearly trying desperately to make things normal.

"She's Josh Nolan's sister." He says my brother's name like everyone at the table would know who that is, and they all do. I feel heat creeping into my cheeks as everyone's eyes turn to me. "And get this. She doesn't even watch football."

I glance around the table at the mix of surprised and horrified eyes as well as a couple of dropped jaws at that statement. I offer a smile with a little shrug. "I'm a unicorn."

Luke laughs and tosses an arm around the back of my chair, squeezing my shoulder. He leans over and presses a loving kiss to my temple, and my entire body warms. I glance at Jack, and I'm not sure why. He's watching the entire exchange. "You're more than a unicorn, babe."

"You guys are so cute," Kaylee says, obviously sealing in my instant love for her with that pronouncement.

I offer a nervous giggle, and before I can come up with some witty reply (which clearly isn't going to happen with the sheer number of intimidating people at this table), Jack speaks up. "Probably a smart move, Luke. The last two fanatics really fucked you over."

Luke pins him with a glare, but Jack just laughs.

We're saved when someone comes to take our dinner orders. I notice that Jack and Luke order the same thing—a medium steak with baked potato and broccoli. Must be some kind of football diet even in the offseason.

"What have you been up to this offseason, Jack?" Carol asks. "We know what Luke's been up to," he says, raising his brows in my direction. When his eyes land on me, I feel...exposed. Branded. Nervous.

My cheeks redden further at his insinuation even though it's not true. Well, except for that one night.

"Stop," Luke says.

"I've been running drills with the new guys," he says, turning toward his mother to answer the question she posed. "Getting to know them and using my position as team captain to instill a sense of pride in our team." He glances at his brother. "But I don't want to give away too many secrets to the enemy."

Luke rolls his eyes. "What you do in the offseason isn't giving away any secrets."

"We understand, Jack," Tim says as if Luke never spoke at all. "We're just so proud of your accomplishments. Do you think the Broncos have a shot to win the big game again?" The way he says it clearly indicates that there's only one son at this table he's proud of, and my heart aches for Luke again.

He has his own accomplishments. He's a successful wide receiver. He plays pro football. He's a genuinely good guy. He's doing so much for me—giving me a place to live, giving me a job...giving me eye candy and thirst traps and spank bank material.

God, who knew that just being a witness to this family dinner could make me fall even more for the guy? I want to grab him into a hug and hold his hand and tell him that someone here cares about him. Someone here is proud of him. Someone here thinks the world of him.

That someone is me.

"More than a shot," Jack says to his father. "We traded for one of the top receivers in the league," he says, his eyes flicking to his brother as if to insinuate that Luke *isn't* one of the top receivers, "and combined with the speed of our draft picks and the skillset of our current team, we'll make an even stronger return. Expect a repeat."

Luke chuckles and shakes his head.

"What?" Jack asks, his tone a bit accusatory for someone who brims with such confidence.

"The Aces are in top shape, man. You'll have a fight on your hands for a repeat."

"Guess we'll find out which team is better twice next season," Jack says with a smirk. This time, it's not confidence as much as it's cockiness. Yet despite that, there's something incredibly charming about the guy. He's being a dick to his only brother, yet he does it with a smile that seems so damn genuine you can't help but think that somehow he's paying Luke a compliment even though he isn't.

My first impression of him is that he's someone who makes everyone in the room feel special just because they get to be in the same room as him. And somehow that includes me, even though he's barely glanced in my direction since he walked in except to make some sort of sexual insinuation about his brother.

I hate that it includes me. I don't want to like him because of how he treats his brother…yet I find myself incredibly fascinated by him. Incredibly attracted to him. Like I *want* him to look at me, to notice me.

His brother sure hasn't.

Jack dominates dinner conversation with tales of his big win and the celebrating that followed while Luke remains quiet. I learn that the Aces lost to Jack's team in the playoffs last year—the game that sent the Broncos to the Super Bowl. I learn that Jack likes women and he doesn't filter his words in front of his parents. I get the sense that Jack flirts with everyone—including our waitress, including a woman who walks by our doorway and recognizes him, including me when his eyes flick to mine from across the table as I sit next to his brother who I'm engaged to marry.

I learn that Luke is reserved in front of his family. He's not like that with me, though, which just tells me he's actually opened up to me even though he seems like such a closed book. I get it now, though—the reason *why* he's closed off. In his own family, he comes in second or third. Never first.

I just haven't figured out *why* that is yet.

CHAPTER 14

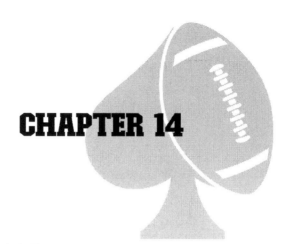

After what feels like an insufferable two hours, dinner is finally over. Jack leaves first, and I have no doubt it's because he has some woman chained to his bed that he needs to get back to. Just watching him cut his steak showed me how controlled and disciplined he is. He seems like the kind of guy who might have a secret kink if you know what I mean.

Tim orders one more cup of coffee even though the meal is over, and I glance at Luke as I'm unsure whether or not we have to stick around for more of this rare form of torture.

"Kaylee, would you mind hanging with Ellie by the lobby bar so I can talk to Mom and Dad alone for a few minutes?" Luke asks.

"I'd love to," Kaylee says, and she stands.

Luke leans over and presses a kiss to my cheek. "I'll be right there."

"Thanks so much for dinner," I say again to Tim, and he gives a short nod.

Kaylee links her arm through mine and we walk toward the bar, thankfully far away from Carol and Tim. "Congratulations on surviving your first dinner with them," she says, elbowing me a little in the ribs, and I giggle.

"Is it always that awkward?"

"Only when Jack and Luke are in the same room together," she says. "I'm sure he filled you in on their history."

"Not really," I admit. We slide onto the stools at the bar, which is fairly empty. "Just little tidbits here and there."

Her brows dip, and I guess as his fiancée, I should be more privy to all the inner workings of his family dynamic.

We each order a mai tai—probably a terrible idea since alcohol makes loose lips and I can't afford to admit the truth to Luke's sister for his sake, but after our first drink, the advantage is that *her* lips loosen, too. I sort of wonder how long Luke will be, but then Kaylee starts spilling all the tea once our second round arrives.

"Luke is my favorite brother, you know. I probably shouldn't pick, but Jack is just...he's Jack. He's my parents' favorite because he's the oldest, I'm the second favorite because I'm the youngest and the only girl, and Luke sort of just falls in the middle. He's such a good guy, so talented in football. But he tends to keep to himself. We could be such a close family. We try. Really, we do. I do, anyway. These annual vacations were my idea. It was the only way I got to see my very busy brothers when I was a pre-teen and they were just getting their starts in the league. And that's still true today. Do you know I haven't seen Luke since we were in New Zealand and I've only seen Jack once since then?"

I'm not sure whether that's rhetorical, and I don't want her to stop, so I just raise my brows and take a sip of my mai tai.

"We used to be closer before the whole Savannah thing went down between those two, and that's when their rivalry really started," she says.

"You mean the articles Savannah wrote?" I ask, proving I know at least a little something about the man I'm going to marry.

"The articles, yes, but all the other stuff, too," she says, lowering her voice. "It forced my parents to choose sides, and Luke came out the loser in all that. It pushed a divide between all of us. He stopped sharing the little parts of himself that he used to with us, it gave him trust and jealousy issues, and it wrecked his confidence."

My brows dip. What other stuff? What made him stop being himself around his own family? The articles probably gave him trust and jealousy issues, but what wrecked his confidence?

Being born into a family with someone like Jack probably set him up for low self-esteem. His own father favors his brother, and clearly his mom does, too. Were they like that his whole life?

Who builds him up when his family tears him down? The awful women he's been with before?

Enter Ellie.

I don't want to admit what I don't know, so I tuck it to the back of my mind for later. But I *will* be asking Luke about it.

She blows out a breath. "Anyway. Tell me about you. I've always wanted a sister and God knows Savannah and Michelle never fit that description."

I laugh. "What do you want to know?"

"Do you work?" she asks.

I nod. "I'm in PR and actually I'm handling your brother's publicity now."

"I saw his Instagram. It's freaking lit, Ellie. Is that all you?"

I nod and give a modest shrug. "Yeah. He didn't want one, but I talked him into it." I refrain from mentioning that he actually *needed* one to hit his goals. I'm not sure how much Luke would want me to share with his sister regarding all that—especially not if it gets back to his mom, and then his dad, and then back to Jack. He's right about the family politics. There's all sorts of shit I wasn't expecting up in here.

"God, if you could get him to do that..." she trails off, but her insinuation is that I'm a good match for him. It feels good that the one family member whose opinion he might actually respect thinks that of us. "When are you getting married?" she asks.

I freeze. It's our news to share together, but this is still his turf. He wanted to wait and tell everyone the night before, and it's up to me to respect that. Another mai tai might not have stopped me, though. "Oh, I don't know. You know Luke." I twist my lips and roll my eyes.

"What's that eyeroll supposed to mean?" the man himself asks. He must've snuck up behind me.

I jump, startled by his voice. "I didn't know you were standing there. Your sister was just asking me when the wedding is."

"Ah," he says, and then he shrugs. "We'll figure something out."

Good dodge, Luke.

"So why do you call him Lu-Lu?" I ask Kaylee.

She giggles. "I couldn't say *Luke* when I was little, so that's what I called him. It just stuck even though he frickin' *hated* it."

"Imagine this," he says, making a motion with his hands in the air. "A twelve-year-old boy with all his buddies over, and his two-year-old sister walks by yelling Lu-Lu! Lu-Lu!" He shakes his head with a chuckle.

Kaylee and I both giggle.

"What did you talk to Mom and Dad about?" Kaylee asks.

He rolls his eyes. "I told them to lay off Ellie. It's not her fault Michelle's knocked up."

"But it *is* yours," another voice similar to Luke's says.

Luke grits his teeth then clenches his jaw as we all turn to see Jack standing behind us. He flicks a finger in the air to the bartender, who dashes over to tend to the man who owns the entire room just because he's in it. It's truly some phenomenon to witness.

He orders a gin and tonic. I've never seen anyone order anything with gin in it before, and somehow it brings another level of sophistication. Luke orders a beer when the bartender's eyes flick to him.

If we were at this same bar without Jack, I can't help but think that Luke would be the man owning the room. He's more laid back than his brother, and definitely not as arrogant, but the brothers do share some of the same qualities. Ridiculous good looks, athletic ability, and those navy blue eyes, for starters, plus this intrinsic charisma—though the brothers express that charisma in totally different ways.

I feel suddenly nervous that he's here. He somehow throws everything into a tailspin with just his presence...even though I have to admit that I'm curious what this dynamic will look like without the parents around.

"Nice of you to join us," Luke says.

Jack slides onto the open stool next to Kaylee. "Figured I could spare some time for a drink with my favorite siblings." His eyes fall onto me, and my chest races. "Plus the future Mrs. Dalton."

Heat creeps up my spine, and I take a sip of my mai tai to try to cool down.

"When's the wedding?" Jack asks.

I glance at Luke desperately for the answer. He gives a similar vague reply. "We're working on it."

Jack barks out a laugh. "That's noncommittal. I thought you weren't getting married again."

It's not a question, but Luke treats it like one. "I wasn't. And then I met Ellie." His arm is around the back of my chair, and it slides to my shoulder. He draws me into a side hug, and it all feels a little territorial—as it should since we're putting on the show now even for his family.

"Seems fast," Jack comments, and the bartender returns with the drinks.

"It is," I admit. "But when you know..."

"You know," Luke finishes, and he pins me with a loving gaze that makes me momentarily forget that Kaylee and Jack are right beside us.

Jeez. If this is an act, Luke deserves the Oscar.

"Finishing each other's sentences already. Precious." Jack's final word drips with sarcasm, and Luke leans over to press a kiss to my temple.

"Jealousy is ugly on you," Luke says.

Jack scoffs with a grunt, but he doesn't respond to Luke's claim, and suddenly I feel like a bit of a pawn in Luke's little game with his brother.

Was that always part of the motivation here? To marry me in front of his family, but more specifically, in front of Jack?

Why would that make Jack jealous? He could have anyone he wanted.

Although Kaylee mentioned something about there being more with Savannah...did Jack want Luke's wife?

Questions swirl around my head, but I have zero answers and a pretty strong buzz from the mai tai.

Luke stands suddenly and grabs my hand. "We're going to head out."

"We're just getting started," Jack says, draining his entire gin and tonic in practically one sip.

"Maybe you are," Luke says, "but my fiancée and I are going to call it a night, if you know what I mean."

Jack raises a brow in a way that totally makes it clear he got Luke's underlying meaning.

"You two are adorable," Kaylee says. "Have fun, kids."

"And be safe," Jack says, eyes forward as he motions to the bartender for a refill. "This family doesn't need another baby scandal."

"Fuck you, Jack," Luke says quietly—venomously—and then he yanks my hand into his and leads me away from the bar.

CHAPTER 15

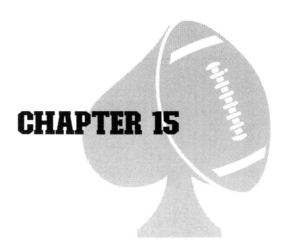

Instead of leading me up to our hotel room, Luke stalks toward the doors that exit to the pool. Clearly he's upset after his brother's words. I see it in the way his shoulders are hunched, in the way he's walking too fast for me to really keep up especially after a few mai tais while I'm wearing heels, and in the pinch of his brows.

He walks past the pool, and finally I yell at him, "Slow down!"

He stops, and I run into him a little. "Sorry," he mutters, and then he keeps walking. When we get to the beach, he slips off his shoes and socks, and I take off my heels. We leave them in the sand, and he grabs my hand again.

He draws in a deep breath, and he blows it out slowly as we stroll slowly toward the water. The beach is deserted at this late hour, but it's lit by the lights coming from the hotel just behind us. His hand isn't in mine anymore, but then there's not really anybody out here for us to continue putting on the show for.

"What the hell am I marrying into?" I finally ask.

He grunts out a chuckle even though it's not very funny, but that's his only response.

"You want to tell me about what's going on between the two of you?" I ask once our toes touch the water.

He clears his throat as he stares down at the gentle waves rolling over his toes. "Not really."

"Kaylee said Savannah came between you and Jack," I try again, "and she made it sound like there was more to it than you told me." I leave that out there for him to expand upon, and he just quietly stares into the water. I let him gather his thoughts, and then because I can't take the silence, I say, "Talk to me, Luke."

He sighs. "I've lived in Jack's shadow my entire life. When Jack wouldn't commit to Savannah, she turned to me to make him jealous. I was young, stupid, and horny. I thought she wanted me for me. Turns out she only wanted my brother."

My head whips in his direction. "What?"

He nods and presses his lips together. "She was with him first. They were together almost a year when he dumped her, and she came to me as a shoulder to cry on. I fell for her. I chose her over my family. That's when my parents chose Jack. They thought I was the dick who stole Savannah away when the truth was that she was a conniving bitch who said all the right things to make me think it was me she wanted all along. That was far from the truth, and now I'm stuck paying alimony to a woman who only ever loved my brother and the spotlight."

"Oh my God," I murmur, shocked by this new revelation.

"See?" he says, and he pats his chest. "I'm no prince."

"She tricked you, Luke," I say. "That doesn't pull you from the prince category."

"As I've been reminded constantly, I chose her over my family. I broke family code when I slept with my brother's ex even though he told me at the time he was okay with it. I felt like shit after the first time I slept with her, but I called Jack the next morning. I was honest with him from the start. He told me he was fine with it, and eventually he agreed to being spotlighted in her articles."

"Why would he do that?" I ask. The waves wash over my feet, burying them in wet sand, and I pull them up out of the sand so the process can start over.

"I don't know. Maybe because he still cared about Savannah. They were together a long time, and he wanted her to have a successful career. We both knew the reach a story about the two of us could have since we were brothers in the league together with a fairly well-known father. Or maybe because he knew I'd come out looking like the asshole and he loved any chance he had to take the spotlight."

"So were you private even before she printed all that stuff about you two?"

He lifts a shoulder. "I guess I've always been that way. We're a famous family, but we're not perfect. We all have secrets we'd prefer to keep hidden."

"What are yours?" I ask softly.

"Aside from marrying Savannah?" He grunts. "Stories for another day."

So there *are* more secrets in his closet. Interesting.

I'm not sure what to do with the revelations from tonight, though.

"What are Jack's?" I ask.

He kicks at the sand. "Not my secrets to tell."

We're quiet a beat, and then because I'm me and my filter often malfunctions particularly after alcohol, I ask the question that first came to mind at the bar. "So this wedding, and me...is this all just a game to one up your brother?"

He clears his throat, and then he blows out a breath. "I wouldn't call it a *game*," he says. "But it *is* an opportunity. We were going to do this anyway, and the timing just worked out. I get to flaunt my happy ending with my beautiful bride in front of my entire family. A bride who, by the way, has no prior affiliation with my brother. She's all mine. It's a fresh start. Besides, what's more romantic than a wedding on the beach in Maui?"

"Even if you don't have real feelings for that bride?" I press.

"They don't have to know that." He shrugs with nonchalance, and it only serves to piss me off.

I nod and press my lips together as I try to process all that. It shouldn't hurt...but it does. I should be thankful for his honesty...but I'm not.

Instead, I'm left wondering whether I should really be doing this. All the breakthroughs over the last couple days, the bonding, the fun...it feels like it was all just part of his plan.

Luke doesn't love me. He doesn't want me. He doesn't have feelings for me, as he just made abundantly clear.

I'm not even totally sure he even *cares* about me.

But how do I back out at this point? He may not have feelings for me, but it's not like I can just shut off mine for him. And even if I could, then what? Move back to Chicago?

It's not like I have a home or a job that doesn't intertwine with Luke Dalton in Vegas. I could stay there, but I'm risking my career all over again after everything that happened in Chicago not so long ago. I finally have a *celebrity* client. This could open up so many doors for me, and all I have to do is just go through with what we already have planned.

But his admission hurts. His words cut. Maybe they shouldn't, but my feelings are involved even if his aren't.

"Glad the timing worked out for your opportunity," I say, and then I spin on my heel, run up the beach, grab my shoes, and head in the direction of the hotel room I'm sharing with him.

I'll call Nicki. She's on her honeymoon, but I need to talk to someone about this. I'm desperate, and if this isn't an emergency, I don't know what is. What the hell am I supposed to do?

I brush away a tear as I pass by the pool.

Should I go through with this ridiculous plan?

I already know what Nicki will say. The obvious answer is *no*. I'm only hurting myself.

I refuse to let more tears fall until I'm up in my room. I beeline for the elevator. I need to get the hell out of here before some other Dalton sees me crying in the lobby after Luke just admitted he doesn't have feelings for me.

But fate apparently has other plans.

Just as I hit the button to call the elevator, a voice sounds behind me. It sounds like Luke's, but it's not. It's deeper. More confident. "Going up to bed alone?"

I spin around, my feet still bare and my shoes in my hand. "That's not your business." My voice is a hiss, and I'm not sure why I'm so defensive when Jack has no idea what just went down between Luke and me. I haven't even had thirty seconds to myself to process whether I'm overreacting, so of course I had to run into him.

Jack smirks, and I wish his face wasn't so goddamn handsome. "You're marrying my brother. Sounds like it *is* my business."

"I'm not Savannah," I spit at him.

"Or Michelle." He laughs, but I don't get the joke.

Or Michelle?

What the hell is that supposed to mean?

Did *Jack* sleep with Michelle?

Is Michelle really pregnant with Luke's baby?

Or is it...Jack's?

Before I can ask that question, he leans in a little closer and lowers his voice. "So he filled you in on our history, did he?" He's close enough that I can smell him, some woodsy and masculine scent mixed with hot danger and gin. He lowers his voice. "Did he tell you *everything*?"

"Of course he did," I lie, and I'm not even sure why I'm lying after what he just said to me out on that beach. I'm angry with him. I'm hurt and I'm sad. Yet here I am, protecting him and our lie as Jack puts me on the spot—a place where I'm incredibly uncomfortable because honestly I don't know Luke well enough to defend him. He hasn't let me get to know him—not the *real* him, anyway.

The elevator doors open, but I don't step on. I'm rooted to the spot as Jack penetrates me with his gaze.

He raises a brow as his mouth curls into a lazy smile, and it's sly and salacious and definitely flirtatious. "Good. Then you know how we like to share. I'm in room twenty-six-oh-nine if you're up for some fun. I can promise you a hell of a good time...better than whatever my little brother gives you."

He gets onto the elevator, and his raised brow is a clear invitation that I should go up to his room with him.

Luke doesn't want me.

But Jack seems to.

I don't want to be part of this game between the two of them, but suddenly I'm sucked into this world I didn't even know existed a few minutes ago. Suddenly I have two brothers pulling at me from different sides, neither of them pretending like this is something more than it is.

I don't know whether I want either of them while I'm sure I want them both. How lucky is Savannah that she got to experience a life with both men? Not just for their talents or how fucking hot they are or their fame or money...but because she got to know each man and who he is on the inside, she got both to fall in love with her, and she got to share a bed with both of them.

And Michelle, too?

That could be me next...except *neither* man wants me for me. They want me for how they could use me to one-up their brother. I shouldn't get on with him. I shouldn't share that small space with Jack Dalton, not with the tempting invitation he just issued when I'm *engaged* to his brother.

I don't know if I can continue this lie with Luke.

Despite how hurt I feel right now, I still want to protect him from his family. I still want to help him with this Michelle mess.

But I'm not entirely sure I can marry him.

To be continued in book 3, **FAIR GAME**.

Fair
GAME

LISA SUZANNE

DEDICATION

To my 3Ms.

CHAPTER 1

I contemplate what to do as I stand in the lobby staring at the closed elevator doors. Watching them close on Jack's face made something snap inside me.

Twenty-six-oh-nine, I repeat in my head, a mantra as I press the call button for another elevator car. *Twenty-six-oh-nine.*

Luke doesn't want me, but Jack seems to. That's where my mind keeps going, an endless loop between twenty-six-oh-nine and Luke doesn't want me.

Twenty-six-oh-nine.

Luke doesn't want me.

And then Jack's voice adds to the mix. *I can promise you a hell of a good time...better than whatever my little brother gives you. Just ask Savannah.*

I can't substitute one Dalton brother for another. It doesn't work like that, though I guess it did for Savannah...and maybe Michelle. I'm not either one of those women, though.

I care about Luke. I love Luke.

So why am I contemplating going up to twenty-six-oh-nine and knocking on the door?

Because *he doesn't love me back.*

That's why. That's what it all comes down to in my head. He hurt me out on that beach with his words. He was so flippant about it when he told me his family didn't need to know that he doesn't have feelings for me as they watch us stand up to be married. So uncaring. So cold.

Is Jack any warmer?

I brush the thought away...but I can't. Not really. Not as the elevator doors glide open and I step on.

I stare at the number board.

Do I hit twenty-seven, the floor where the room I'm sharing with Luke is located?

Or do I press twenty-six instead?

My heart pounds wildly as my fingers seem to take on a mind of their own. They locate a button and press it. It lights up with red behind it, as if to say I'm making the wrong choice. Red equals bad. *Press the other one*, the elevator seems to be saying to me, but I can't make my fingers do it. I stand stock still, alone on the elevator with just my thoughts, but my mind is blank as I stare at the red number board. I don't watch the electronic sign at the top telling me which floor I'm moving past. I keep my eyes trained on that little red circle all the way until the doors pull open.

When I step off, I glance both ways, in part to check which way I'm supposed to go like everyone does when they get off an elevator in a hotel, and in part to make sure the hallway's clear— just to make doubly sure nobody's about to catch me.

Am I doing something wrong? I'm not sure yet...but looking both ways and feeling like I may be caught sure feels like the start of some guilt edging in.

I move toward the room, my heart pounding louder with every step I take down the hall. I look at the numbers posted on each door, counting up by odd numbers until I'm standing outside room twenty-six-oh-nine.

My legs feel like jelly as nerves tingle through me.

Ellie, what the fuck are you doing?

My own conscience screams at me as I lift a fist. My thundering heart races.

Ellie, stop! Turn around. Get back on the elevator. No one ever has to know you walked down this hallway.

Before I can even connect my fist with the door, it opens.

When it swings open as if by magic or some strange premonition, there stands my future brother-in-law wearing just a pair of athletic shorts that hug his hips.

Either I was staring at the elevator contemplating what to do for a much longer period of time than I realized or he ran up here and basically stripped off his clothes.

He's in peak physical shape with contoured muscles creating the perfect specimen of man. The plane of his chest is solid, his skin smooth and his shoulders broad.

I realize I'm staring directly at his abdomen, but you can't have abs that look like *that* and expect people not to stare.

So I'm attracted to him. Big fucking deal. I'm also attracted to Kristoff from *Frozen*.

And Luke, the tiny voice in my head reminds me. My soon-to-be husband.

Jack opens the door as if to tell me to come in, and I stalk past him. I stop in the middle of his room. It's a suite like ours, with a sitting area and a desk and table here in this room and French doors that are currently wide open to give me a peek into his bedroom. His sheets are a little rumpled, like he's already used the bed.

Did he have sex in here?

With who?

Someone from housekeeping? Someone he picked up in the lobby? He's only been here a few hours, and most of that was spent at dinner. Maybe he works quickly.

It's not my business.

He raises a brow at me. "I had a feeling you'd come."

The first words he speaks to me in this room drip with sex, like he means the word *come* in the carnal sense. My cheeks burn as I try to come up with something witty to say, but words elude me. Sense also apparently eludes me.

Why else would I show up here?

I had sex with Luke the night I met him.

Luke doesn't want me.

His words on the beach ring in my ears.

It's an opportunity.

I get to flaunt my happy ending.

They don't have to know that he doesn't have real feelings.

I stand frozen to the spot for a beat. What now?

I stare at Jack as Luke's words bruise my soul.

Why not have sex with his brother the night I met him, too? Another one-night stand. Another notch in my belt. Another story to tell at the next bachelorette party. I can just picture it now.

Oh, you haven't had two separate one-night stands with a pair of hot brothers? Let me tell you, you haven't lived until you've done that.

I take a step toward him, and he remains in place. The look on his face says *you will come to me* and I'm doing it. I'm moving toward him. Why am I moving toward him?

The answer eludes me, but as my feet shuffle another step in his direction, the gap between us narrows.

My eyes flick to his lips.

What would it be like to kiss him?

He's mesmerizing. Something about Jack Dalton is captivating, and he has the power to make people bend to his will without a single word—as evidenced by the way my feet continue to take small steps to close the space between us.

That tiny voice in my head tells me I'm only even considering this at all because Luke hurt me, but it's not like he'd mind since he basically just told me he doesn't really care about me at all.

I'm spellbound by the man who looks like a slightly older, edgier, tougher version of his younger brother.

A pounding at the door startles me, breaking the spell that holds me in his gaze as a sudden dart of guilt pings through my chest.

My eyes widen as I realize what could've just happened.

Jack's smirk only makes the guilt burn brighter.

I shouldn't be here, and whoever is on the other side of that door is going to get entirely the wrong impression. And I already know who it is before Jack even makes a move toward it to answer it.

I blow out a breath as I brace for the impact.

He doesn't tell me to go hide or move out of sight. He doesn't act like we're doing anything wrong as he starts toward the direction of the knocking.

And so I don't, either.

CHAPTER 2

Jack's eyes lock on mine before he gets all the way to the door, and that's the moment reality comes crashing into me.

How dare he do this to his brother?

How dare *I* do this to his brother?

I wouldn't have kissed him. I wouldn't have done that to Luke.

I repeat that in my head a few times so I believe it.

The steps I was taking toward him were to bring me closer so I could slap him across the face.

I'm attracted to Jack, sure...but I'm in love with Luke. No matter what, I couldn't have really had sex with Jack. I couldn't have done anything with him that might jeopardize the friendship I've built with Luke despite the words he said out on that beach.

I blow out a breath as I force the words that suddenly feel like a desperate attempt to save myself even though they're the truth. "I only came up here to tell you to back down." And maybe to get more details about his involvement with Michelle, but I refrain from mentioning that. I'll circle back to that when the time is right. "I'm marrying your brother, and I'm nothing like Savannah. *Nothing.* So you can get it out of your head right now that something might happen between us."

He laughs, and it's a haughty laugh that plainly says he doesn't believe me and my words won't be enough to shut him up or stop his efforts. "I just want to get to know you," he says. "Did you think I meant something else?"

My cheeks burn, and I hate how he has this *power.* He's a pro at twisting and manipulating, and it's easy to see why the Dalton parents sided with him in whatever went down between the brothers. Luke never stood a chance. He's too nice a guy, while Jack here is reminiscent of a salesman who will do whatever it takes to close the sale. Not a greasy one, or a smarmy or dirty or slimy one, but a devilishly handsome one who probably gets by on his good looks alone most of the time.

"What do you want to know?" I finally ask, my tone exasperated because I can't find it in myself to behave any other way in front of this guy who seems to grate on every last nerve I have at the same time I'm so damn fascinated by him.

Someone is still pounding on the door, but Jack ignores it in favor of this conversation. It has to be Luke on the other side and when he finds me in here—particularly after it's taking so long for Jack to open the door—he will get the wrong impression.

But something compels me to have this conversation anyway. He narrows his eyes at me. "Why is Luke marrying you?"

My brows dip. "Don't you mean why am *I* marrying *Luke?*"

His gaze on me is hot and intimidating. "I meant what I said."

Because he needs an out so Michelle can't trap him and to shut up Savannah. Because he wants to show his boss he's committed to someone who isn't Michelle. Because he *has* to follow through with it now that it's out in the media because if he doesn't, it'll look like he made it up to get the woman who's carrying his child to back off and that'll just make him look like a douchebag, won't it? Even if it's the truth...

"Because he loves me."

The words sound fake even to my own ears. I can't force them with any shred of authenticity when he just told me he doesn't and my heart is so freshly bruised.

Jack shakes his head. "You may think I don't know my little brother, but I know him. Maybe better than anyone. He isn't marrying you for love." He points a long finger in my direction. "That much I know."

"I don't know what you're talking about."

He ends the conversation there as he keeps his eyes on mine, and I know he ended it there to leave me a bundle of exposed nerves.

He succeeded. Is he going to come after us? Is he going to blow our cover?

Is he going to continue trying to seduce me? And am I strong enough to keep pushing him away when Luke has made it so goddamn abundantly clear that he isn't interested?

Jack finally pulls open the door.

The way he's looking at me will give the wrong impression to whoever might be standing there, but like me, he's already pieced together who it is.

I stand tall and firm that I'm not doing anything wrong here.

"Ellie?" Luke says, his voice clouded with confusion. "What are you doing here? And why did it take so long to answer?"

My eyes meet his, and I'm about to tell him I only came here to tell his asshole brother to back off when Jack speaks first.

"She wanted to take me up on my offer, if you know what I mean." He elbows his brother in the ribs. "Not the first woman to enjoy the Dalton brothers, am I right?"

I gasp at his words. "That's not true," I hiss.

"Are you going to believe your brother or some broad you've known all of a few months at best?" Jack sneers.

Luke looks between the two of us. His eyes are a little bloodshot like he had another drink or four before he came up here, and instead of answering that question, he shakes his head. "Does it matter who I believe? You're going to tell the tale however you want it heard, and we're all supposed to just take you at your word."

"You didn't seem to have a problem with that when I was covering up *your* mistakes," Jack says, poised as ever while his brother seems to cower a bit.

Luke sighs. "I came here to try to have a conversation with you, but I don't know why I bother. I should know better by now." He seems...tired. Like this entire exchange has aged him a little while wearing him out completely. "Ellie, we'll talk tomorrow."

He turns to walk away, and I glare and hiss at Jack on my way by. I may not be done with this conversation with Jack, but the hell we'll talk tomorrow.

We'll talk tonight. Right the hell now.

I follow Luke down the hallway, and I'm sure Jack is laughing behind us as we move in silence toward the elevator.

I click the button to go up one floor to our room, and when the elevator arrives, I step on first. He doesn't move.

"I need some time to think. Can I trust that you're heading up to the room? Or do I need to worry that I'll find you in Jack's room again?"

I fume as the doors slide shut.

I didn't do anything wrong.

I go to our room and get ready for bed, and then I slide beneath the sheets and attempt to fall asleep.

When Luke finally gets back, it's close to two and anger simmers within me. I need to know where his head is at.

I'm not sleeping. How can I when each scene from tonight replays on a continuous loop in my mind? Luke's hunched shoulders. Jack's intense eyes. Kaylee's genuine friendliness. The parents' attitudes toward their kids. The confessions. The history. Savannah. The want and the pull. Jack's abs. Luke's weariness.

I'm confused, and I'm torn. On the one hand, there's the stable, kind man I've started building something with even though it's just a friendship.

And then there's Jack. He's a mystery. A wildcard. I know literally nothing about him, but he's been clear that he *is* interested in me.

I can't run to Jack, though. It's tempting, but I've somehow fallen for Luke. Even if he doesn't love me back, I can't do that to him...especially not after I learned about the history between the two of them and Savannah. I'd wager there's even more history between the two of them that I'm not privy to yet. How many other women have they *shared*? How many others got stuck in between them?

I don't want to be just another statistic on that pie chart, yet the attention from Jack tonight was some combination of warm and thrilling.

So when Luke finally walks into the room, my only real option is to pretend to be asleep. I'm not ready to face him along with everything that happened tonight...with everything that *could have* happened.

Besides, he waited a long time to come back up. He wanted me to be asleep. He's not ready to talk, either, and if he was, he'd wake me. Maybe. I guess I don't know him well enough to know the answer to that.

I hear the shower turn on. I wait for his side of the bed to dip down when he gets in...but it never does.

CHAPTER 3

When the light of dawn peeks through the curtains, he's still not in the bed we're supposed to be sharing. Of course I already knew this fact since I was busy tossing and turning all night.

I get up and find him asleep on the couch in the main living area. I try to be quiet so as not to wake him, but he shifts as I turn to go back into the bedroom.

"Morning," he says, his voice hoarse from sleep.

"Morning," I murmur. "Why'd you sleep out here?"

He sits up and winces a little, and I can't help but wonder what he did in the time between leaving him on the beach, seeing him in Jack's room, and when he finally came up to the room. He rubs his neck. "Figured you'd prefer it that way."

I sigh and sit on the coffee table in front of him. "It's just a lot to take in," I murmur.

"I know. And I'm sorry for the way I acted last night." He reaches over and takes one of my hands in his. "I care about you, Ellie. A lot."

I glance up to find sincere blue eyes locked on mine, and my heart wants so badly to believe him. My brain is still undecided.

"I don't know if we're doing the right thing," I say, withdrawing my hand from his grip. I don't want to. It's the last thing I want to do, in fact. But I can't hold his hand when I feel the way I do and when I know he feels the way he does. It's too personal, too close, too intimate for two people who are nothing more than colleagues. "I don't want to be a pawn in the games you play with your family."

"You're not," he assures me. "That's not what this is, and the way I said it last night wasn't fair to you. Yes, I admit the reason I wanted to speed this up and do this in front of my family was to find some way to show up Jack. But Jack has nothing to do with the reasons we agreed to this in the first place."

"He hit on me." I knew I wouldn't be able to hide that tidbit from him. How does he do that to me? I'd like to say I'm nothing if not truthful...but clearly that's a lie since we're about to get married as a sham and I'm lying to pretty much everybody in the entire world except for Luke.

Oh, hell. I'm lying to him, too. I'm putting on the act like I'm not *totally* head over heels in love with him when I definitely am.

His face falls a little, but he quickly schools it back to indifferent. He *has* to have feelings about that, and I wish he'd show them. I wish he'd just fucking let me in.

"I ran into him when I left you on the beach," I say, giving him all the details he didn't ask for. "He came up behind me when I was waiting for the elevator."

"What did he say?" he asks, clasping his hands in front of him and leaning his elbows on his legs.

"He told me how you two like to share, and then he invited me up to his room."

"Fucking dick," he mutters. "And you went with him?"

"No." I shake my head. "He went up, and I followed on the next car, and I'm still not sure why. Maybe to tell him to back off. I was only there a minute when you came knocking."

"Telling him to back off isn't enough for him," he says. Then he lowers his voice and mutters, "Nothing is."

I stand. This suite is nearly a thousand square feet and it's not freaking big enough right now. "Well I'm sorry I didn't handle your brother to your liking when I had to get the hell away from you because you were so happy to let me know that you're just using me and you don't have real feelings for me."

He looks a little shocked at my outburst. I turn away from him and look out over the gorgeous view. I glance down to the spot where we're supposed to exchange vows in two days.

One thing he said last night is absolutely true: Hawaii is the perfect romantic backdrop for the wedding of my dreams to the man of my dreams.

But this is neither of those things. For one thing, the man of my dreams would want me back.

"He asked me why you're marrying me," I say, my eyes still out over the beach.

"What did you say?" His voice is a little distant behind me.

"I told him it's because you love me. He was adamant that you don't." I blow out a breath. "This is a bad idea, Luke. I just want to go home."

He's suddenly beside me. I didn't hear him stand or pad across the small distance to join me by the window. "I understand. I knew it was a bad idea from the start. I'll book your flight home. I'll be honest with my family. I'll figure out how to get Michelle off my back and keep Calvin happy without dragging you further into this mess. Actually, as my publicist, maybe you can help me figure out how."

I glance over at his profile as he looks out over the beach.

He's giving me a place to live and a job. He's become my best friend over the last few weeks—my *only* friend since I left everybody else behind in Chicago and Josh and Nicki are off doing their thing as newlyweds. He still wants me to work with him as his publicist.

He's my brother's best friend. I want to help him escape the demon women of his past and brand his image as the good guy the Aces can't live without.

And I love him.

All good reasons to marry him. But instead of saying any of that to him, instead of backtracking, I take the out he's offering. It seems like the only way to protect myself. "Thanks," I murmur. "And I'll start looking for my own place to live as soon as I'm back in Vegas." My heart twists as I think about Pepper and how much I'll miss her when I move out. Debbie, too, and my gorgeous purple and white office.

But most of all, I'll miss Luke.

Tears prick behind my eyes, but I blink them away.

He glances over at me. "You're welcome to stay as long as you need to."

I hold his gaze for just a beat. "I appreciate that," I say, and then I head to the shower, where I scald myself with heat and sob quietly into the water as I feel everything that was so close to my grasp slip away from me.

I only allow myself to feel that for as long as the shower lasts, though. I compose myself. I dry my hair. I apply some make-up. I get dressed.

Luke's sipping coffee in shorts and a flowery button-down shirt. He looks like the typical Hawaiian tourist, not the pro athlete he is. My heart twists again.

"Bad news," he says quietly. "The next direct flight out isn't until Sunday. If you don't mind a connecting flight, I can get you out later today."

"I don't know what I want," I admit. I want to leave *right now* before he has a chance to pin me with that gaze and change my mind. "Thanks for looking into it. I guess I'll just do Sunday." The words are out before I can stop them. *No! Take the one with a connection! Get out of here! Save yourself!*

The thoughts in my mind come too late.

"Do you want to come to brunch?" he asks. "We're supposed to meet my family in ten minutes. We can, uh, tell them the truth together if you want." He's holding in his emotions again, and it only serves to tell me I'm doing the right thing. I need to be with someone who's willing to let me in, and Luke has too many walls up that he's unwilling to tear down.

I'm sure he doesn't want his brother getting ahold of this news, and as his public relations manager, I want to be in control of the narrative...but the sooner we get it over with, the better.

"Okay," I say.

We head down to the restaurant. His parents, Kaylee, and Jack are already sitting at a table. Two open chairs wait for us at a round table, putting Luke next to Kaylee and me next to Jack.

Of course.

My heart races. Not only am I being forced to sit between these brothers who clearly have a sibling rivalry, but we're about to tell the truth about our fake relationship to his family.

My right knee bumps into Jack's as I sit, and he doesn't move his leg over. He's asserting his dominance or flirting or something, but to me it's just another example of what a cocky bastard he is. I glance over at him, and he smirks.

I want to slap that smirk off his face, and at the same time, my heart thumps loudly in my chest. I get it. I understand how he gets every-freaking-thing he wants in life. I can see how easily I'd succumb to his charms—maybe to hurt Luke because he's hurting me, too, or maybe because we'd have a lot of wicked hot fun together.

But I'm not meant to be a part of this family.

"Before we order, there's something I'd like to tell you all," Luke says after the good morning greetings are out of the way.

All eyes turn to Luke, including mine. So we're really doing this, right off the bat. We don't even get to enjoy brunch first, I guess. But this is a good thing. That way I don't have to wait and wonder when he's going to do it. I don't have to fake my way through another meal even though I'm faking far less than he is. I don't have to fight off Jack because once he has the proof that Luke isn't really in love with me, he'll lose interest.

"Actually, it's something we *both* need to confess," he says, glancing at me. I keep my eyes trained down on my ice water because I'm not sure I even *want* to see all the smug, self-righteous reactions on the faces gathered around this table.

Luke draws in a deep breath. "Ellie and I—"

"Sorry about the wait," the waitress says, interrupting what he was about to say when she bounds over to our table as if from out of nowhere. "What can I get for you?"

Luke hisses out a breath, and I glance over at him.

I shouldn't have.

I thought I was making the right decision by backing out, but when I see his clenched jaw working back and forth and his hitched up shoulders from the stress of simply eating a meal with these people and I combine those small things with the reasons why we were going to do this in the first place...I realize I'm back on board.

I can't let him call it off.

The way they treat him just isn't fair, and I want to be the person on his side. I want to stand up for him. Maybe it's because I love him, or maybe it's because he's paying me—but regardless, I *want* to do this.

Luke draws in a breath once the waitress skips away to put our order in. "Ellie and I have something to say." My eyes move to him, and he clenches his jaw for another beat. He opens his mouth to tell the truth...but I don't let him.

Not in front of Jack.

Not in front of his parents.

"We're getting married," I blurt before he can say anything more.

Luke's eyes meet mine. I see a question there, and I nod almost imperceptibly as I blink just once as if to will him to see that it's okay. The wedding is back on.

"We know that," Carol says with more than a touch of exasperated disapproval.

"No," I say, shaking my head with my eyes still locked on Luke's. "In two days. Here in Hawaii."

I glance at Kaylee, who looks nearly hopeful, and then at Carol and Tim, who both look disappointed. I can't force my head toward Jack just yet. I look back at Luke, and I see the question in his eyes melt into something else. Gratitude. Hope.

Heat.

"You're what?" Carol squawks.

Luke nods. "Getting married on Saturday." His voice holds a little bit of wonder, and I'm thankful for an actual show of emotion. Maybe there's hope yet for this guy. "To the love of my life." He leans in and presses a soft kiss to my lips, and damn if butterflies don't batter all the way around my stomach and my chest. "And we'd love to have you all there."

"Of course we'll be there," Kaylee sings. "And we're just thrilled to be welcoming you into the family, Ellie," she says to me with a big smile. "Right, Mom?" She elbows Carol.

"Of course," Carol mumbles.

"Well if that isn't just the happiest news I've heard all morning," Jack says, and his leg inches against mine again.

"Congratulations, little brother." His voice drips with condescension.

I cross my leg at the knee away from Jack and toward Luke. I don't bother looking in Jack's direction. I lean in toward my fiancé and away from the man who seems like he just doesn't care about boundaries.

"We're very excited," I say.

Luke loops an arm around the back of my chair as a show of possession, and I lean further into him. It's not like it's difficult being close enough to smell his scent and feel his warmth, especially not in the presence of all these rather chilly people.

We suffer through small talk with Kaylee doing her best to lead the charge and Jack dominating most of the conversation. Luke is quiet to my left despite our announcement, though there's nothing out of the ordinary about that. I glance up at my future husband as Jack drones on about the Super Bowl again, and his eyes lock down on mine.

Thank you, he mouths to me, and I take the opportunity that's presented to me when I tip my chin up and give him a soft kiss that melts my insides to butter.

After all, we're about to be married. Surely betrothed couples kiss at the brunch table.

Once the interminable meal ends, Luke and I head back up to our room. As soon as the door clicks shut behind me, he lets out a long breath.

"Thank you," he says, turning to face me, and it's somehow reminiscent of our one-night stand when he looks at me the way he is as we stand near the door of a hotel room. "Why'd you change your mind?"

I press my lips together. "You deserve better than how they treat you."

"I don't deserve you," he says softly, his eyes flicking to my lips for a beat.

"You deserve the world, Luke." And by *the world*, I really mean *me.* I give him a sad smile. "The only one stopping you from having it is *you.*"

He nods as he turns away from me, and he heads over toward the slider doors to look down over the beach. It seems to be where he does his best brooding. I move into place beside him.

"So we're really doing this?" he asks.

I nod. "We're really doing this."

A knock at the door pulls him from what was about to be a pretty intense brooding session. He turns to answer it, and I stay where I am, glad for the reprieve from his family.

It's a reprieve that's far too short as I hear Luke's voice. "What are you doing here?"

A male voice I don't know well enough yet responds. "We came to talk about this wedding."

CHAPTER 4

Luke's parents stand in the doorway, and eventually he opens the door a little wider to let them in. They both eye me warily before they help themselves to seats on the couch.

I don't move from my spot where I'm suddenly rooted to the floor.

Luke sits at the table, and he motions for me to sit, too. I hesitate but then I do it in a show of support.

"What do you want to talk about?" Luke asks.

Tim looks at Carol as if telling her to go ahead. She eyes him before she exhales a short breath.

"Why are you two doing this?" she asks.

"Why does anybody do it?" Luke counters.

"Some would say pregnancy," she says, raising an eyebrow in my direction.

"Oh come on, Mother," Luke says. "Do you really want to go there?"

"I'm not pregnant," I blurt. "That's not what this is about."

"I should hope not," Tim says. "Not when you've already got another woman pregnant." He shakes his head, his eyes down like his son is his life's biggest disappointment.

And *that* is why I'm doing this. I can't say that to them, obviously.

"So you two think I should be marrying Michelle, someone I can't stand and neither could you, simply because she's knocked up?"

Their silence speaks volumes.

Luke sighs. "I don't even have evidence that the child she's carrying is mine."

"You haven't asked for proof?" Carol asks, a tinge of surprise in her voice.

Luke shakes his head as his eyes move to the window. "It's complicated. I want to keep Calvin happy, but not at the expense of my own happiness."

"We didn't raise you that way," Tim says, and I have to admit...I'm curious what he means. They didn't raise Luke to think about his own happiness? He answers my question when he says, "We raised you to take responsibility for your actions."

"I am," Luke protests, but his words are weak and tired. I don't know him all that well, but he definitely strikes me as someone parents should be proud of. He's a good, kind, upstanding man, and getting someone pregnant doesn't diminish that in any way. "I've accepted that I'm going to be a father. I've taken action. I'll be attending her doctor's visits with her. I'm appeasing Calvin. I'm trying to do what's right."

"By marrying some girl you hardly know?" Carol asks, and then she pauses before she points a scary finger at her son. "Oh wait a minute," she says, her lips curling up shrewdly as if she's solved the puzzle. "Wait just one minute. That's what this is, isn't it?" She points that finger at me, and I feel like I'm going to throw up.

Luke closes his eyes and shakes his head. "I'm in love with Ellie. Not that it's any of your concern, really, but she's my best friend's little sister and I know her very well, thank you very much. We're walking down the aisle together out of love, and it's as simple as that."

Carol raises a brow at me. "And as for you, my dear? Getting a nice little compensation out of all this?" She circles her finger between her son and me.

I tip my chin up defiantly. I will *not* be intimidated by this woman. Except I totally am and I might pee myself as my next words come out of my mouth. "If by compensation you mean a husband I'm in love with, then yes."

Her lips thin into a pressed line, and my goodness she's scary.

"Well I think Carol has nailed it," Tim interjects. "I think you needed a way to keep Cal from going after you for impregnating his daughter, so you're marrying someone else to keep them at bay."

"That's not what this is." Luke is totally frustrated with having to defend our lie, and I get it. I'm frustrated, too. But I'm also starting to see that maybe his family knows him better than he realizes.

"Your story doesn't add up, son," Tim says. "You told us time and again after the Savannah fiasco you weren't getting married ever again, so why the sudden change of heart?"

"Love," Luke repeats. "I've never felt about *anyone* the way I feel about Ellie, and that's the honest truth. I was young and dumb when I married Savannah. I'm older now, and I like to think a little more seasoned and a whole lot wiser." He turns to me, his eyes locking on mine, and once again I'm struck that if this is all just for show, he's a damn good actor. "You don't just let someone like Ellie go because you made mistakes in your past. What we have has been powerful enough for me to see that I want to spend the rest of my life differently than how I've spent the first thirty-one years of it."

"We will be there, but I can't say that either one of us supports this," Tim says.

"I don't need you to support it, and I don't really care if you're there," Luke says, his voice full of venom. As it should be, really. His parents should support him even if they don't agree with him. My parents certainly would if the roles were reversed...except they don't even know I'm in Hawaii days away from getting married.

Tim stands. "A pleasure as always, son." His tone is full of sarcasm. He glances at his wife. "Ready?"

Carol stands, too. She studies the two of us for a beat, but her expression gives nothing away. As much as Luke wants to be nothing like these people, I suddenly see it very clearly. The way he schools himself to hold in his emotions—it's all there on Carol's face. She does it, too. Tim's the more emotive of the two, but even he really only seems to express anger and disappointment in Luke.

What the hell happened in this family that pushed them so far apart?

And, more importantly perhaps, what happened that made Jack the golden child while Luke was relegated to the outcast?

What the hell am I marrying into...and why am I still agreeing to it?

CHAPTER 5

Luke's hand is linked loosely in mine as we walk up the ramp to board the ship for the sunset dinner cruise Kaylee planned. I don't know if the rest of Luke's family is here just yet, but I can't say I'm looking forward to seeing them—especially not when I see how deeply they affect Luke.

We stroll around the rather large yacht and determine what we think will be the best spot to watch the sunset, and we run into the rest of the Daltons once we move into the dining room for cocktail hour. His parents and his siblings are already seated at a table, and two open seats await Luke and me.

I suck in a breath just as I notice my future husband doing the same. I glance over at him, and we lock eyes. I let out a soft chuckle, and he does, too. Funny how we're both bracing ourselves for whatever this evening has to offer. To say I'm dreading another meal with this family is an understatement.

"Nice of you to join us," Carol says when we take a seat.

"I didn't realize we were late," Luke asks with a touch of exasperation that's nearly borderline implying they should be glad we showed up at all.

Carol purses her lips.

"This mai tai is fantastic," Kaylee says, jumping in as usual to try to salvage what's going on. This whole routine is getting a little old, to be honest.

I glance at Luke. "I could use a drink," I say.

"I don't know if I'll make it through this meal without one." Luke smirks and stands.

"There's the Luke we all know. Substances to numb, right?" Jack says under his breath.

Luke glares at him before he strides away. I have to practically run in my heels to catch up to him as we make our way toward the bar.

"What was that all about?" I ask.

He rolls his eyes. "Just Jack being Jack."

"Substances to numb?" I ask, repeating what Jack said.

Luke stops in his trek to the bar and glances around like he's making sure nobody will overhear us. "I was hurt early in my career and I took injections before games to help numb the pain."

My brows pinch together. "Like painkillers?"

He shrugs. "Toradol. It's basically strong ibuprofen."

"That doesn't sound so bad." And the truth is...it doesn't. Ibuprofen is common after injuries, right? But if it's not so bad...then why did he glance around us before his admission to make sure nobody was listening? Maybe there's more to it, or maybe he just wants this conversation to be on the down low.

"It's not," he says, moving his feet again as we head at a slower pace toward the bar. "Jack has taken it, too. Everybody does. Some guys take it before every game. I only took it when I needed it."

I'm not sure I care for the *everybody does it* kind of argument. It reminds me too much of when I was a teenager and my mom asked whether I'd jump off a bridge if everybody else was doing it when I simply had asked if I could go to a concert with my friends.

For the record, I was the only one out of my group of friends who wasn't allowed to go. Nothing bad even happened, so that's one bridge I could've jumped off of.

"So why'd he call you out on it just now?" I ask.

"Because he's Jack." His tone is exasperated again, and I don't quite like that he's directing his attitude toward me. It was funnier when it was toward his mother.

I order Kaylee's recommendation of a mai tai because, well, when you're in Hawaii, you drink mai tais. Luke orders a beer for himself, and then we head back to our table with his family and I think I'm going to need four or five more of these to get through this dinner.

"So tell us how you two met," Kaylee says to me. "All Luke said was that you're Josh Nolan's sister."

I launch into the story we made up together even though the real one is actually a whole lot more interesting.

Luke's arm is around the back of my chair, and he's turned in toward me as I talk, interjecting little details here and there, and the story actually sounds real. We've told it enough times now that it sure as shit should.

"She couldn't resist my charm, and I've never been happier in my life," Luke says at the end, and he leans forward and presses a soft, chaste kiss to my lips.

I melt.

I. Freaking. Melt.

I wish that kiss was real. I wish his words were real. I wish *all of this* was real.

I try not to gloat as he pulls away. He smiles at me, and the adoration in his eyes looks so genuine that even I am falling for it at this point.

But it's all an act, I remind myself.

We eat, and both Luke and I are fairly quiet as Tim dominates the direction of the dinner chatter with stories of Jack's heroics when it comes to the field. It's all a bit of a bore, if I'm being honest. I already wasn't super thrilled with football talk, and when it's focused on someone other than Luke, I lose interest fast. But I guess I'd rather sit idly by than the alternative of defending our decision to get married even one more time to the Dalton family.

We head outside after dinner to watch the sun as the ocean swallows it up, and the scenery is beautiful. Luke's arm is around my shoulders, and his lips brush my temple, and I squeeze my eyes shut as conflicting emotions crash into me. On the one hand, I relish being so close to him and feeling the love coming from him. On the other...disappointment lances through every part of my being that it's just a show to him. He's just playing the part for his family's benefit.

And when we're not with his family, the show appears to be over. He's quiet again. He retreats back into himself.

The day after tomorrow, we're getting married. These days should be filled with love and excitement, but an impending sense of dread washes over me. I just have this feeling that something is going to go wrong at the wedding.

"I'm going to go for a walk if you'd like to join me," I say once we're back at the hotel room.

"Thanks for the offer. Have a nice walk," he says.

Whatever. I head down to the beach all alone. I could sit up in the stifling room with him as he broods, or I could walk the beach and try to soak in more of Hawaii while I'm here.

We're not even to the halfway point of this trip. I should've taken him up on the offer to leave with a connecting flight. I might not even have had to sit through brunch this morning. Instead, I'd be on my way home and out of this mess.

Even as I think it, though, I'm reminded that *home* is really just Luke's house. There's no escape.

He's paying me well for the publicity. He quadrupled my rate when I signed the contract with the lawyer with the stipulations for our arrangement. He *said* the pay was for my public relations work, but we both know it's a legal way for him to pay me to marry him, and right now that thought makes me feel hollow.

I've taken a bunch of photos of him and with him while we've been here. I should be set with content for the next year. I've posted on his behalf a few times, though nothing indicating we're in Hawaii, and I've gotten excellent feedback, more follows for him, and a handful of sponsorship requests that I've forwarded to his agent.

I sit in a lounge chair by the pool for a few minutes and scroll through my spank bank—I mean *professional photographs*—of Luke. I pick one out and post it along with a question to engage his fans.

I click off my phone with the intention of heading toward the beach for a solo walk where I can lose myself in my thoughts. But before I get the chance to stand, a voice stops me.

"What are you doing out here all by yourself?"

I glance up and find Jack's penetrating navy eyes focused down on me.

He's all alone, too.

And suddenly I feel like I'm very much in danger.

CHAPTER 6

"Oh, uh, hey Jack," I stutter. "Luke was tired."

"So it's just the two of us, all alone. At least we're in public this time." He raises his brows then laughs at his own joke.

I'm not laughing.

He slides onto the lounge chair beside mine, and my heart races. I don't like being alone with him—not because he poses any sort of physical threat, but because I still don't understand the relationship between Luke and him. I'm nervous I'll say the wrong thing.

I'm nervous he'll get me to agree to something I shouldn't agree to.

I glance over at him. He's relaxed on the chair, eyes trained up toward the sky. I wonder how often he gives in and relaxes like this. He doesn't seem much like the type of man who even knows *how* to relax.

"I'm not sure what you're getting at," I say quietly, "but I'd like to make it clear that I'm in love with your brother."

He sits up and turns to face me. His eyes glow in the soft blue light bouncing up at us from the pool, reminding me of the night I met Luke and he first kissed me by a pool.

"I'm not getting at anything, Ellie." The way he says my name makes it sound so...sexual. "Just trying to be friendly as I get to know my future sister-in-law."

I keep my eyes focused on the pool. "That's all I'll ever be to you."

He huffs out a laugh. "Oh come on. We're all well aware that this is just some PR stunt. Aren't you handling his publicity? At least he could've picked a better cover up."

"It's not some PR stunt," I lie, doing my best to defend Luke, but let's be real here. I'm a bad liar.

I think about changing the subject and confronting him about the little Michelle bomb he dropped on me, but he asks a question before I get the chance to bring it up.

"If it's not for PR, then why don't *you* have anyone here to witness this shindig?"

Dammit. He's smarter than I thought. "Because we decided last-minute to do this here. We want to get married before training camp, and we agreed Hawaii was the place to do it."

"Okay, I'll play along. But for the record, you could have me if you want me," he says.

I choke, and he lets out another laugh. I don't even know what to say to that. Do I want him? Maybe. Sure. Of course. He's sex on legs, for God's sake. But he's Luke's evil brother, and I'd never do that to Luke. I couldn't.

I feel like maybe this is my opening to bring up Michelle. He mentioned her in passing, and I need to know if it's true or if he was just pressing my buttons. As a beat of silence passes between us, I can't quite figure out how to broach the topic. *Did you really sleep with Michelle? Any chance you knocked her up and not Luke? Are you the ticket to helping us get her the hell out of our lives?*

I just feel like I'm not quite lucky enough for that last one to come true.

"So why are you really marrying my brother?" he asks before I get the chance to bring her up.

"Because I love him." At least I don't have to lie about that.

"You've known him all of five minutes. You don't know him well enough to love him. And if you did..." he trails off, but his words are a clear indication that I wouldn't love him if I knew him. I feel my hackles rise with the sudden dire need to protect Luke at all costs from whatever Jack thinks he can do or say.

"That's not true," I say. "I know him very well after all the time we've spent together."

He raises a brow and lowers his voice. There's nobody within hearing distance, but I notice how both Jack and Luke ensure their privacy when they say things they don't want anyone else to know. It feels oddly good to be in the inner circle of people on the receiving end of those lowered voices. "So you know about the shit Savannah holds over both of us? Did he tell you about that? Did he tell you about what we did to cover up *his* mistakes? Did he tell you how damning the evidence she has is? How it could fuck up both our careers and how we both pay her to keep her mouth shut?"

"Of course he did," I snap. It's another lie, but it's not like I trust Jack to sit here and tell me the truth. He's just trying to make waves. He's trying to catch me in something and I won't sit here and take it. I stand. "I'm going to bed," I say.

It's not what I had planned. I wanted to go for a walk on the beach. I wanted some time to myself away from anyone who has the last name *Dalton*. Instead, I'm either stuck sitting with Jack as he does everything he can to squeeze the truth out of me or sitting in silence in the room with Luke.

I think I need to go with silence.

Not because it's what I want, but it's why I'm here. It's what I'm being paid to do.

As I walk up to our room, I realize I've now been confronted by Carol, Tim, and Jack—twice—about marrying into this family. I guess three down, just Kaylee to go.

But first...I need some answers.

Luke's watching football when I walk in. He barely even looks in my direction.

Some way to greet your fiancée.

"What does Savannah have on you?" I ask.

He stares at the screen a few beats before he clicks the power off and turns toward me. "What?"

"Jack mentioned Savannah holds something over the two of you. He confronted me just now asking if I know everything, and he made some pretty strong insinuations that you two covered something up that could come back to hurt you both now. So I'll ask you again, what does she have on you?"

Luke sighs and glances away from me, and it's that very moment I realize I don't know him. At all. I don't know if glancing away means he's about to come up with a lie. I don't know if Savannah really does have something on them that she's covering up. I'm marrying this guy, and I don't know truth from lies. I don't know what's real and what's fake. "Jack's just trying to get under your skin," he says.

"Well it's working," I spit. "And you're under my skin, too. I fucking hate all of this. And by the way, Jack thinks this wedding is fake, among many reasons because there's no one sitting on *my* side of the aisle."

"Then we'll pay someone to act like your friend."

I press my lips together and nod slowly. "Right. Good solution. Throw money at the problem." I huff out a sigh. "I'm going to bed. Goodnight."

I'm not tired, but lying in bed seems like it beats talking to Luke or potentially running into Jack again.

CHAPTER 7

My inbox has another Luke Dalton email alert when I wake up—alone again—in the morning.

I click the link, and it's a picture from last night on the boat. His lips are brushing my temple. Our body language says it all. I'm happy to be there beside him. I'm leaning into his kiss, and his arm is around my waist, and if I didn't know better, I'd think I'm looking at a couple very much in love.

I glance through the article. It doesn't mention specifically where we are in Hawaii or the fact that Luke and I are getting married. It's just some hot trash letting everyone know that we sure are cozy on a boat together.

I take my phone out to the main room of our suite where I'm sure Luke's asleep on the couch. My intent is to wake him with the latest article, but he's already up, his eyes trained on his phone. He glances up at me when I walk in, and I flash my screen at him with a smirk. "You see the latest?"

"Good morning to you, too," he mutters. He sits up and winces, and then he stretches his neck like it's stiff. "And yes, I saw the photo."

"Someone's watching," I say, not really feeling all that bad for him that he has a stiff neck. It was his choice to sleep on the couch for another night. The bed is plenty damn big.

He blows out a breath. "Someone's always watching, Ellie. It's a part of this life and it's only a fraction of why I enjoy my privacy. My popularity index is rising with your hunger traps and I'm not sure I like it."

"Thirst traps!" I scream at him. "They're *thirst traps* and you're real fucking welcome for building your platform to make you indispensable to the Aces. You're real fucking welcome for doing everything I can to help you with your problems. You're real fucking welcome—" I stop yelling at him—screaming like a banshee, really—when I hear a knock at the door.

My eyes widen.

How thin are these hotel walls?

Did anybody hear what I was just screaming?

I glance at the door, and then I look back at him. I just rolled out of bed. I'm not in the mood for guests. "You can handle that," I hiss, and then I head to the bathroom to take a long, hot shower.

Once I'm dressed, I find Luke on our balcony, brooding once again as he looks over our view. "Who was at the door?"

He keeps his eyes trained on the ocean in front of him. "Housekeeping. They wanted to clean our room." He glances up at me. "Kaylee texted me a while ago and asked if we wanted to meet for breakfast."

"Sure," I say. "And I'm sorry I exploded at you before. This is just...it's all just a lot, Luke."

He presses his lips together. "I know. And thank you for all you're doing." He clears his throat. "Give me fifteen minutes," he says, and it's his turn for the shower.

That's it. No apology for his words. No hugging it out. No reassurance that we're doing the right thing.

My phone starts ringing as I'm sitting on the balcony waiting for him, and when I glance at the screen, my heart squeezes.

Very few people actually call my phone anymore. If anything, they text...but my best friend is someone I talk to on a daily basis. When she's in the country, anyway.

And I've missed her. I've been going through this alone, and the one time I thought about calling her on her honeymoon to get some advice was the one time I followed Jack to his room and was tempted to make a poor decision that came from a place of anger and pain.

"Hey, Nicki," I answer. My voice is filled with exhaustion even though I'm trying to fake enthusiasm. I don't particularly want to have this conversation, but I'm tired of feeling completely isolated.

"I'm back from Fiji ready to tell you all the stories and imagine my surprise when I saw a headline that you're in freaking Hawaii with Luke and his entire family!"

Shit. I need to be careful not to reveal that we're here to get married. "He invited me to come along on his family's annual trip."

"To show off his fiancée?" she presses.

"Something like that."

"And how's Hawaii? We thought about going there instead of Fiji. Tell me every detail."

I laugh. "We're heading to breakfast in a few minutes but it's great. We'll find time to chat soon. How was Fiji?"

She launches into some story that I'm half-listening to about how my brother kept getting stopped at the airport to sign autographs. I stare down at the beach. I've looked at all this a hundred different ways, but hearing Nicki's voice feels like home, and it's reminding me once again what Jack said last night. He's right. There's nobody here for me.

Luke steps onto the balcony, and I interrupt Nicki. "I'm so sorry, babe, but we're heading out now. I'll call you later, okay?"

"Of course. Love you!"

We hang up. "Sorry. That was Nicki." A flash of alarm passes over his face, but before he can say anything, I say, "I didn't mention anything about getting married."

He nods. "Okay. You ready to eat?"

I stand. "Here's to hoping it's just you, me, and Kaylee."

He chuckles, and we both step back inside. When he closes the glass slider, he stops. I turn back to see what's holding him up, and his eyes lock on mine. "In case I haven't told you recently, thank you. You're an incredible woman, and I appreciate you and all you're doing for me."

I press my lips into a thin smile. "Thank you for all you're doing for me, too."

We leave it at that, and we head down to breakfast. My hope that it would be just the three of us is shattered the second I spot Jack sitting beside Kaylee.

"Good morning," Luke says brightly, reminding me once again of his stellar acting skills as his hand tightens over mine.

"Morning," Jack murmurs, his eyes on me before they slide down to where Luke clutches my hand.

I feel scrutinized with the way he's looking at me. I force my hand more firmly into Luke's, but then we're done walking and we're at the table and it's just awkward for a beat as we let go and sit.

"This is our annual sibling breakfast," Kaylee explains to me. "We do one without Mom and Dad so we can chat about whatever we want without parental judgment."

"She's not a sibling," Jack points out, his eyes on me.

Heat creeps up my neck.

"Close enough," Kaylee and Luke say at the same time, and then they both laugh.

Kaylee smiles at me. "You're getting married tomorrow. We'll count you in as part of the family."

"I won't until tomorrow," Jack says, his eyes edging over to Luke.

"Don't be an asshole," Luke says to his brother.

Jack lifts a shoulder. "Until the vows are spoken, she's fair game."

I glance over at Luke, who looks like he's about to pop a vein in his head.

She's fair game.

That seems to be Jack's motto.

Kaylee clears her throat. "Jack, be a decent human being," she says. She looks at me. "This is just such a repeat of the past. These two have a, um, *colorful* history."

"So I've heard," I murmur. "I'm happy to leave you three to it." I move to stand, but Luke's hand finds my thigh. He puts some pressure there, forcing me back to my seat.

"Stay. Please. Don't let Jack push you away." He leans over and presses his lips to my cheek, and I get a whiff of his freshly showered scent and *God* do I want him a little more every single second.

"Sorry," Jack says, holding up his hands in what might be the most insincere apology ever. "It's just not fair to invite someone to a sibling breakfast when she isn't actually a sibling."

"You want to talk about what's *fair*?" Luke demands.

"You think it was fair to marry my fucking ex-girlfriend?" Jack spits back.

And that's it. That's the root of the problem between these two men.

Jack never forgave Luke for being with Savannah even though he gave them his blessing. And now Jack will spend seemingly every waking moment making Luke pay for that.

"Guys, stop. Lower your voices. People are looking," Kaylee says.

"You're only getting married to somehow come out looking better than me," Jack says, completely ignoring his sister, "but it's the opposite. You look like a mess. We all know you just want to take some of Mom and Dad's attention off me. You're always so desperate for their approval, but it's so obvious to everyone that all this," he pauses to wave his hand between Luke and me, "is just a charade. Some PR stunt. I just can't figure out *why*, but rest assured, I'm working on it."

My heart thumps in my chest. Is this where we drop the act?

Is Luke really so desperate for his parents' approval that he'd go to these particular lengths? I guess he's going to these lengths for his team owner's approval. I wonder for a half-second what that relationship is like. Is Calvin a pseudo-father to him? Another person to try to impress?

"Fuck you, Jack," Luke says.

"Stop it!" Kaylee yells, and silence falls over our little table. She lowers her voice. "Stop it. You know people are always listening. We don't need you two blowing up the media by fighting about personal matters in public."

Luke's eyes move to his water glass, his mouth shut in his own way of conceding to his sister's good point, but Jack is not to be stopped.

"Just admit it," he says quietly.

"The only thing I'll admit is that I have fallen in love with Ellie." His voice is soft, but there's still ice in his tone.

When I glance over at him, his eyes are on me. They're tender and kind, adoring and loving, if I didn't know the truth, I'd believe him. I'm part of the lie and I very nearly believe his sincerity right now.

He leans forward and presses a gentle kiss to my lips.

"I love him, too," I say. My words are my truth.

"You two are the cutest," Kaylee says, clearly approving.

"What a fucking joke," Jack mutters. He stands and tosses his napkin on the table. "I'm out." He stalks out of the restaurant, which is fine by me. I'd rather eat this meal without him here anyway, and I'd bet money Luke would, too.

And all this goes down before we even order our freaking pancakes.

CHAPTER 8

"Why is he so bent on this idea that we're faking it?" I ask, if nothing else to break the intense, awkward silence that falls over us after Jack stalks out.

"That's just Jack," Kaylee says, like that excuses his rude behavior. "He gets an idea in his head and doesn't stop until he gets his way. And in this case, proving he's right means getting his way, so he's going to pick and pull at every thread and push the two of you to the edge to prove his point. For what it's worth, I believe you."

A surge of guilt pulses through me. She believes us, but she probably shouldn't. Jack doesn't, and I wish he would. What a mess.

"Thank you," I say softly. Luke tosses an arm around my shoulders and squeezes me to him. He presses his lips gently to my temple in a public display of affection for his sister's benefit, and I can't help but wonder if he feels the same surge of guilt that I do.

Breakfast is decidedly pleasant once Jack leaves. Luke and Kaylee catch up, and I sit quietly observing as Luke tends to deflect questions back to her. He's friendly as he makes conversation, but he leaves personal details almost completely out of the equation.

Except for Pepper. He lights up when he talks about that adorable pup.

Kaylee is animated and she's the kind of over-sharer who gives every detail about her life—so, in essence, the complete opposite of her brother.

I learn she recently ended a three-month relationship because they had vastly different visions of the future. She wants a litter of children and dogs and he didn't. I learn that Kaylee is in her last year of college and she's majoring in education. She wants to be a middle school teacher—the hardest group of youngsters to teach, I'd imagine, but growing up with two brothers her elders by at least a decade seems to have given her a thick skin. I learn that she and her roommate are in the middle of a fight because her roommate finished her box of cereal...Lucky Charms, naturally.

Oh to be twenty-one again.

"What's on today's agenda?" Luke asks.

Kaylee smiles then makes the motion to zip her lips.

My brows dip. "What's this about?"

Kaylee laughs. "Today is excursion day!" She's positively gleeful as she says it. "Whenever we do these family trips, whoever picked the location gets to plan two excursions. The dinner cruise was one and I have a mid-morning and afternoon surprise planned for today."

Oh yay. So after the awkward breakfast encounter with Jack where he wrote me off as unimportant to this family, I'm so blessed and lucky to get to spend more time with him today. Carol and Tim, too, who gave us that awkward wedding pep talk about how we shouldn't do it. I really just can't wait to spend more time with these people.

Luke's arm is still around my shoulder, and his fingers dig into my flesh for a beat as more than likely the same thoughts run through his mind.

"Do we need to bring anything or wear something special?" I ask.

She shakes her head. "What you're wearing is fine. It's just a fun, relaxing little thing today."

A fun, relaxing little thing. With Luke's family. I'm not sure those two ideas can comfortably coexist.

We head right for the lobby when we're done eating, and the rest of Luke's family is already waiting there for the three of us—Jack included.

"Good morning, everyone," Kaylee says. Everyone exchanges morning greetings and then we stare at Kaylee awkwardly as she taps some things on her phone. I still can't imagine ever feeling awkward around my own family. Even Kaylee must feel it, but she blows past it because she's trying to build memories. Clearly she wants all this to be normal, but it's just...not.

She finally looks up with a smile. I can't tell if it's forced or not. I can't tell if any of these people should've gone into acting instead of athletics or if they actually do have real emotions they can express. "Our car will be here in a few minutes."

We all pile into the luxury SUV Uber that Kaylee called and we're on our way to the surprise location. We only drive for maybe ten or fifteen minutes as Kaylee murmurs about the beauty of the scenery and the rest of us remain quiet when the driver pulls into a parking lot for a beach.

A beach much like the one where we're staying.

Why, exactly, did we need to drive fifteen minutes to get to another beach?

The answer is made abundantly clear as I spot several large, beastly animals tied up to stalls near a shack. It would be a lovely picture of horses on the beach...if I liked horses.

I don't.

They terrify me.

I pray with all my might that the horses are *not* the excursion she has planned, but we all already know that of course it is since this is my life and it couldn't possibly be any other way.

Kaylee opens the door and we all tumble out of the vehicle, and then she claps her hands together. "Horseback riding on the beach!"

My heart races so fast that my chest actually hurts.

My first instinct is to flee. I look around for a place to run away, somewhere to hide until this is all over, but I don't see one except the little shack where we need to go to get set up for our adventure.

I stand frozen to the spot, my eyes focused on those damn horses as all the color drains from my cheeks.

What the hell am I going to do? I can't just bolt. This is a *family* excursion. I'm going to be a part of this family, no matter how temporary that may be. It's part of the job description to go out and bond with them, isn't it?

I just never thought I'd be bonding over *horses*.

Equinophobia. That's my thing. Fear of horses. And that's the only thing I can think of as I ball my trembling hands into fists in some attempt to feel something other than fear as my knuckles turn white.

"Uh, Kay?" Luke says.

She looks up at him. "Yeah?"

"Ellie doesn't care for horses," he says, and my cheeks that had blanched just a second ago now start to burn with mortification.

It's not that I don't *care* for them.

I'm fucking terrified of them.

"Of course she doesn't," Carol mutters, and if I wasn't all wrapped up in my own thoughts about these damn horses, I might be offended by that—I might even question why she'd say that.

But I can't. Instead, all I can do is stare at the animals from where I stand. Why, exactly, do people ride horses?

They're animals. They're wild. They're not meant for us.

I inhale a large breath and hold it for a beat.

I can do this. I won't be trampled. They're just gentle animals. They won't hurt me. They won't buck me off their backs.

I clear my throat as I repeat those mantras that I certainly don't believe on any level. I'm not trying to be difficult in front of his family. I'm just genuinely panicked here.

"It's fine," I say, a tremor to my voice. I clear my throat to try to get rid of the shakiness and press my lips into a small smile.

Luke's brows dip. "It's *fine*?" he says.

I shrug and nod. If these people can all act their way through anything, if they can all wear these facades and masks and hide their real emotions...well I can, too. "Yeah." I say it with a nonchalance I don't feel on any level. "Let's do this. It'll be fun." Random phrases tumble out of my mouth, but I don't really mean them.

"You sure?" Kaylee asks, her brows pinched, and at the same time, Luke says, "You don't have to do this."

"It's fine," I repeat, my fists still clenched as my nails bite into my palms.

Luke tries to grab for my hand as we all turn toward the shack to check in for our ride, and I physically have to make myself unclench my hands to grab his. I think I grasp his a little harder than I mean to.

He leans into me. "Are you okay?"

I keep my eyes focused forward, somehow landing on the back of Jack's head, and I nod. "Fine."

He squeezes my hand in solidarity, and then we're at the shack and it feels an awful lot like there's no turning back now. Why do I continually feel that way around this family over and over again?

Jed, the man who runs this whole operation, leads us out to the beach. He points to six of the eight horses in their stalls. "We have Clementine, Dale, Sugar, Domino, Fiona, and Scout. Pick your horse and we'll get you all saddled up."

He gives a few more instructions, and then Luke asks, "Which one is the gentlest?"

"Sugar. She's a sweetheart. Aren't you, girl?" Jed says, rubbing a palm on her muzzle.

She doesn't look like a sweetheart. She's brown with a little white on her and isn't he scared she's going to bite his hand off when he pats her nose like that? She's a huge beast of an animal easily ten times my size, not some gentle creature.

"Take Sugar, Ellie," Luke says to me.

I blink and nod as I try to reconcile the fact that I'm getting on this thing with the fear that permeates my entire being. It starts in my heart and with every beat, it pulses out into my veins. The pounding synchronizes in my head, ba-boom, ba-boom, ba-boom, every beat setting me further and further on edge.

I spot Jack as his eyes edge over to me, a sly smile curling his lips.

Why do I get the premonition like something bad is going to happen that has nothing to do with the horse?

Everyone else mounts their horses except for Luke, who's still standing beside me. I'm standing a few feet away from Sugar as I try to force myself to get on. Luke grabs my hand and squeezes it.

"You sure you're okay with this?"

I draw in a deep breath and exhale, and then I just do it without answering. I brace one foot on the stirrup and toss my other leg over, and magically I'm on top of a horse. For a second I'm stunned that I made it this far, and then I grab onto the little knobby thing sticking up—I think Jed called it a *horn*—since I already feel like I'm going to fall off.

What if I fall off and the horse tramples me?

It's my biggest fear, and one I really didn't think I'd ever have to face. Certainly not today when I woke up this morning.

I try to draw in a deep breath, but it doesn't seem like I can fill my lungs enough. I exhale short, sharp breaths.

"Ellie and I are going to skip this one," Luke says, patting Dale on the side.

I can't help it when I glance over at his family to gauge the reactions to that. Carol tuts disapprovingly and Kaylee's eyes are full of disappointment.

"It's fine, Luke," I grit out. "Get on your horse."

I guess if anything, I have the option of sitting out by myself, but if this is going to somehow help Luke bond with his family, then I'm going to suck it up and just do it.

Jed unties the horses from their stalls and leads the pack of us down toward the water. We're moving slowly, which I'm thankful for, but somehow Jack ended up next to me—not Luke. Luke is behind me.

I feel Jack's eyes on me, but I can't look over at him. I'm focused forward because if I tear my eyes away from the spot between Sugar's ears for even a second, I might fall off.

"You seem to really enjoy horses," Jack says, and I hate that I can picture his smirk at just the mere sound of his voice.

"Let's just enjoy the ride in silence," I suggest.

"Oh, but where would the fun be in that?" He laughs, and I wonder if Luke can hear our conversation or if he's too far back to catch it over the clopping sound of hooves hitting wet sand. "It's just such a romantic ride on the beach. Just think of it. You ride this horse now, and the invitation to ride the stallion is still open if you'd like to stop by later."

My jaw drops in shock, though it really shouldn't. He's been hitting on me since practically the moment we met, and I'm pretty sure he does it just to get a rise out of me—and to piss off his brother.

I still don't look over at him. "Thanks, but I'm busy. With your *brother.*"

"You know that old saying about being hung like a horse..."

I gasp. "Oh my God, Jack!" I'm about to finish my shrieking with something about how inappropriate that was, but it would appear that gasps and screeches spook poor old gentle Sugar.

I suppose it might've helped if I would've listened to Jed over the rushing fear between my ears earlier as he told us what to do if our horse gets spooked, but instead I was too focused on my fear. As Sugar's front two legs shoot up into the air and she spins to change direction, my brain computes that horses flee when they're afraid.

I'm afraid, too.

Beyond afraid. I'm freaking the fuck out. I don't know what the hell I'm supposed to do as my horse runs along the beach and away from the Daltons at what feels to be lightning speed. I simply grasp onto her neck for dear life and close my eyes, praying that Jed will be able to catch up to us and save me.

Sugar is moving so fast that the saddle is starting to slip around to the side. Maybe she puffed herself out when the saddle went on to give herself more room or something, but it's not snug around her and I'm clenching my thighs to try to keep balance as the saddle starts to move. My body is still on it, and I cling to her neck as my life flashes before my eyes.

I'm not on the beach anymore. I'm not riding the horse. I think I might've blacked out. I don't hear anything except the rushing in my ears. My eyes are squeezed shut tight as fear permeates every atom of my being and pieces of my life flash before me.

I had a good childhood. Josh and I fought, sure, but we were always close. My parents did what they could to give us memories to last a lifetime. Family vacations, barbecues with neighbors, memorable birthday parties, Christmas mornings with so many presents we had to take breaks unwrapping them. And even my adulthood has been pretty good. I've had my share of failed relationships, of assholes, of frogs dressed as princes until I saw what was really on the inside.

There's the good and the bad, and if I come out on the other end of this alive, I'm going to have to take a good, long look at my life.

I thought I was on the right track here. I thought I'd somehow met my Prince Charming and I was heading toward a happy ending. As I flail on this horse that I'm no longer riding (at least in my mind, I'm not, because I would never ride a horse, and instead, I'm just being taken for a joyride on a really scary rollercoaster), I finally realize that I need to come to terms with what's really going on.

Should I really be wasting an entire year of my life on someone who doesn't love me?

Or is it really wasting it if it has the potential to be everything I think it could be?

CHAPTER 9

I finally force my eyes open when the wind whipping around me seems to slow. I realize I'm still riding a horse on the beach with the Dalton family.

That's when I stifle a scream.

Screaming will only spook the horse further, but then I see Luke on a horse beside mine. I see Jed as he grabs the horse's tether on my other side.

I'm saved, and a lump clogs my throat.

Everything comes back into focus, and then Sugar stops completely.

I jump down off this bitch and run up the beach as fast as my legs will carry me.

I collapse onto the sand once I'm far enough away from the horses and I lose all control as the rushing terror starts to melt into something resembling gratitude.

I'm still alive.

I'm off that horse.

Luke was right there to save me.

Like a goddamn Prince Charming galloping in on his steed.

I burst into sobs.

Ugly, gross, wet sobs.

He is a fucking prince. Okay? He just is.

These tears aren't from what just happened. Okay, they're not *entirely* from what just happened. The horse galloped, and I was slipping off, and I got scared.

But I'm marrying the guy who seems to be my prince every single way I look at it except for the one way that really matters in a marriage.

And that's a whole lot more terrifying than some stupid horse.

I wrap my arms around my legs and tuck my head down into the hole to cry in peace. I'm certain the entire Dalton family is watching. Maybe they're laughing, maybe not. Jack is, probably. Luke might not be.

And that's when I feel his arms come around me. He holds me for a beat, and his hands move in soothing circles around my back. "Are you okay, Ellie?" Luke asks softly, and he presses his lips to the top of my head.

"I'm okay," I sob into my little dark hole. "I'm so sorry."

"Hey, hey," he says quietly. "There's nothing to be sorry for. You're okay. I've got you." He keeps rubbing those circles, and see what I mean? That whole thing about being torn between whether this has real potential or I'm wasting a year of my life. It doesn't feel very wasteful when his arms are around me.

"She's fine," he yells, maybe to his family or maybe to Jed. I'm not sure since my head is still down in my little hole. "Go on ahead."

He lets me cry a few beats as he keeps rubbing my back and whispering soothing phrases. "Look at me," he eventually commands softly.

I lift my chin out of my hole, and he thumbs away my tears as his navy eyes bore into mine. His sunglasses are flipped up on his forehead, and concern and apprehension shade his view as he gazes at me.

"You're okay. I'm right here with you, and you will never, ever have to ride a horse ever again. Not for me. Not for my family. Not for anybody. Do you hear me?"

I nod but can't seem to form words around the huge lump in my throat. The horse could've hurt me. But so could Luke, and it's not like I can just hop down and run away from him like I did Sugar.

"Thank you for trying," he says. "You didn't have to do that."

I sniffle and try to draw in a deep breath, but the air comes in short little spasms as I attempt to calm down. I'm definitely letting him think the tears are from the whole Sugar incident, not from this situation I find myself in with my husband-to-be.

I wipe my eyes with the bottom of my shirt and take a swipe under my nose, too, all the while trying to calm my breathing so I can inhale deeply enough to feel satisfied again.

"Can't wait to see what else Kaylee has planned," Luke mutters, and I can't help when a small giggle bursts out of me. I'm riding some emotional highs right now, and I'm not sure if I've ever had sobs turn to laughter at the snap of a finger before, but his words strike me as incredibly funny in the moment.

His eyes lift to mine again, and he chuckles when he sees the fear in my wild eyes replaced with just a hint of merriment.

"What happened out there?" he asks. He hasn't moved from his spot kneeling in front of me.

"Jack said some really inappropriate things to me and I sort of shrieked and I think I scared the horse," I say.

Luke shakes his head and grits his teeth. "I'll fucking kill him."

I set a hand on his arm as I'm finally able to draw in a breath. I don't need family violence over this. "It's fine," I say. "I'm fine. Everything's fine."

"What did he say to you?"

I stare at him for a beat, and then I realize I have zero reason to protect Jack in this. "An invitation to ride the stallion who's hung like a horse," I admit.

"Jesus Christ." Luke closes his eyes a beat, and when he opens them, they're stormy with anger. "I can't believe him. I'm so sorry."

Does it really matter? It's not like you want me.

I can't bring myself to say those words.

It's not like I'd take Jack up on his offer anyway.

"Just forget about it," I say.

My gaze falls across the beach. The rest of the Daltons continue on their adventure, with Jed leading the pack. Our horses are tethered together and near the stalls again. We're safe, and they're all far away and heading even further from us.

Thank God.

And so that's why when Luke leans in and nuzzles my nose with his, a dart of surprise pings my chest.

His family isn't watching. They're riding horses, judging the girl who they assume is overly dramatic and did something to make the horse run away when really it was Jack's fault.

This isn't for their benefit.

His warmth and his proximity and this moment...it all feels like it's just for us.

His lips are centimeters from mine, and my body lights up this close to him. His heat washes over me, and every detail of our single night together rushes back to me. His tongue in my mouth. On my body. His hands gliding across my skin. His fingers pushing into me. Fingertips clawing the glass of the window.

I freeze as I pray he'll kiss me.

Instead, with his lips centimeters from mine, he speaks so softly I almost miss his words. His voice is tortured as he says, "You deserve so much more than him. More than me. I wish I could give you that."

You can.

"You can." The words slip from my lips before I can stop them. I don't want to stop them. I want him to see that we're made for each other. Why can't he just see that?

His lips brush mine as if he just can't help himself, and then he backs away. "I can't." He stands, and he pulls me up with him, breaking the moment we just shared. He doesn't even give me a second to regain my composure or to brush off that kiss that made my knees weak. "I'm glad you're okay."

"Me, too," I admit. "But no more horses. Like ever again. Okay?"

He chuckles. "Deal. I saw a brewery up on the boardwalk. Should we go grab something stiff?"

I raise a brow at his choice of words. I'd *love* to grab something stiff.

Oh great, now I'm starting to think like Jack.

I push that thought quickly away, but Luke laughs at the look on my face anyway as he grabs my hand and we move up the beach toward the boardwalk.

Kaylee's whole idea here was to bond her family, but instead...it feels an awful lot like this horseback riding fiasco has only brough Luke and me closer together.

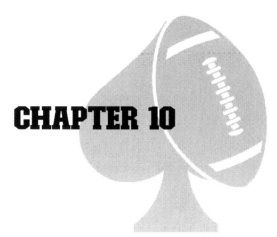

CHAPTER 10

"Double vodka seven," I order.

I realize we're at a brewery and the traditional order might include the beer that's actually brewed here, but even though I'm breathing normally again, my nerves are still on high alert. I'm not quite over nearly falling off a horse for the second time in my life.

And then there was that kiss and his words.

I sigh.

"I'll try your IPA," Luke says, and the bartender slinks away to make our drinks while Luke taps out a text. "Just letting Kaylee know we came up here."

I roll my eyes. "Can't wait for them to join us." My voice is full of sarcasm, and he chuckles.

"This might be a strange time to say this, but I'm really glad you're here," he says. He sets his phone down on the bar.

"You are?" I can't hide the surprise in my voice.

He drums the bar a little with his fingertips. "I don't know how this vacation might've gone if I didn't have you here by my side."

My eyes feel a little misty at that. "Really?"

He lifts a shoulder and keeps his gaze trained down on the bar top. "You see how they are. It's worse when it's just me and them. At least they're civil in front of other people. Most of the time." He shakes his head. "My parents, anyway. Not Jack, apparently."

I reach over and squeeze his hand, and instead of responding to any of that, I throw out the question I need the answer to. "Why are you so convinced that you're wrong for me?"

He's quiet a while, and I give him time to think about that since I popped that question out of nowhere. The bartender drops off our drinks, but I'm not letting Luke out of answering just because we're distracted by drinks.

He holds up his glass to mine. I clink and we each take a sip. Okay, *sip* is a bit of an understatement. I gulp down half mine and Luke does the same.

He blows out a breath. "I'm thirty-one. I don't want another real marriage because I've already tried it and it didn't work for me. I don't want to go through that devastation again." He rubs the back of his neck. "I should know what I want out of my future by now, but I don't. I'll be sharing a child with someone I can't stand, and I don't really know if I want more kids than that. I've got a past, I don't know what my future will look like, and it's all just a lot to burden someone with."

"I get all that, Luke. I do. But *everyone* has a past. Everyone has baggage."

He presses his lips together but doesn't answer.

"You won't even give this a shot," I press. "And you're saying it's because you don't want to burden me?" I shake my head. "You haven't even thought about whether I'm willing and able to shoulder those burdens. That's what marriage is, Luke. It's a partnership."

He stares straight ahead. "You deserve more than I can give you." His voice is nearly robotic, like he's saying the words he's trained himself to say. There's no emotion there, but there rarely is with this guy. He gulps down the second half of his beer.

I nod and sip my drink just to give my mouth something to do other than tear into him because I'm about to unload all my thoughts on that. He doesn't know that. He's given me *everything* I could possibly ask for in the short time I've known him.

Everything except himself.

He's given me friendship. Shelter. A job. Food. He takes care of me. He gets off his horse so he can make sure I'm okay and he rubs my back when I fall.

I feel it, and I *know* it can't just be me.

Every sign points to the fact that he cares about me as more than just a friend...every sign except the only one that matters.

His affirmation.

I drain my vodka. "I deserve happiness," I finally say. "We all do." *And I think you can give me that.*

His drink is empty, too. He motions the bartender over. "And in the long run, I don't know if I can give you that."

I drop the subject before I start to sound desperate...if it's not too late already. I'm not asking for forever. I'm just asking him to give this a real shot because I think it could be something incredible for us both.

"So what does the future look like for Luke Dalton? You'll play football as long as you can, and then..." I trail off as I wait for him to fill in the blank. We've sort of covered this topic already, but he didn't really have a definitive answer.

"It's bad luck to talk about what comes next," he says. "I'll worry about it when I'm there. Despite my age and the statistics, I don't feel like I'm anywhere near the end of my career at this point."

"I didn't peg you as superstitious," I admit.

He chuckles. "I have three rules, Ellie. I eat Lucky Charms and blueberry waffles with peanut butter on them for breakfast on game day. I listen to the same playlist each week to get in the right pregame headspace. And I don't talk about what happens after my days on the field come to an end."

I laugh. "What's on the playlist?"

"That's confidential," he says with a wink and a twinkle in his eyes. "Top secret."

"I'll find out," I promise.

"Good luck," he scoffs, clearly teasing me. "I have two hundred playlists. You'll never get it."

"I only have to be wrong a hundred ninety-nine times, babe."

"Assuming, of course, that you have access to said lists," he points out.

I take a sip of my fresh drink. "All right. Until you confirm otherwise, I will just be over here believing that your game day playlist is a power mix of hits from Celine Dion, Adele, and Whitney Houston."

"Don't forget Mariah Carey," he says, and then he covers his mouth in jest like he just gave away a secret.

I raise a brow, and his eyes continue to twinkle, and it's just another moment that I fall in deeper. I'm going to live to regret this, but there's just no turning back at this point.

"You really won't tell me what's on it?" I ask—mostly because now I *need* to know. He can't dangle something so silly in front of me and expect me not to dig until I get my answers.

He shrugs. "Nope."

"Celine it is, then," I tease.

He narrows his eyes at me. "Hey, you could do a lot worse than Celine Dion."

We're both still laughing when the entire Dalton clan walks in through the front doors of the brewery, and suddenly all the merriment and laughter is sucked right out of the room. I feel it physically drain out of me, replaced instead with a mix of anxiety and irritation...especially when my eyes meet those of a smirking Jack.

CHAPTER 11

"There she is," Jack says as the entire family approaches the bar where we sit. "The horse whisperer."

"Shut the hell up, Jack," Luke hisses.

"Boys, boys, let's give it a rest," Carol says, her voice tired as if she's been telling them the same thing for the last thirty years. She glances at me before settling a disapproving gaze on Luke. "You couldn't grab a table for the rest of us?"

My brows arch and my eyes widen at her words.

She doesn't ask me whether I'm okay.

She doesn't tell us how much fun they had.

Not even a fucking *hello*...but a complaint about our choice of where we decided to sit when we came here alone while the rest of them continued on their adventure right after I almost died.

"I didn't realize you'd all be joining us," Luke says. He glances around and nods to an open table—of which there are plenty in here, for what it's worth.

"Didn't you get my text back?" Kaylee asks, and Luke shakes his head as we pick up our drinks and follow Carol toward the table.

Kaylee falls into step beside me. "I'm so sorry, Ellie. I had no idea you didn't like horses or I never would've planned that for everybody. You okay?"

I nod and press my lips together. What happened was terrifying, but I give the dramatics a bit of a break. "I'm fine."

"You're a mind-reader, Lu Lu," Kaylee says. "This was activity number two. Lunch at a brewery. You know, since I'm of legal age now and all that jazz."

We take our seats at the table and a waitress comes right over with menus. We've been sitting less than thirty seconds and I already miss my alone time with Luke. We were laughing, and he was opening up even if he was saying things I didn't want to hear, and we were pulling closer to one another. And then his family shows up, and it's like he regresses. He's a turtle retracting back into his shell, and it'll take another near accident or an act of God or something to get him to come out again.

I hate what they do to him, and I just want to get away from them.

Especially Jack, who keeps looking at me from across the table. I feel his eyes on me, and I try to ignore it. But every time I glance up, our eyes lock.

He always gets what he wants, right? And right now, he wants to prove that what we're doing is nothing more than a sham. The funny thing is that he *is* right. But he thinks that he can just keep hitting on me and eventually I'll give in.

I won't.

"So what happened out there?" Kaylee asks.

I lift a shoulder. "I guess my horse got a little spooked or whatever and he just took off the other way."

"The way you were holding on, I thought you were practicing for the Kentucky Derby." Jack smirks again.

"Knock it off, Jack," Luke says, his volume rising.

"It's fine," I say. "I can take his teasing." Because I can. That's a way to show affection. It's part of being in most families, right?

Jack holds up both palms innocently.

"This whole thing is your fault," Luke says to him.

Kaylee, Carol, and Tim just watch the tennis match as it unfolds. I sit uncomfortably as I wait for Luke to drop the truth bombs in front of his parents.

Jack's brows arch. "My fault?" he repeats. "How, exactly?"

"You know exactly how," Luke hisses, pointing a finger at him. "You need to stop hitting on my future wife. We're getting married *tomorrow* and she's not interested."

"Why don't you let her tell me that?" he asks, never losing his cool despite the rare show of emotion from his brother.

"I have," I say, finding my voice despite the extreme awkwardness of this situation. "I'd appreciate it if you stopped."

"And speaking of our wedding, our rehearsal is tonight," Luke says.

Carol purses her lips. "So there's nothing we can do to stop this?"

I meet Jack's eyes across the table, and he looks...confident. Arrogant.

I have a sinking suspicion that he has a plan, and the thought scares me almost as much as that damn horse.

Luke's arm moves around my shoulders. "We're going through with the wedding." His voice is firm and holds no space for argument.

"Our little conversation didn't have any impact on you at all?" she asks.

Oh, it had an impact all right.

Luke shrugs with nonchalance, but his fingers digging into the flesh of my shoulder tell a bit of a different story than what he's projecting to his family. "It did have an impact, actually. It made me see how very much I need Ellie in my life."

He leans over and presses a kiss to my temple, and something tells me he's not just tossing out a jab with those words. I think he actually means them. But what, exactly, he means *by* them is a different story entirely.

"You know we all think this is a mistake, Luke," Tim says. "It's too fast." He avoids looking at me, and in that moment, the truth finally strikes me.

I suppose I sort of get it. Tim is trying to watch out for his son—his professional athlete son with a healthy bank account. He doesn't know we've signed papers that keep Luke's assets perfectly safe. In his own twisted way, he's trying to show he cares. Carol, too, I guess. And maybe even Jack—maybe he thinks that he can lure me away and prove I'm not in this for the right reasons.

They have a funny way of going about it, but maybe it's the only way they know how, particularly since Luke is so closed off even with them.

"Leave them alone," Kaylee interjects softly. "Can't we just enjoy our lunch and talk about all this later? Can we stop fighting for two seconds and just enjoy a little time together as a family? This should be an occasion of joy. Luke has found the love of his life, and they're getting married. Let's celebrate that instead of forcing our opinions on them."

I look at her gratefully, and another dart of guilt pierces my guts. I wish we could let Kaylee in on the truth, but it's just too risky.

"Thank you, Kay," Luke says softly.

A beat of awkward silence falls over the table, as if nobody really knows what to say if they're not fighting.

"So tell us what we missed," I finally say. "How was the horseback riding?"

Kaylee launches into their tales of horses splashing through the surf. The four of them are laughing as they retell their adventure that I'm only half-listening to. Instead, I'm studying them. All of them. They moved from the tense argument to laughter on the turn of a dime, and meanwhile I'm over here still trying to play catch up.

And my future husband seems to be, too, as he stares down at his beer in silence.

Gone is my laughing, fun Luke from a few moments ago, replaced with this brooding man. I just wish I knew how to get the other Luke back.

CHAPTER 12

Luke and I have a quick meeting with Alana, our wedding coordinator, in the front lobby regarding details for tonight's rehearsal when we get back from lunch. We're still sitting in the comfy chairs in the lobby when it happens. We watch as a taxi pulls up in front of the hotel, and then two figures get out of it.

Familiar figures. A man and a woman.

It takes my brain a second to catch up with what my eyes are seeing.

"Oh my God!" I screech once it all registers, and then I pop up out of my chair as I run toward the hotel entrance. I toss my arms around my brother's neck. "What are you guys doing here?"

"Hey, Sis," Josh says, and I move to Nicki for the next hug. She's a golden tan from her honeymoon, her blonde hair streaked with even more highlights than usual, and she wears a bright smile.

"Oh my God, it's the bride!" she gushes, and I can't help my giggle as I recall saying that to her not so long ago when I arrived in Vegas for their nuptials. I squeeze her, grateful suddenly to have someone here for me...someone who can sit on my side of the aisle.

I thought having Luke here was enough. He *should* be enough, and he has been...in those few times when he has actually allowed me in.

But now that I've met the family, I realize I need an entire army on my side to get through tonight and tomorrow.

"Didn't I just talk with you on the phone this morning?" I ask her.

She giggles. "We had just boarded our plane when I called you. I was testing the waters."

"What are you doing here?" I ask Nicki since my brother didn't answer the same question. I glance over at Luke. His eyes are twinkling at me. He had to have been the one who clued them into where we are and what we're doing here.

But why would he do that?

As I recall, it was his idea for the two of us to travel to Hawaii before these two got back from Fiji just so they didn't have the chance to try to stop the wedding.

"Josh came to talk you two out of it," she admits softly in my ear. "I came to stand beside my best friend as she marries my husband's best friend. I'm here to support you in whatever way you need support."

Tears spring to my eyes. I needed them both here more than I realized.

"Why don't you two get checked in and meet us in our room so we can talk?" Luke suggests, and the newlyweds head toward the check-in desk while Luke and I go to our room.

We're quiet on the elevator ride since we're not alone, but once the door closes us into privacy in our room, I spring the only question in my mind on him. "Did you do this?"

He shrugs then smirks, and that smirk is so devilishly delicious that it just makes me want to jump his hot bones. "I *may* have had something to do with it."

I toss my arms around his neck. "Thank you," I say, and then I untangle myself before I get carried away. "But why?"

He flops onto the couch where he's been sleeping the last few nights, and I slide into a chair at the little table across from the couch.

"I know this has been hard on you," he admits. "It wasn't just Jack pointing out that you don't have anyone on your side of the aisle. It's the fact that you don't have anyone here *at all*. I know I can be closed off, and that's something I'm working on. I have a hard time letting people in because of how I've been burned in the past even though I'm starting to realize how much I can trust you. I guess I just wanted you to know that even if I don't always show it, I do care about you."

"So you called in the very people we were trying to avoid finding out about this because we thought they'd try to stop us?" I ask, the confusion clear in my tone.

"I told them the truth. They're the only people in the world who know apart from you, me, and my lawyer." He glances out the window before his eyes return to me. "They can try to stop it if they want. But this is between you and me. Do you still want to go through with it?"

I blow out a long breath, my gaze out the window now. "I don't know why, exactly, but yeah. I do."

"I do, too."

My eyes return to him, and he lets off a soft chuckle.

"That almost sounded like our vows," he says.

"You better give me a little more romance than that. At least if you want your family to buy it."

He's still laughing when he opens the door a few beats later. My brother and my best friend are standing there, and I still can't quite believe they're really here.

"So what the hell is this?" Josh asks, walking into the room.

I haven't moved from my spot at the table, and Nicki takes the chair next to me.

Luke blows out a breath and falls back into his spot on the couch. "It was supposed to just be a fake engagement, but your sister said she'd really marry me to shut up Michelle."

"And Todd," I remind him, and Luke nods.

"And Calvin," Luke says.

"Probably Jack, too. Pretty much everyone, really," I admit as I see from yet another angle how this is the only way to help Luke with his public image.

"Calvin?" Josh asks.

"He confronted me about the headline with the pregnancy scandal at the Beating Hunger in Vegas Charity Ball," Luke says. "He's pissed that I got Michelle pregnant and I'm not marrying her. He told me I need to get my priorities in line, and then he reamed me a new one in his office a few days later."

Josh shakes his head. "Oh man," he laments.

"Where *are* your priorities?" Nicki asks, and I'm sort of surprised she's the one jumping in with that question.

"I want to protect Ellie. I want to ensure my child is taken care of. And I want to fucking play football." He ticks off those items, seemingly in no particular order...but I can't help noting that I was first in that list, and his public image is nowhere on it at all.

"My sister better be first," Josh says, catching onto the same thing I did.

Luke sighs. "I'm sorry I dragged you into this," he says to me, and part of me wonders whether he really means it or if he's saying it for my brother's benefit.

"It's not like I put up some huge fight," I say. "Part of what you hired me for was to fix your image, right? Really, that should be on your list of priorities, too."

"But it's a stupid reason to get married," Josh says. "You two can't do this."

"We're doing it, and we invited you here to support us," Luke says firmly.

Josh seems angry. He looks from Luke to me and back again as he tries to form words to reply to that.

"Josh, it's okay," I say softly. "We've been back and forth over this a hundred times. Believe me. But we're both okay with it. We've both signed papers to protect ourselves. We're going in with eyes wide open. Luke has been so kind to help me, and I want to help him, too."

"I knew asking if she could stay with you was a mistake," Josh mutters.

"It wasn't a mistake," I say softly. "This is something we both want. We both benefit from it."

"You don't get married because you're benefiting from it. You get married because you love the other person," Josh says. He glances at Nicki, who's been uncharacteristically quiet during this whole thing. The way he looks at her tells me they're having some silent conversation that only the two of them are privy to.

"There are lots of reasons to get married," I say. "Maybe this isn't the traditional way, but we've talked out every angle. We've had his family trying to stop us for the last few days, so it would be great to feel like we have someone on our side here."

"Are you going to tell Mom and Dad?" Josh asks.

I clear my throat. "To be perfectly honest, I haven't really thought that far ahead."

"Eventually they'll find out, right?" Josh asks. "Once the media gets wind of it, it'll be everywhere. Don't you want to get ahead of that and tell them before they find out from someone else?"

"As soon as it's official, I'll call them," I say. I'm *really* not looking forward to that call.

"Don't you think they'll be upset they weren't invited?" Josh asks.

My eyes edge over to my soon-to-be-husband, who's awfully quiet during this exchange. I'm reminded of the magnitude of what we're doing, but that doesn't change the fact that I still want to go through with it anyway.

"We'll just tell them the truth," Luke says.

"You sure about that?" I ask.

Luke shrugs. "I trust you and your family implicitly." He motions toward my brother. "Obviously, or else I wouldn't have called in these two and filled them in on the truth."

I trust you and your family implicitly.

How come his actions and his words don't match up? He keeps giving off the vibes like he doesn't care, but then he does things that absolutely show that he does.

I guess he's just trying to make this situation more comfortable for me. He cares about me as a friend. He cares about me as the little sister of his best friend.

But despite inviting Josh and Nicki here and little things here and there that make me start to think otherwise, his words have been pretty solidly consistent in letting me know that's where it ends.

Nicki and Josh glance at each other, and then Nicki clears her throat. "Ellie, can we talk somewhere privately?"

I nod and stand. "Bedroom?"

"Oh yeah," Luke says lewdly. "To the bedroom."

"Come on, dude," Josh whines. "That's my wife and my *sister.*"

I giggle as Nicki follows me to the bedroom. I close the door behind her.

LISA SUZANNE

Before I even get the chance to turn around, she says flatly, "You're in love with him."

"What?" I ask, my hand flying to my chest in surprise.

She rolls her eyes. "It's so obvious, Ellie. Just admit it."

My brows dip. "What are you talking about? This is nothing more than a business arrangement. I'm in charge of his branding, and he's paying me to work as his publicist. That's it. His public image needs some help, so I'm doing what he's paying me to do." I'm babbling, and it's *totally* giving me away. I'm a bad liar, and Nicki knows me far too well. I need to shut it before she sees right through me.

"Then why do you look at him with hearts in your eyes?" She folds her arms across her chest. "Why are you doing this? Do you think he's the answer and you're finally going to get your happy ending with your Prince Charming by trapping some guy into marriage?"

That's sort of the thing about best friends, isn't it? They know everything about you, and they're here to point out the things you're pretending like you can't see. I appreciate what she's doing, and I appreciate that she's trying to be here for me in any way she can, but at the same time, I'm so damn tired of fighting everybody off.

"What happened to supporting me in whatever way you can?" I demand.

She sighs. "I don't want you to get hurt." She sits on the edge of the bed, and I collapse next to her.

"Too late," I admit.

"What's really going on here?" she asks. She lies back, too, and we're both staring up at the ceiling.

I sigh. "I have a confession."

"Yes?" she says, drawing out the word in a sing-song tone.

"I'm totally in love with him." I toss my arm over my eyes.

"Yeah, no shit. So what are you going to do about it?"

"There's more," I say. I might as well get it all off my chest at this point.

"More?"

I nod even with my arm still covering my eyes. "You can't tell Josh."

326

She tugs my arm, and when I glance over at her, she's lying on her side, leaning on her elbow as her hand props up her head. "I tell Josh everything, so if you want this to be a secret, don't tell me. But please tell me regardless of that."

Eventually he's going to find out anyway, right? I decide to rip off the bandage. "Remember my one night stand the night of your bachelorette party?" I move to mirror her position.

Her brows pinch together as it hasn't quite clicked yet. "Yeah..."

"It was Luke."

Her eyes widen. "It was *Luke*?"

I nod.

"How did you not know who he was?"

"You know I don't pay any attention to football. Although if I knew the players looked like him, maybe I would." I waggle my eyebrows playfully even though I know this is a serious conversation.

"He didn't know who you were, either?" she asks.

"I guess not. Josh probably just referred to me as his sister, not by name. It's not like he showed off pictures of me to his friends. Quite the opposite, in fact. It sounds like he warned them all off me."

"He didn't," Nicki breathes.

"Oh, he did," I confirm. I move so I'm lying on my back again, staring up at the ceiling again as I recite the story. "And Luke and I..." I trail off and sigh as that night comes back to me.

"Luke and you..." she repeats, prodding me into telling her the dirty details.

"We were strangers who met at the bar in a club even though neither of us is a clubber. We had one amazing, incredible, hot as fire, molten, steamy, unforgettably orgasmic night together, and then we parted ways. I snapped a selfie of the two of us so I could brag to you the next morning, but you were busy doing bride stuff so I held off. And actually, before I even got to your house, I ran into him at Starbucks, overheard him bragging about his conquest, which was me, and we had a little confrontation before I spilled all my coffee everywhere and it was the most embarrassing moment of my life so I told him I wanted to just pretend like I never saw him that morning."

"He was *bragging* about you?"

I nod. "Yeah. To Josh."

Nicki stifles a laugh. "Oh my God, wait until he finds out."

"To be fair, my plan was to brag about it to you, too."

"As I recall, you did. For a minute. But your parents were there making brunch." She laughs, but I'm failing to see what's so funny about my life.

Ah, who am I kidding? It's a freaking comedy.

"So then what?" she asks.

"Then Josh introduced him as his best man at the rehearsal dinner and I about fainted and then we became roommates and it's all backwards and so messed up and I went and totally fell in love with him. He's a goddamn prince."

"Oh, Ellie," she says softly. "How does he feel about you?"

I'm quiet for a beat, and then I answer honestly. "I have no idea. He's so closed off with his feelings that it's impossible to tell, but I keep thinking that he *does* feel something for me. It's just that he's been very clear I'm off-limits, whether it's because of some agreement he has with my brother or some misguided attempt at chivalry or something."

"I'll find out."

I sit up, and I shake my head as I stare down at her. "No," I say. "I don't want you getting involved."

"Too late," she says simply, and I'm a little terrified of the can of worms that I may have just opened.

CHAPTER 13

I stare at the video on my phone that was posted less than thirty minutes ago.

"Oh-em-gee, do I have some *piping* hot tea to spill today," Billy Peters says. The photo I saw this morning in my inbox alert flashes across the screen. It feels like a decade has passed since that moment. I nearly got killed by a horse, had some laughs with Luke at a brewery, faced off against his family for the umpteenth time since they arrived on the islands, and ran into my brother and sister-in-law.

What a day.

And it's not even over yet.

"Here we have Luke Dalton and fiancée Ellie Nolan, sister of the Vegas Aces star wide receiver Josh Nolan." As he talks, a heart forms around our faces. "But get this nugget. Jack Freaking Dalton, Luke's older, more successful, and arguably hotter brother, is there, too. Wait...is he hotter?"

The screen flashes to a side-by-side of the brothers, and no one can deny they share a lot of genes. Both ridiculously handsome, both with chiseled features, both with dark blue eyes. "I can't decide. Sound off in the comments. Anyway, they're all in Hawaii right now, and football star Nolan and his new bride just showed up, too. Any guesses why those closest to this hot couple would be flocking to the islands?"

He pauses, as if waiting for someone to scream an answer at whatever device they're watching this shitshow on. "It's not to get lei-ed." Billy winks. "That's right, peeps. Lukey Luke is there to *marry* his best friend's little sister. But his not-so-believing big brother was overheard questioning the legitimacy of this union. The words *charade* and *PR stunt* were used when Jack accused Luke of getting married for nefarious reasons, including the accusation that he's simply seeking their parents' approval. And believe it or not, there's more! Luke used to be married to...wait for it..." he pauses for a few beats, and then he says, "Jack's ex-girlfriend!" His mouth drops open with over-the-top dramatics. "I'll be digging into that today, so be sure to stay tuned for all the latest." He snaps his fingers and moves onto the next celebrity victim in his line of fire.

"Shit," I mutter.

"I'm so sorry to be the one to show you this," Kaylee says.

I shake my head. "No, don't be. You were the one telling them not to talk about it in public."

She nods as she presses her lips together. "This was why."

"Luke!" I yell. We have a half hour before our rehearsal is set to begin. My hair and make-up are done, and I'm moments away from getting out of my sweats and into the dress and heels I brought along for the occasion.

He appears in the doorway. He hasn't started getting ready yet. I roll my eyes and shake my head as I think to myself, *men*.

"Yes, my love?" he asks, and I swoon at the term of endearment for a beat before I get to the point.

"Did you see the Billy Peters video?" I ask, and he nods.

"The guy's a douchebag. I don't really care what he says."

"That's fine, but we need to hurry up and get ready. We need some pictures of the two of us to post as soon as possible to shut down rumors regardless of whether you care about Billy Peters. Super romantic stuff that shows how much you love me, 'kay?"

He chuckles. "Whatever you need, babe."

Kaylee sighs dreamily. "Gosh, you two. If people would just *see* you two together, they'd know it was real. They wouldn't even question it."

I press my lips into a thin smile at Luke as she heads out of the bathroom and toward the living room of our suite.

They wouldn't even question it.

I'm a *part* of it and I question it daily.

"How can you not care what he said?" I ask when it's just Luke and me.

He shrugs nonchalantly. "Shit like this gets posted all the time. You learn to tune it out."

Will I learn that, though? It sure doesn't feel like it. And it's not just that. I'm worried about Luke. I'm worried about Calvin getting hold of this information. How will he treat Luke at work if he knows this is just some stunt—and will he piece it together that it's a stunt for *his benefit*? He owns a freaking football team. It's not like he cruised into that position without some shred of intelligence.

We need to keep it quiet, and we need to make sure it's believable. Luke's job might be at stake if his boss allows personal vendettas to get in the way of his professional life, and after Luke's "reaming," I'm not so sure of Calvin's intentions.

Luke runs a comb through his hair, brushes his teeth, and gets dressed, and he's ready to go in under five minutes. He zips the back of the navy dress I chose, and I slip on my heels.

He studies me for a beat, and I cower a bit under his intense scrutiny. "You're stunning," he finally says.

So are you.

I wrinkle my nose instead of saying that. "Really?"

He chuckles. "And adorably modest, too." He taps my nose, and I giggle.

We head down to the beach with Kaylee, who is waiting for us in the lobby.

We're first. Alana isn't even here yet, and the sun is just starting its descent into the water.

The lighting is *perfect*.

"Kaylee, would you mind taking some shots?" I ask. I whip out my phone and pass it over.

"Of course not," she says, and she sets to work. Luke turns on the show. He kisses me. He holds me. He embraces me. His fingertips skate down my bicep. His arm comes around my shoulders. It may be a show, but it *feels* real. And all this against the backdrop of swaying palm trees and a nearly setting sun on the island of Maui as the sky boasts pinks and reds and golds.

331

I'm scrolling through the photos, admiring Kaylee's handiwork as well as what an attractive couple we make with Luke's arm tossed casually around my shoulders.

Luke and Kaylee are admiring the sunset beside me when I hear Nicki's voice. "Oh my God, there's the bride!"

I giggle, select one of my favorite images of the two of us with a simple ring emoji in the text, and click the post button before I shut off the screen.

Jack walks in with Carol and Tim a minute later, and Alana strides in last to begin our rehearsal.

"Ellie and Luke, you will stand here," she says. "And since we don't have a maid of honor or best man, it'll just be—"

"Change of plans," Luke interrupts. "My best friend just got back from his honeymoon in time to attend, so if he's up for it, I'd love for him to be my best man."

We all turn and look at Josh, who looks uncomfortable. But rather than blow our cover, he simply says, "Yes, of course. I'd be honored."

Everyone's eyes turn toward me. "And I'd love for Nicki to be my matron of honor," I say.

She squeals before she rushes over and hugs me, and I take that as a yes.

Alana runs through the ceremony, explains where the guests will stand, answers our questions, and releases us to dinner.

It was quick and painless, and to my extreme surprise, Jack stayed in his lane.

In less than twenty-four hours, I will be Mrs. Luke Dalton.

I feel a little weak in the knees at the thought, and I'm just crossing my fingers (and toes for extra luck) that everything goes according to plan between now and then.

But this is *my* life. Of course it won't.

CHAPTER 14

"It's not the bachelorette party I envisioned throwing for you since we were teenagers, but it'll have to do," Nicki says. Our feet are submerged in our own little footie-bathtubs as we wait for our pedicures to begin at the hotel spa after dinner.

Josh whisked Luke away for one last night out as bachelors, and Nicki brought me here.

"Room for one more?" Kaylee asks.

"Of course!" I say, perhaps a bit too enthusiastically as I pray and cross every finger and toe I have that Carol isn't also on the guest list for this little shindig...and that Jack isn't on the guest list for Luke's party. I highly doubt we'd be that lucky on both fronts, though.

Do I really want Kaylee here? No, not really. I'd love to chat unfiltered with my best friend, but it looks like that's not what the universe has in store for me tonight.

I lean back in the chair and work the remote for the massage elements built into the back. Some ball back there rolls up and down my back, and I feel more relaxed than I've felt in weeks.

Probably since before I met Luke Dalton.

My life has tumbled into a chaotic mess since the night we first met by chance at the bar. I almost miss the good old days when I was obsessed with glitter stickers and my bullet journal and had a crush on a boy I worked with who ended up not being very prince-like *or* very charming...you know, like a couple months ago.

"What are we doing after the pedicures?" Kaylee asks.

Nicki shrugs. "Club?"

I wrinkle my nose. "The last time I went to one..." I start to say, but then I trail off. The last time I went to one, I met Luke, and we had a one-night stand, and now I'm marrying him. Nicki knows this after our conversation yesterday, but Kaylee does not, and we don't need Kaylee finding out when we're this close to pulling this wedding off.

"Ooh, what happened?" Kaylee asks.

"I drank way too much," I lamely finish, and Nicki laughs.

"*Way* too much," she agrees, and I shoot her a glare. She turns to Kaylee. "It was my bachelorette party not so long ago. We partied in Vegas and this one could hardly handle her liquor."

Kaylee giggles. "Was Luke there?"

"Oh, Luke was there," Nicki says, and my eyes are bugging out of my head as I fear that Nicki's about to give away our secrets. She doesn't, though. She's a better actress than me. Instead, she says, "Come on, Ellie. It's your last night as a single woman. Let's live it up and have some fun."

I huff out a *fine* since she seems hellbent on this idea. Once my nails and toes are a very lovely, albeit virginal, bridal white, and they've dried the appropriate amount of time under the ultraviolet lights, we head upstairs to change.

An hour later, we're standing at the bar and I glance around the club. Blue and purple lights bounce off the walls, and there's even a few disco balls spaced evenly around the ceiling to make the lights glitter as they move. It's a typical club except for one thing: nobody on the dance floor is actually holding a drink.

The bartender approaches us, and Nicki orders a mai tai for each of us.

Just what I need. Rum.

We all turn to move toward the dance floor when the bartender calls our attention. "No drinks on the floor," he says, nodding toward the swell of people dancing.

My brows dip down. "We can't dance and drink?"

He shrugs. "Maui laws."

Nicki, Kaylee, and I all glance at each other, and then we shrug and tip back our first drink of the night. As I chug, I pray it doesn't make my face too puffy for my wedding day tomorrow, my mother's words from the day after Nicki's bachelorette party fresh in my mind about whether I'd had too much to drink because of how I looked.

Once we finish our drinks, we move to the dance floor. I feel positively ancient next to the young twenty-somethings (like Kaylee) dancing up a storm to songs I'm no longer familiar with, but I put in my best effort.

I'm two or three—possibly four—drinks deep when someone sidles up next to me at the bar while I'm waiting to order another round.

"Hey good lookin'," a deep voice says close to my ear. "You come here often?"

I chuckle.

"The last time I saw a sexy lady waiting by herself for a drink at the bar," the deep voice continues, "she was looking for someone to fuck just for one night."

I shiver at his words. Somehow the hard *k* in the word *fuck* presses my horny button, and an ache pulses between my thighs.

I glance up. My eyes meet Luke's. He's clearly a few drinks deep, too, and I have to admit, I'm semi-inexperienced with a drunk Luke. As I recall, the times we've indulged to the point of excess have ended with either sex, a kiss, or something that leaves me completely and utterly confused.

I glance just beyond him and find not just my brother, but also my fiancé's brother. So Jack *is* on the guest list.

My eyes return to Luke. "Fancy meeting you here," I say, and he chuckles.

"Not many club options on the island."

"Did you find a strip club at least?" I ask.

He shakes his head. "Your brother found a hostess bar, which is essentially the same thing except it wasn't. Maui has some randomly strange laws."

I nod toward the dance floor where drunk people are still dancing sans drinks. "You mean like how you can't drink and dance at the same time?"

He laughs as his eyes follow the direction of my nod. "Yep, that would be one of them."

"That's why I'm standing here by the bar. Then I can get smashed, go dance, and come back for another when I'm ready to cool down."

"Brains and beauty," he says, and he leans forward and plants a kiss on my lips.

My heart races and every nerve in my body seems to light up at once as his mouth covers mine. I can't help it when I grab the back of his head and kiss him like I fucking mean it...because I *do* mean it. My tongue assaults his as he meets me step for step, and if this is just some show for his brother, well, I don't care.

His fingertips skate up my spine, and I shiver in his arms as I tighten my grip on him. I'm kissing Luke Dalton, and I'm in freaking Heaven.

Until Luke stops kissing me at the sound of Josh's voice.

"Get a room!" my brother yells, and I'm sure it's to break up what he thinks is a fake kiss just for show...but jeez, that sure didn't feel fake.

It felt real, and it felt hot, and it felt like holy hell I want more of it.

Nicki appears behind my brother, and she mock-smacks him in the back of the head. He rubs the spot of her offense, but he's laughing when he turns around and takes her in his arms.

Kaylee and Jack stand by a bit awkwardly in the presence of these other two happy couples, but I have a hard time recognizing that it's actually awkward because of the amount of rum I've consumed.

I drag Luke to the dance floor, where I promptly begin grinding on his leg, and it's all just so reminiscent of our first night together. That was back before we knew one another, back before we were roommates and before feelings were involved and before I knew who he really was. It was such a simple time compared to the mess that has ensued ever since.

We dance until the edges of sobriety seep back in, and then Luke has to use the restroom. I head back toward the bar to grab us each another round, and this time my big brother sidles up beside me just as I pick up my freshly poured mai tai.

"I know this is just pretend or whatever, but I have to tell you something," Josh says.

I glance over at him with raised brows that invite him to say whatever it is he needs to say as I sip the sweet liquid that's definitely going to leave me with a wicked headache in the morning.

"I'm pretty sure he's in love with you, Ellie."

Mai tai sprays out of my mouth.

"Classy," he mutters, pawing at his cheek.

"I'm sorry," I say. "But...what?"

"He's different around you. I saw him when he was with Michelle. He was never like this with her."

"Like what?" I ask. I go to take another sip, but Josh puts a hand on my forearm to stop my forward progress. Annoying, yes, but also probably necessary for him.

He shrugs. "I don't know. Happy? It's just the way he looks at you."

"It's an act, Josh. He doesn't want to be with me." I refrain from adding, *partly because of whatever you said to him.*

He shakes his head before he presses his lips together. "He's not that good of an actor."

My tummy somersaults at his words, and then Nicki drags him back to the dance floor. I'm left with that thought as I stand by the bar by myself trying to reconcile what I just heard from Josh with my actual feelings for Luke.

What if this whole time he's been hiding feelings for me, too? What if he's just been waiting for Josh to get back to clear things with his best friend before admitting how he really feels?

Or maybe Josh is just drunk, too. That's the more likely scenario.

I toss back the rest of my mai tai so I can return to the dance floor. I set my glass on the bar, and I haven't even turned around when a deep voice close to my ear sends shivers down my spine...and not the good kind. "Give up the act, Ellie. Don't marry him. I'm the better brother."

I turn to the side and raise a brow at Jack. Just as I open my mouth to tell him how much better Luke really is than him, he stops me.

"You can't deny there's something between us," he says.

My eyes are hot on his. *Is* there something here? Maybe. But would I ever do that to Luke?

Not on your life.

Jack thinks he can take what he wants, but I'm not like the others, as I've told Luke time and again. I will *never* bend for Jack. Not when I'm so close to finally getting Luke to see that we could be everything together.

Jack's a little wasted, too, and he lowers his head toward me like he's moving in for a kiss as he loops an arm around my waist.

He may be charming. He may be sexy. He may be athletic and talented and rich and smell like a dream.

But he's also an asshole. He's rude and demeaning and crude. He takes what he wants without a care to who he might be hurting.

And the worst thing about him? He's not Luke.

I turn my head and move my face toward his ear. For a second, I'm sure he thinks I'm going to suck on his earlobe. I'm not.

Instead, I say directly into his ear, "You need to back off. I love Luke, and that's why I'm marrying him tomorrow. I'm not a pawn in your game. I'm your future sister-in-law."

Rather than listen to my words, he leans in and nuzzles my neck. I pull back out of his orbit, and when I do, I catch him looking with a sly smile over my shoulder.

I turn and follow his gaze, and when I see who he's smiling at, my heart drops.

Luke's staring at the two of us from halfway across the room in what had to look like a very compromising position as I nestled in close to his ear and Jack held me in his arms.

Luke purses his lips and shakes his head before he moves toward the door.

Does he really think I'd go for Jack? Even after the horse incident?

And then I realize...of course he thinks that. He'll *always* think he's going to lose to his brother because *he always has.*

But not this time.

"Shit," I mutter, and then I take off toward my fiancé so I can explain what he just saw.

CHAPTER 15

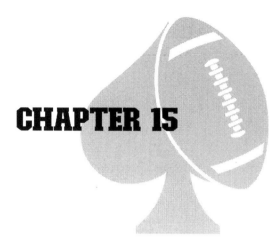

I find Luke waiting out front for a ride.

He gives me the kind of look that stops me a few feet away from him. I can't gauge his mood, not when there are so many variables at play. We're both a little drunk, emotions are high, we're getting married tomorrow...it's a lot.

But anger dominates as it seems to be vibrating off him.

"Figures this would be the time the car takes forever to pick me up," he mutters.

"I can explain whatever you think you just saw."

"Well if that isn't a textbook admission of guilt..." He glances away from me. "No need. This is all just for show. Right?"

I blow out a breath at the reminder. "I guess. I just..." I trail off. I just...*what?* I'm in love with Luke? I can't tell him that—not when he's been so clear that this is just a business deal to him. "I don't have any interest in your brother."

He huffs out a laugh. "Right. Because women are never interested."

I take a step closer to him, and then another. I reach out and grab his hand. I squeeze it even though his remains limp, and part of me is touched that he cares while the other part of me thinks it's just because he's worried our little stunt here will go public.

"I'm not like the others, Luke," I say softly, repeating something I've told him before. "I see what he does. I see how your family treats you. I'd *never* give into him no matter how hard he tried."

"So he tried?" he asks flatly. "Again?"

I press my lips together in a non-answer that says everything.

He nods. "Okay," he says softly.

I squeeze his hand again. "I'd never do that to *you*. I'm on your side. Haven't you figured that out yet?"

"I don't need anybody on my side," he asserts.

"Okay," I say, doing my best to placate someone who's clearly angry and trying to hold it together as he awaits his car. And if I hadn't had five—or was it seven?—mai tais, I might be able to hold back from getting mad at him for the way he's acting. But I did have those drinks, and frustration permeates my blood.

"Fine. Push me away all you want," I spit at him. A dart of dizziness rushes through my head. I think I just need some water. I don't like fighting with Luke, but he keeps pushing me away and frankly I'm sick of it. "The fact of the matter is that we have to live together for at least the next year, and I'd rather do it on friendly terms than on whatever this is."

I spin on my heel to go back inside the club both to get some water and return to the girls who are probably still dancing as they wonder where the hell I went...and I come face to face with Kaylee.

All the blood drains from my face and that dizziness from a second ago gets a little stronger as my stomach heaves.

"Kaylee," I say, wondering exactly how much she just overheard as a buzz plays around my brain. I hear Luke mutter a curse word, but my stomach heaves again. "Uh..."

I'm about to ask her how much she overheard, but I'm never able to.

The mai tais catch up with me, and a second later, I'm heaving an embarrassing amount of liquid right into the hedges by the entrance to the club.

Well, I guess that's one way to avoid the conversation with Kaylee. For now, anyway.

Luke's SUV arrives, and he helps me into the back. "Wait here," he says to the driver. He says something to Kaylee, and then he rushes back inside. He returns less than a minute later and hands me a bottle of water when he slides into the car.

I must pass out, because the next thing I know, sun streams through the curtains in our room and a pounding on the door matches the pounding in my head.

I'm in for a rude awakening in more ways than one.

"Don't do this," Kaylee says when I open the door. I glance around the suite, and I don't see Luke. He's not on the couch, the bathroom door is wide open, and his side of the bed is untouched. The balcony door is open, but I don't see him in either of the chairs out there, either, and it's pretty common for him to leave them open for both fresh air and the soundtrack of the ocean rolling in and out of the shore.

Maybe he went down for an early breakfast, and I don't even know where we left things. As I recall, though, we were in the middle of a pretty heated argument when I tossed my mai tais into the hedges.

"Don't do what?" I croak, my mouth dry from the amount of alcohol I consumed last night. I rustle through my suitcase for some ibuprofen.

"Marry my brother. If you don't love him...don't do it."

I find what I'm looking for and down three with nearly an entire bottle of water. There's no way my skin will have a dewy glow tonight for the wedding, not with rum sweating out of my pores. Six—or was it eight?—mai tais last night was a really dumb decision.

I sit on the couch and look up at my soon-to-be sister-in-law. It's not like I have anything else to lose at this point. He's not around to hear me, and if she runs to Luke with my confession, well, then one of two things will happen. Either he'll finally know the real truth rather than assuming it's just some little crush or he'll assume Kaylee is lying.

"That's the thing, Kaylee," I say softly. "I *do* love him."

Her brows dip. "But last night you said..."

I hold up a hand to stop her. "I'm in love with your brother. I'm not sure what you heard last night, but we'd both appreciate it if you could just keep whatever you think you heard to yourself."

She blows out a breath and walks over to the window. "You're asking me to choose between Luke and the rest of my family."

"No, I'm not," I say, and a wave of emotion plows through me. "I'm asking you to keep quiet about what you might've overheard. All that matters is that by the end of the day, I'll be married to the man I've fallen in love with. And whatever you overheard last night when we were fighting, that's the honest to God truth of the matter."

"But does he love you?" she asks.

"I like to think so," I say softly. And it's true. If nothing else, I think he's come to love me as a friend or maybe by default as the little sister of his best friend. Of course, in my wildest dreams, the things Josh said to me last night would be true—Luke would be in love with me, too.

Maybe I dreamed up that whole conversation. I was pretty drunk at the time.

I glance at the clock. "I have an appointment at the spa I need to get to. Please, please just be on Luke's side for this. He needs someone in his family who he can trust, and I'd love it if that person was you."

She purses her lips as she stares at me for a long beat. "I'll think about it. But Ellie, I need you to think about something, too. Whatever you're getting out of this, just be warned that you're also getting the Dalton last name. Sometimes it's cursed. Sometimes it isn't. If you're marrying my brother today, do it with that in mind. He never wanted to get married again, and there are reasons why."

"Thanks," I say simply, mostly because I don't know what else to say. She walks out the door, and I move toward the shower.

Except just as the door closes behind Kaylee, I hear a noise out on the balcony.

I turn to look in that direction, and that's when Luke appears in the doorway.

"You're in love with me?" he asks softly.

Always double check the balcony before you make big secret confessions, Ellie.

Always.

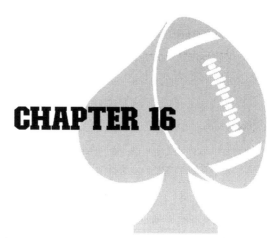

CHAPTER 16

"Yes. Yes, I have feelings for you. Yes I am in love with you. Yes it clouds everything and makes this an even dumber idea to actually marry you, but I'm doing it anyway whether or not you feel the same."

Do you feel the same?

I don't have the nerve to ask even though I just laid my entire heart on the line.

"Thank you," he says softly.

I try not to let it bother me that he doesn't immediately reciprocate my feelings. I've already locked into this for a year, so it doesn't matter. But I can't stop thinking how much better the next year will be if he *does* have feelings for me.

"Sure," I say awkwardly.

"Last night..." His eyes dip away from mine toward the floor and then out the window. "I wanted to tell you how much it hurt me to see you with my brother like that. I wanted to be pissed. I wanted to go back into that club and explode on my asshole brother. But then you got sick and I changed into a different person. I just needed to take care of you. To get you back here safe. It didn't matter what happened with Jack."

"Nothing happened with Jack," I say quietly.

He nods. "I know. But not because he didn't try." His eyes move back to mine. "So thank you."

"Sure," I say, and it's the second time I use that word in the span of a few seconds, and it's not any less awkward this time. I'm sure he has more to say, but I'm hungover and tired and just want to go shower to feel human again before we dig into all this.

"Look, I need to take a shower, but I don't trust your sister. Or Jack. Or any of them, really."

There's a knock at our door.

"Then it's a good thing I have a plan," he says as he moves toward the door.

My brows dip down. "What plan?"

He opens the door, and a woman steps in.

"Alana?" I say, totally confused as to why she'd be here.

"Good morning," she says to both of us, and then she turns to my fiancé. "Luke, I got your message and rushed over here as soon as I could. What's going on?" she asks.

"We'd like to get married," Luke says.

Alana and I both regard him for a moment with confusion, and then Alana says, "Right. Tonight at six."

He shakes his head. "Before then."

My heart thumps in my chest. *What?* Somehow I manage to keep myself from reacting in front of Alana, though.

Luke shrugs. "Between my brother and his ego, her brother not wanting us to get married, and the media already sniffing around, we want a private ceremony so we're legally married before the one tonight at six. Then if anyone jumps in with whatever bombs they plan to detonate, it'll be too late."

She nods, and she holds a hand over her heart in an *oh-my-God-that's-so-romantic* kind of motion. "Of course, sir." Her eyes edge to me. "This is what you want, too?"

I force the confusion off my face. "Yes," I breathe, shocked that *this* is his plan but here for the ride anyway. What difference does a few hours make in the grand scheme of things? "Just give me an hour to make myself presentable."

Luke turns to me, and his eyes sweep over me. "You're perfect."

The words don't feel like an act when he says them with such warmth. He wouldn't *really* need to put on an act for Alana anyway...so is this real? Is he being sincere?

"I'm hungover and I just rolled out of bed," I counter.

Alana laughs. "You two are meant to be. I'll call Manny and make sure he can preside over your early ceremony, but I don't

344

anticipate any problems. Would you like to do this here in your room?"

Luke nods. "Right over here," he says, nodding toward the slider doors that lead onto the balcony. "I'd say on the balcony, but we never know who's listening."

Alana nods and turns to leave.

"And Alana?" he says. She turns around. "Thank you."

She smiles. "Always happy to help a couple as in love as the two of you." She winks and heads out, and I'm about to run to the shower because holy shit, I'm getting married in an hour, when Luke stops me with a hand on my arm.

"Are you absolutely sure this is okay?" he asks me, his voice full of earnestness.

"Yes," I whisper. I nod resolutely. "I'm sure. There's no turning back now. I'm committed to this, and I will be here with you for the next year. We'll get that image turned around. We'll get through the birth of that baby. We'll get Michelle, Calvin, Savannah, and Todd off our backs. And in a year, this will all just be a distant memory."

I refrain from adding the parts about how my bank account will be a little more padded and my heart will be a little more cracked and how I don't *want* it to be a distant memory.

His eyes turn down to the ground. "Thank you," he murmurs. "Let's not tell a soul about this early version until after the wedding tonight, okay? I don't want it getting back to Jack, or worse, to the media. There are too many ears always listening."

I loop my pinkie finger through his. "I pinkie promise."

* * *

I slip on a simple white dress I find in the hotel gift shop, allow my hair to fall straight down to the middle of my back, and brush on some light make-up. I don't look as disgusting as I did less than an hour ago, and I smell a hell of a lot better.

Alana knocks on the bedroom door of the suite, and I let her in without peeking out to see if Luke has changed. She hands me a small bouquet of colorful hibiscus flowers. "I took them from the hotel lobby. Don't tell anyone." Her eyes twinkle.

She agreed to be our witness, and only she, Manny, and the two of us know about this secret pre-wedding wedding ceremony. But this is the one that matters. This is the one that makes our union legal.

"Housekeeping is just finishing up out there," she says, and I nod. I take a few beats alone in the bathroom, spritz on a little perfume, and meet Alana back by the door that leads from the bedroom out to the main area of the suite.

"You ready for this?" she asks.

I force away the tears that spring to my eyes and draw in a deep breath. I never really thought I'd be doing this alone.

My mother may drive me crazy, but she's still my mother. My dad isn't here to walk me down the aisle. My brother, my best friend, other friends...none of them even know we're doing this.

It's just Luke and me.

There's something both romantic and terrifying about that.

"Ready," I say resolutely, and then she opens the door.

The suite has been transformed. Furniture has been moved, but that's not what strikes my attention first. It's the sheer amount of flowers and candles situated around the room, like Luke gave romance a real effort for this.

My heart squeezes.

My chest aches.

I take in the view of this room, the place where I'll take vows with another person that'll only really matter for the next year.

Alana moves first toward Manny, who stands with his back to the slider doors. Luke is on his left, and it's my turn to move my feet until I'm standing beside Luke.

The brightness of the sun is behind him from the angle where I stand, darkening his entire being into a shadow, and I can't help but pray that's not some sort of strange omen.

A song plays from someone's device somewhere as I start walking, just the slow keys of a piano, and it takes me a second to figure out that it's "Speechless" by Dan and Shay.

My hands tremble around the bouquet, and once I step into place beside Luke, I look up into his eyes.

I'm going to regret this.

I'm going to get hurt.

But I still want to do this.

For him.

Everything seems to fade away as our eyes meet, and despite the warnings in my own head about how I'm only going to come out the loser here, I don't care. I love him, and it's as simple and as complicated as that.

"Please join hands," Manny says. Alana reaches for my bouquet, and I pass it over.

Luke takes my hands in his. His are warm, and mine are ice cold.

"You look beautiful," he whispers. My lips tip up in a smile, and I'm about to tell him how freaking hot he looks in his charcoal shorts and black button-down shirt, but Manny cuts in before I get a chance to.

This feels like *us*, though. I'm in a simple dress. He's in something he might wear down to lunch. And maybe that's the thing—when it's for the two of us, it's pared down to the essentials. When it's a show for others, there's more that we're forced to put into it.

"We're gathered here today to unite Luke and Ellie in the bonds of matrimony," Manny says. "I'm going to give you the short version. Do you, Luke, take Ellie to be your lawfully wedded wife?"

"I do," Luke says.

"And do you, Ellie, take Luke to be your lawfully wedded husband?" Manny asks me.

I take a deep breath. "I do," I say on the exhale.

"Luke, please take the ring for Ellie and repeat after me." He gives Luke a beat to reach into his pocket for the ring, and then he continues. "Ellie, I give you this ring as a symbol of our union. With this ring, I thee wed."

Luke repeats the words as he slides on the diamond-encrusted band that fits with my engagement ring.

"And Ellie, Luke's ring?" he asks me. Alana hands it to me. "Repeat after me. Luke, I give you this ring as a symbol of our union. With this ring, I thee wed."

I repeat his words.

"You have consented to matrimony and both Alana and I have witnessed this exchange," Manny says. "By the authority vested in me by the state of Hawaii, I now pronounce you husband and wife. Noho me ka hau'oli," he says in Hawaiian, and then in English, "Be happy."

Luke's lips spread into a smile, and I can't help when mine do, too. He leans forward and plants a gentle kiss on my mouth. It may be soft, and it may be simple, but it's everything. It lights me up from the inside. I want more. I want *everything*, and I want it with Luke.

Is that too much to ask?

CHAPTER 17

"You're sure you want to do this?" Josh asks. He's playing it off like a normal wedding day question to the bride from her big brother in front of the women working on Nicki and me, but we both know what he's really asking.

I can't help but find the irony in the fact that I had to convince both Josh and Nicki they wanted to get married on their wedding day while they're trying to convince me of the opposite.

I don't dare open my eyes as the make-up artist, Leila, dusts a shimmery shadow over them. Nicki is getting her hair done a few feet away by Mia. "Positive."

"Then I won't stop you."

I feel Leila step away, and I open my eyes. "Thank you," I murmur.

He gives me a sad smile. "Mom and Dad are gonna be pissed that I was here and they weren't."

I press my lips together. "Yeah," I say. I don't know what else to say. Would they really want to be present for their daughter's first wedding even though it's fake? Or does this whole thing appear a certain way because of the very fact that they aren't here?

"Just be careful," he says quietly.

"He's *your* best friend, Josh. You're the one who brought us together in the first place. Remember?"

He chuckles. "That's not what I heard from Nicki."

My cheeks flame. "She told you?"

"Of course she did." He reaches for my hand and squeezes it. "Take care of him, and take care of yourself, too."

"We're fine," I say, but his kind words are kind of making me feel like that's not entirely true. *I am not fine, and I'm willing to bet Luke isn't, either.* "Now go and talk to him, too. The guy who never wanted to get married again probably needs his best friend more than ever."

He nods. "See you out there," he says.

"I'll be the one in white."

He snort-laughs. "Like you can really get away with wearing white to your wedding."

I offer him a glare and a middle finger, and he leaves his echoes of laughter behind as he walks out of the room.

Nicki squeezes my hand as Mia and Leila talk to each other a few feet away. "You handled that well, but now it's time to be honest with me," she says softly so the two women don't overhear whatever she's about to say. "Are you sure you really want to go through with this?"

I want to tell her I've already done it. So badly. She's my best friend, and I tell her everything.

Is there really any reason not to?

Just one.

Luke told me not to tell a soul.

Leila and Mia may seem like they're not listening a few feet away...but that doesn't mean they won't hear me.

I keep my trap shut even though it's one of the hardest things I've ever had to do.

I'm *married*. It's a crazy thing to believe. I'm somebody's *wife*.

If you would've told me that I'd be married by the end of June when Belinda walked into Todd's office in Chicago and caught me just as I crashed into an orgasm, I never would've believed it.

And it doesn't really matter *why* I'm married. The fact is that I'm now Mrs. Luke Dalton.

There's a knock at the door, and Nicki runs to answer it. Mia puts a few extra pins in my hair to make sure it's secure, but I'm just about at the point where all I have to do is slip into my dress, buckle my shoes, and put on my jewelry.

Kaylee appears in the doorway. "Can I talk to you?" she asks. She glances at the women packing up their supplies. "Alone?"

I nod. "Can you excuse us, please?" I say to the women, and Mia closes the door behind the two of them as they walk out to join Nicki in the suite. "What's wrong, Kaylee?"

"Don't do this," she pleads. "Don't go through with it. Don't make me choose between keeping your secrets and telling my family the truth."

"Kaylee..." I start, not exactly sure where I'm going with that but sure I don't want to have this conversation. It's too late, anyway. *We're already married. We've already done it.* "You're not keeping secrets. I love him."

"If you love him, think about *him*. He might be my older brother, but he's the one who needs protecting right now. I don't know what your motivation is, or even what his is, really, but there has to be some other way to solve whatever the problem is aside from what you're doing."

"You're absolutely right," I say, surprised we agree on something here. "He does need protecting. From your brother. From your parents. From the ex-wife and the ex-girlfriend trying to drain the life out of him. He has taken care of me, and I'm going to take care of him, too."

That's a promise.

She stares at me for a beat.

"Look, Kaylee. I love him. That's what matters. Why does it matter to you?"

"I told you earlier, there are curses with family you don't want to get mixed into. Especially in your line of work. If the truth came out, they'd both be in trouble, and a simple Instagram post sure as hell isn't going to fix it." Her arms are crossed and one brow is raised as she snarls at me.

"Thanks for the warning, but I can take care of myself. And my soon to be husband." My voice is full of a certainty I'm not sure I feel. "Now I need to get dressed. You can see yourself out."

She purses her lips at me with a glare before she spins on her heel and walks out, and damn it all, I thought she was the one who was supposed to be on Luke's side.

It sure as hell doesn't feel like it. If anything, it feels like Luke and I are in this alone. Just one more thing to bond me to my new husband, I guess.

I don't know if she's running off to tell Jack what she thinks she heard or if she's running to the media, and I don't know *why* she'd do that if she wants to protect her brother. Either way, I'm vibrating with anger.

I have to brush it off, though. I have to appear as the glowing bride because I'm about to walk down the aisle. Even though we're already married, this is the one we'll post pictures of. We didn't even actually *take* any photos at our real ceremony.

This one is the one for show, though. This time, the staff photographer at our hotel will take photos so we can sell them to the highest bidder when the media gets wind of our nuptials...if they haven't already.

CHAPTER 18

"You're a glowing bride," Nicki says with a smile as her eyes sweep down my white lace, chiffon, and satin gown. The top is a gorgeous lacy design with v-neck that fades into a simple bottom with a slit. "If I didn't know the truth, I'd really believe it."

I glance at her. "It's real for me, even if we're not at the marriage stage yet in real time."

"I know it is," she says softly. "And maybe you'll get there."

I nod and press my lips together as I try to ward off the sudden heat pricking behind my eyes.

"You ready for this?" We're standing by the pool, just out of sight from those gathered to witness our little event.

I nod. "This is just a formality at this point," I say.

Her brows dip down. "Because it's fake?"

I press my lips into a small smile and shake my head. I can tell her now, right? There's nobody around us really, and we're seconds away from doing this in front of everybody anyway. "Because we're already married."

This time her brows arch up nearly off her forehead. "What?"

I smile. "We did it this morning. We didn't want to take any chances that the media would find out before we made it legal."

She smacks me in the arm. "And you didn't tell me?"

"I couldn't. My husband made me promise."

Alana comes rushing up to us. "Nicki, you're up," she says, panting like she was trying to wave us down but we missed it due to my big confession.

Nicki narrows her eyes at me. "All right, girlfriend. Let's do this, but later we're going to have to have a chat about how you don't keep these big things from your best friend."

I laugh as she hustles to get into place. "The last time I told you a secret, Josh knew three seconds later," I remind her, and she giggles as she starts her walk toward the aisle.

And then I'm by myself for a beat before Alana will prompt me to start walking.

I don't have to question whether what I'm doing is right since it's already done, and that helps push away any nerves I might've felt in doing this.

I wish my parents were here, but since the *actual* wedding already took place and *nobody* was there, I don't suppose it really matters.

I try to get a glimpse ahead, but I'm around the corner and out of sight so nobody will see me per wedding traditions.

I wonder who's gathered there on the beach, whether Luke called in any more surprises, whether Jack will be sitting there exuding all that sexual energy in my direction like he always does even though I'm literally standing there marrying his brother.

"We made it!" a familiar voice behind me calls in victory. "She's right there."

It can't be.

I turn slowly around and spot two people rushing toward me.

"Dad?" I say softly, those tears pinching behind my eyes again. "Mom?"

"Oh honey," my mom says, and she flies into my arms.

I can't cry. It'll ruin my make-up.

But dammit, my freaking parents are here. This is bigger than just Luke and me and some ridiculous plan. Did Josh invite them here...or did Luke?

Because if it was Josh, well, that's one thing. But if it was Luke...maybe that means something.

It's just a show for the media. For Jack. For the Daltons. That's one possible meaning.

But another possible meaning is that he listened to me. He saw that I had nobody here and he called in Josh and Nicki, and it doesn't feel like that was just for the media or just for show. It feels like it was just for me.

What if he did this, too? Does that mean he cares?

"Luke told us everything," my mom says softly. "And we don't understand the reasons, but you're our little girl, and we will always, *always* support you."

That.

That right there is *family*.

They're not here to talk me out of it. They're here to stand by my side and support me.

I wish Luke had that, too. And he will, now that he's married to me.

"I couldn't let you walk down the aisle alone," my dad says, and those damn tears tip over and I just cross my fingers that I don't have runny mascara raccoon eyes.

"I love you guys," I say to my parents, and they take turns hugging me before they each grab onto one of my arms and Alana signals us to start walking down the aisle.

It's exactly like I pictured my dream beach wedding.

Well, *almost* exactly.

I'm sort of missing the guy who's madly in love with me and the majority of our closest friends and extended families, but at least I have my dad to walk me down the aisle.

Everything else, though? Spot on, from the magical glow of the sun as it descends into the ocean to the calm, rolling tranquility of the waves, to the prince standing up front as he waits for me to walk down the aisle.

I thought I'd be walking by myself.

I thought nobody would be giving me away, and not in some statement of independence on my part, but rather the idea of chucking tradition since this isn't real anyway.

As soon as I turn the corner, I find him in the small group gathered...but then my eyes always seem to search him out. It's as if nobody else is here, and maybe they aren't. I wouldn't know because I can't look away from him, and tears prick behind my eyes yet again when his meet mine. I sense a bit of awe, a bit of wonder...and maybe some heat, maybe some love—or at least some sort of affection. He *has* to at least care about me, right?

I dissect the possibility of heat in his eyes. I certainly look different from the first time we did this just a few hours ago after being pampered and styled by an entire team, but he does, too.

He wears a dark khaki linen suit with a white shirt underneath, his tan skin glowing and his blue eyes shining as he waits for me to walk to him. I move slowly as the same song as earlier plays, and I feel a little speechless myself as I stare into the eyes of the guy who will play the part of my husband for the next year.

A dart of sadness streaks through my chest at the thought of actually parting when this next year is up. And then another pang of sadness creeps in, but unlike the first streak...this one sticks.

It's not like we can't still be friends when it's over, but it means I'll have to move out of the Barbie dreamhouse. It means the fantasy will be over. It means reality will kick in again and I can resume my hunt for Prince Charming.

He's told me time and again it's not him. But when I look at him...I still see the prince. I'm not convinced that he isn't. I still hold onto the night we met, that night when he made me laugh and feel safe even though we were strangers and he pushed my body past any sort of pleasure that it had ever felt before. He was a prince to me that night, but nobody's perfect—not even Prince Charming. I bet even *he* had a past. Even *he* must have made poor decisions or acted out of jealousy or made the princess cry.

I swipe at the tears as they stream down my cheeks. I offer a smile and play them off as happy tears since this is supposed to be the happiest moment of my life.

It's not.

When I join Luke in front of Manny, he stares at me. His eyes don't flick from mine—not even to greet my parents. That just causes another surge of emotion to course through me.

"Welcome friends," Manny says. "We are gathered here today to unite Luke and Ellie in the bonds of matrimony. Who gives this woman to be married?"

"Her mother and I do," my dad says, his voice wavering with emotion, and for a split second I think what we're doing here is all wrong. My even-keel dad rarely shows emotion, and I feel like a huge disappointment to my family as I take vows to someone knowing this is only temporary—knowing that *my parents* know this is only temporary.

But then I look into Luke's eyes as my parents back away, and somehow everything seems right again. He thumbs a tear from my cheek before he takes my hands in his. My smile is genuine through my sadness. I'm happy to be here with him, truly—I just wish there could be a different ending for us...a fairy tale ending.

Manny begins the ceremony. "This is not the beginning of Luke and Ellie's story but rather an acknowledgement of the next chapter they will write together. These bonds are not to be taken lightly, and today they will affirm their relationship both formally and publicly. In Hawaii, we say E hele me ka pu'olo, and that means you make every person, place, or condition better than before, always. This is the sacred Hawaiian way, and as we witness the union here today, we can see that Ellie and Luke make each other better than before."

Luke leans over and presses a soft kiss to my cheek. I'm not sure if it's for show or if it's a rare expression of emotion, a way of thanking me for what I'm doing. I hope I'm leaving *him* in a better place than he was before. I hope what we're doing is for the overall good. But I'm still certain I'm going to regret it.

"With that in mind, if anyone objects to this union, speak now or forever hold your peace."

I hold my breath as my worried eyes meet Luke's during Manny's ridiculously long pause. I can't bear to look out over those gathered here. I'm sure Kaylee has objections—unless Luke got to her. Jack has objections. Even Carol and Tim do, and Josh and Nicki and my parents. And that's it. That's everybody that's here—at least I *think* that's it. And I *think* they're all here, but I'm not really sure. My eyes locked up on Luke's when I walked in and I never looked to see.

It would be far too cliché for someone to actually stand up and object at this point, wouldn't it? We already know everyone here has their doubts. We probably should've had the foresight to tell Manny not to include that line in the script. Their objections don't really matter, anyway, since we've already done this.

"With no objections to this union, the happy couple will now make their vows," Manny says, and I finally exhale. Luke does, too—visibly.

We're past the scary part. It's smooth sailing from here...right? In someone else's story, maybe. Not in mine.

"Luke, do you take Ellie to be your lawfully wedded wife and equal partner, to join with her and share with her all that is to come, and to commit to a life together from now until you part?" Manny asks.

We were careful about keeping that whole *until death do us part* thing out of our vows. Nothing Manny just said is a lie. We both know what we're vowing to here, and when we *part* in a year, we'll both be able to say that we stayed true to our vows.

Hopefully, anyway. I don't plan on taking on any other *partners* in the next year, and I don't think he does, either.

"I do," Luke says.

Manny turns to me, "And Ellie, do you take Luke—"

"Stop!" a woman's voice yells. It's out of breath and loud and screeches Manny's sentence to a halt as we all freeze.

I spot the look of horror on Luke's face as he turns his head before I do in the split half-second it takes for me to turn my head and see a woman running down the aisle toward us. Jack steps out into the aisle with a broad, sly smile on his face. And when my eyes fall on the woman who rushes up toward Jack's side, a pit forms deep in my stomach.

The woman holds a hand over her stomach as she moves toward us, and I'm about to glance over at Luke to gauge his reaction when she yells again.

"Stop the wedding!"

The entire wedding party sits in stunned silence, and then Luke hisses a single word: "Michelle."

To be continued in Book 4, **WAITING GAME**.

Waiting GAME

LISA SUZANNE

DEDICATION

To my 3Ms.

CHAPTER 1

"What the hell are you doing here?" Luke demands.

"I came to stop this wedding," she says. "You can't marry her."

"Why not?" Luke asks.

"Because we all know it's not real," Michelle says, her tone full of accusations. "You still have feelings for me. It's the only reason you'd go through with this. Luke, don't marry her."

My brows dip. It's the only reason he'd go through with this? What the hell is that supposed to mean? Does she think he's marrying me as a show to get her back?

She really is freaking delusional. More reasons why we need a paternity test. Luke needs hard evidence that he really is this baby's father.

Luke snorts before his eyes turn on his brother. "And I suppose you're the one responsible for calling her to let her know I'm getting married?" He doesn't even dignify her delusional words with a response.

"Does it matter *why* she showed up?" Jack asks.

Luke rolls his eyes. "What do you want, Michelle?"

"I want you, Luke. I've *always* wanted you. I'm carrying your baby. Don't marry some girl you hardly know," she says, and I can't help my own very un-bride-like snort.

"And what, marry you instead?" he asks derisively.

She glances at Jack before she turns back to Luke, and I can't help but wonder what that small look was all about. "Yes," she says, and cue the hands on her stomach that's barely even showing. "I want you to be happy. I want you to find something real with someone who deserves you, and that's not her. This baby deserves his or her parents to be together, not for her dad to be with some random chick he just met."

Oh hell no, bitch. Did she just take a shot at *me*?

I'm about to put on my fighting gloves, and I even see Josh fume with anger at her words out of the corner of my eye when Luke steps in again. "Marrying Ellie is what will make me happy. I've fallen in love with her," he says, his eyes locking on mine. "Nothing you can say here will stop us."

Jack loops a protective arm around Michelle's shoulders. "What if I have something to say?"

Luke and I both regard Jack with wariness.

"It has come to my attention that this entire thing is a sham," Jack says. "Apparently they have an agreement for the next year."

Very few people aside from Luke and me know that, so the culprit is most likely Kaylee, depending what she thinks she heard last night.

That damn traitor.

Luke's eyes move to his sister, and when I glance over at him, he looks angry and a little sad. He trusted her. She was the *only* one he trusted in his entire family.

Kaylee stands up, her shoulders hitched up with apologies as she looks at Luke. "I had to do something after what I overheard last night."

"What did you overhear?" Carol asks.

"They were fighting," she says to her mom but also to the group as a whole, "and Ellie said something about how they have to live together for the next year and she'd rather do it on friendly terms than fighting." Kaylee looks back at Luke as all the blood drains from my face. She's tossing out these secret conversations in front of Michelle...one of the main people that pushed Luke into having this idea in the first place, along with her father—Luke's boss.

"I'm sorry. I just...this is all so fast, and I'm just trying to protect your heart." Kaylee's hand is on her chest, which makes me think she's being sincere. She was just looking out for her brother...but running to the other brother in a very intense sibling rivalry couldn't have been the answer.

Luke lets out a heavy breath. "Not that I need to explain myself to you, but what you think you heard..." he shakes his head and lets out a mirthless, slightly maniacal laugh. "I once told Ellie how the first year of marriage is the hardest. If we can make it through that on friendly terms, we can make it through anything. After what I went through last time, I firmly believe it's all about that first year. And that's all she was saying last night."

Kaylee looks like she wants to say more, to jump in with how many times she tried to stop me and how I may have admitted things that don't align with what Luke just said, but the look he gives her silences her.

"It's nice of you to try to protect my heart," he says to his sister, and then he looks at me. "But Ellie already owns it." His eyes burn into mine, and I can't help but think the words he's saying right now are the truth.

I wish with everything I am that they're true...but history tells me otherwise.

He pauses, his eyes on mine, and then he turns to his sister. "But it's great to know where you stand." He takes my hands in his and turns back to Manny. "Can we continue now, please?"

"Of course, sir," Manny says.

"You can't just continue," Michelle spits from where she stands still in the middle of the aisle the two of us walked down to join hands and speak our vows. Her words sound like a child throwing a tantrum.

He turns and looks at her like she's a nuisance, a fly that won't stop buzzing around. He lets out another one of those maniacal little laughs. He's trying to hold his shit together in front of the daughter of his boss, but she's pushing him right to the line. I have to wonder why the hell he ever got involved with her in the first place.

"Why, exactly, can't I continue with my wedding?" Luke asks calmly.

"Because I came here to stop you. You can't just ignore me," Michelle says as if that explains everything. She sounds just like Jack—she came here to stop us, and she always gets her way.

Not this time, bitch.

He chuckles. "Oh, that's right," he says. He squeezes my hand as if to brace me for something. "Whatever you say here doesn't really matter."

Michelle looks confused.

Jack does, too.

In fact, everyone gathered here does...except Nicki.

"Why doesn't it matter?" Michelle asks.

"Well, you see, we had a feeling Jack would do something to try to stop me from actually being happy for once in my life, or the media would show up." He nods to Michelle, as if to imply she's the media since we both know she'll run right back to Savannah. She probably has a recording device planted somewhere on her as we speak. "Or any one of a hundred other things that could go wrong, and this is something we both really wanted...so we made it legal earlier today."

Boom! In your face, Michelle!

God, do I want to scream that out. I refrain.

Her face falls. "You...you two...you're..."

"Married," Luke finishes. His eyes move to mine again. "Ellie managed to do what you couldn't. You might be carrying my child, but she carries my heart. She holds it in her hands, and I count myself the luckiest man in the world that I found her when I did."

I smile at our secret about the night we really met, and he smiles back at our little inside joke. My smile hides the well of emotion inside me as I wonder whether those words are true. He says them so earnestly, and when his eyes are on mine the way they are now, I can't help but believe him. Something's been holding him back, but we're married now. Surely it's time for him to admit the truth.

"Now if you'll excuse us," he says to Michelle, "we have a ceremony to finish in front of our friends and family. We have to pose for photos for the media, and we have to finish the show, which is all this is since the ceremony earlier was the one that mattered. You're neither a friend nor family, so you can go now."

She sputters, and Jack draws her in a little closer. "You can stay as my date," he says to her, and I hate Jack even more. He's doing everything he can to look like he's the good guy while Luke selfishly takes care of his own needs and leaves the girl he knocked up behind and he marries someone he barely knows.

I know that's not what this is, but to everyone outside of our innermost circle, that's how it'll look.

Luke's jaw clenches as Michelle looks over at Jack with hearts in her eyes. He doesn't say anything.

Luke just gives Jack and Michelle a look of disgust. "You two deserve each other." He glances at his brother. "Good luck with that train wreck." Then he turns back to Manny. "Can we continue now, please?"

Manny nods. "Join hands, and we will start over with the vows." Luke nods before he takes my hands in his and turns to me.

"Luke, do you take Ellie to be your lawfully wedded wife and equal partner, to join with her and share with her all that is to come, and to commit to a life together from now until you part?" Manny asks.

Luke nods as his lips tip up. "Yes, I do."

I can't help my own smile at his. Someone in the very small group of our guests makes a noise, but I drown it out as I lock my gaze on Luke and listen to Manny's words.

"And Ellie, do you take Luke to be your lawfully wedded husband and equal partner, to join with him and share with him all that is to come, and to commit to a life together from now until you part?" Manny asks.

"Yes, I do, too."

Luke's smile widens, and mine mirrors his. Maybe more noises come from the group, but I have no fucks left to give. This is between Luke and me.

"We will now exchange the rings." Manny nods to Josh, who hands over both our rings. Manny mumbles a few words over the rings then hands my set to him. "Luke, repeat after me as you slide the ring onto Ellie's finger. Ellie, I give you this ring as a symbol of our union. With this ring, I thee wed."

Luke repeats the words and squeezes my hand when he's done, and then it's my turn.

"Luke, I give you this ring as a symbol of our union. With this ring, I thee wed," I say, repeating Manny's words.

"You have consented to matrimony in front of the witnesses gathered here tonight. By the authority vested in me by the state of Hawaii, I now pronounce you husband and wife. Noho me ka hau'oli a mau loa," he says. "Live happily ever after. You may now kiss your bride."

Luke's mouth tips up in a soft smile that will imprint on my brain for the rest of time, and then he leans in and presses his lips to mine.

And fuck it all, we're putting on a show. I grab the back of his head and go for it.

I kiss him with all the pent-up passion I've reserved for my own private thoughts, and I don't even care that it's in front of these awful people who call themselves his family...plus my brother, Nicki, and my parents.

We haven't even opened our mouths to each other yet, but this is still the most passionate kiss I've ever experienced. Maybe it's because I'm pouring my soul into it just for him...and maybe he's pouring his in right back. It sure feels like it.

I'm about to open my mouth and give him some tongue when I hear a cheer. That's what brings me back to Earth.

Our eyes meet when we break apart, and his have a little gleam to them while we both pant just a little to try to catch our breath after that epic kiss.

"Congratulations," Nicki says, handing my bouquet back to me, and Luke and I link hands while Kaylee and Tim clap for us with my parents, Nicki, and Josh—I do note, however, that Carol, Jack, and Michelle refrain from celebrating our union. They're not clapping or cheering or even smiling.

I bet those assholes will still eat the cake we paid for, though.

CHAPTER 2

It was nice of you to try to protect my heart, but Ellie already owns it.

Ellie carries my heart. She holds it in her hands, and I count myself the luckiest man in the world that I found her when I did.

If those aren't wedding vows, I'm not sure what words would be.

Did he mean them?

That's the question. If he has feelings for me...well, then I guess we could try dating. We could try getting to know one another on another level. We could give a relationship, our *marriage*, a real try.

But if he doesn't, then nothing changes.

I just can't figure out why he'd keep up the ruse when I admitted this morning that I have feelings for him. He never got the chance to tell me whether he reciprocates those feelings, but after the words he said tonight paired with the way I feel about him, I can't honestly believe he doesn't feel it, too.

It can't be one-sided.

It's too strong and too deep to be anything less than real.

We head right for our reception after we're announced as husband and wife, which is really just a small, private room at the nicest restaurant in the hotel. We're seated at a round table large enough for our entire party, and a small dance floor waits behind us. The cake is in another corner and it's all very simple. We're given menus, and I glance it over as I try to decide what the first dinner I have with my husband should be.

Luke reaches over to rest his hand on my leg once he's decided what he wants, and it's another small sign that his feelings might be real. Nobody can see his hand under the table. There's no reason for it to be there on my leg other than that he *wants* it to be there.

I almost lean in to ask if he meant what he said, but there are too many prying eyes around this table. Too many people who clearly would love nothing more than to expose the truth. And that would be extra detrimental for my husband considering Michelle is sitting across the table from us.

What a mess.

He leans over and presses a soft kiss to my cheek, the scruff on his jaw tickling me. I turn and catch his lips with mine. It's what you do when you're the bride at your wedding reception, right? I'm taking every chance I can to publicly let the people at this table know that we're in love.

And the more we kiss and touch each other and hold hands, certainly the more convincing we'll be.

Carol huffs across the table, and then she finally breaks her silence. "So you're the girl my son impregnated?"

She looks at Michelle like she's a big bug that just crawled across the table. Finally, Carol and I seem to agree on something. Michelle's eyes edge to Luke, and mine do, too. I'm pretty sure steam is coming out of his ears.

Michelle clears her throat. "Yes," she says softly, and my goodness is she milking the pregnancy card for every single ounce its worth.

"When are you due?" Carol finally asks her. It is, after all, her grandchild in there despite the horrid woman carrying it.

"December tenth," Michelle says, flashing them a sweet smile.

"Can we save this conversation for another time, please?" I ask. "We're just trying to enjoy our wedding reception, which obviously isn't about Michelle in any way despite her best effort to make it about her."

I smile sweetly at the group gathered, and I see Nicki stifle a laugh at my harsh words. But you know what? I don't give a fuck. The only people I care about at this table are my family and Luke. Everyone else can fuck off out of here, and I mean that in the sincerest way possible.

"I ended up the real winner here," I say, leaning over to kiss Luke on the cheek. "Locked this one into marriage when he said he'd never do it again. I guess he was just with the wrong woman before." I lift my wineglass haughtily to my lips, and Michelle glares at me from across the table because she knows I'm right.

She couldn't lock him down, he dumped her, so she showed back up for a bonus night and found a way to claw herself into his life forever.

God, Luke. He really picks some winners.

Thank God I entered the picture when I did. This poor man needed a decent woman in his life to stand up for him, and I will continue to do that—for the next year, at least. Maybe longer if he lets me.

I turn toward Nicki and Josh and ask about their honeymoon, effectively ending the Michelle conversation. Luke and I chat with them and my parents as they fill us in on Fiji—where, incidentally, I wish I was right now rather than at this table with most of these people. We eat, we laugh, we ignore the Daltons, and then it's time to dance. Luke holds me in his arms as we listen to "Speechless" again, dancing our first dance as husband and wife.

He kisses me, and it feels real.

Josh and Nicki join us for the bridal party song, and I don't care about the rest of them, but they join us for a few songs, too, before his parents call it a night first. Michelle's feet are *positively aching*, so she heads out. Jack and Kaylee leave with her, and I wonder if the Dalton family likes Michelle more than Luke let on.

That leaves the only people who I actually care about, but my parents bow out, then Josh and Nicki decide to call it a night, too. They're newlyweds, after all, and I don't even want to know what sort of freaky shit they're about to get up to.

And then it's finally time for the conversation I've been holding off all night.

It's time to confront my husband and find out if he has feelings for me.

CHAPTER 3

My hands tremble as we get back to our room. Will he sleep on the couch again tonight after everything that went down today?

Or will he at least give me some courtesy sex since it's our wedding night?

Yeah, I doubt that one, too.

He settles onto the couch, where he kicks off his shoes, and I settle into the chair across from him, where I take off mine, too. He's still in his suit. I'm still in my wedding gown.

"Why would Michelle come all this way to stop the wedding?" I ask. "Did she really think you'd choose her?"

He shrugs. "She was already a little unhinged. Pregnancy has made it worse, I think."

"She was unhinged?" I ask. It sounds like there's more to that story.

"She's holding onto something that hasn't been there a long time for me. I can't lie when I admit I'm concerned that she's going to make trouble for me at *the office*," he says, air quoting his last two words to indicate his relationship with her father.

A beat of quiet passes between us, and I glance up at him. "What are you thinking?"

He turns toward the window. "I don't know," he mutters. "I'm not sure if she's going to run to Daddy and fuck up my relationship even more with him."

"Why'd you start dating her in the first place?" I ask. He doesn't strike me as the kind of guy who would choose to mix business with pleasure. Example one would be how I can't seem to get him to admit there's something between us.

Eventually I'll get to that question.

He huffs out a mirthless chuckle. "We first met at a charity event. I had no idea who she was at the time. I knew Calvin had a daughter, but she'd been overseas studying fashion, so I'd never met her. She approached me and asked me out, and I liked that she had the balls to do that. It was one of the first things that attracted me to her. We went out a couple times and we slept together before I learned who her father is. I was pissed that she kept it a secret, but she had a valid point that I never would've dated her if I knew. And then I basically lost two years of my life to her. She treated me like trash, and I didn't know how to end things without pissing off her dad, so I stayed far longer than I should have while things just got more and more broken between us."

"I'm so sorry, Luke. You've had some pretty bad luck when it comes to women."

He nods as he presses his lips together. "Pretty much why I swore off marriage. Until I met you." His face smooths into a smile, and this is my chance. I take a deep breath to ask the question that's been on my mind since he said those beautiful words earlier, but he wrinkles his nose. "But I don't want to talk about Michelle anymore."

"What do you want to talk about?" I breathe. Is this it? Finally?

He shrugs and looks out the window, as if to tell me he doesn't really have a topic in mind. That's when I decide I need to get in the driver's seat.

"I need to ask you something," I finally say.

He glances over at me before he folds his hands and leans his elbows on his knees. "Go for it."

I draw in a deep breath. On the other side of this question lies my fate. If I get the answer I'm hoping for, the next year could be a dream come true—and maybe even beyond. And if I don't...well, I haven't really considered that possibility yet. But either way, I'll know.

I let out the breath slowly, and then I finally say the words I've been wondering all night. "What you said during the ceremony about how I carry your heart and you count yourself lucky...did you mean that? Or were those just more words for the show we were putting on?"

He tilts his head a little, his eyes lifting to mine from where they're pinned down toward his hands. "I meant it."

My chest tightens and my heart races as he stands.

He moves across the small space between us and holds a hand out to me. I set my hand in his, and he helps me up before he pulls me into his arms. I'm pressed against his front, and I take the lapels of the suit jacket he still wears between my hands if nothing else so I have something to grip onto.

"I meant every word," he says softly. His eyes burn down into mine, and my fingers tighten over his lapels. "I'm tired of living this lie. It's exhausting pretending like I haven't fallen in love with you, too."

He presses a soft kiss to my lips while my ears buzz and I feel a little dizzy.

He feels it too?

"I had to push you away. I had to pretend like this doesn't mean everything to me, like *you* don't mean everything to me." His voice is full of passion, a rare show of emotion that I very much trust. "And it's because of Jack. I thought if we got married in front of him, he'd believe me. But he ruins every good thing I have. He can't come in second, ever, and he will try to tear us apart. I thought if I pretended it wasn't real, like I didn't feel anything for you, it would be easier when he succeeded, because Jack *always* gets what he wants."

"Not this time," I say. I grip those lapels a little harder. "He won't tear us apart, Luke, because we were meant to find each other. We crashed into one another before we were supposed to meet because fate put you at the club that night."

"I don't believe in fate," he says. "But I do believe in feelings. I haven't been forthcoming with you, and I apologize for that. I don't know what admitting this to you will do to us over the next year, but, God, I want it to work. I want to take you to bed. I want to wake up next to you. I want it all. With you."

I brush my lips to his, finally letting go of his suit jacket to link my arms around him. His body is flush against mine, right where it should be...where it hasn't been for far too long.

"So why is this suddenly okay?" I ask against his lips, not sure why I'm questioning it but needing the whole truth before I get my hopes up too high.

"Because I'm so fucking tired of pretending. I love you, Ellie. I'm so damn in love with you. We're doing this all backwards, and I know you're my wife now, but I'd love to take you out on a date. I want to get to know you as more than just my best friend's sister, as more than just my roommate, as more than just my publicist." He peppers soft kisses between phrases.

"Hawaii seems like a nice place to get our fresh start," I say, and then there's no more talking.

He kisses me like he did when Manny announced us as husband and wife down on the beach, but this time no one stops us when our mouths open and our tongues brush together.

His grip around my waist tightens, and then out of nowhere, he sweeps me up into his arms and carries me into the bedroom. "Tonight won't be about palms on windows or taking you from behind. Tonight's a night to celebrate this new union between us." He presses a soft kiss to my lips as my heart races and a wave of emotion plows through me.

He sets me on my feet rather than on the bed, and then he spins me around so he's looking at the back of my dress.

He doesn't touch it yet—just merely seems to be staring at it. "Is there a lock on this thing?"

I giggle. The layers of lace on top bury the tiny buttons that close the back, and it took Nicki a good five minutes to get them all buttoned up. I didn't stop to think how I'd get *out* of it, and especially not with such intense need between my new husband and me.

I'd suggest just going up the bottom and getting busy right here in my dress, but the layers of chiffon and silk will make that a difficult feat.

"The buttons are under the lace," I say, and he fingers the back until he uncovers them.

"Jesus Christ," he mutters when he sees the sheer number.

"I'm sorry," I say.

He chuckles as he gets to work. "Don't be. You look gorgeous. The most beautiful bride I've ever seen in my life." I feel the back starting to open as he pushes each button patiently, slowly through each loop. He's calm and collected while the thought of what's coming sends nerves through my entire system.

We've done this before, but that first time, it was meaningless. This time...it's not.

"When I first saw you walking down the aisle toward me, I had a feeling this was how our night was going to end. Whether you asked me about my real feelings or not...I was going to confess them."

Another button through the loop, another thump in my chest.

"It wasn't just your beauty," he says, "but the way you carried yourself with such beautiful, calm, simple grace." He presses a kiss to the small gap he's made as he keeps progressing down the buttons. "It was the way you stood up beside me and I felt like we could face anything together. And we did. We faced my family. We faced Michelle." He slips another button through. "Done," he says with another soft kiss to my back, and he spins me back around.

I slip his jacket off his arms, and it falls into a pile on the floor. I unbutton his shirt, my fingers shaking as I make slow progress. He's patient as I work, and he sets to unbuttoning the cuffs of his shirt. He sets the cufflinks on the dresser behind him as I get to the last button, and then I slide his shirt down his arms and it falls on top of the jacket.

I take a minute to stare at his abs.

Holy shit. I'm married to those.

For the next year, at least.

And now that he's confessed how he really feels, I'm going to enjoy every damn minute of this union.

CHAPTER 4

He slides the straps of my dress slowly down my arms, and it drifts from my arms to the ground. My heart pounds so hard I'm certain he can see it beneath the white lace lingerie set I wore under the gown *just in case.*

I've wanted this to happen again since the first time, and now that it's actually happening, I'm a nervous wreck. It's a mixture of *will it be as good as the first time* and *oh my God we're really doing this* and *holy hell we're* married *now.*

The fear that I somehow won't be good enough for him is real and tangible.

He stares at me for a beat, and the self-conscious side feels like he's studying me. "So perfect," he murmurs, and then moves in toward me and presses a kiss to my neck. "I love you, Mrs. Dalton," he says.

"I love you, too," I say on a moan as his lips move from my neck down into my cleavage. He's moving slowly, deliberately, with love and tenderness—something missing from the first time we did this. It was savage and hot and fiery. There was no fear of what tomorrow might bring because it didn't matter when it was just supposed to be for one night.

But something brought us together. He might not believe in fate...but I do.

We were meant to find one another ahead of time. We were meant to have this history between us as we traveled on our journey, and maybe we're at the destination now. Maybe this is where our happily ever after begins.

It might be naïve to think that way, but it's what I'm choosing to believe tonight.

He sweeps me up into his arms and carries me to the bed, his lips finding mine as he moves the short distance, and if that's not a damn fairy tale Prince Charming move for the books, I'm not sure what is. He lays me down gently and moves so he's hovering over me. His eyes burn into mine for a beat, and then his fingertips run down my torso, landing on my thigh. He settles between my legs, still wearing pants, and he thrusts his hips toward me as he buries his face in my cleavage.

A little moan escapes me. As good as this feels, I want him. All of him. I want our clothes out of the way, and I want him pounding into me as I lie beneath him. I didn't get to feel his warmth over me the first time. I didn't get to look into his eyes, to watch his handsome face screw up with pleasure instead of his reflection in the window.

I'm not missing those things this time.

His lips land back on mine, our tongues battering together as he continues thrusting his hips to mine, both of us moaning as the frenzy between us builds to nearly unbearable levels, an ache pressing between my thighs as needy moans escape me.

He stops abruptly and stands, unbuckling his belt and lowering his pants and boxers. He stands naked before me for only the second time, but it's incredible how different the feelings are this time. I won't need to scrub away the guilt in the morning.

Does it still qualify as a one-night stand when you *marry* the guy?

"Slight problem," he says. "I didn't bring any condoms. I figured less temptation that way."

"I don't have any, either. But it's fine. I'm on the pill." *And I want all of you anyway.*

"This is okay?" he asks before he moves back toward me.

I nod. "This is *more* than okay." That's the green light he needs.

He moves toward me and slides my panties down my legs. It feels like everything is in slow motion, but that's okay. We have tonight, and tomorrow, and forever if that's what we want.

He helps me sit up and unhooks my bra next, which ends up on the ground, and then we're both naked and we're really going to do this.

And then he moves over me. He kisses me again, and he thrusts toward me, and I feel him between my legs, hot and hard against my slit. He reaches between us to pump himself right against my clit a few times, and it intensifies the ache. It's so good as he presses that magical spot, and I'm about to lose it and fly into a climax when he slides himself down and right into me.

Holy shit.

If I thought it was good *with* a condom, it had *nothing* on this.

He's hard as steel as he enters me. A warm feeling rolls over me, heating me from the inside out. He starts moving, sliding in and out, nothing between us but wet heat as we both grunt and moan from the incredible feeling. It's like our bodies were made for one another as he rocks into me.

I can't believe this is really happening. It's like I've entered some alternate universe that I certainly never want to leave.

He kisses me, and he's tender and slow. He reaches for my breasts, and my hands skate up and down his back, leaving scratch marks when I have to grip onto his shoulder because I'm trying to hold off my orgasm. It's close. So damn close. He feels so good, and I can't hold on much longer, but I don't want this to end.

I want him to drive into me for the rest of time. Nobody has ever made me feel this way, and that's how I know this is right.

He leans down to catch one of my nipples in his mouth, and the pain there pairs with the pleasure down below. With my mental state in the right place, too, as love pulses hotly between us, he pushes me right into my first climax of the night.

He comes along with me for the ride, growling incomprehensible strings of curse words along with my name as my own release pushes him into his. We ride the wave together as he continues pushing into me and my hips thrash around, our eyes hot on each other as heat pulses from him into me.

And when it's over, when we've both come down and our bodies are left shuddering with the pleasure we both just felt, he remains inside me for a few beats as he kisses me slowly.

I never want this to end.

I know I only signed a contract for the next year, but I want forever.

CHAPTER 5

That old phrase *cloud nine* has nothing on where I'm floating when I wake up in the morning. Not only am I married, but I'm married to the guy I've fallen in love with...and he's in love with me, too.

When I was fired and Todd dumped me twelve seconds later, I thought it would be a long-ass time before I found happiness again, yet here I am, less than two months later. Happy as a damn clam.

Until Luke wakes up and opens his mouth. "We probably shouldn't have done that," he says instead of something simple like *good morning* or *hey there wife* or even *should we do that again?*

I blow out a breath and get out of bed angrily. "Are you serious, Luke?" I grab a shirt and pull it on because you're damn right if you think we slept naked.

"It's just going to complicate our agreement," he says, like that's any better.

I shake my head sadly as the anger starts to dissipate into pure disappointment. "I should believe you when you keep telling me you're no prince. Maybe you're right. But you sure fuck like one." I mutter the last part and I leave those as my parting words as I head to the bathroom, slam the door, and take a shower.

It's sort of like the last time we were together. I scrubbed and scrubbed under scalding hot water, but nothing could make the grime go away. The same holds true this time.

No matter how hard I scrub, I can't change what he just said.

I can't try to justify his hurtful words.

He knocks on the bathroom door just as I finish drying off. I wrap the fluffy hotel bathrobe around me and open the door. "What?" I spit at him.

He gives me a wry smile, and why does he have to be so goddamn hot? I can't stay mad at him when he looks at me like that. It's like a damn puppy dog with sad eyes.

"I'm sorry. I guess I've just gotten used to pushing people away, but I don't want to push you away. I just don't know how to be in a real relationship."

I weigh my options here. I could give in and set the precedent that it's okay to say mean things to me, or I could stand my ground.

I go with the latter. I have to.

"You're right," I say. "You don't know how. And it might just be part of my job description to teach you."

"How can I make it up to you?" he asks.

"Find another hotel," I say, standing my ground. "Our honeymoon starts today, and it starts away from your toxic family. I want more nights like we had last night and less mornings like we're having right now."

"Consider it done. What else?"

"You once told me that there were two people in your failed relationships. What did you do that caused them to end?" I ask.

"Oh Jesus," he says. "It's too damn early for this conversation."

I raise a brow.

He blows out a breath. "Fine. But can we at least order breakfast first?"

I nod toward the phone and cross my arms over my chest. "You know what I like."

He gives me a look I can't quite decode, and then he walks over and picks up the phone. I grab my clothes and close the bathroom door while he orders.

Time to find out if he's been paying attention.

After I finish getting ready, I pack up my toiletries with a sigh. I don't *really* want to leave this place. It is, after all, where we got married yesterday. But my family is heading out today, and with his family and Michelle here, I can't stay. Not when they constantly hurt him, and not if we're meant to enjoy this "honeymoon." It's a big place, but not big enough to escape all that.

I toss my make-up bag in my suitcase and start reorganizing my clothes when Luke appears in the bedroom doorway holding a cup of coffee. He isn't wearing a shirt, his hair is messy from sleep, and the light is hitting him at the most perfect angle. He looks like a damn advertisement for coffee.

I slip my phone out of my pocket and snap a picture.

"What was that for?" he asks.

"I swear, if you didn't play football, you could model," I murmur, checking out the picture I just took—another one for the spank bank, not that I need it if he's going to deliver like last night again. I push that whole *we shouldn't have done that* thing out of my head and try not to read past what he said.

"I'm ready to talk now," he says, lifting his coffee cup into the air to indicate that he couldn't really get moving on conversation until he had that in hand.

I nod, and I follow him out toward the couch where he *didn't* sleep last night. I set to work on my own cup of coffee, too. He collapses onto the couch, and I sit in the chair across from him.

"So what I said this morning, about our agreement...it's shit like that, Ellie. I work hard to push people away. Sometimes I blame my family for that, and sometimes I think it's just all me."

"Why do you think you do that?"

He lifts a shoulder and looks out the window. "When it comes to women, it's usually because of Jack. But fuck the agreement. I want to give this a real try with you."

"Then I need to understand your past. Start with Savannah." I take a small sip of my piping hot coffee, proud of myself for being blunt about what I need out of this relationship.

"Like I said, it usually goes back to Jack. He was just always there between Savannah and me, and I always wondered if I was good enough since she was with him first," he admits. He sits up a little straighter, palming his coffee cup in both hands.

"Why'd you marry her?" I ask, truly wondering what the answer might be.

He clears his throat, and his eyes move to mine. He regards me for a beat, studies me like he's trying to decide if he can trust me. "I thought I loved her."

"*Thought?*" I ask.

He nods. "We were, uh, sleeping together when I tore my ACL in the middle of my second season."

"I didn't know you tore your ACL," I say, not sure why that matters.

"I was out the rest of the season. I missed most of training camp and preseason my third year, but I was ready for the field by our home opener." He presses his lips together.

"How'd you feel about being out?" I ask.

His eyes turn back to the window. "It was the hardest eight months of my life. Savannah took care of me, and I guess along the way, I developed real feelings for her. Eventually, I proposed."

"So how did you start sleeping with her when you knew she'd been with your brother?"

A knock at the door saves him from answering. "Room service," the voice on the other side says.

Luke gets up to let in the attendant, who wheels in a cart with our food. He signs the receipt and the attendant leaves while I pull the lids off the plates.

I wrinkle my nose at the egg white omelet with a bunch of vegetables including spinach, and I smile at the plate of pancakes, scrambled eggs, and hash browns.

I knew he'd pick right.

"The omelet is for you," he says, coming up behind me and setting his hands on my hips.

I giggle, and he nips a soft kiss on my neck, and somehow any lasting anger I had from his words this morning seems to melt away.

We sit to eat, and I bring up my question from a few minutes ago. "Back to Savannah. How did you first get together?"

"She and Jack had broken up a few weeks earlier." He takes a bite of omelet. "They lived in San Diego, and I went to stay with Jack a few days before our family trip to Vancouver. This was back when we were close. I had literally *just* had a conversation with my brother about how he didn't want the same things she did. She wanted marriage and kids and the white picket fence, and he wanted to play the field and have some fun. He was out, and she stopped by to talk to him and got me instead. She was crying, all upset, yada yada yada. We exchanged numbers, and it started out very innocently but quickly turned into talking every day. Eventually I was in San Diego again and we went to dinner. She took me back to her place, and the rest is history."

"How did Jack react when he found out?" I ask.

"He said he didn't care."

I raise a brow. "But he did?"

Luke shrugs.

I let that slide because the truth is that these brothers will *never* have an even score between them. "Okay, so you dated, got hurt, got engaged, got married. And then things fell apart?" I ask.

"Sort of." He cuts some of his omelet with his fork but sets down his fork instead of eating it. "She didn't just want marriage. She wanted to be a football wife. She wanted money. She chased fame. And I helped her chase that fame when I let her write that series on Jack and me."

I dip my pancake into the syrup. "And you had no inclination about any of that before you married her?"

He shakes his head. "I'm sure this isn't something you want to hear, but I was blinded by the sex."

I raise a brow as I keep my eyes down on my pancakes. I'm not sure what to say to that, so a beat of quiet passes between us while I chew. And then I finally ask, "So what led to the divorce?"

"I've already talked a little about her role in that, but for my own part..." He blows out a breath. "She knew things about my family, so I had to find a way to keep her quiet. At the same time, I started to hate her. I didn't want to be married to her anymore. I couldn't. I didn't fight for us because there was nothing left to fight for. She turned into someone I didn't know, but I did, too. I pushed her away, did little things to piss her off to get her to leave first. She wouldn't budge. Eventually I offered to pay her just to get rid of her. I'm not proud of that, but I *am* proud of the fact that I didn't have as much then as I do now. I threw myself into work, and the year after our divorce was my best season up to that point."

"Don't you sort of *have to* throw yourself into work, though?" I ask, tucking the need to know more regarding these secrets about his family into the back of my mind for now.

"Well, yes and no," he says. He lifts his coffee cup to his lips for a quick sip. "I worked out constantly. More than I needed to. I was in the best shape of my life. Looking back, I did it as a means to escape her and to escape the way she made me feel. I was angry all the time. She put this divide between Jack and me that hadn't existed before. She caused a split in my family. I admit a large part of the blame falls on my shoulders there, too. Then the team offered me my current contract worth more than she and I ever dreamed of. The best part? She didn't get to touch that money. But it led to an even bigger issue with her."

"Why?" I ask, and I think I know the answer, but I wait with bated breath for his answer.

"Because of what she knows."

"What does she know?" I breathe.

He shakes his head and keeps his gaze down. "Enough about Savannah," he murmurs. He's not spilling those family secrets today, but my curiosity burns.

"So we're moving onto Michelle?" I flash him a smile.

"Good try." He finishes the last bite of his omelet. "But we have to save *something* for lunch conversation, don't you think?"

"I figured we'd talk about all *my* failed relationships at lunch."

He wrinkles his nose. "What if I don't want to know?"

"You already know about Todd. The rest were all pretty short-term. Nothing nearly as exciting as yours."

He laughs. "Fair enough. But to be honest, when it comes to why things failed with Michelle, it's basically the same story without the marriage. We tried, we both turned into different people, and it just didn't work out. Rather than allowing family secrets to be the thing holding me back from breaking up with her, it was the fact that she's my boss's daughter. I held on as long as I could, but I think I'm just not one of those people who's destined to have relationships that last longer than a year."

Enter Ellie.

"Hence the one-year contract?" I ask.

He shrugs. "I figured if nothing else, you could put up with me for a year, and vice versa. But that was when we were friends. Throwing sex and feelings into the mix will definitely complicate things, and that's all I meant this morning when I said that. I didn't mean to hurt your feelings, but like I've told you, I don't know how to do relationships. People leave. People choose Jack, and not just women. I've had buddies who chose him. My own damn family chose him." He shrugs. "Why would you be any different?"

"Because I love *you*, Luke," I say, my voice full of all the passion I've had to push away for the last few weeks since I first realized I was falling for him. "I don't give a shit about football. You're my brother's best friend, and you've helped me out, and I fell for the person *you* are long before I met him. I don't care about your job or your money or your brother or your family or any of that stuff. I just care about you."

He stares at me a long beat like he's trying to gauge whether my words are the truth. "I care about you, too."

"Lesson one for an adult relationship. You ready? You listening good?" I ask.

He chuckles and nods.

"Okay. Don't push me away. Don't bow out. Talk to me, and fight with me, and communicate with me. It's the only way relationships work." Not that I'm any expert, to be honest. Just look at Todd.

But Luke and I have the tools to make this work, and now that he's let me into a small part of his history, I'm ready to get on with the honeymoon.

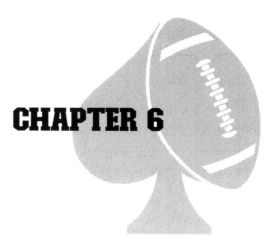

CHAPTER 6

We're standing at the reception desk in the lobby a little before lunch time when we hear Kaylee's voice from across the lobby.

"What are you doing?" she asks. She's in her swimwear, sunglasses perched on her head. I'd feel sorry for her that she's stuck with Carol, Tim, Jack, and Michelle for the next few days, but she betrayed us when she ran to Jack with what she heard, so I can't muster up those feelings of sympathy.

"Checking out," Luke says thickly. He signs the receipt and pushes it back toward the clerk, who hands him back a folder with our suite charges.

"Thank you for staying with us," the clerk says, and Luke nods before we both turn to face Kaylee.

"Where are you going?" she asks.

"On our honeymoon," Luke says, tossing an arm around my shoulders to draw me in closer, "and we can't do that here in a place filled with traitors and people who want our relationship to fail."

"But...but..." she sputters. "Luke, this is our family trip. You can't just leave."

"Watch me."

Carol and Tim, also donning swim gear, saunter up behind Kaylee, and this is the exact reason we're leaving. This place is too damn small to enjoy the time we have left on this island.

Carol's brow is raised. "Where are you two off to?"

"They're checking out," Kaylee says, ever the little tattletale.

"We're going to another hotel to enjoy what's left of our trip. Just the two of us." He leans over and presses a kiss to my temple.

Carol rolls her eyes. "Still keeping up the act, I see."

"It's not an act," Luke says. Our eyes meet, and in this moment, I know he's telling the truth. That's how it started, and we're certainly not in the position for a traditional marriage given how long we've known one another...but at this point, we're both committed to giving it a real try. And that's what makes it so much more than the *act* we each signed up for.

"Okay," she says, her tone full of sarcasm. "So why leave this lovely place?"

"Do you really want the answer to that?" Luke asks. "Enjoy your day at the beach. Enjoy the rest of your trip. Enjoy your life. I don't know if I can be a part of any of it anymore."

A spear of sadness forms in me. As much as my mom drives me crazy, I still love her. I'd never just part ways with her. But watching the way Luke's family treats him makes me see how families can become estranged. I try to think of it from their perspective, and I still can't wrap my head around why they constantly degrade him while building up his brother. It's not right, and maybe now that he has me, he can finally start to see that he deserves more.

Luke sighs as he turns away from his family, and together we walk away from them and toward the restaurant where we're meeting my family for lunch before they check out to head home and we head to our new hotel to check in.

They don't try to stop us. They don't say anything else—not even in response to Luke's words that he can't be a part of their lives anymore.

That spear of sadness I felt before seems stronger. If I feel it, I can't imagine what he's feeling.

At least we didn't run into Jack.

Yet.

"Are you okay?" I ask once we're out of earshot.

He nods and presses his lips together. "Better than I've been in a long time, I think." He leans over and kisses me. It's soft and quick, just a nip of lip to lip, but it feels like so much more. It's sealing our promise. It's a thank you for holding his hand through that. And maybe, above all, it's not for show. He kissed me because he wanted to, not because we're faking for everyone. That one was just for us, just as all the kisses in our future will be.

I just wish we didn't have the heavy cloud of what just happened with his family hanging over us.

Nicki and Josh are already seated and waiting for us when we slide into the chairs across from them. "There's the newlyweds," Nicki says, and I smile. "Did you two have a crazy kinky night?"

Josh wrinkles his nose. "Babe, gross. That's my sister."

"And it's my best friend," Nicki points out. "I need all the details."

"You know it's not real, right?" Josh whispers to her, loud enough for only Luke and me to hear as I wave over my parents when I spot them near the hostess stand at the front of the restaurant.

"Actually..." Luke says, and then he turns to me. His eyes twinkle despite what just happened, and I get the sense that a weight lifted when he said those words to his parents. He seems a little lighter despite the heaviness I still feel.

"Oh my God," Nicki squeals.

"What?" Josh asks.

Luke kisses me again and then turns to my brother. "I'm in love with your sister."

Josh's eyes practically bug out of his head. "You...this is...wait. You are? For real?" He glances at Nicki. "See? I told you!"

Luke laughs. "I am. And I'm sorry. I know I promised you I wouldn't take a shot at her."

Josh looks between the two of us, and he seems to soften a little. "This seems like more than *taking a shot*."

"It is," Luke says softly as he grabs my hand in his.

My parents approach the table and we all stand for good morning hugs.

I still can't quite get over the contrast from his family to mine.

Once we're all seated again, Luke regards my parents. He seems suddenly nervous as he clears his throat. He glances around and sees that we're alone in our little corner of the restaurant before he speaks. "Mr. and Mrs. Nolan, I just wanted to thank you both for being here, and I also wanted to let you know that last night I told your daughter about my real feelings for her. I'm in love with her, and we're both thrilled to be giving this a real shot."

My parents glance at each other, and then they both look at me. "Is this what you want?" my dad asks.

I can't help my grin as I nod. "More than anything." My eyes edge over to my husband. "I'm so in love with Luke."

My mom squeals and claps her hands together. "Does that mean I'm finally getting a grandchild sometime soon?"

I laugh as Luke blanches. "One step at a time, Mom," I say. I jab my thumb toward my brother and Nicki. "Maybe badger these two a while first."

Josh blanches a bit, too, and then Nicki throws the attention back to me by changing the subject as she clears her throat. "So what's next for you two?"

"We just checked out of here and we're going to another hotel to celebrate our honeymoon," I say.

"Away from my toxic family," Luke adds.

"You both deserve to be happy," Josh says. "I'm glad you're finding that with each other. But keep the details to yourself, okay?"

We all get a good laugh out of that. We order, and so far, we haven't had the pleasure of running into the last member of Luke's family that we haven't said goodbye to just yet. My fingers are crossed that we don't...but that would be too easy, wouldn't it?

My parents are at the reception desk checking out. It's as we're hugging Josh and Nicki in the lobby and bidding them a safe trip home—a place that doesn't sound so bad right now—before they head up to pack to catch the flight they're all taking together that we hear Jack's voice.

"The party's over so soon?"

I draw in a deep breath before I turn around. Michelle is right by his side, and the prissy gloating expression on her face makes me want to barf.

"We're heading home tonight," Josh says, and he seems to regard Jack a little warily. I'm not sure if that caution has more to do with the fact that he's professional competition or with how Jack treats Luke. Maybe both.

"And we're heading to another hotel," Luke says.

Jack's brows arch. "Running away?"

Luke grunts out a chuckle. "Hardly. I'd just like to enjoy my honeymoon with my new bride away from my family and Michelle."

"So...running away," Jack says.

"Sure," Luke says, and his tone clearly expresses that he doesn't care what his brother thinks.

And _that_ might just be the deepest dig for Jack. He doesn't know how to respond to his brother's sarcastic indifference, and seeing him sputter for a beat is somehow totally out of character for him while it's incredibly satisfying to watch.

Luke glances between Michelle and Jack. He narrows his eyes at them. "Hope you're enjoying your sloppy seconds."

Jack raises a brow and lowers his voice. "I'll let you know once I get Ellie into my bed." He winks at me.

"That will _never_ happen," I snarl.

Josh steps in to save the day as my parents join us. "Well, you two have a fun honeymoon. We'll see you when you're back home."

I give each member of my family one final hug, and then I wiggle my fingers at Jack and Michelle while Luke gives them a smirk.

"Bye," we say together, and then we head out for the car waiting for us out front to take us to our new hotel.

CHAPTER 7

"What's a *lanai*?" I ask.

Luke types the word into his browser on his phone before reading me the results. "The Hawaiian word for *porch* or *veranda*."

"Well whatever it is, I'm in love with it." I collapse into one of the cushioned chairs on our *lanai* that overlooks the ocean. If I thought the last hotel was nice, well, it has nothing on this one.

This one boasts *nine* pools with waterslides, a lazy river, and waterfalls, seven restaurants, and beach access all in the lap of luxury. Our huge suite has a private lanai, and it's both relaxing and romantic...and, maybe most importantly, it's just for us. We may still be on the same island as the rest of his family, but this separation feels both necessary and much better.

It's ours, and ours alone, for the next week.

We spend our days at the pool and our nights naked. We relax. We fall asleep on the beach. We cover each other in sunscreen. We swim. We ride waterslides and kiss under waterfalls. We learn how to kayak. We snorkel. We get massages. We have sex up against windows and in our bed and in the shower and he even slips it in when we're in the ocean, separated by ourselves yet with people all around us probably doing the same thing.

We spend time together laughing, the weight of his family and their secrets mixed with what started as a lie between us off our shoulders as we truly get to explore everything about each other for the first time.

I don't know if I've ever felt closer to another person. There are still secrets he holds, but they have no bearing on us. Maybe someday he'll be ready to tell me about them, and maybe not. I'm not sure if it matters. They're swept away with history, and I keep telling myself that they don't *really* matter...even though a small part of me hates that Savannah still holds onto a piece of him that he doesn't want to reveal to me.

It's still early days for us. We have at least a year or the rest of our lives.

The seven remaining days of our honeymoon in Hawaii pass in the blink of an eye without drama and without incident, and suddenly I find myself staring out Luke's car window as he pulls back onto his street. We're nearly *home*. When we left, I'd just signed a contract saying this would be home for the next year, and now I have hope that it might last far beyond that.

I'm excited to get back to work. I'm ready to sort through our photos, to focus on our upcoming charity event, to make my new husband indispensable to his team...even to make his team owner see that marrying me was the right choice despite Luke having knocked up his daughter. That might be a stretch, but if anyone can do it convincingly, it's me.

He pulls into the driveaway, and I can't wait to get inside, kiss Pepper on the head, and unpack the luggage. I'm tired of living out of suitcases...but even if I wasn't, it's just in my nature to have everything unpacked, the laundry started, and the suitcases put away within an hour after arriving home.

"Look who's back," a singsong voice from next door calls as we pull suitcases out of the back of the car.

"Hey, Mrs. Adams," Luke says. He doesn't stop what he's doing to acknowledge her, further evidence that he's ready to just be home, too.

"You know you're supposed to call me Dorothy," she reminds him. She looks between the two of us. "I saw the gossip columns, but please tell me they got it wrong. You didn't go and get *married* now, did you?"

Luke holds up the shiny new hardware on the third finger of his left hand. "We sure did." He flashes her a cheesy smile and draws me in with an arm around my shoulders.

"Tsk tsk," she tuts. "Abigail will be so disappointed."

"Tell your granddaughter I'm so sorry, but I fell in love," Luke says, his eyes on me.

"Can I still sit on your lap at least?" she taunts, and Luke laughs.

"No. But if you need a pickle jar opened, you know I'm your guy."

"I hope you two are happy," she says. "As happy as you and Savannah were, at the very least."

"Now, Mrs. Adams, you know that's not a nice thing to say," he admonishes.

She holds up her hands, the picture of innocence. I know she's basically harmless, but that doesn't mean I have to like the way she hits on my husband.

"Mrs. Adams?" I say. She turns her attention to me, and she looks at me like I'm a naughty toddler. "My brother across the street is real good with pickle jars, too." I smile sweetly, and then I turn into my husband and plant a big kiss on his mouth.

Here's to hoping that shuts her up.

Luke lugs the heavier bags upstairs and I take up our carry-ons once he opens the door. I immediately set to unpacking.

"What are you doing?" he asks.

"Unpacking," I say. "Why? What does it look like?"

"Don't you want to relax a little?" he asks. "Debbie's bringing food plus Pepper by in an hour. We can do this later."

I purse my lips and shake my head. "There are two types of people in this world, Luke. We have those who unpack immediately when they get home, and we have those who leave their bags untouched for days. Which are you?"

"The first one?" he guesses, and I nod.

"Good boy. Now get unpacked. There's no relaxing until this is done."

"Yes, ma'am," he says.

"See? Prince Charming."

He laughs as he starts separating his clean clothes from the dirties.

"Doing my best," he says.

I stand and walk over to him. I loop my arms around his neck. "You're doing great. Thank you for a wonderful honeymoon. It was the best one I've ever had."

He laughs. "I know you're just saying that because it's your only one, but it was the best one I ever had, too."

I smile. "That line is *almost* good enough to get you laid, but only after you finish unpacking."

CHAPTER 8

When Debbie lets Pepper off her leash in the foyer, she bounds through the house and heads right for her daddy.

"Pepper girl!" Luke exclaims as she crashes into him. He laughs as she licks his face.

"Hey Pepper!" I say with tons of enthusiasm, ready for some puppy kisses of my own...but she's too busy with her dad.

I roll my eyes, and Debbie laughs. "Just wait until you two have children. Same thing. Dads get *all* the glory."

"You have kids?" I ask.

She nods. "My daughter is twenty-six and my son is twenty-three. They're both still here in Vegas, so I see them often."

"How nice." I scratch Pepper behind the ears. She only comes to me for a courtesy pet, and I don't get the same kisses Luke got. I'll take it.

"Thanks for taking care of her," Luke says.

"Happy to do it." She smiles. "My house is awfully quiet these days."

"You need a dog," Luke teases.

Debbie laughs. "I'll just borrow Pepper every now and again."

We all watch as Pepper jumps on the couch, walks in a circle, and settles in for her afternoon nap.

"I've got food and groceries in the car for you two. Let me just go grab everything," Debbie says.

"I'll get it." Luke moves toward the door before she gets a chance to protest.

"Congratulations on the wedding." Debbie winks at me as soon as Luke is out of earshot. "I know you'll take good care of my Luke."

"I promise." I hold a hand over my heart.

"You're good for him. I haven't seen him smile like he does around you in a very long time. Maybe ever."

"How long have you been cooking for him?" I ask.

She moves into the kitchen, and I follow her. "Oh, six or seven years now I think. He and Savannah were married when I started."

"How'd you two meet?"

"My husband was an assistant coach for years and years," she says. "He'd have meetings with the wide receivers at our house once a week and I'd cook them dinner when they were over. Luke was always such a special boy. So grateful, so kind." He comes back in at that moment with the food from Debbie's car.

"You must be talking about someone else," he jokes, and Debbie laughs as he sets the bags on the counter.

"When my husband passed, I quit cooking for the team. And then Luke offered me a job cooking for him," she says.

"She's like a mother to me." He squeezes her shoulders like he's giving her a massage. "Always telling me what to do."

She bats his hands away affectionately, and I see more mother and son love between these two in this cute little moment than I did between Carol and him the entire time we were in Hawaii.

So Debbie is a mother figure. His teammates are like brothers to him. His coaches are probably father figures at least to some degree. Maybe he was born into the Dalton family, something he couldn't choose...but it seems like he's created his own little family when he was more or less exiled from his own blood relatives.

And now he has me. The princess with her trusty animal sidekick here to save the day—or something along those lines. I guess Pepper is more of a sidekick to *him* than me, but since I know the rules of fairy tales so well, it's probably okay if I break a few.

"Are you hungry?" he asks me once Debbie leaves.

I glance at the clock. I'm still on Hawaii time, which means that even though the clock here says it's seven o'clock, it feels like four. "Sure. What did Debbie make us?"

He opens the fridge, which Debbie stocked while we finished unpacking and started the laundry. "We've got chicken, burgers, spaghetti, chili, fish..."

"Spaghetti," I say, and he takes out the container and sets to work on plating it. I grab some garlic bread from the freezer and get the oven preheating.

"What was your favorite part of the trip?" he asks.

"Definitely the wedding," I say, and I pull apart the bread and set it on a cookie sheet.

"The first or the second?"

I glance up and meet his eyes. "The real one. The one that was just for us, and then the words you said at the second one, and then, obviously, the wedding night. What was yours?"

"All the sex," he murmurs. "I want more."

I laugh. "Way to beat around the bush."

"The only bush I'll be beating on is yours."

"Whoa, Tiger," I say. "At least let me eat first."

He laughs, but when his eyes meet mine, the twinkle turns heated. "Refuel. And then you're mine."

He's not lying about that. We eat, and I brush my teeth because who wants to fuck garlic breath, and then we meet in bed.

Our bed.

The bed we've shared so many nights already while pretending like there wasn't this huge, beautiful thing between us—but we don't have to pretend anymore. It's still there between us, but we've both acknowledged it now.

And there's nothing more beautiful than when my husband strips me out of my clothes, licks his way through my pussy as he sends me to heights I've never visited before, then fucks me into oblivion.

After a hot and steamy session, he runs a bath for me. We luxuriate together in the bubbles, drinking wine as we take turns soaping each other. He holds me in his arms after he slips into bed beside me, and I'm still in his arms in the morning after a long and restful sleep for both of us.

And then it's back to reality.

I spend Monday morning working on the charity event while Luke heads to the practice facility to meet with his coach and teammates. I have under three weeks to launch this event, and four weeks from today, training camp begins for him. I have no idea what life will be like once he's at camp all day, and then a month later, the season starts.

He gets home a little after four, and I'm still in the office chipping away at this charity event. I've sent invitations to everyone on Luke's guest list, which is mostly comprised of his teammates, and I'm staring at the short list of names I came up with.

Calvin Bennett.

Michelle Bennett.

Savannah Buck.

Jack Dalton.

Tim and Carol Dalton.

Kaylee Dalton.

All people Luke did *not* include on his list. All people neither of us really want here.

But also...all people who this charity could benefit from. All people we'd be showing goodwill toward as we also show how happy we are...not that his family deserves any goodwill, especially considering how much of a weight was lifted after we left the hotel we shared with them.

I'm torn, so when he gets home, I decide to ask his opinion.

"Honey, I'm home," he sings, peeking his head into my office.

"Welcome home. Now have a seat," I say, nodding to the chair sitting across from my desk.

He raises a brow but does as instructed. "Am I in trouble?"

I chuckle. "No. I just wanted to give you an update on our event. Invitations were sent out to everyone on your list, but I thought of a few others who you didn't include."

He raises a brow. "Such as?"

"Calvin."

He shakes his head and starts to protest, but I jump in.

"You need harmony with him, Luke. Inviting the entire team and coaching staff and leaving him out looks petty, and besides, it'll give him a chance to see you're serious about doing your part for the baby even though you're married. Happily, I might add."

"The only way it'll show that I'm doing my part for the baby is if we also invite Michelle," he points out.

"Oh, good idea," I say, scribbling her name down like I hadn't thought of it.

"Ellie, no," he says.

"Come on, Luke," I say, sure this is a terrible idea but pressing it anyway. "We need to extend the olive branch. We need to be the bigger people here. And besides, Calvin probably has the fattest bank account of anyone on this list." I don't need to reiterate how *that* fact could benefit our little charity.

He huffs out a breath. "Next you're going to tell me you want to invite my family, too."

I raise a brow. "Now that you mention it..."

"No, Ellie. A firm, hard no."

"At least Jack? Think how great that'll look going into boot camp. You and your brother at a public event? The press will eat it up."

"The press? You mean Savannah, don't you." His voice is flat.

"Yep. Let's get all your enemies in one place and watch the fireworks." I flash him a smile. "Come on, it'll be fun."

"It will *not* be fun."

"You'll be too busy to care what they're doing. You can hang with your buddies, and I'll take care of the rest. Come on, Luke. I'm trying to find a way to make peace between you and your boss. To keep you here in Vegas playing for the Aces. A charity event where you're helping the community while also smoothing things over with those who have wronged you makes you not just the bigger man, but it's what will catapult your status as indispensable fan favorite."

He sighs. "You've already made up your mind, haven't you?"

I nod. "Yep."

"You've already sent them invitations, haven't you?" he asks.

I laugh. "No. I was waiting for your input first."

He narrows his eyes at me. "Were you?"

I shrug. "Not really. I'm going to do it either way, but I'd like to do it with your permission."

He sighs. "I'm never, ever going to say it's a good idea for the two of us, my brother, the girl I knocked up along with her father-slash-my boss, and my ex-wife all to attend the same event, let alone an event with my name on it. Don't you see how fucked up that is?"

"Definitely." I tap my pen on a pad of paper. "And it's also a publicist's dream, Luke. The way we handle this will pave the way for how we handle every single future event. It's telling the world, including your boss, whose shit list you are already on, that raising money for charity is more important than petty differences."

"I don't think knocking up his daughter and refusing to marry her is a *petty* difference," he points out.

"So why'd you really marry me?" I ask, trying to get to the root of this.

He glances away from me, like it'll soften the blow of the truth even though I'm fully aware of what I signed on for. "You offered me the only way out of being trapped by Michelle into something I didn't want. I take full responsibility for the child we'll share. I will love that kid with everything I have. But that doesn't mean I have to be with Michelle. Trust me when I say that the two of us together would be toxic for a child. Whatever happens between you and me, at least we both have an out at the end of it. With her...she wasn't about to let me have that, and neither would her father if he had anything to say about it."

"Then how great would it look for you to invite them both to this thing? To show them they have a place in your life, the baby has a place here, and you can still be one big happy family without having to commit to Michelle?" I set my pen down and fold my hands on top of my desk. "It's the best of all worlds. It smooths things over with her dad, it shows you're making a real effort. But leaving them off the guest list does the exact opposite."

He thinks about that a few beats, and then he finally sighs and nods. "You're right."

I wink at him. "Get used to saying that."

He rolls his eyes, and I shrug innocently.

"Happy wife, happy life...right?" I ask.

"Something like that," he mutters. "But when this whole thing blows up, it's on you."

"I am willing to shoulder that so long as when it *doesn't* blow up and you raise a ton of dough for your new foundation, that's also on me."

"Deal," he says, and he sticks his hand out across my desk. I shake it. "I have more questions. Have you considered holding this event indoors somewhere or is it definitely an outdoor event?"

"Of course," I say. "I found one affordable indoor option since, as you know, it's hot as fuck in the summer in Vegas, but I reserved a local park. Indoors means fancier, and that's not what you said you wanted. This way, people can bring their families, and we can hold it somewhere that's similar to what you want to build for other parts of our community. I'm thinking we can set up tents for the players with extra air coolers, other tents for drinking and hanging out, and maybe a bounce house for the kids. It'll be a charity event unlike any our guests have ever been to. It'll be the event of the season, and maybe next year, we'll find a date when we can hold it in sub-triple digit temps."

"Are you sure you want to rush this?" he asks, folding his arms across his chest.

I nod. "I think we have to. We need this to take place before the season while you have time to do it. We have to prove now what an asset you are to this community. And I promise, I'll do it right."

"I know you will." He exhales. "And on a totally different note, your brother and Nicki are coming over for a date night in an hour."

"Tonight?" I ask. To be honest, I've been working all damn day. I'm tired, and I want a glass of wine and maybe a foot massage from my new husband in the bathtub...but instead, I'm supposed to be entertaining?

"Yeah. Is that a problem?"

"Nope. Can't wait." I smile sweetly. If he can budge a little on the whole inviting all the worst people in the world to his summer outdoor charity event, I suppose I can give up my foot massage in the tub idea. Seems like a pretty even trade. And, to be fair, the night he planned for us sounds like a lot more fun than the thing I'm planning.

CHAPTER 9

We're experimenting with new cocktail concoctions when the doorbell rings. Luke goes to answer it while I taste test the whiskey and tequila mixed with cranberry juice and seltzer thing he just mixed for me. For the record, it's a miss.

I'm still wincing when he walks in with my brother and my best friend. "Not a winner?" he asks with a laugh, and I shake my head as I try to cleanse my palate with some plain seltzer, which tastes almost as bad as the Luke special he just had me try.

"It's a one-way route to Vomitsville," I say.

"Count me in," Josh jokes, and hugs are issued all around.

We end up with four simple whiskey and Cokes, all heavy on the whiskey, and the bell rings a few minutes later with our food delivery—a nice assortment of salads and fried appetizers. We take the food out to the back patio and sit under the pergola, which has landscape lights strung across the top and couches for us to relax on with a table in the middle where we set the food.

The sun has just set and the lights cast a romantic glow over the four of us. The air coolers I bought to try out ahead of our charity event are doing their thing, and so far, so good.

We fill each other in on everything we missed since the last time we saw each other (except, obviously, we leave out the dirty details about *all the sex* we've been having since, hello, this is my brother—but I *will* be filling Nicki in on the goods later). Josh and Nicki are adjusting to life at home as newlyweds, which basically translates to mean that they haven't actually unpacked their bags yet because they've been so busy doing nothing (or maybe they're leaving out the dirty details for my benefit, too—for which I thank them. Profusely).

Luke and Josh head inside to refill our drinks, and that's when Nicki starts grilling me.

"You two are looking awfully cozy," she starts.

I grin. I can't help it. "It's like…God, it's like a dream come true."

"Give me every detail."

I giggle. "Some things shall remain between husband and wife."

"Liar. Is he a boob guy or an ass guy?"

"More boobs, but just because we haven't had a lot of time to really get to know one another yet."

"Josh is a total ass guy," she says.

"Nicki! There are things I don't need to know about my brother."

She laughs, and despite my horror, I do, too.

"Okay, boys aside, are you okay? Work going good? You're enjoying Vegas and staying forever?"

"That's a lot of questions," I say. "But, yeah, everything is going really well. I'm planning this charity thing and it's sucking up all my time. Invitations went out, so now I wait for the RSVPs and then I can really take off." I reach for another mozzarella stick. If there's one thing I can't resist besides glittery stickers, it's fried cheese.

"Consider the Nolans, party of two, there. This is our official RSVP. And tell me what I can do to help. I'm here for anything you need."

"You're the best," I say, munching on my fried goodness. "I will definitely take you up on that."

The boys rejoin us, and with more alcohol comes louder voices and more boisterous laughter. By the time they leave, it's well after midnight and I'm exhausted.

But not *too* exhausted.

"I'm gonna take a shower," Luke says as we finish cleaning up the kitchen.

"Care for some company?" I ask with a raised brow.

He takes a step toward me. "If you're offering, that's a definite yes." He pulls me into his arms.

"Oh, I'm offering. I've been waiting all night for them to leave so I could have some naked time with you." I lean forward and kiss him, and he chuckles before he sweeps me up into his arms and carries me up the stairs.

He sets me down once we arrive in the bathroom and he moves away from me only to turn on the water in the shower to let it warm up. He moves back into my orbit after he peels off his shirt and tosses it to the ground.

I peel mine off, too, tossing it somewhere near his.

He lowers his pants, and I mirror him.

We stand in our underwear, which we both remove next as we eye the other hungrily, and then he pounces. His mouth crashes down to mine as he pulls me against his rock hard body. This kiss is urgent and needy, all the pent-up desire from being apart for much of the day rising to the surface.

I've always loved the *honeymoon* phase of a relationship—that time when you just can't get enough of the other one, when it's all sex all the time and it's hot and fiery. But this is an *actual* honeymoon phase...and I find myself not wanting to ever move out of it as I kiss him back with all the same desire and passion he's giving me.

I know that's not possible. Work is starting up again for him very soon, and we'll have to face a new reality. And so I plan to indulge in every spare moment I possibly can in the meantime.

He moves us into the shower, a stream of hot water beating down on each of us thanks to dual shower heads, and our kiss turns slippery despite the urgency still there. He turns me around, and I reach for the glass of the side of the shower to brace myself as I bend forward to allow him the access he wants. He plunges into me then reaches around to grab my breasts in his hands. I claw at the glass as he pounds away at me. I need something to hold onto, something to grasp as the pleasure drives me closer and closer to the edge, but my hands simply slip on the wet glass. He paws at my breasts, and then he moves one of his hands down to brush against my clit while he continues to drive into me.

And then the flash of white light hits me, and I dive over the cliff into the abyss of bliss, my body contracting over his as his grunts turn into growls. A loud and sexy groan rips from his chest, and then he shoves into me a few more times as he lets go, too.

He slips out of me, and then he soaps my loofah and washes my body. I do the same for him, spending extra time massaging shampoo into his hair and stealing kisses around the stream of water.

He dries me off with tender care, kissing my body all over as he dries each spot, and then we collapse together into bed.

If this isn't sheer perfection, I'm not sure what is. I send up a prayer before I fall asleep that this feeling, this love, and this bond between us will last forever.

CHAPTER 10

I point to the giant white tent on the left. "That's the hospitality tent," I say, and the line of workers holding trays of food disperses in that direction.

I fold my arms over my chest and survey my work.

In the last three weeks, I've slept very little as I've worked my ass off to get this event off the ground. We're scheduled to have twenty-seven members of the Vegas Aces in attendance, eight other football players, a bunch of Aces staff—including the team owner—and, of course, Luke's brother, and most attendees are bringing dates or even entire families with them. I ended up reserving three huge tents and a few smaller ones, too. One of the big tents is filled with sand boxes and toys and smaller versions of the adult cornhole games set up to entertain the kids. We also have two bounce houses—one for kids four and under, the other for kids five and over. The hospitality tent has tables and chairs along with food served buffet style and drinks, and the third large tent is where the tournament will take place.

The smaller tents are the places where cornhole players will register and donations will be taken. The park has bathrooms, so I didn't even have to worry about that part of throwing a party.

Air coolers are set up in each of the tents, and while it's going to reach a blazing hot one hundred six degrees today, the coolers are definitely helping. I'd briefly considered having this event at Luke's house—*our* house—but decided this park was way better. A huge playground sits not too far away from us, and on the other side of the park is a splash pad to cool off the kids. It's a perfect example of the types of things Luke wants to build with the money he raises today.

And it all starts in less than an hour.

I draw in a deep breath as I look around.

I've done all I can do at this point. I've delegated every task I could think of to delegate, including hiring an official event photographer—but I'm still going to focus on taking pictures of Luke. I need as much footage as I can to show the community how much they need him here in Vegas.

Luke is in the tournament tent working with the men we hired to serve as our referees. Josh is with him, and Nicki is in the hospitality tent helping out there. I check on everybody, make sure nobody needs anything, and then I glance up and see the first of our guests as they start to arrive.

This is really happening.

My heart races.

I head to the hospitality tent for a cold bottle of water. It's showtime.

I grab Luke and the two of us walk toward the registration desk hand-in-hand to greet Luke's celebrity friends as they enter the First Annual Dalton Celebrity Cornhole Tournament to benefit the Luke and Ellie Dalton Foundation.

That's right. The Luke *and Ellie* Dalton Foundation.

That's what he wanted to name it. He said it wouldn't exist without my idea or the contributions I've made, and he thought it was important for my name to appear on the marquee.

I was too excited to turn him down, but what happens in a year from now when our *contract* is up? What if my last name isn't Dalton anymore?

I guess we'll cross that bridge when we get to it.

"Hey, Fletch," he says to the guy I recognize as Brandon Fletcher, the quarterback I met at the ball we attended together. A different woman is on his arm, dressed in freaking jeans and heels when we're at an outdoor tournament in a park. For my own part, I'm wearing a Dalton shirt, shorts, and sneakers. It's what Luke wanted, and he's in shorts and a t-shirt, too. We're comfortable, as opposed to the last charity event we attended together.

Luke introduces me as his wife to his teammates, and it's absolutely surreal that I'm even here right now. I recognize Nadine, Krista, and Leah, the football wives who were Nicki's bridesmaids, when they come in with their football player husbands.

When I spot Calvin as he makes his way toward the registration table, the woman on his arm surely can't be Michelle's mother. She might not even be as old as Michelle, to be honest.

I push the negative, judgmental thoughts away. It's not my place to judge someone else's relationship.

It just seems a little hypocritical that he expects Luke to give up his own happiness to be with Michelle when Cal himself is with someone who's not the mother of his own children (but who is probably in the same age range as his own children).

I'm sure they're desperately in love. I'm sure it has nothing to do with his money.

"Mr. Bennett!" Luke says brightly when Calvin gets to the front of the line. "We're so pleased you could make it."

Too much brightness, Luke. Dial it down a notch. We're not *that* happy he's here.

"This looks to be an incredible event. We're always thrilled to do our part to help the community. Isn't that right, darling?" he says to his date.

"Yes, of course," she says.

"Ensuring every kid has a fair shot to play sports is important to me," Luke says.

Calvin gives him an unreadable glance. "As long as your own kids come first," he murmurs, taking a bit of a shot.

"Of course," Luke says simply, and speak of the damn devil, up walk Jack and his date.

I blow out a breath as I recognize the woman on his arm. Michelle.

"You might've chosen a hotter day for this," Jack says in lieu of a hello, and the criticism isn't lost on me. God, I hope Luke hits him in the balls with a beanbag.

Sort of like I did to Luke on accident that time.

"Daddy!" Michelle says, rushing up to Calvin and throwing her arms around him.

"Shelly," he says affectionately, patting her on the back as she clings to him. "Have you been taking your vitamins?" he asks.

"Of course, Daddy," she says, and the sweet factor is beyond fake as she glances over at Luke to gauge his reaction to her even being here. "And I have an appointment this week. Jack said he'd come with me since he'll still be in town. Isn't that so sweet of him?"

Calvin purses his lips. "So Jack, the brother of the father, will be there? What about the actual father?" He glances in Luke's direction.

"Of course I'll be there," he says quickly. "In fact, both Ellie and I are thrilled to go." He grabs my hand.

I knew nothing about this appointment, but I nod and fake my way through it just like everyone else in this conversation seems to be doing. "We just need Michelle to fill us in on the exact time, date, and location." I smile sweetly, and then I completely change the subject. "Thank you all again for being here. We're so excited to raise money for this very important cause." It's my way of ushering them through the line.

And then, as if these people showing up at the same time wasn't enough, Savannah makes her way toward the table.

Why the hell did I think it was a good idea to invite them?

CHAPTER 11

To my extreme surprise, Savannah remains professional through the entire tournament, but I can't help wondering the whole time what, exactly, she has on the Dalton brothers and if I'll ever find out the truth. She basically ignores me, which is fine, and she takes notes throughout the day, which tells me that maybe she'll write an article about the event. I hope she does because any exposure for the foundation is good exposure.

The accountant we hired gives me the final number as the tournament draws to a close. Luke beat his brother, which made my heart absolutely sing (and his, too, I'm sure), but the final big winner of the tournament who will take home the trophy is Jaxon Bryant, star running back of the Vegas Aces.

I give the number to Luke, who takes the microphone the announcers had been using all day during the tournament. "Thank you to everyone who came today, to all the players who paid to be part of this tournament, to everyone who donated their time and money. I'm amazed at what a successful event this has been, but maybe I shouldn't be. After all, my new wife is the one who planned the entire thing while also planning a wedding. I'm proud to have her by my side," he says, nodding toward me and waving his hand in a *come up here* motion. He waits for me to join him on the stage before he continues. "Give it up for Ellie Dalton," he says, and I hear hoots and hollers at the mention of my name. I smile shyly as my cheeks color and I wave to the crowd assembled as they listen to Luke.

He turns back to the crowd. "Thanks to you and your generosity, we've managed to raise over one hundred thousand dollars. We'll continue taking donations today, so that number may still change. Thank you again. We hope you had a great time. I know I did, and if Ellie is up for it, we'll have another one of these tournaments next year. But maybe in, say, February."

That garners a laugh from the sweating crowd.

"Go Aces!" he yells, and his teammates all echo his sentiment with one loud baritone *Go Aces!*

And then it's all over. People say their goodbyes and start making their way back to their cars.

For all the planning that went into this event, as quickly as it began...here we are at the end. We're married. Our charity event is over. Training camp starts next week.

Now what?

I've been running around settling tabs with vendors, and Luke has been a gracious host as he talks to groups of people before they take off. Nicki and Josh are still around helping out, too. So I'm surprised when I see Jack and Michelle still sitting in the hospitality tent as everyone else except Luke, me, Nicki, and Josh has cleared out.

Michelle is talking and Jack looks bored beside her. People move all around them taking down tables and chairs, but they seem oblivious.

And then I watch Jack as his eyes zero in on his brother, who sits alone in the registration tent as he glances through the notebook where the volunteers kept track of donations. Minus the expenses from today, we made a huge chunk of money that will go directly back to the community.

I don't like that they're still here, but at least they didn't cause any problems during the actual event. I head toward Luke to see if he needs any help.

"You know your brother is still here?" I ask him when I get to the tent.

He glances up at the sound of my voice. "Ellie, this is incredible. It far exceeded any of my expectations." He stands and presses a kiss to my cheek. "*You* are incredible. Thank you for the idea, for the event, for being here for me."

One of the papers on the table is swept up in a random gust of wind and flies just outside the tent. "I'll grab it," I say.

It flutters away from me to the backside of the tent, and as I bend to pick it up, I hear another voice join Luke's.

"What do you want?" Luke asks.

"Just hear me out," Jack says. There's a pause, and then Jack says, "I'll triple my donation if you divorce her."

Why would he want us divorced? Why does he care so much about making sure I'm not in Luke's life?

There's another brief pause, and I can't see either of them from where I'm frozen on the other side of the tent, but I still so as not to make a sound. I imagine in that brief pause, Luke does something to indicate they aren't alone. "Forget it. I love Ellie, and I don't need your damn donation. And by the way, you can stop blackmailing me now. I have as much on you as you have on me."

Jack blows out a frustrated breath. "You can't tell her. This stays between you, me, and Savannah. You know it could ruin both our careers if it gets out. Her brother is on the Aces, man." His words clearly show that he didn't get it if Luke was trying to warn him that I'm standing right here overhearing this entire conversation.

"And, may I remind you, you're showing up everywhere lately with my team owner's daughter," Luke says.

"Yeah, we're so in love." The sarcasm isn't lost on me, and I get the sudden feeling the only reason Jack has been hanging around her is so he has something he can hold over Luke...but Luke doesn't really care *who* Michelle hangs out with as long as it isn't us.

"Look, we both have a lot to lose if anyone finds out," Luke says, his voice low like he's trying to be quiet enough for me not to overhear since he knows I'm standing right here. "Ellie is my wife now. I trust her with my life. Look at what she did for me today."

My heart balloons in my chest. I hate Jack a little more now, but I also get that he's trying to protect whatever secret they all have.

It seems like it's a secret they're holding pretty tightly onto...but secrets always have a way of coming out.

I slowly walk across the field toward Nicki, who watches me as I walk. "Were you just spying on the brothers Dalton?"

I shake my head. "No. I was grabbing this piece of paper when Jack walked up and they started talking. I just don't want Jack to ruin what has been such a great day for Luke."

"Why'd you invite him, then?"

I make a face. "His fat checkbook."

She laughs, but I'm not laughing. I want to tell someone what I just overheard...but clearly this is a secret they want to keep. If I mention it to Nicki, then I'll just have added pressure to find it out.

No...I better not say anything. But I might just have to ask Luke later.

Especially if this could affect the careers of these brothers. I'm his publicist now. If making him look indispensable to the team is part of my job, I need to know what skeletons are hiding in his closets so I'm equipped to handle them when they jump out.

CHAPTER 12

I glance at the picture on the wall above Michelle's head.

Four little tiny baby fingers wrapped around a single adult finger, and the thumb coming around the other side. Precious.

I knew my "husband" had gotten another woman pregnant, but I didn't really think about what that meant until this very moment. I know nothing about kids, but once Michelle has this baby, I'm going to have to learn. I'll be a stepmother of sorts to this child.

Part of me even wonders if Luke is going to ask Michelle to move in so he can be close to the baby. He's just the kind of guy who would do exactly that even if it's the last thing he—or his wife—personally wants.

It's weird sitting here, Luke's hand in mine and Michelle sitting across from us and next to Jack. I shouldn't even be here, really, and neither should Jack.

I've always wanted kids, but I assumed they'd be a little further into my future. And, if I'm being honest, I assumed they'd be *mine*, too. I assumed I'd be the mother, not the woman married to the father-to-be.

As we sit here, I sort of start to see the reality of why Luke felt so desperate that the only answer he could see was to marry another woman.

"Michelle?" a woman calls, and the four of us stand. The woman looks surprised as she sees the two lean, attractive men walking toward the ultrasound room with Michelle and me. "Last name?" she asks.

"Bennett," Michelle says.

"Right through here," she says with a smile, and the four of us follow her to the room.

Michelle sits on a table, Jack takes the chair beside her, and Luke and I hang back. The ultrasound technician turns off the lights. "Lie back, lift your shirt, and lower your pants just a little," she says. Michelle does, and she squirts some gel onto Michelle's stomach. She moves it around with a wand, and we all see some movement on the large television screen broadcasting Michelle's uterus. There's a bunch of other information on there, too. Dates and codes and things I assume are in some way related to pregnancy but I have no actual idea.

"There's baby," the tech says, and I strain to see what she's talking about. I really just see some wavy white lines on a black backdrop.

"Where?" Luke asks, voicing my own question.

She takes a mouse and points to the baby on the screen. She circles a blob. "Right here," she says.

"Can you tell if it's a boy or a girl?" Luke asks.

"Not yet with certainty on the ultrasound, but if Michelle had the genetic testing done at ten weeks, the doctor should be able to tell you if you want to know," the tech says. She doesn't leave room for questions—like the one I have, which is whether Michelle already knows if it's a boy or a girl. "I'm just going to take a few measurements. Michelle, you'll feel some pressure, okay?"

"Okay," she says, and it's so weird that we're all looking at the baby chilling in her uterus as the tech moves the wand all around.

Once the tech is done, she hands over a printout of the session. "You can head back to the lobby and the doctor will call you back shortly for your exam."

"Does everything look okay?" Luke asks.

"Growth is on track and the baby looks healthy," the tech says with a smile.

"Thanks," Luke says.

The four of us head back toward the lobby.

"Do you know the gender?" Luke asks.

Michelle shakes her head.

"I want to know," he says.

"Okay. I don't."

"Then I won't tell you," he says thickly. "But I have a right to know."

Michelle just huffs in reply, and it may be kind of a petty argument, but it does give me some insight into why they ended things. They're just not compatible, and if they argue on things like finding out gender, certainly they'll argue over the bigger issues later.

My heart aches for Luke. He wasn't expecting this twist of fate, and he certainly doesn't want to share a kid with this woman he thought he'd written out of his life story, and now because of one drunken night, he's stuck with her forever.

"Michelle?" Luke asks.

"Hmm?" she asks, lazily playing with Jack's hand as she clutches it.

"Why did the chart in there put your date of conception at March thirty-first?"

Michelle blinks in Luke's direction. "Huh?"

"The date of conception," Luke repeats. "We weren't together March thirty-first. We weren't together until that weekend. April fifth."

My heart races.

If what he's saying is true...what if he's not the father?

It crossed my mind when we first found out, but Michelle said he is, and he admitted they had a night, so we all assumed she was telling the truth.

But what if she isn't?

Between the wedding and the charity event plus working on Luke's public image, I sort of let the whole idea of whether Luke is really this baby's father go. But maybe it's time to revisit that train of thought.

"That's an estimate based on the date of my last period. If you want more details, I'd be happy to get them for you. You know, like the length of my periods, how many tampons I go through..."

Luke holds up a hand. "I don't think that's necessary."

A paternity test might be, though.

I don't bring it up in the lobby of the obstetrician's office, obviously.

No...I wait until Luke and I are home, long after Michelle and Jack have slithered off to wherever it is they go. Sheila just left after doing a deep clean of the whole house, Pepper is taking a nap in the family room, and we're enjoying some of Debbie's homemade shredded chicken tacos for dinner.

"So you think it's yours?" I blurt.

Luke chuckles. "I wish I could say I have no reason to believe it isn't...but I don't trust Michelle."

"You mentioned you have some experience with paternity tests. Care to share more about that?"

He blows out a breath and takes a bite of taco before he answers. "I've had two women allege I was the father of their unborn children. For the record, I have no children. I was stupid, but I always wore condoms unless I was in a relationship. I know they're not a hundred percent, but I requested both women take a paternity test anyway."

"And they came back negative?"

He chuckles. "Something like that. They came back and showed I was not a match to the child."

"Can they do one of those when she's pregnant?"

He nods. "They can do a blood draw and compare DNA that way. It's completely safe for both mother and child."

"Then do it. Make her take one," I say.

"It's not that simple," he says. "Aside from the fact that her father would murder me if he thought I was indicating that baby isn't mine, she claims she wasn't with anyone else. She's sure it's mine. And besides, we'd been in a relationship. I wasn't exactly running for the condom box. I never found a condom in the morning, so we can both guess what that means."

"You're assuming you had sex," I point out. I want to eat my taco because it's so damn delicious, but I also need answers. "What if you didn't? Drunk Luke hates Michelle just as much as sober Luke."

"I can't deny that."

"You don't even have definitive proof that you slept with her. Why aren't you putting up a little more of a fight here?"

He stares down at his plate. "She says it's mine. Her father has the ability to take away everything that matters to me. What choice do I have, Ellie?"

I don't have an answer for that. He's right. He's stuck.

"Have you thought about asking her for proof it's yours?" I ask.

"Of course I have. But then I think about how her father would react to that if he ever found out, and something stops me."

"There isn't anything stopping *me*," I say, suggesting I'm happy to do his dirty work for him.

He looks thoughtfully at me for a beat. "I guess I can't really stop you if I don't know anything about it."

"I'm your wife, Luke," I say. "I'm here to protect you, to fight for you, to fight *with* you. We'll get to the truth no matter what it takes."

His eyes lock on mine across the table, and he nods briefly. "Thank you." His voice is soft and sincere and full of emotion.

"Don't thank me until we have our answers."

But I *will* get those answers.

Whatever it takes.

CHAPTER 13

I sit in the backyard with Pepper the next Monday morning. I stare at the empty treadmill that's sadly not getting any use now that Luke is away at training camp.

The Aces rent out some vineyard in California for the first two weeks of camp before coming back home to have the rest of camp at their practice facility. Their first preseason game is mid-August, a few days after they return home from the vineyard.

It sounds like a vacation, but Luke has assured me that it's not. Instead, his days are filled with workouts and practices and new formations and schemes and battles for position. Nights are filled with recovery, and early mornings are filled with cryotherapy and massages.

Still sounds like a vacation to me.

Josh is gone, too, and Nicki and I have already talked at length about how we'll spend every waking moment together. Except I'm awake right now and Nicki's not here, so I guess that promise was a bit of an exaggeration.

I post a picture of Luke and a story with a picture he sent me last night of the vineyard where he's staying. I do some research on how players contribute to the community even when they're in season.

And then, on a total whim, I take a quick glance at local public relations agencies. I need something to do. Handling one client isn't enough to fill my days, especially now that our little charity event is over and he's not even here to create thirst traps I can snap pictures of.

I have nothing on the horizon. In short, I'm bored.

I step onto the treadmill. I think about the hot guy who usually uses it. I click some buttons, but it's useless. I can't even get the damn thing to turn on. So instead, I take a walk around the yard. I toss the ball for Pepper, but she gets bored with me after a few runs across the yard. This is just the first day of this new reality. I need to get out. I need to find a hobby. I need *something*.

The doorbell rings a little before eleven, and when I open it, I find Debbie standing on the other side with bags of groceries.

"Hey Debbie!" I say probably with way too much enthusiasm. "What are you doing here?" I take the bags from her and she follows me into the kitchen. I figured without Luke here, she'd take a couple weeks off.

"Oh, dear, you still need your nourishment. I'll be making your favorites." She winks at me. "Or, at least, the things Luke told me were your favorites."

"You don't have to do all this. You should take this time off while Luke's away." I don't mind cooking, anyway. In fact, I sort of like it...plus it gives me something to pass the time.

"I don't mind. It gives me something to do." She smiles at me, and suddenly I feel a little bond with her. She may have lost her husband when he passed away, which is very different from what I'm feeling, but we're both searching for a purpose. She found hers when she started cooking for Luke.

I have yet to find mine. Maybe I'll look through those local agencies again.

Debbie and I chat while she gets started making the shredded chicken for the tacos—definitely one of my favorites—and it's nearly four in the afternoon by the time she's done and takes off. I text Nicki.

Me: *What are you up to? I'm bored.*
Nicki: *Reorganizing my kitchen. Want to come help?*
Not even a little bit.
Me: *Sure. Be right over.*

"Do you think the plates should go in this cabinet?" Nicki points to one. "Or this one?" She points to another one.

I don't care.

I don't say that, obviously. This is my best friend. But I don't even like organizing my *own* kitchen, let alone someone else's. When I moved into Luke's place and it was already done, I was good to go. As Nicki should have been. She's lived in this house for over a year. Who takes literally everything out of their cabinets only to change which one the plates are stored in after a year of habitually going to the same cabinet?

"That one," I say, pointing to the first one. "It's closest to the oven, which will be convenient for plating your food." Like she ever cooks.

Okay, I'm being snarky. I need to work on that.

"So give me the real talk. What's it like being married to a football player?" I ask, setting down the bowl in my hand to have a conversation with Nicki.

She sets down the wineglass she's polishing and slides onto the stool next to me. "It's wonderful and frustrating and awful and amazing all at once."

"What's a typical game week like?" I ask, setting my chin in my palm as I lean on the counter.

"If they win on Sunday, they get Monday off. Sort of. Coaches will email film for them to study but they don't have to go in. If they lose on Sunday, they go in on Monday. Tuesday is their day off, so it's the one day when they can connect with the community or do rehab if they need to, but it's also the one day they get with you. Wednesday is technique practice and Thursday is strategy practice for the upcoming game. They go hard and intense. Friday is a travel day if it's an away game, and they do light situational practice or strategy meetings when they get wherever they're going. Saturday is a light practice at the stadium and Saturday night they stay in a hotel."

"For away games, right?" I ask.

She shakes her head and picks up the wineglass. "Home or away."

My brows dip. "They stay in a hotel the night before a game even if they're playing at home?"

"Yep." She stands and picks up another wineglass that apparently needs polishing. "They have a curfew to make sure they get enough sleep and are ready to play on Sunday regardless of which city they're in. Every team is a little different, but the Aces do bed checks on Friday nights, too, if they're out of town. I guess Fridays used to be crazy party nights whenever they'd travel somewhere away from home, but Coach Thompson put a stop to that."

"That's crazy. They don't even get to go out?" I ask. "These are grown men."

"Right. And they're getting huge paychecks to play a game. The Aces just want to make sure their players are ready to do what they're being paid to do."

"Don't some of the guys resent that?"

"Thompson is great about spinning it to make it come from a place of caring about each player rather than keeping tabs on them. The younger guys don't always get it at first, but guys have been kicked off the team for repeatedly missing curfew. They take it pretty seriously when they know their job's at stake."

"Wow. Serious business."

She nods. "The Aces are great in the way they take care of their guys. You'll see."

"Fingers crossed," I murmur. I'm still more than a little worried about Luke's future with the team given the owner's feelings toward him.

I'm surrounded by plates and bowls when my phone dings with a new text. I grab it out of my pocket with the hope that whatever this message says will get me out of actually having to put all this shit away.

Luke: *We're free for the next half hour if you're around to talk.*

I glance up and see Nicki reading a text on her phone, too. This must be the official *call your wife* time.

"I'm gonna call Josh," Nicki says.

"I'm going to head home. It's Pepper's dinner time anyway and I just got a text from Luke, too."

She gives me a quick hug. "You can come back here for dinner if you want. I'm ordering Chinese."

"Thanks, but Debbie left me chicken tacos. You're welcome to join me."

She glances around her kitchen and sighs. "Thanks, but I've got a project I can't give up on now."

I laugh. "Check in tomorrow, okay?"

She nods. "I'm actually getting together with the other football wives tomorrow for lunch. Come with me. You're one of us now."

I nod. "Okay. That sounds fun, actually." Not only will it give me something to do, but it actually *does* sound fun. It's time I get to know some people in the area—even if it's not the best idea to get attached to the football wife lifestyle.

I call Luke as soon as I walk in the front door.

"Hey," he answers softly, and his warm voice sounds exhausted.

"How's the first day?" I ask.

"Reminding me why the average age in the league is twenty-six."

I chuckle. "You okay?"

"Let's just say I'm looking forward to the cryotherapy in the morning."

"What exactly is that?" I ask. "You've mentioned it a few times."

"It's cold therapy. I stand in a chamber in freezing temps for three minutes."

I make a face even though he can't see it. "That sounds awful."

He laughs. "It helps with muscle pain. It's worth the three minutes of freezing my ass off for the benefits."

"So what was today like that you're already in pain?"

"It's the first day. Everyone pushes hard to show they didn't fuck around in the offseason. The rookies are trying to prove themselves—well, the ones who don't walk around like they know everything, anyway. And the old guys—that's me—are trying to prove they're still relevant."

"You're still relevant," I say softly.

He sighs. "I like to think so."

"Does the owner go to camp?"

"Not this leg of it," he says. "He'll be there when we're back home, but he doesn't come out here. This is just coaches and players. It gives us a little time to get back into things, to get to know the new guys, and to get back in shape."

"And to use the cold chamber."

"We have a chamber at our practice facility, too," he says. "Out here, they have four. We only have one, and the line tends to get lengthy waiting for it."

"What does a vineyard need four cold chambers for?" I ask.

"Aside from actually freezing grapes, we're not the only guests who frequent this facility. There's a whole therapy wing that gets used pretty much year-round by different athletes."

"Interesting. So what's next on the agenda?"

"Dinner in, well, fifteen minutes now, and then we have meetings with our position coaches. What have you been up to today?" he asks.

"Trying to find something to do. Pepper has been well-exercised and I've realized how entertaining you must be."

He chuckles. "You know, a few guys mentioned to me how impressed they are with my social media presence."

"They did?"

"Yep," he says. "I actually had two who asked me if my publicist is taking on more clients. If you're interested, I'm sure I could rally up more than just two guys. As long as I always come first."

"Seriously?" I'm in awe. I just wanted to help the guy who offered me a place to stay, and now I'm working for him, married to him, and he's pimping me out—in a good, professional way, of course. "What did you tell the ones who asked about me?"

"That I'd talk to you about it. I know you said you don't know enough about athletes to take them on as clients, but from what I'm hearing...that doesn't really matter. You'll research what you don't know, but what you know about PR more than makes up for what you don't know when it comes to the game. So I guess...just think about it."

"I will," I promise...even though it's a no-brainer. Of course I'll take on more clients. He's right. I'll research what I don't know. Are there people better equipped to take on athletes as clients? Absolutely. But I don't know all that much about architecture, and one of my clients was a firm in Chicago. I don't know that much about lingerie, but I learned when I had to work with Todd on a client who needed a total rebrand after a celebrity was caught gifting their goods to a hooker.

And I'll learn more about football, too.

Especially since it'll help make Luke even more indispensable to the Aces, which is my end-goal in the first place.

CHAPTER 14

Leah, Nadine, and Krista are already sitting at a round table when Nicki and I walk into the restaurant.

"I hear congratulations are in order," Nadine says to me, and I grin widely and flash my hand so everyone can check out my sparkly new hardware.

"Good catch," Leah says. "So many women have tried to tie that one down—including Calvin's daughter. How'd you manage to do it? And so quickly?"

I shrug, trying not to feel defeated that Michelle has already been brought up as I slide into an open chair and Nicki takes the one beside me. "We've known each other a while through Josh. The timing was just right, I guess."

"Didn't you just break up with someone?" Krista asks, and I get the feeling she doesn't believe what Luke and I have is real.

"Yep. But when the timing is right with Luke Dalton, you jump at the chance. Am I right?" I get a laugh out of most of the ladies gathered. Not Krista.

"Well congrats, girl," Nadine says. "But now you'll be a one-night stand virgin forever."

Everyone shares a laugh, and I don't correct her. Because I'm not anymore. Not really.

"So tell me everything I need to know about being a football wife," I say, trying to push the spotlight off me and allow these ladies to shine.

Leah launches into the same warnings she gave Nicki about lifting your husband up so some other woman doesn't swoop in, Nadine talks about how important it is to maintain my own identity and have things that are just for me, and Krista tells me who I need to get to know in the staff offices. Apparently there are tons of activities for the wives and families of players, things like ladies' luncheons, community events, charity work, and even Bible study groups if I'm so inclined to be part of any of it.

And I am inclined. I don't just need something to fill the hours...I need a community. But does it make sense for me to become a part of this community only to have to leave it in a year?

I'm scared to form attachments that I won't get to keep. And nothing says I won't still be around in a year. We can stay together forever if that's what we decide, but the contract only stipulates a year.

Even so, it makes sense to immerse myself in this experience. Getting involved and helping anywhere I can, being supportive of my husband—these seem like more ways to prove that this team needs Luke.

"Richard mentioned you've taken over Luke's social media," Nadine says. "How's that going?"

"He hired me as his publicist. I used to do public relations back in Chicago and when we talked about his total lack of media and community presence, I said I'd take him on," I explain.

"What's it like working with your husband?" Krista asks.

I raise a brow. "Have you seen the thirst traps I've posted? It's not hard."

The girls laugh. "Well you've done wonders," Nadine says. "People are taking notice, and not just the social media stuff, but the community outreach. Can you take on Richard, too?" she asks.

I chuckle. "For the right price."

Nadine laughs and winks at Nicki. "I like her."

My chest warms at the thought of building a bond with these women. We sit chatting for hours even after we've all finished our lunches. We sip wine and laugh, and I'm already starting to get that first feeling like I'm a part of something.

I learn that these two weeks are the loneliest of the entire season because even when the guys have to travel for games, they're usually only gone Friday through Sunday.

Leah invites me to go with her to the staff offices tomorrow so she can introduce me to all the key people, and I jump at the chance. Not only will it seal my own place as a football wife, but it's also giving me the chance to get to know Leah. I could certainly do with more friends out here in Vegas since my old ones basically ditched me when I left Chicago.

I think of Brittany. She was my best friend at the office back home, and when she got wind of my tryst with Todd and the way we were both fired, she faded immediately away. If that taught me anything, it's that scandals prove who your true friends are.

I've learned my only true friend is Nicki. She's the only one who has been by my side since we were teenagers, and now she's family. But I'm working on a complete transformation. Maybe it's okay to make some new friends—especially if these are people Nicki trusts.

* * *

"This is Erin," Leah says, stopping in a doorway. "She's the director of charitable contributions. Erin, this is Ellie Dalton, Luke's new wife."

Erin glances up and smiles.

"We've met," I say, smiling at Erin. "Good to see you again. Thanks for all your advice with our event. It went amazingly well."

"I saw Savannah's story in the *Sun*. Great work, Ellie. I never would've imagined it was the first event you organized based on its success."

"Thank you," I say, feeling a little self-conscious at her compliment. "I couldn't have done it without your help."

We move to the next office. "This is Phil, Director of Player Engagement and Development," Leah says. "Phil, meet Ellie, Luke Dalton's new wife."

"Ellie," Phil says warmly as he stands. He sticks his hand out over his desk to shake mine. "Nice to meet you."

"And you," I say. I'm about to ask what, exactly, his job entails when he beats me to the punch.

"I'm here to help players set career goals both while they're with the organization and with what comes after," he explains.

"Oh, yes." I nod. "You and I need to schedule a meeting about what comes next for Luke."

He chuckles. "I've been trying to get that guy to commit to some sort of goal regarding what comes next for *years*. Here's to hoping you have better luck than me."

I press my lips together. "That definitely sounds like my husband."

Leah introduces me to Terry, the Director of Community Relations, and a few other key people. The name plate on the last office we get to says *Monique Thompson*.

"Thompson?" I ask.

Leah nods. "Maybe the most important person you'll need to know in this entire organization...Coach's wife." Leah knocks on the door, and we hear a *come in* a second later. I'm suddenly a little nervous.

"Leah!" the elegant woman behind the desk says. I'd pin her at mid-fifties, but despite the elegance, she has this motherly aura about her. She stands and moves around to give her a hug. "And you must be Ellie," she says to me. She pulls me into a hug, and somehow she's warm and comforting and at the same time gorgeous and stylish in her dress and heels. "I'm Mo, but you can call me *mom* or *Mama Mo*. All the other ladies do." She smiles as she pulls out of our hug. "Now look at you." She eyes me up and down, and then she grabs my hand and ogles my wedding ring. "The one who finally tied down Mr. Luke Dalton. Good work, girl. Make it stick."

God, how I hope I can. Michelle edges into my mind at that moment. She's one of the ones who *tried* to tie down the man I married.

I wonder what Mo's opinion on her is. I know what *mine* is. Was she as friendly to the boss's daughter as she's being to me? Did Michelle get special treatment...or was she even a part of this club? And what happens now that she's not with Luke anymore? Does she just get voted off the island or something?

These might be questions best suited for Nicki.

"You two sit," she says, and we do as she makes her way around her desk. "I'm so glad Leah brought you by. You know, when she and Dave were engaged, it was Nadine who brought her by to introduce me to her, and I love how the torch is being passed." She folds her hands in front of her on top of the desk. "Welcome, welcome, welcome. I'm here for *anything* you need, whether it's a shoulder to cry on because you and Luke got into a fight all the way to a recommendation for where to go when your claws need a pedi."

I giggle at her description.

"I'm the president of the Ace of Hearts Club for the wives and girlfriends of players. You're the newest member of this very exclusive, very private, and very fun club, one that brings a ton of blessings but also a few curses. We're all here for you, and in fact I'm planning a luncheon for next Wednesday. Come. I'll introduce you and you can dive right into whatever you're interested in."

"Thank you," I say. "I appreciate it."

"Do you know many people here in town aside from your brother and Nicki?" she asks, and I love how she already knows this. It makes me feel even more a part of this club she's referring to.

I shake my head. "I met Leah, Nadine, and Krista through Nicki, but that's it. I'm completely new to town."

"Well you've got me now, and all the other ladies. They're just going to love you. And they'll all be banging your door down to take thirst traps of their men. Not for public consumption...just for their own." She winks, and I laugh.

"Luke isn't exactly a tough subject to photograph," I admit.

She laughs. "I don't think you'll get any arguments there."

We chat a little longer before we say our goodbyes, and on my way out the door, she hands me a folder. "All the important contact information you need is in there. Don't hesitate to text me or call me any time of the day or night. Supporting the wives is what I'm here to do." She gives me another hug, and I love her. I love this organization. I love my husband. I love the place I'm settling into here.

I just hope I get to keep it all.

CHAPTER 15

The day has been too good, and I feel that deep in my bones as we make our way toward the exit. My chest is warm and I feel like I've found a place where I belong even though I have no idea how long it'll last.

Does anyone, though?

Players can be traded or fall to a career-ending injury at any time. Separation and divorce run rampant for any marriage, but ones in the spotlight come with different sorts of pressures and complications.

So I'm claiming my place here while I can.

But the day has been the sort of good where I feel something coming to blindside me, and sure enough, just before we get to the exit doors to seal in what I can only describe as a feeling that I'm home, I hear my name.

"Ellie?"

I turn around and blow out a breath. "Michelle."

"Were you here looking for me?" she asks.

I shake my head nicely as I try to act like that's not the most self-centered, egotistical question I've ever heard. "No," I say. "Leah was just introducing me to some of the office staff."

"You must've skipped by my office," she says pointedly.

"You work here?" I ask.

"I figured you two already knew one another," Leah says, a touch of defensiveness in her tone. The boss's daughter really sort of puts everybody on edge.

"Yes," Michelle says, answering my question and ignoring Leah. "I'm currently serving as the administrative assistant to the director of marketing."

"That's wonderful," I say sweetly when what I really want to say is something along the lines of how it must be nice that her daddy gave her a job. Didn't Luke say something about how she'd just gotten back from studying fashion overseas when they first met? Good to see she's putting her fashion experience to good use.

"I'm glad I ran into you," she says.

"You are?" I ask, and I brace myself for whatever she's about to say.

"I was going to swing by the house tomorrow so we could have a chat since I don't have your number."

"A chat about what?" What could the two of us possibly have to talk about?

"About me moving back in."

My brows practically fly off my forehead as my eyes widen.

"Oh," she forces a fake chuckle as she covers her mouth with her hands. "I'm so sorry. Did Luke not tell you? We talked last night and I'll be moving my stuff in this weekend."

I narrow my eyes at her. What's the right move? Is she lying and trying to trap me? I won't play that game. "Luke and I haven't discussed you moving back in. That's not something I'm comfortable with."

"Good thing your opinion doesn't really matter then." She wiggles her fingers at me and flashes me a smile over her shoulder as she turns to walk away. "I'll see you Friday."

"The fuck you will," I mutter to her retreating figure.

I need to have a little chat with my dear husband.

As we walk back out to Leah's car, she's quiet. Once we slide into our seats so she can drive me back home, she starts up the car and glances at me. "You want to talk about what just happened?" she asks.

I twist my hands in my lap. "I hate her."

Leah chuckles. "Tell me how you really feel."

"She's so manipulative. I don't even really believe the baby is Luke's, yet she's moving back in? Fuck that. I need a goddamn

440

paternity test before I even consider letting her move in. And I need to talk to Luke." I barely know Leah, and I should be thinking about whether I can really trust her. She was one of Nicki's bridesmaids. If Nicki trusts her, I'm sure I can, too. Right?

But I have no idea what her relationship with Michelle is.

"But you can't until the little ten-minute window he gives you later tonight." Leah sighs heavily. "I hate training camp month."

The feeling is definitely mutual.

When my phone rings a little after eight, I immediately pick it up. "Hey there, hubby," I say.

He doesn't even muster a chuckle. "Hey."

That one syllable sort of puts me on alert. "What's wrong?"

"Rough day. I'm exhausted."

He doesn't exactly sound like he's in the mood to chat about Michelle, but I need to get this off my chest and find some answers. And I also need to know when, exactly, he made time to chat with her when he can barely fit *me* in. "I ran into Michelle today."

"You did?"

"Yeah. Leah was introducing me to the key people I need to know in the Aces organization and we happened to cross paths in the lobby. And isn't this fresh? She said you gave her the green light to move into our house."

"She said what?" he thunders.

"Yep. She's moving in this Friday. It'll be just the two of us. Isn't that sweet? Oh, and by the way, when did you have time to talk to her?"

He blows out a breath. "We talked last night," he confirms, and I fume.

I've been missing him like crazy. I get all of five minutes of his time each night...yet he somehow made time for *her*.

I blow out a breath. "You made time to talk to her when I barely get a second of your time?"

"She called from Calvin's line at the office. When your boss calls, you answer." He still sounds tired. "And I never said she could move in. I said we'd talk about the possibility."

"So why on Earth does she think she's moving in on Friday?" I demand.

He's quiet a beat, and then he mutters a curse. "I may have said something just to appease her."

"Such as?"

"That I'd talk to you about it. I figured we'd come up with a plan together, and then I had another meeting and to be honest I forgot about it. See? That's what she does. She waits until she *knows* she can manipulate me because I'm not in the right frame of mind."

"What, exactly, did you mean when you said you would talk to me about it?" I ask.

He sighs. "I told her that if you were okay with it, we'd figure something out. She must've taken that to mean that you *were* okay with it and it's fine for her to move in."

"I refuse to live with her until we have a positive paternity test, Luke." My voice is flat and unmistakably clear.

"I get that. It's fine. I'll call her right now and tell her no."

"Please do that. I know you're busy and this is the hardest couple weeks of the year for you, and I know she's your boss's daughter, but that does not give you a pass to let her manipulate *me*."

"Understood," he says. "I will fix this."

"Now. Bye." I hang up with shaking hands as anger fills me.

I realize too late that it isn't Luke I'm mad at. It's Michelle. And I just sent him off to call her, and she's going to lay it on thick and probably make him feel like he might lose his job over this, and it's all because I'm insecure.

She's winning. She's coming between us, and I'm letting her.

I have to find a way to play this game with her. I'm not quite sure what the rules are since she's making them up as she goes, but I guarantee one thing.

I'm going to find a way to beat her at her own game.

CHAPTER 16

I'm just finishing up some scrambled eggs for breakfast when the doorbell rings. I'm a little wary to actually answer it. What if it's Michelle?

Pepper beats me to the door, and when I open it, I see Greg standing there. Luke's lawyer. I only met him once when we had our contract drawn up.

"Hi," I say, my voice hesitant. "Luke isn't home..."

"I know," he says, smiling broadly. "I'm here to see you. And don't worry, I come with good news. God, lawyers hardly *ever* get to say that."

I open the door a little wider to allow him in. "Come on in."

We move to the kitchen since that's the epicenter of where guests hang out in a home, and he opens his briefcase. He slides some papers across the counter toward me.

"Luke believes in your abilities as a publicist so deeply that he wants to gift you your own company. Here I have the paperwork for you to create your own LLC, a business plan, and a check to cover start-up expenses."

My jaw hangs unattractively open. "Uh...what?"

Is this his way of apologizing for our fight last night?

Or was this already in the works? It had to have already been in the works. There's no way Greg could've shown up here that quickly since our fight was just over thirteen hours ago.

Greg chuckles. "You heard me correctly. Luke wants you to create your own agency. He has clients chomping at the bit, but you need a business plan first. And I realize you're a publicist, not a businessperson, so I'm here to answer questions and help you complete the paperwork. Luke wants this to be yours and solely yours." He clears his throat and lowers his voice. "It's something you can take with you at the culmination of your contract."

Oh.

And just like that, the wind is completely knocked from my sails at the reminder. I wonder if those are Greg's words or Luke's, and to be clear, the answer to that does make a difference. It would explain whether Luke still sees the end of our contract as the end of us.

He's giving me something wonderful, and I'm going to choose to focus on that. Those had to have been Greg's words.

"I can't believe he'd do all that for me."

He offers a small smile. "He cares about you, Ellie. Deeply." He seems like he wants to add more, but he doesn't. I wonder if that falls under the whole client confidentiality thing.

We spend the next several hours filling out paperwork. When it comes time to name the company, Greg throws out a bunch of suggestions. "Ellie Nolan Public Relations? Ellie Dalton? Dalton PR?"

"Prince Charming Public Relations," I say emphatically. "PCPR."

This may be my company, but it will always hold the name of the man who gifted it to me.

I just hope I don't live to regret that decision.

* * *

All day I've been waiting to hear from him. I wanted to call him to thank him for the gift, and with an apology for our fight, and with curiosity as to whether he got in touch with Michelle, but I forced myself to be patient so as not to bother him while he's working. I thought about sending a text message, but I want him to hear my genuine gratitude in my voice. So by the time my phone rings a little after eight, I grab it immediately.

"Thank you," I gush in lieu of a hello. "You are the most amazing man on the planet."

He chuckles. "I don't know about that."

"My very own Prince Charming," I say.

He laughs.

"Which is why I named it PCPR."

"PC...for Prince Charming?" he asks.

"Yep. I named it after you."

"Wow, Ellie," he says, a touch of surprise in his tone. "Thank you."

"Thank *you* for everything, Luke. I promise I won't let you down. This will be the most successful public relations company in all of Las Vegas."

"With you at the helm, I don't doubt that. And that reminds me, I have three potential new clients for you," he says. "I sent their information to Greg, and he'll forward it to you once he gets your official email set up. Knowing him, it'll be there by morning."

"I look forward to it. Thanks for talking me up to your buddies."

"I didn't have to. They saw what you did with the charity event. They were there. They see the benefit to what you're doing for me, and if they see it, Calvin will, too. And that's where this all started in the first place, right?" he asks.

"Yeah. That reminds me. The player relations guy...what's his name again?" I ask.

"Phil?"

"Yes, Phil. He said he's been trying to get you to set some post-playing goals for years now," I say.

He laughs. "Yeah, but remember what I said in Hawaii? It's bad luck to talk about the future."

I roll my eyes. "Yeah, yeah."

"Oh, and I called Michelle last night but she didn't answer. I'm still working on straightening that one out."

I sigh. "I thought about it a lot last night, Luke, and I'm starting to think she's doing all this on purpose. She's working hard to come between us. What if we just let her move in? Let her see firsthand that this is real, that we're in love, that she can pick and pry all she wants but it won't matter because we're married now?"

"I think that's a terrible idea," he says.

"I do, too, but what if we also get in *her* head?" I ask. "What if it gives us a way to prove this baby isn't yours?"

"Why are you so sure it isn't?"

I press my lips together. "Intuition mixed with total distrust."

I hear some loud voices in the background. "I hate to get off the phone in the middle of this conversation, but I have one more meeting I need to get to. Do you want me to try calling her again?"

"No," I say. "Let's let her move in. Let's play her game."

"Are you sure?" he asks. I'm sure he wants to say more but he can't since he has to get to his meeting. It's fine. I can handle it.

"Nope. Not at all. But it gives me a week alone with her before you get back, and if she drives me bananas, I'll stay with Nicki."

"Just be careful," he says. "I think this is a bad idea. I don't want her to hurt you. And I don't want anything that happens between the two of you to jeopardize my career."

"It won't," I say, my voice adamant. "I've got this. And thank you again for what you did for me. You can tell me you're not a Prince Charming until the end of time, but I'll keep right on believing you are."

"And I'll keep finding ways to prove I'm not."

We'll see about that.

CHAPTER 17

"Ellie, no. What the hell are you doing?" Nicki asks me.

We're hanging out at Luke's house—*our* house—eating ice cream and I just nonchalantly confessed that Michelle is moving in on Friday.

I shrug. "I don't really know, to be perfectly honest. But it has to be better knowing the devil you're dealing with than waiting for more bombs to drop, right?"

She shakes her head and makes a face. "No! This is a terrible idea."

"I know it's a terrible idea," I admit, "but it's also currently the only idea that I have to protect Luke. That's what this is all about. Starting the moment he hired me as his publicist, and going through our wedding up to now, my goal has remained the same. Protect Luke, whether it's protecting his job, his personal life, or himself, that's my whole purpose here."

"How is living with the woman your husband knocked up and hurting yourself in the process protecting him in any way whatsoever?" she asks.

"It's making him look good to his boss," I point out.

"So does sending a thank you card."

My brows dip. "Was he supposed to send a thank you card?"

She blows out an exasperated breath. "We just sent one for his wedding gift."

"Oh. We didn't get one of those from him," I say. "See? He already hates us."

"Because you didn't tell anyone about the wedding. Remember?"

"Yeah, yeah. And I get what you're saying. There are other, easier ways to look good to the boss. But this is a delicate situation, Nicki. Luke is so afraid of Michelle and her father that he *married* me. He won't stand up to her...but I will."

"Won't that be even worse?"

I lift a shoulder. "You know me. I'll just be sweet and charming."

Nicki snort-laughs. Yeah, I might have my work cut out for me when it comes to Michelle.

"So why, exactly, is this how you're choosing to handle it?" she asks.

"Because this gives me the inside track. It lets me be as close to her as I can be. Keep your enemies close, right?" I ask. "Can't get much closer than living together."

"I guess. But won't you feel like a prisoner in your own home? You can't say anything in front of her. You'll have to pretend all the time. And what if she's listening? What if she plants devices or video records you?"

"All things I've thought of. Luke has a surveillance system already in place, so if she plants anything or even tries anything, we'll know about it. We'll keycode our bedroom door and offices. She'll only have access to the places in the house we want her to. And what if *I* am the one listening? What if I hear her admit that it's not Luke's?"

Nicki rolls her eyes. "Are you really on that train again? This is Michelle. She's slightly delusional, yes, but this isn't some soap opera, Elle. This is real life, and she's not going to *lie* about who the father is."

I press my lips together. "You really don't think so? In your version of *real life*, do families oust one member as the black sheep? Do parents choose their favorite child and make it really obvious when they do? Do sisters betray their brother's confidence on their freaking wedding day? Do brothers sleep with the same woman?"

"I take it you're talking about the Daltons."

I give her a *duh* look and shove a big spoonful of cookie dough ice cream in my mouth.

"I mean, obviously you're looking for a yes, but I just don't think Michelle would do that. Not with her dad's vested interest in Luke."

"That may be true. But don't you think desperate people have done far worse than lying about a baby's true paternity?" I ask.

"Maybe," she concedes.

"I'll get to the bottom of it," I say resolutely.

She points her spoon at me. "Just be careful."

* * *

In a twist of fate that I never would have believed, a moving truck actually shows up at the house on Friday.

And in another twist I still can't believe, I don't send it away. In fact, I welcome Michelle into our home. Not quite with arms wide open, but something along those lines.

The truck arrives before she does, and the movers ask me where to put her stuff. I guide them toward the bedroom off the second family room. It's the furthest away from our bedroom and gives us the most space from her while living in the same house.

My heart races when she walks in the door with the movers on their third or fourth trip in. I didn't expect her to ring the bell, and certainly not when she feels so entitled to be here that she is moving in uninvited, yet I don't like how it feels. I don't like her walking in without me knowing that she's here, but since my big idea is to just let it happen, it's something I guess I'm just going to have to get used to.

"Happy move in day," I say with far more enthusiasm than I feel.

She purses her lips rather than giving me a friendly response. "Where, exactly, are you putting me?"

"I figured you'd appreciate having some privacy, so your bedroom is the one off the second family room. Nice view of the backyard and plenty of space just for you." I smile sweetly.

LISA SUZANNE

"So you're basically separating me from the rest of the house? Putting me next to the dog's room?" She's whining already. Good Lord, this is not what I signed up for.

Except...it is. And I'm still not really sure why.

"The placement of your room is for you as much as it is for us. We're here to help you through this pregnancy, but ultimately we all have our own lives to live. I'm sure you don't want the room right next to the master bedroom so you can listen to everything newlyweds do in their spare time."

"Oh, honey," she says condescendingly. "Your husband won't have any spare time."

I raise a brow. "Excuse me?"

"I've scheduled my appointments for the baby on Tuesdays. And I do expect they'll take all day. I sure hope you've found something to occupy your time since your *husband* will be busy taking care of me." She gives me a smile like she thinks she's won.

Oh, quite the contrary.

"Actually, I do have something to occupy my time. My *husband* recently gave me all the tools to start my own business since he believes so strongly in my abilities. So I'll be quite busy as I launch my new company. I do hope you have something to occupy your time as well since as much as I'd love to sit around and chat all day, I simply won't have the time." I smile sweetly back at her.

When she came up with this demented plan to move in here, she probably thought I'd just lie down for her. Since Luke is incapable of standing up to her because he feels shoved between a rock and a hard place, I'd be willing to bet that with a father as powerful as hers, she's spent her entire life walking over people who fear what she has the ability to do.

But I'm not scared of her. And that's what prompts the next words to fall out of my mouth. I know he won't say it, and I'm here to protect him...to protect both of us. "Oh, and by the way, before you trap my husband further into your web, I'm going to need a paternity test to prove that he's really the father of that child you're carrying."

Her eyes widen and an ugly snarl twists her face. "How could you even insinuate that this child isn't Luke's?"

I take a step closer to her. I'm maybe the least intimidating person in the world, but I refuse to be trampled by this bitch. "Because I don't trust you. Until I have definitive proof that it's his, I'm not participating in the games you're playing." And it's not just that. If I hadn't gone to the doctor's appointment and saw the baby with my own eyes on that screen, I'm not entirely sure I'd even believe she's pregnant.

She laughs like the thought is simply absurd. "Sure you're not. If that were true, would I really be moving in today?"

I give her another sweet smile. "Really gives you something to think about, doesn't it? I have to get to work now, but good luck with the unpacking. Take it slow and don't lift anything too heavy." And with those as my parting words, I stalk out of the room toward my office, slip in my earbuds to drown her out, and get to work.

CHAPTER 18

Five more days.

In five days, Luke will be back home, and I'm praying I don't kill her before then. It's not looking good.

I'm being a little dramatic, but I can't stand living with Michelle. I can't exactly confess that to Luke since I approved this from the start, but she's a terrible roommate. She doesn't just leave wet coffee spoons in the sugar bowl, though she does do that after jumping on the defensive to say she's just having one cup of decaf since too much caffeine is bad for the baby.

She apparently knows everything about everything because she reads blog posts about mom life, she's the first person ever to get nauseous during pregnancy, and she's more worried about whether her child will be attractive than smart.

She also listens to awful music way too loudly—so loudly, in fact, that even Pepper runs outside just to get away from it. It's a huge house, yet I can still hear the beat of the bass in my office. Is that good for the baby?

I'm trying to be supportive here, but I'm realizing far too late that I should've put up a much, much bigger fight about her moving in. Nicki was right.

At least I can still drink, unlike poor Michelle who's apparently also the first person who ever had to give up alcohol during pregnancy and it's just the worst thing in the world—except for her aching feet.

I roll my eyes about four hundred thousand times a day, and I leave the house to work at Starbucks just to get away from her.

Four more days.

In four days, Luke will be back home, and I've had to sit on my hands so I don't strangle her. But Luke arranged for me to go with her to her next doctor's visit today, and I'm going in with a question.

"You don't have to come into the actual exam room with me," she says when her name is called by the nurse.

"Oh, that's okay. I'd love to come." I give her the sweet smile that I've started referring to in my own mind as my *Michelle smile*.

The doctor walks in and eyes me.

"This is Ellie," Michelle says.

"Hi. The wife of the father." I give a little wave.

The doctor's brows dip a little, but she doesn't say anything. I imagine she's seen far worse in this room. "I'm Dr. Pruitt," she says, and she moves to examine Michelle. I turn away to give her privacy.

"Any questions?" the doctor asks at the end of the exam. She glances at me as if to ask if I have questions, too.

"Yes, I have one," I say. "How invasive is a paternity test?"

"Totally non-invasive and safe for both the baby and the mother with a simple blood draw. We'll need the father's blood, too, for comparison. Are you interested?" Dr. Pruitt asks.

"Yes," I say at the same time Michelle says, "No." Both of us are firm.

"It's just...we're not *totally* sure that my husband is the father seeing as how he doesn't even remember the night Michelle says she got pregnant." I wrinkle my nose and say it under my breath like I'm revealing a little hush-hush secret.

Dr. Pruitt nods with understanding. "I see. Michelle, you have to get a blood draw today anyway. If you're interested, they can grab an extra vial for paternity testing while you're back there."

"I, uh..." Michelle says, sputtering a little. "I'm just terrified of needles. I'd rather not."

"You'll be fine," I say, my voice flat. "They have to draw anyway, so let's just get it done, okay?"

The doctor looks back and forth between us. "It's not my place to get involved, but I also can't watch someone coerce my patient into something she doesn't want to do," she says to me.

"I'm sorry," I lie. "Michelle, do you have some reason why you're not okay with getting this test done? I'm sure Luke would love to know."

Michelle sighs. "No, it's fine. Let's just get it over with."

The doctor nods. "You can go back to the lab for your bloodwork. I'll put in the paperwork for an extra vial."

"Thank you, Dr. Pruitt," Michelle says softly.

The doctor glances at me again before looking back at Michelle. "Would you like to talk privately, Ms. Bennett?"

"No, it's fine," she says softly, her tone full of reluctance.

"Would you excuse us?" Dr. Pruitt says to me.

I hold up both hands. "Of course," I say, and I exit the room. They talk for a few brief moments, and then the doctor exits. She brushes past me without another glance.

Michelle emerges a minute later and we walk back to the lab together. She draws in a few deep breaths. She really is scared to get this bloodwork done.

"It's okay," I say to her. "No big deal. Just don't look at the needle and you'll be fine."

She glares at me. Whatever. I was just trying to be helpful.

Her name is called, and she's all shaky when she walks up to get her blood taken. I watch through the window as they put the elastic band on her arm and tap around for a vein. She closes her eyes and turns away when they insert the needle.

"Stop!" she yells after a few seconds. "Stop. I'm going to pass ou..." the end of her sentence trails off as she actually does pass out.

My heart races as I watch the phlebotomists rush around as they get her cold water, removing the needle from her arm and bandaging it up. They reposition her with her head between her legs as she comes to, and my heart rate starts to even out when I see that she's fine.

They only got one vial—the routine one they needed for her test, not the extra one we requested.

There goes another chance to find out whether Luke is really the father, and with the chance goes my hopes right down the drain.

And it's not just that.

I feel like shit for making her pass out.

I drive her car back home, and I make her dinner, and by *make her dinner*, I mean I reheat something Debbie left for us. By the time she's done eating and leaves her plate on the kitchen table like I'm her maid, well, I'm done feeling bad.

And when Luke calls, I'm even more done if that's such a thing.

"You made Michelle pass out?" he asks.

"Is that what she told you?" I feel like he's immediately putting me on the defensive. He didn't ask about me or my day. He asked about *her*.

"Basically."

"And you believed her?" I ask.

"Well? What happened?"

"She had to get her blood drawn. The doctor called in an extra vial of blood for the paternity test, and she passed out on vial one. We didn't get it."

"Babe, you can't push her into stuff she doesn't want to do," he says gently.

"I didn't," I say thickly. "She agreed to it."

"Yeah, under duress. She's pregnant. You have to be more careful with her."

"I'm fully aware that she's pregnant," I spit. "I'm the one currently living with her."

"By your own choice. I told you it was a terrible idea," he says.

"Nice time to throw that in my face. And way to let her come between us. A-freaking-gain." I hang up. It's childish, but I'm pissed.

I hate leaving things that way with Luke, but it is what it is. The distance is clearly getting to us. So is Michelle.

But even though I'm mad at him, I know this is worth hanging onto—at the very least, hanging onto it to make it bearable for the next year. But also for so much more than that...I hope.

Three more days.

Michelle has some friends over. They cackle loudly about how she gets to live here even though Luke is married to someone else now.

I roll my eyes at Debbie, who chuckles, but later she reminds me how she's never seen Luke as happy as he is with me.

Two more days.

Michelle leaves a mess on the stove after making eggs and burns toast so badly she actually set off the smoke detector.

Tomorrow Luke will be home.

Oddly, Michelle spends most of her day at the office. I guess as the Aces get closer to coming back home, work for her starts to get a little busier. Lest anyone's overly concerned, though, Michelle's father cut her hours in half so she has time to rest. Her paycheck is apparently the same, though, not that it's any of my business. Lucky her for being born into a rich family.

And then, after two long weeks apart, the laundry room door opens. "Honey, I'm home," a charming, deep, and very familiar voice calls out.

I scramble from my place on the couch to get to him first, but I'm not fast enough. Pepper runs toward him, and then there's our new roommate.

"Thank God you're here," Michelle says, rushing past me. "Ellie has just been so mean to me!"

Oh. My. God.

I clench my fists so tightly my nails dig into my palms as I watch her toss her arms around his neck, practically kicking Pepper on her way by. Pepper whimpers a little.

"Excuse me," Luke says, untangling himself from her. He gently moves her aside, reaches down to scratch Pepper on the head, then walks past Michelle and over to me. He pulls me into his arms and a certain heat passes between us for a beat. His eyes crinkle as a smile lights his whole face.

And then his mouth crashes down to mine as my arms link around him, and he kisses me—really kisses me good and hard—for a full minute before he pulls away and we come up for air.

"God, I missed you," he says, punctuating his words with smaller kisses to my mouth.

"I missed you, too," I say, my chest tight as I kiss him back. I feel it with every fiber of my being.

This isn't for show. This isn't part of an act. This is two people who spent nearly every waking minute together and then were forced apart for two of the longest weeks of either of their lives. This is two people who desperately missed each other as one held a piece of the other's heart across the miles.

We're both whole again now that we're back together, and neither of us cares that someone is watching. This isn't about her. It's about a husband and his wife and the love that has blossomed between us.

"Get your sweet little ass upstairs," he says softly.

I know she heard, but I don't care. I don't care what her reaction is. Instead, I don't even look at her as I follow his directions.

"I'll be right up," he says after my retreating figure.

Every part of me wants to stay and listen to what he has to say to Michelle, but I give them their moment together. He pushed past her for me, and a feeling of joy rushes through my chest.

He isn't going to let her come between us.

CHAPTER 19

I sit waiting as patiently as humanly possible on the bed. Should I get naked? Or do I let him do it? Is he even coming up here for sex? God, I hope so.

I'm desperate to be with him again. It's only been two weeks, but those two weeks were filled with emotional ups and downs. I don't think I realized how attached I'd become to him until he was gone. And it's not just that physical attachment. I feel it deep in my chest, down into my soul.

I need this time with him. I need to feel him as he pushes into me, to strengthen our bodily connection again as we continue to nurture our emotional one.

I'm giddy as I wait. I bounce up and down a little, and I shake my hands out to try to burn some of my nervous energy. The door opens. My heart races.

He kicks it shut behind him, and he locks it for good measure. He's clutching his duffel bag, which he drops to the floor as his eyes meet mine. And then he stalks slowly across the room toward me, his eyes hot on mine the entire time.

He kicks off his shoes as he walks, and he doesn't waste a single second. He pulls his shirt over his head, tossing it to the floor as my eyes fall to his abs. Those sweet, sweet abs I missed so damn much.

He moves between my legs, gently pushes me back, and climbs on the bed until he hovers over me. Our eyes lock for one hot beat before he lowers his mouth to mine.

His mouth opens to mine and our tongues brush as all the aching need I've felt since the moment he walked out the door intensifies to unbearable levels. I push my hips toward his as I seek some sort of relief, but it'll take more than a little humping to alleviate my burning need.

My nails glide up his back, and he grunts into me as our tongues continue to batter each other's. He deepens the kiss, somehow making it more intense and more intimate as he lowers himself down, his heat warming me all over. And then, out of nowhere, he flips us so I'm on top of him, straddling his hips. He doesn't break our kiss when he moves us, but I do. I sit up on his lap and grind my hips over his. I feel how hard he is for me. I feel how *ready* he is for me, and I'm just as ready.

He groans as I continue shifting my hips over him, and then I reach for the hem of my shirt and rip it over my head. I toss it to the floor and then I unhook my bra, throwing it across the room. He runs his palms along my torso, stopping to cup my breasts. His hands are rougher than they were the last time he touched me, but just the feel of his touch on my bare skin sends me into another stratosphere.

I close my eyes and moan as I lean my head back, jutting my breasts forward automatically to give him a better angle to work with. His thumb brushes my nipples, and I whimper as the feeling sends an arrow of need through my entire core.

He does it again and again, and the whimper turns into a moan.

He shifts us again, setting me to the side of him but only long enough to get rid of his sweatpants. I get rid of my jeans and my panties while we're at it, and I don't think a single word has been spoken since he walked into this room. Our bodies are doing all the talking for us. There will be plenty of time to catch up later. Plenty of time to argue and fight. Plenty of time to make up and talk.

Right now, though, we both need this.

He urges me over toward him so I'm straddling him. I'm about to reach down and fist his cock when I notice the bruises all over his arms and chest. I run a finger softly along one of them on his biceps, and he winces a bit. No wonder why he wants me on top. The poor guy is hurting, but that's not going to stop him—or me—from the release we're both desperate for.

Finally, I reach down, grab his shaft in my fist, and pump up and down a few times. His eyes close as his face twists with pleasure, and then I line him up and lower myself onto his waiting cock.

We both groan at the perfection of his body entering mine. I move over him so he slides almost all the way out before I shove my hips back down so he's as far in as our bodies physically will let him be.

I cry out as he fills me, and then I move up again before slamming back down. "Oh fuck, Ellie," he murmurs, and his curse only goads me on to pick up my pace. Up and down, in and out, up and down, in and out. We find a rhythm together as he holds me under my ass, helping direct our speed. One of his fingers inches over to the tight bud in back, and I stiffen as he presses into a place that I'd still categorize as virgin territory.

I'm already filled in front, and this new and foreign sensation seems to fill me even more. The heat between us mixes with this prohibited, illicit feeling, and it's mere seconds before my body convulses into a climax.

I scream out as pleasure rips through me, and his finger continues to push into the forbidden area as I come and come. The contractions of my body send him into his own release. He growls as his hips jerk up to meet mine, and then he grunts a string of curses that are absolute music to my ears as I listen to him ride the wave of bliss.

It's over far too soon.

I know we'll do that again. I know there's more in store for us. But every time we're in the midst of our passion, I want it to last forever. Despite how good it feels to come, I can't help but feel a little sad when it's over and we're forced to break our sweet connection.

We do, though. I shift up so he slides out of me, and I lie beside him for a few quiet minutes, both of us panting as we try to regain our breath.

"Well that was fun," he says after a few quiet beats pass between us.

I giggle and turn on my side to face him, and I find him already on his side facing me. I run a fingertip over his eyebrow. "I missed you," I say.

His lips tip up. "I missed you, too. No more letting her come between us, okay? And for the love of all things holy, don't fucking hang up on me."

"I'm sorry," I say, heat creeping into my cheeks. He's right. It was childish.

"It's okay. I love you, Ellie."

"I love you, too."

I just hope that love is enough for us to overcome all the obstacles that lie ahead of us.

CHAPTER 20

"Seriously, be a little louder next time," Michelle mutters sarcastically as we walk into the kitchen hand-in-hand after our nice little welcome home romp.

"You're the one who wanted to move in with the newlyweds," I shoot back.

Luke gives me a look of warning, and if we were on the phone, I'd be tempted to hang up on him.

"But we'll try to keep it down," I amend, and Luke gives me a look of gratitude for attempting to keep the peace. This can't be easy on him. She's already ruining the sugar bowl again, and just when he thought he was rid of her, she's back.

Letting her move in was a stupid, stupid mistake, but it takes exactly one more little bitch fest between the two of us for me to realize how very, very stuck we are.

"Stop putting your wet coffee spoon in the sugar bowl," I snarl at Michelle after dinner.

She looks at me in surprise. "I had no idea it bothered you so much. You don't even use the sugar."

"Because it's all hard and crusty from your wet spoon." *You fucking slob.* I don't say that last part aloud, obviously.

"Ladies," Luke booms. We both look at him in surprise where he still sits at the kitchen table. Even Pepper pauses in chewing on her dog bone to glance up at him. "Just stop. Don't pick fights with each other. I just need some peace and quiet at home, and if I can't get it here, I'll go stay with Josh during training camp. Is that what you want?"

"No," Michelle says at the same time I say, "I'm sorry."

"Just knock it off," he says, and he stalks out of the room.

"This is your fault," she says to me as soon as he's gone.

I sigh. "How, exactly, is it my fault?"

"Just shut up about the goddamn coffee spoon." She glares at me like I'm an idiot. "Luke doesn't care about shit like that."

"God, Michelle. You don't know one damn thing about him."

Her brows dip like she doesn't quite get it, and I realize then it's because she *doesn't get it*. The first night we met, he confessed the coffee spoon in the sugar bowl thing. Before we knew a damn thing about each other, that was the first thing he said. He was joking that it was the reason they broke up, but clearly it was those little things that got to him first, and it was the big things that caused the eventual split.

And now he's literally stuck with her for the rest of his life because they share a child.

The only way out of this is finding out it's not his baby...but the odds aren't looking good on that front.

I stalk out of the room and head upstairs. "Can we talk?" I ask when I find Luke collapsed on the chair in our bedroom as he looks out over the backyard.

"Sure," he says. He makes no attempt to move.

"I'm sorry I let her move in."

He sighs. "It's not your fault. It's mine. I should've been clear with her from the start of that conversation."

"Why weren't you?" I ask gently.

"I had a lot on my mind. Camp isn't just about practice and game strategy. It's about fighting like hell for your position. I hate competing against Josh, but it felt like it was the two of us against each other, against the second-string guys, against the new guys."

"Who won the battle?" I ask, genuinely curious about the answer.

He shakes his head. "Nobody yet. We still have nearly two full weeks of camp here at home before we really have a clear answer. Last year Josh and I were the top two. But this kid right out of college is fast as fuck and he's posing a real threat."

"I get it. It's a lot to worry about, and you don't need Michelle and me fighting here when you need to focus on the game."

"No, I don't," he says. "You're right. But you're both here, and we have to learn to live with that. As much as she drives me up the fucking wall, as much as I don't want her here and don't want to live with her, the reality is that she's carrying my child. It's too early for her to be here, but I'd sort of thought I'd ask her to move in when the baby gets here anyway. So I guess we're just a few months ahead of schedule."

"There are ways for you to see the baby without the two of you living together," I say. *If the baby's even yours.*

"I don't want to just *see the baby*. I want to be an active part of its life. I already have a fucked up schedule because of my job, so this is the only way I'll get full access to my own child."

"Unless you sue for full custody," I point out.

"Which I can't do." He gives me a look like I'm insane.

"Why not? You have rights, Luke."

"I realize that," he says with frustration. "But so does she. I can't just take the baby away from its mother. Besides, what would Calvin think?"

For as much as he doesn't give a shit what his own family thinks, he's sure hung up on what Calvin might think. I get it since Calvin holds Luke's career in his hands, but that doesn't make it any less frustrating.

I sigh but I don't really have a response to that.

"I can't exactly kick her out now," he finally says. "Just stay away from her. Do your own thing. Don't let her get to you. We just have to deal with her."

"Okay," I say, trying to keep my own frustration out of my tone. I'm not sure I succeed.

But I *will* succeed in being the bigger person. I won't let Michelle come between Luke and me.

CHAPTER 21

I've been to plenty of football games over the course of my brother's career, but my focus was always on nachos and beer, not on actually watching the game. I went for the social connection, for the fun of being there and people watching while I sat with family or friends sometimes in the stands and sometimes in a suite.

Today we're in a suite, and this just *feels* different than all those other games.

Today I'm going in to actually watch the game, to see my *husband* as he takes the field with his teammates after a couple weeks away for training camp, to hold my breath with every snap of the ball as I pray for an injury-free game.

I guess it doesn't just feel different. It *is* different.

I'm too nervous to eat. *It's just a preseason game.* I remember Josh saying that back in Chicago, like they don't *really* matter compared to regular season games.

But the risk is still there. Every time Luke steps out onto the field, he's putting his body at risk. His safety. His health.

I never cared when it was my brother doing it, but it's a completely different realm when it's the man you love going out there.

We were out the door by ten-thirty after we ate Lucky Charms and blueberry waffles with peanut butter spread on top. We drove to the stadium with Nicki and Josh, and I saw the way she wrung her hands in her lap as my brother drove. I saw the way Luke locked up and got real quiet the closer we got to the stadium. I saw the way my brother focused on traffic. Everyone in the car was silent as we approached the stadium, and Luke gave me a kiss before he headed to the locker room with my brother.

"Go get 'em," I said to him, and he smiled at me, pressed one more kiss to my lips, and turned away. "And be safe, Luke," I called after him. He turned back and winked at me, and it felt like the start of a new tradition, like I will say those words to him hundreds of times.

We watch from our suite as the stands begin to fill. I can't help but wonder what Luke is doing right now. Probably listening to his pregame playlist, and I still haven't gotten out of him which playlist it is or what's on it. He seems private about it, so I will continue to believe it's a power mix of ballads from Celine Dion, Adele, and Whitney Houston until he proves otherwise.

Leah, Krista, and Nadine are in our suite, too, along with Mo and a couple other women who Nicki just introduced me to.

"Does it always feel like this?" I ask Nicki when we're seated by ourselves in the second row of our suite as the others mill around the buffet table behind us.

"Like what?" she asks, glancing over at me.

"Like you're freaking out a little on the inside that he's going to get hurt and you want him so badly to pull out a win and be the big savior of the game and it feels like it's a personal attack against you if all that doesn't happen."

She grunts a small chuckle. "Yeah. Except you'll freak out a *lot* on the inside, not a little. Especially when it comes to the regular season. I'd be surprised if they put Luke and Josh in for more than a quarter today. They have to keep their best players healthy." She keeps her eyes focused on the field. "The worst thing in the world would be for either of them to get hurt during a game that doesn't even matter."

"Yeah," I say absently.

"And whatever you do, don't talk about contracts or give away any inside vulnerable information to the other wives." She says it softly, but it's a clear warning. "You can't put yourself in a vulnerable position, either."

I look at her with brows drawn in together. "Why not?"

She shakes her head. "We'll talk more about it later, but just know that every single time your husband gets out on that field, he's fighting for his spot to play there. And he might be fighting against the husband of the woman sitting behind you. He might be fighting against your best friend's husband. You can be real with me, obviously, but there's a set of unwritten rules we need to follow."

I nod, and it's just then that the women settle into their seats with plates of food in front of us and behind us and Mo slides into the seat beside me.

"How's the first game so far as a football wife?" she asks.

I tuck away Nicki's hushed warnings for now, but I keep them close. "Considering we haven't even started yet, so far, so good."

She chuckles. "You feeling the nerves already?"

I glance at her plate of food. "I can't even eat."

"It does take some getting used to. It's easier now that Mitch is a coach and not player anymore. I don't have to worry about *him* getting injured, but I do have every other man out on that field to worry about. They're all my boys—including your Luke."

I smile. She's really like the team mother, and she's helping me feel more at ease.

"I heard Michelle Bennett moved in with you. Is that true?" she asks, her voice low so this conversation is just between us. That doesn't make it any more comfortable, though. This just seems like the wrong place to gossip about the owner's daughter.

"Yeah, it's true," I admit. I glance around to be sure nobody's listening. "And I hate her." I cover my mouth with my hand.

Oh shit. After Nicki's warning literally five seconds ago, I'm already showing a vulnerability that I probably shouldn't—especially not to the coach's wife, even if she's here for us and heads up the wives' club.

Mo laughs, but she doesn't just laugh. It's a good, solid belly laugh, and she's wiping her eyes by the time she's done. In fact, she's laughing so loudly and so heartily that she draws the attention of some of the women in our suite. They pause their conversations to glance over to see what's so funny.

I guess letting that little vulnerability slip out wasn't my worst mistake.

"I'm sorry," she says as she tries to catch her breath. She leans in close as she calms down and the others return to their own conversations. "You're far from the first person to tell me that. I'll keep my own opinions to myself, but for what it's worth, Mitch has come home raving about Luke's newfound fire. We both attribute that to you. So keep pushing. Keep walking beside him. Keep holding his hand. He didn't have that fire when he was with her. He'll be down on that field playing for *you* today, not for her. Never for her."

It's my turn to wipe my eyes, but not because I'm laughing. I hold her words close to my heart.

A few minutes later, the announcer calls the opposing team to the field. They run out to their sideline, and then the announcer says, "And now, your Vegas Aces!"

The crowd filling the stands goes wild, deafening screams all around for the hometown heroes as they run onto the field.

I find the *DALTON* eighty-four jersey right away as he runs beside *NOLAN* number eighteen, the same number my brother has worn since he was in peewee league. My heart races, and I can't imagine what he's feeling down on that field if I'm feeling it so strongly up here watching him. Is this just something he's used to dealing with? Or does he get nervous before each game?

Is he as worried about getting hurt as I am?

The game starts, and I find myself on the edge of my seat as I start to wonder why I didn't pick up a love for this sport ages ago. I guess I'm a little more invested now that the guy I married is on the field. And Nicki's right. Both Luke and Josh only play the first quarter. They're on the sidelines with baseball caps instead of helmets and towels slung around their necks as they watch their teammates give a real beating to the Seahawks.

I'm relieved when the game is over even though Luke spends most of the time on the sidelines. I do manage to get myself some nachos at the half, but only because he isn't playing.

Nicki leads me down to the post-game room, where wives, girlfriends, kids, and families wait for their players to emerge from the locker room. The first one comes out about a half hour after the end of the game. Nicki explains how the coach says a few words, they head off to showers, and then they have interviews with the media, so we'll usually have to wait about an hour. And she's right on the money. Luke walks out with Josh, both of them looking exhausted as they walk slowly toward us.

Nicki beelines for my brother, and I watch as she inspects a shiny bruise on his arm after kissing him.

Luke pulls me into his arms and leans his forehead down to mine.

"Good game," I say softly.

"Thanks," he murmurs. He draws in a deep breath.

"Hey, you okay?" I back up a little so I can get a look at him.

He leans down to kiss me softly. "Better now," he says.

I melt, and then I mirror my best friend as I inspect his arms for new bruises. I see a few scratches, too. "How'd these happen?" I ask, lightly fingering near them.

"The turf is rougher than it looks. Especially when a lineman slams you to the ground and you slide across it."

I wince.

"It's fine," he says, clearly trying to be the tough guy and especially here, where ears of teammates who want his position might be listening. I never realized how protective he needs to be over his place on the team until Nicki pointed it out just before today's game started.

I glance around at the men gathered. They're all moving just a little more slowly than they were when they pranced in this morning, but it's because they all just took a beating out on that field even though they won. I can't help but wonder why they do this to themselves.

And even though we're not supposed to talk about it, I can't help but wonder what comes next.

CHAPTER 22

The next preseason game is an away game, and I've hardly seen Luke all week since he's been at camp all day every day. He comes home bruised and exhausted, and our conversations are short as he goes to bed nearly immediately after he walks in the door and he's out the door before sunrise.

It's an intense, hard schedule, but it's one he has to keep up in order to keep his place on the Aces. I guess I'm starting to get it now.

He loves this game. It's his life. It's his path and his passion.

But he's in a contract year. He's one bad landing, one hit too hard, one injury away from early retirement. He's one conversation with the boss that goes the wrong way from being traded. He has proven his worth over the last nine years, but no matter how indispensable I make him to the team, ultimately if he doesn't perform on the field, it doesn't matter.

Fans can love him, and we can post his thirst traps, but those things won't keep him here.

He can still contribute to the community wherever he lands. It'll make him attractive to other teams, I suppose. But he doesn't want to go to another team, something he's made very clear.

I keep to my side of the house and avoid Michelle at all costs.

They lose the second preseason game, which I don't attend since it's in New Orleans. Of course we can travel to any game we wish, just as anybody can, but Nicki explained that traditionally wives stay home for the preseason away games. Many of the wives have children, and some have their own jobs, but all have responsibilities back home that make it difficult to take off for three days. Traveling is part of the deal for Luke and the other guys. Their hotel rooms and meals are included, and it's not like I'd be taking a vacation with my husband since it's not really part of the deal for spouses.

But Nicki and I have made plans to go to the first game of the season in a few weeks.

Luke informs me that he played exactly four plays anyway—not because he wasn't needed, but because they benched their top players early to keep them healthy when the other team had scored twice in the first few possessions.

There are two more preseason games, and this coming weekend is at home against the Broncos.

That means Jack will be in town.

I'm hopeful we don't have to see him, but I haven't gotten the official word yet from Luke as he goes into his final week of training camp.

He's practicing at the stadium on Friday when the doorbell rings mid-morning. I'm in my office, and I have no idea where Michelle is—nor do I care—as I stand and head down the hallway toward the foyer.

But apparently Michelle *is* home because she beats me there. I hear voices as I approach that direction, and I quiet my steps. I stop, standing just around the corner from them to listen.

"Is she home?" the voice is low, but not too low to miss his words. I immediately recognize it.

"Yeah," Michelle says softly. I hear the telltale smack of a quick, stolen kiss.

Wait a minute.

Michelle and Jack are *kissing* now?

"You shouldn't be here."

"I know," he says. "I figured it would be easy to play it off that I was visiting my brother."

She laughs. "He's not even home. He's at practice."

What the hell?

And...what the fuck?

How do I even play this little twist?

"Come on in," she says a little louder, and I choose that moment to walk into the hallway.

474

They look up at me in surprise, and I don't have to fake the surprise on my own face. "Jack. What are you doing here?"

"Oh, just came to see my brother, but Michelle tells me he isn't home," he says. He's just as handsome as I remember, somehow so devilishly charming with just a single glance in my direction, but I won't fall for it.

"Well he's not here, so you can feel free to slither back to wherever you came from." I smile sweetly, giving him the *Michelle smile* I've come to perfect over the last few weeks.

"Oh, but I have a whole two hours free, so I'd love to get to know my new sister-in-law a little better," he says.

I give him a tight smile. "Some of us have jobs," I say, glancing over at Michelle pointedly as I wonder why she isn't at hers, "so I'm unable to entertain you at the moment."

"I can entertain you," Michelle says. "I'm free all day."

I wonder exactly what sort of entertaining Michelle is going to be doing, but I really do have work to do. Greg sent me the contact information for three of the Aces teammates who are interested in my services, so I have three plans to draft to try to sell them on why they need PCPR to handle their publicity. Each of the three has slightly different goals, so it's not just some easy cut and paste job. I need to be precise as I tailor plans to each man.

"It's as lovely as ever to see you, Jack," I say with as much sincerity as I can muster. It's true. It's as lovely as ever—which isn't very lovely at all. "I hope you lose on Sunday." I smirk and turn to leave as he bellows out a laugh.

"Oh, silly, sweet, misguided Ellie." His tone is mocking, and I want to slap him. "You really don't know much about the game, do you?" I turn back around at his insult to find him leering in my direction. "Not only are we going to beat the Aces, but we're going to beat them handily. Tell Luke to watch out for Allen Hammond." He winks at me, and I repeat the name three times to myself so I can look him up when I get back to my office.

"Break a leg," I say back, meaning those words literally rather than figuratively. "Oh, sorry. Is that appropriate for football? Or is that more suited for drama?" I shrug and play dumb. "Well, plenty of drama here, am I right?" I leave those as my parting words as I head back toward my office.

The first thing I do is type *Allen Hammond* into the search bar. I learn he's a safety for the Broncos. I look up what a safety does and discover that their job is to stop the offense from scoring at all costs.

And then I look up a little more on Allen. Apparently he's known for his extremely aggressive behavior when it comes to stopping wide receivers. He's famous for launching himself into opponents trying to catch the ball, in particular shoving a shoulder into their chests to knock the wind out of them and hurt them just enough to sideline them for a few plays. He's intentional with his hits, but he doesn't catch penalties since there's nothing illegal about chest hits.

I'm sure Luke knows how to deal with aggressive safeties. It's part of his job, after all.

But this just gives me one more thing to worry about.

CHAPTER 23

The three of us sit down to dinner an hour after Luke gets home. Today's training camp session was slightly less intense than previous days to give players a bit of a break to rest before Sunday's game. Luke's plate is nearly empty, and I'm almost done, too. Michelle takes an hour and a half to eat three bites of pasta, and I don't have the energy to play hostess to her tonight.

Especially not when I need answers.

My plate is empty, and I take mine and Luke's to the sink when I decide I can't sit on this any longer. Rather than talk privately to Luke, rather than stew over it, rather than have a conversation with Michelle, I blurt out the question that's weighed on my mind since this afternoon when I return to the table.

"Hey, Michelle, you want to explain to Luke and me why you and Jack kissed earlier?"

Her eyes widen as she looks across the table at me.

She's caught, and her expression says it all. Not only did I catch her doing something she didn't think I knew about, but I also caught her off guard with my question.

Her eyes edge over to Luke to gauge his reaction.

"It was a friendly greeting," she says, brushing off my accusatory tone. "He's become a good friend to me the last few weeks."

I nod, my expression dripping with sarcasm. "Right. So that's why you told him he shouldn't be here and he said something about it being easy to pretend he's here to visit Luke."

Her brows dip. She had no idea that I heard everything.

"He said *what?*" Luke asks. "He wouldn't come here to see me. Not before a game." He turns his angry gaze on Michelle. "What was he doing here?"

"I told you, he's become a good friend to me," she says. She's maintaining her cool, but there are little things that tip me off to the truth. The way her eyes dart around a little like she's trying to come up with a sufficient lie, for example. The way she taps her fork lightly against her plate without even realizing she's doing it. The way she takes a big bite of pasta to fill her mouth so she can think up more lies.

"How *good?*" Luke sneers, his tone full of innuendo.

"Why do you even care? It's not like you want to be with me."

Luke lets out a maniacal little laugh. "No, you're certainly right about that. But I have a right to know. You're carrying my child and you're living in my house while claiming you're still in love with me. Are you sleeping with my brother?"

She smirks. "Wouldn't that be great if I was? A great way to poke the beast in you. To get you to wake up and see you should be with me."

I roll my eyes. I can't even muster up a good response to that joke of a line.

"You still haven't answered my question," Luke says. "You of all people know where I stand with my brother. You and me may not have ended on the best terms, but when we were together, I let you in. And for you to run to him, even as a friend..." He trails off and shakes his head. "It's a betrayal."

"Luke, no, it's not like that," she says. She's already starting to whine, and I am not here for it.

"Then what's it like?" I spit.

She glares at me before her eyes dart to Luke. "You told him he could have me." There's a bit of desperation in her tone. "You called him in front of me and said he was my problem now. You gave both of us permission."

"Because you called me a *fucking loser* when I got home from the playoff game that sent his team to the Super Bowl," Luke says, his voice increasing to a yell before it falls eerily quiet with his next sentence. "You told me you wanted to be with a winner like Jack instead of a *fucking loser* like me."

Whoa.

I knew she called him a loser...but I did *not* know about the part where she called Jack a winner. What a low blow from someone who claims to love him.

Just more examples of how he has surrounded himself with all the wrong people his entire life.

Enter Ellie.

"Why are you even here?" he asks. "Why aren't you bothering him instead of trying to ruin my life?"

"For the baby," she cries.

He blows out a breath. "I'm sorry, Michelle, but I'm married now, and I'm in love with my wife. I will never love you the way I love Ellie."

"But we're having a baby together," she says, actual tears falling down her cheeks now. "Doesn't that mean something to you?"

"Yeah, it does," he says. He stands. "It means I want a paternity test."

Her brows draw together. "You can't be serious."

"Oh, I'm dead serious. And I want my brother's DNA tested against this baby, too." He points at her. "Your refusal to answer my question about whether you've slept together tells me everything I need to know."

"I did," she finally says. "I slept with him after you and I broke up in January. I was so angry with you, and I wanted to hurt you. I wanted to make you jealous."

He shakes his head and snags his bottom lip between his teeth. I'm a silent observer through this entire exchange. "It didn't work. Don't you see that? I'm not jealous that you slept with Jack." He lets out a little chuckle. "I'm disgusted. Get that paternity test done in the next month or you'll hear from my lawyer. If the results show I'm the father, we'll figure something out. Until then, stay on your side of the house. Stay away from my wife and me or find somewhere else to live." He turns to me. "Come on, Ellie, let's go have sex."

My eyes widen at the whirlwind of his monologue, but I stand as instructed and follow my husband up the stairs to our bedroom.

CHAPTER 24

"Are you okay?" I ask tentatively once I shut the door behind me. He collapses on the bed and lies back to stare up at the ceiling.

"Not really," he admits.

I sit on the edge of the bed then lie back beside him. "Wanna talk about it?"

"Not really."

"Do it anyway?" My voice is a hopeful question, and he chuckles. "You'll feel better." I nudge him a little with my elbow.

"It's just a lot, training camp and preseason games and everything, and we're playing the Broncos this week so the added pressure of the team who beat us in the playoffs. And then to have to come home to *that*—to find out my ex slept with my brother, or maybe she's still sleeping with him..." He exhales a long breath. "I've come to terms that I'm the father of that baby...but maybe I'm not."

"It *is* a lot. And you know, your wife is supposed to help you carry those burdens." I glance over at him, and he turns his head to lock eyes with me.

He doesn't say anything as a bit of heat passes between us. It's always there, but never more present than when we're lying on a bed together.

"Thanks, Ellie," he says softly.

I reach down and grab his hand. I squeeze it. I want to ask how he'll feel if it isn't his baby—or how he'll feel if it *is*. Instead, I ask, "How does it make you feel that she and Jack slept together?"

His eyes are still on mine. "I'm disgusted by it, but they're free to do what they want. They deserve each other."

"Does it hurt?" I pry.

"I was done with her over a year ago, but it took me a little time to get up the nerve to actually end it. I don't know how she thought sleeping with my brother would somehow translate to getting me back, but that's Michelle for you. She's fucked up, but my choices are limited given who her father is." He shakes his head and moves his eyes back to the ceiling. "I wish I would've known who she was from the start. I never would've gotten involved with her if I had."

"So what if she gets the test done and we find out the baby isn't yours?"

He's quiet as he mulls that one over. "I don't know," he says. "I know it's not ideal, especially not with her, but there's still a part of me who keeps thinking about the baby. I figured I'd have kids down the road. I'm still young, and maybe family, kids...maybe that's where I want my focus to be eventually." He's edging around talks about *the future* even though it's a known superstition that brings bad luck in his eyes.

He wants kids *someday*...and now he's married to me for a year, which pushes *someday* further back—unless Michelle really is carrying his baby, in which case *someday* might actually just be a few months away.

What a mess.

"And what about Jack's role in all this?" I ask. I flex my fingers in his.

"If anything hurts, it's the betrayal there. But at least I understand his motivation. He has wanted to get me back for everything that happened with Savannah for years, and he thought he found that opportunity when Michelle came knocking. But even so, I can't help wondering how we even got here. How our relationship got so fucked up that his first move is to try to hurt me."

"I only saw him for a minute today, but he told me to warn you about Allen Hammond." I keep my eyes on his profile as I say those words, and Luke winces.

"Not much I can do about him," he says.

"I looked him up," I admit. "He sounds like a real asshole."

He grunts out a laugh. "He is. He's sidelined me for a few plays. He's left me with more than a few bruises. He's as tough as they come, and he's also one of the few really dirty players in the league."

"Because he intentionally hurts people?"

Luke nods. "Nobody wants to *injure* anyone. You can't take away someone's livelihood like that. But *hurting* them? Taking them out for a few plays or even for the rest of the game? There's still a few guys around with that old school way of thinking, and Hammond is one of them."

"So how do you protect yourself?"

He shrugs. "I play the game. I get out there and defend myself the best way I know how. I catch the ball and run it into the end zone."

"How many career touchdowns do you have?"

"Sixty-seven," he says without missing a beat.

"Wow," I say. I'm not sure if that number is impressive or not.

"I'm in the top hundred of all-time career TDs for a single player. I'm actually one TD away from tying a spot in the top fifty."

There's my answer. "Holy shit, Luke. That's impressive."

He chuckles. "Just doing what I love."

"Speaking of *doing what you love*," I say, trailing off.

He chuckles. "Is that an invitation?"

I sit up and then I turn and toss one leg over him so I'm straddling him. I shift my hips over his. "Well you did invite me up here for sex," I point out.

He chuckles. "Yeah, I did do that, didn't I?"

I lean down and press a soft kiss to his lips, and then I sit up over him as I continue to move my hips over his growing erection. "Whatever happens, Luke, I love you. I'm rooting for you, and I don't just mean from the stands. I'm on your side and I'm here."

He reaches up to pull me down so my lips are inches from his. "I love you, too. Thank you for being you. For being so different from all the mistakes of my past."

And then there are no more words as his lips meet mine.

CHAPTER 25

"You can expect the results in seven to ten business days," the tech tells Luke as he places a bandage over a small cotton ball on his arm.

"Any way we can speed that up?" Luke asks.

The tech gives Luke a tight smile. "Not really but you can still try if you're offering to grease my palm."

Luke chuckles. "Understood. Thanks."

We leave the lab, and I let Michelle take the front seat next to Luke since she almost passed out again and claims the backseat makes her carsick.

"I was hoping we'd have the results before I have to leave for Denver," Luke says on our way home. It was a long shot anyway since he leaves in three days.

"Guess we won't," Michelle says, and I sense more than a little bit of smugness in her tone.

Whatever. I roll my eyes behind my sunglasses. She can be smug all she wants. She's the one who forced her way into our home. She's the one sleeping alone in Luke's house while Luke keeps me warm at night.

We're quiet the rest of the way home, each of us lost in our own thoughts, and it's not until after dinner when Michelle heads out with some friends that I find out what he was thinking.

We're sitting on the couch, Pepper in between with her butt against my leg—of course—and her head perched on Luke's leg. He scratches her absently behind the ears and I'm petting a pattern on her back when he glances at me. "Can I talk to you about something?"

My eyes lock on his. "Always."

"This whole mess with Michelle just has me thinking a lot about what I want out of life. You know?" He scratches a trail from Pepper's head down to my hand, where he links his fingers through mine. "Do you want kids?" he asks.

I nod. "Yeah. Someday. Ideally a few years down the road, and I'd love a boy and a girl, sort of like Josh and me. I want them to be close like we are. What about you?"

"I never thought I did, mostly because I didn't want multiple kids who would grow up to turn on each other. But regardless of what happens with the paternity test results, yeah, I do, too. Kids will eventually grow into adults who can make their own decisions. It's the parents' job to give their kids the tools to foster healthy relationships with their siblings."

"How many do you want?" I ask.

"Two sounds good," he says. His fingers tighten in mine, and my eyes fall to where our hands are connected. "Especially if they're with you."

I glance up at him, and he gives me a small smile. I lower my voice just in case Michelle is around to overhear. "What are you saying?"

"I'm saying I want this," he says, using his other hand to wave between the two of us, "to be real. I don't want some stupid contract laying out our future. I don't want either of us to hold any anxiety about what happens when the term is up. In fact..." He trails off and stands, and he leaves the room. He returns a minute later with some papers in his hand, and then he ceremoniously rips them in half.

It's just figurative since I still have my signed copy, but the sentiment is there, and tears spring to my eyes.

"It's you and me, Ellie. I might be a different person during the season, and I want you to just hold out for the me you know. He'll be back, and we'll have our life back in a couple months, and we'll be stronger for it." My mind immediately moves to overdrive. What does he mean that he might be a different person? How, exactly?

I don't get a chance to ask because he keeps talking.

"I just want all this nonsense," he says, shaking our contract, "to be off the table. This Michelle business is making me see how very much I want kids someday. A family. With you."

He sits back down, but this time beside me instead of on the other side of Pepper. He's close, and he murmurs softly when he speaks again.

"I never thought I'd get married again," he says. "I never thought I'd have kids. And then you tumbled into my life at a damn nightclub of all places and somehow you brought everything I didn't know I was missing. Be my wife, Ellie. For real." He drops a kiss just below my ear on my neck, and I shiver at the feeling.

"You and me," I murmur, and his lips trail over to my mouth.

He kisses me briefly—way too briefly—before he pulls back. "Is that a yes?"

"Oh, hell yes, that's a yes," I say, and then he pushes me back. Pepper jumps off the couch at my sudden movement, but I hardly notice because Luke's mouth is hot on mine, his tongue assaulting mine in the most heavenly way as an ache presses ferociously between my legs.

"Fuck me," I murmur. "Right here. Right now."

He answers by shifting up off me to unbuckle his belt. He fumbles with my jeans before he shoves them down, and I kick off one leg so I have enough room to spread my legs for his lean body. And then he shoves into me without foreplay, and holy hell. My eyes roll back into my head at the perfect feeling of his entrance. He rocks into me right there on the couch, and there's something so simple about having sex with my husband on our couch even though there are so many other complications clouding our relationship.

But those complications don't matter.

We're sealing our new commitment. It's a new promise. It's pure and beautiful with a little magic thrown in, and as he drives in and out of me, he pushes my body to the brink. I collapse over it, freefalling into an orgasm that shifts my world off its axis as the contractions of my body over his sends him into his own climax. He grunts into me. "Oh, fuck, Ellie, yes," he mutters. "Fuck, fuck,

fuck." His words punctuate his thrusts as my body milks every ounce of pleasure from his.

It's over far too soon, and as he pulls out of me and shimmies back into his jeans before helping me with mine, something here feels different. It's a renewal of our vows with a lot more meaning behind them this time. It's a promise that we're both in this. We'll both fight for this.

It's real. Him and me. Forever.

CHAPTER 26

Of all the cities in the world for the Aces to have their season opener, of course it would be Denver. That means a risk of running into Jack and also more anxiety over whether this Allen Hammond guy is going to ram into my husband's chest in some asshole move to sideline him.

The stakes are higher this time, and it's palpable as Nicki and I walk into the stadium. We're wearing our specially-made Aces jerseys showcasing our husbands' numbers, and we get a few leers as we walk through another team's home stadium to our seats.

It's the first Sunday of the regular season, and Luke left Friday to travel with the team to Denver...as did Michelle. She doesn't have a key position with the team, but since her dad owns the team, apparently that means she can do whatever she wants.

Nicki and I took the short flight yesterday morning, and we're sharing a suite at the same hotel where the team is staying. We had a quick few minutes with our men last night and again this morning, but otherwise they've been busy with their team responsibilities as they get ready to play a team who handily beat them just two weeks ago.

But they're ready now. They're serious. This one counts. The starters will be in.

And that's why it feels extra ominous when a strange sensation washes over me as we walk toward our seats. I may not know the details of whatever secret Savannah holds over the Dalton brothers, but for some reason, she slithers into my mind.

I ask Nicki out of the blue, "Does Savannah come to these things?"

She shrugs and purses her lips. "Doubtful, but given her history with both brothers, maybe. She'd probably love to run another profile on the two of them, and what better event to dig up dirt than when they're playing each other?"

Speaking of Luke's exes, I bring up the other pain in my ass. "Think we'll be lucky enough to run into Michelle today?"

She laughs. "We'll definitely see her on the sidelines. Maybe after the game, too, if we go to the team dinner. How's that whole living with her thing going, by the way?"

I roll my eyes. "About as awful as you'd expect. But I'm hopeful for good news when the paternity results come in."

"When are those supposed to show up?" She pauses to look at the numbers at the top of each section in the stadium to find the ones that match our tickets.

I stop with her, and we find our section. "With any luck, they'll be waiting for us when we get back home." We both turn in and show our tickets to the attendant at the top of a long row of stairs.

"I've got my fingers crossed for you."

We opted for tickets we found in the third row near the fifty-yard line on the away team's side of the field. My heart thumps when we slide into our seats, and it starts racing when the announcer introduces the Vegas Aces. Nicki and I cheer like a couple of maniacs, drawing the ire of several Broncos fans sitting nearby.

I spot eighty-four right away as he runs beside my brother, and I can't help but stare at his long, lean frame as he rushes across the field from the locker room they just came out of toward the sideline.

God, he's hot. And I'm *married* to him.

This still doesn't feel real. I didn't even know him a few months ago, and somehow we're living out our fairy tale now. He's in love with me. I'm in love with him. We're giving this a real effort.

I'm a nervous wreck as a handful of players move to the center of the field for the coin toss. The Aces will get the ball first, and a bunch of men line up on either side of the ball for kickoff. I say a little prayer in my head. *Please keep him safe. Please don't let him get hurt.*

I look for eighty-four. "Is he out there?" I ask Nicki, and before she answers, I find him standing on the sidelines as he waits for his turn to take the field.

She shakes her head. "The special teams unit goes out there for kickoff. But he'll be on for the next play."

And then the players are running at each other.

"Go, go, go!" Nicki yells as some guy in a black and red uniform runs with the ball. He makes it to the thirty-yard line before he's tackled, and I wince at the contact. God, that can't feel good.

We watch as a bunch of players run off the field, and then I spot Luke as he runs on.

Number three, Brandon Fletcher, hands the ball off to Jaxon Bryant for the first play for no gain. He does that again on the second play, and this time Jaxon gets away and manages to get a first down. I only know this from the announcer narrating the events.

My eyes are zeroed in on number eighty-four. I watch as he fights off Hammond to try to get free, but he seems unable to escape him.

On the next play, Fletcher throws to my brother, who makes a big gain and another first down.

They don't get much further than that, and the first drive is over for the Aces, ending with no score as it's the Broncos turn to take the field.

I breathe out a little sigh of relief that Luke isn't on the field for a while. I can breathe easier while he rests. I sort of like when the other team has the ball just for that very reason, though I'm sure he's itching to get back on the field to try to escape Hammond.

I watch Jack as he goes to work. I don't know him well, but from the few interactions I've had with him, it's safe to say that he's a confident guy. That translates to the field, too.

I watch as the center snaps the ball to him, and all the linemen protect him from the defenders who are trying their hardest to take him down. He's clearly in his element as he takes his time scanning the field, watching his men move into the places where they're supposed to go based on the strategies the team has practiced over and over. The way he stands there before he throws the ball reminds me a lot of the way he acts in his everyday life. He takes his time, he waits with poise, and then he throws the ball with accurate precision.

A wide receiver catches it and gains a few yards before one of the Aces defenders takes him down.

I can't help but picture Thanksgiving at the Dalton house as Carol and Kaylee made the turkey inside and the boys went outside to toss around the ball. I can just see Jack and Luke making even a simple game of catch into a competitive sport.

It actually sort of helps me understand their relationship now in a way. The competitive spirit has always been there between them, starting with sports but not ending there. Clearly that spirit has infiltrated every aspect of their relationship, and I can't help but wonder if it's beyond repair. They're two stubborn men, and Luke obviously drew the short end of the stick when it comes to fitting in with his own family.

Enter Ellie.

I'm his family now. Josh is. Even my parents are.

I text my mom. I'm sure they're watching the game. In fact, I bet they'll come to Vegas next weekend for the home opener.

Me: *Will you be in Vegas next weekend? Luke and I would love to take you to dinner.*

I'd invite them to stay with us, but we have that whole *Michelle* issue going on.

With any luck, she'll be out of the house by next weekend. Surely we'll get the test results in the next few days, and I'm certain those results will show us that Luke isn't her baby's daddy. And I can't wait. I can't wait to get her out of our house. I can't wait to have Luke to myself. I can't wait to look ahead to our future together—maybe with babies in it, but babies that belong to Luke and me.

The Broncos score, and my chest tightens as some players run off the field while others run on. The Broncos kick the ball back to the Aces, and Jaxon Bryant catches it and runs it all the way to the forty-yard line.

I'm getting pretty good at understanding what's going on.

My eyes zero in on the hottie wearing number eighty-four as he runs into his position. I spot Hammond standing on the line across from him, and something punches me in the gut. I have a sudden bad feeling.

I want Luke off the field.

Maybe it was Jack's ominous threat before the preseason game, or maybe it's just some strange premonition poking at my gut. My stomach twists and I feel like I can't watch as the ball is snapped to Brandon Fletcher.

I watch as Brandon looks around the field for an open receiver. I watch as he spots Luke.

And then I close my eyes as Luke makes the catch.

CHAPTER 27

I regret closing my eyes, but only because in closing them, I heard the crowd's reaction before I saw what actually happened.

The loud cheering and jeering all around me turned to a collective gasp before the entire stadium went silent for a moment.

And it's in that moment of silence that I open my eyes.

I can't see the field because everyone around me is standing. I stand, too, and I see a ring of men surrounding someone on the ground in the spot where Luke caught the ball. I can't see past those men, but I spot Nolan eighteen standing there. Fletcher is nearby, too, as the trainers rush out onto the field. Players from both teams kneel as they wait.

And then Nicki's hand finds mine. She squeezes my hand as we wait with bated breath.

Is he okay?

What just happened?

Should I have kept my eyes open to see? Or will I see it a thousand times over on replay both on television and as it haunts my dreams?

Time seems to slow to a crawl, or maybe it's moving backwards. The stadium remains hushed, but a buzzing in my ears starts to get louder.

And then the big screen replays what just happened.

We watch as Allen Hammond plows into Luke's right knee. It looks like a cheap shot to me, and the bend of Luke's knee looks both unnatural and painful.

I can't watch.

I close my eyes and offer up a little prayer.

Please let him be okay.

Maybe he just got the wind knocked out of him.

"Oh shit," Nicki murmurs beside me.

I see the cart as someone drives it out onto the field, and that sick feeling in my stomach worsens. I may not know much about the game, but I do know that when the cart comes out, it's to clear an injured player off the field so the game can go on.

But how can it go on without Luke?

My heart thumps loudly in my chest. I feel it in my head.

A few players shift out of the way of the cart, and suddenly I can see him just as he sits up with the help of one of the trainers. His helmet is still on, so I can't see his face to get any sort of gauge on how he's doing.

The trainers help him stand. It's hard to see around them, but his knee doesn't look right. I try to suck in deep breaths, but they won't come. My chest feels heavy as I imagine what he's going through right now. His worst fears are being realized. He has an injury that could take him out for the rest of this season, and since he's in the last year of his contract and he's thirty-one and he could need time for rehab, this could be more than just *season*-ending.

And it's happening in Denver. His brother's homefield.

"What do I do?" I cry to Nicki.

"The tunnel," she says. "Let's go find the tunnel. We'll get you down to him."

I nod. I don't know what the tunnel is, but I follow her as we walk down the three rows to the security guard standing on the field near us. "She's his wife," Nicki says, her tone panicked. "Luke Dalton's wife. How do we get to the tunnel?"

The guard looks at her like she's crazy, and then, thankfully, Josh spots us. He rushes over and says something to the guard, and then he lets me onto the field and ushers me toward the tunnel.

Nicki stays behind.

I'm terrified to do this by myself. I don't know where I'm going, and I have no idea what I'm walking into.

Security passes me off to another security guard, who leads me through the back tunnels of the stadium toward the room where Luke is being examined.

This guard knocks on the door, and when we're called in, I spot Luke sitting on an exam table holding a towel pressed to his eyes, his shoulders trembling beneath all that gear. His helmet is off. A team doctor in an Aces polo shirt is typing on a tablet. Luke's injured right leg is stretched out on the table and the left hangs off the side. He's swinging that leg a little in what seems to be a nervous tick.

His tight football pants are pulled up over his knee, which looks like it just got through a warzone. It's already starting to swell, and it just doesn't look right. It doesn't look healthy.

"His wife is here," the guard says, and Luke lowers the towel. His eyes are red and watery, and he's sweaty, and despite all that, a wave of emotion washes over me. Tears spring to my eyes at how damn much I love him.

He's crying, and I can't help but wonder if it's because of the pain or if it's because he knows it's the end of the season and maybe more than that.

I force my own tears away and I stop myself from rushing to his side. I take it slow here. I don't know exactly what he wants from me. Yes, I'm his wife. Yes, we're in love. Yes, we're giving this a real try. But the reality is that we're still getting to know each other.

This is the moment where I need to be strong for my husband—where I need to show him what I'm made of as his *wife*. I offer a smile. "Hey good lookin'," I say. "You come here often?"

He doesn't smile, but a slight tick of his neck calls me to his side.

"Can you help me out of this?" he asks, tugging at his jersey. His voice is soft as he fights off his emotions.

"Of course," I murmur. I tug at it. It's on there tight. I wrestle with it and can't even imagine how he actually got it on. "Dammit," I mutter. "Is there a lock on this thing? Why's it so tight?"

"So defenders can't grab it." His voice isn't just soft. It's hollow and flat. It's missing the element of *him*.

I finally wrestle it off and help with his shoulder pads, and then I reach over and hug his head to my chest. He wraps an arm

497

around my arms, and this big, strong man quivers beneath the hold I have on him as he allows some of his very big emotions out. "What's the word, Doctor?" I ask the man examining Luke, my voice soft and soothing as I hold Luke to me.

"We've got a dislocated knee and possible torn ACL, but we won't get the full picture until we get an MRI," the doctor tells me. "We've got an ambulance on the way now. If it was a kneecap, that's simple, but this is a total knee dislocation, and that requires emergency treatment."

"How long is the recovery on a dislocation?" I ask.

"Nine to twelve months depending whether there's any nerve damage. If we're also dealing with a torn ACL as I suspect, it could be even longer."

Luke lets out a small yelp of protest as he continues to shudder beneath me.

"Does it hurt?" I ask softly.

"Like a motherfucker." His words come through gritted teeth.

"What can I do?" I ask.

"Nothing," he mutters.

He lets go of his grip on my arms as he seems to draw into himself at the mention of potentially being out for a year or even longer.

This injury transcends whatever bullshit he has going on with Michelle and his boss. It's bigger than our "fake" marriage.

A year out of the game at this point in his career could very likely mean the end of it. Not only will he need time to heal and get healthy, but when he returns, he'll be another year older. He may not have the same range of motion with a bum knee. He'll be another year less agile. He'll have another year on the kids joining the team right out of college, which in football is detrimental.

He's scared. I get that. But my job is to be here for him. To be the place he leans while we work together to pick up the pieces, to figure out the plan so he can get back to doing what he loves.

Instead, he's already pushing me away. I feel it.

And I don't know what to do.

CHAPTER 28

I ride in the ambulance with him. I clutch his hand in mine. I mutter nonsense about how everything's going to be okay. I don't know if it'll be okay. We don't know the full extent of his injury yet, and I certainly don't know how he's going to deal with it—emotionally or physically. I don't know what it means for him...for us.

"What's the score?" he asks.

I chuckle. I can't help but think it's *so him* to want to make sure his teammates are okay as he's on his way to the hospital to assess whether he'll be out nine months or forever. I pull my phone out of my pocket and see about a million missed messages and calls. I'll get to them when I get to them.

I search for the score. "The Aces have the lead. Seventeen to ten at halftime."

He doesn't react, and I hate how he's a total blank slate. He's always been private, and he's always done a pretty good job of hiding how he's really feeling, but it's okay to smile when your team is winning. Unless, I guess, you're the injured player on the way to the hospital who can't contribute to that win. The one who can't celebrate that win.

Tears pinch behind my eyes again.

When we get to the hospital, we're checked in through the emergency room. I sit and wait on a chair in a little room with a curtain while he's carted off for his MRI. It's only then I pull out my phone and check my messages.

I see Nicki's first.

Nicki: *What's going on? Is he okay?*

Me: *He's okay. We just got to the hospital. We'll know more after the MRI.*

I check the ones from my mom next.

Mom: *We'd love to visit with you two.*

Mom: *We just saw the hit. Is he okay? It looks bad.*

I don't have the energy to come up with something new to tell her, so I just copy the same message I sent to Nicki. Those are the only people in my circle who really need to know what's going on.

I'm so new at this that I don't even know my place yet. I assume I shouldn't talk to the press...yet I'm more than his wife. I'm his publicist, and handling the press is sort of my job when it comes to him.

I think of all the times Luke had ESPN on to catch the highlights. Any time someone was hurt in virtually any sport, it was the coach's press conference where we learned more. Either there was no new information or the coach gave some indication of how severe the injury is.

Luke returns from the MRI. He puts the game on the television as we wait on the results. He's silent as he stares blankly at the screen.

The doctor comes in with a clipboard a while later. "The good news is that it doesn't look like there's any nerve damage," he begins. "The bad news is that you're going to need an open reduction to reset the bone."

"What's open reduction?" Luke grunts.

"When you have a dislocated knee, there are two ways to put it back into place. Closed reduction means without surgery where we do what we can to shift it back into place. Open reduction means surgery. You've also torn your ACL, which will require surgery as well. I can get you scheduled for surgery this week or you can go home and have it done there."

"I'd like to go home so our team doctors can give me a second opinion."

"Of course," the doctor says. "I understand. But it's a cut and dry injury, Mr. Dalton. I guarantee you'll hear the same answer from your doctors back home."

"Still," Luke says.

The doctor nods. "I assume your team heads home tomorrow?"

Luke nods.

"We'll fit you for a knee brace and crutches so you can travel back with them. No weight whatsoever on your knee until you check in with your doctors back home. Don't let it go untreated for too long or you risk nerve damage."

"Thanks," Luke mutters. I grab his hand as the doctor walks out.

"You sure you want to go home instead of just getting the surgery done as soon as possible?" I ask.

"They'll have me cut open Monday night and I'll be back home by Wednesday," he says. He doesn't look at me as he says it. Instead, his eyes are back on the television screen. The news is on now. The game is over, and we're watching a story about one of the highways here in Denver.

I don't even know what to say to that. I'd rather see him just get it done instead of risking it by going home with the team, but I get him wanting to be back home for it. He trusts the team doctors—after all, they've been his doctors for nearly the last decade.

The curtain opens, and a head appears there. "Can I come in?"

Luke glances at the doorway, and then he shuts off the television as he stares across the small space at his brother.

"What are you doing here?" he asks.

"Came to check on my little brother." Jack steps fully into the room and slides the curtain closed. "You okay?"

I don't know why seeing him here makes the heat press behind my eyes again. Maybe it took this terrible turn of events for Luke to smooth things over with his family. Or maybe not. I don't even know if that's something he wants.

"Dislocated knee and torn ACL," Luke says flatly.

"Fuck," Jack mutters. "Not again."

Luke blows out a breath. "Yeah. Again." His eyes turn red as he fights to keep his emotions away, and then he bites his lip.

LISA SUZANNE

"I was kidding when I threatened you with Hammond. I had no idea he'd really take a dirty hit on you. He'll get a fine," Jack says. He walks to the foot of the bed.

"He'll get a fine and I'm out for the season. My entire career might be over. But at least he'll get a fine." Luke presses his palms to his eyes, and I'm shocked he's showing such vulnerability in front of his brother.

"It'll be okay, Luke," Jack says softly. Soothingly. In a tone I've never heard out of him before, least of all when it comes to his brother. "Better your knee than your neck, right?"

"It's over either way."

"Come on, man," Jack says, gripping the foot of the bed with both hands. I can't help but wonder if he's thinking he may not have too many years left, either. "Don't be so dramatic. You've got your life. You've got a woman who loves you. Life will move on whether or not you get to play again, and you got nine solid years out of the league. That's way more than most. You and I both know NFL stands for Not For Long."

Luke sniffs in response, and I squeeze his hand. "He's right that you've got a woman who loves you," I say. "I'm right here, whatever you need. Through all of this." My tone is fierce.

"You just can't let what happened the last time you tore your ACL happen again," Jack says, still gripping the footboard.

"What happened the last time?" I ask.

The brothers lock eyes for a beat, and some silent communication passes between them before they both turn their eyes back to me.

Jack's expression is riddled with something resembling guilt. Maybe it's guilt for letting something slip just now in front of me...or maybe it's more. I get the feeling it's more. Much, much more.

Something so big that it severed his relationship with Luke. Yet he showed up here again.

He still cares about his brother.

Or maybe he's here as a warning. Maybe he's here to remind his brother not to let whatever happened last time happen again.

What the hell happened?

"Nothing," Jack murmurs. "I, uh, just meant the recovery time." I've never heard this man stutter over his words before. Not once. This is the self-assured, confident man who both speaks and acts with precision and care. Always.

He's lying. Something happened between these brothers the last time Luke tore his ACL, and it was enough to force a wedge between the two of them and between Luke and the rest of his family.

And I'm going to figure out the truth. No matter what it takes, I will fight for Luke.

I have to. He's not just my "husband." He's the man I plan on spending the rest of my life with.

And there's this one other thing.

As I was sitting in the room waiting for Luke to return from his MRI, I realized something as I glanced through my calendar trying to piece together how to handle his injury with the media.

My period is late.

To be concluded in Book 5, **END GAME**.

End
GAME

LISA SUZANNE

DEDICATION

To my 3Ms. You're my End Game.

CHAPTER 1

"So what are you going to do?" Nicki asks.

We're at her house, obviously. I can't have an open conversation at my house since Michelle is still sucking the life out of it.

Our flight got in a few hours before the team's did. They take the bus as a team back to the practice facility, and then they all drive home their separate ways from there. Josh and Luke carpooled, so at least I don't have to worry about how Luke's going to drive home with a dislocated knee.

They should be back home in an hour or so, and I'm starting to get nervous. I don't know what state my husband will be in when he gets here, and I don't know exactly what my place should be.

"Just be there for him as best I can," I say. I keep wondering if I should tell Nicki about what I suspect is happening with my body. I don't have proof. It was less than eighteen hours ago that I first realized I'm late, and I'm too scared to work up the nerve to actually buy a pregnancy test.

I've never done it before. Though, to be fair, I've always double bagged it, so to speak. I've always been on the pill *and* made the guy wear a condom. With Luke, though, things were different. I thought I was fine since I was on the pill.

And now look where I'm at. This is why I double bag.

"I need Michelle out of my house," I say. I lean my head all the way back on the couch and stare up at the ceiling. "That's for damn sure."

"But the timing isn't great," she points out. "He needs to play nice with her now more than ever. He needs to stay on Calvin's good side because injuries are tough. Owners don't want to keep guys around if they aren't healthy."

I nod. "I get that. Luke isn't ready to be done. But between this injury and what's going on with Michelle, I just don't see how Cal's gonna say that they need to keep him."

She presses her lips together. "Yeah, it's not super likely. Would he play somewhere else?"

I shake my head. "He's been here his entire career. He's not interested in playing somewhere else."

"Even if it means he gets to keep playing?"

I lift a shoulder. "I don't know." More proof that I don't know him as well as a wife should know her husband.

A beat of quiet passes between us, and then Nicki says, "I have to tell you something."

My brows dip and I turn toward her. "What's up?"

She draws in a deep breath. "I wanted to tell you all weekend and Josh told me to wait and then Luke got hurt and I don't want to wait anymore."

A sense of alarm flitters through me. I don't know how much more I can handle.

"I'm pregnant," she blurts.

My eyes widen as the alarm turns into something else. My brain takes a half-second to put together that this is *good* news, not more bad news.

"Oh my God!" I shriek. "I'm going to be an auntie?"

Her eyes shine as she nods. "It's a honeymoon baby!"

I lean over to toss my arms around Nicki. Guilt presses on me as I hold onto my little secret suspicion.

"How have you been feeling?" I ask, more than a little curious as to what I might be in for.

She shrugs. "Pretty good for the most part. Tired and nauseous all the time."

"When are you due?"

"February twentieth."

I count backwards in my head. "So you're already three months along?"

She nods.

"When do you find out if it's a boy or a girl?" I ask.

"We're not. We want it to be a surprise."

"Are you hoping for one over the other?" I narrow my eyes and study her to see what she says.

She shakes her head. "As long as he or she is healthy, that's all I care about."

We're quiet a beat, and then I say, "I'm so happy for you guys. How many kids do you want?"

She laughs. "We'll start with one."

I need to take a test. Stat. I need to know if she and I are going through this together, if cousins will be born a few months apart. I need to know if Luke's going to father one child in December and another potentially in March or April. If I *am* knocked up, I have no idea when it might've happened. I don't remember missing any pills, but I know the pill isn't one hundred percent effective.

"What about you?" she asks. "How many kids are in your future?"

My eyes dart to the window almost involuntarily as I try to mask the fact that there might be one on the way. I'm not ready to just blurt that out before I even know if it's true. "God, I have no idea. One or two. Maybe three. Luke and I haven't really put a number on it."

"Aw, look at you! *Luke and I.* You want kids with him."

I lift a shoulder, glad I dodged the bullet of having to explain my current situation. "Well, yeah. I love him. I see him in my future. I don't see Michelle there, but we'll handle it if we find out it's his."

"How do you feel about it?" she asks.

"I can't fault him for anything he did before he and I met. And even after that. We didn't make any sort of real commitment to each other until after we got married."

Nicki giggles. "It's so weird to hear you say that."

I laugh, too. She's right.

"All right," I finally say. I stand. "I should head home. Debbie will be there cooking so at least I'll have a buffer between Michelle and me."

"You need me to come kick her ass?" she asks.

"I love you for asking, but no. You take care of that bun in the oven." I wink, bid her another congratulations, and then I head home.

I find Debbie stirring something at the stove. "That smells wonderful," I say.

"Beef merlot," she says, holding up a bottle of wine. "An old family recipe. You want a glass? I have some extra."

I pause. Oh shit. What if I *am* pregnant? I've been drinking lately. I never thought I might be. I feel fine—everything is totally normal.

I need to go get a test.

I make a face. "Thanks for the offer, but room temperature wine has never been my thing."

She laughs as she moves around the kitchen, and I glance at the clock. The boys will still be a little while, and there's a drugstore right up the road. "I need to run a quick errand. You'll be here a little while yet, right?"

She nods.

Can I even eat something that has wine in it? I have no idea. I know *nothing* about being pregnant or babies or children in general.

Although I *am* living with a pregnant lady, and there's another one across the street. If I need to know something, I'm sure one of the two could answer any questions I have.

Except one, I have no idea if I even *am* pregnant, and two, I'm not ready to tell anyone if I am. Least of all Michelle. Everything I know about pregnancy I've learned from her, and that hardly seems like the winning source of information.

I hop in the car and head toward the drugstore. I stand in the aisle with the tests for a few beats. I have no idea what I'm looking for. I even wonder if I should've worn some sort of disguise or at least a hat. What if someone sees me picking up a test?

I'm not thinking clearly. I'm tired.

All signs that point to what I think I already know.

I grab the test that looks the easiest to read with its digital screen letting me know if the results are positive or not. I take it up to the counter, and I'm lucky it's a teenaged girl behind it. She seems like she doesn't much care at all that I'm buying this when it's a huge freaking deal to me, and she barely even looks at me—surprising considering I'd be curious about every person who walked through my line, but that's me. I'm nosy by nature, I guess.

I pay for the test—the only thing on my ticket—and I take my bag and shove it into my purse. I think briefly about doing this right here in the bathroom of the store, but I'm not seventeen and stupid. I can do this in the privacy and comfort of my own home and still find a way to dispose of the evidence without anyone catching onto my secret.

I head home, and I rush upstairs to my bathroom. I read the instructions, but I don't have a lot of time. I scan for the basics, and then I do my thing on the stick. I cap it and stare at it as I wait for the results. A little hourglass flashes on the screen as the test works its magic, and my heart races as I stare at it.

It must be a million hours of waiting that in real time is only about three minutes.

And in those three minutes, a million thoughts run through my head.

I read somewhere once that an hourglass is a sign that life is fleeting—that pirates used them as symbols on their flags to scare their victims. I get that an hourglass symbolizes *time*, first and foremost, but it's that other symbolism that strikes me now. The sands of time will run out for all of us at some point, whether it's on our careers or a season or our entire life. It's inevitable. The one thing we really can't stop is time, yet it's such a limited, precious thing.

Whatever this test says when the hourglass stops flashing, one thing is certain. I want whatever fleeting moments I have left on this Earth to be spent beside Luke.

Yet I fear for us. This injury and whatever secrets are still held in his past are two things that have the power to come between us.

I'll do everything I possibly can not to let them.

Luke's words come back to me. *I want you to just hold out for the me you know. He'll be back, and we'll have our life back in a couple months, and we'll be stronger for it.*

He issued that warning before the injury. Does it still hold true? Will he be back? Or did the Luke I fell in love with change forever when Allen Hammond plowed into his knee?

That man he referred to when he said *the me you know* is my Prince Charming. That much I know.

The hourglass keeps flashing, and then a single word appears on the screen.

Pregnant.

CHAPTER 2

Tears roll down my cheeks. I'm not sure whether they're happy tears or something else just yet, but whatever the case is, this baby is Luke's without a doubt. I'm having a baby with the man I'm in love with.

Holy shit.

I feel a little dizzy at the thought of it.

I type *what do I do if I'm pregnant* into my search bar on my phone, and it says I should make an appointment with a doctor ASAP.

I don't even have a doctor out here.

Michelle's doctor was a little mean to me, but it was in the interest of her patient. Since it's the only doctor's office I even know about here in Vegas, I immediately call and book an appointment. They can't get in new patients until next week, and I suppose I'll wait to tell anybody anything until I've gone to that appointment and confirmed everything's okay. Then I'll have a due date. I'll have more information, and I'll be equipped to handle whatever Luke's response might be.

I draw in a deep breath, shove the test into the bottom of my purse, and hide my purse in my closet.

I stare at myself in the mirror.

I'm the same girl I was before I left for Denver, yet everything is different. Same dark blonde hair. Same blue eyes. But now I know something about myself I didn't before.

I hear the front door open and close. I swipe under my eyes, and then I hear my brother's voice. "Hi honey, we're home!"

I rush down the stairs. Josh is wheeling Luke in a wheelchair into the family room, where Michelle is already waiting on the couch with a sympathetic pucker on her face.

Josh helps Luke up from the wheelchair and onto the chaise lounge section of the couch, a place where I've laid with Pepper beside me a few times, by far the comfiest seat on the big sectional. I shove a few pillows under Luke's knee to keep it elevated and one behind his back before I sit beside him and study him.

He looks different. Still handsome. Still the man I fell in love with. But different.

His eyes are haunted and ringed with dark circles like he hasn't slept. He probably hasn't.

"How are you feeling?" I ask. I press a kiss to his lips—a kiss that isn't returned.

Just hold out for the me you know. He'll be back.

"Fine," he mutters.

"He's in a bit of a mood," Josh says, moving the wheelchair into a place behind the couch. His cheerful tone is a total contrast to Luke's rather sullen attitude.

"I don't blame him," I say. "Besides, I know how to cheer him up." I wiggle my eyebrows at Luke, but it doesn't even get him to crack a tiny smile. Michelle snorts across the couch.

"You can't just mount him with his knee like that," she says.

"Nobody asked for your opinion," I shoot back.

Luke sighs. "Can I just have some time alone?" he asks.

"Everybody out," Debbie says, her voice authoritative as her gaze falls to Michelle. She doesn't mean me...does she? "I've got my famous homemade chicken soup for you," she says. She sets a tray over his lap with soup and crackers along with a tall glass of chocolate milk. All of that sounds good to me. "Let's give Luke some space to eat in peace, and when he's ready, he will let you all know."

"Thanks, Deb," he mutters. He's doing a lot of muttering.

"I need to talk with Josh anyway," I mumble, and I follow my brother to the front door. "Is he okay?"

Josh shakes his head. "I've only known him for the last year, but I've never seen him like this. Football is his life, and it was just taken away from him for who knows how long."

"What can I do?" I ask, or rather, I *beg*.

"Give him a minute to sort out what he's feeling, and just be there for him. But don't take any shit from him. If you need me, I'm right across the street."

"Anything else I can do?"

"Do you have a guest room down here?"

I nod.

"Make it into your bedroom so he doesn't have to deal with the stairs," he suggests.

"Oh, good idea. Okay. Can I text you if I need any help?"

"Of course." He gives me a look of sympathy. "Luke will waver between wanting to be alone and needing you not to leave him alone. I know that won't be easy to judge when he needs what, but I can help. I know him pretty well. We don't want him to slip into a depression over this, but he very likely will. It's a big hit to him, especially given that it's the last year of his contract. Just be sympathetic and be strong, okay?"

I nod. "I'm nervous, Josh."

He hugs me. "I know. We'll be here for you, I promise. Let me pop home and say hi to my wife, and we'll be back in a bit. We can rearrange some furniture to make things more accessible down here for him."

"But we won't let Nicki move anything too heavy," I say, a touch of slyness in my tone.

He chuckles and rolls his eyes. "She told you, didn't she? I knew she couldn't keep it quiet."

I giggle before I toss my arms around his shoulders. "I'm so happy for you. Congratulations."

"Thanks, little sis." He squeezes me, and I don't know how I keep my giant mouth shut, but somehow I refrain from telling him that his baby will have a cousin only a couple months younger.

I've only been living with this news a couple minutes. I'm not quite sure I actually believe it just yet.

I give Luke some space to eat in peace while I go to work on the guest room. I can't do much since I'm guessing I shouldn't lift too many pounds, but I change the sheets on the bed and grab our pillows from our bed upstairs. I take our comforter, too, and I set shower supplies in the bathroom.

I tackle his office next, pushing the lighter things around to make it easier for him to move. I sit in his desk chair for a minute.

What does this injury mean for his sponsorships? What does it mean for next year? If he knows he'll just be cut after his contract runs out, will he even be motivated to work hard to get healthy?

These are all good questions. I make a note in my phone to email his agent tomorrow. He might have some of the answers I'm seeking, and since I'm his publicist, the agent seems like a great place to start.

I hear the doorbell along with Pepper's barking, and I find Josh and Nicki on the other side. Pepper calms when she sees familiar faces, and she scampers back to the family room to lie in front of the television.

Nicki has a bouquet of flowers with a *get well soon* balloon coming out the top. She brings her gift into the family room where we find Luke watching the game where he was injured. He's rewinding the play as we join him.

He watches as Hammond plows into him. Rewind. Watch. Rewind. Watch. Over and over and over.

It was a dirty shot. It was cheap. I've seen it too many times, and every time my reaction is the same: my stomach turns as I wince.

"The asshole didn't even draw a flag," Luke mutters.

Josh grabs the remote out of his hand and I clear away the tray holding an empty soup bowl beside him.

"What the fuck?" Luke protests.

"Don't do this to yourself, man," Josh says. He clicks off the television.

Luke blows out a frustrated breath.

"We brought flowers!" Nicki says brightly. Too brightly.

This is awkward as hell and I have no idea what to do.

"Thanks," Luke mutters.

"I'll take them!" I say as brightly as Nicki. I walk them over to the end table so we can all see them. "Can I get you anything?" I ask Luke.

He shakes his head, and Josh takes a seat nearby. "You hear from Dr. Charles yet?" Josh asks.

Luke shakes his head.

"Who's Dr. Charles?" I ask.

"Surgeon," Luke and Josh say at the same time.

"He's sort of our unofficial team orthopedic surgeon," Josh elaborates. "He has a private practice and specializes in sports medicine."

"He checked out my knee when we got back to the practice facility," Luke tells Nicki and me. "He has a surgery tonight but said he could get me in tomorrow or Wednesday. His secretary will call to schedule."

As if on cue, Luke's phone starts ringing. He holds it up. "And there she is." He answers the call, and we all listen to his side of the conversation, which mostly consists of grunts and *okays*. When he ends the call, he says, "I need to report to the hospital tomorrow at noon and I can't eat anything between now and then."

Tears pinch behind my eyes. I want this for him—for him to start the healing process, to get healthy again—but I'm terrified of him going under the knife.

I can't believe how important he's become to me in the last couple months...and how important he'll be to our future now that I've confirmed my little secret.

"You've got this, man," Josh says.

Luke doesn't say anything, and my new goal for the night is to get him to unload some of what's inside and also to distract him from what's coming tomorrow afternoon.

CHAPTER 3

"How are you *really* doing?" I ask once we're alone...even though we're never *truly* alone with Michelle nearby.

"It hurts, Elle," he says softly, shortening my name by a syllable. He doesn't look at me.

"You need some ibuprofen or something?" I ask, not sure what to offer or what he's already taken.

He shakes his head. "I've taken some. They don't even touch the pain."

"What can I get you?"

He shakes his head and keeps his eyes on the blank television screen. "Nothing."

"I just want to help."

"I know you do," he says with a touch of frustration that reminds me how very much this isn't about me. "I just want to be alone."

"Even from me?" I ask with too much hope.

"I just want to be alone," he repeats.

So much for my goal of getting him to talk.

I grant him his wish, disappearing to my office for a while. But I can't work. I can't focus. Instead, I think good thoughts and send healing vibes to the man I love.

I give him an hour when I feel the need to check on him. And what I hear in the family room before I even step foot beyond the hallway stops me in my tracks.

It's laughter. Luke's. He hasn't laughed once—he's barely even cracked a smile in my presence—since he got hurt, and he's in there *laughing* right now. The sound of his laughter is a soothing balm to my soul, but then I hear another voice giggling with him.

I'm beyond confused.

I stride into the family room where I find Michelle sitting on the floor with her legs crossed. She's directly under Luke's feet, and she's adjusting his socks for him. That's *my* job.

"What are you doing?" I ask.

"Luke is so damn ticklish," she says, feigning total innocence. "His sock was twisted so I came over to help."

I didn't know Luke had ticklish feet. I didn't even look at his socks to notice whether they were twisted and I had no idea it would bother him if they were. I wonder what other things Michelle knows about him that I don't.

What things exist that *neither* of us are privy to?

"I can help," I protest.

Michelle stands. "All done." She claps her hands together and sort of wipes them like the job is done. "I'm going to bed. Luke, man up." She winks at him to let him know she's teasing him, and I hate how she's being so easy with him when I'm struggling to string a sentence together. "I'll see you in the morning."

I'm about to make some parting shot about when those test results are coming in, but I refrain. I don't want to piss Luke off, and especially not when he's actually smiling again.

I sit on the cushion where his legs are stretched out. "I fixed up the guest room down here so you don't need to try to tackle the stairs," I say. "You ready to go to bed?"

"I'd love a shower, actually," he says. He finally looks at me. "But I'm going to need some help with that."

"I'm here, Luke. For whatever you need."

"Yeah," he says thinly, his voice soft in case Michelle isn't completely out of earshot. "I guess it's in your contract."

His words stab my heart.

I know what he's doing. He's lashing out because he's angry about his injury, and I'm the closest target to take it.

I can't take it personally even though it hurts.

"That's right," I say. "It's the *in sickness and health* part of the marriage pact since I'm not aware of any other contracts you might be referring to." I smile sweetly, and he simply grunts in response.

Well if the reminder that our contract no longer exists since he ripped it up isn't enough, I guess I'll just have to work my magic in the shower.

And I try. Man, do I try.

I help him out of his clothes. He winces a lot. He mutters some curses. He grips onto the countertop for support—or maybe so he has something to clutch to help with the pain.

"Did they give you any painkillers?" I ask.

"They tried," he says.

"And you wouldn't take them?"

He just sighs in response. So it's going to be *that* kind of conversation.

I get it. He's a big, tough man. But that doesn't mean he can't take help when it's needed.

I help him slowly over to the shower, where the glass door is already open for him. It would be easier upstairs in our shower since it's big enough for two—or five—but that's not our current situation. I get undressed too, in part to try to take his mind off his injury and in part because I don't want to get my clothes wet from helping him.

"Do you want me to wash your hair?" I ask.

"I'm not a fucking child," he mutters, and I hand over the shampoo bottle. He's really in a mood.

He washes his face next, and most of his body. I kneel down to help him wash his legs and feet, and while I'm down there, I get a little idea in my head.

I glance up at him, and our eyes lock. A bit of heat passes between us.

Or, at least I *think* it's heat. I move toward his dick, ready to suck it to the back of my throat just to try to take his mind off things and give him a few minutes of happiness again, but he pushes me away.

He pushes me away.

I feel hurt. I feel rejected. I feel humiliated.

But this isn't about me, I remind myself.

So I finish washing him. I quietly get out of the shower and dry myself off, and once I have a towel wrapped around me, I help him dry his legs. He handles the rest himself because, in his words, he isn't a *fucking child*.

He brushes his teeth while I get dressed, and then I help him into his boxers and over to the bed.

He's silent through the entire process. I ask him little questions here and there, and I offer help where I think he needs it without assuming he can't do something for himself. And once he's in bed, I feel a tiny bit of sweet relief.

Once this surgery is over, I'll feel more of it.

"I'm going to sleep," he says, flicking off the bedside lamp.

"Okay." I set the television remote on his nightstand next to a bottle of water and his phone. "I'm going to work a while. I'll be back in a bit."

"Night," he says.

"I love you," I say.

He doesn't say it back. I try not to feel hurt over that. Maybe he's already asleep or something, but somehow I doubt it.

I close the door behind me, and I set a hand on my lower belly as I lean on the wall in the hallway. And then I let the tears freefall down my cheeks.

CHAPTER 4

I can't decide which is preferable: feeling lonely because I'm actually by myself or feeling lonely because I'm sitting beside Luke. Either way, I bury myself in work for a while. I grab a snack, watch a show on Netflix, and then head to bed.

I slip into bed beside him. He's quiet, and I assume he's asleep. I turn away from him and face the windows of the guest room wishing things were different in this moment. We should be holding hands as we brace for tomorrow, and instead I feel like he keeps pushing me further and further away.

"I'm scared, Ellie," he whispers into the darkness. I'm nearly asleep, and for just a beat, I think I might've dreamed that he said those words.

"So am I," I admit, though my admission comes from a completely different place than his.

"I've been under this knife before. The recovery was brutal, and it'll be even worse this time with the dislocation and my age. I don't know if there's any coming back from this." His voice is soft, but I still hear the emotion in it.

Tears pinch behind my eyes. I'm grateful for this midnight confession in the dark. I'm grateful he's letting me in.

I turn onto my back then reach over under the covers to take his hand in mine. I lace my fingers through his, and I squeeze. "You're a fighter, Luke. If you want to come back, you'll find a way."

"Yeah," he murmurs. "But I don't know how much fight I have left in me."

"How come?"

"It's everything. You know? It's my age. It's Calvin making me feel like I'm not good enough, and it's Michelle and this baby trapping me into things I don't want with her. It's my family and the lack of support. It's feeling like an asshole for lashing out at the people I care the most about."

I hope he means me...but I'm not going to assume anything at this point.

"Let's start with your boss. How has he made you feel like you're not good enough?" I ask.

"I don't know," he says. "He just does."

"Any chance you're projecting your fears onto him?"

"Maybe," he mutters.

"Okay, what about the thing with Michelle?" I ask, moving onto the next part of his speech. "What if the baby isn't even yours? We should find out any day now."

"Right, but what if it *is*?"

"Then you'll be an amazing father. You care so much, and you're so kind and giving. You'll roughhouse and play and provide." I realize I'm telling him everything that's been flashing through my own mind since I took that test. I amend my thoughts to include the whole point of what we're talking about. "And you and Michelle will figure things out. You'll build a bridge for that baby. Maybe in different houses, though."

"I guess," he murmurs.

"When you mentioned lashing out at people..." I say, not sure how to ask if he meant *me*.

"I was talking about you. I didn't mean to push you away in the shower," he says, and I can't help but wonder whether he'd be confessing to these same truths if we were face-to-face in daylight rather than lying beside each other in darkness. "I just...I'm not in a place where I'm ready for that. Believe me, I want it. I want *you*. I love you. That hasn't changed, but like I once told you before, I become a different guy during the season. I *have* to. I'm focused on the game, and I can't afford distractions. But when I'm hurt, well, that becomes the center of my focus. I might be a different guy during the season, but I know I'm virtually unrecognizable when I'm hurt."

"You have every right to be," I say softly. "And I'm here for it. For you. I know this is the worst-case scenario, and I will hold your hand every step of the way."

Not just because I'm your wife. Also because I'm carrying your child.

I omit that last part. I can't tell him now—not because I don't want to, because I most certainly do. But because I need to get checked before I spring more news on him, especially when there isn't anything he can do as he goes into surgery tomorrow. It's just one more thing he doesn't need to worry about until I have a chance to see a doctor.

"And as for your family, your brother showed up at the ER after the game," I point out. "Wasn't that support?"

He snorts in derision. "Hardly. He was just covering his own ass."

"For what?" Is this it? Is he referencing this big secret they hold?

"Just making sure I'm keeping my mouth shut."

"About what?" I press into the darkness.

"Let's just get through this surgery. Once I'm on the other side of it, maybe we can revisit this conversation."

I want to push harder. I want to fight for that secret. It's been referenced too many times in my presence, and secrets have this way of coming out one way or another.

But I leave him be.

"So if you're not feeling the fight...what comes next?"

"I guess maybe I set up a meeting with Phil."

I remember meeting the Director of Player Engagement and Development at the Aces facility when Leah took me around to show me the ropes. "Are you leaning one way or another?"

"Maybe coaching," he says dismissively. But then he adds, "I can get a feel for it from the sidelines the rest of this season since I won't be able to suit up."

"I'm so, so sorry, Luke."

He squeezes my hand that's still in his. "I know. Let's get some rest now, okay?"

"Sure. Goodnight."

Neither of us gets any rest, though.

We don't talk, but I toss and turn. Luke is still since he doesn't have much range of movement with his injury, but I can tell he lies awake, too.

When the light of morning dawns, I shift in his direction. His eyes are open as he stares up at the ceiling.

"Six hours until my knee is cut open," he says.

"Good morning to you, too."

He huffs out a little chuckle, and I lean over to kiss his cheek. He turns his head at the last second to catch my lips. "Thanks for our talk last night," he says. "It meant a lot to me to know that you still want to be with me."

My brows dip. "Of course I still want to be with you. I love you, Luke. Broken knee or not."

"I love you, too," he says softly. "Thanks for understanding."

I just pray I can keep understanding as we fight together to get him healthy again.

CHAPTER 5

I stare at the clock on the wall as it seems to move backwards.

I've chewed off every fingernail.

I've been on my phone so much that I killed the battery.

I'm just sitting here now, biding my time in silence as I wait for some news. Any news. I'm desperate to know how he's doing.

The surgery is only supposed to take a few hours. It's been three hours and four minutes.

Nicki and Josh are here with me. It's Josh's day off, thankfully, so at least I don't have to sit here alone. Nobody from Luke's family is here, though.

A doctor walks into the waiting room, and every head in the room swings in his direction as we all wait for updates on our loved ones.

The doctor's eyes land on Josh first and then me beside him. He's an older gentleman with kind brown eyes and graying hair.

"Dr. Charles," Josh says.

He nods at Josh then turns to me. "I assume you're Luke's wife?"

"Yes."

"He's out of surgery. It was a success and I'm confident he'll have full range after physical therapy. He's resting and still under general anesthesia but should be coming out of it any minute. He's in the recovery room and nurses will be moving him to a room for the next two to three days for observation."

"Thank you, Doctor," I say, my voice shaking, and I can't help when I start to weep.

He's okay.

The surgery was a success.

He'll have full range.

I let out a breath.

I feel an arm come around my shoulders, and I turn and cry into my brother's chest. Nicki lightly rubs my back, and I can't help but think what amazing parents these two are going to be.

When I finally compose myself and wipe away the tears, my brother lets out a soft chuckle. "Awfully attached for a fake marriage," he whispers, and I give him a half-smile.

"Not so fake anymore," I say wryly.

A short while later, a nurse pops in to let me know he's awake. "Only the wife can come back to recovery," she says to Josh and Nicki, who sit back down.

I follow her through the surgical recovery room, keeping my eyes on the floor as I feel a little faint. Curtains separate patients knocked out from anesthesia in their beds, and I feel a little queasy as heat creeps up my spine. I've never done well around blood or medical issues in general, so to be back here feels a little terrifying.

The nurse drops me into Luke's bay, and his eyes are closed. Heat presses behind my eyes again as I stare at him. He's pale, and this powerful, strong, lean man who I've seen running on a treadmill so many times looks weak as he lies there. It's not my Luke, but it's my job to help him get back there.

His eyes open and he's groggy as he focuses on me. His lips don't tip into a smile, but his eyes seem to fill with warmth as they land on me. "Hey good lookin'," he croaks. "You come here often?"

I force that dizzy and queasy feeling away as I rush over and press a kiss to his cheek, relieved that the man I fell for is still in there. "How are you feeling?"

"Not great, but this little button that pumps in morphine helps." He indicates a clicker in his hand.

"Can I get one of those?" I tease.

He chuckles. "Doubt it."

He's in better spirits than I would've expected, but he's also high on painkillers.

The nurse comes to transfer him to his room, and she gives me the room number as I take a different route than the medics who wheel Luke's bed through the hallways. I find Josh and Nicki still in the waiting room.

"He's going to be fine," I say, and Josh looks relieved to hear it from me in addition to Dr. Charles. "They're transferring him to a room now. He was even making jokes back there."

"Thank God," Josh murmurs.

They come with me to Luke's room. He's sitting up as a nurse asks him questions while he sips water.

"What's the prognosis, nurse? Is he gonna live?" Josh asks brightly.

She gives him a look like the joke was totally inappropriate, but Luke laughs. It's a relief to hear his laughter again.

"He'll be fine," the nurse says sternly. She glances at her patient. "You need me to kick these jokesters out?"

"Not yet," Luke says.

We all stand around awkwardly for a few beats, and then Josh breaks the silence. "How long will he be in here?"

"Two to three days," she says. "The doctors want to make sure there's no delayed arterial damage."

"When does PT start?" Josh asks, and I'm glad he's here to ask questions since I don't even know where to begin.

"As soon as the swelling goes down and he can stand without significant pain. Two or three weeks probably," she says.

Luke sighs. I'm sure he already knew that, but two or three weeks of sitting around without bearing weight on his knee must sound horrific for someone as active as he is.

Guess it's time to load up on movies and snacks.

The nurse heads out, and Josh and Nicki take off when Luke wants to rest. I sit in a chair in the corner and let him sleep while I look up things to do with someone recovering from surgery. Cards, games, puzzles, discovering new music and movies...there's a list. It's not endless, but we can certainly check off a few things.

I head down to the cafeteria to get some food, and when I get back to his room, Coach Thompson is standing beside Luke asking questions. I'm not sure whether this is a private conversation and I should stay in the hall, but Luke spots me and waves me in.

"Hi, Coach," I say as I move into the room.

"Ellie," he says warmly. "Good to see you again. Luke's been telling me how wonderful you've been, and I can't thank you enough for taking care of my boy."

My boy.

His *coach* is here and his parents aren't. That says something to me. Mitch seems like more of a father to Luke than Tim is. I know the coaching staff at the Aces is fairly new, but clearly these two share a bond.

"I only wish I could do more," I say.

"His smile when he looks at you says it all." He nods briefly at me, like this conversation is getting a little too deep for him, and he turns back to Luke. "I will fight for you with the big guys. You know that, right?"

Luke nods. "I know you will, and I can't tell you how much I appreciate it. I just have no idea whether I'll come back from this."

"You will," Mitch says confidently. "Stronger than ever, kid. Just keep your eye on the ball. Keep your focus, and work hard to get healthy."

After Coach leaves, Luke tells me to go home, but I can't make myself leave.

And so I spend the next two and a half days in a hospital room with my husband.

CHAPTER 6

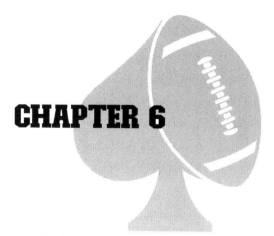

I texted my mom to let her know that we won't be able to do dinner with Luke just getting out of the hospital. She understands, but I also have an ulterior motive.

I'm not sure I can face my parents without them figuring out I'm pregnant.

I know my mom will be thrilled, and I'm feeling that excitement edge its way in, too, but I'm just not ready to face all this. We agree to a raincheck, and I think Josh was right when he mentioned in passing that he thinks our parents are probably looking at houses here in Vegas. They're both retired, and both their kids live in the same place literally across the street from each other while they're back in Chicago.

The only thing keeping them there is their circle of friends and extended family, but they're out here for most of Josh's home games, so it makes sense for them to make the move.

Josh helps me get Luke into the house, and I've never been more grateful to have my brother literally across the street.

As the doses of morphine decreased over the last couple days, Luke's mood worsened. He's back to lashing out, but I thrive on the little moments when the real him flickers through—though he's trying his best to convince me that *this* is the real him, that this is the guy I've dubbed my Prince Charming.

It's late, and we're both exhausted after sleeping in a hospital for the last few days. We head right to the bedroom we slept in the night before the surgery, and I settle Luke into bed with his leg elevated as the nurse showed me before we left the hospital. I make sure he doesn't need anything before I hop into the shower.

It's glorious.

I take my shower upstairs rather than making noise in the bathroom next to where he's trying to sleep, and when I'm done, I flip through the mail Debbie left on the dresser in the bedroom. No test results just yet. She knew to keep a lookout for the envelope from the LV Paternity Solutions Lab and to text me if it arrived, but I thought maybe she missed it.

Or maybe Michelle got to it first, but we didn't give her a key to the mailbox, so that's doubtful.

Exhaustion hits me, and I head back down to sleep beside Luke just in case he needs anything at all. The room is dark, and I creep quietly to the bed before I slide onto cool sheets beneath a warm comforter.

"I didn't marry Savannah just because I loved her," Luke says quietly into the dark.

I startle at the sound of his voice. I thought he was asleep. "What?" I'm confused. Maybe he's been taking painkillers again and he's confused, too.

"I married her because she knew things and I needed to keep her quiet."

"Quiet about what?" I ask softly.

He sighs. "My parents have been married for thirty-four years, but that doesn't mean they set a good example of what a marriage should look like. The Daltons look a certain way. They always have. But nobody knew how my mother manipulated my father. Nobody knew about the whispered arguments between the two of them that all three of us overheard. Nobody knew that they probably would've been happier apart, but they stuck together. Maybe they really do love each other. There are moments of tenderness there, I guess, but it seems like the bad tends to outweigh the good."

He pauses, and I can't help but wonder how the history of his parents links to why he kept Savannah quiet. But I listen anyway. I wait patiently as he confesses these secrets into the darkness of this room.

I reach over and slide my hand into his. He doesn't move, doesn't flex his fingers, doesn't hold mine back. But I leave mine there anyway, and I tighten my grasp.

"My parents showed me one example, and I followed in their footsteps when Savannah knew things I couldn't afford for anybody else to know."

"What things?" I ask.

He's quiet a beat, but then he starts talking. "When I tore my ACL the first time, I took some drugs Savannah gave me. At the time, we were dating. We were just starting to get serious. Whatever she gave me helped me heal, and nobody could believe how fast my recovery was going. The progress was incredible, and I felt great, so I kept taking them. I increased the dose. I asked her for more, and she gave them to me. And then Jack found the bottle. He confronted me. He told me they were PEDs that were banned by the league. I had no idea they were illegal, but I knew I could get into a hell of a lot of trouble if I was caught."

"What are PEDs?" I ask stupidly.

"Performance enhancing drugs," he says. "I stopped taking them as soon as I learned what they were. Savannah claimed she had no idea they were banned, but she's a sports reporter. She played dumb, and I believed her. She wouldn't have given them to me on purpose if she knew what it could've done to my career. And then a few days later, I was slapped with a random drug test. Hindsight tells me she had something to do with it, but it didn't matter. There was no way I'd pass. PEDs can linger in your system for up to four weeks, so I was fucked."

"What did you do?" My voice is soft in the quiet room.

He clears his throat. "Jack stepped in. He, uh, took the test for me."

"Oh my God, Luke," I gasp. "Isn't that illegal?"

"Very. It's considered fraud. But he did it to protect me. He confessed to my parents when my test showed up clean, and that's when I was pushed aside as the family outcast. The fact that I let my brother put himself at risk when he was a rising star was unacceptable to them."

"Does Kaylee know?"

"No," he says quietly. "My parents. Jack. Me. Savannah. And now you. That's it."

"I don't get it," I say stupidly. "Why did she do it?"

"My guess is so that she'd have something over me. Insurance, if you will. She's a master manipulator, and looking back now, I know she only married me for money. She divorced me knowing she'd get more out of me with the evidence she held."

"Why are you telling me?" I ask, truly curious as to what his answer might be.

"Because you've shown me what a real marriage looks like." He's quiet a beat. "You've been there for me in ways nobody else has ever before in my entire life."

"So why did you marry her if you didn't trust her?"

"She'd been pushing for a ring, though I'm not totally sure she cared if it was from me or my brother. I think she gave me those drugs so I'd be dependent on her, regardless of whether she knew what she was giving me." He lowers his voice. "I did love her even though I didn't fully trust her, but I looked to my parents for the example. They didn't trust each other, either. I was young and dumb, and I thought I needed to marry her to keep her loyal."

"And you divorced her..." I prod.

"When I could no longer take being manipulated by her." He doesn't mask the hostility in his tone. "I did what my father never could when it came to my mother. Savannah just wanted money and the last name of an NFL star to seal her career as a sports reporter. To make it look like she had the inside track, which she did. For years. She had total inside access first to my brother and then to me. She got to see the inner workings of three different teams. She got to see inside the heads of two players in different positions, including one who was traded while they were together. And she made out with plenty of cash."

"What would happen if the truth came out now?" I ask.

"The league would open an investigation, I suppose," he says. "There could be fines or suspensions or even worse."

"How would a suspension work with you being injured?" I ask.

"I don't really know. It would depend how the news came out. If it was public, the punishment would be harsher. If it's within the organization, it would probably be swept away like everything else."

"What's the suspension for something like that?" I ask.

"First time offense for substituting a specimen would be two weeks for Jack. For attempting to substitute a specimen *and* having evidence of the drugs, which Savannah has, it'd be six weeks for me. But those are penalties for guys currently doping, not who did something eight years ago. I don't even know if there's a statute of limitations on something like that."

"Did it happen in Nevada?" I ask.

"Yeah."

I grab my phone and look it up. "The statute of limitations for fraud in this state is four years." I click off my phone and set it back on the nightstand.

"Well at least we're clear legally then."

He yawns. I can't see it in the dark, but I can hear it. "Get some rest. We'll talk more tomorrow," I say, though I'm not sure why I'm ending this conversation when he's finally telling me everything I've been wanting to know.

"Okay," he says.

"Thanks for letting me in," I say, settling my hand back into his. "Thanks for trusting me with your secrets."

"Thanks for being someone I can trust." He flexes his fingers in mine, and then his breathing evens out as he falls asleep.

My mind is buzzing now, though. I can't just go to sleep after that confession.

What if the truth comes out? Savannah knows, and she wasn't the nicest person when I met her. She can't be happy that Luke knocked up one woman and married another and she no longer holds his attention. She might even be worried about the money he pays her.

We need to find a way to make sure she keeps this story to herself. I know it's been eight years, but my gut tells me she's just waiting for the right moment.

I can't let her kick Luke when he's already down.

CHAPTER 7

I'm tired when I "wake up" in the morning, and I use that term loosely since in order to wake up, you're supposed to fall asleep at some point. Dawn is just starting to light up the room.

Between Luke moving and shifting all night as he tried to find a comfortable sleeping position and my mind reeling at his midnight confessions in the dark, I couldn't find a way to calm my thoughts enough to actually sleep.

I need a plan.

I need pre-damage control.

But I also need to let Luke's loyal fanbase know that he's okay. I haven't posted anything yet. I've been waiting for him to be in the right mood to give me a statement, and that hasn't happened.

I'm still shocked he confessed his little story last night, to be honest. Maybe it's the painkillers or maybe it's the fact that I didn't run just because he's hurt.

I turn over and find that Luke's awake, too. He's staring blankly up at the ceiling.

"Did you get any rest?" I ask.

"No." He doesn't move his gaze from the ceiling, and I can't help but look up there, too. I don't see anything. "You?" he asks.

"Nope."

"Sleep upstairs tonight," he says. "You shouldn't miss out on sleep because of me, and I can call you if I need anything."

"You *can*," I say. "But you won't."

He shifts a little then winces.

"How's it feeling?" I ask, sitting up.

"Like hell."

"I'm sorry. Want me to get you some pain meds?"

He blows out a breath. "I'm trying to do this without them given what happened last time. But not taking them will make me crabby."

I narrow my eyes at him. "Who, you?"

He lets off a soft chuckle.

"You've been crabby since the morning after I met you. Maybe even that night."

His brows dip. "I was *not* crabby the night we met," he says crossly.

"You whipped out a stack of condoms that were enough to nearly scare me away and you complained about how your buddies had been ribbing you all night about it having been too long since you had sex. You were *totally* crabby."

"Whatever," he mutters.

I giggle. "See? Crabby. Let me make you breakfast. Or give you some morning sex?"

It's his turn to narrow his eyes. "You know I can't have sex."

"Why not?"

He rolls his eyes. "How do I thrust when I can't use my knees?"

Heat crawls up my neck as I think about him thrusting. "You let me do all the work," I say, though to be honest I'm a little scared of bumping his knee the wrong way.

"Let's give it another day or two. But I will take you up on the breakfast offer. Can you just help me out of bed?"

I don't feel quite as rejected as the other day in the shower. That's something, at least.

We make it to the kitchen and I help Luke settle into a chair at the table. I set another chair across from him to prop his leg up. "Do your stretches," I say. He has a whole list of things he's supposed to do four times a day to help rehab his knee. I set to work on the task of making breakfast, glancing up at him every few minutes to check that he's doing his exercises.

He isn't.

I want to badger him about it.

I don't.

I set scrambled eggs, toast, and bacon on plates for us and join him at the table.

"This is going to sound weird, but I feel closer to you after our talk last night," I say. I dive into the scrambled eggs. I might not be the best chef in the world, but I do make a mean egg.

"Not weird at all," he says. "And I feel the same."

I want to ask more. I want to expand on that.

But Michelle still lives here, and she's the last person we'd want finding out about Luke's past. I get why the brothers are so careful with their secret. If it ever came out, it wouldn't just make them look bad. It would make their teams look bad...maybe even the entire organization.

The doorbell rings, and I head over to answer it. The mailman stands there with an envelope marked *Certified Mail.* "Is Luke Dalton home?" he asks.

"He is," I say. "He can't come to the door. Would you like to come in?"

He looks a little uncertain.

"He just had surgery and can't walk," I explain. "I can bring you to him in the kitchen."

He nods. "Fine."

I try to get a good look at the envelope but I can't see who it's from. It *has* to be the test results. I didn't realize they'd come certified, so it's a good thing Luke is home from the hospital.

My heart races. My chest tightens. My stomach turns, and I very nearly catch myself resting a hand on my lower belly.

This is it. The moment of truth. Either Luke Dalton is going to father two children a couple months apart or potentially just one pending my doctor's appointment on Thursday.

I show the mailman out and when I return to the kitchen, Luke is eating his eggs while the envelope rests beside him on the table. He's staring at it.

"You ready to open it?" I ask.

He shrugs but doesn't say anything. How can he sit there so casually when in many ways, the fate of the rest of his life lies inside that envelope? This will tell him whether he can kick out the toxic woman trying to suck the life out of him...or it'll tell him he'll be co-parenting with her.

"You need me to?" I press.

His eyes lock on mine. "There's just a lot riding on what's inside that envelope, and I'm not sure I'm in a place to handle any more upheaval."

I reach across the table and squeeze his hand as my heart pounds loudly in my chest. He doesn't want any more upheaval...but I've got my own little secret that will send both of us into a tailspin once it's confirmed. At least it'll be a *happy* tailspin. I think. "I get that. But you know what? Regardless of what the paper in there says, either things stay the same or they get easier. Right?"

He nods, and then he shoves the envelope toward me. "You do it."

I don't hesitate. I tear open the envelope and pull out a small stack of papers.

I scan the top page, a little note thanking us for using their lab. I flip to the next page, where I see a chart with a bunch of numbers on it. I spot Luke's name at the top, and then at the bottom I read the statement to myself.

My head buzzes as the results register, and then I read it aloud to Luke. "Based on an analysis of the STR loci listed above, the probability of paternity is seventeen-point-three-three-three percent."

Luke's brows dip. "Seventeen percent?" he asks. "But that would mean..."

"You share *some* DNA with the child, but not enough to conclusively state that you're the father."

Our eyes meet across the table and mine widen as I realize what this means.

"Jack," he hisses.

CHAPTER 8

I clutch the paper as I stand from the table, anger permeating my veins and seeping into my bloodstream. How could she do this to him? And *why* would she do this to him?

I stalk furiously through the kitchen so I can go to her room and give her a piece of my damn mind when Luke's voice stops me. "Wait."

I halt in place and turn around.

"Let me handle this."

"I was about to head to her room to kick her the hell out of here," I say.

"I know exactly what you were about to do," he says thinly, "and this is *my* problem to handle. I don't need you tackling it for me."

"It's *our* problem," I remind him as hurt stabs at me that he wants to do this alone when we've been in it together the entire time, all the way back to when I first saw the headline when I woke up one morning and was the one who told him he was having a baby with her as he was dripping with sweat from running on the treadmill.

God, those were such simpler times.

I set my hand on my hip. "Fine. Want me to go get her?"

"She'll slither out eventually. Until then, I plan to enjoy my eggs in peace knowing that I didn't make the biggest mistake of my life." He holds up his glass of orange juice like he's about to make a toast. "Dodged a bullet there."

I hope he's talking about sleeping with Michelle and not about having children in general.

"Aren't you mad?" I ask, walking back to the table to sit. I push my plate aside. It's not like I can enjoy my half-eaten breakfast now that I have this information.

He nods. "Furious. But she's still my boss's daughter. I can't have you making things worse."

"That's not what I was going to do!" I protest.

"Oh, come on, Ellie. Yes it was. You were going to go kick her out of the house with *joy*."

He's not wrong there.

"Look, I've got enough problems. I don't need you making one more."

I glare across the table at him. "Fine. Enjoy your breakfast." I stalk out of the room and head to my office to pout there.

Maybe I'm being mean. He'll need help when he's done eating. He can't get from the table to anywhere else, especially not with how far out of his reach I stored his crutches once he was in position at the table—not to be mean, but just to get them out of the way.

I'm sure Michelle will come along to help.

I hate my bitter thoughts where she's concerned, but I can't help it. I want her out. Now. She's provided enough distraction for Luke. Maybe if none of this had ever happened, he wouldn't have gotten hurt. I realize that's a real stretch since it was the fault of another player doing something dirty, but maybe he would've seen it coming if he hadn't been distracted, if he would've had just a little more focus instead of being pulled in a million directions in his personal life between his family and Michelle.

And me, I suppose.

I heave out a breath.

I can't get mad at him for wanting to handle things his own way. I've heard of pregnancy hormones before, and maybe this little spat is my first real experience with them.

I draft up a statement to post on his social media, and after a while I head back to the kitchen to show it to him and get his final approval before posting. He hasn't asked for approval since my first few posts, but I feel like this is one he'll want a little control over.

He doesn't apologize for his comments when I slide into the chair across from him, but I guess I didn't really expect him to. Instead, I let it tug at my thoughts. Letting these things build without confronting him is going to get ugly, but he's recovering from major knee surgery along with the devastating loss of his football season—and potentially his entire career. I'll give him a pass on a stupid comment that I'm sure he didn't even mean.

"I drafted up a little thing to post to let your fans know you're okay," I say, and I shove the paper in front of him.

He glances over it, and before he gets a chance to respond to my hard work, Michelle waltzes in. "Good morning, everyone," she says brightly. She has no idea what we know.

"Morning," Luke mutters. I glance around the table and don't see the envelope with the test results. How'd he do that? He couldn't have gotten up from his chair. He must be fucking Houdini. My gaze finally lands on his, and he shakes his head just slightly to remind me to keep my mouth shut.

"Good morning," I say sweetly. The last *good morning* you'll be spending here, you evil bitch.

She sets about making herself a bowl of yogurt with some berries, and then she joins us at the table. "How's the knee, big man?" she asks.

Big man? Is that some pet nickname I never knew about? Gag me.

"Hurts. Where were you on March thirty-first?" he asks without preamble.

Her eyes dart from her yogurt to him and back again to her bowl. She looks guilty. "I don't remember, Luke. That was almost six months ago."

He narrows his eyes. "Stop acting like you don't know. Tell the goddamn truth for once."

Her brows dip. "What, exactly, are you accusing me of now?"

Luke blows out a breath. "You know, I thought it was strange when you showed up in Hawaii with my brother. Even stranger that you were *so adamant* that this is my baby. But the strangest thing of all is that there's no way I was so drunk on the night of April fifth that I would've had sex with you, especially not when I

543

was so angry with you after we broke up. So you either need to tell the truth about that night we were together, or you need to tell the truth about who else you were with at the end of March."

"I, uh..." she stutters and stammers a bit. "You and I were together, Luke."

He shakes his head. "You know, the more I think about it, the more convinced I become that we weren't. What I think happened, and you feel free to correct any details I might get wrong here, is that you were with someone else, had a feeling you might've gotten knocked up, and decided to use that to try to get me back. You came here that night, and you slipped me something that made me pass out because I sure as hell wasn't drunk enough to fuck you. Then you found a way for us to wake up naked together and you left me to make assumptions."

Her jaw drops. "How could you even say that to me?"

He pulls the papers from his lap where apparently he's been hiding them. "Because these DNA results show that there's only a seventeen percent chance I'm your baby's father, which tells me that either you and I are related or you fucked someone in my family."

Her eyes widen as she realizes for the first time that she's caught.

A sense of vindication washes over me.

"You might want to have Jack's DNA tested," he says. "And since I can't throw these papers at you before I storm out of the room thanks to my fucked-up knee, you can see yourself out. Oh, and move the hell out of my house by the end of the day."

She stares across the table at him, and then she looks at me. "It's her, isn't it? She did this. She turned you into this monster I don't even recognize."

"No, Michelle," he says. "That was all you."

"My dad will be hearing about this," she says, standing up as she tosses her spoon down on the table.

Real classy, Michelle. Use your damn father against a man whose career might be over anyway.

"You do that," Luke says, his voice escalating. "You make sure to tell him how you used me, lied to me, and manipulated me. I guarantee I won't be the one to come out of that looking like the asshole you'll try your hardest to paint me as."

She glares at him. "Your career is over. I'll make sure of it."

"You have no power," he says dismissively. He's not scared of her threats, and I've never been prouder of him. He shifts in his chair and winces at the movement. He hasn't had his pain pills yet this morning, and he probably needs them even more after this conversation with Michelle.

"Get out," I say to her through a clenched jaw. "Luke needs a calm home to recover in, and you're not welcome here in it."

The look she gives us both tells me this isn't the last we've seen of her before she spins on her heel and stalks out of the room.

"I hear Denver's real nice in the winter," Luke calls after her retreating figure.

If our suspicions are true and Jack is actually the one who knocked her up, then she'll still be part of Luke's extended family. But who knows what that even means at this point—it could very well mean that he *might* see his niece or nephew once a year, or maybe not. Maybe he doesn't want anything at all to do with his family anymore—especially not when Jack went behind his back and helped Michelle keep up the lie.

"You okay?" I ask, nodding toward the hallway she just disappeared down.

"Fine," he mutters.

"I just mean about the news."

"I know what you meant," he says shortly. "And it's fine."

Few things are more unconvincing than his tone, but I let it go.

Seems I'm doing a lot of that lately. I'm starting to wonder how many things I should let go before it's one too many.

CHAPTER 9

I'm in the kitchen cleaning up our breakfast dishes less than an hour later when Michelle comes slithering back in. "Can we talk?"

I helped Luke move to the couch a little while ago, and he's still angry. Now isn't the time, but I guess she thinks an hour is enough for him to cool down. Maybe I know him better than she does, because I know it's not nearly long enough. Forever might not even be long enough to forgive what she did.

"About what?" Luke grunts, and it's nice to have his moodiness directed at someone other than me.

She stands in front of him with her arms crossed over her chest, and it's maybe the most vulnerable I've ever seen her. But it's still fake. It's a game, and that's all any of this ever was to her, which is a real shame considering there's a baby involved.

She glances over at me, and then she lowers her voice—but not so low I can't still hear her (maybe since I'm literally hanging onto every word she speaks). "I'm sorry. I just so badly wanted it to be yours. I wanted a life with you."

"And you thought trapping me with a baby was the way to do that? That's really fucked up, Michelle. Even for you."

She starts crying, but I can't muster any sympathy for her. I doubt Luke will, either.

"What I did with Jack...it was a mistake." She sniffles and seems to tighten her arms around herself. "I know that now. I just thought you'd fight for me."

"You played a game, and you lost," he says flatly. "After what happened with Savannah, you should've known better. And I don't really care what you and Jack did. I'm just glad I'm not going to be tied to you for the rest of my life."

There's a knock at the front door, and I move to answer it.

When I open it, I'm shocked at who's standing on the other side. "Calvin," I whisper.

His lips thin. "May I come in?"

"Of course." I open the door wider and I lead the way to the family room where my husband and his daughter are currently duking it out. Or as Michelle stands there looking all apologetic and Luke lies helplessly on the couch.

"Daddy!" Michelle says when she sees him, and she rushes toward him. He pats her back gently as he gives her a hug.

"Mr. Bennett," Luke says, sitting up a little straighter.

"How's the knee?" Calvin grunts.

Luke clears his throat. "Fresh off surgery that was a total success. Dr. Charles says I'll get complete range of motion back with a little PT."

Well that's certainly a more optimistic picture than he's been painting for everyone else.

"Glad to hear it," he says. "I came to help Michelle get her stuff out of here. She'll be coming home with me a while."

Does that mean he knows the truth? Did Michelle actually confess to her father that she's a manipulating bitch who slept with brothers just to make one of them jealous?

If he wasn't standing here in my family room, I wouldn't believe it.

An awkward beat of silence passes, and then Calvin gives Michelle a stern look before he glances at Luke. "I'm sorry for what she's put you through." His voice is gruff, and Michelle looks absolutely miserable. She didn't just lose Luke. She also disappointed her father.

A moving truck comes by later in the afternoon, and Calvin takes off with very little interaction aside from when he first walked in.

And that's it. Michelle is out. She's gone, and that's all I care about.

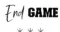
Luke is propped on the couch with pillows elevating his knee on Sunday at ten when the first game starts in our time zone.

The Aces are playing at home, which apparently means the afternoon game, and I guess it also means it's Football Sunday just as it's been my entire life.

At least I sort of understand the game now, though not watching Luke strut around in those tight little football pants will definitely make it a whole lot more boring.

We watch the Broncos game first, and he watches both his brother and Allen Hammond, who's back on the field like nothing happened last Sunday. It reminds me that today is the first Sunday Luke doesn't get to play, and the thought makes me sad. He won't get to play for the entire rest of the season. The Aces are projected to do really well. This season could be his shot at a Super Bowl ring, and while I believe he'll still get one if the team wins the big game, this certainly wouldn't be how he'd want it. Maybe they won't even get there with one of their key players out.

My heart breaks for him.

Luke studies every play. I set a bowl of popcorn beside him, but it sits totally neglected as he pauses and rewinds live TV so he can focus on what certain players are doing and then watch again to see what other players are doing in reaction.

It's not really the most entertaining way to watch the game, but it does tell me he'd make a good position coach. I still want to get him to talk about the future, but he's so focused on his injury right now that it's just not a good time.

I head to my office. Two of the Aces guys have signed up for publicity with me and both are looking for community outreach ideas, so I research some different opportunities that take place on Tuesdays since that's their only day off.

I drown myself in work for a couple hours, and then I grab lunch for both Luke and me around noon. I set a sandwich and salad on the couch beside him, and he hardly acknowledges me.

I go back to the office, and when I emerge at one to watch the Aces game with him, I see that his sandwich and salad still sit untouched beside him.

"Eat," I command.

He doesn't even look at me. "Not hungry," he grunts.

"Eat it anyway, or Pepper will." I go for a light, teasing tone.

He pushes the plate away.

"Come on, Luke," I beg. "You need your strength to get healthy. At least do your leg exercises if you won't eat."

He sighs. "What difference does it make? We both know this is the end of my career."

"Regardless of what comes next in your career, you're young. You still need to get healthy. Are you just going to sit on the couch with your knee propped for the rest of your life?"

He purses his lips, and I wonder what he'd do without me. Maybe sit on the couch forever.

I'm not allowing that.

"I know it's a tough road." I take his hand in mine. "But I'm right here, okay?" I know it's not enough, that *I* am not enough, but I still need him to know he isn't going through this alone. And when I say that I'm right here, I really mean we—both me and this baby I think I'm carrying. "We'll get through it. You'll come out stronger once you're able to start therapy."

He pulls his hand away. "You and I both know that's not true."

I pick up his plate and set it directly on his lap. "I know it's true. I just need you to believe it, too. Having a bad attitude isn't going to change it."

He lets out an exaggerated sigh, like I'm an annoyance who's just in his way. And then the Aces game starts, and that's the end of our conversation as he laser-focuses on it.

"Coach put in Higgins," he mutters as soon as he sees his team take the field. "I knew he would. That kid was just waiting for something to happen to either Josh or me. Man, did he luck the fuck out."

"You getting hurt isn't lucky for anybody," I say, doing my best to keep the tone positive in here.

He just gives me a look like I'm dumb. Maybe I am for believing the best in people, but I guess it's true. Tristan Higgins wouldn't have gotten this opportunity today if Luke was on the field.

I sit beside him as we watch a little bit of the game, and he yells at the television. A lot. I've never seen him get so passionate about anything before, and if we weren't sitting here because he's hurt, it would be hilariously entertaining to watch him.

But the truth of the matter is that we *are* here because of an injury.

Higgins makes some unbelievable catch, and Luke mutters a curse.

"Why's it a bad thing he made that catch?" I ask.

He gives me that same look as before, and then he sighs. "This is his chance to prove he's more valuable than me, and he's doing it. Handily. They won't negotiate a new contract with me because they won't need me anymore." He shakes his head and keeps his eyes focused on the screen.

"Not even as a back-up?" I ask. I don't know how this works.

"They're not gonna pay me to be a back-up."

"But someone else might," I point out.

He lifts a shoulder. "Yeah." He's made it clear before that he doesn't want to play somewhere else. He wants to stay with the Aces. But from what I've learned from the other football wives, these men don't really get much of a say in it. It's a business, and transactions are made based on that fact.

"I wish I could fucking be there today," he says. He glares down at his knee as if that'll change things. It doesn't.

"Do you still *want* to play?" I ask.

I get the look. Again.

"Then eat your damn sandwich," I scold.

He flattens his lips and his nostrils flare, but then, miraculously, he picks it up and takes a bite.

I don't want to treat him like a child, but if he's going to act like one, then I will.

After all, now's as good a time as any to start learning how to deal with children since I might have one of my own soon.

CHAPTER 10

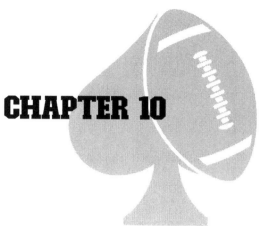

The road to Thursday is long.

I'm nervous about my doctor appointment, and I'm keeping it close to the vest so I don't even have anyone to talk to about it. I almost slip to Nicki when she talks about how she's nearly at the second trimester, which is supposed to be much smoother sailing than the first, but I manage to cover it up.

I almost slip again when Josh asks if I want a glass of wine one night when they come over for dinner. I tell him I'm not drinking in solidarity with Luke, who isn't supposed to be mixing alcohol with painkillers.

With Michelle out of the house, we can rest easy knowing any conversations we have are safe—provided she didn't plant a bug, which I wouldn't put past her.

Still, though, with everything going on, I feel like it's best to just keep quiet about it until it's confirmed by a doctor and not a drugstore test.

It's Wednesday night before I finally get Luke to talk.

He just took his pain meds, and he's in a better mood than he has been the last couple days as I've let more and more slide when it comes to the way he treats me. I often think back on Josh's words not to take any shit from Luke, and I'm afraid it's too late. On the other hand, I also think back on Luke's words to be patient with him. I know the man I fell in love with is in there underneath this grumpy exterior, and I'll get him back. He just needs a little TLC.

"You haven't really talked about how you're feeling about the fact that Michelle's baby isn't yours," I begin as we sit down to Debbie's world-famous shredded chicken tacos.

He grunts and takes a bite of his taco, and I wait patiently for his answer. I stare across the table at him with raised brows, and when he glances up and catches my eye, he sighs.

I know he doesn't want to have this conversation, but it's important to me. I need to know where he stands on having kids in general. He mentioned to me that he wants kids with me sometime down the road...but that was before the injury.

"Relieved," he finally says.

That was sort of my fear, but before I read too much into his answer, I get him to clarify. "Why?"

He clears his throat and looks past me out the window. "You know I want kids someday down the line, but I never wanted them with her. I guess I'm just relieved I won't be tied to her for the rest of my life." He shakes his head and his eyes move to mine. "In some ways I will be if it's really Jack's, but at least she won't be *my* problem. You know?"

I nod, satisfied with that answer. Until he continues.

"But it's not just that. Right now...it's not just bad timing. I've got rehab. I've got a long road ahead of me. I don't know what next year will look like, or even beyond that. I need a stable future before I can even begin to think about kids. And I need to be selfish to get healthy. Worrying about her pregnancy and delivery and then having a newborn, it's all just too much. But it's Jack's problem now."

I press my lips together and force any emotions tightening my chest away.

I get what he's saying, but he's saying these words a little preemptively. And now I'm even more terrified to go to this appointment tomorrow. When I get the official confirmation and due date and it all becomes real instead of some abstract idea...then what?

How do I tell him?

I clear my throat. "Jack's problem?" I repeat. "Has he taken the test?"

Luke nods. "Confirmed. It's his. Ninety-nine percent match."

"How'd you find out?" My brows dip.

"He texted me this morning."

"I didn't know you two texted." I take a bite of taco.

"Well we do. I guess there's a lot you don't know about me." He says it like he's musing, but it's true—and it cuts deeper than it should.

* * *

I pre-filled out the paperwork online, so when I arrive for my appointment, all I have to do after I check in is leave a urine sample then sit and wait for my name to be called.

The urine sample thing sounds pretty self-explanatory, right?

It's not. Nobody really tells you what to do, and in true Ellie *falling into the pool at my brother's wedding* fashion, I have no idea how to do this.

I'm nervous and anxious about this appointment, particularly after Luke's words last night, so I'm distracted. And distracted Ellie is never a good thing.

I hover over a cup and do my best work, filling it about a quarter inch. I hope that's enough because I didn't know I was going to have to do this and the tank is empty.

I set the cup on the floor once I'm done so I can pull up my pants, and when I move to flush, I kick it over on accident.

My quarter inch spills all over my shoes.

I gasp as I stare at the floor, and then I heave out a heavy sigh as I try to clean up both my shoes and the floor with some combination of toilet paper and paper towels. The floor is mostly dry, but it smells like ammonia in here.

I chug some sink water, which nearly makes me gag, and force out another sixteenth of an inch, careful not to knock it over this time.

And the best part? I get to tell the lady at the front desk the bathroom floor needs some disinfecting.

As my brother would say...*only you, Ellie.*

Once I'm back in the waiting room and nobody sits by me because my shoes smell, the ultrasound technician calls me in.

I sit on the table just as I saw Michelle do not so long ago, and the tech squirts the same jelly on my stomach. She moves it around with her magic wand, and I see a bunch of lines on the screen.

Then I hear a *whoosh-whoosh-whoosh* sound.

"There's the heartbeat," she says.

Tears spring to my eyes. *Whoosh-whoosh-whoosh.*

This is the first time this has actually felt real since I took that test. I know it said positive, but when you don't really feel any different and you can't see inside there, it's sort of hard to believe, or it's easier to believe it's a false positive.

But this right here is hard evidence.

She takes some measurements. "You're measuring at seven weeks, four days."

"Seven weeks?" I blurt. "I've been pregnant for *seven weeks?*"

She nods and smiles. She must hear exclamations like that all the time.

"Everything looks great." She prints out some pictures and hands them over to me. I stare at the wavy lines. One of them has the word *baby* with an arrow pointing down to what looks like a little jellybean.

My little jellybean.

"You can head back to the waiting room and your doctor will call you in shortly," she says, and I'm just supposed to get up and walk into the waiting room?

But I'm pregnant! Is that safe?

Okay, I'm being dramatic. But the point is that I have no idea what this means. I have no idea how to take care of a pregnant body. I wasn't real sure how to take care of a regular body, either. Or shoes, apparently.

And I express that as soon as I'm called back. The tech takes my blood pressure and records some things on a sheet of paper. "Congratulations," she says.

"Thanks. So what do I do?" I ask.

"What do you mean?"

"How do I take care of myself?" I ask, or rather, I beg. "How do I keep this baby safe?"

She smiles. "The doctor will have all sorts of information for you as well as resources to help you. But during my first pregnancy, I asked my sister *everything*. She had two kids. Do you have someone like that you can go to?"

Nicki pops immediately to mind. "My best friend is pregnant."

"Aw, you two can go through this together. So sweet."

I smile. She's right. It'll be a lifesaver—or at least a sanity saver—to have her nearby.

The doctor comes in, and the tech was right. She gives me an entire bag of stuff for newly pregnant mothers (*mothers!* I'm going to be someone's *mother*), and I'm going to need to find somewhere to put this until I figure out a way to tell Luke about this little secret.

She gives me a quick exam and taps some stuff onto a tablet. Before she leaves, she asks if I have any questions.

There's one question that keeps flitting through my mind. I guess this is my chance to ask it. "I've been on the pill for years. How did this happen?"

"There are lots of potential reasons," she says, sitting on a stool to explain. "The pill is ninety-nine percent effective when it's taken perfectly. For most women, that's a little closer to about ninety-one percent, and lots of things can affect it. For example, if you take it at different times, or if you miss one, or even if you drink too much or take certain medications. Do any of those sound relatable?"

"Possibly the drinking thing," I admit. And there may have been a day or two where I took it later than usual or when I missed it altogether. It's all sort of running together now, and for the first time, I'm starting to feel a little queasy.

"And you're aware of all your options?"

I nod. We all learned of the options back in our high school health classes, right? And regardless of how this happened, I feel a sudden fierce protection over whatever's growing in there. Something I've never felt before in my life tugs at my conscience, something that tells me I will stop at nothing to ensure this baby is safe, protected, and loved.

"How soon can I find out gender?" I ask. It's a boy. I can feel it.

"Usually around twenty weeks, but if you decide to get the genetic testing done, that can be done as early as ten weeks and it screens for gender with ninety-nine percent accuracy."

My brows dip. "What's the genetic testing?"

"A noninvasive prenatal test that screens for certain genetic disorders," she explains.

"Am I supposed to get that done?" I ask.

"That's a decision for you and the father, if you're including him in the decision-making."

"I am," I say quickly. "I just have to figure out how to tell him we're having a baby."

She smiles. "Are you going to do something special?"

"I don't know," I murmur.

"Read through the new mom packet in the bag I gave you, and feel free to call the office at any time with any questions," she says. "We'll see you back in a month, or if you want the genetic testing, a bit sooner."

I nod, and she leaves.

I make my next appointment for a month. Once I figure out how to tell Luke, we can discuss the genetic testing.

Holy shit.

I'm having a baby.

With someone who counted his blessings just the other day that he's *not* having one.

CHAPTER 11

"I'm pregnant."

I say it into the mirror, and it still doesn't feel real. Now that it's confirmed, I should tell Luke. I just have no idea how to break this news to someone whose entire life is already in complete upheaval. This will throw him into a tailspin, and somehow I can't help feeling like it's my fault. I realize it took two of us to create this life, but I assured him I was on the pill. I thought we were safe. I even urged him to forego the condom.

And despite this totally unplanned surprise, that's exactly what it is—a surprise. It's not a mistake. It's not a problem. It's not an accident.

It's a baby.

A baby that's part me and part the man I love, and when we said our vows that we'd join together in all that is to come, well...this is part of it. Our vows were real even though our intent wasn't.

I just hope he'll feel the same.

I don't have a plan other than to just go down there and blurt it out.

But when I get to the family room, he's still engrossed in football. Instead, I take Pepper outside. We sit on the patio for a little while, and I confess my secret to her. Her ears perk up. Her life's about to change, too, and the pup doesn't even know it.

I lose my nerve. Friday morning means a doctor appointment for Luke at the Aces' practice facility, where a team doctor talks to him about his progress.

"Have you been doing the stretches they gave you at the hospital?" he asks.

Luke nods, but I jump in with the accurate information. "Not as often as he's supposed to."

Luke glares at me for telling the truth, but I don't care. Go ahead and get mad at me, dude. This is about recovery, not about pretending to be an angel.

"The swelling is much better," the doctor says, "but since you still can't bear weight without pain, we'll hold off another week on physical therapy. Potentially next week, but possibly a little longer yet. No walking and no bearing weight until you see me next Monday, but you *need* to do the stretches. You won't be ready for PT if you don't start rebuilding the muscles and movement. Understand?"

Luke is obviously disappointed, but he nods.

"Coach will be in shortly," the doctor says, and he leaves.

"Thanks for ratting me out," he snarls at me once the door clicks shut behind the doctor.

I just smile sweetly.

Coach Thompson knocks on the door and lets himself in. His eyes edge over to me before they land on Luke again. "Can we talk?"

Luke glances at me and then at him again. "Yeah." He nods and doesn't dismiss me from the room, and for some reason my heart lifts a little at that. He trusts me enough to be in here while this conversation happens, whatever it might entail—and that means something to me.

Coach blows out a breath. "Cal was breathing down my neck about next year before your injury, but about a week ago, he seemed to let up a little. Any idea why?"

"Michelle's baby isn't mine," he admits.

"Thank God for that," Coach mutters, and I stifle a laugh. "What do you want next year? This is you and me, kid. Be honest."

"I want my fucking knee back," Luke says.

"Then you gotta work for it," he says, and I hope his words get through to Luke. If they don't, I'm afraid Luke will fall into a pit of despair where he won't bother taking care of himself because he doesn't see any reason why he should.

I have a reason.

"What else?" Coach asks.

"I want to play."

"Another thing you gotta work for. I hate to break it to you, but that Higgins boy is *fast*. You need to keep up with him despite the bum knee or you need to take out Nolan." My eyes lift to Coach's at the mention of my brother. "I know that's not an option. But might I remind you that as much as we're a family, we're still cutthroat, Luke. It's still every man for himself out on that field, and I don't know whether the man upstairs is issuing a contract to an injured player who's been in the league nine years already."

"But I put up record numbers last season," Luke protests. This is his shot to plead his case, and clearly he's jumping at it. "If this injury hadn't sidelined me, I would've done it again. You have to fight for me, Coach. I need you."

Coach presses his lips together. "You know how I feel about you, Luke." His voice is gruff. "You're a son to me. I'll do what I can, but I can't make any guarantees."

"That's all I'm asking," Luke says.

"How's the progress?" Coach asks, nodding to Luke's knee.

Luke's eyes move to his knee, too. "Doc said the swelling has gone down but I can't start PT until next week at the earliest."

"Then you sit on your ass until you're able to start PT, and you put in the work to get better," Coach says. "It's the only way you've got even a half a shot at coming back next year."

Luke nods. "Understood."

Coach blows out a breath. "We miss you, Luke. The locker room isn't the same without you."

"You just miss the granola bars," Luke says, and Coach laughs. "I'll have Deb whip up a batch."

Coach claps him on the shoulder. "I'm sorry this happened to you. It's the shit end of the stick. But get well soon, kid. We need you back."

"Thanks," Luke says, and he seems a little emotional at his coach's words.

Josh is waiting for us when Coach leaves, and he helps Luke from the exam table and into a wheelchair. And then we head home—all three of us, which makes telling Luke about the baby a little more difficult.

I guess I'll just put it off a little longer.

CHAPTER 12

"What are these granola bars Luke mentioned to Coach Thompson?" I ask Debbie on Saturday morning.

She chuckles. "I make these homemade granola bars and the boys all go crazy for them. Luke brings them in every Thursday since that's their hardest day of practice."

"Can you make some for Luke?" I ask. "I think they'd really cheer him up. And I want to try them too."

Debbie laughs. "Of course, dear." She lowers her voice and nods toward the family room, where Luke is watching—surprise, surprise—football again. He's far enough away and engrossed enough in the game that he can't hear us. "How's he doing?"

I lift a shoulder. "Good days and bad. More bad. Mostly I just try to be helpful and kind of stay out of his way."

"Is he being nice to you?"

I laugh at the question, but it isn't long before I get sort of serious. "No, not really."

"That's how he was the last time he was hurt, too. He was extra grumpy with Savannah, though he was always sort of grumpy with her."

"So what do I do?" I ask.

"You put him in his place. I've known Luke a lot of years, and I know he loves you. You can't let him walk all over you. That's not the strong woman he fell in love with, is it?"

I shake my head sadly. "No, it isn't."

"He'll never tell you when he needs anything. He's too hard-headed. So you just have to do your best to read his mind." She winks at me, and I giggle.

"There's just so much on his plate that I don't blame him for being a little grumpy."

She nods. "But no matter how much is on his plate, that doesn't give him a right to take it out on you."

"True," I concede, and I have the sudden urge to confess my little secret to her. "Can I tell you something that stays between us?" I ask, lowering my voice.

"Of course you can."

I glance at Luke. He's still watching the game. I glance back at Debbie.

"Oh," she says, her mouth dropping open. She covers it. "You're not..." She nods toward my belly with wide eyes.

I nod, and I can't believe the amount of relief that flits through me at *finally* unloading this very big secret on someone. I'll never know why it's Debbie I choose, but she's a pseudo-mother figure to Luke, so that makes her this baby's pseudo-grandmother.

"Oh my goodness!" she exclaims quietly so as not to draw Luke's attention. She grabs me into a hug, and then she drags me into the laundry room so we can talk without worrying about him overhearing. The smell of detergent rushes to my nose, and my stomach feels suddenly queasy. "Congratulations! How are you feeling?"

I shrug. "Pretty good. No real symptoms like you hear about."

"And you haven't told him?" she asks.

I shake my head. "Every time I try, another bomb is dropped. I just found out a few days ago myself. I haven't figured out how to tell him."

"Oh, honey," she says. "You need to tell him. This could be exactly what pulls him out of this horrible funk. It'll give him purpose."

I nod as tears pinch behind my eyes. "He was just so relieved that Michelle's baby wasn't his..."

She gives me a stern look. "He was relieved he wasn't going to be tied to that horrible woman for the rest of his life. But it had to come as a blow that he thought he was having a child and then that was taken away from him."

"He just said he was glad, and that's made it even harder to figure out how to tell him." I set a hand on my lower stomach to try to ease the queasiness. I need to get out of this room. I always loved the smell of detergent, but suddenly it's putrid.

"Has he talked to you about his feelings at all?" she asks. "Not about Michelle, but about the loss?"

I shake my head.

"Then you don't really know how he's feeling. I suspect he's numbing more than just his knee with those painkillers."

"But this baby doesn't make up for the loss of that one."

"No," she says, shaking her head, "it doesn't. You're right. But it gives him something new. It gives him a future to look forward to with the woman he loves."

"I'll talk to him," I promise. "And now I need to get out of here. This detergent is making me nauseous."

She laughs. "Oh, I remember those days. Just you wait."

I emerge from the laundry room with hope, and I gulp in breaths of air that's not filled with the perfumed scent of detergent. I march right to the family room because she's right. Luke and I need to talk about his feelings. He needs to unload whatever he's holding inside, and then I can give him our good news, and fingers crossed he'll see it as good news, too.

When I get to him, he's watching football. It's some game he recorded, and he rewinds and studies the same play over and over. At least it's not the one where he got hurt.

Pepper's head rests on his good leg, and he absently strokes her ears with one hand while working the remote with the other.

"Can we talk?" I ask.

"After the game," he grunts.

"After the game you've seen a thousand times?"

He doesn't even acknowledge me.

I wonder if he'd even notice if I moved out...not that I have anywhere to go.

"Have you done your stretches?" I ask.

"No." He rewinds the same play to watch it again.

"So, to be clear, you'd rather watch a game you've already seen than have a conversation with me about something important."

He finally glances over at me. He raises both brows. "Uh, yeah. That about sums it up." His eyes return to the television.

I know this is the knee injury talking. This is his pain talking. This isn't him. This is the exact attitude he warned me about, and Josh warned me about, and even Debbie, to some extent, when she warned me that I need to be the strong woman he fell in love with.

She's right.

And I refuse to take his shit any longer.

I grab the remote out of his hand, and his brows dip in surprise. "Hey!" he exclaims.

I turn off the television and throw the remote out of his reach.

"What the fuck?" he says.

"This has to stop," I yell at him as I fold my arms across my chest.

He stares at me like I've grown two heads. Before he gets a chance to protest, I get a little more passionate.

"I've let your bad attitude slide because you had my sympathy. But I refuse to be your punching bag, and I refuse to sit meekly by while you treat me like garbage. Josh told me not to take your shit, and he's right. So you're going to do your damn stretches and you're going to talk to me while you do them."

He looks surprised. "You can't tell me what to do," he says. I figured he'd put up a fight.

"Uh, yeah, I can. If you can't bear weight on that knee yet, you're pretty dependent on me. And if you can be a dick to me, I can be a bitch back."

He huffs out an annoyed sigh, a signal I've won this battle.

I sit on the edge of the chaise lounge and help brace his foot so he can do his knee exercises. In other words, I'm *forcing* him to do his knee exercises by basically doing them for him. He winces as I lift his leg, but he pulls it up to an angle to stretch it anyway. "You haven't told me how you're feeling about finding out Michelle's baby isn't yours."

"Yeah I did," he says. "Relieved, remember?"

"Right, relieved you won't be tied to Michelle, but what about the actual *baby*?"

"Oh," he murmurs. I watch his eyes carefully. They're focused down on his knee as he holds the stretch we're supposed to hold for a full minute. "I guess I was sort of excited about the idea of it, but I didn't let myself get attached since I never really believed it was mine."

"And how about finding out it's Jack's?" I ask.

"It was Jack's way of getting me back for sleeping with Savannah." His tone is bitter. I don't say anything because I sense he's going to say more, and he does. "When I ended things with her, she told me she was going to fuck my brother. I told her to go for it, and I told him to go for it, too. She said it to hurt me, thinking in some twisted way I'd grab her back into my arms and defend what we had. But I never felt about her the way she felt about me. I'm just glad she's his problem now."

"What a mess," I say. I help him straighten his leg out. "Do your heel slides now."

He pushes his heel forward and flexes it back as we continue our conversation. "Where's all this coming from?" he asks.

"I just don't want you to hold all that inside." I watch his leg as he keeps flexing his heel. "I want you to know you can unload those things on me and I'm here to help you deal with them."

I glance up at him, and his eyes meet mine. For the first time in days, they soften. "Thank you," he murmurs. "You're a good person, and I'm quite sure I don't deserve you."

I give him a small smile. "You deserve everything, Luke. You've been hit with one thing after another, and we're married. That means we share in both the joy and the sorrow."

"You got any joy in there? Because the sorrow seems to be taking over lately."

My heart races. This is it. The *right* moment to finally tell him. "Um, yeah. Actually, I do have something," I say.

And just as I open my mouth to finally unload this happy secret, the doorbell rings.

CHAPTER 13

I spot a manilla envelope on the porch leaning against the front door when I open it. I glance around, but there aren't any cars or people around, so I have no idea who just rang the bell and left an envelope. I grab it and see a post-it note stuck to the top of it.

Luke—
It's about time this came out.
XO, S

Something feels wrong. My gut tells me who the S is, and if it's Savannah, my gut is also telling me that what's inside has something to do with the secret truths she holds—secrets that could hurt not just Luke's reputation and career, but also his brother's.

More upheaval.

But we need to know what's in that envelope. We need to brace for whatever it is that *S* thinks needs to come out.

I hand Luke the envelope. "This was on the porch," I say as I sit beside him.

He glances at the note stuck to the top, and his eyes move to meet mine. "Oh, shit."

He rips open the envelope, and we both look at the words printed across the top of the page.

For Immediate Release

The headline is printed immediately below that in bold letters:

Fraud, Illegal Substances, and the Dalton Brothers

And the subtitle paints an even worse picture: *Video Evidence Emerges in Dalton Brothers Scandal*

"Shit," Luke says. He sits up a little and winces. "Is she fucking kidding me? Get my phone. I need my phone."

I jump up and look around for it. "Where is it?" I yell, and he reaches into his pocket.

"I have it," he mutters. "Goddammit." He pulls up a contact, and a few beats later, he starts yelling. "What the fuck do you think you're doing?"

I've never seen him so angry. I can tell he wants to get up and pace around, but he can't. He's a caged tiger, and I don't know what sort of ferocity he's going to unleash.

Just when we had a breakthrough. Just when things were finally looking up. Just when I was about to tell him the truth about our baby.

Impeccable fucking timing, Savannah.

I go immediately into publicist mode despite the fury searing through me.

Damage control.

What can we do to fix this? How can we get ahead of it? Is it already released? Is it coming tomorrow? Or is this simply a threat?

Whatever the case, I need to set my emotions aside. Luke needs me to be calm because he certainly isn't.

"If you send this to the press, that invalidates our contract. No more bonus checks, princess." He listens to whatever lies she spouts for a beat.

"You'll pay for this, Savannah," he hisses, and then he ends the call before he throws his phone across the room. It hits the wall and leaves a dent. "Fuck!" he yells. He grabs his hair with both hands and pulls.

"What did she say?" I ask, trying to keep calm for him. I pick up his phone. It has a nice new crack in the screen.

His fists are clenched and his nostrils flare. His chin is tipped up, revealing an angry vein in his neck. He's fucking *livid* right now, and I have no idea how to calm him down.

He draws in a deep breath.

"I need some whiskey," he says.

"You shouldn't mix—" I begin.

"I know what I should and shouldn't do. I need a fucking glass of whiskey."

Whoa.

I scramble off the couch and pour two fairly tall glasses before I remember *I can't have one.*

I hand him one. I'll take care of the other one later.

He gulps it down and winces. "More."

"Luke," I plead.

He nods to the cup, and I bring him the other one.

Once that one's empty, too, he finally says, "She already sent it to the press because, according to her, she doesn't need my money anymore."

My brows dip. "Why not?"

"Because she's engaged, and she won't get my alimony checks anymore when she remarries. Checks that, by the way, have a little extra in them each month to keep her quiet about this." He holds up the papers, and then he rips them to shreds and tosses them on the floor.

I don't blame him, though I'm certainly annoyed by it since he's not the one who's going to have to clean them up.

"Who the hell would marry her?" I ask.

"A young, dumb kid who believes she can help seal his spot on the Aces," he mutters. He glances up and his eyes meet mine. "Tristan Higgins."

"Tristan Higgins? Isn't he, like, twenty?"

"Twenty-three," he mutters.

"And she's..."

"Robbing the goddamn cradle at thirty-three," he finishes.

Sort of like Luke is, I refrain from pointing out. There's ten years between them. There's six years between us.

"But why would she print this trash?" I ask.

"Because it'll hurt my reputation and solidify Tristan's spot on the team." His tone is pointed, like he doesn't really get how I didn't put that together myself.

"How?" I ask, my brows drawing together in confusion.

"She's been holding onto this shit for eight goddamn years. She was waiting for the right moment, and now that I'm hurt, she can stoke the fears that I'll do the same thing this time. She'll kill my rep, make everyone think I cheated to get healthy, all my sponsors will drop me, and nobody will want me on their team." His tone is full of exhaustion, his speech is starting to slur, and I'm a little scared that he just drank all that whiskey while he's on pain meds. That could be a dangerous combination.

"Why, though? Why would she want to hurt you after all this time?"

"Because I married you. Because I moved on. Because the way she sees it, I'm happy and she's..." He shrugs, but it's half-hearted. He seems worn down. "Her name is fading from the media because she isn't married to a football player anymore. She's crying for attention, and she's hoping this story will get her name back out there. She was just waiting for me to get injured again to blow this shit up."

"Well, good thing you've got a publicist to fix all this," I say. I'm definitely biting off more than I can chew with that statement, but I have to give him hope.

Maybe a baby could give him hope, too? Something to look forward to in the not-so-distant future?

Now's not the time, obviously. And especially not after his next statement.

"Jesus, I can't imagine one more damn thing piled on top of me." He shakes his head. "At least Michelle is out of the picture. But what the fuck is coming next?"

What the fuck is coming next, indeed.

CHAPTER 14

"Hmm, how to get in front of this..." I say aloud, pacing my office. I'm going to wear a path in the purple rug if I don't stop. And then it hits me.

I stop and stare out the window for a few beats as the idea takes root. Luke is going to *hate* it, but hearing from the source himself before the press release hits the news is the only way to get ahead of it.

My phone pings just as I think it.

Too late, I realize as I check the notification. He's already hit one sports news website, and more will surely follow. And that just means we need to set my idea in motion quickly.

I find Luke on the couch watching football in the same place he's been for the last week and a half except for bathroom breaks, sleep, and the occasional meal at the table.

"It already hit one news outlet, so we need to act fast," I say.

"Dammit," he mutters. "I was hoping it was just some sick joke."

"Afraid not, my friend."

"So what's your plan?" he asks.

"I need you to get on camera. Go live in your Instagram stories. Tell your fans that you made a mistake when you were younger, but you won't do the same thing this time. I can draft you a statement to read from or give you talking points, your choice."

He shakes his head. "Abso-fucking-lutely not."

I roll my eyes. "It's a double whammy, Luke. You'll be showing everybody that you're still alive, and you'll be responding to a story that's just starting to hit the press. This way *we* tell the narrative instead of Savannah."

"Let her do her damage," he mutters. "It's all over anyway."

"What's all over?" I ask.

He just glares at me.

Fine. If that's how he wants to play it, then I need to call in the big guns. I think of the person Luke seems to respect most in the world. I need him here.

I head back to my office and make a call.

"Ellie?" the voice on the other end answers.

"I need your help," I say. I explain everything, and an hour later, the doorbell rings. When I open it, I find Coach Thompson and his wife, Mama Mo.

"Please talk some sense into him," I tell Coach, and he nods as I let them in.

"Who was at the door?" Luke yells when he hears the door click shut.

"Me," Coach says.

I spot Luke sit up a little straighter and pause the television as Coach walks into the room. He sits on the edge of the chaise lounge where Luke is propped.

Luke's eyes flick to me, and I swear I see a bit of a glare there...but I don't care. This is for his own damn good.

"What's going on, Luke?" Coach asks.

"You already know or you wouldn't be here."

"Don't you dare give me attitude after I came for a house call," Coach warns.

Luke blows out a breath. "My second year playing, I got hurt. I was young and dumb and took some pills from someone I trusted, the same woman who penned the article hitting the news right now. I didn't know they were a banned substance. I got slapped with a random drug test the day after I learned they were illegal, and my brother switched the sample for me."

"Stupid," Coach says. "On both your parts." He shakes his head. "But you were young. I can understand how you were scared. Your brother, though, should've known better."

"We both know that now, and believe me, this has torn our relationship apart. My relationship with my entire family...it's been eight years, and we're still not past it. We're still not half as close as we used to be."

Mo grabs my hand and squeezes it while Coach whistles through his teeth. "You know the league's going to open an investigation."

He nods. "Yeah, I know."

"Only because it's public," Coach amends. "My guess is you'll both get maybe one game and a fine."

"Jack's going to fucking kill me if he gets suspended."

Coach stands and paces a little in front of Luke. "He's not innocent if he took the test for you."

"No," Luke concedes, "but he did it to protect me."

Coach sighs, and Mo squeezes my hand again as we stand quietly bearing witness to this conversation.

"What's the best course of action here?" Luke asks.

Coach shrugs. "Are you denying it or admitting it?"

"I won't lie," Luke says, and there's the man I fell in love with. The one who's brave and noble and truthful.

"Then get ahead of it. Do what your wife is suggesting. One of the most powerful things you could do is admit you made a mistake in the past and show people how you've learned from it." Coach glances over at me. "It's a smart move. There's a reason she's the publicist."

"Fine," Luke mutters.

Thank you, I mouth to Coach. He nods once and presses his lips together.

"Now where are those granola bars?" he asks.

Luke laughs. "How'd you know I have some?"

Coach's brows draw together. "How do you think Ellie bribed me to come over?"

We all enjoy some of the most delicious homemade peanut butter chocolate chip granola bars I've ever tasted in my life while I go over the talking points I want Luke to hit, and suddenly I understand why Coach has been missing Luke in the locker room.

Well, the granola bars plus Luke's sweet, sweet ass...I mean his *talent*.

Yeah, his talent.

I have him practice his statement a few times and I coach him on tone and delivery. Then Coach and Mo help me get Luke into his office, where he takes a seat behind his desk with his leg propped. He wears an Aces t-shirt and a ballcap, still a freaking hot thirst trap if I've ever seen one, and behind him are plaques and trophies and books.

Coach, Mo, and I stand behind my phone so Luke can pretend he's just having a conversation with us. We all nod encouragingly, and then I hit the *live* button for him to start talking.

"Hey everyone." His voice is subdued. "I've never gone live before, but I wanted to come on here today for two reasons. The first is to let you know I'm doing well. Doctors are confident I'll be able to start my physical therapy in the next week, and the swelling is nearly gone. My wife has been forcing me to do my leg exercises to help get me strong and healthy." He glances at me and waves me over. I shake my head, and he says quietly, "Come on."

This was not one of the talking points.

I walk over and smile and wave at the camera, wishing I would've at least had time to fix my hair. I hear my mother's voice in my head. *Put on a little lipstick!*

I get out of the shot as soon as I can.

"That was her, and she's been amazing through all this along with my best friend Josh Nolan and Coach Thompson." He draws in a deep breath. "The second reason I wanted to come on today is to talk about something my ex-wife is publishing in the news. I guess she has some evidence of a mistake I made early in my career, and I just want to address it before it hits the gossip sites. Eight years ago, I took some meds I didn't know were banned. I trusted someone I never should have trusted, and it got me into trouble. I'm sorry for anyone I've disappointed because of this, and most of all, I'm sorry to my family and friends. I'm sorry to those who've kept this secret for many years, and I'm sorry I wasn't truthful about it sooner. I will take whatever punishment the league decides I deserve, and if you feel the need to judge me, do it by my proven performance on the field and the character I've demonstrated over the last eight years." He presses his lips together. "I can't wait to return next season stronger than ever because of the hard work I will put in to get healthy the right, legal way. Thank you."

I end the live chat and click off my phone before any of us talk. He did what he was supposed to do, and he made no mention of Jack. That way, his brother can address the news however he wants.

And now we wait for the proverbial shit to hit the fan.

CHAPTER 15

"Time for your stretches," I call from the kitchen. It's Sunday evening, my night to cook, and this week I went for an easy pork tenderloin with rice and roasted vegetables. I've just finished cutting up the veggies to put them in the oven and I have a couple minutes to help.

I head into the family room, where Luke's on the couch watching football as he has been all day (–slash—all week). The Aces won today, and handily against what Luke proclaimed to be the worst team in the league as he yelled at the television.

"Stretches," I demand, and he huffs out a sigh. I widen my eyes pointedly. I'm not really in any mood to deal with his petulance.

He caves with reluctance as he gets his leg into place for the first exercise. I help him hold it there. All the exercises together take about ten minutes, but you'd think it takes all day based on how hard it is to get him to do them.

It's been a fairly quiet weekend given what Luke confessed to on his Instagram live the other day, and I keep waiting for the phone to ring.

It hasn't.

Or maybe it has and Luke has ignored it. On the other hand...maybe it has and Luke just hasn't told me.

Though the people who'd call have been a little busy with things like, you know, football games. Now that the day games are over and the Sunday night game is set to begin in just forty-five minutes, most of the teams are either home or traveling back, and the league can start looking into this scandal.

At least, according to Luke they can.

And no sooner do I run all that through my thought process than Luke's phone starts to ring.

He checks the screen and mutters a curse. "Hey, Jack," he answers. He puts it on speaker and sets it beside him on the couch as we start the heel slides.

I hold my reaction inside, but anxiety darts through my chest.

"What the fuck have you done?" Jack's voice is accusatory through the phone.

Luke lets out a sigh, and when he speaks, he sounds exhausted. "I got ahead of it and decided to let you handle it your own way."

"You didn't think of letting me know it was hitting the media?" he demands.

"I assumed Savannah took care of that," Luke says.

"Well she didn't. It was the talk of my locker room this morning, and it was enough of a distraction that we lost."

Luke raises his brows and can't hide his smile, which thankfully Jack can't see because I could imagine him punching it right off his little brother's face with how angry he sounds. "Nice. Blame me for your entire team's loss. I'm sure it had nothing to do with the fact that the Chargers are just a better team."

"Oh, fuck you, Luke. You want to hear something even richer?"

"Hit me with it, big man," Luke says. "Can't get much worse over here."

I'm a little more aggressive than I should be when I help him slide his heel down again. I don't mean to be, but I'm really getting tired of him bellyaching about how bad he has it. So he hurt his knee. It'll heal. So his career might be over. He's got a wife who loves him and a baby on the way he still doesn't know about. He still has a future. He still has the entire rest of his life ahead of him, and I'm sick and tired of him acting like his life is over because of an injury.

His brows turn down and he winces.

"Sorry," I mutter.

"My coach has informed me that the league has opened an investigation. Since it's in the media, they're going to make examples out of us," Jack says.

"Goddammit," Luke mutters. "I'm sorry."

"That doesn't change the fact that I might get a suspension because of your stupidity."

"Ream me out all you want, Jack, but you didn't have to take that test for me, and you also didn't have to fuck my ex-girlfriend and knock her up. So save the holier than thou speech. Neither of us is innocent, and we're both going to face whatever consequences the league issues."

"Michelle has nothing to do with this," Jack hisses.

"Oh, doesn't she? You mean you didn't revenge fuck her and accidentally do something you can't take back now? Talk about consequences. Enjoy your life with that nightmare. I'll be going now." Luke cuts the call and tosses his phone against the wall again.

"Goddammit, Luke!" I yell at him. I drop his leg, and he hisses through the pain. "Stop throwing your damn phone!" I pick it up and toss it at him, and then I run into the kitchen to get the hell away from him.

My emotions are big right now, and they're all over the damn place. I'm mad at Luke, and I'm angry with Jack, too, for calling just to put Luke into another funk. I'm tired of everything, but mostly I'm tired of keeping this secret. I'm tired of going through this alone except for a few days a week when the one person I've told does what she can to take a little extra care of me for the few hours she's around.

He's fuming from Jack's call, and while I've already started to learn there's absolutely no ideal time to give him this news, I also know this moment right now certainly isn't even close to a possibility.

Tomorrow.

I'll tell him tomorrow.

Luke's phone rings again, and I hear him answer it. He puts it on speaker again, and it's loud enough that I can hear it from where I stand in the kitchen.

"Hey, Coach."

"I'm calling to let you know the league has opened an official investigation. I'm sorry, Luke."

Luke sighs. "I heard. What's your guess?"

"It happened eight years ago. If it wasn't in the media, they wouldn't even give it a second glance."

"Fucking Savannah," Luke mutters.

"It should be pretty cut and dry. I'd guess you'll know before the end of the week."

"The end of the week is when I'm supposed to start PT," Luke says. "If I'm cleared, anyway."

"Right, and if you get a suspension, you won't have access to our staff. Dr. Charles recommended a few private practices for both doctors and physical therapists, and I've got Mo narrowing it down to the best ones just in case. We'll have your information transferred to them in the event you need to start and can't do it with the team doctors. I'm hopeful it won't come to that."

"Thanks," Luke murmurs. "Can you level with me a second?"

"Of course."

"How bad does this look to Calvin?"

Coach lets out an audible sigh through the phone. My buzzer beeps on my tenderloin, so I take it out to let it rest a few minutes while I strain to hear what he says.

"It doesn't look good, Luke, but I think what you said in that live thing hit where it was supposed to. You were young, and Cal is judging you by your current commitment and performance, the injury notwithstanding."

"That's helpful at least."

My heart soars that my idea actually worked to sort of get Luke back into Calvin's good graces. Between that and the fact that Michelle isn't carrying his kid, there has to be some way to mend their relationship so Calvin isn't searching for ways to get rid of Luke. "Keep me in the loop."

"As long as I can, kid. As long as I can."

"Thanks, Coach." The call ends, and I pull out the vegetables, slice the meat, and make our plates.

"You want to eat in the kitchen or in there?" I yell.

"Kitchen," he yells back.

I help him up, and it's only then I realize I don't know if it's actually okay for me to be helping to lift him. I'm not supposed to lift more than twenty-five pounds according to the literature I read in the *welcome to being pregnant* bag I got from the doctor. I may be bearing more than twenty-five pounds of his weight as he uses me as a crutch to stand.

He hobbles over to the table with his arm around me, and it's good to see him up and moving around. Once we're seated and I've turned off the television, I start up a conversation.

"So what did Coach say?" I ask.

"Like you didn't hear," he says.

I narrow my eyes at him. "Look, I'm trying to be nice and make conversation. You can either choose to participate in that with me or you can be rude."

His brows dip. "What's gotten into you lately?"

A baby is the answer to that question. A baby is *literally* what has gotten into me.

"Oh, did you want me to go back to being your punching bag? Because I'm tired of it. Everyone keeps telling me not to take any shit from you, so I'm done. You want to act like a child? Go for it. I'll treat you like one."

His brows lift a little. It almost seems like he *likes* when I'm mean to him.

Well buckle up, babe. My emotions are hot right now.

I've got a whole lot more where that came from.

CHAPTER 16

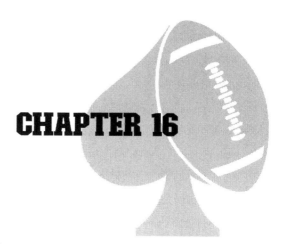

When I said yesterday that I'd tell him tomorrow, I had no idea that *tomorrow* would bring the league's decision about his punishment. It's when I'm done with my morning shower, dressed and ready for another day of taking care of Luke in between work, when I learn what just happened.

I hear Luke yelling, and I rush down to see what's going on.

I spent the entire shower rehearsing how I'd say the words. I even mouthed them to myself as I put on my make-up and dried my hair.

I was so ready to tell him, so hopeful after a nice breakfast where I felt like things were moving in the right direction for us...but the yelling tells me I won't get to.

He throws his phone *again* just as I walk into the room.

I don't bother picking it up, but there's another dent in the wall and probably another crack in the screen.

His arms are folded across his chest as he fumes, and he glares at me and then at his phone. "Well, I can't get up and punch a hole in the wall, so that's how I'm taking out my aggression. Move on or deal with it."

"What the hell happened from breakfast to now?" I demand.

"Coach just called to let me know I'm suspended for two games and I have to pay fifty grand," he spits. "Jack got one game and the same fine."

My brows dip. I'm a little slow here. "I know this isn't the news you wanted, but is it that big a deal when you can't play anyway? Isn't it better to be suspended now than when you're playing?"

He blows out a frustrated breath. "I still get paid on the injury report. I don't get paid when I'm suspended."

"So fifty grand plus..." I trail off and wait for him to fill in the blank.

"A little over a hundred and sixty K for two games."

My eyes widen. I had no idea what his salary was...and I guess I still don't. So a mistake he made eight years ago is going to cost him over two hundred grand. Those numbers are unfathomable to me.

"And worse, I can't have any contact with the entire Aces organization, which means I can't go there for my exam or to start my PT later this week."

"I heard Coach say something about that to you. He's setting you up with a private practice, right? This won't delay your recovery, Luke."

He purses his lips. "He can set me up wherever he wants. I'm not going."

"Stop it," I say like I'm dealing with a child. "Yes, you are."

"No, I'm not. I want to work with Dr. Charles. I want Adrian, the team trainer, taking me through my therapy. Not some stranger."

"It doesn't matter who it is," I say.

He looks at me like I'm dumb. "I trust those people. I don't trust some random therapist I've never even met before."

I sigh as I'm faced with yet another obstacle from a very stubborn man.

His phone rings again. "That'll be Jack." He nods to his phone. "Can you hand it over?"

All Jack is going to do is shake Luke's anger even more. I spot the incoming call: *Jack Dalton.*

I raise a brow and shake my head before I walk past his phone and breeze out of the room. "I told you to stop throwing it. And do your damn exercises. I have work to do."

I hear him mutter something under his breath. Oh, did I make him mad? Well good. He needs to step up and start acting like a man.

But over the course of the next couple days, that's the last thing he does.

He refuses to do his exercises.

His agent calls. One of his sponsors dropped him, just another event in a long succession of things that digs in to hurt a little more.

He wallows. This isn't fun or enjoyable, but it's what I signed up for. I love him despite his poor attitude, and maybe it's my job to help bring him back to himself.

On Thursday morning, I catch him attempting to *walk*.

"What the hell are you doing?" I yell at him.

"I'm fine," he mutters.

"You are not fine. You just had major surgery and your doctor told you not to bear any weight until your next check. And even when you are allowed to put weight on it, you'll need to wear a brace."

"What difference does it make? Between my age, my injury, and my reputation, nobody's going to want Luke Dalton playing for them. It's too expensive and too risky."

I don't know what to say to that, but I do help him back to the couch, where he can continue sitting and wallowing.

Mo calls me with the information for the doctor Luke is scheduled to see on Friday.

He refuses to go.

I call Mo back on Thursday evening when I'm sure he won't leave the house.

"Then I'll get this doctor to make a house call," she says.

"Won't that be expensive?" I ask.

"Ask your hubby."

On Friday morning a little before his appointment, I find Luke stretched out on the couch. His knee is no longer elevated, and when I ask him why, he tells me it's because it doesn't hurt anymore. When the doorbell rings, he looks at me with narrowed eyes. I just shrug innocently and greet our visitor at the door.

"Dr. Shepard?" I ask the mid-forties man standing there, and he nods. "Come on in. Luke doesn't know you're coming, so we're all in for a nice surprise."

The doctor laughs and follows me into the family room. "I have a visitor for you," I say brightly.

Luke doesn't move, but he does pause the game he's watching.

"I'm Dr. Shepard. Monique sent me over since you refused to come in person. Can I take a look at your knee?"

Luke sighs, and I think for a second he might tell the doctor no...but eventually he relents after letting us all know that *this is bullshit.*

The doctor examines his knee. "Stand up for me and walk," he says after a while, and Luke does. "And sit." Once he does, the doctor gives him the assessment. "You're healing well. I'm officially clearing you to start your physical therapy. Any time you're up and moving around, you need to wear this brace." He pulls a brace as if by magic out of his bag. "But you can start slowly regaining strength. Take it easy, and listen to your physical therapist. If you want to get better in time for next season, I suggest you keep doing your exercises and attend your doctor's appointments."

"Yes, sir," Luke says sullenly. I thought he'd be a little more excited about being cleared to start physical therapy, but I guess this is where the real work begins.

He can't just wallow on the couch anymore with the doctor's permission. Now he needs to work to regain the strength and movement he had before the injury.

But at least maybe he'll get his ass off the couch—and maybe, for the love of God, we can watch something other than football once in a while.

CHAPTER 17

The physical therapist visits us later in the afternoon, and he gives Luke a whole new list of exercises to do. He calls it Luke's *homework*, and it includes stairs one at a time with the sage advice of *up with the good knee, down with the bad*.

Luke is *thrilled* to leave the guest room behind to sleep in the master bedroom again, and I waste no time in moving our comforter and phone chargers back upstairs once he's done his first round of homework by climbing the steps.

I find him standing in the closet with a folder in his hands when I'm done plugging in his charger.

"What's this?" he asks softly.

My eyes widen as they zero in on what he's holding.

Welcome to Motherhood!

The letters are big and bold on the outside of the folder.

"I, uh..." I say, all the blood draining from my face. "I can explain."

And here's the explanation: I didn't feel the need to hide the bag since nobody was actually entering this closet except me.

He nods as if to encourage me to explain, and he's back to hiding his emotions. I have no idea what he's thinking. None. I can't tell if he's tired or sad or wary or happy or indifferent.

"Um..."

"Are you...?" he trails off.

I swallow as I try to get past the sudden lump in my throat.

I don't know how he's going to take this, but I haven't known all along—which is why I still haven't said anything. Our emotions are frayed. He's in a fragile state right now.

But it's time for the truth to come out.

My chest races with anxiety as I whisper, "Yes." I'm terrified as I say the single syllable that will mean an entirely new world to us both.

Will I have to do this alone?

Will he be part of this with me?

Will this be the thing that pushes him over the tipping point? Or will it miraculously be the thing that not only brings us closer together but makes him see that his future is rife with possibilities?

His eyes dip down to the folder before they move back to me. "How far along?"

"Almost nine weeks," I say, tears heating behind my eyes.

"Nine—" he stops himself short as if he's counting backwards. "That's right before training camp started."

I nod.

"So you're due..."

"April nineteenth." I tip up my chin nervously.

"It's mine?" he asks cautiously.

I should be insulted by the question, and if it were anybody else, I might be. But I know this man has had at least three women claim that they were pregnant with his child when they weren't. "I've only been with you since the day I met you," I murmur. "Nearly twenty-four hours a day, too."

He doesn't react with a chuckle like I'd expect.

"And I'll take a paternity test to prove it. I have nothing to hide, Luke. It's yours, no question and no doubt."

He blows out a long breath, and it almost feels like he's biding time because he doesn't quite know how to react. His eyes move all around the closet before they land back on me.

"I just..." he begins. "I need a minute."

I nod, but his words kill a huge part of me. I wanted him to react with excitement. Nerves, sure, and maybe a little bit of fear— those are natural, of course—but I wanted the dominating feeling to be one of happiness.

That doesn't appear to be what I'm getting.

"I'll leave you alone," I say, and I walk out of the closet as tears pinch behind my eyes.

I head downstairs and fall onto the couch, where I cry for this baby and for myself and for how freaking *alone* I feel in this moment.

I cry for him finding out in a way I wasn't expecting. I wanted to be the one to tell him, to find some special way, and now I won't get that.

And he needs a minute.

I don't even know what that means. It could mean one minute, or it could mean forever. The one comfort I have to hold onto right now is that he didn't kick Michelle out until he had evidence the baby wasn't his. I'd imagine he'd at least extend the same shelter courtesy to the mother of his *actual* child, especially given that I'm his best friend's little sister.

But maybe this is all just too much for him. He's already overwhelmed, and he's exhausted, and he's been so down about the future. I was hopeful that this would be the good news to pull him out of that, but with his completely blank expression, I have no idea where his head is at.

It's more than a minute when I hear his voice at the top of the stairs. "Ellie?"

I move over toward the stairs and find him slowly descending them. Good leg first, bad leg second, one at a time, and pausing between steps like just taking a stair is taxing for him. It probably is. He's basically laid on the couch for the last two weeks, so this is a lot of movement.

"Do you need help?" I ask.

He nods, and I move toward the landing and help him move slowly down from there to the bottom. We move toward the kitchen, and he leans on the counter.

He studies me for a beat before he asks a question. "How did this happen? I thought you were on the pill."

My heart drops.

That is his first response? *I thought you were on the pill?*

I don't think he wants this baby, and I don't think he wants me, either.

A pang of devastation stabs my chest.

"I *was* on the pill," I confirm, my voice shaking with emotion. "And I stopped taking it when I found out. The doctor said there are a lot of things that could make it ineffective. My best guess is either alcohol or allergy medication."

"I'm sorry," he says.

"For what?" I ask, glancing up at the ceiling as I try my hardest to ward off the tears I feel pinching behind my eyes.

"I should've known." His words incite the first glimmer of hope I've felt since he found the folder in the closet. It's so *him* to be hard on himself over something that was completely out of his control. "I should've seen the signs. I shouldn't have been so wrapped up in my own misery that I couldn't tell something was going on with you."

"You couldn't have known."

"It's all so obvious now." He sighs softly. "That's why you asked how I felt about the *baby*, not about *Michelle*." He says the words as if a sudden lightbulb goes off, like he's connecting the dots of the last few weeks.

I nod.

"And *supporting me* by not drinking? I should've known then."

I can't help a tiny smile. "Don't be too hard on yourself. I've been pretty good about keeping it quiet."

He presses his lips together. "How long have you known?"

I clear my throat. "Officially? About a week."

"But you've suspected since..." he trails off and waits for me to fill in the blank.

"Since the night you got hurt," I admit. "I realized I was late as I was scrolling my calendar."

His eyes widen. "That's almost three weeks. You've been going through this for three weeks by yourself?"

I nod.

"Does anybody know?"

"Debbie," I admit.

"Debbie?" he repeats, clearly shocked that she's the one person I've told.

"It just sort of came out one day," I murmur.

He narrows his eyes. "When were you going to tell me?"

I lift a shoulder as a tear splashes over my lid and onto my cheek. "I went to the doctor the day before Savannah released her article. I wanted to tell you a million times, but it was one thing after another. First the article. Then Jack being an asshole. Then the suspension. I didn't know how to pile one more thing on top of all that, especially not when you were so grateful Michelle's baby wasn't yours."

"I was grateful I didn't have to deal with Michelle," he notes quietly. "I'm sorry I made you feel like you couldn't tell me, but the paternity test results were devastating. It was the third time I felt like a baby was taken away from me because of someone else's lie."

"And now?" I ask, settling a hand on the belly that's only a couple weeks away from growing more and more until I deliver the sweet baby developing inside.

"This feels different than the other three," he says softly, and his words send a pulse of relief through my spine. "This feels like mine."

He shifts to move in a little closer to me, and he rests his hand over mine where it lies on my stomach. He leans down to press a kiss to my lips, the first real sign of affection in days. And then he wraps his arms around me and pulls me into him. I rest my head on his chest as the world seems to spin a little differently now.

He still has a long road ahead of him. We still have to deal with ex-wives and ex-girlfriends and people who should support Luke but don't. We still have to deal with the fallout of his suspension and fine, and the hit to his reputation, and whether his career is really over or if he'll get the chance to continue playing.

But together we've created something, a bond that will come to life in seven short months, and we will hold hands and hold each other as we face all those obstacles together.

At least that's my hope in this moment as I finally blow out the breath it seems I've been holding since I first noticed I was late. I hold onto the moment as long as I can before he shifts a little and hisses.

"You need to sit," I say, and he nods.

"So do you," he teases, and it's a tiny glimpse of my Luke, the one who has been missing in action for the last few weeks. My Prince.

I help him over to the couch, where I prop his knee on the same pillows I've propped them on for weeks now. "I need to show you something," I say once I get him into place. I head to my office and fish through my purse, and then I head back toward the couch.

I sit beside him and hand him the picture from my first ultrasound.

"This is it?" he asks, and I nod.

"That little jellybean thing right there is our baby," I say, pointing to it.

"Holy shit," he murmurs as he stares at the little black and white photo. He glances over at me. "How have you been feeling?"

I shrug. "Fine. I honestly don't know that I would've even suspected anything if I hadn't realized the timing."

"I'm sorry I've been so selfish. That changes now."

"You *should* be focused on yourself. You just had major surgery, Luke. It's okay to be selfish. You need to recover and I'm here to take care of you."

"I should've been here to take care of you, too," he says. He pulls on my shoulder so I lean back, and he kisses the top of my head. "And I will be. From now on."

"I'm holding you to that," I say, and I settle back on his chest so we can both stare at our little jellybean.

CHAPTER 18

As I navigate the car onto our street after Luke's second week of physical therapy, a sense of gratitude washes over me.

I guess the folder was meant to be left out in the closet, or I might still be holding onto my secret. Instead, Luke seems to have found the wake-up call he needed. He's been focused on getting himself back together. I found him lifting weights the other day, and he's dedicated to his therapy sessions. We have one more week of intense therapy, and then we start the in-home phase of his healing.

We're getting there. It's an uphill climb, but today's not just the last day of his suspension—it's also the last day of therapy outside of the Aces' facility.

Josh and Nicki are waiting on our front porch when we pull in. We still haven't told anybody about the baby, mostly because technically Luke and Josh weren't supposed to have any contact with each other during the term of Luke's suspension. That hasn't kept *me* away from them, but we want to tell them about the baby together.

The rules are lifted now that he has served his time, and I've been sort of a messenger between my brother and my husband over the last two weeks.

And now we can tell our best friends that we'll have babies just two months apart. I can finally ask my best friend for advice about what the hell to eat since apparently right around week ten was my threshold for feeling good.

I'm exhausted all the time. I haven't gotten sick, but the nausea has been horrid. Mostly I've spent time lying on the couch beside Luke when I'm not driving him to his PT appointments.

If only I felt a little better, maybe we could hit the sheets together. *That* still hasn't happened since before his injury.

"Come on in," I say to Josh and Nicki, and I unlock the door.

"I brought green chili enchiladas!" Nicki says, and she tears the foil off the top of her pan once we're in the kitchen. I want to gag at the smell of the sauce.

"Thank you," I say. I try to inject some enthusiasm, but it's definitely not there.

"What's wrong?" she asks me. "You look a little green."

Luke's eyes widen as he looks at the tray of food and back at me.

"Can we tell them now?" I whisper to Luke.

He chuckles and nods.

"I'm pregnant," I blurt, and the entire room goes quiet for a few beats. "And I haven't been able to eat anything green for the last week," I add into the silence.

And then there's the eruption.

"Oh my God!" Nicki shrieks. She runs over to me and squeezes me.

"Is she serious?" I hear Josh say to Luke over Nicki's squeals.

I giggle at the commotion and the excitement and the *love* in this room.

This is just everything I ever wanted out of life, all coming together in this one room.

"When are you due?" Nicki asks.

"April nineteenth."

"Oh my God, our babies are going to be cousins *and* best friends!" She's giddy with excitement.

"Way to knock up my sister, man," Josh says to Luke, punching him in the arm.

Excited chatter falls over the four of us as Nicki and I talk about everything from morning sickness to baby room themes and I listen to the boys as they discuss financial security and Josh chips in his two cents on the best car seats on the market.

This is family, and when I was dumped and fired on the same day back in Chicago just a few months ago, I never could've imagined this would be my future. When I bumped into a hot guy at the bar and ended up taking him back to my hotel room, I never could've imagined that a few months later, I'd be married to him and having his baby.

I've always been a one door closes and another one opens kind of girl, but I never would've guessed all the doors that would open simply by moving from Chicago to Vegas.

Life moves incredibly fast.

Maybe it took Luke's injury to slow us down a little, and if there's one silver lining to look for, one door opening, it's that.

As I look at the laughter in this room, I'm just glad I've slowed down enough to enjoy the ride.

* * *

When I told Luke about the genetic testing, he didn't want to get it done.

"Will the answers on that test change anything?" he'd asked me, and when I really thought about it, I knew he was right. No. Whatever those tests say, we will love this baby with everything we have.

But when I told him the test also tells us gender a full two months earlier than without the test, he was all in.

And so he goes with me to my next doctor's appointment. He wears his knee brace under his jeans and a ballcap pulled down low, and we head into the exam room when the tech calls us back. She takes my weight and blood pressure, and the doctor comes in a few minutes later.

"Want to hear the heartbeat?" she asks.

"Of course," I say.

She squirts the same jelly they use for the ultrasounds on my stomach, and Luke sits in the chair beside me. He reaches for my hand as the doctor moves her wand around, and nerves flit through me at the silence.

Why is it so quiet?

She moves the wand a little to the left.

Is everything okay?

She clears her throat.

I glance over at Luke, whose eyes are glued to the wand, and I'm just about to voice the questions in my mind when the sweet little *whoosh-whoosh-whoosh* calms every fear.

I let out a breath. "There's baby," she says softly. We listen for a few beats. "Baby's heartbeat is one-forty-seven. Perfectly normal."

I let out a breath of relief, and Luke does, too.

We head back to the lab for my blood draw that'll get sent out for the genetic testing, and that's it. We head home after the lab techs let us know we'll have results within a week.

Within a week we'll know if it's a boy or a girl. Blue or pink. Dinosaurs or Minnie Mouse. Football player or cheerleader.

It doesn't matter. I'm excited for either, and if our little boy loves Minnie Mouse or our little girl wants to play football, I'll do everything I can to give them what they want in this life.

And I can't wait for all of it.

Five long days later, I get an email with the lab results.

"Luke!" I yell from my office. He appears in the doorway a minute later.

"Yes, dear?" he asks, and I giggle at his response.

"I got the results," I say.

He grins. "Have you looked yet?"

I shake my head. "I waited for you."

He walks around the desk and stands behind me, and I stand, too.

"What are you thinking?" he asks.

"Boy. I've felt boy since the minute I peed on a stick."

He wrinkles his nose. "Thanks for that visual."

I giggle and lace my arms around his waist. "What are you thinking?"

"Boy." He presses a kiss to my lips.

I pull back and smile. "Ready for this?"

He nods, and I move the desk chair out of the way. I navigate the mouse to the results.

"Do you have a preference one way or the other?" I ask before I click it.

"Healthy. That's all. I feel like with a boy, I'll have a little adventure buddy. With a girl, I'll be your typical protective father. Either way, I'll be thrilled."

"I feel the same way," I say. "Do you have any names you like?"

"Just click the button," he says with a touch of exasperation, and I laugh as I press it.

The very top of the page says *Low Risk* in large letters, and I breathe out a sigh of relief. I hadn't realized how nervous I was that there could be problems until I felt that rush of relief.

And immediately next to *Low Risk*, the *Fetal Sex* is listed as *male*. We both seem to spot the news at the same time. "Boy!" we both exclaim in unison.

Tears fill my eyes as I realize for the first time that we're having a healthy little baby boy.

We both straighten as we embrace each other and the fact that this is getting more and more real with each passing day. We're getting closer to meeting this little boy, and the closer we get, the more excited I feel about it.

And the more in love I fall with his daddy.

He cups my neck as his eyes find mine. "Congratulations," he says softly.

"Same to you. So, you got any names picked out yet?" I'm teasing, but the mood shifts dramatically from the excitement of what we just found out to something much, much hotter.

He chuckles. "Not yet. You?"

"Maybe one or two," I admit.

"I love you so much, Ellie," he murmurs. His lips brush mine, and after several long weeks apart, I'm finally getting the sense that we're both in a place where we're ready to show each other that love through physical actions.

"Take me upstairs," I say against his lips.

"I was planning to just fuck you right here in your office."

"That'll work, too," I say.

He opens his mouth to mine, and just kissing him brings every feeling I have for him right to the surface. A hot need aches through my entire body. I'm ready for this. For him.

He pulls me more tightly against him, our bodies flush together, and my desire for this man is off the charts. He pushes his hips to mine, and all the stresses and worries of the day melt away here in his arms.

Except one.

How will we actually do this so I don't hurt his knee?

As if he's reading my mind, he leads me over to the couch. He sits, and he indicates that I should lower down on his lap as if he's testing whether that'll work.

"This won't hurt the baby, right?" I ask as I throw one leg on either side of him to straddle him. I shift my hips over him as I get into place, and he moans.

I know the answer to that question I saw in the booklet from the doctor's office and the internet, but I'm still seeking some confirmation from Luke. I'm not sure why. Maybe because he seems to know everything. Maybe because I trust him with my life.

"It won't hurt the baby," he murmurs, and he reaches for the back of my neck as he pulls my mouth down to his.

We kiss there a while, and then he pulls back. "Get naked," he says, and I laugh.

"What a line," I say, but I still get up off his lap and do as I'm told.

He lowers his pants while I remove mine, and then I get back on. I slide down as he holds himself up for me, and we both groan at his entrance. I move over him, up and down, and he holds onto my hips as we find the rhythm that's been missing from our lives for too many weeks.

The connection between us is intense and passionate, and my chest tightens with love as he moves in and out of me. It's pleasure on top of love, and when his eyes meet mine just before he starts to come, I see all the same emotions reflected back at me. It's not just desire and lust, but it's this commitment to each other that formed out of something else entirely.

We're both in this forever, and as he starts to come, he thumbs my clit and pushes me into my own climax. I yell my way through the pleasure as I fight the contractions of my body, and when I come out on the other side, I'm sated and exhausted.

He lets out a long, satisfied sigh when it's over, both of us panting as we try to regain our breath after that powerful ride. He slips out of me, but neither of us moves for a few beats. He just holds me in his arms there on the couch, and I never want this moment to end.

I finally have my Luke back, and I just hope he stays this time.

CHAPTER 19

It's strange sitting in the same suite with the same women but without the fear stabbing my stomach.

My worst fears were realized when Luke got hurt, but he'll heal. He'll live. It could've been worse, and I'm thankful it wasn't.

My parents are in the suite this time, too, and we all cheer as the Aces' kicker kicks off the first quarter against the Cardinals. Instead of watching the game, I watch my husband on the sidelines. He sits on the bench beside the wide receivers, and he points out things on a tablet. He's not a coach, exactly, but he's helping out where he can.

"Would he want to coach in the future?" my dad asks, nodding toward the field, and I shrug.

"He told me it's bad luck to talk about what comes next, so he hasn't really mentioned it." It's so weird to carry on a conversation with my dad like everything is totally normal. I haven't told them about the baby yet. I'm planning to do it tonight at dinner, but it's all I can think about.

"Ugh!" Nadine snorts behind us. "My husband says that, too. They all have the same superstition, and it drives me crazy. I'd love *some* insight into what my future might look like."

"Right?" I laugh. Part of me wants him to keep playing just because of this club of women I've found, but even if he does, this little club isn't guaranteed. Any number of these players could be traded or cut, and new members could make their way in. The dynamic here will change constantly, and I'm not sure whether that's something I'm cut out for.

I'm just thankful for a friend like Nicki, someone I know will stick around long after the lights turn off on the field.

"Seems to me he'd make a good coach," my dad says.

"I think he would, too," I admit. *By the way, I'm pregnant.*

"Will he keep playing?"

"I don't know," I murmur. *But he did knock me up.* "Depends on his therapy. He's doing great, but he has a long road ahead of him."

Josh catches a ball halfway down the field, and everyone goes wild. I'm thankful for the distraction because I don't know how much longer I can sit here carrying on a conversation without telling my parents about the baby.

The game is long, and I eat a lot of popcorn, but eventually it ends with a victory and we head toward the tunnel and find our players. They're still in the locker room when I spot Savannah.

I assume she's waiting for Tristan, and my blood boils. She doesn't deserve to be back here, not after the way she betrayed Luke.

She has a lot of nerve showing her face here, and I feel a sudden fierce protectiveness wash over me. Maybe it's for the baby and maybe it's for my husband, but something propels my feet in her direction.

I set my hand on my hip as I try to be intimidating, which I'm really not at all, and she blinks over at me like I'm an annoying fly buzzing around.

"Can I help you?" she asks.

"Why would you do that to him?" I demand.

She lifts a shoulder. "He had it coming."

I glare at her. "How? Because he divorced you? Smartest thing he's done aside from marrying me."

She grunts with derision. "Oh, honey, you just go right on believing what you want to believe. He'll treat you like a princess for a few months and then he'll drop you like he always does. Mark my words."

"Like he did to you? Ever think it's because he couldn't stand being with you? That he only stayed as long as he did because he didn't want you blabbing what you knew to the media?"

She narrows her eyes. "Is that what he told you?" She lowers her voice. "I suppose he left out the parts about the wild sex we used to have all over that kitchen counter." She winks at me and lowers her voice to a whisper. "Ask him about *that*. I don't miss being a Dalton, but I do miss that gorgeous cock of his." She tilts her head and gets a faraway, dreamy look in her eye. "His brother's too."

I clench my jaw at her words, and I'm about to issue a very loud, very angry *fuck you* even though my parents are a mere twenty feet away in their own conversation with Nicki when the locker room door opens. I spot Luke, and the words die in my throat as a wave of emotion for this man pours over me.

And *that* is what matters. *We* matter.

Savannah is insignificant. She can try her hardest to tear us apart, to take down Luke, to try to prove he isn't my prince...but she will fail.

Every time.

His eyes scan the room as if he's looking for something, and as soon as they land on me, they soften. He spots who I'm talking to and beelines in my direction.

"So nice of you to chat with the media," Luke says to me. "But we save our comments for respectable news sources, not this trash." He grabs my arm and guides me away from her as she calls out some insult behind us, but I miss it. It doesn't really matter what she says, anyway. What Luke and I have can't be broken by a jealous ex.

"Are you okay?" he whispers in my ear.

"Fine," I mutter.

"She can be a lot to handle." He presses a kiss to my temple.

"She can do her worst, but she won't take us down," I say. I turn my head and catch his lips with mine for a quick, soft kiss that means everything.

Josh is hugging my parents, who congratulate him on an amazing game, and then we all head out. We meet back up at Josh's place—all six of us—for dinner. Nicki has prepared an amazing feast with no green food with the exception of salad, and I stifle a giggle as she winks in my direction while she sets out a bland chicken noodle casserole. She sets a spicy pork dish beside it. I opt for the bland chicken with some focaccia bread, as does she.

"So when are you moving out here?" Josh asks my parents as we all settle into our food.

"We actually looked at a few houses a couple weeks ago when we were out," my mom says. She glances at my dad.

"And our offer was accepted on one about two miles from here," my dad finishes.

"Congratulations!" Josh says, and my eyes widen.

My first thought is that, well, having my parents in Chicago hasn't been half bad as I've been running around having one-night stands and getting knocked up. But my second thought is that it will be freaking amazing to have them nearby as I go through pregnancy and have a baby. There's nothing more important to me than family, and those are values I want to instill in this baby boy—especially given Luke's damaged relationship with his own family.

As much as I don't care for them or the way they treat him, one of my greatest hopes is that someday we can mend those fences. I'm not sure even how that would work, especially since Luke hasn't expressed that as something he wants, but I can't imagine a world where my baby grows up not knowing both sides of his family. I won't push it, though. I've met the Daltons, and I'll understand and respect if Luke has wishes different from my own.

We all express sentiments similar to Josh, and then I ask, "So when do you close?"

My parents glance at each other. "We did. Yesterday."

"What?" I gasp.

"We're just so excited to be here every step of the way as our first grandchild is on its way," my mom looks lovingly at Josh. She turns to me. "And, you know, eventually maybe you'll have kids, too."

I roll my eyes, but then I blurt, "Eventually? Or like two months after Josh and Nicki?"

Her eyes widen and my dad coughs.

"What?" she gasps, mirroring my reaction a few seconds ago.

I laugh and set a hand on my stomach. "I'm pregnant with your second grandchild."

My mom leaps out of her chair to give me a hug, and my dad follows after as my mom embraces Luke. "Oh, honey, I'm so happy," she says as she sits back down.

"And we already know the gender," I add.

"We do too," Josh admits.

"I thought you weren't finding out!" I say.

He shrugs. "We weren't, and then the doctor asked if we wanted to know, and we did."

I laugh. "Well?"

"Let's say at the same time," he suggests.

Luke nods. "One, two, three!"

"Boy!" Josh and I both say at the same time, and my mom starts crying.

Two new baby boys are joining the Nolan clan in just a few months. My mother who has pressed me for grandchildren for at least the last four years is in freaking heaven.

If only this blissful feeling could last.

But I guess it wasn't meant to.

Luke's phone starts ringing just after we walk in the front door from our visit across the street. The smile he's worn most of the night fades as he sees who's calling.

"I already said I'd pay your fine," he answers, and his words paired with his feisty tone tell me it's Jack on the other end of the line. He goes silent, and then all the color drains from his face. "Oh."

I try to wait patiently. Of all the times he *doesn't* have his phone blasting on speaker, it's this one.

"Uh, thanks for letting me know," he says. "I'll be there."

When he hangs up, he stares into space for a few beats, and then he turns to me. "Want to take a trip to Michigan with me?"

My brows dip. "What? Why?"

"My father died."

CHAPTER 20

"What?" I gasp.

"Apparently he had a brain aneurysm." He says it without emotion, but regardless of how close their relationship was, he has to be feeling *some* sort of way about this.

"Oh my God, Luke," I murmur. What do I do? How do I be what he needs in this moment? Those are my first thoughts. I have no idea what this is going to do to him. I'm worried the weight of even more on top of him is going to crush him. But he's strong, and he's got me to hold his hand as we navigate this news. "I'm so sorry."

He ignores my condolence and instead repeats what Jack must've just told him as he stares down at the blank phone in his hand. "Kaylee is with my mom. Jack is flying out tonight. They're planning the arrangements tomorrow." He draws in a breath.

"Are you okay?" I ask. My first instinct is to go into planner mode, to grab us a flight and to get packing, but something tells me he has more to say.

He leans back against the counter and his eyes finally lift to mine. His are filled with shock.

He shakes his head. "No," he says softly. "I'm not."

"Talk to me," I say, matching his tone.

"I just..." he trails off and shrugs. "I figured we had more time. I thought someday we'd fix things. I thought I'd get a chance to apologize and he'd apologize back and we'd put the past behind us. I never thought he'd just..." He stops as if he can't make himself say the words, but then he finishes, "Be gone."

I grab his hands in mine. I have no idea what to say. I've never dealt with losing a parent, and even though my relationship with my parents isn't always perfect, it's still good. It's definitely not broken. And now Luke has to live with that for the rest of his life.

"You can't fix what happened with him," I say, "but maybe that's the lesson. Life is short and precious, and you still have time with your mom and your sister and your brother. If you've ever thought about fixing things, now might just be the time."

His eyes seem to mist over, and he closes them as he bows his head for a beat in what seems like a silent prayer. When he opens his eyes again, they're red.

I step into him and wrap my arms around him. He pulls me closer, clinging to me, and it doesn't matter if they were close or not...this hurts him, which means it hurts me, too.

"I'll get us a flight," I murmur into his chest.

"Thank you," he whispers, and I pull away to get to work.

I book us on the nonstop redeye since it seems like he'll want to get there as soon as possible, and then I run upstairs to pack. I toss in his suit and a demure black dress for myself along with the essentials that'll get us by for a few days.

"Do you want me to book us a hotel?" I ask once I've finished packing.

He shakes his head. "We'll stay at my parents' house." He pauses a beat, then amends his statement to, "My *mom's* house."

I push away how weird that might be for us when his family made it so clear they didn't want us together. I look up whether it's safe for pregnant women to travel, and I find the answer is yes.

We head toward the airport and we're boarding a plane a few hours later. I texted my family to let them know what happened, and Josh made sure to request I send him the information on the arrangements as soon as I have it. I promised I would. I know he has a game to play out of town this Sunday, but I'm sure Luke would appreciate the support of the people he's closest to as we say goodbye to his father.

We land in Detroit a little after three in the morning, which is a little after midnight at home. I'm exhausted, but, then, I'm *always* exhausted lately. I guess it comes with the whole pregnancy territory thing. I'm nauseous, too—something else that's pretty standard these days.

We rent a car and he drives us the half hour to his mom's place, a sprawling mansion in the Detroit suburb of Birmingham. He has a key to the house, and he lets us in. He must've called her to let her know we were on our way since she left a light on, but the house is mostly dark and quiet as we move quietly through it toward the stairs. Together we haul the suitcases up since neither of us can really do it alone, and then he leads me toward a bedroom.

He flips on the light, and I never really thought about what sort of room a young Luke might've grown up in. I wonder how long his parents have lived here, and when he last lived here, and even when he last stayed here.

The furniture is dark wood and the bedding is navy blue. The walls are painted a light blue and are covered in framed jerseys. All Dalton, all number eighty-four, but in several different colors that probably represent high school, college, and eventually the Aces.

If they weren't proud of him...those Aces jerseys would never have made it to the wall. I refrain from pointing that out.

Instead, I wander over to his dresser, where trophies litter the entire dark wood surface. They seem to go on double in the reflection of the mirror. Each trophy has a different figure at the top, but one thing is the same on all of them: every single mini person holds a football. There are a few medals set on top of the dresser, too, and there's no dust, which tells me that even if he hasn't been in here for years, *someone* has.

The medals appear to be from marathons. I didn't even know he was a runner.

I glance at him in the mirror, and I watch as he walks over to the entertainment center. He picks up one of the two photographs set on top and stares at it, and I'm curious enough to walk over to look with him.

I spot a young Luke, maybe early-teens, and a mid-teen Jack. In the middle is Tim, his arm around each of his son's shoulders as Luke holds up a huge fish with a grin. They seem to be on a boat, and they look like the Three Musketeers.

"Did you catch that?" I ask.

Luke nods. "My dad was so proud of me." His voice breaks a little at the end. "It was the summer before my brother started high school. I remember feeling like everything was about to change." He sets the photo down and walks over to the queen bed. He sits on the edge of it. "And it did. That's the last time I can remember feeling like my father was proud of me. All his attention landed on my brother when he nabbed the starting quarterback position as a freshman. Between his own coaching position and my brother, he didn't bother with me. In fact, he basically pawned me off on one of my high school coaches." He shakes his head a little. "I guess I never realized my resentment went back that far."

"Sometimes it takes tragedy for us to weed through our feelings," I muse as I sit beside him.

He glances at me like I just said something very wise, and then he leans over and rests his head on my shoulder. "It doesn't feel real."

"That he's gone?"

He nods. "Feels like a joke. Like he'll walk through the door any minute and tell me this was all just a way to get me here so we could get things back to how they used to be. And now..." He sighs. "He won't even get to meet his grandchildren, and they won't get to meet him. That's a real shame because he would've been the best grandfather."

I try to picture the Tim I met in Hawaii as *the best grandfather* and I'm having a hard time reconciling those two very different images.

"All my memories of my childhood are good ones," he says. "It was never me versus Jack back then. It was just one adventure after another for the three of us. It was bonding over a love of the same game. It was fishing and golfing and running marathons."

I press my lips together. "I'm so sorry, Luke."

He sits up. "I know. Let's try to get some rest. Tomorrow won't be easy."

He's right. I get ready for bed in the bathroom connecting this room to Jack's, and then I crawl under the covers. He goes after me, and he returns two minutes later.

"When was the last time you slept in this bed?" I ask once he joins me in bed.

"Right after I graduated college and before I moved to Vegas. Then I ran to Vegas and didn't look back."

We're both quiet and I lean over and press a kiss to his cheek in the dark room. "I love you," I whisper. "Whatever you need, I'm right here."

He clutches my hand in his. "Thank you," he whispers. "I love you, too."

CHAPTER 21

The room is empty when I roll over, and I check my phone. It's a little after eight, five our time. Luke emerges from the bathroom a minute later, and I'm thankful I don't have to navigate this house or his family alone.

"Good morning," he says softly.

"Morning," I say. I sit up. "You ready for this?"

He shrugs. "Nope. You?"

"I'm ready for whatever you need."

He presses his lips together. "Thank you."

"Can I take a quick shower?"

He nods. "I'll wait for you."

"You can go down," I say.

He shakes his head. "It's okay. Take your time."

I don't. I take a speed shower, make myself presentable, and when I emerge, I find Luke staring at that same photo he'd been studying last night.

He sets it down and glances up at me. "How are you so beautiful?" he asks.

Heat creeps into my cheeks. "Stop it," I say with a little smile.

He chuckles as he stands and walks over to me. He takes me into his arms and holds me a few beats, and I squeeze him back, like I'm transferring all the strength I have to him so he can navigate this day.

Carol and Kaylee are sitting together on the couch when we walk into the expansive family room. Their heads are bent together over a photo album, and Kaylee sniffles and wipes away a tear.

Carol doesn't express any emotions, and it's not the first time I see a bit of a resemblance between her and Luke. Normally he's pretty good at hiding what he's feeling, but he's been surprisingly open since he first got the call from Jack last night.

"Hey," Luke says tentatively as we walk into the room, and I can't imagine walking *tentatively* into a room holding my family members.

Kaylee stands and rushes to her brother's arms, and Carol remains seated. I study her for a quick beat as her eyes fall onto her children. She should feel a sense of pride there. Kaylee cries as Luke hugs her, and Carol should feel *some* sort of way about that. And I'm sure she does, but she's schooled herself not to show those feelings—just like she taught her son to.

Enter Ellie.

Between the way we feel about each other and the fact that we have a baby on the way plus everything in between, I've finally started to break down the walls Carol carefully constructed.

"Breakfast is in the kitchen," Carol says. She nods to the counter behind her, and I spot dishes and bowls in that direction through the open floor plan.

She doesn't have words of wisdom and she doesn't stand to hug her son. Instead, she remains stoic, and I finally start to see her for who she is. It must be the baby I'm carrying and the deep dive of my own mind into what sort of mother I want to be that helps me come to these realizations.

Or maybe it's some of Luke's late-night confessions whispered into the dark. Regardless of how she felt about him, or how he felt about her, they were still married for a long time and she just lost him.

Standing up to hug her son will fill her with emotion she isn't ready to handle...and maybe they're at a point where she isn't even sure a hug would be welcome. Maybe it wouldn't be, but the Luke I know is affectionate and loving. In this moment, he needs a hug from his mother, but she can't read that and he doesn't know how to tell her.

It comes down to a simple lack of communication.

Mentioning that food is in the kitchen is taking care of him in the way she knows how. She's doing the best she can under the circumstances as she's trying to navigate what she broke with her son, and I can only hope that she'll see over the next few days how much more he deserves. I can only hope that he'll forgive her and they can mend what's left so he doesn't have to go through this same sort of self-blame when eventually she joins her husband.

It's morbid to think that way, but it is what it is.

We find a spread of breakfast casseroles and danish on the counter, clearly the food of friends and neighbors who want to help but aren't sure how as the Dalton family reels from this shocking loss.

I grab some cheese danish and a slice of the casserole, as does Luke, and we stand at the counter separating the family room and the kitchen.

"What are you looking at?" Luke asks before he shoves in a forkful of casserole.

"Remember the Mexico trip when I was four?" Kaylee asks. "Because I don't, but you would've been a teenager."

Luke chuckles. "Yeah, I do. I was fourteen and Jack was fifteen and somehow he got his hands on a bottle of tequila. We got so sick and Dad was pissed."

I giggle at the thought of two teenaged boys getting wasted in Mexico on a family vacation, and Carol glances over at her son before pointedly saying, "I remember the dinner cruise and the markets downtown. I guess I blocked out the memory of my delinquent sons drinking underage."

Kaylee elbows her mom. "You were busy taking care of a little girl."

"A very active little girl who loved to climb everything to impress her brothers," Carol says, and she purses her lips.

"And we were always impressed with her climbing abilities," a deep voice says. I glance up and watch as Jack strides into the room. Even here in his family's home, even now under these circumstances, he holds this air of confidence and control.

"Jack!" Kaylee says, and she flies into his arms like she just did with Luke.

Kaylee proved where her loyalties lie when she told our secret at the wedding, but looking back, even I can see that she was just trying to protect her brother. And she should. That's what families do. As much as I hated it, hated *her* at the time, she only wanted what was best for her brother.

"Good morning everyone," he says.

Carol stands, but she doesn't move toward her son, and it's comforting to know that she doesn't fly toward Jack, either...that her parenting style is more of the *let them come to me* variety rather than choosing one son over the other.

Kaylee lets him go.

"Breakfast is in the kitchen," Carol repeats to Jack.

"Get over here, Mother," Jack says with affection, and unlike his little brother, he closes the gap between himself and his mother, who makes a small effort to move toward him as well. He pulls her into a hug and squeezes her tightly, and I watch this moment unfold as Carol's carefully crafted façade starts to crumble.

She sniffs and brushes a finger under her eye, and this is why she's been stoic. She doesn't want to lose it in front of her kids. She's putting herself in the lead position of this family now.

But letting each other in isn't just part of the process of grief. It's part of what makes a family *a family*.

And I suspect that by the time we're on the other side of the next few days, Luke's idea of family will transition once again.

CHAPTER 22

"How's the knee?" Jack joins us in the kitchen and circles the food, and I can't help but feel a little anxiety over what might happen between brothers. Will Jack brush his suspension and fine into the past given why they're standing in this room together?

"Getting better every day." Luke takes a bite of danish as we continue filling our plates.

"Glad to hear it."

"Still pissed Hammond didn't even get a flag for it," Luke says.

"I watched the tape, man." Jack shakes his head. "He should have. If it makes you feel any better, he got fined by the team."

"It doesn't," Luke says pointedly. He's out for the season, and Allen had to give up a few bucks. Doesn't really seem fair.

"And I gave him a shiner when I socked him one," Jack adds.

Luke chuckles. "Now *that* makes me feel a little better. You hit him?"

Jack adds a slice of casserole to a plate and grabs a fork. "And I told him he better not fuck with my little brother or I'd give him another black eye to match the first one."

When I glance up at Luke, his eyes are shining with a little bit of pride and maybe a little bit of admiration. It's plain to see these two care about each other, but they've let too many outside forces come between them.

If there's any sort of silver lining to the reason why we're here, maybe it's that it'll give these men some time to examine their relationship. Maybe they'll find a way to be as close as they once were.

And despite the fracture between Luke and the rest of them, I can't help but think that's something his father would have wanted.

Luke and I carry our plates over to the table, and Jack joins us a few beats later.

After a breakfast filled with meaningless small talk, we join Carol and Kaylee in the family room.

"What's that?" Jack asks.

"The album from our trip to Disney World when I was six," Kaylee says.

Jack sits beside Kaylee to flip through, and he chuckles at the first photo he sees. "Remember when Dad took us golfing?" he says to Luke.

Luke laughs. "We had to be sixteen and seventeen, right?"

Jack nods.

"It started *pouring* down rain, and the three of us got stuck in a flood on the course," Luke explains. "The golf cart died and we either had to abandon our golf bags with it or lug them as we waded through knee-deep water."

Jack laughs. "The lightning was crazy, and the clubhouse ended up sending out a little party bus to pick us up. When we got back to the hotel, the girls were getting manicures in the spa and didn't even know it had been raining."

Kaylee lets out a little giggle. "All I remember was the three of you were soaked and Mom just told you not to get the carpet all wet."

Carol purses her lips primly as she raises her brows. "Nobody likes a wet carpet."

I stifle another laugh, and they pull out another photo album while Luke flips through the Disney one beside me.

And that's pretty much how the day goes. Photo albums and memories with casserole and snacks peppered in. From all accounts, this seems like a picture-perfect happy family, though death isn't exactly when you bring up the bad times.

From what I can piece together, it seems the fracture started when Jack entered high school and really intensified around the time Jack went off to college. He was playing quarterback, and Tim was promoted to the quarterback coach at Michigan, and it just made sense that they'd bond over the position. Luke was cast aside for Jack, and maybe Tim thought Carol would pick up the slack there, but Carol had her hands full with a small girl at the time. Luke got good grades and stayed out of trouble, so he sort of fell off the radar.

After dinner, Jack asks the question it seems like everyone has been avoiding. "Do we need to start making arrangements?"

I'm doing the dishes just to do *something* to keep myself occupied, but I glance up at Carol. She's still sitting at the table with Jack and Kaylee. Luke excused himself from the room a few minutes ago, and I have no idea where he went.

"Bentley is taking care of it," she says. "I gave him your father's final wishes. It was all outlined in the will."

Bentley? Is there another brother I don't know about?

"Do you have the details yet?" Jack asks.

She shakes her head. "I told him you need to be back in Denver by Thursday."

"Thanks," Jack murmurs.

"He said he'd get back to me tonight."

Luke reappears just as I finish the dishes, and he's holding a stack of board games. "Look what I found," he says. He sets them in the middle of the kitchen table.

Carol lets out a small chuckle. "Your father *loved* game night," she says. "We haven't had one in years. Probably since you went off to college," she says to Kaylee.

"He's definitely the one who instilled a healthy sense of competition in us," Jack says.

"Monopoly, anyone?" Luke asks, and he opens the box.

Jack immediately grabs for the car, Luke goes for the shoe, and Kaylee takes the horse.

"Ellie?" Luke asks. "Want to play?"

"Sure," I say, and I slide into the seat beside him. I take the iron.

"Mom?" Kaylee asks.

She presses her lips together and allows the sides of her mouth to go up infinitesimally. "I'll just watch you for a bit."

621

"You sure?" Luke asks. "The thimble is still available." He holds it up and shakes it around, and she lets out the smallest grunt of a chuckle.

"You kids play," she says.

We get started, and it's actually quite a rousing game of Monopoly. It seems like Jack and Luke automatically team up against Kaylee first and then me once she's out. Carol watches her sons in silence as they team up to get me out.

"Your dad would be so proud seeing you two like this," she murmurs as it turns into a fierce competition between brothers.

A moment of silence passes over us all, and I breathe in what feels like peace in this room. It feels like the start of the mend.

After what seems like hours, Jack emerges the winner.

It seems like Jack is *always* the winner. From football to life to something as silly as a board game, he's a champion.

Carol's phone rings, so she bows out of the room for a few minutes, and she rejoins us just as Luke finishes cleaning up the play money from the game.

"That was Bentley," she says. "Your father didn't want a wake. He wanted a simple church funeral with a brunch afterward since it was his favorite meal. The funeral is tomorrow at nine with the burial at the cemetery following. We'll head to the restaurant immediately after that. Bentley will meet us back here after that to read the will."

"Tomorrow?" Kaylee asks. "So soon?" Her eyes sparkle with unshed tears as she glances around at her family, and I'm reminded how the annual family trips were her idea, her way of seeing her entire family together despite the rifts between them. "We don't even get another day together like this?"

Carol presses her lips together. "You're all free to return home after the funeral, or you can stay as long as you'd like. It's your choice." She turns and heads out of the room, and I assume it's because Kaylee's question triggered something in her. She had to run out because God forbid she shows even a shred of emotion in front of her children.

I wonder what sort of healing powers her tears would have for her and for everyone in this room. I wonder how powerful it would be for them to see how hurt she is by this.

That's not her, and from what I can gather, it's never been her. But it's never too late to change.

The three siblings share more memories around the kitchen table, and as much as Luke will say he did it for his sister, I can see it in his eyes. He needs this, too. He needs his family, especially in a time like this. Luke never spoke about wanting to fix things with his family until he got the call that it was too late to patch up his relationship with his father, but I can see it in his eyes.

He's grateful for these tiny moments with his family.

It's a breakthrough.

CHAPTER 23

Kaylee heads to bed next, which leaves Luke and me with Jack.

"You're playing the Cowboys this weekend?" Luke asks.

Jack nods. "I studied film on the plane and Coach is sending me some plays to go over on the plane home."

"I'm glad Bentley arranged the funeral for tomorrow," Luke says.

"Who's Bentley?" I finally ask.

"The family lawyer," Luke and Jack say at the same time.

"Ah," I say, nodding. Of course the Daltons have a family lawyer. There's a lot about this life I'm still learning, I guess.

"I'm glad, too," Jack says. "I love what I do, but missing my own father's funeral to play a game would've been..."

"Tough," Luke finishes. "But if anyone in the world would've understood that, it's Dad."

Jack huffs out a chuckle. "Yeah, he's the one that instilled my work ethic, that's for sure. And he's the one who taught me that you don't have a choice in this career a lot of times."

"It's all part of it," Luke murmurs. "You have to take the good with the bad, I guess."

"What should we do about Mom?" Jack asks, changing the subject suddenly.

Luke raises a brow. "I was wondering the same."

I'm in the dark. What do they even mean?

"I'd think she'd want to be near her grandchild," Luke adds, and I assume he means Jack's kid.

Jack nods. "But she'd hate the weather in Denver. She always talked about how much she hated it here in Michigan."

"You think I should ask her if she wants to come to Vegas?" Luke asks.

Whoa, whoa, whoa.

Hold the phone.

Is he serious?

Carol...in Vegas?

That's a hard no from this camp. I think it might be an even worse idea than Michelle living with us.

Jack twists his lips. "No grandchildren there," he points out.

"Um," Luke says, and he glances at me. My eyes widen, and Jack clings onto that.

"You're not..." he says, his eyes on me.

My eyes meet Luke's, and he nods.

"I am," I say.

Jack whistles then shakes his head. "Wow. I guess you were serious when you said this wasn't just for show."

Luke chuckles. "Admittedly that's how it began." His honesty is shocking, and it sends a dart of anxiety through my chest. But then he reaches over and takes my hand in his, and somehow that manages to calm every fear inside. "But that's not where we're at now."

"Congratulations," Jack says. He glances at our joined hands. "Looks like you won this round."

Luke's brows dip down. "What do you mean?"

He studies us. "You seem good for each other." He blows out a breath. "I thought about trying with Michelle since we're having a kid, but, Jesus Christ, how did you put up with her for as long as you did?"

I can't help my snort-laugh at that.

"I was blessed with a lot more patience than you," Luke says. "Plus I drank a fuck ton of whiskey to get through it."

Jack laughs. "I don't drink in season," he admits. "Except for special occasions." He stands and walks over to the enormous walk-in pantry, and he returns a moment later with a bottle of Macallan and two short tumblers. "You okay to have some?" he asks Luke.

Luke stares at the bottle for a few beats before his eyes meet his brother's, and then he nods without a word.

"I take it this bottle has some special meaning?" I ask as Jack uncaps the bottle and pours two short glasses with no ice.

"The Rolls Royce of single malts," Luke and Jack say at the same time.

Luke grunts a soft chuckle. "Our dad loved a good single malt scotch, and that's what he always said about this one. His dad gave him a bottle when my parents got married and told him it was only for special occasions. So he had a glass the night Jack was born, and me and Kaylee, too. He had one the night Jack got into USC, and the night I got into Wisconsin."

"Not always the happy occasions, either," Jack says. "Just the big life events. When Uncle Larry died, he had some. After grandpa's funeral, and grandma's, too."

Luke nods. "Our cousin Jackie's wedding."

"When we won the state game in high school," Jack adds.

"When you were drafted," Luke says.

Jack nods. "And when you were."

"At your wedding?" I ask Luke, and he shakes his head.

"No, not that night. At least not that I know of." He glances at Jack then down at the glass sitting untouched in front of him. "I think he knew it wasn't going to last. I think that's just a small part of why he was so hard on me."

"He was hard on you because he loved you," Jack says softly.

Luke keeps his eyes down on his glass. "He had a funny way of showing it."

"Be that as it may, he talked to me a lot about how you were your own man. He always thought you'd take flight away from my spotlight. He didn't know how to coach a receiver like he could a quarterback, so that naturally pushed us together." His voice seems to get a little emotional, and seeing his carefully crafted exterior start to crack causes *me* to get a little emotional, too. I swipe away a tear.

"I know you always thought he pawned you off on Coach Sterling," Jack continues, "but he did it because he thought you had the best chance at becoming pro with someone else's help. He couldn't provide that for you, so he got someone who could. He gave you space to thrive on your own away from me."

Luke's eyes seem to mist over a little, but he keeps his face down to hide it. I can't help but wonder how these revelations make him feel. A little better about their relationship? Or even worse that he can't fix it now—that it's too late to get the actual truth from his dad's mouth?

Jack clears his throat then holds up his glass. "To Dad."

Luke sighs heavily, but then he picks up his glass too. He taps it to Jack's with a *clink*. "To Dad," he repeats.

I get the sudden feeling like these two men have a lot more to talk about, so I head up to bed.

I don't know how much time passes, but I wake when the bed dips as he gets in. "You doing okay?" I ask into the darkness.

"Yeah," he says softly. He leans over and presses a kiss to my lips. "Tonight was..." He trails off as he searches for the right word. "Healing, I think. For Jack and me. It felt like old times, laughing and talking about the past. Drinking Dad's Macallan. He told me he's happy for you and me, and we talked more about Michelle and how he feels about the baby. We needed it." He sniffs.

I reach over and pull him into me. I hold him until his breathing evens out, and then we sleep in each other's arms. Tonight was healing, and tomorrow will be difficult, as will the days that follow...but my last thought before I drift to sleep is that through this tragedy, Luke just might have gotten his brother back.

CHAPTER 24

I remain close to Luke's side throughout the morning as we attend the funeral, where we sit in the first row as we listen to a preacher read words from the Bible that are supposed to provide comfort to those gathered. I spot my brother and Nicki toward the back of the church, and I'm so thankful for the friendship he and Luke have formed. I'm thankful he's here for Luke. I see Coach Thompson and Mo sitting near Josh. It's another relationship of Luke's I'm grateful for.

I part from Luke long enough for him and Jack to join some other men I don't know as they work as pallbearers. I hold his hand as we travel with Jack, Kaylee, and Carol to the cemetery, where we watch the casket as it's lowered into the plot.

And it's there, after the preacher is long gone and friends have dispersed to the restaurant for brunch and the immediate family of Daltons is all that remains, when Luke breaks the silence as they all stare at the casket.

"Life's too damn short for all this anger between us."

Nobody moves for a beat. Nobody says a word.

But then Carol speaks. "You're right," she says softly.

She doesn't apologize for the way she's treated any of them, but just the admission that she agrees with her son seems like a huge leap in a new direction. And maybe in a few days they'll each get back to their own lives and go on living the way they have been. On the other hand, this could be the wake-up call they all needed.

I've already seen a change between Luke and Jack.

They can be competitors on the field and brothers off it, but it seems like somewhere along the line, they lost that brotherhood.

Carol turns toward Luke, and I let go of his hand as I urge him toward his mother. She hugs him, and he clings to her, and both of them shake with silent tears. Kaylee's tears are a little louder as she sniffs, and even Jack seems to get emotional. He hides it by hugging his mother from the other side, sandwiching her between her sons. Kaylee hugs Luke from behind, too, and while this moment doesn't fix *everything*, it does go a long way to mend what was so broken for so long.

Luke introduces me as his wife to family and friends whose names I'll never remember. I spend a little time with my brother and Nicki, but mostly I stick by Luke's side in case he needs anything.

We're asked a thousand times why we didn't have a big wedding, and I realize that these are all people who care about Luke. I have the same network of family and friends of my own who also missed out, and now that we've transitioned from *fake* to *real*, I'm starting to feel the sting of what I missed out on.

I always dreamed of the big fairy tale wedding. The dress. The shoes. The hair. The tiara. The veil. And most of all, celebrating the love I share with the man of my dreams as we seal our commitment in front of everyone who matters to us.

I didn't get that. Neither of us did.

I think it's time to revisit the idea of a wedding. It might be a little late, and I might be a little knocked up, but it's something I didn't realize I wanted as badly as I do until we were reminded over and over today that we never had it.

After brunch, we head back to the home where Luke grew up. Bentley is waiting in the office when we arrive, and it's time for the reading of the will.

"This is for family only," Bentley says, and he glances at me.

"Ellie's my wife," Luke says, his hand tightening around mine.

I sit between Luke and Jack on the black leather couch. Carol and Kaylee chose the plush chairs facing the desk, and Bentley slides into the executive chair behind the desk.

"First and foremost, let me express my condolences," Bentley says. "You lost a husband and a father, and I lost my best friend. I'm devastated, but I'm glad to be here to carry out Tim's final wishes. As you know, he did well for many years as an investment banker, and he gave up that career to coach football. His knowhow in the field of investments left him with a rather large sum." He turns to Carol. "You're the main beneficiary. You'll keep the house, and you have enough investments and assets to live more than comfortably for the rest of your life. Only a portion of Tim's net worth, which is a rather healthy sum, will be split amongst Tim's three children provided they meet certain conditions."

"Conditions?" Kaylee repeats.

Bentley nods. "Tim provided for you when he was alive, but in his death, he wanted to ensure you met certain criteria in order to receive an inheritance in the sum of ten million dollars each. These are simple requests that are meant to encourage you to take the path he thought you'd be happiest going down. We'll start with you, Kaylee." He puts on his readers and glances at a paper in his hand. "You will receive your sum upon earning your degree at your graduation. Your father wanted you to use the money to buy a house and get started on your adult life as you begin your first career in a field he hopes you love."

He glances at Jack next. "Jack, you'll receive your sum after you've been married for one year." Jack snorts with derision beside me. "Your father had high hopes that you'd settle down and find someone who could both put up with and take care of you, and he felt that a year would be long enough to seal your commitment."

And then he looks at Luke. Anxiety pulses in my chest. "Finally, Luke. Your father recently amended your condition. Initially, you and Jack had the same stipulation. But when he saw you marry someone you hardly knew with the accusation that you were only planning to be married to her for a year, he had concerns that you knew about this provision of his will."

Luke shakes his head. "I don't care about the damn money," he says. "I have my own. And I had no idea about his conditions."

Bentley looks sternly at Luke. "Shall I continue?"

"By all means," Luke says snidely.

Bentley clears his throat and reads from another paper. "This is from an email your father sent to me. 'Because I want my sons both to experience the joy of fatherhood and I'm not sure whether his marriage is real, Luke will now receive his sum after the birth of his first child. He will be an incredible father, more than I ever was to him, and while I know he can and will provide for his family, I never want him to worry about their futures. I ask that he either use this money for his family or, if he doesn't want my money, which I would certainly understand, that his portion is donated to the charity he recently started.'"

Luke keeps his eyes trained to the ground.

Is this when we're supposed to tell everyone gathered that I'm actually currently growing that first child? That Luke's inheritance is a mere six months away?

"As you can all see, these are simple conditions made in the interest of the kind of life he thought you each wanted. And I think he knew you all better than you gave him credit for." He looks around at everyone as he speaks until he gets to that last sentence, when his eyes train on Luke. "I'm the executor of the will, and as soon as you have met the conditions, please call me and we'll immediately start the transfer."

Bentley excuses himself after no one in the room has further questions, and Carol walks him out. When she returns, the four of us are still sitting silently in the office as each of the siblings works through their own reaction to their individual conditions.

"He knew exactly what I wanted," Kaylee says to her mother through her tears. "Exactly what I *needed* to start my life."

"I'm not really sure he knew me at all," Jack says, a hint of surprise in his tone. "I don't want to get married."

"Ellie's pregnant," Luke murmurs.

CHAPTER 25

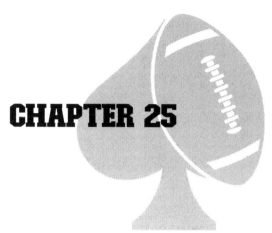

"She's what?" Carol asks.

"Pregnant," Luke repeats.

"Oh, Lord," Carol mutters. "Are we absolutely sure it's yours?"

If we didn't just go through the same thing with Michelle and if I was a little less understanding of Carol's personality, I'd be totally insulted by that comment.

But this is the Dalton family. That's all the explanation necessary to see that her question makes perfect sense.

"We are one hundred percent sure," I say pointedly. "No other possibilities." I nearly go so far as to say he's the only man I've had sex with since Todd dumped me back in May, but I leave that part out.

Carol stares at Luke for a few beats, and then her eyes edge over to me. I see the skepticism written on her face, and Luke must catch onto it as well.

"This is real, Mom," he says. He glances at me, and I nod. He grabs for my hand. "It didn't start out that way. It started as a way to get Michelle off my back." He glances at Jack, who nods his encouragement for Luke to continue. "But something changed along the way, and Ellie is the woman I'm going to spend my life with. I've never been with someone who put me first. Who cared about me more than herself. Who cared about my future more than my present."

He says the last part thickly, and it's a stark reminder that both Savannah and Michelle and probably countless others cared more about the fact that he's a pro football player than anything else. And that strikes me as incredibly sad.

I've gotten to know the man beneath the shoulder pads over the last few months, and he's a star in more ways than just on the field. Simply put, he's the Prince Charming I've been searching for.

And I'm glad for his past relationships. They helped make him into the man sitting beside me right now. The man I love.

"She takes care of me," he says. "She changed my bandages after my surgery and she makes sure I'm doing my exercises. She keeps up my social media and makes sure fans know I'm okay. She loves me fiercely, and she's taking such good care of the baby by eating right and learning everything she can. She's not just the woman I love. She's the best friend I've ever had, and she's going to be a phenomenal mother to our lucky children."

My eyes fill with tears at his words, and I squeeze his hand. He turns toward me, and I mouth *I love you* to him. He squeezes my hand back.

Carol raises a brow, and the room is quiet as everyone awaits her response expectantly. And instead of congratulating her son for finding the love of his life and on the upcoming birth of his first child, she stands and walks out of the room without a word. The door clicks shut behind her, and we all sit in stunned silence for a second.

Heat creeps up my back as anger sparks deep inside and explodes through every nerve ending in my body.

Is she freaking serious?

Hell no, lady.

I don't care if she's my mother-in-law. You don't respond to your son's bleeding-heart confession by walking out of the room without a word. You don't respond to your son's words that his wife is pregnant with silence.

I may be starting to understand the Dalton family, but what she just did isn't okay.

I stand as heat pricks behind my eyes. My fists are clenched as I walk toward the door. I think Luke says something, a feeble attempt to try to stop me probably, and maybe Jack and Kaylee say something too...but the rushing in my head prevents any of their words from registering.

I'm going to give Carol a piece of my mind, and I move with speed before I can change my mind and before anyone can stop me.

I throw open the door, and I open it with such force that it bounces back against the spring doorstop and slams shut behind me again.

I find Carol standing in the hallway a few steps away from the office. She faces away from the door.

"You have nothing to say to your son?" I ask, my voice full of venom.

She doesn't turn around. She doesn't even acknowledge that I spoke.

But through my red haze of anger, I see her shoulders shaking. She sniffs as she finally turns around, and her hand is over her mouth as she cries into it. Her eyes are red as tears stream down her cheeks.

"Thank you," she whispers. She brushes the tears away. "For taking care of my son. For being everything he needs."

Understanding dawns on me. She ran out so nobody would see her like this. I'm sure I'm the last person she wants to cry in front of, and yet somehow it must be better than crying in front of her children.

The tender heart in me can't stand to see anyone crying, so it's natural as I move toward her and open my arms for a hug. I'm surprised when she moves her hand from her face and moves into my arms, and I hold her for a beat as she lets out the pent-up emotions she tries so hard to hide from everybody.

"This is hard," I say softly. "It's okay to let your kids see that you're struggling."

She seems to pull herself together at my words. "No, it's not," she says, moving out of my arms. She sniffs again and wipes her cheeks with her fingertips. "They need to know they can come to me with anything and I'm strong enough to handle it."

I shake my head. "They need to know you're human. They need to see that you have emotions, too, and that it's okay to express them. Luke *still* has a hard time showing me what he's feeling. He learned that from you. I don't want either of you to feel like you have to hide what's inside because you know what?" I hold my hands out wide. "There's more room out here than in there." I point to her chest at the end.

She sighs. "It's just not who I am."

I shake my head. "But it's okay to run out of a room when your son finally opens up to you?"

She presses her lips together. "I'm just so happy for him. He's doing well despite everything we did to mess him up."

"You didn't mess him up," I say. "He's a wonderful man, and you'd know that if you bothered to get to know him."

She stares at me a beat, and nerves rattle around inside until she speaks. "He's right, you know," she says. My brows dip because I don't know what she means. "You're going to make a wonderful mother."

She leaves the hallway with those words, and now it's my turn to cry by myself for a minute.

CHAPTER 26

Jack stands on the top rung of a ladder in the front hall while Luke hands him a replacement bulb for the one burned out in the chandelier.

"How pissed would the Broncos organization be if I accidentally tipped over the ladder while you're on top?" Luke teases.

"At least I can get on a ladder," Jack retorts.

"Too soon," Luke says, laughing as he shakes his head.

I'm still making him do his exercises while we're here in Michigan. Most of his therapy has transitioned to home care at this point, anyway. He still has a limp, and his knee isn't strong yet, but he's getting better and better every day. His next appointment with the doctor is in a week, and I'm interested to hear what the team trainers have to say about Luke's potential for next season. I'm also interested to hear what Calvin might say.

"What else, Mom?" Jack asks.

"I told you I can hire someone to do that stuff, boys," she says, her tone one of scolding but her expression one of pride.

"Why hire someone when we're right here to do it?" Luke asks, and Jack nods.

It's funny seeing Jack and Luke team up this way. They both want to do little odds and ends around the house. They both want to make life a little easier for their mom. They're working together after working against each other for so many years.

It feels like it's been a long time in the making, and if it feels this good for me, I can't imagine how it feels for Luke and Jack.

The men go through their dad's closet together. Carol pops in to check on them, but mostly they take care of it both so Carol doesn't have to and also so they have time together to dig up old memories. They each keep a few items that are meaningful to them, and Kaylee walks away with some mementos as well.

I sort of wonder how Jack feels about that money. Luke indicated that he doesn't care about it. He said he has his own, and Jack does, too. But that doesn't change the fact that I'm grateful the money will be set aside for our kids. Luke may have plenty, but it's comforting to know we have insurance should anything go wrong between the two of us. I don't anticipate it will, but we have no idea what the future may hold—just like we had no idea he'd take a hit that ended his entire season and potentially his career.

Jack takes a call from Michelle later in the evening, and we can all hear her bitching about being pregnant over the phone. He rolls his eyes and heads upstairs to talk privately, and once we all hear the door click shut to Jack's room, it's Carol who speaks up first. "There are two types of pregnant women. The miserable ones who hate being pregnant," she says, glancing upstairs to indicate Michelle, and then her eyes land on me. "And the glowing ones who seem to have it all together."

Did Carol just...dare I say...*compliment* me?

Kaylee loses it to a fit of giggles at her mom's words, and I can't help my *glowing* smile.

Later in the evening, we're all sitting together in the family room when Luke looks at his mother. "What do you need this big old mansion for?"

She lifts a shoulder. "It's been home for a lot of years."

"It doesn't have to be home forever, though," Luke says. He glances at me, and as much as I still think this is a bad idea, that moment in the hallway earlier today was a breakthrough for Carol and me. I think I'm learning how to deal with her. It seems like I earned her respect when I stood up to her by standing up for her son, and I guess that's what every parent wants for their child, isn't it? Someone to love them so much that they'll stand up to the scariest monsters to defend them.

"Move to Vegas," Luke says, and Kaylee gasps. "You can get to know your grandchild, and Ellie, and even me. We'd love to have you close by."

I have to admit, I appreciate that he said *close by* and not *in our house*...but *love* is a little strong.

She glances around. "Oh, Luke," she says softly. "I don't know. There are so many happy memories here. And, I guess, not so happy ones as well, but that's what makes it a home, doesn't it?"

"Like when Jack jumped over the bannister?" Luke says, nodding upstairs to the bannister in the hallway that overlooks the family room.

Carol purses her lips. "Oh, you mean when he sprained his ankle and couldn't play baseball?"

Jack shrugs innocently. "Or like when Luke hit the mailbox with a baseball bat?"

"How about the time you walked in on Jack *naked* on the couch with Sandi Meyer?" Luke counters.

Not to be outdone, Jack adds, "How about the time you caught Luke in *your bed* with Jamie Keck?"

I turn to Luke with a raised brow, and he looks like he wants to kill Jack. Really, Luke? In your *parents'* bed? Does it get grosser than that?

Kaylee turns red and Carol shakes her head. "Always one adventure after another with you two," Carol mutters, and I giggle.

"Just think about it," Luke says to Carol, getting back to the point of the conversation.

She nods. "I'll think about it."

They may not be perfect, but this is certainly what families are made of. I think back to our time in Hawaii when I was so certain I wasn't meant to be a part of the Dalton family.

I wasn't—not *that* family, anyway. Not the one with hurt and pain and scars between them. They're still there, and they always will be, but it feels like Luke has jump over a lot of hurdles to finally find a place where he can be close to his family again. It's unfortunate that it took a tragedy to get here, but I've learned that tragedies have the power to birth wonderful things.

So I'm part of the Dalton clan now.

It feels good. It feels right.

And I'm so excited to start my own little family with my Prince Charming.

* * *

"I want to redo my will when we get home," he says as we settle onto chairs in the first-class lounge at the airport.

"Oh?" I ask. These are exactly the necessary types of morbid conversations I dread.

"You're carrying my child. You're my wife. You and the baby deserve it all if anything happens to me."

"That's nice of you to say, Luke, but nothing's going to happen to you." My tone is adamant. I can't have anything happen to him. I can't even imagine my life without him.

"What happened with my dad...it just goes to show that you never know. He was here one minute and gone the next, and it was totally unexpected." Tears fill my eyes as he talks because he's absolutely right. We never know what tomorrow will bring...if we're lucky enough to have a tomorrow. "I want to be prepared if the worst should ever happen. It's just insurance," he says, and he squeezes my hand.

"Whatever you want," I say. It's such a weird conversation to have. He earned everything he has well before he met me...and yet he wants me to have it all if anything ever happens to him.

"Whatever *we* want," he amends. "It's yours now anyway. I'm going to have Greg create some new paperwork for us if that's okay with you."

"I don't want to talk about this stuff," I say.

"I know." He rubs my leg over my jeans, and I'm glad we're headed for home because the button on these things barely clasped this morning and I think it's about time to start shopping for maternity clothes. "But they're the type of grown-up conversations we need to have."

"I know you're right, but the thought that something could happen to either of us...I just can't think about it. Not with a baby on the way. All I can think about is a future with us holding hands as we stare down at him with all the love in the world."

"That's all I want, too." He leans over and presses a soft kiss to my lips as he sets his big hand over my stomach. It's just starting to bloat a little before the big swell comes, and I can't wait for every moment that lies ahead. "I want to live life to the fullest because we don't have any guarantees that we'll get a tomorrow."

"In that same vein," I say, finally just going for it, "I want to have a wedding. A real one. Call it a renewal or whatever, but I want a ceremony, and I want a party, and I want my friends and family there as well as yours. I want to celebrate this love we share with everyone important to us before the life we created arrives."

"Then you'll have one," he says, and his words are so simple that I feel like I could ask him to reach up and grab the moon for me and he'd do everything in his power to grasp it. "Start planning, or hire someone, and just tell me what you need me to do."

"Show up and wear the tux I pick out for you," I say, and he chuckles.

"Consider it done, wife."

I smile at his endearment. "I like when you call me that, husband."

He grins at me. "It's really starting to feel like it, isn't it?"

I nod. "Just wait until this baby gets here. Then our lives will be flipped upside down once again."

He squeezes my hand again. "I can't wait."

CHAPTER 27

"I think I'm ready to talk about what comes next."

His words whispered in the dark when we're back home in our own bed come as a shock. We both fell under the covers with exhaustion once I emptied the suitcases and separated the laundry, and I assumed I'd be drifting to sleep after a quick kiss goodnight.

But his words wake me with a start.

"You are?" I ask on a gasp.

"I've been thinking a lot about it over the last few days. I know I said it was bad luck to talk about the future, but I haven't really had a string of good luck lately despite my best efforts to fill myself with good luck charms."

"Good luck charms?" I repeat. "You mean...Lucky Charms?"

He chuckles. "You figured me out. My grandfather nicknamed me Lucky Luke because of the copious amounts of Lucky Charms I ate as a kid."

I giggle. "That clearly carried over to adulthood."

"It gives me that warm, comforting feeling of childhood every time I pour a bowl. So, yeah, it carried over, and I'm not embarrassed by that."

"You shouldn't be." I reach over and squeeze his arm. "I think it's one of the most endearing things about you."

"You know what's one of the most endearing things about *you*?" he asks.

"Hm?" I murmur.

"Your tits."

I smack him in the arm, and he laughs.

"I was nearly asleep when you started this conversation by saying you wanted to talk about the future," I remind him. "You're not getting out of that by seducing me, so get talking, Dalton."

"Yes ma'am." He sighs. "I keep thinking about what happens next if I *can't* play. It's a real possibility. I'm working hard, and my knee is doing better, and I want it...but there are no guarantees I'll wind up with a contract on the other side of this. So I've been thinking over my options."

"And what conclusions have you come to?" I ask.

"This all hangs on my recovery, obviously, so I don't have a timeline...but I was thinking I could coach."

"You'd make an incredible coach," I say. It's a relief to hear that he wants to coach—and not because it means he'll still be a part of the game he loves so much, but because it's a decision. It's a future.

"Thank you. But I don't think that's what I want."

His words shake my relief. "It's not?"

I think he shakes his head, but it's dark in here so I'm not sure. "No. I think I'd love it, but I think there are other ways to still be involved with the game that I'd love more."

"Like what?"

"Big life changes mean big priority changes," he begins.

"Such as..." I trail off and wait for him to fill in the blank.

"Such as *you*. I've never loved a woman more than I love the game. But then I met you."

Tears fill my eyes at his words.

"You flipped my entire world upside down, Ellie, and I love it. I love *you*. I want to be around for you and the baby."

"Luke..." I say, the tears in my eyes splashing over as my chest tightens with love. "I love you, too." My words are whispered through the emotion clogging my throat.

God, I love him.

I turn in toward him and I kiss him. He welcomes me into his arms as he deepens the kiss and pulls me against him. He flips me so I'm on my back and he's hovering over me, and I know we're in the middle of an important conversation, but somehow this seems to be a part of it. I want to know what he wants next out of life, but I also want to feel his body as he enters mine. We can talk later. For now, our bodies will do the talking.

He's different as he kisses me. His focus is fully on me—and it's always been there, but he had things holding him back. The game, or the injury, or his own personality where hiding his emotions was ingrained by his parents. But if the last few days taught us anything, it's that he never has to hide from me.

Our clothes fly in different directions, and he flips us again so I end up on top of him so he can rest his leg. It's dark in here, but there's enough light from the moon edging in around the sides of the curtains that I can see where he is. He reaches up and caresses my breasts as I lower down onto him, both of us moaning at the now-familiar feel of nothing between us as I begin to move. I reach down and stroke my own clit as he moves in and out of me, our bodies rocking together in a perfect rhythm that I don't think I'll ever get enough of. He bats my hand out of the way and takes over my clit, and the way he knows exactly how to handle my body sends me into a mind-blowing, earth-shattering climax far too soon.

He follows soon after, growling his way through an epic release as my body milks his, and when it's all over, I lean down to kiss him while he's still inside me, love and lust and satisfaction all swirling thickly around us. He holds the back of my head for a few beats as he deepens our kiss, and there's one thing I know for certain. I will never, ever get tired of kissing this man.

Once we've both cleaned up and returned to bed, he picks up our conversation where we left it off.

"As I was saying before you came onto me—" he begins, and I interrupt him.

"Um, excuse me? *You* came onto *me*."

He snort-laughs. "Hardly. You turned into me and sent off all the signals!"

"Whatever!" I tease him. "You totally kissed me first!"

He laughs. "Well, I got mine and you got yours." He laces his fingers through mine beneath the covers.

"Truth. That was a good one."

"It was. But with you, they're all good ones."

He leans over for a kiss, and before our lips connect, I say, "Let it be noted that *you* are the one starting it this time."

He laughs and nips my lips with his. "As I was saying before, I want to be here for all his milestones, and I want to celebrate them with you. Combine that with your passion for public relations, and I started dreaming up some different possibilities."

"Possibilities?" I echo.

"What would you say about working together?"

My brows dip. "Working together on what?"

"I have two ideas, and I'd like your opinion on both."

"Go for it." What I really want to say is that he just knocked every last bit of energy right out of me and I'm ready to fall into sleep now, but he sounds so excited that I don't have the heart to say it.

"Well, for one thing, we could run our charity together," he says. "And for another...I'm thinking about starting up my own sports agency to run alongside Prince Charming Public Relations. You could be the publicist for my clients and we could work hand-in-hand to secure endorsements and negotiate contracts."

"Oh, Luke," I say. "I love the idea. But I don't know anything about sports. I already feel like I'm struggling with my clients, and I'd be terrified of letting you down."

"Enter Luke," he says.

CHAPTER 28

"Your knee is making excellent progress," Dr. Charles says at Luke's two-month post-surgery checkup a couple weeks later. "How has it been feeling?"

"A little pain when I take stairs or try to walk for more than a few minutes," Luke admits.

"There's still some mild swelling. Have you been icing?" the doctor asks.

Luke shakes his head. "I've been doing the exercises, though." He points a thumb in my direction. "She makes me."

"Good work," Dr. Charles says, nodding toward me. "Ice it three to four times a day for twenty minutes. The swelling is very mild but that will likely eradicate it. Keep doing those exercises. It'll help with your range of motion, and the harder you work on it now, the quicker we'll see you back on the field. But take it easy, too. No running. No marathons. We'll get there."

"Thank you, Doctor," I say. He leaves after he makes sure we have no further questions. When we get home, a large box sits in the entryway.

"What's that?" I ask.

Luke grins. "Open it and find out."

"What have you done now?" I ask, narrowing my eyes at him. He just shrugs innocently.

I tear the tape off the cardboard and flip open the box. "Clothes?" I ask. I pull out tops with plenty of room and jeans with tan belly bands around the waist and panties and bras and pajamas.

"Maternity," he says. "You've been saying for two weeks that you want to get some maternity clothes, and I had Debbie help me figure out what to order when you cried the other night that you could no longer get your jeans to button."

I laugh at the memory as I shake my head. "Man, the emotions are *strong* sometimes." I look at the box again and my eyes fill. I swipe away an escaped tear, and he chuckles. "Thank you. This is so kind of you."

He reaches for me and pulls me into his arms as he thumbs away another tear that tipped over. "You've taken such good care of me, Ellie. It's the least I can do to try to pay that back."

"It's not about being even or paying back. I take care of you because I love you."

He presses a soft kiss to my forehead. "Right back at you."

I melt into a puddle right there, and I'm trying to pull myself together again when the doorbell rings. We're both still standing in the foyer.

"Are you expecting anybody?" he asks.

I shake my head. "It's probably Josh stopping by to see how your appointment went."

"I bet you're right," he says, and he moves toward the door and tosses it open as I sink down into the pile of clothes as I hold up a gorgeous white sweater made out of the softest material.

I wait to hear my brother's voice, but instead I hear Luke say, "Mom?"

Mom?

Carol?

What the hell is she doing here?

"Hi," she says, and her voice sounds tentative. Carol Dalton has never been tentative about anything a day in her life.

"Come on in," he says, opening the door wider.

She glances down at me in my pile of clothes as she walks in. "Am I interrupting something?"

I giggle. "Your son just surprised me with all this. He is just the sweetest, most wonderful man in the world."

Luke looks embarrassed, and Carol looks proud. "How kind," she says.

"Mom, what are you doing here?"

"Don't I get a hug first?" she asks, and I almost laugh at the question. She's *never* started a greeting with a hug.

It's been three weeks since we last saw her, and I study her as her son wraps his arms around her. She looks tired. Worn down. Defeated.

Different.

I hug her next even though she didn't ask for one. She seems like she could use one anyway...maybe I could, too.

"Can I get you something to drink?" I ask.

"Some water would be lovely," she says.

"Of course. Come on in." I pile the clothes back into the box and head to the kitchen.

"So...are you going to tell us what you're doing here?" Luke asks once we're sitting around the kitchen table.

She clears her throat. "I thought a lot about what you said, about how I don't need that big old house all to myself, and you're right. I don't. All my friends in Michigan came by way of your father's job. Everything there reminds me of him. Every corner I turn, I see mistakes I made. And now it's too late to change them, but it's not too late to change other things, to fix other mistakes."

She pauses, and my chest tightens. Is she moving here? In with us? Can I even handle that?

No. The answer would be no.

I love Luke, and I want him to thrive and to succeed. I don't want him to be pulled down by the weight of his past and the mistakes of his family, and I'm terrified this will only lead to disappointment all the way around. People don't *really* change. Some tragedy happens, and everyone acts differently for a little while, but then things go back to the way they were. That's just life.

"I'm moving to Las Vegas...if you'll still have me," she says, and my heart drops into my stomach.

I school my expression to blank, but I'm not sure how successful I am in keeping the horror off my face.

"Of course we'll have you, Mom," Luke says. "You're welcome to stay here a while if you need to. Right, Ellie?"

I nod as I'm supposed to. "Of course," I murmur.

Carol glances at me. Gone is the look like I'm some annoying nuisance, and at least that is a small comfort. At least maybe now she realizes I'm sticking around.

I try to look at the bright side. My parents have already moved here, she's moving here, and we'll have people fighting over who gets to babysit when we want a date night. I'm sure we won't feel smothered at all after living without our parents this close for so damn long.

Right. And if I keep telling myself that, maybe I'll start to believe it.

I shake off the selfishness I'm feeling. I want Luke all to myself, but that's not reasonable or possible. He deserves this second chance with his mother—*if* she has truly changed and is ready to make amends.

Either way, whatever happens, I'll stand by his side and hold his hand.

"I put the house up for sale last week," she says softly. "I went to Denver to visit with Jack. I've talked to Kaylee every day. But something is calling me here." She pauses and focuses on her son. "I'd like to get to know you and your wife. I can't wait to meet your baby. I think Jack will need my help more than you will when it comes to the babies, but I don't know where that baby will be. Could be right here in Vegas since this is where Michelle is based." Her eyes edge to me. "I don't want to be a burden to either of you, but I'd like to try to make up for some of our lost time."

Luke reaches across the table to take her hand in his. "I'd love that, Mom," he says.

My tight chest seems to loosen at his words. If he'd love it, then I will, too. "We both would," I echo.

She nods once. "Thank you both," she says, and she seems to shift back to the prim woman I first met. Then she seems to think twice about it and she thaws a little. "I'm looking at some houses today if you'd like to come with."

"I have a meeting with one of my coaches in a bit," Luke says. "I'm so sorry."

I have a stack of paperwork to go through, a take two wedding to plan, and about four hundred emails to go through, but I guess it all can wait. "I'd love to go," I say.

After all, the sooner we find her a place of her own, the sooner I can stop worrying that she'll want to move in with us.

CHAPTER 29

They say the second trimester is like a vacation, sandwiched between the exhaustion of the first and the discomfort of the third. I don't know if I'd call this a vacation, exactly, but I feel good. Most of the time.

I'm finally starting to show a little, and I'm thankful every day for the clothes Luke ordered for me since my waistline is expanding. And it's with that in mind that I approach my husband with a very important question. I find him on the couch with his knee elevated and ice on it.

"When should we have the wedding?" I ask, plopping down next to him.

"We're already married," he grunts, and I giggle. "But any time you want is fine with me. I'm pretty wide open for the next eight months or so."

"Eight months?" I ask, my brows dipping.

"Training camp," he clarifies.

"You think you'll be going to training camp?"

He shrugs. "It's been my routine for the last decade so I have to make plans with that in mind. When were you thinking?"

"I wanted to do this before the end of the year, but there's no good time with the holidays approaching and Michelle's due date looming right in the middle between Thanksgiving and Christmas."

"Why do you want to do it before the end of the year?"

I lift a shoulder. "Because I'm excited." The end of my sentence sounds more like a question than an answer.

"You sure about that?" he prods.

I blow out a breath. "Because I want to feel beautiful in my dress and if I'm all huge and pregnant I won't."

He reaches over to toss an arm around me, and I snuggle into his chest. "You are growing our child," he reminds me. "I can't think of anything more beautiful than that."

I look up at him, and his eyes are heated as he looks down at me. "How'd I get so lucky to land you?"

He chuckles. "I'm a real, live Prince Charming."

"I'm so glad you finally see it, too."

He smirks at me. "Why don't we wait until after the baby gets here? We'll have our very own little ring bearer."

"*After* the baby?" I repeat. I hadn't really considered that as a possibility.

"What if we do it on our one-year anniversary? It'll be a fresh start, no contracts, just us."

I sit up and turn toward him. "Our one-year anniversary," I whisper.

His brows dip. "Bad idea?"

I shake my head, and I lean forward and press a kiss to his lips. "It's perfect," I murmur against his mouth. I don't even know how I didn't think of it, but the symbolism of reciting our vows to one another all over again on the day when our legally contracted time together would end seems like the perfect way to celebrate our very real love for one another. And to do it in front of family, friends, and our little one...well, I can't think of anything more beautiful than that.

With our date in mind, I get planning. The baby will be almost two months old, plenty of time for me to work off the baby weight—at least I hope so. I find the most adorable onesie that looks like a tux and I can't wait to see him in it.

Time marches forward, and we give thanks around a table with Josh, Nicki, my parents, and Luke's mom, who rented a house about fifteen minutes from our place for now. She wants to make sure she likes living here before she buys.

A week after Thanksgiving, Jack texts Luke to let him know Michelle went into labor early. Jack Alexander Dalton Junior, or JJ, is born with both his parents there. Michelle's parents, Carol,

Luke, and me all hang out in the waiting room for the news, and Jack's eyes shine as he tells us it's a boy.

Gone is the persona of the victorious champion making waves on the field, instead replaced with this brand-new dad. We head in to meet the baby, and Michelle runs a hand along the baby's head. That's when the shiny rock on her hand gleams in the light.

My eyes widen, but I don't say a word.

"This is Jack Junior," she says softly so as not to wake the baby.

I squeeze Luke's hand. For a long time, he thought he would be the daddy in this room. I can't imagine what he's feeling right now, but I'm proud of him for showing up for his brother despite their sordid history on top of the lies and manipulations from Michelle. We can only hope she changes her selfish ways for the sake of this baby, and seeing her hold him the way she is tells me there's already been a monumental shift in her.

I guess motherhood will do that, and I'm excited to find out how it'll affect me in the coming months.

Carol washes her hands at the sink by the door then moves toward Michelle. "May I touch him?" she asks, and she gently tousles the baby's soft fuzz on the top of his head. "He's precious," she says, and she pauses a beat before she lets out a soft gasp with a surprised, "Oh! Your ring..."

Carol's eyes edge over to Jack, who shrugs. "It's Grandma Rose's ring," he admits.

"Are you two..." Carol trails off.

"Engaged?" Michelle finishes. She glances up at Jack. "Yes."

Jack nods and glances down at Michelle.

What?

I try to piece together what's going on, but I can't figure out his intentions here. Just a few weeks ago, he was telling his brother how he has no idea how Luke put up with Michelle for as long as he did...and now they're engaged?

Is this because of the baby?

Because of the inheritance?

Or does Jack actually love Michelle so much that he wants to spend the rest of his life with her?

Do fake marriages run in the family? Is that genetic?

These are all questions I *want* to ask, but social norms prevent me from actually voicing them.

I guess time will tell.

* * *

When I wake up on Christmas morning three weeks later, I can't help but reflect on everything that's happened since last Christmas. I was so excited when I selected Todd in my office Secret Santa. I'd been hardcore crushing on the guy since we started working together, and I was thrilled when he admitted he had feelings for me, too.

We rang in the new year together and I was so hopeful that I'd finally met my prince.

Little did I know just how much my life was going to change. Little did I know that my *actual* prince was right around the corner and I just needed to be patient.

The best thing that ever happened to me was getting dumped and fired in the same day. It sent me flying toward rock bottom, and I never would've moved to Vegas if it hadn't happened. I wouldn't have taken the one-night stand bet with the girls at Nicki's bachelorette party. I still would've met Luke since we were walking down the aisle together, but I doubt we would've ended up together since Todd would've come with me to Vegas as my date to the wedding.

Yet here I am, tangled in Luke's bajillion thread count sheets with his arms wrapped around me. I stare at the lights on the tree we put up here in the bedroom. It was his idea, not mine—but there's nothing more romantic than making love under the glowing lights of that tree.

Last night I wondered how good old Todd was doing along with my former best work friend, Brittany. I haven't spoken to either of them since the day I was fired. On the one hand, I don't blame her for wanting to keep her distance from me since she still has to work with Belinda every day. On the other hand, my life changed at a whirlwind pace. It's not like I was scrambling to the phone to call her, either.

So I looked up Todd on Facebook. We're not friends anymore, obviously—especially not after he went to the media early in my relationship with Luke to disprove our engagement's legitimacy—but I spotted a picture of him *with* Brittany. They looked awfully cozy for former colleagues.

But the thing about it is...I didn't feel an ounce of jealousy. A year ago, I would've lost my shit if my best friend started dating the guy I had a crush on forever, but I've ended up in the right place. And so all I can do is hope for the best for them, too.

"Good morning," Luke says, his deep voice raspy from sleep. "Merry Christmas." He leans over and presses a soft kiss to my neck, and chills run down my legs.

"Merry Christmas," I whisper back, and I turn in his direction. He tightens his grasp around me, and after a Christmas morning romp that's truly a gift, we lie panting beside one another.

"How different will Christmas morning next year look?" Luke asks.

"Very," I say as I try to picture it. "We'll have an eight-month-old."

"And you'll probably be knocked up with number two."

I smack his arm. "Let's just take it one baby at a time. What was your Christmas last year like? And did you ever think this one would look like it does?"

He laughs. "It was...interesting. And no. I never could've dreamed up this one."

"What does *interesting* mean?"

"It's an adjective. It means catching someone's attention," he deadpans.

I purse my lips at him and wait for him to get to the truth.

"Michelle was here. We were still together. I had Christmas Day off, but I had practice the day before and the day after, and then we had a home game the day after that. We went to her mom's house for a Christmas luncheon and it was over the top extravagant. Calvin bought Michelle a car, which put my diamond earrings to shame. It was just...nothing I am. I spent the day pretending to be happy when I was miserable. Everyone in the Bennett family grilled me as to why Michelle and I weren't engaged."

"How'd you field those questions?" I ask, tracing a circle on his chest.

"I told people I wasn't getting married again, that I'd been through it once and wouldn't do it again."

"Enter Ellie."

He laughs. "I couldn't resist that cute little ass of yours."

"You married me for my ass?"

"And your tits." He reaches for one of them. I purse my lips, and he lets out a soft chuckle. "I wouldn't have had the idea to do it even for pretend if I didn't like *everything* about you the second I met you."

Heat prickles behind my eyes at his words. "That might be the sweetest thing you've ever said to me."

"A true Prince Charming," he jokes. "Speaking of which, let's go see if Santa came."

I narrow my eyes at him. "You think he did?"

He shrugs as his eyes twinkle, and I feel like I've reverted back twenty years or so as excitement races through me on this Christmas morning.

We head down to the family room, where a ridiculously large tree sits in one corner. We have five trees up in different places throughout the house, and since Luke has a bum knee and I'm pregnant, we hired help to get them all up along with lights decorating the outside of our house.

I think about his words from this morning and how different next year will look. Will we have Paw Patrol characters on our front lawn? Mickey Mouse? Snoopy?

Maybe all three.

Pepper lays near the tree, but when she spots us, her tail wags out of control as she gets up and races over to Luke. He chuckles, and I stare at the bottom of the tree.

This Christmas morning is different from my others as we start our own traditions together. I always went to my parents' house and spent the day with them—which we're doing, but they wanted us to have our own family Christmas mornings first, so we're going over in the early evening to celebrate. Carol will be joining us, and Michelle has even said she might stop by so baby JJ can see some of his extended family on Christmas along with his Grammy Carol.

Jack is playing today, so he won't be stopping by—another one of those life events that the guys on the field have to miss out on. While I want Luke to play if that's what he wants, I'd hate for him to miss his son's first Christmas. I think back to Nadine's words of advice to Nicki at the bachelorette party that football careers are short and retirement is long, and I can't help but wonder what Luke's thinking as his knee gets stronger and stronger every day.

He hands me a box, and I unwrap it to find a canvas print from our wedding day. It's a beautiful shot of us on the beach as the sun sets behind us, and despite everything that happened that day, it's still a beautiful memory. It was the day he admitted he had real feelings for me even though we didn't enter our marriage the traditional way.

He opens the matching daddy t-shirt and baby onesie I bought—the leprechaun from Lucky Charms for Luke, naturally, and a pot of gold for the baby.

We both open too many gifts from each other, from jewelry to books to electronics, and he hands me a small box last as we sit in the middle of a mound of wrapping paper that Pepper skips around happily in. I lift the lid off the box and find an envelope, and I pull out a stack of papers from it.

First is Luke's amended will with me as his primary beneficiary.

Second is a business plan for Dalton Athlete Management along with an LLC by the same name.

Third is a piece of paper that simply says, "this is only the start" in Luke's neat handwriting.

My brows draw together in confusion as I look up at him. "The start?" I ask.

He stretches out his knee. He bends it then straightens it again. It's doing so much better even though he still has more therapy to get it back to playing shape. "I've had a lot of time to think over the last couple months," he begins. "And I know what I want my future to look like."

My brows rise in surprise.

"I never thought beyond the game, and not because it was bad luck but because there was nothing else I loved more. There was nothing I cared about more than playing. And then I met you. It's as simple and as complicated as that. I want to be with you and with him." He nods toward my stomach. "I haven't even met him yet and I already love him more than whatever happens on the field. And if I could love someone that much before I even meet him, then I know I need to be around for all of it."

"All of it?" I echo.

He nods. "I'm going to work my ass off to get healthy for you and for him, not to play. Even if Coach and the GM and Calvin get together and invite me to play again...the answer will be no. Because this is only the start of our life together, and I won't let football or injuries or families or crazy exes or *anything* come between us. I'm retiring."

"Wow," I say softly, not sure what else to say as my heart thumps in my chest. "You're...you're giving up your career for me?"

He shakes his head. "For us. It's not guaranteed anyway, and I'd rather go out on my terms than dick around for the next eight months with unknown answers. We don't have time for that, not when we could be building our business as we wait for our baby's arrival."

We don't have time for that.

He's talking excitedly and with animation in terms of *we* and the future, and it's honestly the most beautiful gift anyone has ever given me. My heart squeezes with love for him.

"Are you sure about this?" I ask, not because I want him to rethink it or because I want him to play but because I don't want him to make a rash decision when playing is all he's ever wanted out of life. I think back to his reaction when Savannah sent the story about his drug test to the press and how his first concern is that it would kill his reputation and nobody would want them on his team. He wanted to play as little as a couple months ago, but something changed.

The baby.

He nods slowly. "There's too much risk. If I take another hit to my knee, it would be devastating. I take unnecessary risks every time I step out onto that field, but it didn't matter when it was just me. I can't continue to take those risks when I have two people who need me."

His words are so simple, yet they tell me everything.

He isn't just giving up the game. He's giving up everything he loves because he found something he loves even more.

Our game plan may have started with a fake engagement, but happily ever after is our end game.

EPILOGUE

We're lying around lazily on my parents' couch in their new Vegas place later that evening. Too many presents have been unwrapped, the mass of wrapping paper has been cleaned up, and the food has been eaten.

We're all in turkey comas since my mom always makes a Christmas turkey, and we're sipping hot chocolate with marshmallows as we stare into the crackling flames of the fireplace. The tree glows with lights beside it, and piles of open presents litter the floor (both babies made out pretty well). I'm leaning into my husband's chest as we simply relax.

Josh and Nicki are beside us while my parents clean the kitchen. I asked a hundred times if I could help, and I even tried to start the dishes, but my dad bumped me out of the way and told me to take a load off my feet. I gladly accepted, and I haven't felt this content in a long time.

It's nice having my mom and dad close, and I know that'll only continue to ring true once the baby arrives.

My mom sits on one of the easy chairs across from the couch, and my dad takes the one beside her. They both hold their own mugs of hot chocolate between their hands.

"Time for the annual Nolan Trip down Memory Lane," my dad says.

"Best memory of the year?" my mom asks. She glances around as she waits for one of us to answer.

"Marrying Nicki," Josh says.

"Aww," Nicki says, and she leans in for a kiss. "Mine was finding out about this little nugget," she says, rubbing her stomach. She's due in under two months now.

"Thanks a lot," Josh says.

"Marrying you goes without saying," she says, elbowing him playfully as he narrows his eyes at her. "Okay, let me amend that since apparently it doesn't go without saying. Marrying you, the honeymoon, and finding out about the baby. In no particular order."

"Moving to Las Vegas. It's a new adventure for us," my dad says, looking at my mom, "and it's wonderful to land so close to both our kids."

My mom nods. "I can't choose one, but the weddings, the grandbabies, and moving here." She glances at me. "Which reminds me...we never got to have that big celebration for *your* wedding."

I sit up a little. "Hey, you're right. Why don't we have one next year?" I ask, turning to Luke.

He grins. "How's June twenty-first sound?"

I pretend to think for all of a half a second. "That sounds like *perfection*."

We both laugh, and my parents look at us like they don't get the inside joke.

"We'd like to formally invite you to our wedding, round two, on June twenty-first," I say. "I want your help planning and picking out a dress," I say to my mom. "I'd be honored if you'd walk me down the aisle," I say to my dad. I turn to Nicki. "I want you to be my maid of honor."

"And I want you to be my best man," Luke says to Josh. "Again."

"Our baby boy will be there, and so will his cousins, and it'll be the most perfect way to celebrate our first anniversary with a real wedding in front of all our family and friends," I finish.

My mom claps her hands together with excitement and my dad looks proudly at the two of us. We share a round of hugs before my dad turns to me. "So tell us your best part of the year."

664

I smile softly. "It's a tie between the night Luke ripped up the contract for our fake relationship and the day he found out about the baby."

Luke's eyes twinkle as they land on mine. "Same. And when we found out he's a boy."

"Speaking of these boys," my mom says, "do either of you have names picked out yet?"

I laugh. "We haven't talked about names yet."

Luke shrugs and shakes his head.

"We have one," Nicki says, raising a hand. "Are we telling?"

Josh shrugs. "Go for it."

"Good, then your sister can't try to steal it."

I hold my hands up innocently. "I'm not going to steal it!" There's a name that I keep coming back to in my mind, and I guarantee Josh won't pick it. "Tell us!"

Nicki and Josh exchange another glance, and then Josh says, "Warner."

"Warner?" my dad asks. "Like the great Kurt Warner?"

Josh chuckles. "Yeah."

"Warner," my mom says, turning it over. "Warner Nolan. Oh, that's cute!"

"Middle name?" I ask.

"James, after Dad."

My mom's hand goes to her chest like it's the most adorable thing she's ever heard.

"Dang it!" I mutter. "I wanted James for a middle name."

"Ha ha, we're first so you can't steal it!" Josh singsongs.

"Enjoy going into labor first," I say, and I smirk at Nicki.

"Hey, don't involve me in your weird sibling stuff," Nicki says, and we all laugh.

I guess it's time to start thinking about names.

* * *

We're snuggled together on the couch watching the early Times Square coverage on New Year's Eve with Pepper lying on the floor nearby when he asks, "What was your last New Year's Eve like?"

I lean into him a little more, and he tightens his arm around me. "I was with Todd. We'd just gotten together about a week earlier and we were trying to keep it on the down low because of the office's fraternization policy. But we went to a bar with a big group of friends and he snuck in a kiss at midnight. I drank way too much and was stumbling around wasted. Slightly different from this year."

His arm is wrapped all the way around me and his hand rests on my stomach, and I rest my hand on top of his for a beat.

"How about you?" I ask.

"I was with Michelle. She dragged me to a charity ball. I had to wear a tux." He makes a gagging sound, and I giggle.

"Sounds like torture." I draw a little circle pattern on the back of his hand.

He lifts a shoulder. "It was. I'd been wanting to end things with her but it was just one thing after another. You don't break up a relationship nearly two years strong over Thanksgiving dinner, you know? Or right before Christmas."

"This low key celebration tonight might be the best New Year's Eve I've ever had."

"Same. But I know how to make it even better," he says.

I turn and look up at him, and he looks down at me with that familiar heat in his eyes. "How?" I ask.

He chuckles. "Like you don't know how."

"In front of the dog?" I whisper.

"Pepper!" Luke yells, and the dog startles as she lifts her head. "Go to bed."

I sit up and giggle, and it turns to even bigger laughs when Pepper actually does saunter out of the room. "I think we're alone now."

He reaches for me and pulls my head down to his. He kisses me with passion, with love and adoration, and it's the kind of kiss that makes me see how the lust and the butterflies are still there even after everything we've been through, but there's more. There's a solid base and a real foundation that came from starting with friendship and working through some of life's biggest challenges together.

I pull his shirt over his head and then my own, and it's mere moments before we're both naked and I'm moving over the top of him as gasps and sighs of pleasure fill the room. He thrusts into me, and as our bodies rock together one last time in this year, I give into the pleasure as a climax plows into me with brute force. He follows right behind me, and it's as we're both panting and coming down from the throes of pleasure that I think about the future we're building together. The intimate moments on our couch may be fewer and farther between as our baby starts to grow, or even as the house is filled with more babies. But that just means we'll find new ways to be adventurous and new places to express our passion for one another.

We kiss at midnight, but neither of us tastes even a drop of alcohol as we ring in the new year. I always think of this day as the perfect time to reflect, and while this year has certainly brought me an incredible array of ups and downs, I wouldn't change a moment of it. All those little events added up to this one big emotion I have in my heart for the man beside me, and I'm thankful for every blessing and every challenge that we've gotten to face together.

Whatever tomorrow brings, we'll still have that.

And, by the way, tomorrow brings *good* news for a change.

"Guess what?" Luke says as he saunters into the kitchen. I'm just making scrambled eggs, and he moves toward the coffee pot.

"That's decaf," I warn him. I'm sticking to decaf since I can't give up my coffee addiction altogether but I also can't have too much caffeine.

"Thanks," he says. He pours a cup anyway. "I'll repeat. Guess what?"

I laugh. "What?"

"Savannah married Tristan last night."

My brows dip. "What?"

He nods.

"And how do you feel about that?"

"I feel like celebrating," he says. He does a little dance in the kitchen, and I can't help my laugh. "No more alimony checks! What a way to start the year."

"Well congratulations. Seems like everything's falling into place."

"Except for poor Tristan Higgins," he says. "I tried to warn him, but apparently he didn't listen. He's got a nightmare on his hands now."

"Maybe she's blackmailing him, too," I suggest, and he looks at me like he hadn't thought of that.

"Interesting theory," he says, and his brows dip as he considers it. "He seemed like he was hearing me when I sat him down and told him about my history with Savannah, yet he still married her. Whatever the case, she's someone else's problem now."

"What does that mean?" I slide some bread into the toaster.

He shrugs. "I hope for his sake they have an airtight prenup that protects the nine million signing bonus he got when he was drafted along with his salary." He takes a sip from his steaming coffee mug.

"Best wishes to them," I say. "I hope it's true love."

"So do I, but I doubt it." He walks over to the table and if he wasn't wearing his brace, I'd hardly even know he's recovering from major surgery on his knee. "There's something strange about the two of them getting married so fast."

"The same could be said for us," I point out.

"I guess you're right." He shrugs as he slides onto his chair. "Oh well. Not my circus, not my monkeys."

"Speaking of monkeys, what do you think of that as a theme for the baby's room?"

"Monkeys?"

I nod as I divvy the eggs out onto two plates.

"Will monkeys make you happy?"

I nod again and smile.

"Then they'll make me happy, too. Happy wife, happy life."

"Man, I really leveled up when I married you." I walk a plate over to him and set it down with a fork.

He nods toward his plate. "Thanks. And don't you forget it."

* * *

We're watching the Aces fight for the AFC championship on a Sunday afternoon a couple weeks later when the back of my brother's jersey catches my eye. The game is tied at three in the middle of the first quarter, and Luke has been vocal about this particular game. He wants to see his team succeed even if he doesn't get to be on the field, and since it's an away game and he's still out, he didn't travel with the team.

"Hey, have you thought of any baby names?" I ask during a commercial break. I haven't really thought too much about it since Christmas at my parents' house, but I'm due three months from today and we still haven't discussed what we're going to name this little jellybean. While Jellybean is cute, I think we should come up with something slightly more traditional.

He shrugs. "There's a few I like. You?"

"I keep coming back to one, but I feel like you're going to hate it. What names do you like?"

"Emmett, Troy, William..."

"Football names?" I ask, wrinkling my nose.

He shrugs innocently. "I have a bunch more if you hate those. What's yours?"

I clear my throat as I get a little nervous to tell him. It's how I've been referring to him in my head whenever I'm not referring to him as Jellybean. "Nolan," I finally say.

He pauses a beat, and he tilts his head like he's rolling it over. "Like your maiden name?"

I nod.

"Nolan Dalton," he says, trying it on for size, and my heart races as I wait for his reaction. "Middle name?"

I shrug. "I was thinking James after my dad, but if I get first, you can take middle. Just please not Troy. I may not know much about football, but I was raised in a Bears' house, not a Cowboys'."

He still hasn't reacted to my name other than to repeat it, and his eyes edge to the screen as the game comes back on.

He laughs. "I actually have a middle name in mind, and it isn't Troy."

"What is it?"

"Oh shit!" he yells as his eyes widen at the screen, and even though we're having what I deem a very important conversation, I glance over to see what he's oh-shitting about.

Someone in a black uniform with red lettering is down, but I can't tell who it is. A ring of players surrounds him as the trainers rush out.

"Who is it?" I practically screech as I pray it isn't my brother.

"Tristan."

I send up a little prayer in my head that he'll be okay. I know now what it's like to help a football player heal, and it's been hard enough helping someone who was nearing the end of his career anyway. I can't imagine the level of disappointment for a kid in his rookie season to get hurt. I pray that whatever it is won't keep him down, that he'll sit out a play or two and then get right back into the game.

That doesn't happen.

The broadcasters show the replay, and my stomach turns over as I see the angle at which his ankle bends. It's not natural. It's not supposed to move like that.

"Fuck," Luke mutters as he shakes his head.

"How long will that keep him out?" I ask.

"Depends on whether it's a compound fracture." We watch as the cart comes out to help haul Tristan off the field. He's covering his face with a towel, and after they move him onto the cart, he lowers the towel to wave to the crowd and let them know he'll be okay. His eyes are rimmed in red and the emotion is written all over his face. This is a devastating blow to Tristan and also to the entire Aces' organization.

"What's a compound fracture?"

"When the bone breaks the skin," he says, and I get a little queasy at that description.

We listen to the broadcasters. "The Aces already lost Luke Dalton to a season-ending injury, and it's looking like Higgins will be out a while, too. You think he'll be back in time for next season?" one of them asks the other.

"Hard to tell, Al, but I'd guess he'll be down a few months. I was talking to Mitch Thompson last night and he said Luke Dalton is making great progress. They're hopeful he'll be ready at the start of next season, but I gotta tell you, I've been hearing rumors about retirement."

"I wouldn't blame the guy," the other broadcaster says. "He's in his thirties now, he's been injured twice. That's a lot to come back from."

I glance at Luke and wait for the broadcasters to cut to commercial before I ask my question. "Are you going to talk to Coach sometime?"

He shrugs. "I'm on contract through the end of this season. My decision doesn't matter right now, and I'm not going to burden him when they're in the middle of playoffs."

"But you *are* going to tell him, right?"

He chuckles and he reaches for my hand. He squeezes it. "If you're worried I'm going to change my mind, I won't. I'm done playing. Not forever...I mean, I'll toss the ball around with Nolan, and maybe I'll coach his peewee league team or middle school or even high school."

My eyes fill with tears as I gaze at him. "You called him *Nolan*."

His eyes twinkle back at me. "That's his name, isn't it?"

I can't help when I attack him with a very aggressive hug.

The future is looking beautifully bright for Luke, Ellie, and Nolan Dalton.

BONUS EPILOGUE #1

Less than a month later, we're back at the hospital, but this time we're in the maternity ward again as we wait to meet Josh and Nicki's baby. We got the text late last night that she was going into labor, and a mere fourteen hours later, we got another text that the baby had arrived.

I try not to cringe at the *fourteen hours* part. It's not that long for everyone the first time...right?

Warner James Nolan was born February seventeenth at ten in the morning, weighing a healthy nine pounds, four ounces. We haven't seen a picture of him yet, but I already know my little nephew is perfect. After all, he does have Nolan blood running through his tiny little veins.

We're waiting beside my parents just after lunch time, and I only have two months to go until I'm back here in this same maternity ward to deliver my own baby. It's surreal and a little terrifying and awfully exciting all at the same time.

Josh comes to get us. He barely looks like the brother I know. He looks tired, and he looks a little lost. He has a heavy weight on him now—the responsibility of fatherhood. "They just transferred Nicki to a room. Come meet Warner," he says.

We follow him through a series of hallways, and when he opens the door, we find Nicki on a bed in a hospital gown as she holds the baby. She looks exhausted, and she must not have slept all night...yet a look of pure contentment is on her face as she looks down at him.

She glances up at us when we walk in. "It's the whole Nolan side of your family," she says softly to the baby, and maybe she's only been a mom for the last two hours, but I can already tell she's a natural. She was made to be that little boy's mama.

I wash my hands first and move toward him. I know the grandparents want a turn, but I'm being selfish. This isn't just my brother's firstborn. It's also my best friend's first child, so it feels doubly special for me.

"Oh, he's just perfect," I say as Nicki hands him over. I stare down at his little button nose and the shock of dark hair on the top of his round little head. His cheeks are pink and his eyes are closed as he transitions from his mom to me, and it's so crazy to think that Nicki is a *mom* now.

This is the girl I've known since high school, the one who was boy crazy in high school even though she was fairly harmless and innocent through most of those years. She's the one who went through a period where she was obsessed with the NBA and only wanted to date basketball players, the one who was too shy to ask Jordan Hewlett to the Turn-About Dance our sophomore year, the one who loved heavy metal music and hated country, the one who cheated on every history test we ever took and who did her homework three minutes before class began but still managed to pull decent grades.

And now she's married to my brother. She's someone's mommy.

Funny how all that stuff that was so important to us a decade ago is meaningless now. All that matters are the people in this room, and family and friends, and relationships.

My mom steals the baby from me while I ponder all this, and Nicki's parents and brother sweep into the room next. A quiet excitement bubbles around the room for the new parents and this new life.

The next two months are filled with babies. We're either visiting with Warner or we're prepping for Nolan's arrival. I rest as much as I can—it's not easy walking around with a watermelon for a stomach, and from everything Nicki tells me about being a new mom, I should definitely take all the rest I can now because I won't get much once the baby's here.

It's harder and harder to sleep as the baby kicks my ribs and my stomach grows even larger. I sleep on the chaise lounge chair of our couch most nights, and Luke has to help roll me off in the morning. But Pepper has been great about keeping me company, cozying up next to me like she knows things are about to change. We won't have this quiet house for much longer. Soon it'll be filled with soft newborn cries that turn into a thunderous infant, and I've never met a quiet toddler before in my life. Maybe Nolan will be the first.

Somehow I doubt it.

As mid-April approaches, I go to the doctor more often, and it's at an appointment the week of my due date when the doctor informs me that my water is leaking and I should get to the hospital.

I stare at the doctor with wide eyes. "Are you serious?"

She chuckles. "Yes, Ellie. I'm serious. You're in labor."

Luke is with me, but my overnight bag is not.

"Can I stop home to get my bag?" I ask. I feel a little panicked that I don't have my bag. How can I go to the hospital without my bag? It has everything I need for the birth plan that I so painstakingly pondered for weeks if not months before I committed to it and wrote it up.

My water leaking and going early was *not* part of the plan. Do babies *ever* do anything according to plan?

No. The answer, as I'm sure I'll discover over the next few years, is no.

The doctor shakes her head. "I wouldn't."

"Josh can bring it," Luke says gently. He's maintaining a level head and why isn't he panicking with me?

Oh, right. Because *someone* needs to be the calm one here.

He helps me out to his car, and he's driving again which is great because there's no way in hell I'd be safe behind the wheel of a car right now. He drives well over the speed limit to the hospital, which is normally a ten-minute drive but he gets it done in about five, and he drops me at the entrance while he parks the car. I stand there looking a little lost.

Holy shit.

I'm about to have a baby.

So many emotions course through me. Is this going to hurt? I can't wait to meet this little guy. What's life going to be like with a baby? I've seen a little preview of it when we visit with Josh and Nicki, who are handling things well...but that's them. They have an easy baby, at least according to Nicki. He's only two months old and he's already sleeping through the night for eight hours. Will this baby be like that, too? Or will I be up every hour feeding him?

Time will tell. I know that'd be Luke's answer to all my questions, but I don't want some practical (dumb) cliché. I want the truth, and I want someone to give it to me straight, and I want it now.

I don't get any of it now, though. Instead, I get a contraction.

Seventeen hours later, a baby is born.

It turns out the doctor was wrong. My water hadn't broke, and the hospital almost sent me home but said I was dilated enough to stay. It took some time, but the baby arrived safely at three twenty-six in the morning on April fourteenth.

Luke, who coached me through the whole thing, cuts the umbilical cord, and the doctor lies him on my chest for skin to skin time immediately after he's born. I cry tears of joy that he's here, and Luke does, too, as he clutches my hand in his. We're responsible for this perfect little life with ten tiny fingers and ten little toes. Together we'll raise him and teach him and give him siblings.

"What's the baby's name?" the nurse asks.

"Nolan," I say. I spell it.

"And the middle name?"

I look over at Luke, and he clears his throat as he seems to get a little misty-eyed. "Timothy."

"After your dad?"

He nods, and my tears fall a little harder as I realize it's his way of making up for the things he couldn't when his dad was here with us.

"It's perfect," I whisper.

Luke squeezes my hand. "So are you, and so is he." He presses a kiss to my forehead as his palm finds the baby's head, and despite the exhaustion and the hunger and the anxiety over what comes next, I don't think I've ever been so happy in my entire life.

BONUS EPILOGUE #2

The happiest day of my life was the day Nolan was born.

I think today might be the second happiest.

I worked my ass off to fit into the perfect wedding gown that my mom and Nicki helped me find. I've spent the morning being pampered, and my hair and make-up are on point. For the first time in the last two months, I *feel* gorgeous. I'm wearing something other than sweats, and I even took a shower. I *love* being a mom, but today I feel like something a little more than that.

Nolan's wearing his tux-onesie, and I've never seen a cuter baby in my entire life. I literally can't stop staring at him, and I think it's because I see such a strong resemblance to his father. And speaking of his father...

I'm marrying my husband all over again today. Luke has proven to be an amazing daddy to this little one. He's been so helpful to me as I've started navigating motherhood, and he seems to intrinsically know when I need a break before I even realize it. He changes diapers and gives baths and helps with feeding when he can. It has just been the most blissful couple months.

And today we celebrate all that bliss with everyone we love.

For real this time.

It's been real for the last year for the two of us, but today is still a symbolic new beginning, and I think it's one we needed.

Josh is Luke's best man, and Jack is a groomsman this time around. I chose Nicki as my matron of honor, and Kaylee is also standing up with me to make this a real family event. Luke's two siblings were so sure we had the wrong intentions the first time, so to have them standing up with us and lending us their support today means the world to us both.

The Broncos didn't make it past the division championship game this year. The big game went to the Bears for the first time in a whole lot of years.

Luke's one big regret is walking away from the game without a ring, but technically he still hasn't announced his plans for retirement yet, which creates quite the interesting dynamic since we learned just after Nolan was born that Jack was traded...to the *Aces*.

I don't *think* Luke will change his mind, but as we inch closer and closer to when training camp is set to begin, I can't help but wonder whether he's reconsidering. Of course he'd want to play on the same team as his brother, especially now that they're close.

I wouldn't blame him if he was thinking twice about his decision, and it wouldn't diminish his love for me or for his son if he did.

In fact, I wrote a little something about that in my vows to let him know that I support whatever decision he makes—even if that means changing his mind and changing our plans.

"It's time," our wedding planner, Olivia, says, and Nicki and Kaylee head out to walk down the aisle. We're doing this thing at the same place where Nicki and Josh held their wedding. The Cosmopolitan hotel on the Vegas Strip has so much meaning for the two of us, and we couldn't pass up the chance to mark another meaningful event in our relationship right here.

It is, after all, where we met a little over a year ago when we were both at the same club. It's where we reconnected the next night for the rehearsal when we had no idea who the other was, and it's where I first realized he was a real Prince Charming when he rescued me from the pool after I nearly drowned in a bridesmaid gown the night after that at the wedding.

I shake my head with a little chuckle at the memory.

"What's so funny?" my dad asks, narrowing his eyes at me as we get ready to leave the little bridal room where we've been waiting for the ceremony to begin.

"Just thinking back to when I fell in the pool at Josh and Nicki's wedding," I say. I get into place and link my arm through his elbow.

His eyes twinkle as he looks down at me. "I saw they covered the pool today."

I nod and give him a wry smile. "When Olivia told us they had a cover that would turn it into a dance floor, we took that option without even discussing it."

He laughs. "You ready for this?"

I shrug. "Nothing to be nervous about today, but even if I wasn't, I would still be ready. He makes me happy."

My dad seems to get a little misty at that. "I'm glad, my sweet girl," he says. "You deserve the best."

"I found the best when I found him."

We head toward the aisle. Luke stands waiting for me in his tuxedo, the truest Prince I've ever seen in my life, and I swear to God I'm not going to make it through this entire night without ripping that straight off him. Surely we could find a spare minute or two for a quickie, right? He's ridiculously sexy all the time, but put him in a tux and forget about trying to have any sort of coherent thought for the rest of the night.

My dad hands me off, and we asked Debbie to preside over our vows. She's special to us both, and she's been a godsend in helping us out with Nolan. She's his surrogate third grandma, and he loves her to pieces.

Her voice starts off a little shaky with nerves, but she calms once we get going. It's a short and sweet ceremony, and we arrive quickly at our vows. "The first time Luke and Ellie said their vows, they simply repeated the words of the officiant," Debbie says. "Today they have decided to write their own. Luke, you may begin."

Luke reaches into his jacket pocket for his notes. He glances up at me, and our eyes lock. He slides the paper back into his pocket, and then he reaches for my hands. "When we met a little over a year ago at this hotel, I had this strange feeling my life was about to change. I didn't know it wouldn't just *change*, though. Like a whirlwind, you came into my life and upended everything I thought I knew, from never wanting to get married again to being uncertain about having kids to not even having an Instagram account." The last part garners a little chuckle from our guests.

He pauses a beat before he continues. "But that's the thing about love. You're bumbling through life, sure you know everything, and then you bump into the one person who shares the other half of your soul, and you'll do whatever it takes to make sure they stick around. Ellie likes to tell me I'm her Prince Charming, and I like to tell her I'll do what I can to prove I'm no prince. But if I'm a prince, it's only because she's my princess. She's the center of my universe, and she grounds me in a way no one else ever has. She's given me the most important gift in our son, and she continues to inspire and amaze me every single day. So today, in front of our family and friends, I vow to keep trying to be the prince you deserve. I vow to open up to you even if it's in the dark, and I vow to love, honor, and cherish you and our son and any other future children we may have together for as long as we both live. I love you today and always."

"I'm supposed to follow *that*?" I say, and I swipe at a tear.

He grins at me, and Debbie laughs as she says, "Ellie, you may say your vows now."

I draw in a deep breath. "A little over a year ago, I lost my job and my boyfriend in the same day, and I moved to Vegas thinking it would be a great place for a fresh start. I couldn't have known then that it wouldn't just be a fresh start. It would completely change everything. I met the person who gets me like nobody else, the one who makes me laugh even though he also knows how to press all my buttons. We've been through a lot together in the last year, and each event has only bonded us closer. One of the most important lessons we came away with is how short life is, but when I'm with you, I know I'm making the most of the time we have on this Earth. We don't know what the future holds."

I pause to squeeze his hands, and then I get to the part I've been a little nervous to say, the part where I basically let him know that we'll be fine if he wants to change his mind about playing next year. "But it's okay. It's okay to work together, and it's okay to change our minds, and it's okay to try new things or to stick with what we know. It's all okay because every single one of those steps will happen with your hand in mine. And that's what matters. So today, in front of our family and friends and our baby boy, I vow to support you and encourage you. I vow to love, honor, and cherish you. I vow to hold your hand through all of life's biggest decisions, blessings, and challenges. All this I vow all the days of my life. I love you today and always."

I love you, he mouths to me.

I swipe another tear.

Debbie says a few words about marriage and a few words about us, and then it's over. He kisses me to seal our renewed commitment, and then we smile as we hold hands down the aisle. We'll take some photos and then it's party time.

He leans over just as we pass the end of the aisle. "Hey, good lookin'. You come here often?"

I laugh and shake my head.

He leans in a little closer. "I need to get you out of that dress," he mutters into my ear.

I look over at him and raise a brow, and then I move in toward his lips. "Well I need to get you out of that tux."

He kisses me softly. "Should we run up to the room real quick?"

I glance back at the clapping crowd of our closest family and friends.

Hors d'oevres are coming up, and the bar's open. They'll be fine.

"Only if we can do it up against the window."

His eyes light with heat and excitement as we're both transported back to the night we met right here at this hotel.

"That's a promise," he says. He grabs my hand and we rush toward the elevators.

I giggle while we wait for it to come get us. It's sort of anti-climactic after the way we just ran out of our own party so we could head upstairs to have sex.

We step onto the car loaded with people, and everyone stares at me in my dress.

"Runaway bride," Luke quips, and some of the people in the elevator give an awkward courtesy laugh. I smack him in the arm.

Last time we did this, I was soaking wet and super attracted to him but he was trying to keep his distance because of my brother.

But this time...we're married.

We have a child together.

We stop on various floors so people can get off, and eventually it's just the two of us as we ascend to a floor nearly at the top of the hotel.

Just the two of us. My Prince Charming and me.

"Tell Her Tonight"

A SHORT STORY PREQUEL TO
THE VEGAS ACES SERIES

Originally published in the
LOVE IS IN THE AIR ANTHOLOGY

Josh Nolan is in love with his sister's best friend. Will he get up the nerve and finally tell her tonight?

CHAPTER 1

I'm going to tell her tonight.
I'm going to tell her tonight.
I'm going to tell her tonight.
Fuck that. I'm *not* going to tell her tonight.

My little sister has been best friends with Nicki Blair since her sophomore year of high school, and even back then when I was a senior, I thought she was hot. You know, for a sophomore.

I'll never forget the first night she spent at our house. I heard giggling coming from Ellie's room, and the sound of Nicki's laughter rang in my ears for days after.

The second time, she snuck down to the kitchen for some popcorn after Ellie fell asleep, and I happened to be in there looking for some Doritos. We got to talking, and we sat at the kitchen table until the sun came up.

I was a senior, though. It didn't matter that I thought she was hot. She was too young for me. Too sweet and too innocent. Too much Ellie's best friend for me to be anything more than a friend to her, too. I knew better than to come between high school girls. Hell, I'd already done that with a few different pairs of best friends my own age.

She was fifteen, and I was seventeen—a few days away from my eighteenth birthday, when having a relationship with her was a stupid idea. The last thing I wanted was to end up on some offender's list for life when I had a bright future ahead of me in football, so I wrote it off as a dumb crush.

But we're not in high school anymore. She's not a sophomore anymore.

Actually, technically that's not true. She's a sophomore in college now, and I'm a senior. I've got my entire future ahead of me, and my dumbass is hung up on a girl two years younger than me who's been best friends with my sister for the last four years.

My dumbass has been hung up on her for a long, long time.

Ellie invited me to hang out for the weekend at Illinois State where she and Nicki share a dorm room. It's an easy one-hour drive from the University of Illinois, the school I attend and play football for. Go Illini.

I'm guessing she invited me because I'm twenty-one now and can buy them beer, but since I have a rare free weekend, I'm down for hanging out with my sister.

And her best friend.

I'll get to that World History paper when I get back home Sunday night. I'll study for my stats test Monday morning.

This weekend is for fun.

When I pull into the parking lot, Ellie is waiting outside the double doors that let us into the dorm. This is hardly the first time I've been here visiting, but something tugs on the borders of my consciousness that tells me this time will be different.

Because you're going to tell her tonight, Dumbass, my brain reminds me, but I shut that thought the fuck up as I grab my duffel and follow my sister into her building after greeting her with a hug.

My heart races as we take the elevator up to Ellie's floor and walk down the hallway toward her room. I wonder if Nicki's in there. Maybe she's studying, poring over a textbook as her shiny blonde hair falls across her face. I wonder if her hair still smells minty like it did that summer day when I caught a whiff of it as we bumped into each other in the small hallway leading to the bathroom at my parents' house in Chicago.

I shift uncomfortably on my feet as the thought of her hair turns me on in an unexpected way.

After four years of knowing the girl and pretending like I don't have feelings for her, I have to admit...I'm tired of pretending.

What's the worst that could happen? I tell her, she rejects me. Ellie doesn't understand why and cuts off their friendship. They have to live out the rest of their sophomore year in a tiny dorm room hating each other. Ellie can't take it and ends up shacking up at some guy's place just to get away from her, but he's from the wrong side of the tracks, so to speak, and he gets her involved in nefarious activities and she ends up in jail after she throws her entire life away because of her druggie boyfriend.

But at least I admitted to Nicki how I really felt.

As a side note, Creative Writing is the one class I'm currently pulling higher than a C in. Coach tells us to make sure to have a minimum of a C average, and that class alone is putting me into the C+ range. Not that it matters since my college playing days are over, but my parents would kill me if I failed out my last semester.

This is a terrible idea.

When Ellie sets a hand on the doorknob to the room she shares with Nicki, I blurt, "Can we talk a second?"

Her hand slips from the doorknob and her brows dip as she fixes her gaze on me. "About what?" She studies me a beat then narrows her eyes. "Is this about the alcohol? Because I don't need a *lot* but a couple bottles of rum and vodka should do the trick. Just buy them at different stores so nobody gets too suspicious that you're supplying your underage sister with liquor."

I laugh. Leave it to Ellie to break the ice. At least some of the nerves in my chest have dissipated. "Nah, it's not about the alcohol."

"Then...what?"

I shake my head. "Never mind."

She shrugs as if to say *suit yourself* and opens the door without warning, and my heart feels like it might explode. Those nerves are back, and they're rattling around as my eyes search the small room for Nicki.

It's empty.

Where's Nicki?

I want to ask. Maybe she's just out for lunch or something. Out at a friend's. At the gym. It's not like she's waiting around here for me.

"You can take Nicki's bed. She went home for the weekend."

My heart drops as my chest aches a little. "She went home for the weekend?"

Ellie nods. "Yeah. She's been seeing this guy and he lives up there. She's been commuting back and forth every weekend, but I'd rather have her go there than him come here." She pulls a face like she just got a whiff of something gross.

My hackles rise as I think about Nicki with someone else...someone who isn't me. "You don't like him?"

Ellie shakes her head. "He's okay. He's just...he's not the right guy for her." She slides onto the chair at her desk, and I collapse on the futon that sits under Nicki's lofted bed.

"How do you know?"

She studies me a long time, and then she sighs. "Never mind."

"No, Elle. Not *never mind*. Tell me."

She lifts a shoulder. "It's stupid."

My brows dip. "What is?"

"I just...I guess I always pictured her with...I don't know."

"With what?" I prod.

She draws in a deep breath. It's not unlike my sister to string me along a little, but this is pure torture. "With someone like you," she finally says.

I want to revel in those words for a minute, but the sweet feeling of victory is far from my grasp knowing that she's with somebody else.

My jaw slackens as I think about admitting how I feel about Nicki to my sister, but ultimately I stop myself. If she knows, it will become her life's mission to do something about it. And if Nicki's dating somebody and she's happy with him...

I let that thought trail off. I just want her to be happy.

But I want her to be happy with me.

I'm two months away from my life potentially changing forever. Rumor has it that a pro football team will select me to play for them in the first round of this year's draft in April, and if that's true, then there's a good chance that pretty much overnight I'll go from college boy to pro football superstar.

Every time I think of that, I get a little anxious. Every time I get a little anxious, I think of the same person I've thought of for four years when I need something to pull me out of it.

And that person is my little sister's best friend.

Only she has no idea.

And neither does my sister.

But I think that has a lot to do with the current timing of my feelings. I don't want to be the guy who sleeps with a different woman every night just because I'm on television every Sunday. I want to be the guy who settles down with one girl. One girl who I trust. One girl who has been part of my life for four years. One girl who doesn't care about fame and contracts and how much time I get on the field.

I've already met a few of those and I don't even have a contract yet.

"Someone like me?" I repeat, my hand bumping into my own chest in surprise.

She shrugs. "She'd kill me for saying this, but she's always had a massive crush on you. She thinks you're, as she puts it, one decadent slice of man cake."

"Man cake?" I repeat, shock flitting through me at my sister's admission.

She giggles and slaps a hand over her mouth. "I can't believe I told you that."

I laugh. "I can't, either." I try to categorize this new information, but I'm having a hard time reconciling *man cake* with the pretty blonde girl who smells like mint.

"Don't tell her I told you," she says.

"It's not like she's here for me to ask her what the hell that means anyway." I sigh. Maybe next time I come visit I can ask what, exactly, a *man cake* is.

CHAPTER 2

We can't go to the bar since my sister is only nineteen, so instead she takes me to a party at some off-campus house. It's rowdy when we walk in, and she walks me right over to the keg, where we each give the guy standing next to it a five-dollar bill to offset the cost of the beer and grab a red Solo cup. I fill the first cup to the brim, an expert in getting beer from a keg without that thick head on top, and hand it over to my sister.

Aside from my moves on the football field, a good, clean cup of beer from a keg is one of my talents in life.

I fill the second cup for myself and gulp down half of it in a few sips. It tastes like piss-water, which tells me it's not one of my preferred brands. But it's cheap beer and I'm here to hang with my sister, so I don't mention it.

My sister is one of my best friends, and our parents would be glad to see us hanging out together even though we attend different schools. I've tried letting go of the little cloud that settled over me the moment Ellie told me about Nicki and the guy she's seeing, but I've been unable to shake it.

Ellie introduces me to some of her friends, and one of the dudes recognizes me.

"Holy shit!" he says. "You're Josh Nolan!"

"That I am," I say.

"That catch you made at the end of that game against Nebraska...it was in-fucking-human, dude!" he says. He's an exclaimer.

"Thanks, man."

"I heard you'll go in the first round of the draft. Is that true?" he asks.

"We'll both find out in April," I admit. I'm confident someone will pick me up, even if I don't go in the first round.

"Who are you hoping for?"

I'd love for it to be my hometown team, the Bears. I won't admit that to this guy, though, or else it'll be all over the news. I may not have a publicist yet, but I'm no dummy. Plus Coach has trained us for questions like these, and he helped me find my agent, who has also been training me. "I'll be happy if *any* team picks me. I'm ready to work and I'm honored to even be considered."

"Sounds like an agent's already gotten to you," he says, and I just press my lips into a smile.

More guys approach me with their questions, their women give me eyes they shouldn't be since they're here with boyfriends, and I even get a few invitations from single ladies, but I can't seem to get my mind off the one girl who isn't here. I don't want any of these women.

I want Nicki.

We have a few more beers before we head back to Ellie's dorm at my request. I'm a big dude at six-feet-five inches and a little under two hundred pounds, but I'm coming off a season where I didn't drink much, so my tolerance isn't what it used to be.

I'm not wasted or sloppy, just tired and a little disappointed, so when we get back, I climb into Nicki's bed to just pass the hell out.

The sheets smell like mint, and a wave of arousal washes over me.

Dammit.

Then another emotion crashes into me, too. That familiarity that comes with someone you've known a long time...that feeling of warmth and comfort. I breathe in the scent, boners be damned. I can take care of that when I'm back home.

Ellie's phone rings, and the guy on the other end is talking loudly. The din of the party we just left is still in full swing in the background. "Why'd you leave?" he yells.

"My brother was tired," she says quietly, like I won't be able to hear her even though I'm literally ten feet away.

"What?" he yells.

She repeats her words but louder, and I sigh.

"Do you want to go back?" I ask, forcing one eye open.

She shrugs, and now I feel bad for taking her from the party where she was having fun.

I sit up and bang my head on the ceiling. "Goddammit," I mutter. I swing my legs over the side. "I'll walk you back if you can find a way home."

She says a few more things over the phone and hangs up. "Thanks, Josh. Trevor is coming to walk me back."

"And we trust Trevor?" I ask.

She smiles. "We trust Trevor. He's just a friend."

"Sure he is," I tease.

I lie back down and I'm pretty sure I pass right out.

But I wake up when the light flicks on and the door slams. It seems like four seconds have passed since I teased Ellie about Trevor, but a quick, bleary-eyed glance at Nicki's clock tells me it's been more like two hours.

I squint down in the bright lights, and my heart races as my eyes focus.

That's not Ellie.

Blonde hair flies around as the most gorgeous girl I've ever seen wrestles out of her coat. She slams it down onto her desk, huffing her way around the room. She's angry, and if I don't say something, she'll have the daylights scared out of her when she climbs into her bed and finds me in it.

"I don't want to interrupt whatever you're doing," I say, my deep voice breaking into the quiet of the room as she jumps, startled, "but I wanted you to know I'm here."

She spins around and looks up as her terrified eyes meet mine. "Holy crap," she says, clutching her chest. "You scared the shit out of me."

I chuckle. "Sorry. I was trying to avoid that."

"What are you doing here? I figured since Ellie was still out, you would be, too."

I sit up, and—you guessed it. "Goddammit!" I say, rubbing my head where I hit it on the ceiling *again*.

Nicki giggles. "Not a lot of clearance up there."

695

"Especially not when you're six-five." I climb down from her bed. "Sorry for making your bed smell like me. I'll take the futon tonight." I close the gap between us and give her a quick hug in greeting.

She lingers for a beat, mint pressing into my senses, and I want to pull her into me and hold her. I want to calm the angry crease that still rests between her brows. I want to be the reason she smiles as I take away her frown.

"Don't be silly. Your six-five frame won't fit on the futon. You can take my bed."

Only if you're in it with me.

"It's all right. What are you doing back here?" I ask. "Ellie said you were with your boyfriend."

She smacks her lips together and sticks a hand on her hip. "He is *not* my boyfriend. We were kind of seeing each other, but we're not anymore."

A pang of relief hits me in the chest. "Is that why you're slamming doors and throwing your coat like it did something wrong?"

"You saw that?" she asks sheepishly.

I lift a shoulder.

"Yeah, that's why," she admits. She moves to pick up her coat and she hangs it while I slide onto the futon. "I wanted to kick the chair, too, but I realized it's not the chair's fault that Cam is a dickhead."

"Maybe it's because his name is Cam." Northwestern's cornerback is named Cam, and he's a real douchebag. Big as a house and always trying to flatten me.

I pat the empty futon seat beside me. "Come sit and tell me what happened."

I toss my arm casually over the back of the futon, but ultimately, if she sits next to this piece of man cake, I can easily slip my arm down and around her shoulders. Goals.

She narrows her eyes for a beat, and my breath catches in my throat. She's so *pretty*, so kind, and she deserves better than whatever just happened. She walks toward me and sits, curling her legs under her frame and turning in my direction. I shift to turn toward her, too, even though my preference was to leave my arm across the back of the futon and pull her into me.

"I drove all that way, over two hours to see him and surprise him, and get this. He had *some other girl* over. In bed. Naked."

"I'll kill him," I mutter.

She chuckles. "Thanks for the support."

"Were you exclusive with him?"

She shrugs. "I guess we never defined it, but I wasn't seeing anybody else and we've spent just about every weekend together for the last two months. Usually with me driving up there."

"How'd you meet him?" I ask.

"He's a friend's cousin. He was down visiting one weekend and we hit it off." She ducks her gaze like she doesn't want to admit exactly what *hit it off* means, and it's okay because I'm not sure I want to hear it.

"He's an idiot." My words are plain and simple. He's an idiot for hurting Nicki. She deserves more.

She chuckles mirthlessly.

"I'm serious. I've just never understood the concept of sleeping around. Why risk sticking your dick in a bunch of different places when being in a relationship feels so much better?"

Her eyes meet mine, and hers are a little dreamy.

My dick starts to protest painfully in the basketball shorts I chose to sleep in.

Not tonight, big boy. She's hurting. Just be there as a friend.

But tomorrow...I'll tell her tomorrow.

Maybe.

"You're like..." she sighs as she glances around the room, and I hang onto her words as I silently urge her to finish that sentence. "Just like the perfect guy." She shakes her head. "One of a kind. Most guys aren't like you. They're like Cam. But you're not just hot as hell. You're so sweet and you're funny and—"

I cut her off when I lean in to tuck a strand of hair behind her ear, her fresh minty scent striking my senses. She stops talking at the movement as her gaze lifts to mine.

"Hot as hell?" I repeat, my voice a deep, low murmur, and I'm treated to a delicious coloring of her cheeks as the meeting of our eyes turns into something hot and nearly indecent. Her eyes flick to my lips, an open invitation if I've ever seen one.

Kiss her you idiot!

I can bend down to the line of scrimmage facing off against some of the largest opponents, future NFL prospects, and not feel the same type of fire racing through me right now.

And that's what tells me that this is my chance.

I need this woman in my life. She somehow calms the tempest, and it's going to get stormy over the next few months. She's the perfect person to hold my hand through it all—the *only* person—and she doesn't even know it yet.

But she will.

Nerves rattle around in my chest as I slowly lean in, closing the gap between us so I can brush my lips to hers, and I'm inches from the promised land when the door opens.

I jump back like I'm guilty of something even though I'm not, and Ellie prances into the room. Her brows dip when she sees the two of us sitting together on the futon. "What are you doing back?" she asks Nicki. "And what are you doing awake?" she asks me.

I heave out a sigh, and if I'm not mistaken...so does Nicki beside me.

"Cam's a dickface and I'm already over him so I came back here," Nicki admits.

"Oh my God! What happened?" Ellie squeals as she bolts across the room to sit on the floor in front of Nicki like she didn't just interrupt a moment between the two of us.

Nicki shrugs. "We just had different ideas about what we were, I guess. And I woke up your poor brother when I came bounding into the room. I figured you two would still be out so I wasn't quiet about it." She glances at me again, and I sense the disappointment in her eyes. I think it's because we were interrupted, not because of what went down with Cam, but maybe I'm projecting my wishes onto the situation. "Sorry about that."

"No problem." I stretch my arms up and hit the bottom of the lofted bed above me—Nicki's bed, where I was sleeping not so long ago. Where I want to be tonight...but not with my sister in here. And speaking of my sister, I direct my attention to her. "How'd your night end up?"

She blushes. "Good. Really good."

Nicki raises a brow. "*Really* good?"

"Well, not *that* good," Ellie admits. "I mean I did come home, so there's always room for improvement. But Trevor *finally* kissed me and it was ahhhh-mazing." She's all dreamy and shit and I'm sure there's more details an older brother doesn't want to know that will grace my presence anyway.

"I thought Trevor was just a friend," I protest.

Ellie laughs then rolls her eyes. "That's just something you say to your big brother so he doesn't go all caveman protective."

"Caveman protective?" Nicki asks, nudging my leg with hers. "That's sweet." I don't miss the repetition of her term of endearment—a reference to our earlier conversation.

"I've been told I'm a delectable piece of man cake, too," I say, and that *might* be the beer talking.

Nicki's eyes widen as they turn on my sister, her cheeks filling with color again. Ellie looks sheepishly at Nicki. "Sorry!" she says. "It slipped out."

Nicki covers her face with both hands, and I can't help my rumbling laugh.

God, do I want to hold her in my arms tonight.

I force that thought away. She just broke up with another guy. Tonight's not the night.

Tomorrow, though...all bets are off.

CHAPTER 3

My neck is stiff when I wake in the morning, and it's likely from sleeping on a futon...something I haven't done since...well, since the last time I visited my sister, I suppose.

And why didn't I tell Nicki about my secret feelings that time? She was dating some other guy.

Why didn't I tell her the time before that?

I was dating some other girl.

The timing never worked out, and it almost didn't this weekend, either. But she's newly single. I'm not seeing anyone. I'm not even interested in anyone aside from her...and I haven't been, not really and truly, possibly ever. I've tried writing it off as a crush, but after the way my chest lit up in her mere presence last night, I think it's time to acknowledge the truth.

I've known this girl for four years, and I've been in love with her for three and a half.

She's nineteen now. I'm twenty-one. There's nothing illegal anymore.

And it's more than a crush.

I've always felt like crushes are for people you don't really know. They can develop into more or less once you have a real conversation, and Nicki and I have had those over the years. There were late nights in high school when she and Ellie had sleepovers, or after school when she came over to do homework with my sister.

We haven't had as many since I headed off to college, but when we get a chance to see each other at the holidays—it's never small talk with her. It's always something deeper, and that's something I haven't found with girls my own age who only want to hang out with me because of my place on the field.

I'm going to tell her tonight.

I'm going to tell her tonight.

I'm going to tell her tonight.

I really am going to tell her tonight.

If I can wait that long.

I'm up before either of the women, and the room is quiet as I pick up my phone and scroll through the headlines on my various sports apps just like I do every morning. Nicki is sleeping literally right above me, and all I can think about is how I want her closer. I want her body physically on top of mine rather than the six feet or so that it's currently resting above me. She's so close, yet so far.

When my phone vibrates with a text while it's in my hand, I nearly drop it. And when I see who it's from, I can't help the smile that forms on my lips. I procured her number a few years ago when I was trying to surprise my sister for her birthday.

Nicki: *Good morning.*

Me: *Good morning. How'd you know I'm awake?*

She leans over the side of her bed and our eyes meet. She chuckles softly and my chest aches at her beauty. She just woke up literally moments ago, and she's as gorgeous as I've ever seen her.

Nicki: *I could hear you tapping around on your phone. It sounded like angry scrolling.*

Me: *Hope I didn't wake you. That's just my big fingers.*

Big fingers that want to touch every centimeter of your body.

Nicki: *You didn't wake me. I don't think I ever fell asleep.*

Me: *Sorry. Was it my snoring?*

Nicki: *<laughing emoji> No. You weren't snoring. My mind was just wandering all over the place.*

Me: *Want to talk about it? Or...text about it, I guess?*

Her answer doesn't come right away, but I can hear her softly tapping out a message on her phone in the quiet stillness of the room. I can't help but wonder how many times she types and backspaces and retypes before her message comes through.

Nicki: *I want to ask you a question but I'm nervous about your answer and I sort of feel like asking via text is less embarrassing than face to face.*

Me: *We've known each other a long time. You can ask me anything.*

This one also takes a while to come through, and those familiar nerves I get around this girl clatter around again.

When the text comes through, I'm surprised at the candid nature of her question.

Nicki: *Did you almost kiss me last night?*

Okay, Nolan. This is your chance.

I'm going to tell her tonight...nope, looks like I'm going to tell her right now.

Me: *Last night, last month, that one time when you were fifteen. Yeah, I almost kissed you. More than once.*

It's my turn to feel a little embarrassed by my admission, but I've learned something in the last four years playing football at the collegiate level. Playing safe gets you safe results. Taking risks, calculated or not...that's what unlocks the big wins.

I see Nicki's face again as she leans over the side of her bed, and our eyes meet in a conversation of their own. It's the way my parents have silent conversations across the room, the way my buddy Eric looks across the room at his girl, the way anybody who's ever been in love can have those meaningful moments without words.

And it's in that moment that I know I don't have anything to fear when it comes to spilling my real feelings to Nicki. I glance over at my sister's bed. She's still fast asleep, her breathing even.

"I wish I could kiss you right now," I whisper into the quiet room.

The most beautiful smile widens her lips, and I know without a doubt that before this day is over, I'll feel those lips moving under mine. I'll know what it's like to have her fresh smell of mint filling my nose as I taste her for the first time. And maybe, just maybe, I'll get the chance to let my fingers dance along every sweet and gorgeous crevice of her body.

"I've wanted you to kiss me since the day I met you," she whispers back.

I raise a brow. "Then get your cute little ass down here so I can make your dreams come true."

She giggles out loud then slaps a hand over her mouth as we both glance over at my sister.

It's too late. The giggle seems to have awakened the beast...er, I mean, *my sister*, as that little cock-blocker stirs over on her bed.

"Later," I mouth to Nicki, who nods as our eyes do one more of those little tangos, and then she moves back onto her pillow and I do the same as my sister wakes up.

*   *   *

"So obviously I'm going to need every single detail about this Trevor kiss," Nicki says once we've placed our brunch orders at a nearby restaurant. My sister hardly ever goes out to eat, mostly because our parents are paying for her meal plan in the dorms, but whenever I come visit, it's tradition to head out to brunch. As far as I can recall, Nicki has always come with, a breath of minty fresh air every single time.

I order pretty much the meatiest platter on the menu while Nicki and Ellie settle for pancakes and eggs.

"I'm good on those details," I interject, and both ladies laugh.

"She's been working on this for like a year," Nicki says. "Let her bask in the glory of the long game."

I laugh at how short a year sounds when I compare it to four in my own mind. "Okay, then. How was it, Ellie? Is he your Prince Charming? Your happy ending?" I think twice about that last one. "Wait. I don't want to know if you gave him a happy ending. That's way too much information."

My sister is forever going on about finding her Prince Charming. Between her notebooks filled with pink, glittery stickers and her penchant for fairy tales, she's the epitome of the Disney Princess who deserves her happy ending someday. But, like, the *real* kind, not the sexual one. I don't want to know about that.

Now Nicki, on the other hand...I'll take any happy endings she's willing to dish out. Sexual or otherwise.

I realize they're nineteen and young, and I'm only twenty-one, but I've been thinking a lot about the future as I get ready to graduate and move into the next phase of my life. It's hard *not* to think about that stuff, and as exciting as having women in every city calling my name sounds, that's not the life I want.

I know what I want. I think I've always known it, too. I've wanted to play football professionally since I was ten, and I worked my ass off to make it happen.

I've wanted Nicki Blair by my side since I was seventeen...and I'm going to work my ass off to make that happen, too.

Ellie's eyes widen a little on a chuckle. "Josh!" she berates playfully. She clears her throat and rolls her eyes. "I don't know if he's prince or frog material just yet. It was one slightly drunken but very steamy kiss one night after over a year of knowing each other. But all signs point to prince."

My eyes flick to Nicki's lips as I think about a slightly drunken, steamy kiss with her.

My dick tries to poke his way into my internal dialogue, and I force my thoughts to getting smashed by a defender. Some guys think of baseball while others think of apple pie to tame the beast, but for me, it's football. Obviously, considering it's my entire life and has been since I was six and will be until the day I retire...with any luck, anyway.

Our server drops off some coffee and juice, and I drink down half the orange juice in one long gulp. "So what's the plan for the rest of the day? You got more plans to see Prince Trevor?"

It's my not-so-subtle way of figuring out how to get Nicki alone. And speaking of Nicki, my eyes edge over to hers while my sister obliviously chatters on. She's looking at me, too. A heated moment passes between us.

"Maybe at another party tonight, but since my big oaf of a brother is visiting, this afternoon is out."

I turn toward Ellie and raise a brow. "Oaf?"

She lifts a shoulder. "I thought it was nicer than *ogre*."

"Did you just compare me to Shrek?" I glance over at Nicki, who's watching our exchange with a playful gleam in her eye.

"You have, like, the biggest hands I've ever seen and you're six foot five," my sister tells me. "You're basically a monster."

"I think I might've preferred *ogre* to *monster*," I admit. "And just to prove I'm not a monster, please don't let me stand in your way of seeing Prince Charming. I'm happy to find something to entertain myself." My eyes flick to Nicki again, and a little color stains her pretty cheeks. "In fact, I have a big paper due Monday that I haven't even started, so if you want some Trevor time this afternoon, I can work on that."

"That's the most boring thing I've ever heard. You come to visit your sister for the weekend and you're going to hang in my room working on a paper?" Ellie asks.

I shrug. "I'm just being the gentleman who's opening time for you to chase your man."

And opening up my chance at a moment alone with Nicki. I refrain from mentioning the ulterior motive.

Ellie twists her lips. She pauses, and then she shakes her head. "No. Forget it. I can't ask you to do that."

"It's fine, Elle," I say, shortening her name to make myself sound even more sincere. "Really, I don't mind. I'm tired after a long week anyway. Workouts have been grueling ever since Coach hooked me up with a former pro player to get me league ready."

She sighs. "Are you sure?"

I glance at Nicki. A small smile plays at her lips as I answer my sister. "I'm sure."

CHAPTER 4

"I just got a text and he said I should meet him at his house," Ellie says once we're back at her and Nicki's room. She looks frantically through her closet. "What do I wear? What the hell are you supposed to wear to an impromptu afternoon date at someone's house? Is this even a date? Like, is he going to kiss me again? Or are we going to get naked? Do I need sexy underwear?"

"Brother still in the room," I remind her, and Nicki giggles at the two of us before she takes charge in the sexiest way I may have ever seen.

"You," Nicki says, pointing to me. "Get your laptop out, put your earbuds in, and get started on your paper. You don't need to hear our conversation right now. And you," she says, pointing to Ellie while I do as I'm told. "Take a deep breath."

Ellie freezes and breathes in deeply.

"Good." Nicki nods, and then she grabs Ellie's hands. "Oh my God, you're going to Trevor's for an afternoon date!" They allow a moment of a girly freak out dance, and I can't help my chuckle. Then Nicki says, "Wear your lucky pink sweater and jeans. Keep it casual." I slip my earbuds in, so I have no idea what they say next, but I really do get to work on my paper as I sit at Ellie's desk.

A half hour later, Ellie yanks an earbud out of my ear. "Text me if you need anything, okay? Otherwise I'll be back by dinner."

I hold up both hands. "Don't rush on my account. If you're not back and I'm hungry, I have a car. I can find a place to eat."

She tosses her arms around my neck. "Thank you," she says, and she bounds toward the door. I slide my other earbud out the moment the door clicks shut behind her, and Nicki glances over at me, her cheeks pink and her lips parted and her chest moving up and down with each breath she takes.

I close my laptop and stand. I gaze across the room at her. "I think we have a conversation from this morning to finish."

She clears her throat but doesn't answer, and I can't help but wonder if it's because words elude her or if there's some other reason. But I know I didn't misread the situation. She told me she wanted me to kiss her...and now I'm going to.

"I like you, Nicki," I say softly. I take a step toward her, and she takes a step back.

"I like you, too," she murmurs. The door is mere inches behind her, and she moves until she's against it with each step I take—not because I'm a menacing threat, but like she wants to prolong this chase between us.

Once this happens, everything changes.

"I've liked you a long time, and as hard as I try to get you out of my head, I haven't been able to." Another step.

Her eyes soften in surprise. "The feeling's mutual."

Another step. She's out of room and I'm out of patience.

I've been waiting a long, long time for this moment. My heart races erratically in my chest. It's more nerve racking than taking the field even though she told me she wants this, too.

I finally reach her, and she looks up at me as I stand within inches of her. She's tall at five foot eight, but I still tower over her with nine inches on her. And I've got another nine inches waiting for her somewhere else if she wants it.

Her blue eyes are clear and a little anxious, too, and I want to know what's on her mind. I tuck some hair behind her ear like I did last night. "What are you thinking?" I murmur.

She blinks rapidly a few times, like she's scared to tell me, but then she blurts it out. "I've just wanted this for so long that I can't believe it's really about to happen. What if it doesn't work out? What if it feels like I'm kissing a friend? Will it make things weird with Ellie?"

"Is that a risk you're willing to take?" My voice is low and raspy, a sexual sort of deep that I didn't even know I had the power to do.

She doesn't answer with words. Instead, she loops her arms around my neck and pulls me down to her, and our lips brush together with the sweetest, most tender touch at first.

It doesn't feel like I'm kissing a friend.

It feels like I'm kissing the only woman I'll ever kiss again.

I wrap my arms around her waist and pull her tightly against me as the tender brush of lips turns a little hotter, a little more urgent. Our mouths both firm as I open mine, my tongue moving out to tangle with hers. It starts slow, but the passion builds as the arms looped around my neck move to explore. Fingernails trace down my back and slip under my shirt, and the feel of her chilled hands on my warm back are at once rattling and calming.

I break the kiss long enough to murmur, "Jesus Christ, your hands are cold."

She chuckles and moves them further up my back as our mouths meet back up again. I slip my hands under her shirt, too, and she stops kissing me long enough to pull off her shirt and toss it to the floor. She's taking the lead, and I'm letting her move at the pace that's comfortable for her—which is far faster than I would've taken it, but I am one hundred percent on board with it.

She pulls my shirt off, too, and runs her hands along the ridges of my abdomen.

We kiss some more, both of us without shirts, and I unsnap her bra and toss it to the ground. My hands have a field day on her breasts, the perfect cupful in my palms, and then I lean down further to give my lips a taste. She moans and leans back against the door as I suck her nipple into my mouth, my tongue swirling around the tight tip, and then I let it go only to hoist her up. She wraps her legs around my midsection and I carry the two of us over to the futon, kissing between her breasts as I navigate my way through the small room.

I lie her down then climb over the top of her, and we make out there for a minute or an hour. Time doesn't matter when Nicki is in my arms. It becomes this inconsequential thing that passes way too quickly anyway.

Her hands are warmer now, and they trail down to the buckle of my belt. I sit up a bit to let her have her way with me, and she opens my belt, flicks the button of my jeans, and lowers the zipper before reaching in.

"Fuck," I hiss as she strokes me, and then she reaches her other hand in and cups my balls. I'm about to lose it, but shooting off early wouldn't be nearly as much fun as driving into her for the next hour.

I move my hips back, and she lets go of me. I need a minute to recover, and while I do that, I slide my hand into the space between her skin and her jeans. I keep going further until I find the silky top of her panties, and I go lower until I slide a finger across her wet clit. I dip inside her, driving my finger in and out as I watch her face twist in pleasure. She snags her bottom lip between her teeth, moaning as she gives into the pleasure.

"I want you," she pants.

That's the signal. I give the lady what she wants.

I pull her jeans down her legs along with her panties and toss them to the side.

"There's condoms in that little jewelry box on my dresser," she murmurs, and I find one and shove my own jeans down just enough to release the beast. I roll it on in the space of about four seconds.

I return and hover over her, my lips colliding again with hers, and she reaches down to guide me to her entrance. The fact that she's so confident in her movements just makes her even more beautiful to me, and my chest tightens with emotion that this is actually happening.

I slide into her, and as her warmth squeezes me like a vice, I get this feeling like I'm home. No matter where in the world I am, as long as she's by my side, it'll be home.

I drive into her, the futon hard and unforgiving beneath us as our moans mingle in the air into a symphony of passion and desire. She flexes her hips to meet mine, and the nerves dissipate as they're replaced with something rich and meaningful.

I'm only moving in and out of her for a few short minutes when I reach down to thumb her clit between us. That's the magic button, and her entire body clenches onto me. Her pussy squeezes my dick, and my balls draw up as I feel the familiar release edging its way toward me. I grunt and growl, and then I roar as the pleasure overtakes me and I fly into an intense, mind-numbing climax.

It's over far too soon, but my gut tells me that won't be the only time we do that this weekend.

In fact, as I settle onto the futon beside her, my legs too long for it as my body scrunches into a strange angle to fit, I see our entire future before us.

"Whoa," she murmurs as we both fight to regain our breath.

"Yeah. Whoa."

She chuckles. "That was..." She trails off, suddenly timid when she wasn't before.

"What?" I prod. I lean up to look at her face. Her cheeks are flushed and her lips are swollen and her hair is a halo around her head. I don't think I've ever seen a more beautiful sight than a freshly fucked Nicki.

"The best," she says simply, and I grin.

"You're damn right it was."

Once we're clothed again and standing awkwardly across from each other, I have this sudden urge to be fully honest with her. I clear my throat. "That was..."

She holds up a hand to cut me off. "The best," she finishes. "It really was." She looks away, her eyes melancholy. "And I get it, Josh, really. You don't have to say any more. I know you're heading off to the NFL and graduating college and the last thing you want is some college chick holding you back. I promise it won't change anything between your sister and me now that we've gotten that out of our systems."

"Out of our systems?" I repeat.

"Well, yeah. The sex. We've done it, and now we can move on. Let's just put it behind us so we don't have to have the awkward conversation, okay?"

I grab both her hands in mine and duck down to try to catch her eyes. "No, Nicki. That's not okay."

Her brows dip, and it's her turn to be confused. "You want to talk it out?" She gives me a doubtful glance as she moves to pull her hands out of my grasp. I don't let her, instead tightening my hold there.

"I don't want it to be a one-time thing. You're not some college chick holding me back. You know what's holding me back? Lying about how I really feel about you for the last four years."

The crease between her brows deepens. "How do you feel?"

I press my lips together as anxiety pierces my chest. I clear my throat. *Tell her. Just tell her.* "I'm pretty sure I'm in love with you, and I want you to be a part of my future. I want you by my side when I get taken in the first round of the draft. I want you cheering me on in the stands when I play. I want to see where this can go and what sorts of mountains we can climb together."

"Together?" she repeats.

I nod as I finally drop her hands and pull her closer to me. "Together." I lean down, and I'm centimeters from taking her mouth beneath mine again when I murmur, "But only if it's what you want, too."

I back up enough for our eyes to lock, and a pretty smile graces her lips. "It's all I've wanted for four years, Josh Nolan."

One side of my mouth lifts up, and then my mouth crashes down to hers.

We're interrupted when the door opens with such brute force that it knocks loudly into the wall, reminiscent of the way Nicki walked into the room last night when I was asleep.

"Oh Jesus," Ellie mutters, catching the two of us mid-embrace. At least she walked in *now* and not ten minutes ago when we were both naked and fucking on a futon. "Did you two *finally* admit how you feel about each other? Because I've been waiting for *years* for that to happen but does it really have to be right this second?"

Nicki laughs gingerly as she backs away from me, and I feel a wicked sense of loss. Though I guess if she's still got two years in college and I'm playing pro football, having her move out of my arms is something we're going to have to get used to.

Ellie wrinkles her nose. "Did you two have sex?"

Nicki turns bright red as she changes the subject without answering. "What are you doing back here so soon?"

"Turns out Trevor's *not* Prince Charming," she mutters. "Total frog material. A big, fat, warty frog."

"Oh?" I ask. "Why's that?"

"Would Prince Charming casually grab your hand and stick it on his pants to show you that he's hard literally less than ten minutes after you walk through the door?" she asks. She wrinkles her nose again. "It was just...not sexy. At all. It was rude."

"God, Ellie, I could do without the details." I make a face. "But no, he doesn't sound like a very nice guy. Remind me of his address so I can kick his ass before I head back to U of I."

Both ladies laugh, and that familiar laughter of my sister and my girl is one I know I'll hear time and again.

Now we just have to work on finding Ellie her own Prince Charming.

"The Secret Santa Crush"

A SHORT STORY PREQUEL TO
THE VEGAS ACES SERIES

Originally published in the
WINTER LOVE ANTHOLOGY

Ellie has a huge crush on a coworker, and she just happens to draw his name in the office Secret Santa gift exchange. Will she get up the nerve to finally confess her feelings?

CHAPTER 1

I stare at the name on the little slip of paper.

Todd.

Or, as I call him in my own head, *Hot Todd.*

I read the rest of the details on the paper.

Likes: strong coffee with a splash of cream, maple donuts, and dark beer.
Dislikes: unoriginality, water slides, and peanut butter.

Dislikes *peanut butter?* What the hell is wrong with this guy? Who doesn't like the creamy deliciousness that is peanut butter? Hell, most mornings I grab a couple spoonfuls from the jar (if I'm feeling fancy. Other times I just scoop with finger-forks) and call it breakfast.

I look across the conference room at him. I set my chin in my palm as I sigh and stare a little dreamily.

Nothing. *Nothing* is wrong with him.

His dislikes were supposed to be warnings of things not to get him in the Secret Santa shindig the office is holding, but instead he had to write things like *unoriginality*...which makes me think giving him the things he wrote as his *likes* on the list wouldn't be very original. And I want him to like me. I want to impress him.

Why?

Because I love him.

Okay, *love* might be a little strong, but look at him. Jesus Christ. He's a Prince Charming if I've ever seen one. He's got the glowing blue eyes, the perfectly coiffed longish-on-the-top dirty blond hair, and the lean frame that surely holds the kind of six pack you don't drink.

I sigh once more, and then I tear my gaze away when Brittany nudges me.

"What?" I whisper.

"Stop staring," she whispers back.

I giggle, and the big boss, Warren, gives us one of those cursory glares that are usually reserved for teachers trying to silence unruly schoolchildren. He's introducing some lady but I'm too preoccupied by what's on my slip of paper to bother listening.

We're both quiet until the end of the meeting, and when we're released back to our offices, Brittany follows me into mine.

"Who'd you get?" we both say at the same time, and then we both burst into laughter.

"Hot Todd," I confess.

She narrows her eyes at me. "How'd you manage to fix that one?"

I shrug innocently. "I didn't! I swear, it was total luck of the draw, but honestly, Brit, I don't think it's all that lucky. Now I have to find ways to impress him every single day next week. Are you even kidding me with this? It would've been better if *he* drew *my* name."

"I got Karen," she says, and we both roll our eyes.

Karen is Warren's sister, true nepotism at its finest, and she's not only the office tattletale but also the office gossip. She picks and picks until she gets a tiny nugget of information and then she blasts it back to the big boss who, most of the time, doesn't even care...but it still makes the rest of us look bad.

"What are her likes?" I ask. "Wait, lemme guess. Um, insider information, working for a sibling, and..."

"Gossip?" Brittany supplies. We both laugh again, and she shakes her head. She reads off the little slip of paper she drew. "No. She likes red wine, nachos, and hot chocolate."

I raise a brow. "Sounds like someone's angling for a happy hour invite with those first two."

"At least those are easy. What does Todd like?"

I've already memorized my slip of paper, so I repeat the list from memory. "Strong coffee with a splash of cream, maple donuts, and dark beer. But he dislikes unoriginality, so I feel like I shouldn't get him those things."

She shrugs. "But if he likes them, at least you can supply a daily treat. We'll brainstorm and come up with something really ducking good for the Friday exchange."

I giggle when she says *ducking*, our auto-correct and when-we're-in-the-office professionally correct choice curse word.

"What are you getting Karen for the Friday exchange?" I ask.

"A little classiness, but I haven't figured out how to wrap it yet," she deadpans.

We both cackle, and then Warren appears in my doorway. Brit and I exchange a quick wide-eye glance as our laughter simmers down pretty quickly.

The woman by his side is the one he was talking about in the meeting when I wasn't paying attention. She's a woman with a stern look on her face that says she means *all business* and clearly isn't impressed by the fact that two adult women are cackling like hyenas in this office when we should be pumping out work to earn more money for this firm.

"Ladies," Warren says, his voice a total warning that we need to pull it together. "I'd like to introduce you to Belinda. As I mentioned in the meeting, she's our newest team member and your new boss. Belinda, this is Brittany, whose office is down the hall, and Ellie." He indicates each of us as he says our names, but wait just a hot second.

Our *new boss*? Son of a duck. I didn't even know we were in the line of that particular fire.

We have a boss. Darryl. What happened to him? Dammit, I really need to pay attention in those meetings instead of staring across the room at Todd.

But he's just so dreamy.

"Lovely to meet you," Brittany says sticking out a hand toward Belinda and immediately schooling her features to professional. Seeing the quick transition almost makes me dissolve into laughter again, but I attempt to do the same.

I clear my throat. "Sorry for the loud laughter in here," I say. "We were just discussing who we got in the Secret Santa gift exchange."

Belinda's brows dip. "Secret Santa?" she repeats. "Shouldn't that be...a secret?"

Okay, so this lady already hates me. "Well, yeah," I say, back peddling, and then because I'm a ducking idiot who can't think clearly when I'm on the spot, I blurt, "but I got the guy I have a total crush on and I don't know what to get him so I figured Brit could give me some advice."

Brittany's jaw drops. Warren looks uncomfortable. Belinda looks like she sucked on a lemon.

Yep, no good way to get out of that one.

I just admitted to my new boss that I have a crush on a coworker, that Brittany and I are friends who will use work time to talk about personal matters, and that I blurt out stupid shit when I'm on the spot.

Looks like good ol' Belinda and I are starting off on the wrong foot.

"Let's save the water cooler chatter for after work, yes ladies?" Belinda says, and we both nod. "And let's get back to work. I'll be dropping in on both of you today to discuss your current projects, and since we're already here, I'll start with Ellie."

"Of course," Brittany says, and then she rushes out of my office probably so she can prepare to look good in front of the new boss.

Traitor.

Warren takes off, too, and my heart starts thumping. Oh God. Am I going to lose my job?

I won't get to see Hot Todd anymore if I do.

I mean, that shouldn't be my *top* concern, exactly, but it's the first thought that comes to mind. Maybe I should think about how I'll pay my rent on my tiny Chicago apartment without a job, or if I'll have to move back in with my parents who are close by in the suburbs, or maybe I could relocate to Las Vegas, where my brother, who's engaged to my best friend, plays pro football. But I don't think about those things. I think about Todd.

"All right, Miss—" Belinda begins as she takes a seat in the chair facing my desk. I sit behind the desk.

"Nolan," I supply, and she nods.

"Miss Nolan. Fill me in on what you're working on."

I want to ask why she's my new boss and where the hell Darryl went. I suppose that's something Warren covered in the meeting, but the second I saw *Todd* at the top of my Secret Santa draw, my attention bowed the hell out.

I draw in a deep breath and dive into the subject matter I'm passionate about. "I'm at different stages on several projects. My forte is branding and social media, and I often work hand-in-hand with others in the office who provide other facets of publicity to a project. Today, for example, I'm researching the ideal client for Arcadia Architecture, and I'll pass my findings off to Paul, who will create a pitch. He'll run that by me, and together we'll come up with a narrative by which we'll enhance and build the company's reputation based on their goals." I try to hit all the buzzwords as I go into more detail about some of my other projects, and at least she has stopped looking at me like I'm an annoying nuisance by the time I'm done going through everything.

"Impressive, Miss Nolan. I'll be sending out some questions regarding your personal goals and how you can work to achieve them. Give it some thought, but I'd like your responses by tomorrow morning." She stands and pushes in the chair as she turns to leave.

Goals and how I'm going to achieve them by morning. Excellent. I'll just drop everything so I can get that for her. "I'll have it to you tonight," I say instead. I add one last thing. "So great meeting you. I'm excited to work together to reach those goals."

She purses her lips and raises a brow, and then she leaves while meanwhile I'm left to decode what that final look was supposed to mean.

I don't get much time to ponder it, though, because Todd's hot, lean frame fills my doorway just as I turn to my computer to resume my research.

I mean, honestly, it's a wonder I get anything done around here with all these distractions.

"Hey, Ellie," he says, and I memorize the cadence of his deep voice as it wraps around my name so I can replay it tonight when I'm home alone in my quiet apartment.

"Hey, Todd," I say. "Come on in."

"Did you meet the new boss yet?" he asks.

We've become friendly with one another over the last year or so since he started working here. We share the occasional flirty conversation, but mostly we've kept it professional. *Mostly.* Sometimes those fun group happy hours turn into raunchy territory when we've all had enough to drink, but he's never made a move.

I want him to make a move.

I want *him.*

I nod. "She just left my office about three minutes ago. What happened to Darryl?"

He laughs as he steps into my office, filling it with a brightness that wasn't there before. Or maybe some heat. Definitely some heat. "Don't you ever pay attention in meetings?"

I refrain from pointing out that it's actually *his* fault I wasn't paying attention.

"Sometimes," I mutter. "But honestly, what happened in that meeting that we couldn't have done over email?"

He slides into the same chair Belinda occupied moments ago. "Well, introducing the new boss while explaining what happened to the old one, for one thing."

I laugh. "And? Survey says?"

"Sounds like Darryl was in line for a promotion for months. This has all been happening behind the scenes and Belinda left a competitor to come work with us." He swings his head just a little so his hair re-aligns into that perfect coif. God, he's hot. "But I didn't come here to talk about Darryl and Belinda."

"You didn't?" I ask, and I know there's way more hope in my tone than there should be, but I can't freaking help it.

This is it.

I cross my fingers that rest in my lap, and my thighs clench together at just the *thought* that he's finally going to ask me on a date. I've been waiting for this moment for months.

My lips form into a smile and I'm rehearsing all the ways to say *yes* in my mind.

He shakes his head, his hair moving just a little, and his blue eyes continue to glow in my direction. "No. I came to ask where you're at on the Carlisle Jewelers rebrand."

"I'd love to!" I say with way too much enthusiasm, and his brows dip in confusion as his eyes meet mine. What he actually asked versus what I heard in my head finally registers. I clear my throat and amend my reply. "Uh, I mean, I'd love to update you."

My cheeks burn. My stomach churns.

I never learn.

CHAPTER 2

Brittany spends the weekend at my place and together we sort through the complete enigma of what to get Hot Todd for the Secret Santa thing.

The rules were that we give a smaller gift each weekday, and we give a bigger gift on Friday at the office holiday party, which kicks off our annual holiday break. I'm always thankful for that break, and not just because we get a week off work. Also because if I make a complete fool of myself at the holiday party (who, me?), we have a nice little time buffer where we don't have to see the people we work with.

It was completely optional to participate in the Secret Santa and limits were set for each gift—no more than twenty bucks on the small gifts, no more than a hundred on the big one.

Still, though, that leaves me with wide open options, limited time, and zero ideas...except for strong coffee with a splash of cream, maple donuts, and dark beer, of course, to show off exactly how unoriginal I am.

"Okay, but you *know* him," Brittany says. "You've studied him more than you've studied some of your clients, so tell me everything you know and we'll figure this out."

I look up at the ceiling as I name all the things I can think of off the top of my head. "He seems to like the color blue because he wears it almost every day *and* all his desk supplies are blue, probably to match his gorgeous eyes or maybe because he's a big Cubs fan and everything is Cubbie Blue. Every time that waffle food truck drives by the office, he runs down to be the first in line. He listens to music while he works. He puts hot sauce on tacos. He drives a BMW. He smells like the forest after a fresh rain mixed with chopped wood."

Brittany holds up a hand. "Okay, I think we're good," she says. "A mini waffle maker, a selection of hot sauces, fancy earbuds or some kind of earbud holder, and then fill in the gaps with whatever's left on his list." She ticks off each item as she says them.

I stare at her with my jaw hanging open. "You're a lifesaver. And what for the big gift?"

"Do you have any ideas?"

"I could spread myself out somewhere and he could do whatever he wants to me," I suggest, my brows raised in hope.

She laughs, and she pulls out her phone. "You think that's valued at a hundred bucks?" she asks, and I shoot her a wicked glare. "Kidding, kidding. Something with the Cubs maybe?"

I look at her blankly. I'm not much of a sports girl despite having a brother who plays professional football for the Vegas Aces.

"Okay, let's see here. Gifts for men under one hundred dollars." She taps around as she searches. "I'll read some and you stop me if you like one of them. Pocketknife, clothes, shoes, whiskey, water bottle, phone charger, flashlight, flask, decanter set, man box—"

"Man box?" I ask, interrupting her.

"Yeah, like a big crate filled with all sorts of gifts."

"That would just mean I have to come up with even *more* ideas." I wave a hand and make a face. "Pass."

"No, there's a whole place where you just pick out what you think he'd like. So if he likes dark beer, they have boxes that have different kinds of beers in them."

"Interesting," I murmur. "How fast can they ship?"

She finds the site and looks around. "It could be here by Thursday with priority shipping."

"What about a man box with a little coupon booklet from me?"

Brittany bursts into uncontrollable laughter. "Oh my God, Ellie," she says when she finally composes herself. "Like this coupon's good for a kiss? What are we, twelve?"

"I thought it was a cute idea," I grumble, my cheeks burning at the thought that a kiss was *exactly* the sort of thing I had in mind. I like the idea of letting him know I'm interested through these gifts.

"Maybe a decade ago. But Todd is a man."

"Okay, fine," I concede, pretending like I'm not totally offended by her judgment. "Then how do I both impress him and let him know I'm interested?"

"The waffle maker and hot sauce and earbud ideas. Things that show you've been paying attention. He'll get the hint," she says.

"Will he? Guys aren't always that observant, Brit. I've been sending off all the vibes for months and I'm still getting nothing back."

"Trust me," she says.

Famous last words, am I right?

Thank goodness for the quick shipping that comes with online ordering, because on Monday morning, I have a wrapped mini waffle maker that put me out twelve bucks plus a little bag of waffle mix. I wrapped it last night and even included a little bow, and I decided to just go for it as I typed out a label to fix onto the gift: *To Todd, my Secret ~~Santa~~ Crush.*

When I say I decided to "just go for it," what I really mean is that I printed the label and didn't use it. But I have it in case I want to use it later in the week.

I chickened out. Instead, I just wrote *Todd* on the first gift.

I stealthily drop it on the front desk when I walk into the office, and Myrna, the receptionist, will make sure he gets it. When I walk into my office, I can't help my wide smile.

My blinds are already open. Letting light stream in from the window is the first thing I do every morning when I walk in.

A venti Starbucks cup sits on top of a wrapped box on my desk. As I get closer, I also see a bit of red and green glittery confetti in the shape of Christmas trees, and I read the label on the cup.

Venti nonfat white mocha extra whip.

Yeah, I get it. Brittany *always* makes fun of me for getting extra whipped cream with a nonfat drink, but I feel like they cancel each other out.

I can't help my wide smile, and I also can't help but wonder if Brittany lied about who she got. Who else would know my particular Starbucks order? I didn't write it on my card.

In fact, I scribbled some nonsense on my card.

I like fluffy socks, popcorn, and glitter.

I dislike banana-flavored food, horses, and turtlenecks.

To be clear, I love bananas. But fake banana flavoring? Not my thing. And you'd dislike horses too if you were thrown off one when you were a child. Okay, that's dramatic. I fell off, but still. I'm not a fan.

See? Nowhere in that list do we find my Starbucks order.

I take a sip and practically melt back into my chair. I don't care *who* my Secret Santa is. I just love whoever it is. Even if it's Karen.

I go for the present next because I'm a child who can't wait through reading a card to see what's inside the gift. I tear the neat Christmas paper from the box and rip the cardboard to get inside faster, and I pull out a pair of the softest, fluffiest hot pink socks I've ever seen. I want to slip off my heels and walk around the office in them for the rest of the day, to be honest.

But I feel like Belinda would have a thing or two to say about that.

I finally go for the card.

As Christmas comes closer you'll find out who
is your Secret Santa and has a thing for you

I roll my eyes.

Yep. It's *definitely* Brittany. I just don't know how she managed to get me to believe her lie that she drew Karen. She's usually easier to see through than that.

Even if I *wanted* to believe it could be someone like Todd, I know it isn't for one very obvious reason: he's a loud and proud Dunkin drinker. He'd never be caught dead picking up a drink for me from my preferred coffee vendor.

I don't get time to dwell on it because we have a standing team meeting on Monday mornings. I haven't even powered up my computer yet to check my email, but I don't want to be late. It'll be the first meeting Belinda is running, so I'm anxious to get there on time and not make a fool of myself, but knowing me, I'll manage to find a way.

And I definitely do.

I stride into the conference room with my Starbucks cup in hand, and everyone already gathered in the room turns to look at me...including Belinda, who cuts off in the middle of a sentence.

Wait a minute. I check the clock on the wall. I'm three minutes early.

Belinda stops talking. She looks sternly at the cup in my hand before glancing back up at me. "I see you had time to stop for coffee," she scolds, and I feel about three inches tall.

"I'm so sorry," I say. "It's a Secret Santa gift."

Her stern look seems to deepen. "Get to meetings on time or don't bother coming at all."

I slide into the open seat next to Brittany as my cheeks flame. I shoot my best friend a special glare. "Why didn't you tell me it started earlier?" I hiss once the attention isn't on me anymore and Belinda resumes whatever I interrupted.

"I emailed you," she hisses back. "Didn't you get it?"

"No!" I whisper-yell. "Who emails these days?"

"Someone who accidentally left her phone at home."

"Ladies," Belinda warns, and oh my God could this day get any worse?

Yes, yes it can. I look up and my eyes meet Todd's across the table. He smirks at me, and I just bet he's Belinda's number one guy while I'm on her shit list. He's *laughing* at me, and I'm over here feeling like a complete and utter idiot. An unprepared, misinformed idiot.

At least I have my coffee.

CHAPTER 3

"You didn't get the email?" Todd asks. I squirm in my chair, but it's not because of his question.

It's just the fact that he's here in my office. Among other things, that fact is making me hot. For him.

While I just want to curl up with my cozy socks from my Secret Santa, I can't. Todd and I were given a project to work on together, and while we have many projects in the works, for some reason this one feels...different.

While my niche is branding and social media, Todd's is damage control. This career sometimes has a negative connotation to it—like clients only need us when they need to turn their image around. That may be true for the bad boys of Hollywood, but there's a lot more to it. Clients turn to us when they want to build or protect reputations, not just when they get themselves into trouble. But when they *do* get themselves into trouble, nine times out of ten, Todd's the guy with the answer.

When we acquired a company that needed quick damage control and a total rebrand, it was natural to put the two of us on the project together.

So what's making me hot?

It's for a lingerie store.

They're all over the news since some actor slept with a prostitute and photos leaked with him holding bags from their store while he ushered the woman into a hotel. While all press is good press...this is a high-end store that wants a classy image, not a dirty one associated with paying for sexual encounters.

It's up to Todd and me to turn that around for them.

Yes, you heard that right.

I have to talk about prostitutes and lingerie and probably sex with the guy I have an enormous crush on in a professional environment, and that's why it's hotter than hell in my office right now. I swear to God, this would only happen to me.

"I rushed in late this morning because I was wrapping my Secret Santa gift and didn't have a chance to check my email. Who starts meetings early on a Monday morning, anyway?" I grumble.

"I do," Belinda says from my doorway.

Oh ducking hell. Seriously?

She steps in. "And I expect you to be at them. You missed several important points, including the fact that our team meetings will start at eight-thirty now and they will take place on Mondays, Wednesdays, and Fridays. Timeliness is important to me, and I don't work well with people who don't take their responsibilities seriously."

"I take them very seriously," I protest, but she just purses her lips at me.

Fine. She's already judged me, she's berating me in front of my crush, and she hates me. Whatever. I can't get out of this one.

Prince Charming swoops in to save the day. "If I may, Belinda, Ellie is incredible at her job. In fact, we're meeting now to discuss the Clandestine account and she has some excellent rebrand ideas."

I try not to blush too hard at his compliments. Belinda raises an eyebrow with some sort of harrumph noise.

"I'd like to start over with you, Belinda," I say, extending an olive branch, because let's be honest here: I don't much care for her, either.

"I'm afraid that's impossible," she says. Who says that? I'm fuming as she continues. "As a professional in public relations, you of all people should know that first impressions are everything. With that said, I'll expect you to be on time and for your focus to be on work rather than gossip. Todd, have a report to me by the end of the day on the Billings account, and Ellie, have a report to me by the end of the day on Masterview. I'll expect the plan for Clandestine on my desk in two hours."

She spins out of my office, and Todd and I look at each other.

"Two hours?" I repeat.

He chuckles. "She really hates you."

I'm not laughing as the two of us get to work...but I *am* still squirming.

* * *

The next morning, I set the wrapped set of hot sauces on Myrna's desk, and I find another gift on my own desk.

More coffee, this time with two cake pops (which take all of about six seconds to scarf down), and another small box. This one has a gorgeous winter scarf inside, and the card has a cute little poem again.

This little gift (and the coffee) is just for you
from your Secret Santa...bet you can't guess who

On Wednesday, I drop off the earbuds I ordered for Todd. I still chicken out on giving him the special tag I made, and I think for a second about how cute the poems on my own cards have been. But I don't want to be a copy-cat. On my desk is coffee again and a box with a matching hat and mittens for yesterday's scarf. The poem today reads:

I can't give you any hints to who I might be
But pretty soon you'll get to see

Thursday is the random gift I bought as I tried to be original based on what I know about him. I got him some Cubs pint glasses that he can use with the dark beer I ordered in his man box. Waiting for me Thursday is more coffee, a stationery set with a monogrammed E in glitter along with various glittery stickers and pens. It's a thoughtful and original gift from someone who seems to know me pretty well (Brittany). I can't actually wait to add some of the glitter stickers to my bullet journal, which goes everywhere with me. And, of course, there's another poem.

Tomorrow I will be revealed
No longer will I be concealed
I'll finally tell you just who I might be
But only if you agree to a date with me

I still one hundred and fifty-five percent believe it's Brittany. Or, like, at least ninety-eight percent.

On Friday, I bring in a Dunkin coffee with a splash of cream and some fresh maple donuts for Todd, and on my desk is another Starbucks cup along with a small box. I tear off the paper and find a silver necklace with a sparkly elephant charm.

Nowhere on my paper did I write that elephants are my favorite animal, but they are. Brittany managed to combine glitter *and* elephants in one fell swoop, and I have to admit, I'm impressed. I tear open the card.

I know you think I'm just a friend
But tonight is where that friendship ends

Where our friendship ends? Brittany has been taking this secret admirer thing a little too far. I get that she's trying to make a joke, trying to make it look like she's a he and he's got a thing for me...but I can't think of a single person in this office who I really believe would write poems like this for me, nor is there a single person aside from Todd I'd accept a date from. They're either old, married, or not my type.

Since it's the day of our holiday party and the day before our week-long break begins, Warren always sends a memo at noon that we're released from work early. It's a little extra gift from him and it allows us time to get ready for the party.

I'm waiting on pins and needles for that time to come, staring at the clock and fingering my new elephant necklace when an email from Belinda comes through two minutes ahead of Warren's.

Ellie,

I'll need three new ideas for the Masterview logo rebrand before you leave for break. The client wants more options.

-Belinda

My jaw drops open.

Three new ideas two minutes before the big boss emails us to let us know we can leave early?

Is she ducking kidding me?

CHAPTER 4

I don't have time for the fancy treatment I wanted to do to my hair, but I manage to slip into the glittery red dress I chose for this event. I rush into the party only a few minutes late, my hair straight instead of curly where it falls to the middle of my back. I beeline for the bar and find Brittany, who stopped by my place to pick up the man box and my dress since I was stuck at work until nearly our regular quitting time of five o'clock. The man box is actually a cute little wooden crate that says MAN BOX all over it, and inside there's a nice selection of twelve different dark beers plus a random selection of downloads for six "manly" movies.

"You look gorge," she says to me, already sipping some red wine.

I opt for white, placing my order before I turn to my friend, who went with a green dress that sets off her green eyes. "You do, too. And hey, thanks for stopping by my place."

"Of course," she says. "He's going to love the box. And Karen is going to love her hot chocolate assortment." She giggles.

"You can be honest with me now," I say. I've pretended all week like I didn't think it was her. "I know you really got me and not Karen."

Her brows dip, and she shakes her head. "No, babe. I have Karen. I literally bought her a hundred dollars' worth of various hot chocolate mixes."

I tilt my head and stare at her in utter confusion. "But if it's not you..." I trail off, not sure where I'm going with this.

She winks at me like she has a secret.

"Oh my God," I say. "You know who it is! It's Kevin, isn't it? Tell me. Is it Kevin?" Kevin's this super nice guy in accounting who's three years younger than me and a little on the guy who loves video games, *Star Wars*, and Capri Suns too much side for me. In other words, he's too young for me and not my type at all.

But he stares at me in meetings the same way I stare at Todd.

She shrugs. "Guess you'll find out when you open your gift."

"You're the absolute worst," I mutter, and she just laughs.

When I turn around, I literally bump into a broad, warm chest.

"Oof," I say stupidly, while the offending chest lets out the sexiest little grunt I think these ears have ever witnessed. I look up into Todd's eyes, and I'm lost for a beat. He chuckles a little, and I'm torn between grateful I didn't spill my wine on him and melting into a puddle of lust as he grips my bicep to steady me. I could really just sink right there into his chest and cuddle in for a while.

I snap back to reality, though.

"I'm so sorry," I say, and I'm suddenly nervous. Was the man box a good idea? Was it stupid? Was it enough? Am *I* enough?

I blow out a breath as I brush away those insecurities. There ain't no room for them here at this party.

Although one question still plagues my mind. Should I have confessed my feelings for him in the card I wrote? I didn't, for the record. With Brittany's help, I wrote about ten different versions of cards ranging from friendly to raunchy, and I gave her one on the tame end to include with the gift.

Todd grins down at me. "No need to apologize."

He still hasn't let go of my arm, and did it just get about a thousand degrees hotter in here? In the middle of the moment we're having, goddamn Belinda walks by.

"Didn't realize you two were so close," she murmurs loud enough for us both to hear. Todd backs swiftly away after he makes sure I'm not going to fall over with my wine after bumping into him.

"Yes, we're friends," Todd emphasizes, and if that isn't a dagger right to the heart, I don't know what is.

"I'll remind you of the company's fraternization policy," she says.

"Yes, ma'am," Todd says. "I'm very familiar with it, and as I understand it, friendships and relationships are not prohibited provided they follow the guidelines set forth in the policy."

Her lips tip in what I can only assume is a bit of a smile at Todd. "Have fun tonight." Her words are directed more at him than me, but it's still basically the least-genuine wish of fun I've ever heard. I've never seen anyone smile like that before. It legit looked like a strain on her face to have to tip her mouth upward.

She turns to the bar, orders herself a cranberry juice, and I bolt away from both her and Todd, who apparently has the office fraternization policy memorized and probably thinks it's a horrible idea to date a colleague, particularly one like me who has such an obvious crush on him.

Why did I have to draw his name in this ducking Secret Santa thing?

We sit for dinner, and I spot Todd two tables away at what I can only describe as the Boy's Club table. All the twenty-something guys in our office sit together. I tick off each one in my head as I glance around: Kevin, Joe, Carl, Steve, Brad, Greg, Jeff, and, of course, Todd are all laughing at something as salad plates are placed in front of them. I glance around my table, a sort of Girl's Club I suppose with Brittany, myself, Claire, Myrna, Vickie, Nancy, Karen, and an empty chair next to me, which Belinda slides into as the salads are served.

She looks at me and sighs, and then she turns to the other side to chat up Claire and Myrna.

Well, whatever. She's the one who took the chair.

I give Brittany a look and focus on just eating my salad as I try not to let the nerves press to the surface—not the nerves of having my new boss who hates me sitting beside me, but the nerves for the unveiling of the Secret Santas.

I'd sort of forgotten that someone has been sending me gifts, too, and as much as I still think it's Brittany, she swears up and down that it isn't. So does someone in the office really have a crush on me? Or is someone playing a prank?

Brit and I both grab another drink before the main course is served, and then one more for good measure before dessert. I'm slightly tipsy and totally turned in my chair toward Brit and away from Belinda as we await the big speech Warren makes every year.

He finally stands and moves toward the Christmas tree at the front of the room. Presents are piled around it, courtesy of Myrna, who takes the lead on *everything* in our office, and Warren starts talking. "Happy Holidays, Windy City Public Relations!" he begins, and a whoop rises up from those of us who've had one or two more drinks than necessary.

It's me. I whoop. Brit does, too.

"Thank you for another outstanding year. Market trends show we're outperforming our competition, and we've got publicists banging down our doors to get a chance to work with us. That's on everyone gathered in this room, so thank you for all you do. Because of your efforts, you'll see a nice year-end bonus deposited with your next paycheck." He holds up a glass. "Congratulations, and keep up the excellent work. Cheers." He takes a sip of his amber liquid while the rest of us partake. Even Belinda takes a tiny sip of her cranberry juice.

"Without further ado, let's get to the Secret Santa gifts!" he says, and my heart starts pounding. "In keeping with tradition, we'll dismiss table by table. Come up, find your gift, and return to your table. Once everyone who has participated has their gifts, you may open them. We'll start with the table closest to the windows."

That's the Boy's Club table. I watch as Todd gets up, scans the gifts, and picks up the rather large box from me. He glances at the card with his name on it. I typed up the label on the envelope (just as I have all week so he wouldn't recognize my handwriting), and he returns to his table.

"Stop staring," Brit says, elbowing me, and I roll my eyes.

"I wasn't," I hiss. I was. I *totally* was.

Each table is dismissed to get their gifts, and my table is last. I find my name on a rather large box, and when I lift it, I find that it's actually pretty heavy. I'm excited to see what's inside as I take it back to my table. I pass right by Todd on my way by, and when I glance over at him, he's looking at me.

I swear to God, this *heat* passes between us. I'm positive I'm imagining things since I have such a monster crush on him, or maybe it's the wine, but I've never wanted something more to spark between us than I do right now.

I have to take a shot tonight. When he comes over to thank me for the gift, that's when I'll do it. I'll hit on him. I take a bolstering sip of my wine, and I'm grateful when I spot Belinda over by the bar instead of in the seat beside me. She didn't get in on the Secret Santa stuff since she started the same day we picked names, but could you even imagine if I pulled *her* name instead of Todd's?

"That's everyone," Warren says once we're all seated again. "Go ahead and open! And once again, happy holidays."

Everyone claps politely even though we're all like children who can't wait to rip into their presents on Christmas morning.

You'd think that for the first time this entire week, I would start with the card if for no other reason than to prove I'm right that it's been Brit all along...but that's not the girl I am. I'm an open-the-present-first kind of girl through and through.

I tear off the paper and see a box similar to the one I wrapped for Todd...except this one says WOMAN BOX all over it.

I can't help my laugh as I look over at Brit, who's reading her own card. She freaking ordered the same thing for me that I ordered for Todd? So original.

I open the box and find an assortment of wine bottles inside along with all different sorts of popcorn and popcorn toppings. There's also some spa stuff in there, bubble bath and loofahs and scrubs and glitter bath bombs, and more goodies to use on my bullet journal.

It's beyond perfect, clearly customized for the things I like, which was an option on the man box website, but I went with the pre-selected dark beers instead of choosing the custom option. I'm about to lean over to squeeze Brit for being so thoughtful when I realize I still haven't opened the card.

Imagine my utter shock when I finally do get to the card and see the name at the end.

It's finally time to reveal myself

741

I guess I'm not Santa's little elf
I'm just a guy who wants a date with you
But I don't know how to ask out of the blue
I've been nervous since we work together
But I've wanted to ask you out pretty much forever
I'm done keeping up this friendship façade
Because guess what? My name is Todd.

I stare at the card and read it again, and then I read it again and again as I try to reconcile what I'm reading with the thought that my Secret Santa wasn't just Brit all along.

"Oh my God," I whisper, and Brittany leans over me and reads my card.

I look up at her, and her eyes widen when they meet mine. "Todd is yours?"

I lift a shoulder, still not sure this is computing in my brain. "It looks like it."

She grins at me. "Totally meant to be."

"And he wants to ask me out on a date?" I gush. "Is he even kidding? Of course I'll go out on a date with him! He's only the hottest guy I've ever laid eyes on in my entire life!"

"You really think so?" a deep voice close to my ear asks.

My heart stops beating for a second. Just literally stops.

My cheeks flush as I close my eyes. I can't believe he heard me say that. I want to disappear...and yet...

He made it clear on his cards this week and tonight that he's interested. Is it really so bad that he knows I think he's hot?

"Because I'm incredibly attracted to you, and I'm also very interested to know what you meant by this." He holds up the card that I printed, and it's not the card I thought I attached to the gift.

All the blood that just rushed into my cheeks? Yeah, it all drains right out of my face. I feel a little buzz in my head and I think I might pass out.

I thought I gave him the card that said:

Todd,
I'm your Secret Santa! Wishing you a very Merry Christmas and an amazing new year.

Ellie Nolan.

That's the nice, tame one. The friendly one.
Not the raunchy one he's holding out to me.

Todd,

I've had a crush on you since I first met you. I'd love to take this opportunity to drink some dark beer with you, let you ride my water slide, and maybe enjoy some maple donuts when we wake up.

Xoxo,
Ellie

"What, exactly, is your water slide?" he asks.
Oh sweet baby Jesus. I want to ducking die.
"I, um..." I stammer. I cover my eyes with my hand as he slides into Belinda's vacated chair beside me. "You weren't supposed to see that card."
He laughs.
"I just thought I could change your mind about water slides," I mutter.
"Well if it's *yours...*" he says, trailing off. He pulls my hand from over my eyes. "Hey, thanks for everything this week. Your gifts were incredibly thoughtful and totally original."
I'm grateful for his change of subject as I laugh. "Not *that* original since you got me the same thing I got you."
He chuckles. "The man box is awesome, and somehow it pairs exactly with what I got you. This is probably a terrible idea since we work together, but what would you say if I invited you over to my place tomorrow night for dark beer, wine, popcorn, and maybe *Fight Club*?"
"Change it to *Die Hard* and you've got yourself a date."
"Deal," he says, and he sticks out his hand. I giggle as I set mine in his to shake on it, but the laughter ceases pretty quickly when our hands touch. Electricity passes between us, and if hand on hand gives me that reaction, I can't wait to see what lip on lip (or, even better, body on body) might do.

743

Guess there's a chance I'll find out tomorrow night when friends might turn into something else.

CHAPTER 5

I'm nervous as I drive over to Todd's place, and it's not because of the weather. He texted his address to me this morning, and I spent hours this afternoon on both Zillow and Google Earth stalking him...I mean *looking up where he lives* so I don't get lost.

His place is literally two miles from mine. I could have walked, but it's twenty-four degrees and snowing.

Even if it was seventy and balmy, I wouldn't have.

We agreed on eight, so I spent the day prepping. Before I left, I tossed a little overnight bag in my car as a just in case, which I'll leave there unless he invites me to stay the night. I also brought my woman box along even though I was tempted to eat the popcorn all day.

I hate driving in the snow, and even worse is when I have to parallel park on the street in front of his swanky rowhouse. I get out of the car and step right into a puddle of slush, naturally, and then I have to wrestle with the woman box to get it out of my backseat. By the time I slip and slide up his steps to ring his bell, I'm panting and afraid I might tumble right down the stairs from the patch of ice I'm standing on.

He opens the door, and somehow that just makes everything okay. The rush of heat from inside has nothing on how freaking hot he looks. He's wearing jeans and a t-shirt, so casual compared to his typical work style of black pants and a collared shirt, and he's wearing socks with no shoes. There's something sexy about that. He looks relaxed as he reaches out a hand to take the box from me and help me in, and his easy demeanor calms the nerves that've been quaking inside me both from the drive in the snow and the thought of what this night could mean for us.

I step inside, and he motions to follow him in. I look around at the house I already saw on Zillow. It looks different in person. He painted since he moved in, obviously, and the décor is both simple and masculine. Everything is dark wood and dark colors, with the occasional surprise pop of Cubbie blue.

We walk through the entry toward the kitchen, where he sets my box on the counter, and I glance over into the family room. *Die Hard* is already pulled up on the television. He has a stack of empty bowls set out for our popcorn, a Cubs pint glass, a wineglass, and a corkscrew. A fire crackles in the fireplace beneath the television, a blanket rests on one side of the couch, and all in all it looks like he thought of everything.

"So this is what Todd's house is like," I murmur as I shimmy out of my coat. He holds out a hand to take it, and he drapes it over one of the kitchen chairs to dry. I set the gloves, hat, and scarf on top of it, take my shoes off, and look up at him. He's smiling at me.

"I like that you wore those," he says, nodding to the winter gear he gave me, and then he takes a tentative step toward me. "Can I ask you a question?"

I nod, the nerves suddenly back again.

"Was what you said on your card true?"

My brows dip. "That you could ride my water slide?" Is that *really* where he wants to start this conversation? Maybe he isn't the Prince Charming I thought he was.

He chuckles. "No, the first part. That you've had a crush on me since you met me."

"Oh!" I say, my cheeks flaming. "Yeah. Definitely true." I pat the hat I just set on top of my coat as I try to find something to do with my hands so I don't start wringing them together.

He leans back on his counter like we're not having the most awkward conversation about how cute I think he is. "The feeling's mutual."

I glance up at him.

"It's more than a crush, though, Ellie. I have real feelings for you. I've learned in the past it's not a good idea to get involved with colleagues, but I can't keep denying what I want."

The fire crackles loudly, a nice metaphor for what's brewing between us. He has real feelings for me? Suddenly I feel like we've wasted a whole lot of time...especially because I don't particularly subscribe to the no-colleague rule. If anything, it just makes the workplace that much more fun. "What, exactly, do you want?" I ask softly.

He takes a step toward me, and then another, and then he's close enough that we can reach out for one another, but neither of us makes that move just yet.

"To ride your water slide."

I giggle, and then he reaches for me. I rush into his arms, and suddenly I'm very much *home*. His embrace is warm and inviting, and I tilt my head back because I really just want to make every single one of my dreams come true tonight, and it starts with his arms around me and his lips on mine.

When they move down to meet mine, they certainly don't disappoint. Sometimes friends turn into something more and it's awkward at first...but that is not the case here. At all. I'm feeling zero awkwardness as he kisses me. I'm just feeling hot and needy.

Those Prince Charming lips are soft and firm, and he opens his mouth to mine, his minty tongue brushing against my own. He kisses me confidently, sensually, and yet there's a sweet factor there, too, as he moves slowly with me. He holds me in his arms, and this feels like a perfect start to our first date.

And if he kisses like this, well, I can't wait to see what the *end* of the date will bring, if you know what I mean. Wink, wink, nudge, nudge.

He slows the kiss first before pulling away.

I smile even though I didn't want him to stop, but I feel like he's doing it to be a gentleman. We're going to have a *date* first, and then we'll get to the good stuff.

He helps me choose a bottle of wine, I help him choose a dark beer, and we head to the family room with the popcorn. We put an assortment in different bowls, and he picks one up. We sit beside one another on his couch, our thighs touching, and we share popcorn as we start the movie.

And as soon as he presses play on the movie, we start talking rather than paying attention to what's on the screen.

"Are you into these kinds of action movies?" he asks.

"Sure. I mean I prefer a rom com, but I'll take some old school Bruce any day. You?"

"Definitely action over rom com. Sorry."

I roll my eyes. "Such a typical guy."

"To add to the stereotypes, I also like beer, working out, and sports," he says.

"Okay, so tell me something that's not stereotypically manly about you," I challenge.

He stares at me for a second like he's debating how much to reveal on this first date of ours, and then he grins. "I get monthly facials."

I burst out laughing, and he narrows his eyes at me.

"Tell me something non-girly about you."

"I feel like that's way less embarrassing for me than it is for you," I counter. I take a sip of my wine as I try not to get *too* excited about how much I'm enjoying our banter. "Um, okay. I like *Die Hard.*"

"No fair," he complains. "I already knew that one *and* you only like it because of young Bruce. Give me something new."

I grab some more popcorn and shake it around in my hand. "Fine, but you have to get another bowl now so we can try a different topping. This ranch one is pretty good but I bet the cinnamon sugar one is even better."

He nods and switches the bowls as he says, "I'm waiting."

"Okay, okay." I hold up a hand in surrender. "I like beer, too. But not *dark* beer." I make a face.

"You're missing out," he says, taking a long drag from his glass.

"I'll stick to my wine."

"Suit yourself." He stands to grab a second, and he refills my glass on his way by.

We talk about mutual friends at the office, things we like and dislike, and overall the conversation is easy between us. About an hour into the movie (which really just means we've been chatting for an hour), he asks, "Do you like working for Windy City?"

I nod as I reach into the bowl on his lap for more popcorn, the thought not lost on me that I'm practically touching his dick even though it's beneath the bowl. Maybe it's why I keep reaching for more. "It's a great job. I'm lucky to have a good job a field I love. But honestly my dream is to work with celebrities, so sometimes I feel like this is a steppingstone."

"Same. I want to do damage control for larger corporations, though, not work with celebrities. I want to fix problems for people."

I chuckle, and he narrows his eyes at me.

"What?" he asks.

"You want to fix problems. You're such a Prince Charming."

He laughs. "Hardly. Does Prince Charming like beer and sports?"

"You've got the hair, the eyes, the body, and the spirit. It definitely fits you."

"Is that what you're looking for?" he teases.

I shrug as I shove some popcorn in. "Isn't it what every girl is looking for? A man who treats her like a princess but can still be a tiger beneath the sheets."

Oh mother ducker. My goddamn brain to mouth filter is malfunctioning again.

He raises a brow. "A tiger? I would've assumed you were looking for some sort of water dweller."

"Huh?" I ask, not getting what he's laying down for me.

"Tigers probably aren't as adept, as say, a whale," he says, keeping with whatever metaphor he's making. "I don't know if I'm a tiger, but, on the other hand, I can be a fucking whale when it comes to riding the water slide."

"Oh my God," I shriek as I finally get where he was going, and then I smack his arm. He laughs, and then he grabs my wineglass and sets it on the table next to his pint glass and the popcorn bowl.

And then he sets to proving just exactly how adept he really is.

It's mere seconds before I'm pinned beneath him on his couch, his eyes hot on mine as he hovers over me. His lips crash down over mine, and then he's thrusting his hips against me and we're making out in front of the fire while Bruce is *yippee-ki-yay-motherfucker*-ing on the screen.

I reach for his shirt with the intention of slipping my hands under it to feel his skin. He takes it as a signal and pulls it over his head and tosses it to the floor, which is perfectly fine with me since we were heading that direction anyway.

Oh dear.

My eyes pop out as I take in the hard cuts of muscle he keeps hidden beneath those collared shirts on a daily basis. He likes working out indeed. And my dreams of a six-pack beneath his work clothes have nothing on the reality. There must be like eight or ten there. He was born with extras.

I run my fingertips along the carved muscles, stopping to play with the top of his pants as I look coyly up at him. When our eyes meet, I see all the lust he's kept hidden for as long as we've known each other. I'm sure my own eyes are hooded with the same lust reflected back at him along with a total sense of awe that this is actually happening.

He reaches for my shirt, and I help him pull it over my head. He leaves my bra in place as he trails kisses from my mouth, down my neck, to my cleavage, where he spends a little time, and then he helps me sit up so he can unhook my bra strap with one hand. He pulls it off, tosses it to the floor, and lavishes my breasts with attention, sucking on one for a few beats while he palms the other and switching back and forth. All I can do is lean back and moan as I give into the sweet pleasure.

He trails a hand down my torso, pops the button on my jeans, and slides his hand down, cupping me over my silky panties with a sexy groan, and then he reaches in and slides a finger into me.

Oh God.

My eyes roll back as he pulls his finger out and slides it back in, his mouth back on my breast, and if it was any other guy I don't know if it would all feel this good...but it's not, it's Prince Todd Charming, the guy I've had a crush on for a year, the guy who has feelings for me, too, the guy who wasn't just my Secret Santa but also my secret admirer, and now this is actually happening.

My moans get a little louder as I feel the buzz of an impending climax already starting to crash into me. I wrestle with the button on his jeans because I want in his pants, too. He stops fingering me only to help me with his jeans. A true gentleman, he even pulls himself out for me.

Whoa.

He's big. And thick. And hard.

Really hard.

All the coherent thoughts leave my being entirely as cavewoman urges take over. I've always thought he was hot, but this is something else entirely. It's carnal need, like I won't be satisfied until *that* is up in *here.*

I stroke him a few times, and he closes his eyes with a grunt, and then he pulls back. He reaches into his jeans pocket and pulls out a condom, and he looks at me with a silent question in his eyes. I nod quickly, giving the green light that I want this, too, and he rips the packet and rolls it on before I even have time to say *fuck yes, I'm ready to romp.*

He leaves his jeans on but helps me out of mine. I'm still lying back on his couch, and now I'm completely naked except for the fuzzy socks he gave me, which I leave on because hello, it's winter in Chicago.

He hovers over me, kisses me again, and then he slides into me, and it's even better than every fantasy I ever had, better than every time I touched myself imagining it was the object of my crush, better than I could have dreamed.

He pumps into me, our bodies syncing together in a rhythm of total need and want and desire, and he leans down to catch one of my nipples in his mouth. It's all too much. He'd already gotten me three-quarters of the way there, and now with the sensations he's driving into me down below paired with my breast in his mouth and the sounds of our sex and his grunts and the crackle of the fireplace, I fly over the edge into a brutal orgasm.

He continues pumping into me as he keeps sucking on my nipple, and mere moments later, his body stiffens and he growls out a sexy little noise as he flies into his own release.

And then it's all over much too quickly. We both come back down from the climax and he slips out of me. He helps me relocate my clothes along with his own, and we get dressed. He shows me to the restroom, where I take a minute to clean up, and then I glance at myself in the mirror. Fluffy hair, flushed cheeks, swollen lips stretching into a wide smile...yeah, I definitely look like I just got laid.

When I emerge from the bathroom, he's all cleaned up, too, and sitting on the couch with his beer. He hands me a bag, and I read the label on it.

"Clandestine?" I ask, narrowing my eyes at him.

He shrugs. "I figured it wasn't appropriate for the office Secret Santa, but if we need to prove they have classy products, then we should probably take them for a test drive."

I laugh, and he shrugs innocently, and then I pull out a lacy red negligee and thong. "Totally classy," I say.

We spend the rest of our holiday break test driving lingerie from Clandestine, *getting to know* each other, and putting on action movies with the occasional rom com slipped in while we make out on his couch or sometimes on mine.

I don't know what tomorrow will bring, or what things will be like when we have to return to work, but what I do know is that I have hope in my heart that my Secret Santa brought me my very own Prince Charming.

ACKNOWLEDGMENTS

Thank you to my husband for everything you do. The support, encouragement, and love are what makes this possible. Thank you to my kids, and thank you to my parents who love hanging out with my babies so I can get some computer time in.

Thank you to Autumn Gantz of Wordsmith Publicity, my ARC team, Team LS, and all the bloggers who read, post, and review.

Thank you to Trenda London from It's Your Story Content Editing, Diane Holtry and Alissa Riker for beta reading, Najla Qamber for the gorgeous cover design, and Katie Harder-Schauer from Proofreading by Katie.

Thank you to you, the reader, for taking time out of your life to spend it with Ellie and Luke. I hope you enjoyed what you read, and I can't wait for you to read what's next for Jack Dalton!

xoxo,
Lisa Suzanne

ABOUT THE AUTHOR

Lisa Suzanne is a romance author who resides in Arizona with her husband and two kids. She's a former high school English teacher and college composition instructor. When she's not cuddling or chasing her kids, she can be found working on her latest book or watching reruns of *Friends*.

ALSO BY LISA SUZANNE

VEGAS ACES:
The Quarterback

VEGAS ACES:
The Tight End

60013680R00446